THE FIRST BORN
CRUSADE

THE FIRST BORN
CRUSADE

BENTLEY L DEAN

VIEUE MOSAIC

2016

TO THOSE I'VE LOVED.

TO THOSE I'VE LOST.

SESON MIDWAY

DIMYCLES FELL TO his knees and his rattling chains echoed off the walls of his cold cell. Too weak to stand, his legs gave way, and when he hit the ground, a foul body odor clouded around him. He sniffed over himself until he found the epicenter of the stench on the back of his forearm. It tasted like rotten almonds when he probed it with his tongue. After gnawing on it for several minutes, his teeth tore away the diseased flesh, and he spat the frozen bits of skin onto the floor. In his final moments, he shook his head in disbelief, not understanding why he bothered to stay alive.

"I wonder what other criminals think when facing their execution," he said.

The stray light revealed only half of his pale and weathered face. The shell of a man looked up at the stars through the tiny window. Yaliz was there. Every curve on her body told a different story from his life. Dimycles assumed he'd welcome the end, but the woman that gave him courage robbed his soul.

"Others criminals know they earned their punishment," she told him.

"And what about me? Did I not earn this?" He demanded. "Did my actions not flood the graveyards?"

"You flooded the graveyards with your actions, but not with your heart," Yaliz replied. "Being guilty of a crime is more than just an act. Intent... conviction. These things matter too."

"Because of my ignorance..." he breathed. "Moral innocence cannot free me from being criminally guilty."

"No it cannot," she agreed, "but moral innocence can give you the freedom to embrace your death."

He adjusted his furry hat and put his hands on his lap. The floor was cold. Four long heavy chains connected to a wall and the opposite ends of the chains pierced his skin, went into his back and clamped around his bones. He pushed his mangled fingers down between his thighs to warm them.

The Seson Midway prison was a barbaric place.

All Dimycles had in his prison cell was a window. At night the stars illuminated his dark world. The stars also freed his mind. With the stars, he counted, with counting he could do mathematics, and with that, he could make shapes. He drew pictures in the stars, and with them, his imagination made stories. The stories allowed him to stave off the pain of reality, as the darkness confused him and made him lose his mind.

Yaliz was a woman—at least the shape of a woman—traced in the stars. To his mind she was more than a constellation; Yaliz was his companion. Of all the constellations, she was the only one that spoke to him, and he heard her as if her mouth touched his ears. He never intended to escape the reality of his incarceration; he merely hoped to find a way to retain his sanity through the lonely nights. When his only reason to live was a pure fabrication of his imagination, the lines of rationality embraced a more savory means of survival.

The biting cold was bad enough, but the chains in his back kept him from ever having a moment of peace. He'd been wide awake when they sliced through his thick back muscles and clamped the ends of the chains around his ribs. They taunted him for being strong, but he paid the price for his strength as his blood clotted a metallic callous in place of every mortal wound he received.

Now he felt drained and could barely breathe. His sight grew dim in the bowels of the dark prison. His body, which he regarded as his temple, had been dotted in metallic scars threatening to overtake the living tissue. Though his skin was dry, flaking and sallow from infections, he loved it, because it felt alive. Feeling anything at all only meant that Dimycles had not yet reached the moment all questions have no meaning; when he could finally stop asking himself, "Why did I do it?"

With Yaliz, he didn't feel trapped, and he didn't feel alone. Yaliz freed him, and often, she sang to him.

When you search for a star, what you seek is the light

Let it grow wings, and watch it take flight

Parade its soul, and never betray

For the might of the beast will always obey

It will always submit to what its nature will say

Let it bare its teeth, for the thirst, for the blood.

It knows no taste.

Better than the prey it was born to chase

So focused, it insists to carefully hone

The privilege to exist in a league of its own

Under the tension of those who kill to ignore

The truth, locked away, after closing the door

Suits the king as a slave to a life you don't choose

What is the brave and the unafraid willing to prove?

He tried to learn the riddle of her song.

She understood his frustration and explained, "If the words made sense, then it wouldn't be poetry."

"Two years," Dimycles nodded and said as the sun crested the horizon. The new light threatened to steal away his companion.

A sudden noise interrupted their conversation, and the cell door creaked opened. Dimycles turned to face two armed guards wearing night vision goggles. Each grabbed one of his arms. As they jerked him up, Dimycles felt his shoulders give.

The guards disconnected his chains from the wall and escorted him through the hall in complete darkness. Their footsteps echoed hollowly off the cold, unseen walls.

Dimycles felt blind and all of his other senses heightened by the loss of his sight. Yaliz's twinkles faded from his vision. She'd left him, and soon he would die alone. He could not accept this. He decided that he would rather die fighting than have the guards drag him to the gallows.

Dimycles pushed his shoulder into one of the guards, driving him into the wall. The prisoner pounded with chained fists on the other guard. The first guard recovered and cracked Dimycles in the side with a baton. Dimycles fell to the ground. Footsteps echoed from all around, as other guards came to assist.

As Dimycles tried to push himself up from the floor, pain seared his side where the baton had hit him. He collapsed. He tried to raise his left arm, but his chest hurt, so he rolled on his side and pushed up with his right elbow. He stumbled to his feet, swinging wildly in the dark at the escorts. They paid him no mind. They could see, while he couldn't, and he was too frail to cause any real damage. As he got tangled in his chains, the jailers quietly restrained him. As a worker grabbed him from behind, Dimycles tried a hip toss but buckled under the weight. All the guards backed away and let him flail. Dimycles swung at air, exhausting himself until he couldn't even stand up under the weight of his chains. They robbed him of an honorable death.

One leaned into him and asked, "You want to go outside?" Other guards snickered as Dimycles quickly shook his head 'no'. The guard continued, "Why fight? You want a warrior's death. You think that what you did counts as heroic? Hmm? You are no warrior. You are a murderer. Your victims wait for you on the other side!" The guard grabbed a chain hanging from Dimycles' back, and gently twisted it. Dimycles screamed.

"They can't hear you," the guard hissed. "Everyone on Earth has covered their ears to anything you have to say. Why else would they send you to a prison on Mars?"

As they dragged Dimycles away, his chains clanked on the grated floor; their metallic echoes closed in on him as he neared the lift. Gears clanged, and doors creaked open. Stale air rushed out of the lift as the guards pushed him inside. The lift sealed everyone inside and began to move sideways. Dimycles looked down. The large freight elevator jerked and started its descent. Dimycles counted the floors. As the fifth floor passed by, Dimycles thought of his sister, and his jaws trembled. He wanted to tell her how sorry he was for dragging her to this place.

He screamed, "Damyae!"

They stopped at the ground floor and took him to the holding cell at the edge of the prison hall. The guards clamped the ends of his chains to the ceiling, then pushed him down onto a chair.

One guard commanded, "Man the turrets. Wait for the command."

Footsteps marched out of the holding cell, and then the door shut with a loud clang when it locked, and sealed him inside. He heard their strides fade behind the weak heating system that churned away.

"No lights. No stars." Dimycles whispered to himself as he sat alone in a chair in the middle of the room. "No stories."

He waited. The room was warmer than he'd expected. In the stillness, he became more aware, and his breath divided the measures from the rhythm of his beating heart. Something warm dripped onto his cold hands. He was bleeding. As he shifted to wipe the blood from his face, his chains clanked and echoed off the walls around him. He realized the room was bigger than he'd imagined.

He probed the space in front of him and felt a table. He guessed that there must be another chair on the other side. That would be for his legal representative, who was supposed to come in to discuss the final moments with him. No one was there.

The Seson started off as a Martian colony. The midway point for human expansion to Jupiter's moons was an ambitious corporate undertaking until Humans disbanded all Martian colonies. That didn't stop private prison companies from buying the territory for their own use. Dimycles looked around and wondered if anyone in the Seson ever survived to experience their execution.

"Is this what it is like for you, dear sister?" Dimycles lamented, "The only time you see the light is when you are sleeping."

When he'd first arrived, the darkness touched him like someone grabbed his eyeballs and squeezed them. His eyes no longer felt that strain which supported his notion that his eyesight had faded. But then Dimycles realized that he saw something move in his peripheral vision—one of his fingers. He cocked an eyebrow in surprise. There was the dimmest yellow light permeating the room. It was barely discernable. He didn't know if the light grew brighter, or if his eyes were adjusting.

"Dimycles," The voice of a woman spoke firmly.

For some reason, he thought it odd that she did not refer to him to by his prisoner number. The light in the room increased slightly. Footsteps came from behind him. Barely making out the shape, he saw it was a woman as she passed. Soon he saw that her hair was dark and fell to her hips, with the tail of her outfit following behind her as she walked. Dimycles had gone crazy long ago from the dark incarceration, and as a result, his mind made up images when his sanity slipped away, but the woman held something in her hand: a small rectangular transparent screen. That was oddly specific for an illusion.

"Is it true, you are from the planet Covarra?" she asked, her back turned to him.

He looked up at her: hearing the name of his homeland alarmed him. "How do you know that name? What have you heard?"

"I heard about the Six War," she said. "And how it ended with you, in prison on Mars, looking out of a window you dare not break."

When she turned back to him, he saw that the light in the room came from her eyes. The darkness was thick in the holding cell, but everywhere she looked her gaze cast a glow as if her face was a beacon of light.

"There isn't much more to me or that story," Dimycles warned.

"There is always more to a story. You joined the Six, yet you are not human. You followed Lotus with every loyal beat of your heart until you killed him?" The woman aimed her gleaming eyes at him. "Why'd you ever go to Earth?"

Dimycles blushed. "I was lost." He spoke offhandedly as if to distance himself from his words. "Lotus told me a lie that I wanted to believe."

"The humans know nothing of what's outside their system. You went to their planet, delighted by their innocence and intoxicated by their passion. Yet how did you go from being lost to annihilating so many for the sake of a lie?" She asked.

"Lotus had to pay for his crimes as I will now pay for mine."

She scoffed, "There is no sweeter judgment than the one coming from the executioner."

"I am no judge," said Dimycles. "Just... no one else dared to chase the devil into the abyss of hell."

"But you did!" she charged. "You followed the devil and your ego killed him."

"Not ego!"

"What then, honor?" She mocked.

"It is all I had left."

"You are delusional if you think you had anything left. How much honor can you have if it won't allow you to embrace the penalty of your actions?

"Death is easy to embrace. It's the death of every man, woman, and child Lotus hid behind that I can't accept."

"Lies! You burned the entire city in chemical fire, and you didn't even let the innocent ones flee."

"No!'

"Yes!" She shouted. "Die with pride!"

His voice crackled in pain. "No!"

"Why can't you admit it?"

"I admit it was my coup, but I killed no one but the man himself."

"How does that make you any better than Lotus. Those dead because of his command are no different than your pile."

"Except for why they died," Dimycles pleaded her to understand while his chin fell into the furry coat that covered his feeble body. He shook his head slightly. "I am nothing like Lotus. No one died because of my ambitions of power."

The woman seemed intrigued by his response, "What reason do you have to detest those with ambitions of power? Only a bitter pawn, stuck on its square, complains of the king's ambition."

"I don't have a problem with ambition. I hate the source from which leaders derive their control. It is by fear or by force, if not from the will of the people." Dimycles shrugged and looked up. The light hurt his eyes. "You can't give yourself authority because then that is just power." He looked away, troubled by his thoughts. "And power without authority leads to slavery."

From the corner of his eyes, he saw the woman grip the air with her fist. "Do you hate him for what he did to you?"

Dimycles recalled nights in his cell, chained to the walls, screaming at the stars. He'd truly hated Lotus. He hated himself for his decision. Was he a mass murderer who knew better or a slave of ignorance? Suddenly, Dimycles felt empty. He shook his head - no, concluding: "He lied to me, just as he did to everyone else."

"Mmm... how noble," The light bearer acknowledged. "Let's not pretend. Unlike everyone else, you had a reason to believe him."

The temperature dropped. The chains in his body cracked and popped. His skin tingled as the room began to freeze over. The cold made him tremble. He tried to rub warmth into himself, but his icy fingers needed it more. Every move agonized his senses until a numbness crept over him. When he opened his mouth to speak the only sound that emerged was the chattering of his teeth.

As she watched him shake, she said: "I would be lying if I said I didn't find your grasp of nobility amusing, at least on a primitive level."

Dimycles felt ice form behind his eyes. His hat froze, sticking to his long brittle hair. He could not speak. He looked up and saw her. Ice lined her thick lips and coated her smooth, flawless skin. Her dark hair glistened in the frigid temperature. She studied him through the haze.

"Covarra was once part of the Sunil," she observed. "I don't care about Earth. I don't care about the Six. You may tickle me with your rhetoric, but when ask you a question, and you ignore it, death is what you will have whether you're ready to embrace it or not."

Dimycles felt pain and thought his blood might crystallize. He fell out of the chair in shock, but the chains held him up. He could not tell if the pain he felt was from the biting cold, or because the chains pulled against his bones.

She asked again, holding out a sparkling hand: "Are you from the planet Covarra?"

Dimycles looked into her eyes and thought their glow might burn out his retinas. Before his body went completely numb, he nodded yes. The table in front of him froze, and the joints cracked.

"I am Wuyan," she said.

Dimycles felt the room warming up again as he hung limply from the chains. He'd lived with the deaths that he'd caused for too long. Now she'd given him closure. He knew why he'd fought. His reasons had been foolish, yet honorable, and now he couldn't let go. Listening to her was like reading a new chapter, and he could not bear to close the book. He lifted his head. "No...one knows."

She blew off the excuse. "Why would you keep such a thing a secret?"

"If I..." His arms twitched as the feelings returned to his body, "didn't... I'd be dead a long time ago."

"If you kept it a secret any longer, you'd be dead now."

She walked past the chair in front of the table. "Do you know how to find a hidden planet?" she asked.

"You..." He positioned his knees under him to take his weight off the chains. "You're after a hidden planet?" He used the chair to support himself. "Do you not understand why they are hidden?"

She nodded. "The Sunil are hidden because no one has found them. They sit comfortably enjoying the benefits of their sacred knowledge, yet none of it belongs to them."

"Something disastrous happened to the galaxy. They will make sure history doesn't repeat itself," he said. "When terrifying threats once again plague the Realm, the Sunil will be the only ones that can stop it."

"I doubt it," Wuyan said. "Their anonymity is their protection and their vice. What difference does it make what happens to the rest of the galaxy if the Sunil are hidden and safe? They would never jeopardize their way, unless, of course, someone brought the threat directly to them."

Dimycles gasped, "You want to attack them?"

"They have something I want." She came toward him out of the amber haze. "I have something you need."

She took his hand and placed a key inside of his palm.

Dimycles wrapped his feeble fingers around the key, and weighed his options carefully, "You want me to choose between death and dishonor? What do the Sunil have that you would risk everything to get?"

"The hidden planet of Calare has the core to the Midnight bomb," Wuyan explained. "And I want it."

"A Midnight bomb?" Dimycles whispered. He shook his head, confused.

"The core," Wuyan clarified.

It was even worse than he'd thought. To Dimycles it looked like death, no matter what he chose. He raised himself up and sat back in the chair.

"It would be the end of you," he said. "Perhaps by refusing, I may save your life. They hide those kinds of things for a reason."

"The only reason is power," Wuyan said, as she began to pace. "And what right do the Sunil have to these weapons?"

Dimycles raised his head. "To question the Sunil is sacrilege!"

"And you know that you can't give yourself authority! Isn't that what you told me when you felt the need to posture on your nobility?" She reminded him. Her aura scolded his dignity. "Anytime someone gives themselves authority, the people in their shadows suffer."

The light in her eyes made his choice ever clearer.

"You detest Lotus for his expression of power," she said, "but you defend the Sunil for the same reason. It seems your honor is not without prejudice."

"I can neither live nor die without my dignity!" he claimed, "You offer to remove this crushing weight, only to replace it with another?"

Wuyan approached him and leaned close. "Here you are, wanting to hold on to your last shred of honor before going to the same grave where you sent so many others?"

She touched his bearded chin and lifted his face to hers. He could smell her scent. Hers was not the metallic odor of his chains or the stench of frozen feces that permeated the halls. She was fresh with a touch of sweetness.

"Show me this honor," she said, "when you die for your crimes." Her eyes dimmed as her body glowed and transformed into thousands of sparkles. Dimycles shielded his eyes from the brightness. An icy breeze invaded the cell, scattering light into darkness. All went black.

He blinked several times. His pupils flexed involuntarily trying to catch the last glimmers of light. She left a tiny glow that did not go away. The small screen she carried fell to the floor, and it lit up with a slideshow of pictures near his feet. As the pictures flashed, one after the other, he realized it was surveillance photos of the bank tower before the massacre. He dropped to one knee and held the display up to his eyes.

He saw the images of his righteous coup and the moment he killed the man who preyed on his vulnerability - except it wasn't Lotus.

Wait...

Because the display showed Lotus down below setting the charges.

That's impossible.

To facilitate his escape.

W- who did I kill?

While Lotus's men indiscriminately murdered everyone inside.

"Not my crimes," Dimycles whispered.

He thought he heard a voice say, "*It's far too late for apologies*," but no one was there. In his panic, he looked around, unsure if the fear made him delirious again.

"Who's there?" He shouted in the dark.

He heard the voice again. "*Die for what you've done!*"

Dimycles started sweating trying to decipher what was real from his hallucinations. His hand shook, as the words overwhelmed him. Despite the muffled roar of the heating system, Dimycles heard footsteps.

Feeling a deep anger, he stuttered to himself: "No, I didn't do it!"

Dimycles stood up watching the images on the screen start over again. The footsteps slowed as they neared the holding cell. He heard the guards' hands touch the door locks. He became light-headed, tumbling around in the dark, but the chains held him. He was trapped.

The sealed locks on the door released. The door echoed as it opened. Several sets of footsteps came into the room.

He waved the screen in the air, screaming at them to show he was innocent. Dimycles pointed at the image of Lotus. "He's still alive!" The proof was right there, and Dimycles put it in their faces, but the guards ignored his protest because nothing was in his hands.

Guards tightened his chains to the ceiling and forced the hysterical prisoner to hang from his bones.

"He orchestrated this!" Dimycles shouted in pain, waving and pointing to his empty hand.

A man stood in front of him and spoke. "As commander and chief of the Seson Midway Correctional Facility, I hereby sentence you to death for the crimes of genocide, illegal use of biological weapons, and conspiracy to murder in the act of mass destruction."

"Not my crimes!" Dimycles shouted like a mad man. His feet struggled to touch the ground.

The commander continued, "As of this moment you will be exposed to the elements until dead."

Dimycles breathed heavily, shedding tears as his mind struggled to focus coherently on the time and place. He looked down and spoke: "I don't know what you want with a Midnight core."

The commander paused, then continued, "Does the prisoner have any last words?"

Dimycles looked up and said, "No one steals from the Sunil."

"Very well. May God have mercy on your soul."

The boots marched off, the cell door slammed shut, and Dimycles opened his palm and inside of it was the key Wuyan gave him. He heard the commander give the order to open the gate.

"But I can," Dimycles promised, alone in the dark.

He unlocked his chains from the ceiling, and as his feet touched the ground, he felt a surge of energy. His swollen knuckles tingled, and his gnarled fingers felt alive. Inside, his heart charged up ready to burst, and from his mangled skin, he felt the hair on his body straighten.

The sound of bending metal came from the far end of the room and rumbled under his feet. Dimycles gasped, as he felt the last burst of vitality within his body. The energy wasn't much, but then it happened, and Dimycles knew, it was all he'd ever get.

A bright light filled the room and sent him stumbling. He grabbed for any support he could reach. The cell doors popped open. A powerful, low-pressure, vacuum sucked him out the door, knocking the air from his lungs. The table and chairs went too, and he briefly got caught in them. The Martian air tore him to the bone.

The guards realized Dimycles was out in the open. From the armed turrets above, patrols shot exploding canisters that hit and blew rocks in his face.

Dimycles' skin bubbled as he gasped for air. Staggering to his feet, he ran. The light gravity impeded him. Without intending to, he leapt high into the air, then twisted an ankle when he landed. His eyes burned. He settled onto his knees. Ahead of him lay bodies of prisoners workers that once mined the landscape - vaporized from the Martian atmosphere. Jumping through a barrage of artillery fire, he ran until he reached a body. He stripped the corpse of its mask, then rolled low to avoid more shots. The soil beneath him was hot enough to burn his skin. He secured his newfound mask, but it had no air in the capsules. His chest burned. He tried to force a breath and grew dizzy. Something squeezed his lungs.

On the cliffs ahead, next to the cargo shipments, light reflected off a freighter capsule. Like water in the desert, the round spacecraft called to him. Dimycles' legs moved. As his heart pumped, his brain set off an alarm.

I won't make it.

He detoured to an abandoned land-rover, jumped in, and sealed it. Dimycles kept punching the steering column waiting for the vehicle to normalize the oxygen pressure. The indicator barely reached yellow before he gulped air. As he waited for the green light, he coughed.

The gunners from the tower found him. Their shots damaged the land rover. The hope of fresh air steamed out through the cracked hull. Armed troops in protective gear hopped out of the prison to finish him off.

The guns blew a larger hole in the Mars rover. Under his mask, Dimycles held his breath again. The guards reached the rover and ripped off the door. Dimycles bolted, attacking them, and a guard yanked the chains in his back, pulling Dimycles to the ground. As his feet went into the air, his head slammed rocks. The guards poked at him with electric rods.

Dimycles dislodged one of the rods and gutted a guard. The man's insides blew out, boiling in front of his eyes. As the guard fell, a mist of blood and organs settled on top of him.

Dimycles grabbed two guards by their necks, slamming one into the Mars rover's door. As the first guard's body sheared in half, Dimycles ran, tossing the other guard as if he were a doll. The body flew through the thin air. When it hit the ground, the helmet came off, fast-freezing the guard's head as his eyes appeared to boil. Two disembodied hands groped for a now useless mask.

Holding his breath, Dimycles turned purple. He took a huge leap, clutched the side of the cliffs, and realized his senses were fading. He hopped up the rocky side until his eyelids drooped. He collided with the Martian capsule pod. The gracious machine opened up for him, and he fell into the tiny interior, his skin on fire. As he lost consciousness, the door shut. Just as he felt his eyes beginning to melt, he heard a voice:

"Show me this honor, when you die for your crimes."

Then it all went blank.

Wednesday, 8am.

Four years ago...

THE GREATER EVIL

NICOLE BRUSHED THE strands of hair from her face and clutched her husband's arm as they stepped lively through the open foyer of the Austin-Bergstrom airport. The air rushed past. Nicole breathed in the natural scent of her husband's body as her shoes echoed with every step.

She tried to smile, but her eyes dripped with sadness. Nicole leaned in on him and said, "He's afraid of something."

"I'm not trying to comprehend his motive," Bishop answered, urging her along. "We must first plot our course in this matter, and then worry about the rocks along that path. Only then can I take away whatever means he will have to hurt you."

"The monsters that haunt his dreams have now become a nightmare for me," Nicole said as they both stopped. "Silent tears with each lullaby."

"Find your contact, give them the zenomites," Bishop instructed. "I'll lead your monsters away."

Nicole didn't like the sound of that. She touched his chest and ran her fingers up to his shoulder, taking the bag he held, and coldly walking off.

Catching up with her, Bishop took her hand and sweetly spoke "I'll be ok," he insisted, but only a frustrated pain seeped through her eyes in return. "I just want to buy you some time to get rid of it. I won't do anything crazy," he promised.

Somewhat reassured, she kissed him and left, walking toward the airport's interior.

Nicole chose the airport for security reasons. The sensors in the terminal continuously scanned all occupants for any danger, and if someone were after her, security personnel would surely get them first. Nicole, along with her husband, were part owners of the Barlow-Kennedy airline, so her credentials allowed her to access the interior of the airport where she was supposed to feel a lot safer. That's how she planned it. It seemed like the best choice at the time, but at the moment, it felt ineffective.

Nicole didn't feel safer because when she arrived at the rendezvous point, her contacts weren't there. She walked along the corridor - puzzled. Footsteps were matching hers; she stopped - it stopped. Someone was behind her.

Are they pulling this shit here?

Nicole hitched her thoughts to a horse, and a stampede ran through her mind. She could feel the heat from someone's body behind her, like a static force crawling on her back. The odd metallic clinking sound of perhaps a knife agitated her.

Stab me?

She spun around to the right moving her elbow low to protect her liver. The only person behind her was an old man who stood bent over having trouble picking up a coin. The stubborn stratch of money wouldn't allow his stubby fingers to grasp it. Nicole saw him fumbling around, and she walked toward him. Quickly, she bent low to retrieve it for him.

She stood up straight to look around for her contacts. Nicole sighed then detoured to the commons area to buy a bottle of water, also coffee, and she sat at a table, listening to a live band playing happy tunes. The songs made time drift by, as did the bad memories. After several musical sets, the band took a break, dampening the festive atmosphere.

A woman sitting nearby, with short hair dyed purple, said: "You haven't touched your coffee. Nervous?"

"The coffee isn't very good," Nicole answered without looking up.

"And your water?"

"It isn't cold."

"Airport accommodations aren't the best. May I?" the woman asked, changing seats to join her. "The water is overpriced, but at least the coffee's free."

Nicole glanced up with a smile, "I am forever in their debt," while slowly reaching into her bag to pull out a reinforced metal pen for a weapon. Nicole eyed the slender neck of the strange woman.

"I detect an accent in your sarcasm. Is that French?" the woman asked.

What a small neck to stab. I might miss. "I have no idea what my accent sounds like to you, but I do speak French, among other things."

"It sounds beautiful. Where are you from?"

Can I get it through her chest? "Originally? Algeria."

"Do most people there look like you?"

Her left. My right. "Africans look like everyone."

"Yeah, but everyone certainly doesn't look like you." She smiled. "Your husband is a lucky man."

"How do you know I'm married?" *I might have to gut you twice.*

"One hardly has to be told; I can read it on your face. Is that where you're headed? To see your family?"

Make a move, bitch. "I wish. This visit is hardly of a personal nature."

"Business?" she asked. When Nicole nodded, the woman asked: "It wouldn't happen to be in beauty products, would it?"

Beauty? What's her deal? "No."

"Oh, I supplement a lot to keep my skin clear. I love how yours is a smooth golden, with a warm glow. I want that. I figure you must know some tricks."

Why do you care about beauty products? You have purple hair! "Only what my mother taught me. Coconut oil, lots of fruit, and lots of water."

"Yeah, that works, but some people are allergic to fruits. Too many pesticides."

"That's true. My friend sells a product that gives you the same antioxidant effect. Hypoallergenic." *She seems nice. Maybe if I flinch, I can see if she's feeling froggy.*

"Really?"

Nicole snatched her pen, but the lady across from her just steadily smiled. Nicole wrote down a number, and slid it to her, "She swears by it. You should try it." *Nicole, please don't make a scene in this airport.*

"I knew you had beauty secrets!" In turn, the woman wrote her number on paper.

She's sweet. Austinites are quite chatty. "I have friends who have beauty secrets."

"Well, that's certainly worth checking out. My face breaks out if I eat too much fruit," the woman said sliding her number to Nicole and standing up. "Thanks for the tip."

As the woman left, Nicole started to take another sip of coffee but then pushed it aside. *She probably poisoned my coffee.*

Two security agents approached Nicole.

"Ma'am," one official said.

Nicole looked at the uniformed women. "Can I help you?"

"Are these your bags?" the second agent asked.

"Yes, they are."

"Sorry, we missed the rendezvous. There's been a mix-up. Would you mind following us?"

Nicole stood up, grabbed her things and followed them to a private screening area.

DRIVING FROM THE airport, Bishop turned off Highway 21 and took the back roads to Rockne. Green stubby trees dotted the grassland, and cows grazed in the shade. Bishop passed acres of empty fields between the houses until he came upon an isolated manufacturing complex and parked in the lot.

Bishop looked in his rearview mirror to see an extremely conspicuous unmarked van creep slowly down the road. Bishop left his vehicle and walked through the halls of the facility. It looked like an aging school, with long halls, cream-colored floors, and ancient radiators. The air conditioning sapped the air of moisture, making the place feel empty. Bishop found the door to Sheppard's office and opened it. The old man sat behind his desk reading some notes.

Sheppard looked up. He had a neurological twitch that made him shake his head as if he were constantly saying 'no.' "Kennedy? I didn't expect to see you here."

"You didn't think I'd find out?" Bishop asked, approaching the desk.

"I expected to see HER!" Sheppard shouted, pounding his fist on the desk. "Besides, I don't think I keep office hours for my grad students anymore."

"Former grad student, you aren't a professor of anything anymore."

"Thanks to Nicole," Sheppard scoffed, with his head shaking. "She's the whole reason I'm in this shit!"

"Don't blame her for stopping your unethical behavior." Bishop felt a wave of disappointment. "You sold my work to pharmaceutical companies to change people's DNA! It killed a lot of people in very gross ways! You deserved more than just firing!"

"That's all on you," Sheppard said, pointing at his former student with a trembling finger. "You gave me incomplete designs. If you would have been straight with me, I could've cut you in on the deal, but you made it impossible for them to reverse engineer your work! Then when Nicole got me busted..."

"You killed her friend!"

"Her ditzy friend didn't like having freckles!"

"Her skin rotted off of her body."

"Like I said, incomplete designs... all your fault. The authorities purged everything from me, all of that research was bit-blasted and destroyed. Troves of knowledge...gone. Well, most of it, right? Nicole couldn't bear to see your life's work go up in digital smoke and she secretly stole back your zenomites, and now she has an entire terror organization after her for them. I hope you can live yourself for that."

"They were your buyer," Bishop reminded the old man. "They wouldn't have known about it if it weren't for you."

"I did try to warn her."

"Warn her? Seriously, you didn't think she'd notice people were trying to kill her?"

"Kill is a strong word," Sheppard corrected. "I think they just lack protocol. They aren't the asking type."

"I want to find them."

"You think I have their address in my file or something?"

"They were your clients."

"Yea, they were my clients. So what? I'm no good to them anymore. They've grown into a whole organization now. They've infiltrated governments, business; they're everywhere. I've got nothing they can't get themselves." Sheppard eyed Bishop with a shaky look and added, "Including zenomites."

"They won't even have them soon as we dispose of it all."

"You think purging all of the zenomites will help? You can't get rid of the product if you don't plan on getting rid of its creator too?" Sheppard dared. "They'll force you to re-engineer it. How long do you think you can run before they track you down and make you give them what they want?"

Bishop scoffed and reached into his breast pocket. "You don't get it do you, I'm not running from this." He pulled out a container encasing a zenomite.

Sheppard shot up from his desk and backed against the wall in terror. "You brought it here!" The old man looked for a way out, or a place to hide "Are you crazy? Get it out of here!"

Bishop stalked him around the office, holding the container in his outstretched palm. "You set Nicole up; I'm just changing the targets."

Sheppard tried opening the window to escape, but the ancient panes were sealed shut from decades old paint. "You'll change her into a widow waving that thing around. What do you want to do? Make them chase me. I'll never take."

"But they will," Bishop revealed.

"You let them follow you here, didn't you?" Sheppard gasped. "That ain't right."

Bishop had barely processed the words when a spray of bullets shattered the window and crashed into the wall. Bishop ducked and sat down. He flipped the container over and engaged a tracking device, then he ran out the door, and back through the corridors. Bursting through the front door, he ran into three men, backed by several more. Bishop punched one in the jaw, and the man crashed to the ground. Bishop slipped through the other two, disarming them, then decked them both with a quick combination of jabs and punches.

Another larger man moved in, but Bishop chopped at his throat, leaving the man gasping. Bishop spun to meet the others but froze at the sight of a gun pointed directly at him.

The man shouted, "Stop!"

"Not a chance!" Bishop yelled, but all the others had weapons trained on him. He relented, and carefully drew the small container from his breast pocket, giving it to the man who seemed to be in charge.

The men walked away, but one of them was bright enough to scan it. "It's bugged," the man complained. "Remove it from the case."

Bishop felt defeated as he saw his plan fail. Disappointment turned to horror when he saw them prying it open. "No, no stop!" he shouted. "Stop!"

They paid no attention to his pleas, so Bishop ran to his car, started the engine, and floored it. In a panic he turned off-road, crashing through the wired fence. He drove across a field into a stand of trees.

Once the men popped open the container, the zenomite leapt into the air, creating a vacuum, as it pulled all nearby matter toward it, then unleashed an explosion that dug up enough earth to make a fair-sized crater.

TO NICOLE THE Austin-Bergstrom airport's detainment area seemed small: a stale white room with little echo. An ice cooler sat across from the table. A large bin housed what looked like probing and scanning devices. A lime green curtain hung in the corner so occupants could disrobe in some privacy.

As the two agents closed the door, Nicole sat down at the table.

The one who'd identified herself as "Agent Barbara" asked, "Is it here?"

"Who are you? Where is Ike, where is Derek?" Nicole wondered nervously.

"Sorry about that, they were reassigned. I'm Agent Swati; this is Agent Barbara. You are very safe here," Swati assured her. "May I offer you something to drink? Water, coffee?"

Nicole looked around. "Is the water cold?"

"Yes."

"I'll take that," Nicole said. "And thank you."

"Don't thank me yet," Swati said, pulling a bottle out of the cooler and handing it to Nicole. "I only hope it will end this battle. You can't keep looking over your shoulder."

"Wars like this have no treaties," Nicole said.

Barbara immediately went into Nicole's bag and dumped the contents onto the table. A canister rolled out, and the agent's eyes went wide.

"Maybe now that we can destroy this canister, it will bring you peace. This is not a war you should fight alone," Barbara grabbed the canister. "I'll be right back," Agent Barabra said before leaving the room.

Nicole's arm twitched watching Barbara leave the room with the canister. "So... soon it will finally be over?" Nicole asked. "Never again to resurface?"

"Do you go by Barlow or Kennedy?" Swati asked.

Nicole shrugged, "Sometimes I feel like a Barlow, other times I feel like a Kenney. Sometimes I feel hyphenated."

"How do you feel now?"

"I feel like I never want to see those zenomites again," Nicole said and took another sip of water.

"You and your husband have redesigned aviations impact on consumer travel," Swati sat down in front of Nicole. "You've given the next generation of engineers the platform for innovation, how can you hide technology, while pushing the envelope of free thought?"

"Just because we are pressing innovation, doesn't mean everything of ours is suddenly community property," Nicole claimed. "I don't see how concealing zero point energy technology is harmful to the greater good."

"Do you think Lotus is harmful to the greater good? Or just you?"

Nicole's fingers wrapped around the water bottle and the condensation dripped between her fingers. "I think he's afraid of something and thinks technology will fix it," She said. "I'm just an ends to a means for him. Whether I'm alive or dead, he doesn't care, as long as he gets it."

"Did you ever think that whatever Lotus is afraid of should make us all afraid? What if he needs the sacrifice of the greater good to save us all from a greater evil?"

Nicole's toes curled inside of her shoes trying to hide her nervousness. "I never really got an opportunity to listen to his side of the story." An empty silence troubled her, and Nicole looked at the table and all the contents of her bag on top of it. She eyed her purse, and next to it was the piece of paper the woman with purple hair wrote a phone number. Nicole said, "Agent Barabra is certainly taking a long time."

Swati turned around and glanced at the door. "She's ok."

"You sure?" Nicole wondered. "Could you please check on her? I want to know everything is ok. She left the password to unlock the canister." Swati's eye's lit up seeing the piece of paper on the table. Nicole added, "I know they are just gonna dispose of it, but if she needed to open it, ya know?"

"Of course, Ms. Kennedy," Swati said, taking the paper, and shutting the door as she left the room.

When the Swati left the room, Nicole took another sip of her water and put the cap back on. It took a few tries for her to screw the top on, her fingers nervously shook. She reached on the table and grabbed her phone, dialing Bishop several times, Nicole continually received a voicemail. *Where is he?* She panicked and felt her heart in her throat. *Please be ok.* "Hey babe! I'm at the airport. Come get me, please!"

Nicole closed her eyes and reassured herself: *No one is trying to stab you. No one is poisoning your coffee.*

She opened her eyes and watched the door in silence. *These people are here to help you. You're just paranoid. You're safe in here.*

Nicole took the deepest breath she could muster and slowly let it out, grabbed her phone, and blotted out of the door.

SWATI BARGED INTO the control room demanding to know where Nicole fled to, and the responses came with blank looks. Swati asked about canister and received the expected news that the cannister Barbra had was a dud.

Swati paced around the control room. She looked over the monitors and asked, "Where is the real cannister?"

NICOLE RAN BACK to the live band area where she met the woman with purple hair and retrieved the real canister hidden from under the table. Next, she tried to access several exits, but they were all guarded.

"Excuse me," Nicole said to a ticket agent. "Any seats left on this flight?"

"I'm sorry, bookings close 45 minutes before departure," The ticket agent responded

SWATI CONSULTED WITH her staff. The control room was filled with dead bodies from the original operators. Several of Swati's agents were stacking the bodies and bagging them. Swati thought of a plan: "Maybe we can bait Nicole out. She was planning on meeting Ike and Derrek, right?"

"Who's Ike and Derrek?" They asked.

"The... her contacts! Dammit, was she lying to us since the beginning?" Swati realized. "Lock down the exits, use the sensors to track her. She knows this airport so she will know all the spots where we can't track her."

The operator said, "No need, her phone is on WIFI. She's in the nursery."

Swati snapped, and Barbara grabbed a team and stormed into the nursery to find a little girl sitting next to a nursing mother playing games with Nicole's phone.

"She ditched her phone," Barbara radioed to the control room.

Swati then asked, "If she has the cannister, is there anyway she could destroy it before we get to her?"

"No way," The controller replied back. "She can't destroy the zenomites, at least not here."

"Why not?" Swati asked, watching the monitors and noticing all the people boarding their flights.

"Well, you don't want to see what happens if that container cracks and even one of these erratic zenomites get out of their enclosure," he reported back. "She's definitely looking for a way to get out of here."

Swati rubbed the back of her head and wondered, "What would it take to ground all these flights?"

Her lead controller looked up and said, "An act of terror."

A DIRT-COVERED crater was all that remained of Sheppard's office and the surrounding area. Even a couple of hundred yards away, Bishop had to dig his way out. The ringing in his head quieted down, and he groped through dirt to find his phone. It was shattered and unresponsive.

Bishop got to the road quickly to distance himself from the devastation. He winced at the sharp pain running through his hip and his right knee and hobbled for about a mile to a public checkpoint. There he summoned a cab.

In the back seat, he borrowed the cab's phone to check his messages and the first one was Nicole, "Hey babe! I'm at the airport. Come get me, please!" Followed by a hasty disconnect. Bishop quickly returned the call several times but only received her voicemail. "Hey, hon," he said to

Nicole's messaging system. "I got your message. I'll be there in about ten minutes."

As he neared, Bishop checked his other messages. One came from Julius, who was out in the field with scientist testing a device Bishop designed to identify Earth samples. Being in the middle of nowhere, Julius had terrible reception and the message Julius left was incomprehensible. So Bishop called the lab to speak to him.

"Thank you for calling the Harold Amos Geosciences office, this is Stacy, how may I direct your call?"

He looked puzzled, "Stacy? Hey, this B.K, where's Jules?"

"Julius is... they haven't made it back yet?"

"You're kidding me," Bishop said. "All right, thanks."

He hung up and dialed a different number to get Julius. "Hey!" Bishop heard wind and construction work in the background, "Are you still at the dig site?"

"Yea."

Bishop sighed and brushed off layers of dirt onto the cab's floor. "I was hoping I could get you here to Texas. I really... really need your help."

"Well, what do you want me to do? Stay here and promote this device you made, or go to Austin and help you get rid of a different one?"

Bishop thought for a moment. "Why are they keeping you?"

Julius groaned, exasperated. "Can't leave until these guys agree on who owns the fossils."

The fossils? "I thought that would be pretty straight forward," Bishop wondered out loud.

"I thought so too. The Geoscientist insist that the fossils formed from prehistoric lightning strikes in the sand, but the paleontologist are saying the fossils aren't fulgurite at all, but a calcareous exoskeleton."

"What does the analysis say?"

"The spectrometer you gave them says it is a blast, but one that came at much lower energy level than a lightning strike. It also detected evidence of microbial fossilization."

"It sounds like a sweet find. They on the verge of uncovering something big. You should stay. We want to help them as much as possible. I'll just call Adrian."

"I take it you are on the way to your old professor," Julius guessed.

"I'm just leaving."

"Oh. How'd it go? Did they take the bait?"

"Yes, and then they blew themselves up with it."

"Oh man, so much for tracking them down. Are you okay?"

"Barely. My car was destroyed, as was everything else around."

"You'd think getting rid of something would be easier than making it. But perhaps after this incident, they will just let it go."

"They aren't going to let it..." Bishop's voice trailed off. The cab crept along the airport through the heavy traffic surrounding the terminals. Bishop became worried and impatient. He hopped out and entered the crowd to look for his wife.

"B.K, what's going on?" Julius said, but no one was there to answer. "B', where are you?"

Where are you? Bishop wondered about Nicole as he had no way to contact her. The airport was busier than he expected, with seas of people, all annoyed, scattered about. "What's going on?" Bishop asked a frantic attendant

She answered without looking at him or his dirty clothes. "I understand your frustration sir, but it's going to take some time... We're doing everything we can but all flights are grounded now."

"Grounded?" Bishop asked.

"There's been some sort of incident."

Bishop looked up at the screen displays. Every flight showed: "CANCELED."

NICOLE'S NERVES WERE frayed, and she closed her eyes and sank into the plush seats on Flight 522. The airplane lurched into the air, climbed through the atmosphere, and water droplets formed on the windows.

Just as quickly they were wiped away by the wind. Nicole thought it odd that she could hear the drops of water hitting loudly. An uneasy murmur arose among the passengers. It sounded as if pebbles were hitting the plane.

Her attention quickly turned to a ruckus in the back.

Yelling. Screaming.

Terrorist!

A team of masked men ran through the aisles of the airplane shouting and forcing confusion while telling everyone to face forward or *cash out*. Air marshals quickly rose from their seats, armed, screaming back until shots rang out. The first hijackers to get hit fell to death and the others dropped to the ground with their hands up. The air marshals moved on them to secure the situation, with knees on the terrorist's backs, they yanked off the masks and cuffed their hands.

"Lotus," Nicole gasped when she saw him, and despite his prostrated state beneath the knee of an air marshal, she didn't feel safe.

"Enemy secured," the air marshal radioed to the pilots.

A dread came over her.

The passengers still seemed unsettled, and their murmuring among themselves added to the uneasy feeling that something was very wrong.

"Do you copy?" The air marshal asked the pilot.

The noise rattling on the outside of the plane bothered Nicole the most. When she turned her attention from Lotus, she saw a horde of insects crawling over the hull.

What is that? Water Striders?

There was a loud pop, and the nose of the plane came loose and fluttered by. As passengers panicked, the insects attacked, eating through the aircraft's alloy skin.

Nicole's eyes went wide, and she vacated her seat and fell to the floor with Lotus.

When the bugs pierced the fuselage, a rush of air punctured the cabin, and blew shrapnel into everyone's faces. Insects, luggage, and other items flew around the cabin.

Distress calls never left the cockpit. The insects had eaten into radar and communications. Now they went for the engines.

Nicole raised her head to see Lotus running off with the canister. She quickly chased after him, pushing forward through the panicked aisles, and she grabbed the canister in his hands. Her feeble tugs couldn't liberate the device from his grip, and Lotus backhanded her away.

The drag from the high winds and damaged plane forced Flight 522 into a stall. The plane fell from the sky, tail first, as the pilots wrestled the controls to get it to level off.

Lotus threw his helmet over his face, finding the side emergency exit door, and there he attached an explosive device to it. He punched in a code to charge it, timing it to blow the door off.

Nicole tumbled backward into a chair. She sat up and swatted away insects. After she crushed a few bugs, she looked over the remains to realize they were actually tiny mechanical drones. She watched them tearing the plane apart, eating into the seats and shorting themselves out while they chewed through the headrest monitors.

Monitors!

Nicole stood up, put both of her feet on the back of a chair and ripped out a T.V screen from the headrest. She ran after Lotus as he waited for the exit door to blow. She touched him with the exposed terminals and electroshocked him.

His body jerked violently, and the canister flew from his hands, and the G-forces from the fall tossed him to the front of the plane.

Nicole noticed air marshals wildly fighting with the remaining terrorist. A bumbling elderly man, who didn't seem to know what was happening, found himself stuck between the melees. She wedged the canister in-between the nearby seats and hurried down the aisle toward them. In one smooth motion, she grabbed the man and yanked him out of the way.

Free and clear, the air marshal drew arms and shot the terrorist.

Lotus cleared his head and looked around. Passengers were in a full panic, jumping between seats, and trying to swat insects from their bodies. He noticed the abandoned canister, and he ran straight for it, hurriedly pushing everyone aside.

Nicole saw him running, and she raced toward it as well.

Lotus neared the canister.

Nicole tore a seat cushion from its place and threw it. The seat cushion hit the explosive charge on the emergency exit door. The door blew off, and the instant draft from the wind sucked both of them out.

Nicole's tiny hands held on to the railing by what was left of the demolished emergency exit door. The wind blew in her face, her eyes shut tight, holding on for dear life, her fingers bled.

At around 18,000 feet, sensors on the airplane's evac system tripped. The parachutes deployed, as designed, and the plane calmly floated along. Though the outside of the damaged plane seemed stable, inside was a frenzy. The insects attacked and damaged everything in sight.

Nicole pulled herself back inside of the airplane and retrieved the canister from its wedge between the seats. She was worried: *If this canister ruptures, everything in sight will be obliterated.*

She gripped the canister, trying to decide what to do, but the insects decided for her. They pulled it from her and carried it through the remains of the jet. Horrified, Nicole stumbled after them through the panicked passengers to swat them away with a tennis racquet she found. The insects tried to make it through a hole they bore, but she blocked their way out with the netting of the racquet and snatched it from them.

Nicole held them off with the racquet until a contingent of insect drones flew outside of the plane to cut into the chutes by chewing through the couplings.

Two parachutes came loose. Nicole was thrown into the ceiling. After orienting herself, she saw that the pilots had initiated an evacuation. She helped a panicked passenger, but more chutes came loose, slamming her against the rear wall. She pushed off, shoved another passenger into an evac, and launched it. Passengers stumbled around the plane, confused. As she extended her hand to one, she heard a loud pop.

Two more chutes came loose.

As Nicole helped a mother and child into a station, someone pushed her. A large man barreled through and launched himself to safety. Nicole led mother and child to another location, but most of the remaining evacs were damaged. Finding an active pair, she forced the woman into the seat against her protest.

"The child will be next—can't fit with you!" Nicole screamed over the noise. She strapped the woman into the harness and launched. Next, she did the same for the child.

Wind whipped through the torn cabin. Drones chewed the nose chutes off. Nicole swatted her way through insects and passengers trying to find a way off, but the remaining stations were damaged. Finally, she stumbled upon an active seat. The last chutes tore off, and the plane plummeted. There wasn't much time. She sat down, clutching the canister, and strapped herself in. She hit the ejection and braced for impact.

The pod signaled an error: *To prevent serious bodily injury, the adult harness must be secured.*

The harness had torn from its junction. She tried to fix it, but the plane shook violently.

Nicole strapped the child harness around her small waist and hoped the g-forces wouldn't rip her in half. She hit the ejection button.

The pod errored, again.

To prevent serious bodily injury, this passenger must wear the adult harness.

Frantically, she looked around for another evac. She saw a little boy hanging on to a torn chair, his eyes blank. Nicole tore herself from the station and tumbled forward toward him. She grabbed the boy, carried him to the evac. Nicole sat the boy down, buckled the child harness around him... the evac flashed a green ready light. Nicole gave him the canister and ejected him from the plane.

She watched the evac take the boy away as Flight 522 crashed.

FOSSIL

HOLDING A LARGE fossil sample in one hand and a phone in the other, Mason hustled to the front of the Harold Amos Microbiology Lab and plopped the fossil into a ceramic pot on a table. With her free hand she adjusted a bandana holding her puffy black hair down, and then she allowed the machine to scan her finger to identify any particles she left on the fossil. The yellow beam of light reflected an eerie glow off her dark brown skin.

"Mom, I don't know where Aunt Kay got that from," Mason said into the phone. "What makes you think I told her?" She listened as she pushed the fossil into a heated enclosure and closed the divider over it. "Well, I feel like I should be able to talk to any of my family members. Why are you trying to control what I say? I didn't tell her why you needed the money; I didn't tell her anything about you needing money. She tricked you into admitting it!" After starting up a scanning device, she watched the display's readout information on the sample. "I think you just got in a fight with her. You're mad, because she never listens, and you're just looking for someone to take it out on! I can't talk about this right now. I'm at work... Yes, work! Even at this hour. I happen to like what I do!"

The display listed several possible matches among plant life specimens. Mason sighed and shook her head. "Why do you want me to feel guilty about it? I went to school; I got a job. That's it. No one is trying to leave you alone and destitute. Of course, I'll send the money."

Footsteps sounded from down the hall.

"I- I have to go. I have an appointment. Yes. Why do you suddenly sound happy? No! It's not a date." Mason let out a sigh. "Yes, mom. If I get pregnant, I promise you'll be the first to know."

She put down her phone, trying to compose herself for the entrance of one of her interns - Tina.

"Where are the others?" Mason asked.

"Right behind me. What did you make of the fossil?"

"It isn't from a plant."

"Really? The computer thinks it is."

"I know. Everyone thinks it's something. The Geo's figured it was fulgurite, but they were wrong. The paleo's figured it microbial, but they weren't right either." Mason recalibrated the analysis machine, which responded by misidentifying the fossil as a bird claw.

"What natural disaster or animal would it come from?" Tina wondered.

Mason sighed, "This is never going to work if we are trying to identify this thing based on preconceived notions of what it should be." Pulling the fossil from the machine, she handed it to Tina. "Take it down the hall, and get me a date on it. We need to start from scratch."

Tina took the sample. As she left the lab, three others entered. A short Asian woman with two uniformed workers carried credentials from the International Counter-terrorism Police force. "Thank you for seeing us on such short notice," said the woman.

"Hi, Sing! Of course. What can I help you with?"

"We were behind the clock trying to find answer to problems I would deem classified," Sing said, glancing around the lab. "In the process, we lost an agent in the Congo."

"The Congo? Why would you send anyone to a habitat for cloned dinosaurs? I thought the ICP only deals with terrorist."

"I should explain," Sing uploaded slides to Mason's computer and brought up a photo. "Do you know this man, Lotus Daniels?"

Mason looked at the screen and shook her head.

"He's been flying under our radar for some time now. We had no idea how expansive his organization had become until almost a year ago when this happened," Sing switched to another photo- one exceedingly more graphic.

Mason viewed a wreckage so expansive she couldn't make out what she was looking at. Sing explained it was the Flight 522 crash site and the people walking among it were rescue workers rummaging through the debris.

All Mason could say was, "Horrific, how did this happen?"

"There has been no shortage of rumors, and speculations. Some survivors claim insects flew into the engines."

"Insects? What insect is fast enough to catch an airplane?"

"Well, I didn't say the rumors were well founded. Some say terrorist, but even that doesn't explain why the plane crashed."

"Yea, I thought parachutes would prevent that from happening."

"Then there are several lawsuits claiming that the crash was a result of the parachutes malfunctioning and deploying mid-flight, thus ripping the plane apart. We are inclined to believe that whatever the cause, Lotus had something to do with." Sing zoomed into the picture on one rescue worker holding a canister. "This man, holding the canister, was a partner to Lotus."

"And who is that?"

"We don't know. Perhaps a mentor, or spiritual guide," Sing admitted. "After Flight 522, we dug into their organization, and we uncovered a vast network they've built worldwide stockpiling and developing weapons while building a massive army of biomechanical armor. This canister would give his weapons untold destructive power. We tracked this strange man back to the Congo, where one of our agents went missing. And we found this." She motioned for the men to open the crate. A dry foul stench emerged.

Mason peppered her nose, donned gloves, and shoveled the sample onto her table. "Let's see what we find out."

After studying it through instruments, Mason commented, "Offhand it looks like either unprocessed fertilizer or just raw manure."

Sing said, "Some of our analysts suggest it's the biochemical makeup of a weapon, and not from any animal."

Mason repeated, "This is just manure."

"I wouldn't question the judgment of something as specialized as yourself, but the type of technology we've uncovered from Lotus has us questioning a lot. Perhaps, if you could look at it with a more open mind?"

Mason began further analysis. Within the soiled sample was ground up vegetation. Mason zeroed in on it, and commented, "This is the remains of plant life from a digestive process. It came from a big animal—a dinosaur."

"So it's not toxic soil from chemical weapon processing?"

Mason didn't answer. She studied the analysis charts on her screen.

Mason continued, "Either the animal was sick, or this sample came posthumously. I show advanced stages of cellular autolysis, but no signs of larvae or oviposition. I see indications the insects were already eating away at it while the dino was still alive."

"What would a DNA test tell us?"

"We don't have advanced DNA test for cloned animals here, but the basic test should be enough to least identify which bio plant manufactured it and if it is a weapon or an animal." When Mason ran the analysis, the screen listed the pertinent DNA in percentages:

Tetanurae: 18%
Zupaysaurus: 12%
Spinosauridae: 7%
Unknown: 63%
No known bio-lab matched. Please provide a complete sample.

"This is indeed strange. I'm gonna need more time," said Mason.

Sing nodded. "Perhaps, I should leave you to it," As Sing turned to her her men left. "You have my number if you find anything new."

Tina returned. "I took the fossil down the hall and..." She glanced around. "Why does it stink in here?"

Mason didn't respond; her head was down studying the sample of dung. She isolated the unidentified DNA strands for a deeper analysis.

Tina started: "I got a time sample, but I think it's going to be difficult to..." her voice trailed off, seeing that Mason's attention was elsewhere.

As Mason finally sat back, she murmured, "The polypeptides are contaminated with a synthetic bond making them form non-functional proteins." She looked up, suddenly seeing Tina. "What time is it in Germany? Get Christian on the line. Tell him we need to transfer a sample for their analysis." She stared at the screen. "Whatever this was, it was more weapon than animal."

Tina hustled to a station to contact the team in Germany.

In the meantime, Mason stared at the photo Sing had left. She'd never seen photos from an airplane crash site before. She tried to empathize with the victims, but the destruction was so total that she couldn't visualize the experience. There were no bodies, only red stained soil and torn articles of clothing everywhere. The horror didn't seem real. Workers sifted through the wreckage, shoveling dirt that contained traces of human remains. The evidence of the dead was only apparent in the workers faces as any flesh from the passengers had been so thoroughly shredded and pulverized, only the birds and insects were detailed enough to pick it away.

That is where Mason got curious. All of the rescue workers wore protective gear, yet the man Sing had pointed out wore none.

She zoomed in on him.

Mason took notice of his canister briefly, before realizing the man wore no gloves or any other protection beyond regular clothing. He looked very dark, with strong-boned features and a large head. She saw matching tattoos, barely visible over his dark skin, from his neck to his hands.

Tattoos?

Mason grabbed the fossil from Tina. Holding it up to the picture, she squinted, comparing the fossil markings to the man's tattoo.

"Who dug this up?" Mason asked.

"Kara's Geoscience team."

Mason turned the fossil, counting lines and curves etched into the stone. It matched the man's tattoos. "They find any more like it?" Mason asked.

"Well, no. They halted the dig. Who's gonna pay for it."

"And how old did you say this fossil was?" Mason asked.

"66 million years." Tina cleared her throat, "As I was trying to explain, there was so much happening during the K-T extinction; it's going to be difficult to determine what type of plant or animal caused it."

"It may not be either," Mason said.

Tina looked over Mason's shoulder and saw the comparison of the possible fossil with the man's tattoos. She shook her head. "That's impossible."

Mason squeezed her eyes shut. "Behold the impossible and there enters science."

Tina became flustered. "You're suggesting the fossil came from something man made?"

"I am suggesting," Mason answered, "That the first match of this pattern came from something on a man's hand." Mason quickly called the ICP head back. "Hi, Sing. Is there any way I could get a chance to speak with that rescue worker from the picture?"

"You want to speak with one of the heads of the most dangerous terrorist group in the world," Sing chuckled.

"Oh, it's just that rescuer could provide us with some answers."

Sing sighed. "Well, I'm sorry, but you can't talk to him."

"I know there's protocols, but in the interest of science, I just want to know where he got his-"

"Mae, he's dead," Sing answered. "Sorry, I probably should have told you, but I was concerned more with the sample. I think if that man were still alive, we'd all like to ask him a few questions."

Mason bit her lip at the dead end and hung up with a Sing.

"What's she say?" Tina asked

Mason turned to her understudy and answered, "Kara's got more digging to do."

OPEN LETTERS

ADRIAN BLACKWELL TURNED his car sharply into a subdivision, finally slamming on the brakes in a quiet neighborhood. The tire squeals rousted a few birds. He hadn't meant to pump so hard on the brakes, but he was anxious. He ran through a lawn full of weeds, to the front door of an unkempt home. Even when he'd knocked several times, there was no answer. He tried the knob; it was locked. Knowing someone was inside, he ran to the rear of the house, hopped the fence, and entered through the sliding door leading into the kitchen.

A pungent odor singed his nostrils. Adrian fell back on his medical training. Did that aroma carry the scent of decaying flesh? He saw old stale water in the sink. Maggots infested every unwashed bowl, while fungus grew from plates of half-eaten vegetables. In the living room forgotten clothes littered the couch alongside empty liquor bottles.

He headed up the stairs.

Physically, Blackwell looked more like a football player than a medical doctor, and his steps rumbled the vacant stairwell. He was a well-built, dark man, with black hair and brown, piercing eyes. His soft face sat on a muscular neck, and he kept his hair all one length- freshly cut low, and finely edged. Still, in his early thirties, his body had the maturity of experience. He had the awareness and resolution men carry when they are responsible for the lives of others.

Hundreds of open letters were scattered about the game room upstairs. Adrian saw a faint light lining the bathroom door and tiptoed through the sea of papers to rap lightly on the door.

"B.K?" Adrian whispered and poked his head inside after receiving no response. He sighed in relief.

Bishop sat naked in the tub. Despite all of Adrian's clatter, his friend made no response. Bishop just stared down into the water at his hands.

Adrian spoke to Bishop, in an Arabic-inflected African dialect of English. "Did you fill it with your tears?" he asked, nodding at the tub.

Bishop's soft afro curled from its soaking. The water beaded off his muscular shoulders and ran down his tan back.

"There is a saying where I am from: When the tiger is drunk, he forgets about the hunter," Adrian told him. "And you are drunk with rage."

Bishop spoke into the water. "You're not going to bring her back."

"I wasn't trying to bring her back! I wanted to bring you back. Look at you now!" Adrian grabbed a towel off the rack. "The airline won the wrongful death suit because you didn't show up to fight it! Now they have hundreds of lawyers ready to shove it up your ass to make it look like your evac system caused the crash."

With a grimace, Bishop said, "But you will make them pay!"

Adrian realized Bishop was neither listening nor responding to him. Bishop seemed to be aiming his comments into the water like a prayer.

Curious, Adrian stepped forward. "What are you looking at?" Adrian stopped, startled by what he saw in the water. The liquid was blood red. Bishop gripped a sealed canister – the zenomites.

"What have you done?" Adrian demanded.

"A rescue worker found it after the crash," Bishop shook his head slowly.

"Who did you kill? The rescue worker?" Adrian let out in grief. "To spill a man's blood in vengeance scars your soul forever."

"Life has a way of scaring people, revealing both their strength and their suffering," Bishop said. "You should know."

Adrian looked at himself in the bathroom mirror. As a boy, he'd gotten branded with two facial scars in the shape of a 'T'. This had happened during a coming-of-age ritual near a demilitarized buffer zone in Africa.

"I've learned to live with my scars," Adrian admitted, touching his face. "You will never learn to live with your suffering if the world believes you are the terrorist."

"They built a machine to transfer the zenomites to a human host-"

"Listen! The wrongful death charge has to be appealed!"

"Did you hear me?"

"I heard you, but don't you want them to know the truth? You owe it to yourself, and every family member that sends you hate mail?"

Holding up the canister, Bishop shook his head.

"What do you want me to do?" Adrian asked. "They are too dangerous to keep and your parole states you aren't even allowed to touch an electronic device. How will you ever make a machine complex enough to control them?"

"I don't need to," Bishop grimaced. "I stole theirs."

Adrian saw Bishop's eyes were swollen from tears. The man in the tub had rubbed his face so much, it chaffed. The air stunk of filth and pain.

Adrian reached out and took the canister.

BARLOW & KENNEDY was nothing without Nicole. Bishop liquidated the company he built with his wife and infused the zenomites. Julius told his brother Adrian that the operation was as painful as it was pointless. Outside of the sensation of having hypodermic needles shoved into their bone marrow, nothing happened.

The trio couldn't save anything: not the world from terrorist nor Bishop from litigation. Adrian and Julius spent their nights in painful agony from the surgery's aftermath, while their days wasted away by dragging Bishop's depressed body to the courthouse. Mistrial after hung jury, the brothers did more to battle Kennedy's lawsuits then the disgraced engineer cared to do for himself.

As time went on, the childhood friends fell apart. The brothers left Bishop to wallow in despair alone, sitting on the floor, in the upstairs room of his home, surrounded by open letters.

MORAL SLAVERY

IT WAS ALMOST midnight in downtown Austin, and a drunken crowd filled 6th Street. Live music poured from the bars, mixing with the drunken chatter of the people. As a group of medical practitioners stumbled through the crowd, Adrian heard some identifiable notes.

"Coltrane!" he shouted, looking around for his colleagues David and Coleen.

"You wanna take the train?" David shouted back.

"No! Coltrane!" Adrian repeated, almost falling into his friend. "B.K. loved this song!"

"It's jazz!" Coleen shouted.

David's confusion gave way. "Oh! Music! Who is B.K.?"

"Bishop!" Coleen screamed.

"Whatever happened to him?" David asked.

Adrian shrugged.

"Oh come on, don't be like that," David said, with a heated breath of liquor.

The alcohol pushed a wave of depression over Adrian, and he slurred, "The mental exhaustion from helping him battle constant litigation drained me to the point that I no longer wish to speak his name."

"Damn. It's shitty how best friends don't stay that way," David swore.

"Let's go!" Coleen said, pulling them toward the music. They entered the pub, and she headed to the bar.

"Hey, where's your brother?" David asked.

"I don't know! I thought... I thought he was right behind me."

"No, he must've left."

"To where! He doesn't know this city."

"Okay, we - we gotta find him. Can you call him?"

Adrian tried on his cell but failed.

"Maybe he got drunk, and got lost?" David wondered.

"He's no lightweight!"

"Maybe he picked up a girl," David suggested. "Or two if we're lucky!"

"That sounds more like him."

Coleen returned with a tray of tequila shots and beers.

"Shots!" she shouted, handing the drinks out to her friends.

Adrian closed his eyes, took the shot, and let the liquid fire rush down his throat. He listened to the intricate music from the live band. Though the music soothed him, Adrian felt an emptiness he wasn't trying to admit. He painted a hollow smile on his face and chased his shot with more beer. His feet became wobbly, and he felt dizzy. He found it increasingly difficult to stand.

The music stopped.

Adrian opened his eyes and realized he was on stage with the band. He stood there awkwardly with a beer in his hand. As musicians stared, the bar angrily booed this intrusion. Drunken audience members chased Adrian off the stage and out of the bar. On the way out a bouncer yanked the beer bottle from his hand. Everyone was shouting at him, but Adrian couldn't make sense of what they were saying.

In a drunken stupor, he stumbled down the street to the next intersection. He couldn't focus on anything, and people seemed to swirl around him, objects bending eerily in every direction. He felt as if he could see all sides of objects: buildings, cars, signs, and anything else in his line of vision. The ground seemed to give way under him, and as he fell, everything seemed to bend toward him.

A fire truck pulled out of a station and headed down 5th street. The sirens echoed as if they were in an empty room. As he grew frightened and nauseated, panic rose up inside him. Suddenly he saw a toilet. His body materialized in the bathroom of a nearby restaurant. He fell to his knees in front of the bowl and vomited.

Adrian composed himself and got to his feet. He washed his face and left the restaurant. On the corner of 5th and Trinity, he found an empty cab and fell into the back seat.

"Where to?" The cab asked.

"Home," he said weakly. He swiped his driver's license against the display to set the destination.

With a whir, the car started through the city. Adrian's mouth felt dry, and his stomach rumbled. As they passed a pizza parlor, Adrian lifted his head. "I'm hungry," he mumbled.

Once again, the world seemed to swirl around him. The park, roads, and even the interiors of nearby stores surrounded him in a sphere. Suddenly he and his cab teleported into a restaurant, destroying the place. He regained consciousness just long enough to see himself rolled into an ambulance.

Adrian awoke on a hospital bed. He groaned. A ribbon of sun poked through the window blinds and stabbed him in the eyes. He squeezed his eye closed, then opened them to see a shadow eclipsing the sun. It was Julius standing between him and the window.

Adrian groaned, "Thank your big head..."

"You got full smashed last night?" Julius said, with a slimmer and more athletic body than his brother's. "You look like shit."

"Wha... happened to me?" Adrian rolled and saw his face in a mirror. "I look like shit. You look like... wait, you look like you did last night! You didn't come home?"

"You aren't home," Julius said. "And I stayed up all night looking for you. I was worried."

Adrian looked at his brother with supreme disbelief.

Julius corrected himself, "I went to get an Indian dessert."

"Oh, Jules. You mean you went back to see that waitress."

"Where's your car?"

"Wha..? My car?"

"Get up," said Julius. "Take me to the airport, or I'll miss my flight."

"Mmm." Adrian teetered between consciousness and hangover; then he back fell asleep.

"Sometimes I envy you, first brother," Julius said softly. "I have to go. Take care."

As Julius left the room, Adrian was starting to snore. A moment later he suddenly jerked up, wide awake. "Shit!"

He pulled out the IVs, hopped up, threw on his clothes and ran out. The nurses stopped him, and made him check himself out, but as he started again, he glanced outside and saw Julius getting into a cab. Adrian ran out and hopped in after him. "You can't get on a plane."

"Why not?" Julius asked as the cab started moving.

"Last night. It happened!"

Julius eyes got big. "The zenomites?"

"Yes!"

"Wow! What'd it do to you?" Julius asked. "How'd it work?"

"It... I don't know. Have you felt strange lately?"

Julius shrugged. "I feel good and relaxed."

"No, I mean," Adrian paused, trying to get his thoughts in order. "You could kill a lot people if you go on the plane."

"I didn't kill anyone when I flew here."

"Zenomites are dangerous."

"And?"

"And they're inside us!" Adrian shouted.

Julius shook his head. "If I recall, you said it doesn't stay inside our bodies, Doctor!"

"No, no, I don't know."

"You don't know?"

"I based my reasoning on nanomites. I figured they'd be gone in a few days. What B.K made is entirely different... plus it went into our bone marrow."

"Don't remind me!" Julius said with an angry face.

"I think it did something, or has been doing something to us physiologically this whole time."

Julius looked blankly.

Adrian stopped talking and looked at his brother. "Why do you smell like curry? Did you take a shower?"

"Oh, sure, a shower," Julius sneered, then complained. "How am I supposed to take a shower if I'm sitting in a hospital waiting for your ass?"

"You reek!" Adrian shouted. "You filthy swine!"

"I'll take one at the airport!"

"What about at the girl's house? You could have taken a shower at her place. And how the hell does her house smell like a restaurant-" Adrian stopped realizing the truth. "You didn't even leave the restaurant, did you?"

"We barely left the kitchen."

"*Merd*! My favorite restaurant, ruined! I'm never eating there again!"

When the cab pulled in front of the airport, the two got out.

Welcome to the Austin-Bergstrom Airport. Please stand at the doorway a moment while we retrieve your reservation.

As they walked into the airport, the doorway scanned their bodies. Near the entrance, a boarding pass printed out. Julius threw his bag onto a conveyor belt, and the two walked on.

Please proceed to gate E-12. Enjoy your flight... Julius... Blackwell.

As they walked, Adrian continued his lecture: "When we spend our lives looking at the world one way, we forget all the unseen dimensions and energy. The universe is so much more than what we experience with our five senses. When I got drunk and lost control of my senses... the zenomites took over."

A voice called out: *Only passengers allowed beyond this point.*

"So you don't want me to get drunk?" Julius asked.

"Just... try not to experiment on the flight."

The brothers embraced, and Julius kissed Adrian on the cheek before walking off.

"E-Gate is the other way!" Adrian said.

"The Admirals Club is this way," Julius shouted back, "They have showers."

Adrian chuckled and turned, then realized that he had no ID or money for the return cab. When he ran to catch his brother, airport security descended on him.

One of the agents grilled him. "Where are you going so fast? Where's your boarding pass?"

"I don't have one," Adrian said.

"Then why are you trying to board a plane?"

"I wasn't, I just need to get some money."

"Show me ID."

"I didn't bring it."

"You came to an airport without ID? Where's your car?"

"I didn't drive."

"What do you do?"

"I'm a doctor."

"You're a doctor, but you can't afford a car?"

"I have a car; I just didn't..."

"But you didn't drive it here? You came here with no way to get home, and no ticket to get out? Then why are you here?"

"Do you have a bomb on you?" asked the second man.

"No, I do not!"

The agents detected an accent. "Where are you from?"

"Here!"

"Yeah right, where are you really from?"

Adrian hesitated. "Africa."

"What are those markings on your face?"

"Why do you look so nervous?"

"It is very important that you answer this," said the first agent. "What do you know about the Six?"

Adrian looked confused, "The who?"

The agents hustled him into a secured room and locked him in.

"You can't keep me here!" Adrian shouted. "You can't keep...me." He stared at the walls and said to himself: *They can't keep me.*

A COURIER TRANSPORT plane crossed out over the tarmac awaiting clearance for take-off. Adrian appeared in its cargo hold behind a stack of packages. He stood still for a moment, in disbelief at his success. After reading the crates, he realized he was on a DPX transport plane. A courier specializing in transporting goods from defense contractors.

To Adrian, it meant no passengers.

"Yeah!" He chuckled and peeked out behind the crates. He could see to the front of the plane. The pilots taxied to a halt on the runway.

Adrian nodded in self-congratulation and his cheeks burned with excitement he smiled so big. He turned around and fell silent when he saw a man dressed in the DPX's official uniform sitting down behind him.

The two stared at each other.

Adrian froze like a statue not knowing what to say- his mouth hung open. He attempted to speak, and the man looked back at Adrian waiting to hear something that would explain what happened.

Their eyebrows danced back and forth as Adrian raised his and the man scrunched his eyebrows in return. Adrian looked off to the side, and the man looked at Adrian with one eyebrow raised high.

The worker reached down and pulled up a beer can, and held it out to Adrian, who refused, saying, "That's how it happened the first time."

The man shrugged. "When I drink I wake up in strange places too," he said cracking it open. "Didn't know that's how I got there."

Adrian sat down in an empty seat in front of the drinking worker, "Is that... is that legal?"

"Look, I'm gonna need this to believe whatever story you're about to tell me," He said taking a huge swig.

"Well," Adrian added. "It is a long story."

"It's a long flight. When we land, security combs the cargo bay with a fine tooth comb, so you better hope you're a fast runner, because they will skin you alive when they catch you."

"Where are we headed," Adrian looked closely at the man's name tag. "Brad?"

"Vegas," Brad said. "Delivering parts for Uncle Sam?"

Adrian didn't get it.

"Nevada Flight Command?" Brad repeated, took another drink. "You sure you aren't an alien?"

"I'm human. A very confused human right now."

"Yeah, the United States' drone army is controlled by the Flight Command outside of Las Vegas," Brad said, "A place you can make good use of your talents. You could rob a casino in seconds if you can do that trick again."

"I'd rather use it for something a bit nobler than money."

"Noble," Brad laughed, "What's nobler than living lavish in a crooked casino, funded with the money you stole from them?"

"I'm a doctor, not a thief," Adrian smiled.

"You a fighter?" Brad asked, looking him up and down. "You should enlist. Fight in the Six War."

"I've seen the bullets and the lives they take."

"Drones save lives," Brad said, pointing behind Adrian to the crates. "Those are gonna turn the tides."

"So it's true."

"What?"

"Lotus has better tech than the United States does?"

"Whatever. He won't for long."

"That's why he's attracting so many people."

"He's attracting so many people because humans really love raping, pillaging, and killing, a lot more than anyone is willing to admit. Lotus is just giving people an opportunity to do what society suppresses in the back of their mind."

"Not everyone has that kind of mind. At least not those of us who've seen it up close."

Brad pulled out another two beers and tossed one to Adrian. Adrian leaned in to catch it. A stray light beamed across his cheek to reveal one of the 'T' scars on his face. Brad asked, "What have you seen?"

"Massacres, mutilations, death... it really isn't a thing a healthy person can love."

"You've seen it all," Brad noticed. "Were you a slave?"

"What?"

"Whoa, hey, don't get upset, I'm just saying. Slavery is a thing," Brad said. "The Earth has always had quite a strange relationship with slavery."

"By strange you mean encourage?"

"Not encourage. Codependent, if I were to classify it," Brad said. "We have a codependent relationship with slavery."

"That's why we divorced ourselves from it."

"Yeah, but we still pay alimony, until we decide to remarry sometime in the future. History always repeats itself, doesn't it? It's not like we woke up ten thousand years ago, and suddenly the concept of slavery was born. It's gotta be part of some physical, universal law..."

"Slavery is a universal law?"

"Yeah," Brad claimed. "Because power is a universal law. In order to reach the top of the stairway, you need a step to put your foot on. Without a step, you have no means of attaining a higher level. The step is your slave, so to speak, as it provides a means for you to attain a higher state of being. Sometimes it's the animals we eat or the trees we cut down. Sometimes it's the people who live along side us that are there to help us, as a whole, attain a higher purpose. Fighting slavery is fighting against nature itself."

"You suggest certain people recognize their place and choose to help the human race thrive by being a stepping stone for others?"

"Yes! You get it. I'm glad I can talk to you about this without you getting upset!"

"If they have a choice, then it isn't slavery."

"You're missing the point. You're arguing a case for morality when it is nothing more than a feel-good concept we invented. Morality doesn't exist, only power," Brad nodded. "The ancient world knew it to be true. When Rome was powerful, all other civilizations contributed to their advancement. When the Assyrian empire ruled, all other civilization would have to offer tribute, or support the Assyrian prosperity or be annihilated."

"We lost an immeasurable wealth of knowledge due to indiscriminate slaughter like that. There are civilizations we will never know existed, and there are troves of knowledge and artifacts forever lost because of it. That lack of morality has hurt us; we would be further along had they dropped their imperialistic attitudes and worked together."

"For what? Those people were barbarians, inferior, and did not use whatever knowledge they had to better the superior human race. They had to be slaves, or be erased from all history."

"I argue it would be more efficient to share the knowledge, and work together. Barbaric conditions and enslavement kept human society from reaching these higher steps you claim justify mass slaughter," Adrian spoke. "It took us thousands of years to sail across the ocean, yet it only took us eight to get to the moon."

"The point is, we love killing, pillaging, and doing all that stuff you say a healthy person shouldn't love because we desire power. Our thirst for power supersedes our moral compass."

"Our thirst for power is wasted without it."

"I would like to agree with you my friend, but I'm afraid, when this plane lands, you'll realize that your precious morality demands you abide by at least one form of slavery we have yet to abolish – prison," Brad told him, and then asked. "Will you abide to morality, or to power?"

AN ALARM BLASTED at the DPX station in the airport. Armed personnel and security got to their feet and started locking down the hangar area. Adrian appeared inside of a bathroom, disoriented, he stumbled into a wall and hit his toe.

Where are my shoes?

Adrian hopped out of the bathroom on one foot and heard footsteps chasing down the hallway. He ran. Turning corner after corner, he heard footsteps in front and back of him. He gathered his thoughts for a jump, and he wound up on the street in the city. He ran down the sidewalk.

His feet hurt from running barefoot on concrete. He stopped at an import car dealer. Looking in the wide windows, he saw the luxury cars–forbidden toys of the super-rich. As he teleported inside, he felt the dominating power that goes with breaking barriers. He grabbed the keys to a red Ferrari and ran his fingers along the chassis. The mechanical beast faded, turned translucent, and he teleported it into the street. Hopping in, he sped off, flooring it.

Las Vegas Highway Safety alerted the police. Robotic cycles chased him down. The drones forced him off the road; he lost control, and the car flipped over. It exploded into flames. The fire department arrived and put it out, but they never found a body.

Adrian sat down in dried out weeds a distance outside of the city and pondered how to fix it all.

A voice came from behind him: "Dr. Blackwell?"

Adrian turned and looked.

"I'm Omar Jacobs, operations director for the International Counter-Terrorism Police," The man said.

"Is the ICP putting me under arrest?"

"After what you did at the Austin airport? That shouldn't surprise you," Omar said, then shook his head. "I'd love to brag that we are that efficient, but as much as I hate to admit it, I was already keeping an eye on you for a mutual friend."

Adrian looked him up and down. Omar Jacobs was a thin, cream-skinned man, covered from head to toe in tattoos. His ink displayed a variety of skulls, snakes, and flags covered in revolutionary quotes. He had a shaved head with both ears liberally pierced.

Adrian stood up.

Omar said, "We have a need for someone with your talents."

"What sort of need?" Adrian asked.

Omar looked at him barefoot, in the grass, and asked, "What do you know about the Six?"

"IT'S BEEN MONTHS since we sent you this sample, and we haven't gotten any further in determining what it is," Mason complained to the video conference line. "The biochemical properties assure me this came out of an animal!"

"Yes, but," The man on the other end said, "This is not what you call, a complete specimen, though."

"Don't give me that, Christian."

"What you sent amounts to a failed stew of DNA. It's like someone threw metal together, and you are asking us what the make and model of the car was."

Mason's personal phone buzzed, and she silenced it.

The man continued, "Sure, it has some traces of cloning, but that's probably because dinosaurs roamed the area and contaminated it."

"So it's a chemical weapon?"

"I didn't say that."

"It has to be something."

"No, it really doesn't. We've even reported it to the authorities, who've scanned the area and haven't reported back any unusual activity in that area. This could be a collection of a number of things. The least of which is a living dinosaur."

"What about the sheep sample?"

"I'm sorry?"

"North Africa herders reported several maulings. I sent samples of the bite and slash marks on the sheep carcass."

"Dr. Kinoah, are you really going to send us every animal that dies, and every drop of poop it makes? What is this fascination? The Harold Amos Lab has never asked us for such outrageous favors before. What do they want with the findings?"

"It isn't for the Harold Amos; it's a third party."

"Perhaps you'd be willing to share a bit more on this third party?"

Mason was quiet.

The man on the teleconference asked again, "Perhaps you would explain your own fascination?"

Mason shook her head. "I don't know what it is, and not knowing bothers me. We have an animal who is made up of unknown DNA, and I can't accept that."

"You realize dinosaurs are in a very controlled space in the Congo, they mate all the time. Perhaps new species are developing as we speak. Besides what's the worse that you think will happen? That dinosaurs will rule the Earth again?" The man laughed. "A paleontologist wet dream, and worse nightmare."

Mason turned when she thought she heard something topple over in the back of the lab.

"Is everything all right over there?"

Turning her attention back to the teleprompter, she answered, "Yeah, I think some of my plants are getting fidgety."

"You are a fascinating scientist, and your work on plants is amazing. You have my word; we will run the numbers again. What time is it where you are? We will have our final report sent to you first thing in the morning."

"I look forward to it," Mason said, disconnecting the line.

She went to check her missed call and heard the noise again.

Something definitely moved in the back.

She set down her phone and walked toward the end of the lab, making a right at the wall toward the cage opening. Dark heat came out of the large plant nursery behind it.

She punched in a code on the wall to close the gated partition and breathed easy. She gathered her belongings at her desk and as she reached for her keys her phone rang again.

"Hey, Mason," A dreary female voice spoke. "I figured you'd still be at work."

"Hi Kara, I'm just setting up to leave."

"I got your message about the fossil, and it's a bit too early to tell."

"But it doesn't make sense. What the Geo's once thought was a piece of fulgurite, turned out to be an entire, intact, monumental fossil. The paleontologist dig team has uncovered 80% of the artifact, and it looks like a mask!"

"That's why I say it's too early to determine what it is. It could very well be a molted shell."

"A molted shell... with artistic designs?"

"The latest assumption we have is that ancient civilizations found Marginocephalia fossils and constructed ceremonial art commemorating what they saw."

"Kara, I had that fossil dated. It is well over sixty-six million years old."

"We are well aware of the date discrepancy..."

"Discrepancy? If you put sixty-six million years on a timeline, the entire human history would barely be a dot on the paper. It is a huge mistake to assume that this is simply some ceremonial piece made by ancient man when it has military grade durability made with an intense heat source!"

"There is no other reasonable conclusion! Dinosaurs had neither the mental capacity nor dexterity to design military garments for their bodies. As they had no need to do so!"

"They might not need it, but someone else would have. Look, this fossil exists. Point blank, it's here, and a piece of it is in my hand. It's real. Whether or not you can fit a believable story for why it exist should not be relevant. Ancient civilizations did things like this all the time.

Humans trained elephants and horses as beast of war and made armor for them. That's what this looks like! This is decorated armor to charge a beast into war."

"There were no elephants or horses sixty-six million years ago, Mae! As you pointed out, there were no humans either. So, no one existed who would want to put armor on a ceratopsid, much less manufacture the materials to..."

"Listen..."

"Even if, by some strange reasoning we could imagine they did... who would they be fighting? Something is inherently flawed about your argument if you want to claim both the design of an armor without the designer's existence."

Mason sighed. "I admit there are flaws to both of our arguments. I'm merely suggesting we consider alternate and more open minded theories. Besides me, did you tell anyone?"

"Of course not!"

"Kara, you have to tell this to-"

"I don't have to do anything! I'm not about to stick my neck out and ruin my professional career over some wild idea that sounds like it came out of a tin foil gift shop!"

"Fine! I get it."

"You really have some nerve. You are the expert on plants, and no one better dare say a thing to the great Mason, or you will read them left and right about how you know your shit."

"Okay!"

"Yet, you are all up in my field, trying to tell me what I should and should not be seeing."

"You're right!" Mason conceded. "Professionally, I was out of line, and for that, I apologize."

"And personally?"

Mason heard something in the back of the lab fall on the ground. Her heart skipped a beat.

"Mason? Everything cool?"

Mason looked at the entrance, and the door's security still showed locked. She thought for a moment, and said, "Yes, my wayward plants knocked something over. I need to secure it before I have to deal with a mess in the morning."

"Sure, well, I'll let you know what else I find, but for now, don't get ahead of me on this."

"Thanks. Have a good evening."

Mason crept back toward the lab's end, and to the left, a lab mouse scurried out from under a broken cage.

"What the freak!" Mason shrieked.

She took a moment to catch her breath and then knelt down to pick the cage up and retrieve the animal. It ran away from her and into the supply room – whose door was cracked open. Mason stood up and dropped the broken cage. She took a step back. When she turned to run toward the entrance, she saw a man breathing hard, and sweating as he was bent over one of the lab tables.

She shouted, "Who are you?" and quickly walked foward.

"Please!" He mumbled, barely standing.

"What are you doing here? What do you want? I'm calling the police," Mason threatened.

"Good!" The man mumbled. "They need to shoot these plants!"

"What did you say?"

"Your plants are homicidal!"

"They are not!"

"And evil!" He said gripping his arm.

Mason gasped, "Humans are evil!"

The man barely had a response, knocking equipment off the table trying to stay standing.

"Are you hurt? You're hurt! Oh god, were you in the nursery?" She asked, grabbing medical supplies out of the cabinets.

She took the man to her station and quickly injected a serum into him than she began wrapping his arms.

"Are you – are we melting?" The man asked, with a serious tone, but vacant eyes. His head wobbled from a combination of the injected drugs and reeling trauma.

"You don't belong here," Mason warned. "This lab is a very dangerous place."

"My head is spinning."

"Well, powerful toxins require a powerful antidote," She said. "How'd you get in here, anyway?"

"What? Oh. No wonder," He said, with a nonsensible draw to his voice. "I got in through the door."

"What?"

"Huh?"

"You're not making any sense," Mason said.

"So are you vegan?" He asked.

"I'm not having this conversation."

"Why are you vegans so stuck up?" He asked, "Because clearly, your plants eat meat!"

"Clearly, you don't know how to read. The signs say 'Do Not Enter'," Mason told him. "Why are you here?

"To see the plants."

Mason chuckled, "So you were stupid even before I injected this antidote into you? The Harold Amos is not visitation center."

"Power plants."

"Sorry to burst your bubble, but there are no power plants here."

The man closed his eyes and attempted to balance himself from falling off the chair. "They're gonna destroy the world."

Mason chuckled nervously midway through completing her dressing. "How is clean energy gonna destroy the world?"

"No, no... yes... because it's energy!" The man said, opening his eyes. "Because of Lotus."

Mason froze at the name, slowly reaching back for her phone. He grabbed her hand tightly and pulled her phone from her hands saying, "I can't let him have it."

Mason swung at him, and hit him in the face and then repeatedly jammed her keys into his skin, cutting him.

"What is this medicine you gave me? Cuz I barely felt that," He told her. "Give me the power plant designs, and I will go!"

"No!" Mason struggled to get away, and he struck her.

"I'm not trying to hurt- dammit why won't you fucking listen! Sit still!"

Mason's hands trembled after he slammed her on the lab table. She remained motionless, not sure what to do, and after a few seconds, the man went berserk. He threw tables, plants, and devices over the room and repeatedly smashed a metal tray on the table until it was warped beyond comprehension.

Mason complied. She pulled up diagrams on a nearby computer and showed him the files he asked for.

"These aren't it!"

"This is a power plant!"

"No, no," The man said frustrated. "It's not here, is it? You – your laptop is at home. Isn't it? Let's go."

He dragged Mason out of the lab, while she continued hitting him, but he pulled her like a rag doll, and the heavy security doors closed shut behind them.

"Stop!" She shouted, "I have to lock up, or some other idiot like you will get hurt by the plants."

She tried to use her key on the scanner, and quickly her hand darted out toward the emergency button. The man slapped her hand, and the keys flew away.

"If you set off an alarm, I'll kill you!"

She hobbled outside in a rush and got into her car.

"Take us to your home," He demanded.

Mason pressed the button on her car, and it started up.

"Who do you work for?" She asked.

"For a dead man."

Mason tried to compose her shaky hands, but her voice still trembled under the guise of control. "Power plants are pretty well documented. You can make them yourself. The tutorials are on the internet. I don't have anything no other scientist has..."

"Shut up! Yes, you do!" He said. "Nothing delivers the amount power like the ones you are making. If he gets them, we're finished. I know you think I'm a bad guy for this, but... I'm really a hero. I'm trying to keep you from-"

Mason's phone rang. She looked over at his hands – he was still holding her phone.

"Forget about it," Her kidnapper instructed.

Mason's hand twitched, and she snatched the phone quickly from his hand to scream for help. The two wrestled with the phone as it rang, and Mason screamed as the car swerved across the road.

The man overpowered her and tossed the phone backward.

He grabbed her by the neck to push her face into the window while accessing her control panel and directed the car to go "Home." The car automatically realigned itself with the road and drove on.

They arrived at her house, and she stayed still, refusing to move. The man reached over and grabbed her. He dragged her out of the car from the passenger side, and with an arm around her neck, dragged her to the front door. It opened for her.

"Quit stalling!" He shouted.

"Get out of my house!" Mason screamed as she ran away.

The man chased her through the house to her room. He kicked the door in and stormed into the dark. "Why won't you do as I tell you! Dammit!"

He slapped her and pulled her up off the ground. Her shirt tore under his aggression. He lifted her up high above his head and slammed her to the floor.

Mason lied motionless. Her head rang with pain.

The man ripped her clothes off and threw her to the bed.

She saw stars from her head being slammed into the ground. In the darkness, she choked and writhed as powerful hands squeezed her neck. He flipped her and pushed her face into the mattress. She felt hands sliding over her flesh, and then a heavy body crushed her. Her attacker violated her.

ADRIAN SPED DOWN the streets of Washington, D.C. The night felt strange.

Next to him lay a tablet with strange writing on it, and his phone received a call from a strange number. He answered.

It was his brother.

"Where are you calling me from?" Adrian asked.

"Honestly, I don't know right now," Julius responded

"You don't know where you are?"

"No, I – I have no idea where in this entire world... I am. How about you?"

"You stupid, you know that?" Adrian told him. "I'm back in D.C now; ICP had me on another one of their special missions. It was just really strange."

"Yeah?"

Adrian looked down at the tablet. "I had to... acquire something."

"You're getting better at that it seems. What's it like? Ya know, when it happens?"

Adrian thought about it. "Nauseating. It's like I'm in a bubble, with an infinite set of rooms, and the place I think about comes to me, and then suddenly I'm there. It feels like being on every ride in the amusement park at once. It's great, and horrible all at once – I don't like doing it on a full stomach."

"I know what you mean."

"What? No!"

"Yup."

"How? What happened?"

"I got sent back to the dig site."

"Shit."

"Yeah, just my luck. The paleo guys have it almost dug up now. Looks like a mask, but, for a dinosaur. It's weird. Well the winds came, and they covered it up so the dust wouldn't ruin the dig. The clamps broke, and they left to get more. So I sat on top of the covers so it wouldn't blow away while they were gone. The wind was strong, and I got bored sitting... waiting for them to come back, and after a while, I noticed the horizon was slanted."

"Wait, say that again. Slanted?"

"Yes! It's supposed to be straight; I was like yo, this is trippy, the horizon was at a diagonal, and I look down and realize that I'm floating in the air."

"Whoa."

"It was cool at first; I thought the wind was lifting me up until I realized that my body had dematerialized. So I wasn't really floating in the air, the Earth was just rotating away from me."

"The fuck!"

"Is exactly what I screamed. I panicked, and the Earth kept moving away. I was so high in the sky, I turned and looked and thought sure I would die in outer space! I finally figured it out and materialized back solid, and fucking... fell!"

"Damn!"

"Like a rock! So I had moments to figure out how to phase again before I splattered on the ground, and then it got worse. I phase, fell through the ground, and saw nothing but black, and rocks. I didn't know which way was up and was scared I was gonna go to the center of the Earth. I ended up at the bottom of a lake, and then hours later on dry land," Julius explained. "So when I tell you, I don't have a clue where on Earth I am... I don't have a clue!"

"So, you need me to scoop you up?"

"I'll figure something out. I just wanna keep my feet on the ground for now. What about you? You hear from ole' girl?"

"Nah, I'm heading her way right now."

"I think you missed your chance."

"Don't curse me. You don't know that."

"Yes, I do. She gave you the look, but that 'look' is usually temporary, that means she was ready then, at that moment, but you didn't jump on it."

"I'm not like you."

"That's cool, but I'm just saying, you missed your chance."

"If she was down for me once, why can't she be again? I don't know. Maybe you're right; I lost my chance to get with her, but then now it left an ache in my heart that constantly tells me she was the one that got away. Maybe she'll reject me this time, but that's so much better than living with regret."

"Good luck."

"Nice. I'm here. Later."

Adrian got out of his car and walked around the Harold Amos building searching for her office.

He rehearsed it in his mind what to say, but all the office doors were locked. The building appeared empty as he walked through. Adrian turned to leave and noticed a set of keys on the ground. He picked them up and looked them over. There was a "Plant Goddess" key tag with a picture of a flower petal in the shape of a heart attached to it.

"Mason?"

He thought for a moment and reasoned Mason drove off without her keys. Quickly changing plans, he picked up his phone and called Mason instead, but there was no answer. Knowing she wouldn't be able to start her car again without them, he drove to her house. The night was quiet, and he saw her car parked out in the street.

He went to the front door, and raised his hand to knock but, feeling weird; he stayed his hand.

"This is awkward," He said to himself and began rehearsing how he would explain to her how he knew where she lived- and why he was there so late at night. He paced around trying to put it together but couldn't figure a smooth way to explain it without sounding like a stalker.

He turned and walked away from the house and opened her car door to peer inside. He put the keys in the center console. Before returning to his car, he turned back to look at the house. "She'll find them."

MASON LAID ON her bed frozen in horror. Pain branched out from her center through her body paralyzing her with fear. Her attacker pushed himself into her repeatedly.

Mason squeezed her eyes tight, trying to bear through the pain. Her eyeballs fell so much pressure it forced tears from the cracks.

She wished it would end quickly, but Mason couldn't passively hold in her disgust. She yelled a blood curling scream and threw her arms backward trying to hit her attacker.

Suddenly, the weight on top of her doubled. She looked over her shoulder, and, in the darkness, she saw two men instead of the one.

Mason gasped.

Then they both vanished in an instant.

A CAMERA BEEP echoed in a hollow room, as the lens snapped a shot. An incandescent flash burned Mason's eyes.

"Turn to the left please."

The photographer paced around, eyeing Mason's naked body. An examiner pushed her hair up with white-gloved fingers, revealing bruises on the back of her neck that hid in the camouflage of her dark skin tone. The examiner pointed; the photographer shot.

They both examined her thoroughly. As a red dot danced, then settled on her private parts, the examiner used it to line up his ruler. The camera beeped, followed by a burst of flashes. Mason shuddered at each one.

"Take a seat please."

Mason walked across the cold floor, her shivering arms crossed over her bosom. She sat on a papered medical bench. The examiner touched Mason's knees, and lightly pushed her legs open to swab out her genitals. Mason looked off to the side and felt the tingly sensation of the material rotating inside of her. The examiner nodded to the photographer and held the lips of her vagina open. The photographer kneeled between her legs and got a few more shots. After dropping each swab sample into a bag and marking it, they both left.

Next to Mason sat a cup of water, a pill for emergency contraception, and a release form should she chose to take it. With a trembling hand, she picked up the pill and swallowed it down with a gulp of water. With the back of her arm, she wiped water residue from her mouth.

Two officers arrived and took her to a quiet room. Mason sat, covered herself in a medical gown, and watched them situate their paperwork. Mason's haggard face revealed exhaustion. She looked at the two women and waited for her cue.

"I'm Detective Kelly Taferty," said the older woman, "And this is Deputy Anna Melnikova. First I'd like to say that you have our deep condolences. We're sorry you went through this, but in order to get to the bottom of it, we have to be as thorough as possible. So please be detailed in your answers. If you don't wish to answer a question, just let us know, okay?"

Mason nodded.

Kelly adopted a neutral demeanor, neither helpful nor abusive. She glanced over the paperwork, sighed and looked up. "Well, we have good news."

Mason's tired eyes lit up.

"The blood test came back negative for all harmful pathogens, and virus. You didn't catch anything from the incident. Also, your bruises are quite superficial, and will heal within the week," Kelly said. "You suffered a slight concussion, and the doctors have prescribed medicine to alleviate the pain as you heal."

Then there was silence. Mason leaned forward. The detective shuffled in the chair and scratched the side of her head.

Mason looked back and forth from the officer to the detective, and she asked, "Who... who was it?"

"Well, we have your description of the man, and he left quite a trail of physical evidence in your home. After we gain access to your lab, I'm sure there maybe even more evidence we can use to determine who it was."

Mason looked confused.

Kelly continued, "He touched your car. There shouldn't be very many finger prints on your car, so hopefully we can pull something from that as well."

"I don't understand what do you mean by any of this? I think DNA alone should... should end any debate, right? I mean, it only takes a few minutes."

Kelly took a deep breath. "Dr. Kinoah, there was no DNA."

"What?"

"We have lots of fibers, and a lot of data to pour over leading up to your home, but the lab tests found no foreign DNA on or in your body," Kelly explained. "There is no evidence that anyone touched you, but yourself."

"T-th-they swabbed me, and... and shaved me."

"No hair follicles, no skin... no semen."

"How's that possible?" Mason asked, bewildered.

"We were hoping you could tell us."

Mason was silent.

"Doctor?"

"You... you think I made this up?"

"We believe you Dr. Kinoah," Kelly explained. "We just can't find any physical evidence that anyone touched you tonight, and you told the officers that the men just 'disappeared.' That doesn't help us make a case against anyone."

"I'm just telling you what happened. How can I make you believe me?" Mason asked.

"Doctor, you certainly must understand our need for evidence. We can believe you, but if, we have no evidence that your attacker sexually assaulted you. We need to determine how to classify this case you are bringing to us. Someone rapes you, and not only does he disappear, but he takes every hair, skin cell, semen stain, and fiber with him. That's a hard case to type up, Dr. Kinoah."

"You mentioned he was after your plant designs? Is there anyone who'd want those?"

"He was, he was crazy, I don't even know if he knew what he was talking about!" Mason cried. "I don't have any designs!"

"Maybe, but he thinks you do," Detective Kelly nodded her head in sympathy. "I think we still might have a chance to catch him."

WHEN MASON GOT back to her house, she couldn't sleep. She tossed fitfully, then sat up, terrified. She got a long sharp knife from the kitchen and set it by her bedside. She sat there trembling, with all of the lights on. She stared at the door until morning came and brightened everything around her.

ADRIAN LOST IT. He teleported to a junkyard near Mason's home. He tried to interrogate the man responsible for hurting her, but his words were silenced by the intense hatred.

Adrian beat the man and tore his limbs off with various tools. He wanted to know who the man worked for, but the vision of him on top of Mason shut all thought process down until Adrian killed him.

Adrian drove home angry. He looked in the mirror, but he didn't recognize himself. All he saw was his facial scars. Each cheekbone displayed the wounds from of his rite of passage. Each 'T' reminded him of tribal warfare, his parent's death from pillaging, and his grandmother's daring escape. The scars reminded him of persecution.

They reminded him of evil.

He recalled how they held his boyish head back and pierced his face with a hot glowing knife. He heard chanting and saw people in mask dancing around him. The blade had scraped across his cheeks, slicing and sizzling as he screamed.

What were they chanting?

He saw himself in a black room with a door partially opened at the far end. A light broke through the crack, and constantly changed colors. The chatting echoed louder.

Adrian splashed his face with cold water so his mind would snap back to reality.

Adrian paced around his home and then he called Omar and asked, "What's so special about Mason?"

"What do you mean?" Omar asked.

"I mean how valuable are her experiments to ICP? What does she know?"

"Nothing. She's more of a consultant than a member," Omar said, and then asked, "Why?"

"I just..."

"Do you know what happened to her tonight?"

Adrian froze. He didn't know how to respond to knowing something he shouldn't know. "Tonight?"

"Adrian, someone broke into her home, attacked her sexually," Omar said, "And...disappeared."

Adrian felt a sinking feeling in his stomach. "Omar..."

Omar cut him off. "Why are you asking about Mason? Seems odd timing you are asking about her. Oh, did I mention that her attacker disappeared? That kinda training sounds really familiar," Omar accused. "What'd you get into tonight after your mission?"

"Nothing! I didn't know that happened to Mason until you just said it!"

"Don't fucking lie to me! You think I can't track where you go?" Omar screamed. "You stay away from her!"

"It wasn't me!"

"If you want to abuse your power, go back to Vegas where I found you!"

"Omar!"

"This is the last we will talk about it."

Omar hung up, and Adrian punched his mirror. The glass shattered, and the wounds on his knuckles healed.

"I'll stay away!" Adrian screamed to the shattered reflection of himself. "She dies, it's on you! It's on you!"

Adrian retreated to the recesses of his home and sat in the dark, brooding to his diary – jittery at his actions, unable to peel the mental image of what he saw from his mind. Using a flashlight, he opened to a blank page, and wrote:

The rapier. It wields itself.

Studiously, I have mastered it.

To the hilt, I have thrust it.

My arm remains stretched out.

I cannot break ground.

The scabbard is empty.

The rapier. It wields itself

Adrian gritted his teeth defiantly and stormed out of his house, mounted his car, and peeled off down the road to Mason's during the night. Everything was quiet.

He teleported himself inside. There sat Mason, in her bed, upright with a knife loosely in her grasp. She was sleep. Careful not to touch anything, he used the edge of his phone to move the sharp tip of the knife away from her body. He stood there for several moments and looked around.

"They want me to stay away," He whispered.

Mason woke up; she heard someone in the room, and her heart raced. She clutched her kitchen knife, turned and swiped into the air, but no one was there.

A THOUSAND WORDS

MASON LOOKED AROUND her bedroom, and it took her a moment to realize she was still awake. There was a pulsating throb around her head, and even though her eyes hurt, they still detected a blinking light in her peripheral vision. She reached for her phone.

Twenty-four missed calls.

Mason hadn't slept in the three days following her attack, neither could she remember what she did during that time. Her laptop was on the floor with no power.

I haven't been to work.

After pacing around her room with a brush in her hand for a few minutes, Mason walked down to the kitchen, pulled out some milk, bread, and cheese and set it on the counter while she tugged aimlessly at her hair; then she went back to her room. There Mason stood for a moment - forgetting why she walked in there. Not to waste the trip, she put on some clothes, picked up her phone and laptop, and left to go to work. Everything she pulled out of the fridge was still sitting on the counter top.

The traffic along the Hwy 29 seemed light, but she squinted her eyes trying to remember how to get on 395. Glancing at her map, she realized she passed her exit and was going the wrong way. Mason commanded her car to take her to work, and it went back around East to the Harold Amos. While it drove, she called her mother.

Voicemail.

With a raspy voice, Mason said, "Hey, mom. Thanks for the card. I got the money; I told you I didn't need you to pay me back. Just let me know if you need anything. Love you."

Mason sat in the parking lot outside of the lab and looked at the security guard pacing in front of the doorway.

Her drowsy eyes blinked, and she sighed.

The lab was full of chatter, yet none of it made sense to Mason. She aimlessly moved lab samples across the room. When she sat them down, she caught a glimpse of herself in the mirror to see a dark purple swelling developing under her eye. Her dark skin that once showed a chocolate color seemed gray. Lightly, she touched her faced, and her intern came up and startled her.

"Did you see what Christian sent?" Tina asked.

"Ah! Uh, no? What did he send?" asked Mason with puffy eyes. Everything smelled like copper to her.

Tina walked to the terminal and began accessing Christian's report. "Christian sequenced the DNA strands you sent him to isolate the synthetic bonds contaminating the nucleotides. Then he created an algorithm to ignore all the synthetic bonded material."

Paula, another worker, walked up to Tina's display. "Synthetic bonded what?"

"I think he's bullshitting us," April, Mason's partner, said to Paula. "What does he consider synthetic DNA?"

The intern presented the data findings: "He said he realized this strand was similar to the structures that enable frogs to secrete poison from their skin. So he made algorithmic adjustments with the other unknown strands," Tina reported. "After he got a working sequence, he even instructed the system to recreate what the creature looked like."

"What it looks like?" April asked. "As in, using the DNA we have a picture of the dinosaur?"

Tina opened the sketch file.

April noticed Mason hadn't said a word the whole time, and Mason's head hung low. "You all right, hun? You look sick?" April asked.

"I knew it! He's full of shit!" Paula shouted out loud to the others as soon as she saw the image. April rushed over to have a look.

"Are you kidding me? They're making fun of us. Why are they so immature?" April wondered.

"Because they think it's funny," Paula said, chastising Christian's digital reconstruction of the animal. "We'll get them back."

Tina shrugged, looking sideways at the picture- a hybrid dinosaur with human-like features. "It's a clever drawing."

"Belongs in a comic book. I knew he wasn't serious," Paula huffed.

"So what's that mean," Tina was confused. "It's not an animal?"

"It means he's patronizing us. We kept insisting it was a dinosaur, so he sequenced the DNA until he got something to shut us up." Paula examined the picture further. "That's not even a dinosaur; that's a... I don't know what that is."

Tina left the station to tend to her routine, and she emptied out a large crate filled with potted plants.

Mason couldn't muster the energy to argue, so she found solace in the restroom where she was only accompanied by the sound of a leaky faucet.

She gripped the sink and hung her head. The sound of dripping water resonated in her mind. The paint on her fingernails looked brittle and chipped, and her wild hair looked a mess. Finally, the breaths came easily. Her head drooped, and she almost fell asleep where she stood as the rhythm each droplet made plopping on the ceramic hypnotized her.

"What's that noise?" she cried, hearing louder popping sounds from outside the restroom.

From the adjacent room, she identified screams and...

Gunfire?

When she peeked out the door, armed mercenaries were shooting up everything in the lab. She saw Tina jump inside an empty crate to hide while witnessing Paula's face split open from bullets. Mason nudged the door shut, fell to the floor, and crawled about looking for a hiding place.

After she stuffed herself behind a toilet, the gunfire and screams abruptly ended. As her heart beat wildly, she heard footsteps getting closer to the door. She silently got up and edged toward the entrance of the restroom.

A hand touched the door. It creaked open. Mason bolted out. She knocked the invader backward and ran through the lab screaming at the top of her lungs. Another hand snatched her by the neck and slammed her to the ground.

The armed mercenaries then killed everyone in the lab, except for Mason, yet their dominate reign was short lived. ICP officers stormed the building right behind them and barged into the microbiology room. They kept low, with their guns hot. Shots rang out, and Mason covered her face as bullets shredded the area around her.

The man pinning her down shot back, but the ICP officers stood behind robotic drones that functioned as shields, allowing them to mow down the mercenaries efficiently. The bodies of the terrorist fell to the floor as their return fire merely ricocheted off the robotic protection. ICP quickly gained ground and pushed the armed terrorist back.

A gust of air blew into the room, and with it, insect drones ambushed the police. The insects honed in on the officers and swarmed on them- feasting ravenously. The ICP tried to shoot back, but there was too many, and each insect they shot self-destructed and exploded into tiny shrapnel. The officers eventually fell to the ground, screaming, and rolling in their own blood as the insects tore flesh from their bodies.

The surviving terrorist found Mason hiding and went to snatch her. Mason grabbed a metal tray and threw it at one of them. He swatted it away. She kept grabbing things and throwing them.

"Get her!" they shouted.

Mason ran, slammed into a wall, pushed herself toward the gated nursery, scanned her badge to run inside. She pulled her lab coat over her head and covered herself as she curled tightly on the floor.

Chasing after her, the invaders inadvertently incited the plants inside the secure nursery. The vines rustled. Long stems grabbed the men, and twisted thorns pierced their veins. The plants sensed Mason and went to grab her as well but stopped when they tasted the lining of her lab coat.

More vines from the plants snatched everyone coming near them. As for Mason, the vines reached out but didn't hurt her as she cowered under her lab coat.

As the ruckus ended, the plants covered Mason's body in a thick cocoon of bark. She worked to control her breathing. That's when she heard a strange voice. "Where is she?"

She peeked through her coat, and beyond the vines, she saw the man who was speaking. The same man Sing had warned her about: "Lotus?"

A mercenary pointed at Mason's cocoon and reported, "Target is secure."

"Good," Lotus smiled. "Now go and get her."

"Sir, we can't, not with the plants in the way."

Lotus grabbed the man's neck. "Then how is she secure?" He pushed the soldier into a crop of plants that instantly coiled around him and devoured him.

"What... why are you...?" Mason said, frightened.

"I'm feeding your plants."

Mason noticed Jalyn, one of the Six, approach Lotus with a briefcase. Jalyn opened the case, and Lotus reached inside to pull out a small container. A panic of being helpless overcame her.

"It's fine," Lotus assured Mason. "They're just insects."

Mason watched as Lotus opened the container, and real bugs flew out. They settled on the plants around her and began eating them.

Lotus spoke.

"The problem with us humans is that we lack spatial reasoning. We can't truly conceptualize time. We can only think in the present because we cannot feel the past, and the future cannot etch itself into our minds. We are forged by the now, and once it is gone, the person we were is no more. What I mean to say is, everything that happens to you now, will be the past of your future."

As the insects chewed through the plants, they cleared a path to Mason. Lotus walked toward her, saying: "Insects were here long before we were, and when we die, they'll still be here picking the flesh from our bones. That future may come to pass sooner rather than later."

As Lotus knelt next to her Mason emerged from under her lab coat. "Why are you doing this?" she asked weakly.

Lotus caressed her face. "You don't look well. Let's get you cared for." He stood up and turned to his troops. "Take her."

"Yes, Mr. Daniels."

As Lotus walked away from the nursery and back up through the lab, he noticed several potted plants scattered across the floor near a large crate. It was far too conspicuous not to capture his attention. A container large enough for someone to hide in that miraculously had been emptied of its contents. Even a child would be keen enough to find it. Lotus tiptoed toward the crate wondering what play thing he would find cowering in the dark. He reached forward to open it.

The computer image Christian sent was still open on the nearby display, and as enticing as the crate was – the picture firmly grabbed his attention and flooded him with dread. Lotus turned toward the image and curiously looked at the drawing of the sequenced human-dinosaur hybrid on the screen. The picture spoke a thousand words. He reached over the controls and clicked curiously through the data - the DNA sequences, the notes, and returned to view the picture.

The picture seemed crude as it was merely a digital sketch a computer made based on DNA alone. Lotus was not quite impressed with the work of art, but it did, nonetheless, move him. He heard his guards coming back around, bringing Mason in with them. Lotus quickly hit delete on Christian's data. The screen cleared, and Lotus walked away.

Heart and Home

ADRIAN ARRIVED AT Dulles Airport and slowly stepped through the entrance scanners. The system assigned a boarding pass to everyone ahead of him, however, when he walked through, it only asked questions.

I'm sorry, but I can't find a reservation for you, are you here for an arrival?

"No, I have a flight."

Did you say 'no'? Okay, I will help you purchase a ticket. Where would you like to go?

"I don't want to purchase a ticket! I've got one!"

I'm sorry, I didn't quite understand that.

"I said, I have a ticket!"

I still didn't quite get your destination. Hang on; I know who can help you.

A smiling lady approached Adrian and asked: "May I help you, sir?"

"I have a reservation for a flight to North Carolina," he said, showing his identification.

"Oh! Of course, let me get you squared away," she said, happily escorting him to her station. As she settled behind her terminal, she glanced at his ID again and began typing away. "For what day? I don't see a reservation for you."

"Are you serious? Today." Adrian groaned. He checked his calendar and pulled out his corporate card. "I don't have time; the flight closes soon. I'll buy another."

"Of course." The attendant quickly processed his request but looked up sadly. "I'm sorry, but the card has been declined."

"My card isn't working, you can't find my reservation, look again!"

"Sir, please calm down. Being aggressive is not helping."

Adrian looked to the ceiling and shook his head: *Airports.*

"Listen. Clearly, you don't see my name, and I can't pay for a ticket. I must be mistaken," Adrian said as sweetly as he could muster. "My card please?"

"Um... one moment sir, I think... I just need to check on something," She said and trotted off to the back.

Adrian waited a moment, before picking up his phone and calling another local ICP member. "Joel?"

"Yeah," the man said on the other line.

"Hey," Adrian thought for a moment, then asked. "Have you had any issues with your project funds?"

"Me? No, this reorg hasn't caused me any difficulties."

"Reorg?"

"Yeah, we've had endless meetings about the reorg, or should I say, Restructuring Act... whatever that means."

"That means a layoff," Adrian mumbled.

Joel chuckled. "Well, it can't be a layoff, right? We aren't exactly a corporation or even a legit company. Which is what Sing was saying, right?"

"What'd she say?"

"Some members have used our team as a means to violate the law."

"Some members?"

"I didn't understand it either. Sing was real cryptic about some of us using our training to hurt other people, and she said ICP was turning into the bad guys. So she wants to restructure the organization to work more with the governments to stop terrorism, instead of working around them, and becoming the terrorist. Seems fair to me, but whatever, I'll send you the slides so you can read them and catch up."

Adrian received the slides and took a moment to look them over. The slides covered the restructuring plans and staff reorganization. Adrian didn't see his name on the list of operatives. Every project he owned had a red "X" through it.

Making a call to Omar, Adrian waited for an answer. When a woman approached Adrian, he hung up and turned toward her.

"Dr. Adrian Blackwell? I'm Detective Kelly Taferty," She showed Adrian her ID and then pointed to the man standing next to her. "This is Officer George Wilson."

"Look, it's really not that deep. I just checked with my team; we had a big mix up. I got it resolved," Adrian told them, shouldering his bags and stepping away quickly.

"It's okay, this isn't about your flight," Kelly continued as she and Wilson followed Adrian out the exit. "Perhaps, we can give you a lift home?"

"Why?"

"We need your help," George insisted.

"Not interested. I'll catch a cab."

"It's about Mason," Kelly spoke up.

Adrian stopped. "Mason?"

"She's gone," Kelly answered.

Adrian's heart leapt. "What do you mean... gone?" he demanded.

"Lotus took her. He trashed her lab and dragged her away. Killed everyone else. Her intern Tina saw the whole thing."

"Lotus?" Adrian shouted. "I have to help her."

"Then," Kelly insisted, pointing to her car, "let's go!"

Adrian hopped inside with them, and they drove off.

Adrian thought of Mason and felt his nerves fraying. The car moved too slowly. With a couple of jumps, Adrian knew he could be on top of Lotus in a flash. Contemplating a plan, he said: "How long ago? Where is he?"

George initiated a video screen that played a report, and he explained: "The ICP's been hunting the Six for a long time, and now they finally cornered the terrorist ground in a bank tower in Kennesaw, Georgia."

What? Georgia is several states away. Adrian thought, checking his phone. *Why haven't they told me? Why did they send local D.C cops to escort me?*

George continued, "Federal and local police are supporting the ICP. It's a tense standoff with about sixty-two hundred hostages inside."

Adrian felt a wave of confusion, knowing he could infiltrate the bank and pull hostages in a snap. His confusion turned to heartbreak.

"Mason's in there," Kelly said, "She's part of the hostages, so right now we can only hope they will bring her back safely."

"Who is 'they?'" Adrian asked weakly. He felt rejected realizing the ICP simply didn't want his services, and then the ultimate question hit him. *If ICP doesn't want me, then why did the police come for me?*

"The Six have nowhere to run anymore," Kelly said, "The ICP takes their jobs seriously. As do we. Especially in cases of sexual assault."

The words shocked Adrian. "Assault? This is about assault?"

Kelly nodded. "Do you know what home means to people, Dr. Blackwell? No matter where you go in the world, there is an invisible string on your heart, pulling you back to the place you belong. Right now, no doubt, Mason's heart is pulling her back here, back to her lab, back to her plants, her home. When she's safely returned I want to be sure assault is no longer a concern for her."

George added, "Mason filed a complaint about an intruder, possibly multiple intruders. She claimed she'd been sexually assaulted. We gathered all the physical evidence and know two people were with her the night she got raped."

"Which leaves us with two problems," Kelly added. "The first man left a mountain of evidence, but somehow we can't find him..."

Adrian knew, before she finished her sentence, that he had to get away. He leaned forward, looked around and gauged where he would teleport.

"The second man," Kelly continued. "Well... we can't prove how or if he entered the premises. If we had that piece of the puzzle, I think we'd have the whole picture."

Adrian's eyes widened when Kelly revealed that she didn't know how he got inside her home. He leaned back in his seat abandoning his escape.

"You see what we are getting at?" Kelly asked.

"You know there was a second person in her house, but you can't figure out how he got there. It sounds like you suspect I'm the second man? I can't say I admire that sort of detective work."

"Your fingerprints are on her car and keys. The tire tracks from your car were identifiable, but you're right. We were never able to put you inside her home."

"Then your interest in me is less than flattering."

"I'm just interested in your shoes," Kelly stated.

Adrian nervously chuckled, "The ones I'm wearing?"

"The ones you were wearing that night."

Adrian took a deep breath. "Okay. Just tell me which pair."

"My apologies," Kelly corrected. "We want them all."

Officer Wilson produced a warrant to search Adrian's property and confiscate any footwear. "Saves me the trouble of stapling it to your door," Wilson said, thrusting it into Adrian's chest.

Adrian looked out of the window to see police cars lined up in front of his home. Officer Wilson got out and joined his deputies as they exited the house carrying plastic boxes of shoes.

Kelly opened the rear door.

As Adrian climbed out, he said, "I'm sure she had a security recordings which would prove what happened."

"Oh, she did, but there was no video of what happened once she was inside her bedroom. That's why we installed another."

"Another?" Adrian went pale.

"When I met Mason, I couldn't believe anyone could do that to her," said Kelly. "Her story seemed confusing at first, but when I stepped back from the situation, I realized it didn't have to make sense. The attacker wasn't after her; he was after her work. I guessed that if he wanted her work that badly, he'd be back."

"Curious," Adrian breathed. "So if my footprints are in her home...?"

"Footprints fade so easily, and are impossible to date, Doctor," Kelly responded. "No, we laced her carpet with a special substance."

Adrian frowned.

"And like clockwork, he came back," Kelly finished. "I realized I didn't have to prove how he got inside her bedroom if I could demonstrate that he was indeed there. Why do you seem so nervous, Dr. Blackwell?"

"I'm only delighted that whoever hurt her will soon be brought to justice."

George Wilson emerged from the house with a pair of shoes in a plastic bag. Adrian looked at the shoes blankly.

"Got it?" Kelly asked.

George held the shoes by the scanner. "It's a match. Adrian Blackwell, you are under arrest for the sexual assault of Mason Kinoah."

They read him his rights and cuffed him for processing.

GEORGE SAT IN the passenger seat of his patrol car as his Ukrainian deputy, Ana, drove them back to the station. They led a convoy. Blackwell sat, locked away, in the rear armored truck, four units behind. George turned on the dash display, showing reports of the tense standoff at the Kennesaw State Bank in Georgia.

"The Six is finished," Ana noted.

George agreed, "Never thought I'd see the end of this war."

"I never thought we'd catch Mason's rapist," Ana said. "We had nothing."

"How sad that she will have to deal with this when she gets back here," Wilson said. "Hopefully, this will provide her closure."

"It won't be an easy case," Ana admitted. "Kelly's gonna have her hands full if those shoes are all she's got on him."

"I don't know," George countered. "I've seen her work miracles with less. She was clever enough to trap him, and desperate men make mistakes."

"Maybe we owe her an apology, ya know? Not gonna lie, even I had my doubts," Ana suggested. "I can just see a bunch of law students poring through our databases, finding an open sexual assault case that ends with us telling the victim she's crazy."

"You didn't say that," George noted. "You just never found any physical evidence of rape." George glanced at the news on the screen and raised the volume on the notifications.

... that's right, the entire city! Police are trying to evacuate Kennesaw after discovering chemical weapons armed under the tower...

"This is bad," George said.

All are fleeing the vicinity. The roads are in chaos as everyone tries to evacuate.

The lead patrol car stopped as did the others following behind. A line of protesters marched down New Hampshire Avenue in front of them. The 3D mapping popped an information alert.

"What's this?" Ana asked.

"Student protest. March against the energy bill that will divert social security funds."

"Should we intervene?"

"No, just go around it," George commanded. "It's under Drone Compliance."

Ana diverted the car, bypassing the march. George did a double take when the notification switched from green to red in that instant.

Violent protest.
Officer down.

Ana shot him a look. "What just happened?"

George reached forward and lit the siren. "Renner!"

"Dammit!" Ana changed course, and they sped back toward the demonstration.

They pulled up by a crowd of bystanders who were watching protesters fighting with police.

"Let's go!"

As they ran into the melee, Ana got on the comms. "We need crowd control on 21st and M. Hostilities all around, code blue."

They heard screams. A rioter slammed into George and tried to take him to the ground. George hopped back, flipping over his assailant. George mounted him, rolled him over, and hog-tied his attacker with zip ties. When another came at him, George repeated the process.

"Stay there," George said, spying Officer Renner's bloodied face in the distance.

When a bystander charged Ana, she flipped him over and tased him.

George reached Renner, "What the hell happened?"

Renner was stomping around, trying to calm himself. "Fuck! Damn kids!"

Ana ran up, saying, "Drones said the protesters were under compliance!"

Renner scoffed, "No way! That drone can go to hell! I had to wrestle him to the ground! We all did."

"Wrestle! Wrestle who?" Ana demanded. "The drones reported compliance. Shit! The press is coming. We need to close this block off."

Renner continued, "Fuck that drone and anyone who says differently. Someone stepped out of line and attacked us first! I tackled him; four other officers cuffed him, and he hit me! So I was forced to subdue the assailant with maximum efficiency!"

"Oh my god!" Ana put her hands on her head.

"Wait, how'd he hit you if you restrained him?" George asked.

"I don't know; he punched me! That's how my face got bloody!"

"That doesn't make sense! The drones reported compliance." George insisted, "You can't touch citizens under drone compliance!"

"He must've of slipped passed the drones. He got in my face and hit me. When I opened my eyes, I thought I saw him walking away."

"You thought?"

"He was walking away! He turned, locked eyes with me, and ran!" Renner shouted, "Like how they do in the pen!"

"You're not a correctional officer!" Ana shouted. "These kids aren't prisoners! Oh, Lord! This is going to be a nightmare. The press is here!"

Ana left them to close off the street.

George turned back to Renner, "You tackled a protester because..."

"... he attacked me. It's like he appeared out of nowhere! Everything was clear, and then suddenly this big black guy is in my face!"

George nodded, "Okay, that's a start. So your body camera is gonna show that compliance with a drone put you in harm's way?"

"Damn right!"

"Show me your video feed," George said.

Renner went silent, then said, "My body camera is gone."

"Fuck!" George screamed. "You can't-"

"I didn't take it off!" Renner shouted. "Whose side are you on?"

"The law," George insisted. "You took your body camera off, and that could be the only evidence that proves you didn't overstep your authority!"

"You don't think I know that! One minute the streets are clear, the next minute I got a guy in my face!"

"With your body camera missing?"

"Ya know what? We have a job to do out here, and if we don't band together, the criminals and thugs like him get their way!"

"You don't even know him. How did he suddenly become a thug?"

"He assaulted a police officer!"

"While under drone compliance?"

"Well, you're just gonna have to have my back on this whether you like it or not," Renner snapped. "We're in the same boat. If I go down, then you aren't safe either, so you better wise up! If we lose control, society goes to hell! These people have to respect us no matter what!"

George shook his head, and said, "We are always in control!"

Renner wiped blood from his chin. "Yeah? You tell that to your little girl when you finally get to see her."

"You fucking asshole!" George rushed his "wounded" comrade

"Oh, you wanna break the law now?" Renner said. "Get off me."

George stood there as Renner stormed off. He turned and saw Ana approaching.

"What?" George challenged. "You know about my past, just like I know about yours."

Ana stared at him for a moment, trying to recover her train of thought. "I just gotta call from Kelly; she wants to know when we're bringing in Adrian."

George resumed his calm demeanor. "Tell her we're... we have to control this block. Get the convoy to take the armored truck in."

Ana gave the orders, then turned back to George. "Don't you ever snap at me again!"

"I didn't snap, I'm—"

"No, you snapped at me! How dare you threaten me. What about my past?"

"I said I'm sorry," George reiterated.

A deputy ran up to Ana. He shrugged, mouthing: "Not there."

She turned to George. "Where are the shoes?"

"What do you mean? In the back seat."

"He says the shoes are gone."

"Impossible!" George ran to his car and rifled through the back seat. He found the shoes on the floor next to his seat.

As Ana examined them, she said: "These aren't the shoes. These are brand new. The laces aren't even tied, and the tag is still on them. These aren't the ones we got at Blackwell's!"

When George looked at the shoes, he screamed, "He switched them!"

"How?" Ana asked.

A thought hit George, and he said: "Same way he got into her house! The same way he got in Renner's face."

George stormed down the line of patrol cars to the armored truck. The guard standing in front stepped aside. George flung the doors up.

Inside, Adrian sat calmly, shackled to the floor. George didn't like the smugness in the man's eyes, knowing his prisoner was up to something.

Ana ran up and grabbed George.

"What is it?" George demanded.

Ana pointed at her handheld feed. "She's gone!"

"He's right here!"

"No! She's gone!"

George heard the news:

The Six tried to flee after police abandon their position to evacuate the city. Rebel members of the Six staged a coup and hostages were slaughtered in mass.

Demolition charges detonated under the bank tower, igniting chemical weapons, which have now incinerated the city of Kennesaw.

Adrian raised his head. His smug countenance melted into horror as he listened.

Drone surveillance shows only the cloud of fallout. The chemical atmosphere is toxic to both man and machine.

"This is our fault!" Ana screamed. Realizing the extent of the tragedy and blaming herself for not protecting Mason.

George stopped her self-depreciating thoughts, "No one could have saved her, Ana!"

The media provided not stop updates about the genocidal massacre in Kennesaw.

Adrian listened painfully to the news and shuttered when he heard George reassuring his partner.

No one could have saved her.

GOD YOUR POWER

ADRIAN SAT ALONE in his home while battling the weighted guilt he refused to accept. He put his thoughts on paper to prove his innocence, yet the story was always the same; to protect his own interest, he left Mason to die. Chastised by the pages of his feelings, Adrian fought against accepting the truth: he could have used his power to aid Mason rather than satisfying his superficial whims, but he didn't want to look guilty. By being deceptive, did it make him responsible for what happened? The more Adrian pushed the thought from his mind, the more each line incriminated him further.

Not able to stomach the cold-hearted man he wrote about, Adrian changed the words of the diary and then published a book to help people learn how to accept who they are. His book counseled others to use their personal abilities to beat their addictions. Forcing a golden version of himself to the public while hiding the truth in plain sight was supposed to ease his conscious. It didn't, but on the bright side; the book fixed a million others.

The Washington, D.C. public library bustled with the delighted faces of patrons hoping to meet the author who changed their life. Adrian's eyes showed signs of fatigue as, one after another, people approached and handed him copies of his book – "God Your Power."Adrian opened the front cover of the book, signed it and waited for the next.

He wore a V-neck short-sleeved shirt, a blue sports coat, brown loafers, and a permanent fake smile he dug to the depth of his soul to display. Each lie he told required more lies to cover his story as he tried to pretend he was the man in the book.

Someone new approached the table; Adrian said a few words, got the reader's name, signed the book, and waited for the next eager face to tell him of their new found strength to oppose the inner voice calling them to give in to their addictions. All they needed to do, was learn how to control it and God their power.

After the library had cleared out for the night, he looked down at his sales and realized he sold every book. The librarian helped him tear down the boxes, and in the midst of his cleaning, his watch beeped with a message. It was Omar, and Adrian ignored it. Relentlessly, Omar messaged until Adrian turned his watch off. Then the librarian received a message.

"I - I think I have to go," Adrian said, tired and apologetic. "I have another appointment."

Adrian turned his watch back on and messaged Omar that he would rendezvous with him within the hour. A light autumn rain fell through the night and sprinkled over Adrian's dressy attire as he left the building. On his way to the car, George Wilson came out of the night dressed in plain clothes and stopped him

"I read your book," George shouted, closing in on Adrian. With the rain lightly sprinkling over his umbrella, he pulled out a copy of Adrian's book and handed it to him. "Do you mind?"

Annoyed, Adrian took the book, shielding it from the weather, he signed the front flap and handed it back to the officer. "Sorry you missed the book signing."

George sheathed the book, and apologized, "I got sidetracked."

"Welp," Adrian nodded, attempting to leave, but George cut him off again.

"Beating addition by treating it as a superpower? Novel idea," George stated happily, then curiously added, "What gave you that inspiration, because honestly, the book reads as if you actually had a super power."

Adrian spoke in the professional mode from the prior event, "Well, what is a super power? It's the ability to do something extraordinary. Everyone has a superpower. Maybe being a cop is your super power? As such you must be careful because the authority you have gives you power. If you don't have control over yourself, then that power can be dangerous."

George watched him speaking. Unmoved.

Adrian asked, "Have you ever had an addiction?"

"Everyone has addictions even if it doesn't come in the form of a pill." He answered. "But yes. My ex-wife would be the first to tell you stories about how I found myself at the bottom of a bottle every night. She would find me on the side of the road half naked, drunk off my ass. She would drag me home, clean me up, only to watch me do it all over again. One time, she got me home. Showered me, fixed me a dinner, laid me down to sleep and kissed me good night. That was the last I saw her."

"Sorry to hear that, addiction can tear families apart," Adrian sighed, brushing water droplets off of his shoulders, again speaking mechanically the words he says to every fan of his writing. "I'm sure you, more than anyone, can appreciate what it takes to control your addiction."

"Well, that's just the thing. Nowhere in your book did I see where you had an addiction," George claimed. "It seems as though you wished you used your power for a better purpose. That's not the same thing."

"Isn't it?" Adrian shrugged.

"I know what beating addiction looks like. This ain't it. When's the last time someone put your vice in front of you? I put a bottle of Whisky in my passenger seat and drove around for a month. Never once touched it. I had the power to drink anytime I wanted, and chose not to," George boasted sternly. "The book reads like the bottle wasn't there. I don't call that a win. Your book sounds like regret."

Adrian looked at his watch after getting yet another five notifications.

"You should be a critic," Adrian weakly told the officer, as he sleepily walked away, "I have to go. I am expected."

"What happened a few years ago? At a pizza parlor in Austin, TX?" George hollered out.

Adrian stopped and turned around. The wet asphalt grounded beneath his feet. "I was drunk; I don't really remember. Apparently, the cab I was in drove right into a restaurant and trashed it. Just an accident."

George responded, "Dr. Blackwell, I am no book critic, and I am no fool. I had to go to hell and back to find remnants of the surveillance video, and I looked over the technical GPS reports. That was no regular accident. It didn't exactly drive into the place, did it? Mason deserved better. Don't think I closed that case just because she's gone."

Guarded, Adrian asked, "If you are here to arrest me, what are you waiting for?"

George scoffed, "I'm just waiting for you to show the world your real super power."

George let Adrian escape to his car and drive away through the misty night. Adrian parked on a side street near a two-story house: the home of Omar Jacobs. From the outside, it looked big and elegant, with its dark wood trimmings, and manicured garden.

He trotted through the drizzle to the front door. Inside, Omar constantly glanced out awaiting Adrian's approach. Before Adrian's finger touched the bell, Omar opened the door.

"Adrian, please come out of the rain," Omar insisted. "I'm so glad you took the trouble to come."

"It's been a while," said Adrian, dryly, looking around.

Omar took Adrian's coat and hung it up, then he looked around his house and said, "Thanks, I've had a lot of work done. Pulled up all the floors, changed the counters. Blew out the walls and restructured it to my liking." They walked through the short foyer to a fork, where they turned left, into the kitchen. Omar poured Adrian a glass of bourbon, then one for himself. He handed the first glass to Adrian with a hint of a smile that offered eyes of gratitude.

Omar toasted, "To your book." After taking the first sip, he added, "I hope you don't mind, but Sing is joining us soon. I think the weather held her up."

Adrian took a sip. "What's this all about?"

"It's about Mason," Omar started.

Adrian smothered his consternation and took another sip of his drink. He leaned back against the counter. "Omar, we should put this behind us. You were wrong, and so was I. She paid for it."

Omar nodded. "I agree, it's impossible to go back in time, and this whole matter should be buried, but that's the thing. We only had a funeral for her, we never actually buried Mason."

Adrian paced around. "Why are you bringing her up? You sold me out! You burned me, and I was too comfortable to-"

The doorbell rang.

Omar quickly asked, "Listen. Did you see the news?"

"No, what happened?"

Omar put a small display on the counter and played the media feed, "Just... just watch it." As Adrian watched, Omar ran off to get the door.

Adrian saw the report:

NEWS UPDATE: A military freighter from Mars was set to return today, and the SARA space station has lost contact with the pilot. SARA estimates that the probe will enter the Earth's atmosphere and crash in the northern part of Pennsylvania. Authorities are asking everyone on the Eastern seaboard to stay indoors as debris from the falling spacecraft may be harmful.

As it ended, a small Asian woman walked into the kitchen with Omar. Sing's hair framed her jaw on one side and fell almost to her collar on the other side. This created an oval frame for her face. When she saw Adrian, she looked relieved.

She covered her mouth, and in deep sorrow said, "Oh my, thank you so much for coming. We were wrong, and it's taken too many years for us to apologize..."

"I'm not the one who needs the apology."

"Quite right. Look, I know we have had our differences, but this is... well, we need you. Did you see the news?"

Adrian nodded. "Yes. Martian freighter headed to Earth, no response from the captain." He shrugged. "Probably dead."

"But they're lying," said Omar.

"About what?" Adrian asked.

"About the freighter," said Sing, "That's no naval captain piloting it."

"He's a fugitive," Omar concluded.

Adrian set down his drink. "A fugitive from where? Seson Midway Prison? No way. How could anyone escape a place like that?"

"That was my question until I realized the correct question is 'who'?" Omar showed Adrian a picture of the fugitive. In the image he was Dimycles.

Adrian instantly stormed off.

"Stop!" Omar shouted.

"What are you expecting? A confession out of him?" Adrian wondered. "Those pods are only meant to dock on the SARA space station or Mars. Earth's atmosphere will tear it apart on reentry. Even if, by some miracle, it makes it through the atmosphere, he will be vaporized on impact with the surface. Dimycles is a dead man."

"But," Omar started. "This dead man isn't coming back because he missed home. He's coming back for revenge."

"We have a chance here," said Sing. "To make it right, the whole thing. Help us!"

Adrian turned back and listened.

"Show him," she said, nodding to Omar. "Here... look."

She signaled Omar, who made the display show Adrian video of the Kennesaw State Bank attack. "This is what's left of the video feed."

Adrian glanced at the video. "This is when Dimycles killed Lotus. Right before the charges leveled the building?"

"Except that's not Lotus!" Omar exclaimed, pausing the video as it showed Dimycles lifting up a body.

"How you figure?" Adrian asked.

Omar changed screens and showed Adrian the lower level of the bank, near the garage. "Who do you think set the charges?"

In clear view, the camera showed the same face.

"Lotus," Adrian gasped. "This... how?"

Sing added, "No one was allowed to access ground zero for more than two years due to the quarantine. No one could possibly get the real surveillance video. The video on the cloud was altered."

Adrian took the tablet. "Lotus faked his death?"

"It never occurred to me to look for another version of the video until Dimycles busted out of the Seson," Omar admitted. "I mean, that was the only reason I could see him coming back here- to finish what he started."

"Where..." Adrian mumbled.

"Lotus has been underground these last two years. He's up to something- using Mason no doubt," Omar continued.

"Where is he?" Adrian shouted, startling Sing.

"Germany," Sing answered. "We tracked him through shipment of plants and drones into the Sudan..."

"Drones?"

"Insect drones," Omar shrugged.

"We have a team in Berlin hunting for him now, but you are the only one we can count on to quickly extract Mason, once we know for sure." She watched Adrian's expression as she continued, "I know we've asked you to do some shady things in the past, but we all sold Mason out to protect ourselves. If she is alive, we're all she's got. No one else will be looking for her. We need you to be in with us on this."

"For Mason, that's as far as I..." Adrian trailed off. He touched a knuckle to his lips, turned, and walked out of the kitchen. He stood just outside the back door, staring into the darkness beyond the patio.

Sing followed him, asking: "What's wrong?"

Adrian signaled her to be silent. Omar joined them. After a few moments, Adrian whispered, "You feel that?"

"No."

Omar glanced back into the kitchen. "It's just the rain; sometimes it vibrates the—" At that moment he felt it too.

A rumble went through the house. Something thumped through the walls, as dishes shook. Adrian looked up at the night sky.

"Oh no," Adrian whispered.

The roar of military jets filled the sky. The thumping of propellers on the attack helicopters was deafening.

"What is this?" Sing gasped.

Sing leaned back and turned slowly, watching the night sky. The blanket of bombers passed over them. "You think this is because of the Lotus?"

"Lotus has been building weapons for years," Adrian shook his head, "It looks like he's finally going to war."

Omar led them back into the house, saying: "I'll need time to find out."

Adrian's thoughts turned to Mason, and he felt sad again, as well as nervous. He nodded, saying, "Get me a flight to Berlin. I think, despite all of this, Mason is a top priority." He grabbed his coat.

As Adrian drove off, he started imagining all the things Lotus might do to Mason and banged the steering wheel with his fist. He wanted to cry but could shed no tears while driving to the corner store. As he hopped from his car transport planes and air carriers flew low overhead. In the store he bought a bouquet of flowers, and then he headed to the city. As he climbed the steps to St. Mary's Hospital, he had to cover the flowers, protecting it from the stiff autumn wind. Adrian passed people waiting in the lobby. He signed in at the visitor's station and headed to the elevator, where he pressed the button for the fourth floor. A nurse got on after him, on her way to the tenth floor. The doors closed.

"Pretty flowers," the nurse commented.

"Thank you. They're for my grandmother," Adrian replied.

"Fourth floor?" The nurse looked him up and down then guessed, "Dorothy... I mean, Dot?"

"Yeah!"

"Such a sweet lady, and a tough one too."

"Yeah, don't cross her," he said as the doors opened.

The hospital air felt chilly as he walked toward room 418.

"Knock, knock!" He announced. His grandmother was sitting up in her bed, crocheting. She'd recently suffered her third stroke, so seeing her alert and active was encouraging. "Who's that lady in the bed?" he asked.

Dot's face lit up. It was hard for her to speak, but her happiness at seeing her grandson radiated through the room. "Oh, my lord..." she managed. "You better quit...baby... baby Adrian, come here, let me look at you," She raised her frail arms to hug him. "All dressed up. You gotta date?"

"Of course! You!" He hugged her gently and put the flowers on the table next to her bed.

She swatted the air. "Don't play."

Adrian instinctively checked the contents of her IV bag and looked at his watch. "You're right. No date. More like a house party with friends."

He pulled out a dedicated medical tablet and scanned her body, starting with the legs. The bones looked fragile but fine. One knee showed some arthritis.

"What are you doing?" She demanded.

"Just checking everything out," he said, "making sure they're treating you right."

"Stop that, right now!" she cried, weakly pounding her hand against the mattress. "I swear, boy!"

"Sorry, it's hard for me to trust you to other people's care. I worry."

"You got to learn to let go. I chose this hospital, not your hospital!"

Adrian put his tablet away and sat down in the chair on the other side of her bed. "I thought you choose this place just to see if I'd make an effort to see you."

"I-I come here so you won't be checking up on me, and doing exactly what you were doing," she said. "I'm your grandmother, not your patient."

"I apologize. I know better," he admitted.

"Don't think you too old to get spanked. I still put you over my knee," She pointed a shaking finger at him. "You and your brother, Julius. Got too much sass. What's he doing?"

"Jules? He's doing a bit of everything. He's a full-time adventurer these days traveling with a paleontologist, hunters, and whoever's got a reason to leave the country. I believe he's back in the city now. He spends his days at the gym training with B.K."

Dot looked confused for a moment, "B.K.? Oh, the li'l yellow skinned boy. Kenley!"

"Haha. Kennedy, grandma. Bishop Kennedy. Why you always insist on calling him Kenley?"

"He looks like a Kenley," Dot shrugged. "Ya'll three used to run around in...my yard playing with your little space... toys. Until that- that little rascal... set my house on fire!"

"He didn't set the house on fire; he just built a little rocket that burnt a corner of your rug."

"Rug is – is part of the house right?" Dot asked. "Is Kenley doing better ever since...?"

"No. He's... changed," Adrian sighed. "Ever since Nicole died..."

"Aww, baby. Poor Nicole. That was the sweetest, nicest girl. Kenley found himself a winner," Dot squeezed her grandson's hands. "So sad. When that... plane crashed... I just about died at the thought."

"I tried to help him get over it, but I believe I just made things worse."

Dot touched Adrian's cheek. "Sometimes you gotta let people mourn. Let them grieve. It took me... forever to get over losing your mother. My sweet daughter meant the world to me."

Dot lightly rubbed her finger over the T scar on his left cheek. "You never got rid of them?"

Adrian touched her hands and shook his head. "I need them. I have to know where I came from, and what you survived to get us here. So I will never become like that."

"But your heart, baby, did it... survive? I still don't see a ring on your finger. You don't ever bring... a date around." Dot sat up straighter, "Sometimes I feel... like... I saved you, but your heart... still died. They killed your soul. Just like Kenley. Now you two are really... brothers."

"We aren't that close anymore. After the plane crashed, Bishop went into seclusion. He got violent and fled into the Appalachian Mountains for a long time. He lives in the city now, but all he does is train all day. He doesn't invent anymore – legally, he can't touch a computer. Jules travels the world, and I'm busy working at the ER eighty hours a week. We aren't really friends like we used to be. Things change."

"When you get my age, you will look back and wish you never let them." Dot grabbed her yarn and shuffled through the different colors. Her hands started shaking again. "Young people waste time because they think there will always be tomorrow. When you get my age, you realize... that tomorrow never comes... then you die... your job isn't going to stop... That ... your funeral... when you lay in your casket... your money isn't going to stand over you and say nice things... about you... When you get my age you realize that you wasted a lot of time on things that weren't... weren't about who you are.

"I'm gonna crochet something for Kenley, to help him to... remember that he has to... forgive himself. I've survived three strokes now. They keep fixing my... brain, and I keep on going. I'm never gonna look back and regret... spending all of my time working, and not with the people that I love."

Adrian had a thought but elected to listen.

"I'm never gonna close my eyes at... night and be afraid... to die in my sleep because I forgot to... do something that made a difference." As she spoke, she grasped balls of yarn. "Every time I look at you... Julius... I remember... I carried you two out of that tribal... hellhole... and out of Mali. The killing and the raping. I remember the look... on your mother's face when those men... took her, and the look in her eyes. She was at peace... in a terrifying situation. She knew she gave... her life... to free yours. If all you want to do is work, then that's your choice, but make sure you won't regret. You hear me, honey?"

"Yes, ma'am," Adrian sighed.

She patted his thick arm, and said, "You do well. You and baby Julius." She chuckled with her eyes, and added, "And Kenley too. Even though his head... his head ain't right... his mind is in the clouds... oh! You heard about the ship- spaceship... from Mars?"

The news feed brought up a picture of Pennsylvania and placed a dot where they expected the alleged military pod to land. Dot shook her head, "Pennsylvania's got nothing... but crops anyway. I hope they aren't sending the military to fight the people on Mars."

The image kept Adrian's attention, but his grandmother's remarks broke his stare. He turned to her. "The capsule pod will most likely burn up in the atmosphere as it reenters. No one lives on Mars anymore, 'ma."

She barely processed his response before adding more yarn to her crochet work. She reached into her bag and pulled out a fresh set of strings. She looked around the room for some inspiration and remembered when Bishop was a boy wearing overalls - sporting a head full of curly hair. He was the adventurer, always getting Adrian and Julius into trouble. That's how she remembered him, and that's how she wanted to think of him.

Adrian looked down at his phone and read a message from Omar. He answered it.

Omar: The nation is at war. Everything is code red.

Adrian: Who are we fighting?

Omar: I don't know. U.S Military doesn't share information with ICP. I have to hack my way in, but I can tell you this much, whatever Lotus is up to, we are about to find out.

Adrian looked up from his typing. His grandmother's frail fingers knitted in silence. She paid no attention to the news flash update. She was trying to piece together her scattered memory.

"Why don't people live on Mars anymore?" she asked.

Adrian sighed. "Because... we killed them."

...repeat! This is Hellas Basin Colony!! Please! Why are you attacking us? Don't leave us like this! Repeat! This is Hellas Basin...

VALLEY OF DEATH

A CONE-LIKE CAPSULE floated down and landed softly on the surface of Mars, close to the decommissioned Hellas Basin Colony. As the small ship depressurized, a dusty wind blew across its bow. When the doors opened, Lotus hopped out wearing a dark gray protective suit. His tall, lanky frame landed softly on the ground. Poised, he walked forward- his feet kicking up rust-colored dust with every step. His dark sun visor mirrored the dark red sky and a mountainous landscape of dirt and rocks. He looked to the East. The first haze of light edged over the horizon. He walked through the rocky crater until the ground got more even. Something ceramic smashed under the weight of his foot. Lotus lifted his boot and shook the pieces from the bottom of his sole. As he walked on, his visor reflected rows of broken flowerpots blended in with the brown, speckled dirt and copper-toned dust that surrounded the area. He hesitated, looked down, and stepped over a body.

Though Lotus kept his emotions in check, the decayed, frozen bodies sent chills up his spine. For the first time in fourteen years, he felt something: hurt. These bodies seemed barely human. Leathery, blistered skin covered frozen limbs. The constant melting and freezing had turned their faces into balls of clay.

As he approached a large building, he walked out of the sun into a shadow. Finding the keypad on the side of the door, he typed in a code. The door opened, and he entered a decompression unit. When his footsteps triggered the motion sensor, the solar-powered building whirred to life. Lights came on. Lotus looked at his wrist, focusing on the red indicator. He waited, but the light did not change color.

The air is bad.

Inside his space suit, Lotus breathed deeply. He exhaled slowly to the thumping of his heart, expecting to see something perverse, as he stepped out of the decompression unit. The main hall had vaulted ceilings covered with spectacular paintings conveying the story of man and imagination. The ceiling tapered down from a central point, creating a dome with an air duct ring. Frail shriveled stems from a once bounteous hanging garden covered the walls below. The commons area boasted a sea of bodies whose owners had died amidst a modern spread of handcrafted furniture. The sealed hall had preserved them well. The corpses formed a diorama of madness and panic. The bodies seemed posed, miming a scene of tragedy where all morality was lost in a dark abyss. Empty eye sockets and half-decomposed corpses sat in the stillness, blunt objects puncturing their skulls. Lotus walked on. He saw the dead frozen in the midst of cannibalism. The body of a small boy rested in a woman's embrace and pieces of the child's arms in her mouth.

Lotus could see the souls of the dead pleading for mercy, demanding retribution. It pained him that so many had no voice, nor had any scribe been there to write their story. A whisper came from the distance, echoing softly from the walls, like a ghost floating through a haunted house, pleading for freedom. Lotus walked towards the sound, which led him to a communication room. The corpse of a woman lay hunched over a desk with two other male bodies on top of her- naked. Their skin, robbed of moisture, merged into one, forming them into a glue-like lump of putrid art. A commemoration of hate.

As Lotus looked around, the call radio reflected in his visor. It played the same message over and over. When he turned the volume up on the comms, the whisper grew louder.

"...I repeat! Two supply freighters arrived with armed men! They are taking hostile actions against the colony! Repeat! This is Hellas Basin Colony!! Please! Why are you attacking us? Don't leave us like this! Repeat! This is Hellas Basin..."

Behind the voice, he heard the wild pandemonium in the background. It sounded like animals, but Lotus knew it was the death throes of mindless people facing their end. He heard the dull sound of bodies torn apart. He heard another noise and turned down the comms. The generators shut down, and central power returned. A quiet whir emitted from the vents as a steady stream of air started circulating through the room.

It turned into a stiff breeze blowing through the building. The electronics sparked. Materials, untouched for years, cracked under stress. When the red indicator light on his suit turned green, he took off his helmet and set it on the desk. Lotus shifted the helmet so he could see his reflection in the visor. His pale hair, matted with sweat, stuck to the cream-colored skin of his face. Broad shoulders topped his thin frame. His square jaw tightened as he looked back.

A set of dark clawed feet with dense padding appeared - the rest of the body still in the shadows.

"For 14 years, I've only seen this place in my dreams," Lotus breathed, his back to the shadowy figure. The once vibrant colony looked something like a wax museum's chamber of horrors. Lotus pulled a newspaper clipping from his suit and placed it on the table.

The headline read: "Hellas Basin Colony Attacked."

"If you've ever seen men from neighboring countries slaughter each other with hate, then you can imagine what they did to us being on a different planet," Lotus said, exasperated. "It's like a light switch went off in their minds and panic spread like wildfire. Earthlings instantly feared us with a deep-seated horror. They felt our very existence on Mars meant the extinction of humanity on Earth."

Rex Gedeon spoke to Lotus in a profound and proper voice: "Maybe they were right."

Lotus shrugged like he didn't care, but the hurt in his eyes betrayed him. "To send us here as heroes, and then sentenced us to death as villains?"

"Even brothers can be enemies," Gedeon told him.

Clawed feet came into the light revealing muscular legs with coal-black feathered scales. In the darkness, a razor-sharp tail swayed back and forth.

Lotus choked in a whisper. He turned around and looked up at the daunting figure behind him. "Even enemies can be allies."

Inside the newspaper clipping was a tiny microchip.

Cold red eyes gazed at him. Rex Gedeon finally stepped into the light. At eight feet he stood more than eighteen inches above Lotus. Gedeon had a layer of wild scales feathering over his frame. The scales looked like tough pointy skin, and it often changed color. In the shadows, Gedeon's scales turned black as camouflage. When he stood in the light, they turned dark bluish-gray. Gedeon saw Lotus as merely a heat signature in infrared, then his diamond shaped pupils morphed into a circle, allowing him to take in Lotus in perfect color. His mouth formed a sinister smile, as two fangs glistened among a row of sharp teeth.

Gedeon gestured a clawed hand. "How old were you when Tiego found you?"

Lotus could smell the dead remnants of his childhood.

"I was 12. Old enough to know what was happening, still too young to comprehend the level of hate fostered against me." Lotus pointed into the corner and explained. "When soldiers from Earth stormed our compound, they killed everyone. A handful of kids my age were going to be the last to die here. Tiego found us in the closet, huddled together. There were six of us."

Gedeon commented. "One noble act deserves another, I suppose."

"You still don't trust me?" Lotus asked.

"Tiego is dead, and I find it reasonable that you are more than willing to take up your savior's cause." Gedeon noted, "Your commitment to our invasion of Earth is pleasing. Nonetheless, while it's a righteous betrayal, it's still a betrayal."

"I'm betraying no one!" he snapped. "I'm not an Earthling. I am Martian."

"I sense your conflict because you are still human."

Lotus gazed at the rotted corpses. "What is human?" he asked.

Lotus turned back to the comms radio. The last plea for help played quietly from the disavowed colony's radio. He looked down at the newspaper clipping and picked up the microchip.

"You know what the problem with people is? They lack spatial reasoning. Humans have the amazing ability to look back at a tragedy and pretend they are fundamentally different than the ones who committed it. Only after we were supposed to be dead did the voices of reason emerge. Only after they killed us all did they say 'we'd never do something like that now',» Lotus scoffed with disgust. "As if, at this very moment, they wouldn't abandon their code of ethics at the slightest hint that a Martian was still alive.

"The Hellas Basin massacre was such an embarrassment they let this final message play and dedicated an open channel as a tribute. You can tune into it and hear it on Earth. It's supposed to honor everyone who died here. That is how humans deal. They damn their past to be a sinner and praise their future to be a saint. They memorialize their humiliation, and swear that the past was a different time until they relive it again."

Lotus held out the microchip to his companion. "Your military might be powerful in space, but inside of the atmosphere, your bulky ships will never stand a chance. Earthlings have air superiority, and they fight with drones! They will crush your invasion with barely a loss, but this—" Lotus thrust the microchip forward "—will shut all that down."

Lotus dropped the chip into Rex Gedeon's clawed paws. At that, Gedeon's smile melted away into a serious demeanor – his eyes morphed in shape to examine the chip.

"As we discussed before, your starship is complete, but this chip you give me is only half of the deal. This will disable their air superiority, but we also need to sabotage their ground units," Rex Gedeon said, his red eyes cold and focused.

"Mason completed the devices."

"And for a demonstration?"

"She cannot... demonstrate it. Your science officer took her!"

Rex Gedeon's scales started to change to a reddish color. "What?"

Lotus backed away, his heart skipped a beat.

A sleek feminine shadow appeared in the vaulted doorway. Lotus thought she had the figure of an angel, but the talons and the beak of a bird. Kalet Nefrew stood ten feet tall. Her enormous golden brown wings were tucked neatly across her back. The light green and white tones of her face framed yellow eyes. Her entrance drew a gasp from Lotus. Kalet fluttered her feathered wings and spoke a few indistinct words to Rex Gedeon.

Gedeon turned to his human conspirator. "Eyes are upon us."

"Eyes?" Lotus questioned.

Gedeon's turned away and walked off. To Lotus, this sudden abandonment felt like a warning as their priorities shifted quickly. Lotus grabbed his helmet and followed them through the house of corpses.

Lotus put his helmet on, secured his suit, and exited the Hellas Basin Colony behind the two Reptilites. Gedeon and Kalet stepped out into the harsh atmosphere poised for skirmish. Kalet stretched her wings. The golden brown twenty-foot wingspan cast an enormous shadow. A small rod in her hand extended at full length; a glowing blade emerged at the end. With a powerful leap, she launched into the air.

Lotus looked around, and Rex Gedeon was gone. Abandoned, he stood confused for a moment until he saw dust kick up over the horizon. He ran, making huge strides across the Martian landscape, toward his space capsule.

Large shadows overtook him.

The ground rumbled under his feet.

Rovers!

Kalet rained down explosive balls of energy from the blade of her scythe. Pieces of debris flew everywhere at the devastation of her bombardment, causing shrapnel to hit Lotus as well. Dust from the explosive impacts made it difficult for him to see. He lost his footing, and fell to the ground, sliding along the rocks. A mechatronic arm reached out to grab him. When Lotus looked up, an invisible force plowed into the tanker, and he watched the assailant break apart from the seams. He realized Rex Gedeon was camouflaged.

Lotus hopped up and ran away from the epicenter of battle; reaching his capsule, he shut himself inside. The display lit up, but the debris on his visor hampered his ability to operate it. He removed his helmet, and quickly initiated the liftoff. The capsule rumbled, and as it engaged, a mechatronic raider tore into it. Lotus felt the Martian air slam into his face; his ears popped, and he threw his helmet back on, pressing it down with all his might. A large robotic arm grabbed him out of the wreckage and prepped thrusters to fly away.

Gedeon decloaked and landed on the rocks above, his scales a deep purple. The mechatronic thief raised a cannon at the Reptilite; Lotus felt the heat from the yellow glow. Kalet attacked from above; her talons dug into the robot as she smashed down on it, driving the blade of her scythe through it, and blowing it up from the inside. Gedeon leaped over them both, intercepting two remaining units coming up to reinforce.

After tearing the marauders apart, his pupils shifted. Gedeon observed the landscape for any remaining threat and then turned to the others.

"This atmosphere is weak," Gedeon said, in a shallow voice. "The Kaiman is vulnerable to bombardment from space."

Lotus quickly secured his helmet, got up, and trotted carefully behind Gedeon until they approached the Kaiman. The intimidating mother ship looked like the skull of an alligator. On either side, the Kaiman's wings curved up and swept back giving the ship the appearance of a sinister smile. The Kaiman received its high commander and rose from the surface of Mars.

Kalet circled in the air, watchful for any attack while the mother ship was vulnerable. She then entered the Kaiman before it blasted off into space.

Lotus walked through the long, spacious, tubular halls. The surfaces of these walls were not smooth. A mixture of bark and bone matted the walkways. As the Kaiman escaped into the space beyond Mars, Lotus floated. He grabbed the lumpy walls, pushing himself through the halls to the bridge.

He floated at the entrance to the bridge—a spherical node—getting a peek at all the commanders. As he traveled further into the bridge, no one paid him any mind. The large holographic display found a signature match for the residue left behind from another ship. The Reptilite's claws tightened, and he muttered a despised name: "Wuyan!"

The image zoomed in on a small capsule pod zipping through space.

"Where is it heading?" Gedeon asked.

"Earth," Kalet replied. She tried to target it, but the weapons system failed to lock onto the tiny ship. Kalet turned about and looked out of the window. Her eyes focused like telescopes. They zoomed in through the vastness of space onto the capsule. "I can shoot it from here."

"Wuyan may be lying in wait for us to reveal our position," Gedeon said, effectively denying her request. He turned, and beckoned another officer. "Jain!"

Lotus saw a smaller black and yellow Reptilite come to attention. Her stripes were flecked with hints of red and blue. She turned toward Gedeon.

"Rex," She reported.

"Intercept the pod."

Jain grabbed ahold tubes intertwining the bridge. She acrobatically flung herself forward to float off into the bowels of the ship.

The Kaiman flew a circle around Mars, gathering momentum, and sped on toward Earth. Rex Gedeon looked around and caught sight of Lotus creeping through the node. Again he demanded the Martian deliver a demonstration.

"I can't," Lotus replied. "Not without Mason."

"Sarek!" Gedeon shouted.

Kalet took a deep breath and said, "Sarek is on Earth."

Gedeon turned to Kalet, "On Earth?"

"He is in the Congo, I believe. With Krome and their contingent," Kalet responded. "I will contact him immediately."

Gedeon pushed off from the center command and entered the tunnel next to Lotus.

"Come," he told the Martian.

Lotus waved his arms frantically trying to move toward the tunnel in zero gravity. He pushed off one of the intertwining tubes to catch on to the walls and pushed himself forward behind the leader. Slowly, while he floated through the tunneled halls, Lotus felt himself grow heavier. Finally, his feet touched the surface. He trotted to catch up to Rex Gedeon.

JAIN WAS A soldier; she acted with purpose and thought of nothing else. She exited the lift into the shuttle bay at the bowels of the Kaiman. She passed a row of ships and boarded an Interceptor. She sat herself down in the egg-like ship with the cone-shaped bow. The hydraulics pushed the Interceptor out into the center lane. She strapped herself in and signaled to the bay.

The bay door opened. The vicious vacuum of space snatched her ship, and the bay door snapped closed behind her. As the Interceptor floated out, she engaged her thrusters to push beyond the Earth's moon. Her display targeted the pod, but the small capsule moved too fast. She pushed her little Interceptor to top speed, hit the side thrusters twice, and turned the ship around. She floated backward toward the pod as it barreled toward the dark side of Earth. The cone on her bow opened; as the pod passed by, she engaged her tractor beam.

As Jain nailed the pod, it yanked her ship in the opposite direction. The pod towed her to the other side of the moon. The Kaiman left her line of sight, and she couldn't tether back to the mother ship. Jain nudged her side thrusters, putting her directly behind the pod as they both headed toward Earth. Her system alarmed of intense heat and magnetic shielding around the planet Earth. She intensified her tractor beam and tried to escape with the pod. The momentum was too great. Then she reversed her engines to slow down from her suicidal speed. She was forced to correct the angle of decent until the system predicted a safe planetary entry. On reentry, everything glowed red as waves of plasma engulfed the two capsules.

Earth's media covered the whole thing, but their prediction of landfall in northern Pennsylvania proved wrong. Jain had thrown the pod off course. Officials on Earth watched a red line cover 800 miles on their radar screens. It went over the Atlantic toward the Eastern shore.

Dimycles woke up in the pod. He looked around, dazed, barely recalling what had happened. He looked down and saw he was cruising over a dark body of water. At first, he felt trapped, and then his memory returned. The lights of the East Coast came into view. Dimycles's hands groped for the controls. He tried to engage the piloting system, but everything was out of order. He triggered the chutes. The system signaled an error: too much weight.

"Too much what?"

He looked around his tiny enclosure, trying to identify the problem.

"What weight?"

He heard an external explosion, and the hull cracked and starting tearing apart. The ship could not withstand Earth's atmosphere. He continued to wrestle the controls to get control of his descent. The ship broke apart around him, letting in the intense heat. Desperate to escape, he kicked open the capsule. The front fluttered off, and Dimycles grabbed a chute harness and jumped. As the pod disappeared from view, he released the chute. His descent slowed dramatically. Through the night air, he looked over the city lights to navigate a safe landing. Suddenly his chute folded in on itself.

Jain jumped into his chute, and Dimycles felt the material covering him. He punched and kicked his way out from under the chute. Jain cut him in the mid-air assault. He grabbed her neck and tried to toss her away, but her claws dug into his back, and she bit him. He screamed. He bit her too and kicked her off. Her tail whipped around his foot, she pulled herself back onto him, resisting his efforts to kick free of her strong tail. He grabbed her wrist, stopping her from clawing him again. She snapped her jaws at his head, but Dimycles dodged.

His chute bundled up, and the ground came up fast. Dimycles reached up to fix it.

Jain swatted at him as her claws tore one of the chute lines. Angrily, he punched the black-yellow terror. Her tail wrapped on his foot, keeping him from controlling his chute, and the pull flipped him upside down. She gnawed on his legs. He gathered himself into a ball, and then with all his might, he kicked her completely off.

A hard wind blew over him, and he could see the city lights of Washington getting closer. He flipped himself around. The lines to his chute were tangled, and some were cut. He climbed the rope to the main chute, but his leg was snared. Quickly, he pulled in the whole chute, bundling it close to his chest. He gripped the cut lines and released the chute again. He'd done just enough to engage it. It caught him, yanked him up, and then the air draft pulled the lines from his hands.

Dimycles landed on the roof of a church off Marlboro Pike and Penn Crossing. He crashed straight through to the floor. Worshippers screamed. He slowly stood up – dazed. His clothes were in tatters as he worked his leg free from the tangled chute. When he turned around, the worshippers saw the chains in his back. They ran out of the building screaming.

Jain dropped through the roof and collided with him. They slid across the floor. As they came to a stop, he hopped up. She kicked him, spun him with her tail, punched him, and bit his shoulder. Dimycles tore free, and repeatedly slammed her massive body onto the ground. He hurled her through the pews to the back of the church and leapt after her. She hit the wall and rolled away, but Dimycles was on top of her. She double-flipped, landing on top of him, then she pulled a dagger.

Dimycles dodged her thrust and shouldered her to the ground. He pounded her through an exterior wall onto a children's playground. He ripped a mechanical horsey from the ground and slammed the nimble Reptilite. Spinning around, he tried to hit her again, but she leapt high in the air, landing behind him. She swung her tail, clipping his legs from under him. As he fell, he threw the horsey at her, but Jain ducked just in time.

Suddenly, lights were everywhere. Floodlights illuminated the scene while flashing lights identified the newcomers as police and fire department. Jain hopped back twice and disappeared into the darkness.

FROM ORBIT, Kalet stared out of the window. Her eyes peered to the surface of Earth, watching Jain hide away in the dark. All was silent. Earth's uniquely powerful atmosphere acted as a shield to protect the planet. It prevented any bombardment from space, and worse, the ionosphere hampered any communication from space to the surface. It was a nightmare of a planet to invade.

So with her powerful eyes, she just watched.

A young Reptilite groomed Kalet's wings and brushed away the frozen debris from the Martian attack. Kal Sarek stood at the opening of the bridge. White stripes ran around his sides with an array of horns decorating his spine.

"You told me to rush back, yet our commander is absent from the helm?" Kal Sarek asked, sarcastically. "What a surprise."

"With you absent, our commander is with the human," she said, gracefully floating down toward him. "Where were you?"

"Conducting experiments."

As Kalet passed him, she hissed: "Experiments? Have you prepared the beacon?"

Sarek followed her down the hall, talking bitterly to her back, "Prepared? Yes, but it is meaningless. I can't activate the beacon without Tiego's tablet... and Lotus hides it."

Kalet shook her head, saying, "Our leader will not be happy to hear of it."

"There is no leader here. Just a confused freedom fighter taking us on a pointless trip through space?" Sarek explained. "If he were a true leader, the Martian would not be so bold as to keep the tablet from us. How did we ever end up in the service of such a weakling?"

"Hold your bitter tongue."

"Or what? We do not belong in space; we are warriors, not explorers! We look stupid out here."

"If you want war, war is what you will get. If you want to go back to the squalor he found you in, be my guest, run back to Reptilia!"

"Reptilia is no squalor!"

"But it isn't Earth!" Kalet shot back.

"Only a fool would invade an entire planet with no hope of reinforcements. How can you have confidence following someone so reckless?"

The two entered an intra-ship transport.

"We aren't out here because it's easy. We're here because we have to be. One minute you are saying he's weak, next he is crazy! Make up your mind; you're spewing the same nonsense they fed you back on Reptilia," Kalet finally told him. "Gedeon has vision. For all your ingenuity, why can't you just wake up?"

"Vision? You cannot honestly confuse vision with delusion. The mission is just, but the leadership is lacking," said Sarek. "I would feel more comfortable if Apex sanctioned this. Apex has ships and the backing of the State. He can win any war if he chooses. Gedeon only has mercenaries, freed slaves, and barely an element of surprise."

"Gedeon has conviction," Kalet said, "Something Apex would know nothing of."

"Once Apex realizes what Gedeon is up to, that will be plenty enough conviction!"

Kalet's wings fluttered as she pointed at him. "Careful, my friend, your treasonous tongue may find itself missing."

"Treason? Treason! Gedeon is committing treason, is he not? We are still Reptilites. Reptilia is still our home. Don't you dare forget that! If any— and I mean any—of this leaks to Apex, he will execute us all! I can't believe I have to explain it. It's as if I'm the crazy one. Apex thinks we're patrolling the borders. Have you any idea how that wears on me? Every day I have to prepare a report to Apex. I tell him that everything is quiet to ease his mind. And every day it troubles me."

Kalet led him out of the transport to their commander's quarters.

Sarek continued, "What if everything isn't quiet? What if Wuyan is preparing an attack? The Akolytes will catch Reptilia blindly, and it will be our fault! No! My fault! My own people will die. Where will we go? Not here. Not Earth."

"Earth is our rightful home!" Kalet replied. "We would still be there, had we not been taken from it, and bred into..."

"Bred into what? The beautiful, intelligent creatures that we are? I feel like I really am going insane. No one sees how obvious it is. For a species so young, humans have made enormous scientific progress. They've even cloned many of our...our ancestors." Sarek scratched his head. "I hate to even admit to being related to something so perverse. Have you seen those dinosaurs?" He raised his arms high. "Big, smelly, clumsy, and stupid! Every time I look at them, I want to vomit? They don't even taste good."

Kalet gasped. "You ate them?"

"Look at me?" he said, flaunting his rows of teeth, "Of course I ate them."

Kalet stormed off down the hall.

Sarek hurried after her. "Sorry, but I don't see any 'vision' in the big, clumsy, beasts of yesterday... especially when our people face bigger dangers today. Now I hear Wuyan has sent a probe to Earth. She must know we are here now! How do I handle that? How do I tell Apex that Wuyan knows of Earth when I'm not supposed to be here myself? How do I keep it a secret?"

"You tell Apex nothing! I can't believe I'm even speaking to you of this. You'll get both of us killed!" Kalet stopped and faced Sarek. "You speak of Apex as if he is some benevolent king. You don't know what a monster he is."

Kalet's feathered wings fluttered slightly. She walked to the door of Gedeon's study.

Rex Gedeon stood in his study, pondering Earth from his portal. His pupils formed triangles as his red eyes focused on that long sought-after jewel. He watched the waves it produced.

"The humans once thought the Earth was the center of the universe," he said as if speaking to the air. His pupils morphed into shapes. The Earth's colors shimmered and changed as he viewed the planet through the different light spectrums. He didn't want to miss a thing.

"How foolish of them to change their minds," he muttered. Earth appeared as a pulsing ball of heat in his infrared view. His pupils twisted ever further. "Do we really hold your own planet in a higher regard?"

Rex Gedeon turned to his private terminal and waved his powerful claws. A holographic display zoomed in on Earth. The image rotated, as the glow filled the eerily lit room.

Gedeon allowed Kalet to enter, then instructed her to upload any new data from Sarek. Kalet nodded, backing away to allow Sarek in. Lotus stood up and walked into the corner. Kalet closed the door behind her, leaving the three others alone.

"Why were you in the Congo?" Gedeon asked Kal Sarek.

"Collecting samples," Sarek answered.

"Of what kind?"

"Human," Sarek responded.

The data from Sarek's ship streamed onto Gedeon's screen. The display of the Earth disappeared, replaced by the image of a woman.

"Is this the scientist, Mason Kinoah?" Rex Gedeon asked, turning to his science officer.

"Yes," Sarek said, and then bragged, "My efforts with the human woman have enabled me to translate three languages, and I've developed many inoculations from the antibodies in her blood. I even have ways to enhance their-"

"You will kill her with your reckless experimentation," Rex Gedeon noted, pointing at Lotus. "Release her back into the custody of the Martian."

"You don't understand, w-we need these inoculations! Besides, the project on Earth is nearly completed," Sarek protested. "She's no longer any use to him! She must be... improved."

"By whose authority?"

Sarek started to speak but thought better of it. "I apologize, Rex. It was a gross oversight on my part."

"When will the beacon be completed?"

"The beacon is already completed. We only need the microchip the human promised, and of course, the tablet." Sarek glared at Lotus.

"Why the tablet?" Gedeon asked.

"Tiego's tablet. Without it, I cannot unlock the chip's code. I've had much better luck just—"

"What is the meaning of these logs?" Gedeon interrupted, looking over Sarek's new data.

"Simply reports of the humans," Sarek explained. "Details of their infrastructure, anatomy. We are indeed ready to strike."

"We are not ready until I say we are. I will not go into war until the devices Mason created are tested." Gedeon gave his command: "You will give Dr. Kinoah back to her captor until that is confirmed."

Gedeon scanned all the data from Sarek's ship, and his eye's glanced over an unsent report to Apex. Gedeon waved his claw and played the message:

"Supreme leader Apex, for too long I have kept from you the true whereabouts of our leader, Rex Gedeon..." The words of the probe data echoed through the room.

Gedeon's eyes tightened, and his scales turned red. "Treachery!" He grumbled.

As Sarek heard the recording, he panicked. In his rush from Earth, he forgot to redact his latest probe updates. Now he was left with no choice. He attacked Gedeon from behind. Gedeon's tail whipped, striking Sarek's legs, flipping him. Gedeon grabbed Sarek's leg and bit. Instantly, Sarek's leg went numb, as he was flung across the room. The poison set in as he tried to get up, paralyzing his leg and causing the left side of his body to tingle in pain. Gedeon stomped on his waist, pinning Sarek to the ground.

Gedeon leaned in on his prey. "The leader of Reptilia will die in time, and the Earth will spin long after the flesh has been picked from his bones."

Gedeon thrust his tail into Sarek's chest. Sarek grabbed the tail and held on, but the power quickly overwhelmed him. The sharp point of Gedeon's tail slowly pierced through his tough skin.

"Fear. Impatience." Gedeon purged Sarek of these fatal flaws, telling him, "When I found you, I nursed you from my own cup. I bathe your body, and tended to your wounds." Gedeon's razor sharp tail cut into his victim's fingers. Sarek's hands bled, and the paralysis spread through his body. He lost his grip and the tail cut through his heart.

"How could you spit the water of my cup back into my face?" Gedeon finally asked.

Sarek gasped, and his vision faded.

Gedeon stood up. The end of the message played.

"... in the end, there is no room for disobedience or civil war. We have but one ruler, and only he shall govern us. Hail, Apex!"

Gedeon knelt over the corpse, shaking his head in disappointment. "I could not protect you from the mental exhaustion secrecy brings," he told the dead creature. "The guilt wore you down; I freed you from its burden." Gedeon exhaled, and his scales turned bluish-gray. He turned his attention to Lotus, who stood in the corner looking pale.

"Who is Apex?" Lotus asked weakly.

As blood dripped from his mouth, Gedeon turned away from the cowering human, ignoring him.

Lotus insisted. "Tiego told me what happened to the ancient dinosaurs millions of years ago. That breeders would go to Earth and abduct them for genetic engineering. He told me how they used your kind as beast of burden, and slaves for war, but he never mentioned Apex."

The mourning Reptilite answered. "Apex is the Supreme Leader of Reptilia."

"I take it you are not loyal to the Supreme Leader?"

"Apex is no leader, he is a pawn of the Galactic State," Gedeon responded. "He was set in place to keep Reptilites in subservience. He cares only for himself, and not the prosperity of our kind. He would rather see the yokes return to our backs than sacrifice the lofty position and army the State has granted him."

"Then how did you amass such an army without his approval?"

"Though Reptilites were granted emancipation many years ago, we are still enslaved in many parts throughout the Realm. Through no easy task, I traveled the Realm and led revolts to free my kin from the chains of slavery. That is how I now own the Kaiman. That is how I command a powerful army, loyal to me, independent from the flag of the Reptilites." Gedeon rose from mourning over Sarek. "But this power has made Apex nervous. He fears that at any moment I will lead an incursion, with the aim of ruling Reptilia myself."

"To the Supreme Leader's credit, that does indeed make you all the more dangerous," Lotus said, nodding.

"Indeed, however, Apex, like most Reptilites, are ignorant of our history, and he has mistaken my motive; it is not Reptilia that I wish to rule. It is Earth."

"Then the Earth is the Holy Land for us both," Lotus observed, allying himself with Rex Gedeon.

"I do not understand this concept of a holy... land."

"Of course you do," Lotus countered. "Why this fascination with Earth? Resources? Water? You can get those anywhere. It's Earth's unique meaning. You Reptilites may be bred as warriors, but you cannot hide from your emotions because those emotions pull you to this planet—a planet you have little chance of capturing. The reward so outweighs the risk, that it becomes divine."

"True," said Gedeon. "The soil of Earth warmed the eggs of my ancestors, so it must be what you call a 'holy land.' We Reptilites stepped out of the marshes and ruled as kings for the first time on this blue and white spectacle. We did so millions of years ago before humans existed. I worked for years on a plan to reclaim this planet, and now that it lies just beyond my ship, I feel the righteousness at the tips of my claws."

"Then our purpose is one," Lotus added.

"The day you reach out with your hands and accomplish your purpose is the day you become king of your realm," Gedeon conspired, "You will take control of the scientist, Mason, and keep her until you have conducted a full-scale test, assuring I can nullify Earth's ground forces. You will deliver the tablet to me, to enable the beacon that will shut down the human drone defense. If this is not done, I will not see you alive again."

Lotus nodded and hurried from the room. Kalet entered. Her face saddened upon seeing her old companion's corpse. Gedeon turned to her.

He thought aloud to the winged creature. "On the verge of our invasion, Wuyan's presence near Earth is alarming. Kal Sarek's betrayal is most unfortunate. I cannot ignore these setbacks. We exist between two worlds with no home, and it leaves us supremely vulnerable." Gedeon pointed to the data from Sarek's ship, and commanded: "Find me another science officer to disseminate this information, and get my beacon activated!"

"Yes, Rex Gedeon."

"What news of the capsule?" he asked.

"I saw Jain engaged the capsule, but lost sight of them through the skirmish. I expect to hear the results of her interception shortly," Kalet responded. "The capsule did not appear to contain a probe, but... a man."

"A man? Wuyan sent a human to Earth?"

"It was one of the Exiles, from the Sunil."

"We will not underestimate her intentions," said Gedeon. "We must assume the Akolytes are aware of our involvement with Earth, so we must tread carefully. Once we begin our invasion, we cannot risk an ambush.

"The Chungassi are her only allies who have achieved space flight. With no spies near Chunga to determine their intelligence, we will find out the hard way what they know of this planet. Take us to the Chungassi."

"Yes, Rex Gedeon."

Gedeon turned from Kalet. "Get my area cleaned."

Kalet looked at her once eccentric companion. She stifled any expression that might reveal her aversion to his death.

Gedeon looked at Sarek's chewed body. It worried him that treachery could exist at such a high level, so close to him. "There may be others ignorant of our right to rule."

Before she could rush off to complete the orders, Gedeon called her back and promoted her.

"You are my new Kal," Gedeon announced. "Purge any doubt from their minds. We are the First Born of Earth, and we shall rule it!"

Young Reptilites scurried into Gedeon's quarters to cleanse it of Sarek and his blood. When they finished, they bowed and exited.

Gedeon went down into a deep squat to meditate. He felt the Kaiman cast away from Earth's moon and fly over the dark side of Earth. After it swung over the sparkling lights of the night to the other side of the planet, the Kaiman enaged thrusters. It passed Mars and the abandoned human colonies. The souls of the dead still knelt in the dirt on the rust-colored planet. Their souls reached high, still begging, still hoping that someone would avenge them.

As the Kaiman closed in on light speed, it flashed by Europa and her robot-operated observation base. Jupiter's gravity pulled on the spaceship. The Kaiman engines engaged the anti-mass field and blasted into hyperspace. They were off to the water world of Chunga.

NIGHT TAKES BISHOP

AFTER JOGGING THROUGH the D.C. streets, Bishop came to a stop near the Metro Center Station. Squatting, he brushed debris from his white-and-gray compression pants and leaned back against the wall. His sand-colored skin glowed red from his run. His breathing eased, and his powerful muscles relaxed. The autumn wind blew chilly through his fluffy hair, and his sweat-dampened compression shirt began to dry. Bishop had soft and kind eyes and long eyelashes. He stared across the street.

He stayed in that position for a while, then pulled two electronic dice from the sleeve of his shirt. Shaking them in his palm, he whispered the words of a calypso song he learned as a boy in the islands:

"...Johnnie watch the pot... don't let it get too hot..."

Bishop tossed the dice on the concrete between his feet, snapping his fingers when they landed.

A passing car stalled on the road. Impatient drivers behind it honked before passing around the immobilized vehicle on G street.

Bishop picked up the dice.

The politician in the car's backseat had shaggy, unkempt hair, a small chin, and a security detail that insisted he stay put. They walked around the car and looked under the hood. Bishop gave his dice another roll. As they came to a stop, interior lights blinked, and data transferred.

When backup approached, the politician's security looked around- their eyes suspicious. By that time, Bishop was gone.

Bishop slipped the dice back into his sleeve and jogged further west. After a block or two, he slowed down, anxious to look at the data, but he noticed a car idling along the road behind him.

Bishop ducked into a diner. He threw the dice into the nearest trash bin and headed for the counter. After he had scanned the menu, he ordered four sandwiches from the cashier. A few men in suits entered. Their attire was out of place in that casual atmosphere. A lanky man grabbed Bishop's arm, and another patted Bishop's shoulders, arms, and the small of his back.

Bishop looked shocked. "Can I help you?" he snapped as he pushed them off.

A few patrons stood up, and the atmosphere became agitated. The men examined Bishop's phone. It was so out of date that all it was good for was emergency calls and rudimentary text messages. The men looked Bishop up and down, but his athletic compression outfit didn't allow many hiding places.

"I'm very straight," Bishop insisted.

"He's must've dumped it, Fox!" one of the men said to the lanky one.

The security started to search the restaurant until the manager threatened to call the police.

"Let's go," Fox said, tossing a trash bin back into place before they left.

Bishop took the sandwiches he'd ordered. On his way out, he knelt down to tie his shoes and retrieved the dice.

He walked back west and found three homeless men huddled near the entrance to an alley. Bishop handed them the sandwiches, and then took a step back, and saluted them. As they returned his salute, Bishop noticed the car again. It was rounding the corner.

Bishop trotted northwest to K Street and aimed for the closest thing he had to a home - the South Street Mackey Gym. Though it was a small facility, it was known worldwide. It had been designed for an extreme level of training and kept its membership to a minimum. The best fighters tested their might in the gym's boxing ring. The ring had just enough space on the main floor to share with a cage. Off to the side hung a short row of heavy bags for conditioning fists and shins. Mat grapplers and wrestlers came there to hone their explosive ground games.

This was anything but a country club. It was a concrete jungle, mortared together by the blood, sweat, and tears of its members. There were no juice bars, TV screens, or even air conditioning. A lone ceiling fan creaked above the sweating patrons, giving hot air a nudge, but nothing more. Bags, packed densely with sand, gave payback to anyone who dared hit them. The ceiling gave a little at the corners as if it were ready to fall. It wasn't. It was as tough and sturdy as the rest of the structure.

Bishop poked his head in and glanced around the place. A whiff of hot air hit his face, and he felt as if he were suddenly in the jungles of Thailand. Sounds of shuffling feet and tumbling grapplers echoed through the hard interior. Exhalations, thuds, grunts and crashes created the South Mackey soundtrack. The lady at the front desk looked up.

"Bishop?" she gasped. "Not again..."

"I just wanted to do a little training," he said, giving her a puppy-dog look.

"I- I don't know..." She hesitated. "I mean, it's fine with me, but-"

"Oh, thanks!" Bishop cut in. He gleefully trotted to the grappling mats.

Julius was about to enter the ring when he caught sight of Bishop walking through the gym. Like Adrian, Julius had the black hair, dark eyes and strong nose of their mother. Unlike his brother, Julius had been too young to receive the tribal branding on his oval face. Julius looked more like their jovial father. He was thin, with the sleek muscles of a gymnast.

He waved off his opponent and stalked toward Bishop. "What are you doing here?"

"Just trying to get in some mat time," Bishop said, kicking off his shoes.

"Mackey said not to come back for at least a month," said Julius. "You can't keep doing this. People think you're on gear. You're gonna get us busted."

"I'll tone it down," Bishop insisted. "People can beat me up. I'll play it cool. If I act like I'm actually getting tired, no one will know!"

"That's not the point."

"Come on Jules."

"You're hurting people, B.K.! These guys rely on this. It's how they eat. Fighters can't afford to miss fights just because you want to inflict physical pain on them to channel your emotional hurt... Hey, you okay?"

"Yeah," Bishop answered, rubbing his head. When he grabbed clumps of hair in his fingers, he revised his answer to: "No."

Julius gritted his teeth, and said, "I think you should go home."

Bishop felt heat rising into his face. He punched the mat, and stormed off, saying, "I don't have a home!"

"Sure ya do!" said the iron-jawed champ, Rod, from inside the cage. Bishop ignored him, as he sat on the floor and started putting his shoes back on.

Julius told Rod, "Let him go; he's not right in the head today."

"None of us are right in the head," Rod shrugged. "Otherwise, we wouldn't be here. It's the only place a fighter can reveal his true nature. When you fight, everything you hide from society comes out, and who you are shines through. If you're shady, you fight shady. If you're brave, you fight like a champ. Then, of course, you got people like B.K..." Rod's voice faded, as he added: "...who's just a convict."

Bishop stopped and glanced over his shoulder. "Wha...? You talk the most shit, Rod."

"I'm just real," Rod claimed. "You walked up in here; I'm just calling it out. Martial artists have a code. You don't! You're just a convict thug, ruining everything we're about. You come in acting like you believe in this shit, but I see straight through you. The only reason you come in here is because you're hiding from what's out there!"

The gym quieted.

Bishop saw only accusing eyes. "I've never backed down from anything in my life."

"Then how come you got no friends? Either they left you, or you backed away from them," Rod sneered. "Just creepin' around the streets because you got nothing going for you."

"I'm just trying to find you a girlfriend."

"Yeah? Probably cuz you got your last one killed," Rod remarked.

"You mean your mom?" Bishop said. "She's still alive, and she think's I'm swell guy. She also said to tell you not to talk about shit you don't know."

"I know how you fight, and that's all I need to judge a man," Rod asserted.

"You judge a man by how he handles defeat."

"I wouldn't know. Referee keeps raising my hand in victory," Rod retorted. "Come back when you're defending a title like I have. You haven't defended a title? Oh? I guess that means never."

"You know what, you right," Bishop grabbed a pair of 4-ounce4oz gloves, and threw them on. "But you still gonna get your ass whooped for talking shit."

"Come on, bruh. I been waiting for this," Rod said excitedly in the cage. "I want to know what kind of man you are."

"The kind of man I am will split you in half."

"What're you saying? I'm easy work?"

"I'm saying you don't want to catch these hands."

"You're worn out," Rod claimed.

Bishop hopped up into the cage.

Rod squared up and said, "Mental stress takes a toll on a man's body, and your mind hasn't been the same since-"

The bell rang. Bishop launched a straight right into Rod's face. It caught the big man with his mouth open, and he stumbled backward. Rod aimed a bicycle front kick at Bishop's face. Bishop slipped the foot. The moment Rod's foot touched the ground; he did a spinning back kick. Bishop shuffled closer, finding safety behind Rod's right knee.

Rod spun left, concealing a heavy right hook, but before he could unleash the punch, Bishop countered with a left hook. The counter dropped Rod to the canvas, but he hopped up as if he were made of rubber.

"Having nice hands doesn't make you a fighter," Rod taunted, circling. His tone was still confident, but his knees were starting to wobble. "The ring is full of businessmen."

He reached out to clinch. Bishop pushed him off, circling away.

"The cage is full of phonies," Rod claimed, peppering his opponent with quick, but ineffective jabs. "Sometimes you find someone without a heart. Then you know you found a killer." He launched a hard kick.

Bishop caught the kick and floored Rod again with another straight right.

Rod rolled on the ground and covered his head. He rolled to his back and kicked wildly, thinking Bishop would swarm. Bishop paced back and forth instead. Rod got to his feet, but when he started to say something, Bishop's front kick caught him in the chin, and he stumbled backward. He bounced off the cage as if he meant to, but Bishop was already in the air with a flying knee. The blow forced Rod's face into the cage, and a low kick started his knees wobbling. Bishop slipped in a wild jab and followed with a three-three counter to the midsection. Rod reached wildly, clinching Bishop. They pummeled for position. Bishop threw a left knee to Rod's mid-section and broke away.

As Rod cocked back to throw a right hand, he suddenly clutched his liver. Bishop's left knee had been brutal. Rod collapsed into a fetal position, and lay on the ground, shaking.

The bell rang, but it was too late to save Rod. He panted, smacked his lips, and gasped.

Bishop adjusted his four-ounce gloves and pumped the air with two jabs. Looking down at Rod, he said: "I don't hear you talking."

A minute went by. The bell sounded. Rod rolled over and crawled to the edge of the cage. Bishop shook his head. Other men ran into the cage to help Rod up.

"Shit, you okay?"

"I'm fine, get off me," Rod panted. He clawed at the cage but got nowhere.

Seeing Rod's crippled state, Julius spoke to him through the links. "How about you help me clean the mats," he suggested.

"I think Bishop needs another round," Rod replied, as two men helped him to his feet.

"Yeah," Julius agreed. "He needs a couple of rounds at the bar."

Rod got to his feet, doubled over, and stumbled toward the chairs.

Julius grabbed the cage and stared at Bishop. The cage sat on top of plywood, raised eight inches off the ground. Julius and Bishop came eye-to-eye. Bishop looked at his taller friend. Talking quietly through the links, Julius asked Bishop: "Damn, did you have to shrink him like that?"

Bishop didn't have an answer. He looked at the concrete walls, blue-green with black and yellow stripes. His afro was damp, and his curly hair framed his confusing face. His soft brown eyes were often offset by a scowl topped by a wrinkled brow. He was a man who didn't know how he had reached this point.

Julius looked his broken friend in the eye, and said: "You didn't kill her."

"I didn't save her," Bishop exhaled, and exited the cage. He grabbed his shoes, walked out, and crossed the parking lot. His walk became a trot; then a light jog turned to a run. Maybe a high would clear his mind.

Bishop ran down K to the end and turned right on 9th. He slowed for a moment, placing both hands on his head. He kept walking with his eyes tightly closed. As mist turned to drizzle, he stopped. Something shivered through his body and soul. The ground beneath his feet moved, giving off a distant rumble. He glanced up at the night sky and saw military jets and gunships cutting through thick puffy clouds.

In an island accent, he murmured: "Well, mudoes..." After brief hesitation, Bishop ran south. Cars pulled up to the curbs. Their occupants got out and stared at the sky. Fleets of military trucks rolled through. Bishop felt as if he stepped into a war zone.

He took Pennsylvania Avenue, traveling in the same direction as the military traffic. He pushed low-hanging branches out of his way. Once he crossed the Anacostia, he ran until he neared the Maryland line and slowed down. As he wondered where the planes were going, he passed a beat-up motel called the Deluxe Inn. When he saw a familiar-looking man disappearing behind the building, Bishop cut across the parking lot. He passed junked gas-powered cars, and a homeless man hobbled through, speaking only to the air, "D-Don't call my name!"

Passing through odors of urine and liquor, Bishop rounded the corner of the building. There was the familiar face: a street hustler most people called "Logical." Bishop greeted him.

When he recognized Bishop, Logical nodded, "What are you doing out here? I haven't see you for a li'l while."

"Jogging," Bishop answered.

"Ain't the time, or the damn place for that," Logical said, shifting a large backpack on his shoulders. "Get your shit pushed back for no reason out here."

"Don't you usually keep to the streets around Capitol Hill?" Bishop asked him.

"Yeah, that's where the money is. Politicians got the real dough, and police drones don't bother them."

"Why are you on this side of town?"

"Every road to freedom is a good road," Logical replied, pointing to the sky, "Do you not see this shit? It's about to get real. I don't want to be close to the White House. That's the first place shit will go down."

"What are you doing out here then?" Bishop asked.

"Trapping. I heard about a month back the hunger is real around here, so I figure now is a good time to cash in on it."

"I thought you quit doing this?"

"You can't quit the game. I got bills. My kids go to school," Logical shrugged. "They can't eat the books."

"Probably because books aren't for eating. I mean, they can't eat that either," Bishop insisted, pointing at the backpack.

"A G-pack is better than a book." Logical patted his backpack, "Money is guaranteed. Fiends are always hungry."

"True," Bishop affirmed. "Where's wifey?"

"Is that what they call 'em these days?"

"Logical, you live with her, and she had both your kids. What else you wanna call her?"

"She straight. Holding me down. Like she supposed to. You know? Look here, lemme tell ya something. You shouldn't be out here. A lot of hunger come through this time of night."

"Where am I supposed to go? I'm on the streets just like you."

"Yes, you're on streets, but you're not street."

"What's that supposed to mean? I got fucked by the same system that fucked you!"

"Don't get me wrong, that was fucked up what happened to you, B.K.," Logical added. "Guys like you don't just stand on a corner and serve the fiends. Your mind starts wandering; your brain starts calculating."

"Isn't that what it's for?" Bishop asked in frustration.

"You don't respect the street for what it is. I know you, man, everything with you is an equal sign, and sometimes you don't stop to think. You just do whatever it takes to balance the equation. Gotta respect the game. Me, I'm out here, I hold my block, and I get my respect," Logical said. "Cops know what I do, but they don't mess with me because they are looking for the big fish, the ruthless cats."

Bishop didn't quite agree. "You are fantasizing... if I was anywhere near that dangerous, I wouldn't be standing here."

Logical stopped him, "Bull shit... then why are you standing here?"

Bishop went silent.

"B.K, what've you been doing?"

Bishop nodded, and asked, "Did it ever seem weird to you how the Six came to power so quickly?"

"Oh damn. I knew it!"

"Listen!"

"This is exactly what I'm talking about!"

"Since when has a homegrown terror group ever gained that kind of power within the United States?"

"Never?"

"Yet, only after Lotus started manufacturing weapons did they decide to clean house? And the first thing to go-"

"Privacy laws, you preaching to the choir on that one," Logical claimed. "I don't own a single device they can track. My shoes, my watch, everything- chip free."

"It's not that. It's that they purposefully let citizens die and used the tragedy to push legislation to overturn privacy at the expense of citizen lives," Bishop said. "That's not right."

"You'll never prove that." Logical heard a noise and looked around the corner.

"Yeah?" Bishop pulled the dice from his sleeve pocket and showed it to Logical.

"What? You wanna roll dice? You don't have pockets deep enough to go in on-"

"It's a chip! With secret data on it."

"Secret from who?"

"Senator Donald."

"You mean, 'Clean Energy America' Donald?"

"Yes."

"B', get rid of that shit."

"I think he's dirty."

"Fucking hell, he's a politician! America's favorite politician at that."

"Yeah, but I think he was working for them."

"For who?"

"The Six."

Logical took a deep breath. "The Six are dead. You are negative two steps from being charged for treason. You already can't leave the state, and you are banned from getting on a plane. How will you escape the country when every branch of government comes hunting for your head and execute you as a traitor to the land?" Logical warned. "When Nicole died, your soul went away, and shit like this will not fill the abyss that her death left behind. Don't do this to yourself."

Bishop looked away, admittedly ashamed, "... I'm – I'm breaking down, hurting myself, hurting my own friends. I – I just need to do something to fill the void."

"Well, you better figure something out, cuz that's how it starts. Half the addicts walking the streets were just like you. Normal motherfuckers. People with jobs. People with families, and then something went wrong that killed them inside. Then a pain grows within them that they can't get rid of, and that's when they find a guy like me who has exactly what they need to deal with the shit," Logical said, patting his backpack. "Make you forget everything; even ya' own mama."

"I don't want to forget Nicole, but it's like... it's like I lost a limb, an arm or something, and I can't wrap my mind around it because all my life, it's been there, and suddenly it's gone. I can still feel it, ya know, the arm. When I want to pick something up, it feels like I can, but I can't. I think I'm losing it... maybe... we work together we could help each other. A business?"

"Mm... nah. I can't go back to Babylon," Logical argued.

"What do you mean? Aren't you doing that now? You don't own that product." Bishop pointed to Logical's backpack. "Stop being a front man for this. Be my front man for something better. You can't do this forever."

Logical paused, then said, "That's some cold shit, but you right. I can't do this forever, but it's a game you know? I can't quit it." He got distracted. "It's a paradox." He spoke slowly because he heard footsteps splashing through water on the other side of the alley wall. He peered behind Bishop, and saw a lanky figure, followed by three larger men. "B', break out!"

It was the senator's security guards.

One of the men grabbed Logical, slamming him against the wall and holding a gun to his head. Logical struggled, but his attacker just pinned him tighter.

The other two went after Bishop. He disarmed one, holding the attacker's own gun against him. "Let him go!" Bishop shouted, holding the second goon hostage.

"Who the fuck sent you?' Logical cried.

Fox snapped his fingers. The man holding Logical pistol-whipped his victim into silence.

"Cut the bullshit!" Logical said through a mouth full of blood.

Fox put away his gun and pulled out a scanning device. It beeped when he held it toward Bishop.

"He's got it!" Fox announced.

"Bishop Kennedy?" A voice came out of the darkness, and Senator Donald stepped forward. "You have something that belongs to me?"

"I don't give a fuck," Bishop shouted, and aimed the gun at Logical's attacker, "Touch him one more time!"

When Bishop changed targets, Fox and the third goon advanced on him. Bishop step sideways.

Fox reached for his gun. Bishop lunged, pinning Fox's arm, as he kneed him in the sternum. Bishop felt the man's rib cage crush against his knee as Fox fell to the ground. Bishop came up with Fox's gun in the other hand, and fired three shots with both guns, felling the other thugs.

Bishop turned and held up the senator.

Senator Donald stood still staring Bishop in the eye, beyond the barrel of the guns. A car drove up behind him. Fox coughed up blood and struggled to pick himself off the ground. A new team of security poured out of the car, and Bishop took a step back, dual wielding the guns threateningly.

"Boyacobas will be avenged," The Senator claimed, getting into the car with his security. The windy silence lasted only for a moment after the car drove away.

"Yes! Yes!" Logical screamed, jumping in the air. "Fucking yes! That was cold! You kilt that stanky bitch!"

Bishop stared at the car driving off into the night.

"That's how we do it! B', dump the heat!" Logical screamed at the top of his lungs. He grabbed the guns from Bishop, and, after wiping them, he squeezed them back into the dead men's fingers. While Logical was down replanting the guns, he went through the men's pockets, pulling out stacks of cash. Bishop gave Logical a look.

"My kids can't eat books," Logical reasoned. "Fuck it; these guys don't need it."

Bishop seemed disturbed.

"Damn this spot is hot!" Logical claimed, out of breath. "Who's Boyacobas?"

Bishop shrugged, "I don't know."

"How many people have you killed to not know?" Logic asked, standing up, "You got a senator out for your blood."

"Flight 522 killed a lot of people. Someone's always gonna be out for revenge. That's life for me," Bishop cringed at the thought and shook his head. "I get death threats all the time. My home is full of letters."

Logical became insistent. "It is imperative we break out. Drones will be hot on our tails from that gunfire.

"Where should I go?"

Logical shrugged, stashed the cash, and left the scene saying, "Fuck it, go home! Read some letters!"

Bishop looked around, and the word echoed through his head:

Home...

Trying to focus, Bishop walked behind the motel, to the corner of Pennsylvania Avenue. Reluctantly, he headed back west. As he jogged in place at a light, a car pulled up next to him. The young couple inside had their child in the backseat. They seemed to be singing something, but Bishop couldn't hear what it was. The couple kissed. At that moment, Bishop weakened and changed his mind. Instead of waiting for the light, he turned left and jogged through the park.

Ten minutes later, he was in Sherwood Forest, a neighborhood full of huge old trees. He went down 36th.

Oddly enough, the streetlights were off. Trees blocked stars and moonlight. Everything was dark. Bishop found his way to a house and jumped the fence. The ground was moist from autumn rains. He walked to the rear of the property and jumped the back fence into the yard behind it. There he crouched, hidden in the dark. Then he slowly stood.

Bishop inched his way up to a rose bush that blocked the back patio. Through the kitchen window, he could see an older woman making a pie. She was in her sixties, with pale skin, and bright blue eyes. Her hair was white and curly, and she wore large round glasses. Nervously, he pulled the dice from his sleeve and tumbled them in the palm of his hand.

As Bishop watched the woman bounced around the kitchen, humming. He bit his lip, and his eyes watered. He slowly inhaled. An older man hobbled into the kitchen, snuck up behind the woman, and hugged her. She turned, and they kissed. The man stood behind her, holding her as she swayed and danced—all this while working on her pie. Bishop felt a smile forming, but suddenly that feeling died.

Something's not right.

He crouched, and pushed the dice down into the soil. He scurried to the front gate, hopped into the front yard, hit the ground, and rolled forward. He trotted to the sidewalk along 34th. That's when he spotted them.

Drones!

One put a spotlight on him and commanded him to halt. Three more drones arrived, followed by a patrol car. An officer inside used his loudspeaker: "Approach the vehicle please."

"I'm just out for a walk," Bishop said, his white and grey compression outfit glowing in the spotlight.

Two officers stepped out. "Put your hands in the air, now! Down on one knee! Now! Put both hands on top of your head. Sit on your ass. Cross your feet."

One of the officers jerked Bishop's hands behind his back and clamped the plasticuffs on him. The cop patted Bishop down, taking his cell phone, and then backed away. The commanding officer walked over. By the time he got to Bishop, three other squad cars had arrived.

The commander stood over Bishop, looking down at him. Bishop stared up and read the man's name: George Wilson. Deputy Ana approached and said, "The drones detected an unregistered encryption device on him, but we searched him and found nothing. He doesn't even have ID. Just this old cell phone. It isn't even locked."

"Doesn't matter. I know who he is," Wilson replied, taking the phone and returning to his patrol car. Two more patrol cars pulled up, one stopping, so its driver was opposite Wilson's window.

"Who you got there?" the driver asked.

"Bishop Kennedy," Wilson answered while typing on his dash computer.

"How you know?" asked the driver as he looked past the car. "Drones didn't get an ID."

"Flight 522," Wilson said. "It was all in the news a few years ago."

"Holy shit! That's him?" The driver turned to get a better look. "I thought he'd be taller."

"TV does that," Wilson confirmed, reading Bishop's profile. "Yeah, here he is. Looks like he isn't supposed to operate any electronics as a part of his probation agreement."

Ana noticed the phone. "I guess that phone is clear violation of his parole."

Wilson examined the phone and noted that it was a pre-approved device. It bore an electronic seal to show it had not been tampered with. "Nah, it's okay. This drones were just detecting the seal."

"Makes sense," said Ana. "They couldn't find anything else in the area... just a couple of electronic collars on pets."

Wilson eyed Bishop. "What were you up to, Kennedy?" He glanced at Ana. "Do me a favor, and find out who lives in that house." He got out of his car and approached Bishop. "Where's your car?"

"Don't have one," said Bishop. "Not supposed to drive."

Wilson nodded. "What do you do?"

"Am I being arrested?"

"You talkin' back to me? What the fuck you do?"

"I train. I teach."

"What do you train, what do you teach?" Wilson demanded, looking at Bishop's stout figure. "Fighting? Gymnastics?"

"Yeah, a mix of those things."

"Well, there's no gym around here. You a private tutor?"

Bishop stood, nodding at nothing.

"You went to college? You a smart guy?" Wilson queried.

"I went to college."

Wilson looked past Bishop to the house and finally asked the key question. "You know the people here?"

Bishop looked at the ground, then at his folded legs. "Nah."

Wilson had already established a pattern of responses, and the way Bishop hesitated on the last question raised a flag. "You're walking by their house; your footprints are in their yard. You must know them."

No response.

Wilson touched his radio and asked Ana, "Who lives there?"

"A Mr. Arnet and Jacquelyn Peterson. Looks like a couple in their sixties."

"Oh, that's sad. Get on your feet, Kennedy," Wilson ordered. "You scope out the seniors and rob them? That's your deal now? That's what you went to school for? That's why you train in the gym? To beat up old folks?"

Wilson pushed Bishop along the pathway up to the front door and knocked. The front porch light turned on, and the door creaked open. A blue-eyed, white-haired lady opened the door—Jacquelyn Peterson. She seemed shocked at the sight of uniforms.

Wilson nodded. "Ma'am, sorry to bother you this late in the evening."

"Oh my goodness, is everything okay?" Ms. Peterson asked.

"Oh, of course, ma'am, I'm a police officer, George Wilson. I just wanted to know if you recognize this man?" Wilson nudged Bishop forward.

Ms. Peterson examined Bishop, and slowly shook her head, "No, I'm sorry, I've never seen him before."

A man came to the door—Arnet. As he swung the door wide open, Ms. Peterson gave him a quick rundown of what was happening. When Wilson asked if Arnet knew Bishop, the old man studied Bishop's face. "Never seen him."

Wilson nodded. "Okay, we caught him walking around near your home, and we just wanted to make sure this wasn't a misunderstanding. Sorry to bother you."

Wilson pushed Bishop back to his patrol car. Leaning in close, Wilson said: "I watched your trial, and I know your story. I know everything about you. You're thinking this is you against the world; it's not. You think you gotta steal because you're down on your luck; it's not like that. We got laws, and you have to follow them. You want to hurt a lot of people—"

"I didn't hurt anyone."

Wilson straightened up, "Hey! I talk, you listen. Ya' understand? That's the deal? You want to talk; we can take it downtown." Wilson looked at Bishop for a second, and continued, pointing at him, "You hurt a lot of people, and society has to take you out of the picture. You're smart, so you must be thinking you should be working some big top secret job on Capitol Hill. But you're not, so you think it isn't fair. You think you should be up in the SARA space station, and you're not. So you think it isn't fair. Let me tell you; two-hundred-and-three people lost their lives on Flight 522. That, my friend, is what isn't fair."

Bishop shook his head slowly, "That case was closed a long time ago. I didn't crash the damn plane."

Wilson scoffed, "Yeah, but you know what did."

"Cap!" Ana ran up. "Check this out?"

Ana showed her captain a list of Bishop's known affiliates, including Adrian Blackwell. Wilson's stern face turned sour.

"Get... in... the car." George said.

As the words escaped from his throat, another patrol unit screeched around the corner and stopped.

"We gotta go! They're screaming for backup! They found him!" the deputy screamed from behind the wheel.

Wilson grabbed Bishop by the shoulder and put him in the front passenger seat. Ana drove. Wilson slid into the backseat on the driver's side so he could get a good look at Bishop while he talked to him.

The darkness gave Wilson's dark complexion a vintage look. It was as if he emerged from the shadows of an oil painting, and settled into the back seat. He removed his hat, and placed it on his right knee. From beneath bushy black eyebrows, he observed Bishop's attitude and movements. Though Bishop's hands were cuffed behind his back, he didn't fidget. Uncomfortable situations didn't seem to faze this guy. Bishop stared out at the passing city. Wilson guessed Bishop to be a loner. He noted the man's posture: straight spine, shoulders back, personally confident. Wilson saw a man who chose to be alone. Bishop's legs were thick and strong, betraying regular gym time.

"You look pretty tough for a smart guy," Wilson said.

"That's because I'm not that smart," Bishop replied.

"Mmm," Wilson nodded. "The engineering community called you a disgrace and the entire STEM field received a black eye because of your design. Embarrassment and failure don't mean you're not smart."

"Wow," said Ana. "That's harsh, what'd he do?"

"He designed the parachute and evacuation systems for a startup company making airplanes," Wilson told her.

"Sounds like a good thing," said Ana.

"Yeah, sounds that way. Except it didn't work," Wilson said, watching Bishop frown. "The chutes malfunctioned. They deployed mid-flight on 522, tearing the plane apart. Two hundred and three people lost their lives because of him."

"Sounds like a disgrace to humanity!" Ana exclaimed.

"Nah, at least not yet," Wilson poked Bishop in the shoulder. "What you're doing now—creeping around in backyards, preying on senior citizens—that'll make you a disgrace to humanity."

As Wilson finished, a voice on the radio said something about an officer's car door being torn off; then someone had thrown the door at the officer.

Ana stared at Wilson. "What the fuck?"

"Turn that up," Wilson shouted.

The voice blared: "Officers down. Suspect is violent and engaged. Possible fugitive from Seson Midway prison. Requesting backup, and drone engagement."

"What the hell is going on?" Ana asked.

"Just drive," Wilson screamed.

The car sped through city streets, tires screeching as they took Marlboro Pike. A blockade of patrol cars had formed around the shopping strip on Silver Hill. Cops ducked down behind their car doors as they fired. Ana slammed on the brakes, and both cops bailed out of the car. The trunk popped open. They got out their gear.

Bishop leaned forward to see. The cops were definitely engaged. Their prey was a large, naked man. Bishop shifted to get a clearer view. Everything appeared foggy in the streetlights. Then the perp picked up one of the officers and tossed him into three others.

To Bishop it hardly seemed a fair fight: a large man dressed in his own blood, fighting a team of armored police. But the bloodied man was holding his own. It was Dimycles. The police were in this battle for the law; Dimycles was fighting for his life.

Bishop saw Dimycles tear himself from the tasers. The naked man fled, but then caught several shots in his left leg and fell. He rolled, avoiding further gunfire. Dimycles flopped onto the wet asphalt of the parking lot and hid behind a large trash bin. The clatter of lead on sheet metal hurt his ears. The air reeked of garbage and urine. Dimycles saw that the bin had wheels, and started pushing it.

Bishop watched as the man lifted the huge bin over his head. As Wilson and Ana finished suiting up, Wilson stuck his head in the car and shouted: "Don't even think about running! I know who you are. I know everything about you!"

Bishop watched Dimycles throw the trash bin at officers too stunned to move. As he watched Wilson run, Bishop whispered: "You don't know shit about me."

Bishop's cuffs broke, freeing his hands. As he raised one arm, a shock wave formed, intercepting the soaring trash bin. The officers stayed low and still, seemingly waiting for death. The bin fell harmlessly to the ground.

Taking advantage of the miracle, Dimycles hobbled off. He ran into the shopping strip, the police giving chase. As he slipped through an open door into a building, they followed.

Bishop hopped into the driver's seat and put the car in reverse. On the PB radio he heard: "Officer down!" and "Send backup!" Bishop hit the gas, drove into the alley behind the shops, and the screaming radio stopped like a buzzer had sounded, ending a game.

Bishop idled down the alley looking for the victor. He saw a shadowy figure limping.

When Dimycles saw the lights approaching, he ran—right into some cops. As he tried to stop, he slid. He spun on his good leg, caught the officers with the back of his fist, and knocked them sideways. He grabbed one, slamming him into the brick wall, cracking the man's helmet. He punched another hard in the chest, cracking his rib. Suddenly Dimycles tired. Though everything was hazy, he willed himself to chop into policemen's bodies. As he started limping away, he fell. Bishop slowed, shining the car's spotlight on Dimycles. Grabbing the police first-aid kit and his phone, Bishop hopped out.

Dimycles was scooting away on his butt. Bishop saw fear, loss, and purpose in the man's face-- pain and suffering beyond reason, and a thin hope of survival. Bishop knew the feelings well.

Suddenly, the alley was flooded with lights. Drones zoomed in. Dimycles backed against a wall.

"Surrender," a loud voice demanded. Dimycles supported himself against the wall. Bishop realized Dimycles hadn't been escaping; he was trying to stand up.

Dimycles pushed his back against the wall and kept trying to stand. The left side of his face was wet with soot. He finally managed to support himself in a one-legged squat. His good leg trembled. The drones kept calling for his surrender. Bishop assumed that Dimycles either did not understand the demand or refused to obey it.

The drones triggered their weapons. Bishop raised his arm, balling his fingers into a fist. Crushed drones fell at Dimycles' feet.

Dimycles collapsed to his knees and fell on his side. Bishop walked over and knelt next to him.

"Should I call you a lawyer or a doctor?" Bishop asked, reaching for his phone. "Let me call you a doctor. A good doctor." Bishop hit a button and made the connection. Somewhere another phone rang. When a voice came on the line, Bishop snapped: "Adrian! Working tonight?"

Bishop could hear Adrian's grandmother speaking in the background, then Adrian's voice replied: "That depends. What do you want me to work on?"

"I need a secure line," said Bishop.

"Give me a moment." As Bishop listened to rustling on the other end, he opened the first aid kit and started tending to Dimycles's wounds. He heard beeps- Adrian typing a code, then he man on the other end said: "Okay, proceed."

"I gotta body here," Bishop announced, wrapping gauze around torn flesh. "I need you on it."

Adrian responded, "Well, just call the cops."

"I – I just stole a cop car."

"Why?"

Bishop moved to the torso. "Long story, they busted me by the Petersons', then drove me here..."

"Oh God."

"I know," Bishop said with embarrassment.

"No, you don't!"

"I know. I fucked up."

"This isn't healthy, not in the least. The Petersons? This is destructive to your psyche. You can't keep doing this."

"I fucked up! I know!" Bishop shouted.

Adrian took a deep breath and exhaled. "Tell me a little about the body so I know what to prep for."

"Wretched."

Adrian's accent strengthened. "I need more than that."

"He's a beat-up version of a man who's seen better days."

"That's what I imagined when you said wretched."

"He's got long hair, hasn't shaved. Big and pale."

"Russian?"

"I don't just mean pale like white, but pale as if his skin has never seen the sun," Bishop clarified. "I can't tell if he's beat up young man, or a fit old geezer. He has weird metallic looking tattoos, or maybe its metal skin grafts. I've never seen something like this. He's got chains in his back, and, well, his bleeding has slowed. I'm still trying to clean most of it off him."

"Oh no! Don't touch the body! Are you wearing gloves? Wash your hands this instant!"

Bishop rolled Dimycles over on his stomach, "His chains though."

"Yeah, I got that part, chains on his back."

"No, no, not on..." Bishop corrected, "The chains are in his back. They look like they're broken, torn off."

"Sexual deviant?"

"No, not like piercings. I don't even know how to describe this," Bishop said, caressing the chains. "It's like someone cut open his back, and pushed chain links through his muscle tissue and-"

"Wow! That's horrific!"

"He's having trouble breathing. You have to come."

Adrian froze, "I thought you said he was dead,"

"No! Why would I call you in a rush for a dead body?"

"I don't know! You asked for a secure line; I figured you took somebody out! You haven't been the nicest guy recently!" As Adrian's mind woke up to the situation, his body quickly followed. He finally got moving as Bishop's description found a match in his memory. "Is this the fugitive?" he snapped as he ran. "If he's still alive, call it in! Call it in!" Adrian rushed out of the building, "I'm on my way. I'll make sure it gets to me!"

Adrian hung up.

Bishop heard the click and cursed. "Shit! I just told you, I can't call it in!" The line was silent.

Fugitive?

Bishop dragged Dimycles's massive body to the squad car and pushed him into the back seat. Bishop got behind the wheel and drove down Silver Hill back to Pennsylvania Avenue. He got back to Sherwood Forest and drove aimlessly. The streetlights were still off. He looked back at Dimycles. It appeared the bleeding stopped.

A few blocks away from them, a street worker drove along the sidewalk in the moonlight recalibrating the sensors. Bishop hopped from the car and pulled Dimycles onto the road, where he laid him out. Bishop then drove around the corner and waited until he saw the street worker reach the body and stop. The driver jumped out of the vehicle, found a stick nearby, and used it to poke the body. When the driver pulled out his phone, Bishop left.

Before leaving the neighborhood, Bishop drove by the Petersons' again. He snuck into the backyard to find the buried dice. He stopped, holding the dice, as he looked through a window. He saw both Petersons passed out on the couch. They fell asleep watching a movie. Bishop nodded, and finally cracked a smile. He felt relieved knowing they were safe.

He ran off.

He drove out of Sherwood Forest, steering with his knees. His hands were occupied as he connected the dice, flattening them into a single rectangular chip. On the chip, a row of lights flickered. He inserted the disk into the dash computer and accessed the police database. He chuckled as he slid his hand over the dash like a convict who hasn't known his lover's body in years. In the time it took for the stoplight to turn green, Bishop disabled the car's security features, then hacked into the precinct's records, and accessed his file. He found his recent stop and deleted the data. He removed searches on the Petersons' address and the officer's notes on the Petersons and himself.

Just for fun, he pulled up file on his friend, Adrian Blackwell. It looked clean.

"What a loser," Bishop complained. When he finally found Adrian's citation for driving a non-licensed vehicle, he laughed.

"I'll leave this on there," he said to himself. "You can afford it, Dr. Blackwell." Then Bishop pulled up Adrian's brother, Julius. Julius had several moving violations, including speeding in a school zone. "What a loser," Bishop repeated, deleting just a few of the charges. He stopped at the one for public indecency. "What the—okay, I'm leaving that one."

Bishop found his own name coupled to a series of restrictions. He couldn't fly, or even leave the state. He freed himself from that bondage, removing his name from the databases. Outside of the most secret files, Bishop took himself off the grid.

Bishop drove the police cruiser to a remote lot in Maryland and wiped it down. Before leaving, he accessed the dash computer and sent the documents he stole from the senator to several press outlets.

Though with his mission accomplished, he felt no virtue from the act of justice. It the moment of completion, he realized it did not ease his pain, nor did it fill the void within his soul.

Logical was right.

His hand hovered over the dash, poised to type again. He sighed, and in his mind, he told himself not to do it. Feeling the threat of tears, he typed in a name: "Kilee Nicole Barlow." He gasped when her picture came up, her skin the color of warm honey. He remembered grazing her lips with his finger, following them to the sharp edge where her cheek began. He recalled gazing into her green feline eyes. He wanted to reach out and touch her. Then he saw the message below her name: "Status: Deceased."

Bishop let his fingertips brush over the words. Police documents and unreleased photos of Flight 522 appeared, and he forced himself to look at the shredded remains of the airplane. He clicked through several photos. The rescue workers looked sad. He zoomed in on one, a dark bony man with tattoos, who was holding a canister—the zenomites. Bishop ran a trace on the rescue worker but came up empty. He typed in the name Boyacobas, but it didn't help the system identify the worker.

"So much death," Bishop sighed. He flipped back to Nicole's picture and stared at it one last time, wondering if Logical was less of a drug pusher, and more of a community servant, giving fiends a way to deal with their pain. To Bishop, it seemed almost worth it to erase the horrible past from his mind. As he pulled the chip from the dash, the screen went blank. He abandoned the car. His fingers balled the chip into his fist. He crushed it. The wind scattered the dust as he cried.

SHADOW OF THE SIX

KYRA GARRET COVERED her face with her hand, shielding it from the sun. The Asian mercenary sat on the floor in the cargo hold of a transport plane as it started a rapid descent over North Carolina. Sunlight beamed through the window, catching her face in deep meditation - searching for answers. She ignored the plate of half-eaten food on the floor next to her. In the palm of her other hand, the heavily tattooed guerrilla held a ring; it no longer fit her thinning finger. When the turbulence hit, she let it fly away.

In front of her, soldiers suited up for the mission. Steve, one of the mission commanders, shouted something to her. She looked away as if the engine noise drowned his voice.

At the bottom of the drop, they would intercept the town of Lasker— home base for ICP's robotics division. Steve walked to the far end of the cargo bay and powered on the attack drones while the mercenaries checked their weapons - ready to strike.

Kyra stood up, using a thin tube, she wrapped her long black hair into a bun, securing it with an elastic hair tie. She finished shimmying her body into an armored suit, along with the rest of the team.

As the plane started its steep descent, Steve grabbed the sidebar for support and approached her. He looked over the map of Lasker. "ICP has a staff of about 1200," he said.

"That's all about to change," Kyra quipped.

"You seem oddly invested in this hit," Steve commented, as he and the team prepped their weapons. "Never seen you take a one so personally."

"This is for Boyacobas," said Kyra, putting on her helmet and mask.

Air pressure stabilized. The plane jerked, and leveled off. For a moment there was only engine noise. Suddenly the floor dropped out of the aircraft. Two aerial drones fell out and engaged their thrusters.

The drones dipped low to the ground, cruised around to the front entrance of the ICP robotics building, and unleashed a volley of shots at the guards. The guards returned fire as they retreated into the building. Alarms blared.

A set of cylinder drones ejected from the plane, went to the roof, and started burning holes through it. ICP engaged their defenses. Their robots leapt to the top of the building to counter the cylinder drones. As the plane flew over the rooftop, it released another set of aerial drones, then banked around for another pass.

Robots battled on the roof as ICP reinforcements kept coming. Once a cylinder drone had successfully burned a hole, the plane made another pass to drop the human team. They came down wearing their jet packs.

"This won't last long!" Steve shouted into his com. "Keep tight! Let's go!"

The team dropped through the hole and flew down into the building. Disabling their jet stream, they leapt from wall to wall, attaching chains to the inner walls at intervals. When they reached the seventh floor, Kyra shouted: "This is it!"

The team positioned itself around another set of cylinder drones that burned a hole through the seventh floor. Kyra dropped down into the room below and kicked a man in the face. Someone grabbed her from behind. She flipped him over but lost her helmet in the process. As one man tried to flee, she chased him down, shoved her shoulder into his back, grabbed his chin from behind, and slammed him to the floor. The force of it knocked the wind out of him. Kyra pulled out her knife and sliced off two of his fingers. She left him howling in pain.

As the rest of Kyra's unit dropped in, an explosion ripped off the door from the other side. ICP guards poured in after them.

"Kyra! Let's go!" Steve shouted, pointing at the wall, "Move! Move!"

"Hold the door!" Kyra cried, running to the far side of the room.

She slid across the floor, tore off a wall panel, and found what she was looking for: a safe. She pulled a piece of paper from her breast pocket, entered the combination, and then pressed the tips of the severed fingers against the lock.

Nothing happened.

"Kyra!" Steve shouted. Bullets and blast fragments flew through the opened doorway. Steve and the crew, pushed back, emptying their clips. "We're outta time!"

Kyra pulled the tie from her hair, letting the bun fall apart. Her black hair fell to the floor. She wrapped the tie around the base of the severed fingers, stopping them from deflating and wrinkling the fingerprints. She used the excess blood as glue and stuck the paper to the safe, where she could read the numbers. Kyra held the two fingers against the lock scanner, as she retyped the combination.

The safe opened.

Pulling a small tablet from the safe, she inspected it, set it on the floor and rummaged through the rest of the tiny vault. She found nothing. "Where's the damn canister?" she whispered.

"Kyra, are we good?" Steve called through the chaos.

Kyra tried to think. Despite the raging battle, she didn't flinch.

"Kyra!"

"Yeah!" she cried automatically and mumbled under her breath as she stashed the tablet into her backpack.

Her crewmembers threw grenades. A couple of them grabbed her and leapt onto a small platform. Cylinder drones pulled them through the hole, back to the seventh floor. They retreated into the inner structure, latched the chains onto their belts, and then the retracting links yanked them onto the roof. They engaged their jet packs and intercepted the circling transport plane.

Once aboard, they nursed their wounds. As Kyra walked forward, Steve ripped off his helmet and threw it at her. It missed, bouncing off the cargo hold wall.

"What was that?" Steve shouted.

"What was what?" Kyra shot back.

"Did you get the damn tablet? You just sat on the floor while we were fighting and dying. Colin died back there!"

"People die! Shit happens, if you can't hack it, go to college! Get a job!"

"This shit happened because you act like the lives of your team members don't mean shit to you!"

"They don't!" she shouted, aiming her words like weapons. "You don't! I don't give a shit about any of you!" She stared at the floor as she shook her head. "Look- Don't get your feelings hurt."

Steve curled his lips. "You run your mouth too damn much."

Kyra turned around to meet Steve's fist in her face. Her knees buckled, and she hit the wall. When he tried to hit her again, she stopped him with her foot. She thrust her hips up, trapped his head and arm between her thighs, and choked him. He pulled a knife, but she flipped him over, and the weapon flew from his hands. Her legs squeezed tighter. His eyes closed. He lost consciousness.

Kyra got up, brushed herself off, and walked to the front of the plane. She stared out of a portal at the passing scene below. Behind her, Steve was regaining consciousness. After a few moments, he pulled himself up and approached her.

"Lotus lied to us," she said bitterly.

"Yeah, well, you tell him that," Steve demanded.

Kyra shifted her gaze from the portal and looked toward the cockpit. "Where are we going?" she asked. "Why are we over water?"

Steve touched his swollen face. "Germany," he said.

"Why Germany?"

"You're making the drop in person. Lotus wants that tablet to go through as few hands as possible. We're not refueling, making any other stops. The tablet isn't to leave your possession until he has it." Steve started changing his jacket.

"Still, he lied to us," she said.

"Like I said, you can tell him that."

Kyra looked at the tablet. "This isn't right. We should be after the canister. Why this stupid tablet?"

"Cuz that's what Lotus ordered!"

"Since when?" she demanded.

"Since you got cut out of the loop. Cuz you're so obsessed with Boyacobas. Get over it; he's dead!" Steve enjoyed saying it.

"Shut your mouth!" she barked at him.

"Look who's talking. A minute ago, you didn't care who died for you. Now you care about your old mentor all of a sudden?" Steve laughed.

"It's about honor," Kyra proclaimed. "You wouldn't know anything about that."

"Bullshit," Steve shot back. "It's cuz when he died you ended up losing your damn mind. I don't know why you're up here with us. Go work your daddy issues out on a street corner somewhere."

Kyra shot Steve in the head. When he crumpled to the floor, she huffed. "I don't have enough middle fingers for you right now." She dug through her pack and pulled out some clean clothes. The comrades on the plane looked on in shock, as she stepped over the corpse on her way to the back.

THE CABS IN Germany were sleek, stylish capsules. The windows were tinted just enough to keep the cabin cool, and efficient enough to capture usable solar energy. A cab fit six people, three in front, three in back, with the two rows facing each other. Kyra took the taxi from the airport alone. She didn't want to be alone, but she wasn't in the frame of mind to be around anyone else.

"Destination?" the cab asked.

"Train station," she commanded, and the cab whirred off.

A tear ran down her cheek. She wiped it off with her knuckle, as she whispered to herself that it wasn't fair. She watched the city zip by until she reached the train station. Kyra walked through the mixed crowd, her face blank. During the flight, she curled the ends of her dark hair and changed into denim jeans, and a white laced top.

Later that day, Kyra's train arrived in Berlin. She got off and started through the Stuttgarter Plazt. She hurried through the bustling people until she reached the corner, where she turned left. She crossed the Windscheidstraße and slipped through the row of parked mopeds in front of a cafe. A cab with heavily tinted windows slowed as it approached. She leaned forward, looking at it, but it passed her by. She started to cross the Leonhardtstraße, but a bus stopped, blocking her. She glanced up at the faces in the bus windows. Each seemed to carry a story behind a blank look. Did they see her? Could they even guess at her sadness? The bus passed, revealing the dark car that had pulled up to the opposite curb. Kyra trotted across the street. The door swung open. A tall, balding man with a small forehead and a big crooked nose stepped out. He greeted her and held the door open for her.

For a half hour, they rode in silence until they reached what looked like a typical gray warehouse. She got out of the car and entered the building to feel it was abnormally warm and humid inside—an atmosphere conducive to plant life. The building was an arboretum. Rows of plants with transparent leaves lined the walls and floors. The moment she entered two women stood up. Swati said: "Mr. Daniels is expecting you."

Swati and Barbara walked Kyra through a plant-lined hall.

"This is... beautiful," Kyra said, grazing her fingers along the veiny see-through leaves.

"Please, do not touch," Swati insisted.

Kyra passed her hand behind the leaves and watched her fingers move.

Barbara said, "Ma'am, they are very delicate!"

"Every girl loves flowers," she answered.

"This kind of plant will never bloom," Swati said, "So if you don't mind?"

Swati directed Kyra into a private room with a washing station.

"I already showered," she complained as she entered.

Ignoring her objection, Swati said, "Don't take long," and then shut the door.

Bright lights shone on Kyra as she undressed, and took another shower, unsuccessfully attempting to keep her hair dry. It got wet, which required extra time with the blow dryer.

As Kyra finished, she looked in the mirror. Tattoos covered her body from head to toe. Most people found them fascinating. Her thin body was like a canvas that displayed the masterpiece of a genius, with scars beneath the images—wounds from battle, and needle marks from a past too painful to remember. She noticed a long white robe they'd left, and quickly put it on. After Kyra had emerged from the room, her escorts, also dressed in robes, walked her to a clean room hidden in the back. Lotus sat at the end of a long table, looking over documents. He stood up, straightened his robe, and motioned for her to sit.

Lotus was blond, broad-shouldered, and had a devious face. When he smiled, his pale cheeks crinkled upwards, and his eyes gave a sinister glow. Kyra didn't care. He'd always looked like that.

She sat, in silence, staring off to the side.

"How are you enjoying Berlin?" Lotus asked. "I trust your flight went well."

"I've never been to Germany before," she told him. "I feel like I'm in the 19th century. Everything's old here. Sorry. I know I should appreciate it more."

"Never apologize for your opinion of another culture," he responded, giving her a stern look. "I suspect you have what I want."

"Yeah," she assured him, then added weakly, "I got it."

"Good." Lotus relaxed, and motioned to his guards.

Barabra relieved Kyra of the stolen tablet.

Kyra could not hold her tongue. "He didn't have the canister, just the tablet," she blurted.

"I see. It is unfortunate, but the tablet is the highest priority for us at this time." Lotus spoke into the paperwork he was examining. "I felt confident you would bring it back safely."

Kyra glared and leaned toward him. "If he didn't have the canister then he didn't kill Boyacobas! Did you know it wouldn't be there?"

Lotus collected all the paperwork into a folder, and replied, "Boyacobas will be avenged in due time, but first, there is an urgent matter that must be addressed."

Kyra stomped her foot. "You keep doing this! I've waited so long to avenge his death. You said..."

"What did I say?" Lotus replied, standing up while gripping the folder. "Boyacobas died years ago. He's dead today, and he'll be dead tomorrow. Vengeance for a dead man doesn't take priority over my very live plans!"

"I don't understand!" Kyra cried. "The Shadows aren't your personal bodyguards! I'm no hired gun—not for the Six. I want the man who killed Boyacobas! That was our deal! You wanted the canister of zenomites. The man who killed Boyacobas has the canister of zenomites. How does a stupid tablet come into any of this? We're supposed to be working together, but everything I do is for you and your... your plant cult!"

"And what? I've done nothing for you?" Lotus shouted, "Boyacobas sheltered you into a bed of roses. It's thorns, Kyra! Life is nothing but thorns! Drugs wrecked you! I saved you, for Christ sakes! You've been clean, ever since I scooped you up. You should be thanking me! I haven't deluded you, but I want nothing to distract you."

"And nothing to ease the pain," Kyra concluded.

Lotus raised an eyebrow. "Pain? What pain? Does killing hurt? Who does it hurt? The dead don't feel pain. An Earthling is but a pound of dust." Lotus gripped the folder.

Kyra looked disgusted. "Why do you call people that?" she asked. "Earthlings? Who calls them that? Boyacobas had everything planned. This is just nonstop killing. I can't do this sober anymore."

"You need drugs?"

"Yes!"

"How does it feel when you kill?"

"Thrilling," Kyra said, her voice laced with shame. "Powerful... then shitty, guilty, horrible...depressed. I feel as if I lost a piece of myself. How do you do it? How can you kill people so calmly, and easily? I just can't anymore...I feel like... I'm going..."

"You aren't strong enough yet," Lotus insisted. He paced around, still grasping the folder. "When Boyacobas took you under his wing, he shielded you from the harsh realities of the criminal world. I'm honing you to be better than that."

"Honing me? Find someone else. I'm done," Kyra said, getting up. She walked to the door where Swati and Barbara blocked her. She eyed them. "You do realize how many people I've already killed today?"

Lotus waved them aside and called after Kyra, "You're my best assassin, but you're not ready to face the one who killed Boyacobas."

"Wait." She turned around. "You know who killed him?"

"I know his killer was good enough to do the job. I know I found you in the gutter after Boyacobas died. After you OD'd they had to replace your liver. They couldn't clone it you had so much drugs in your system. You needed a fresh, human-grown liver! Do you know how hard it is to find an organ donor these days? It's nearly impossible! I had two people killed to get that liver. You'd still be in a sewer, dead and rotting, had I not saved you." He approached her, and his tone softened. "You were dependent on Boyacobas. I'm honing you to be everything you've dreamed of."

"You are honing me to become insane. Just like you."

Lotus touched her hair, caressing her head. "You're already insane. Stop fighting it."

"If you know what his death did to me, why won't you help me close that chapter?" she asked.

"Kyra, don't go hunting tigers unless you're riding a really big elephant." Lotus held the folder out to her. She took it and quickly skimmed the pages, pausing at the image of a soft-faced young lady.

"She saw us, a few hours ago," said Lotus.

"Who is she?" Kyra asked.

"Mason's old student, Tina."

Kyra threw the folder to the floor, scattering pages. "I don't care about Mason or her student."

Lotus turned away from her and balled his fist. "If you don't take care of this you can forget about revenge! It will find you and your pathetic drive!"

"I'm not stupid!" she shouted. "You're still using me for your own plans. I do your hits, run your clients, but what do you do for me? You don't give a shit about what I want! I thought Boyacobas was a father to you."

Lotus pushed everything off the table. Papers, photos, and folders hit the floor. He and pointed at her. "The only reason you're still alive is because I respected that man more than life itself! If you weren't so close to him, I would have let you rot! Think, Kyra! I got you off those drugs so you could use whatever brains you haven't fried yet! Everyone thought that the Six was dead. Now that ICP knows that I'm alive, they'll know Mason's alive too! Now that Tina saw us, they know where we're stationed! Our cover here is blown. If you don't eliminate this girl immediately, we will all end up like Boyacobas!"

"I'm not stupid," she breathed.

Lotus turned and walked to his empty table. Kyra watched him, then she knelt, and started gathering papers and photos. Gripping the pictures she wanted, she stormed out and slammed the door.

Lotus calmed himself and gave orders to the guards: "Prep the evacuation. I want this whole place cleared out by morning." He then turned to Swati. "Do we have it?" he demanded.

"Yessir!" Swati displayed the pictures she took of Kyra naked in the shower.

"In war, this is the time when generals have to make hard decisions," Lotus told her. "After Kyra completes this task, she'll be a liability. Once it's done, get rid of her."

AFTER KYRA CHANGED back into her clothes, she touched her puffy eye and asked Barbara for something to ease the swelling. Once alone, she roamed around the arboretum, thinking. She asked a worker about the plants but got no answer. She melted into the background and watched workers at their holographic terminals as they accessed classified data. She replayed what Lotus had just told her.

Don't go hunting tigers, unless you're riding a really big elephant.

When she found an unoccupied room full of terminals, she slipped in and put down her folder on the desk. She waved her hand, but nothing popped up. All the terminals were locked. She punched the desk in frustration and picked up the folder in front of her. She darted from the room, summoned a cab with a text from her phone, and snuck out a door. She caught the attention of a group of guards. When they approached, she slipped back into a shadowy corner. The first guard neared her, but couldn't see. Kyra struck him in the chest, spun, and disarmed him from behind.

"Shit!" He said turning around.

As another guard closed in, she crouched and rammed her fingers into his throat. As she twisted and ducked beneath his arm, she kneed him in the groin and kicked the inside of his knee. He buckled. When the other guard tried to clinch and knee her in the stomach, she blocked it with her forearms, twisted her small shoulders, slipping through his grip, and butted him in the midsection with her hips. Spinning back into him, she single-legged him to the ground.

As the cab she called for drove up, Kyra leapt for it. Once she was in the cab, she wiped her face and opened her fist. She gazed at the passkey she lifted from the first guard.

THE CAB PULLED up to Maxim, a well-known bar catering to young professionals. Kyra hesitated before exiting the cab. She twirled the passkey and eyed it with a pained expression. She inhaled, closed her eyes, and slowly exhaled. She put on a happy and flirty smile, then walked into the bar as if she owned it.

The girl with the soft face sat in a booth to the right of the bar. She was the girl in the photo.

"Mind if I join you?" Kyra asked her.

"I'm waiting on a few people," Tina replied.

"So that's a piss off?" Kyra laughed.

"It's not that," Tina pleaded.

"I get it all the time. No worries." Kyra started to move on.

Tina noticed Kyra's bruised eye, "What happened to your face?"

"Everyone wants to know my problems," Kyra snapped. "All I want to do is to drink to forget—not be judged... Never mind."

"No, no, sit," Tina insisted, "What's your name?"

"Kyra." She looked at the girl and slowly fell into the seat opposite her. "Kinda plain."

"No, it's not. I'm Tina! Nothing special about my name either."

"First time in Berlin," Kyra asked.

Tina mistook it for a question. "No, I'm here for school."

"I meant that it's my first time here," Kyra corrected. "So you go to school. What do you study?"

"Botany," Tina answered, "I—"

"You study the trees and shit. I know, I'm not dumb," Kyra laughed, and cocked her head, then waved at the bartender, calling for a drink. He immediately went to pour it. "So, you went to college for that?" she asked Tina.

"Yeah. Still go. Berkeley. I'm here doing research for my dissertation."

"California, eh? Fancy. Who's your sponsor?"

"Dan Weatherford is my dissertation advisor. Before that, it was a woman named Mason Kinoah," Tina said.

Kyra raised an eyebrow, and then coolly asked, "Another Botanist?"

"More than botanists—genius microbiologists."

Kyra received her drink from the waiter, took a long sip, and said, "I bet you do good research for them. I have an eye for brains, and you're smart. Smarter than me."

"Well, it's only Dan now," said Tina. "Mason's gone."

"What do you mean?"

"She disappeared over two years ago. We don't know where she is."

"Who's 'we?'"

"Everyone... people in general."

Kyra finished her drink quickly. "Maybe she just got fed up. Just because people are good at something, doesn't mean they like doing it. They get trapped. Maybe she just ran away. It's what I'd do." Kyra set down her empty glass and signaled for another.

"She didn't just run away," said Tina. "She was kidnapped."

"Why would anyone kidnap a botanist?"

"Wish I knew..."

"Crazy..." Kyra said, as her second drink arrived.

"Yeah, I'm trying to hold up, but to be honest, I'm kind of depressed about it," Tina said. "The semester after she disappeared I failed all my classes. I had to file an appeal so it wouldn't tank my GPA. I wish whoever took her would bring her back. I wanna look into his eyes and tell him how many people he's hurt. Make him feel the guilt and the pain he deserves. He think's he's so smart."

Kyra chuckled.

"I'm serious, he went for entomology," Tina stated. "Weirdo."

Kyra gave Tina an inquiring look. "How do you know all of this?"

"He studied bugs..." Tina explained. "He killed everyone in the lab, and kidnapped Mason. I know because I saw him do it."

Kyra gasped, "I feel so stupid."

The waiter arrived with a third drink, and Kyra gulped it down before he returned to the bar.

"It's okay. You didn't know," said Tina. "Where are you from, and what do you do?"

"Right now I'm from nowhere. I'm hoping Berlin will be my new home. People are a bit more liberal here."

"How are you gonna make money? Or live?" Tina asked.

Kyra shrugged, "I don't know, I'm not as smart as you. All I got is what my mama gave me. A nice ass!"

"Oh come on," Tina sighed.

"Girl, I'm Asian, and I got a nice booty. That's gotta be worth, like a Bachelor's Degree or something."

"That's not funny. I'm serious!"

"I'm serious too. Some of us just don't have it like that. I tried going to school, but, well, it just didn't work out."

"You don't have to go to school, but you don't have to get by on your ass either," Tina protested. "Didn't you just say you'd run away if you felt trapped? I'm not judging you. Every woman thinks about it. I've thought about it myself. When Professor Kinoah disappeared, I would've done anything to numb the pain, but I pushed through it."

"I know what you mean," Kyra commiserated. "I lost someone too. He was like a father to me. A mentor. After I got out of prison, I got caught up in dangerous gangs. He found me, and it was like wind to my sails. After he was murdered, I felt abandoned. Ya know? I really miss him so much. The guy I'm working with now just likes to fuck with my head. He's a liar—so full of shit. If I had one wish, I'd find the man who killed my mentor, look him in the eyes, and end his life. I'd want to watch the blood drain from his body before he died."

Tina's eyes got big. "I feel what you were saying, but that last part- that's a little graphic, Kyra."

"We're just two different people."

"I-I guess you're right," Tina left her empty glass, grabbed her things, and stammered: "I r-really am sorry for your loss... Looks like my people haven't showed, so I'd better go. It was nice meeting you, Kyra. Enjoy your stay in Berlin."

Kyra stood up and helped Tina with her coat.

"Ow!" Tina complained.

"Sorry, my ring must've snagged your neck there."

Tina looked back. "You're not wearing a ring!"

Kyra sat back down as the other woman hurried out the door.

"Beautiful girl. She has her whole life ahead of her," Kyra muttered. She finished another drink and again signaled the waiter. This time, he left the bottle. Kyra peered out the window as Tina hailed a cab.

"Destination, please?" said the cab voiced.

Tina quickly pulled out her phone to make a call and poked her head inside the car to give a destination, but her words were gibberish.

"Destination, please?" The cab repeated.

Tina's gibberish became hysterical, then stopped. Her head fell back, and she collapsed onto the curb. People screamed. A few passersby tried to help her, but all they could do was lay her lifeless body onto to the sidewalk. Her cell phone fell from her hand.

When Kyra finished the bottle, she pointed for another, but the bartender was gone. He joined the crowd surrounding Tina. Kyra stood up and walked behind the bar. Grabbing a bottle of Scotch, she exited through the kitchen. Before she went out the back door, she took a handful of food and stuffed it into her mouth.

She stepped into a dark, narrow alley, and it seemed like another world. The street, the girl, and the bar were out of sight, out of mind. She needed a quick way to soothe her conscience. She was about to leave the alley when she noticed a man. He stood idly near the corner. When he nodded in her direction, she faced him. Her curiosity was a weightless thing, like a ballerina gliding across the stage of her mind. She looked back over her shoulder, then back at the man.

He nodded his head slightly.

How does the ballerina move so gracefully? She wondered. It was as if her curiosity could go anywhere, but never land on anything. As Kyra neared the man, the beautiful ballerina seemed to be dancing toward her. No... it was the man walking toward her, holding up two fingers. It was inviting, it felt right, but all wrong. She shook her head and turned away. Kyra closed her eyes and shut out the dancers, but then the music started to play, a lovely innocent tune, jolly, and gay. She paused for a moment then turned back to him.

He shrugged.

The music went away. The dancers disappeared. A misty darkness arose, with a voice calling to her from deep within her soul. She raised her fingers, signaling: one, five. He nodded, reached into his pocket, and pulled out a small ziplock bag holding bluish-white powder. Kyra stared at it and breathed slowly. She felt the chill of an autumn breeze and the numb rush on her skin. Her mouth hung open, and her hand twitched.

Her hand reached forward, but her feet sent her backward. It was as if her body had split apart. She shook her head and ran out of the alley.

Later that night, Kyra returned to the arboretum. Workers loaded large trucks with soil and plants. Kyra snuck into the back of the warehouse and pulled her gun. She crept past employees and guards and was soon tip-toeing down the halls. Dust and fertilizer caused her to stifle a sneeze. She found the right door, and burst through it, her gun drawn. The clean room was empty. Lotus was gone.

Kyra looked around and wondered why Lotus made the inner chamber of the warehouse so ceremonial, as if he were trying to mimic something she couldn't grasp. With the help of her stolen passkey, the table lit up, giving her access. She sat down, keeping her ears open for guards or anyone else. As she did a search for the zenomite canister, she found a photo of Nicole—a familiar face. Kyra found pictures of Nicole holding the canister before boarding Flight 522.

"Hmm."

Kyra copied the data to her phone and then accessed images of Flight 522 after the crash. Further down, she found images of Boyacobas holding the canister. She searched for Boyacobas's personal data, but the passkey lacked the proper permissions. There were only a few photos of him, one taken with her when she dyed her hair purple. She looked happy.

"I look stoned out of my mind."

Kyra's eyes misted as she went to the next screen. She flipped through documents and knew she'd gone too far when she ran across profiles of talking dinosaurs.

"What the hell?" She swatted in the other direction. "You boys and your cartoons. Grow up."

She heard a voice as someone passed the door. She pulled her gun and aimed it, but the voice faded away. When she turned back toward the display, she noticed a message alert. She opened it and read an update from Fox after losing three men in Washington, D.C. to Bishop Kennedy.

She accessed Bishop's profile and saw a wealth of information that she found rather tedious. She skimmed through it quickly until she saw the status of the zenomite cannister listed in Bishop's possession.

"What?" She stopped scrolling to read the surrounding information. She muttered: "I thought ICP had it. Dammit Lotus, what haven't you lied about."

She found a note from Nital Bradford, one of the Six, regarding Bishop. When she tried to bring up the data the computer blocked her. Again her passkey lacked the permissions to see material concerning the Six.

She returned to reading the non-restricted information about Bishop and confirmed the truth – Bishop was last seen with the canister.

"It can't be him," Kyra told to herself. Refusing to believe the troubled engineer could be a capable killer of any kind. "What was so special about those zenomites, and what's so special about that damn tablet?" she said out loud.

She searched through the database for the tablet until she ran across pictures of Lotus talking about his home to different alien beings. "Reptilites... what the hell? Are you kidding me?"

She tried to make sense of it: Lotus with human-like reptile aliens. For a moment, she could not believe it, but then she realized the pictures were taken on Mars. *Mars...home?* Her breathing stopped. She leaned back from the table and heard more footsteps. People were coming to the door, talking about getting the table. Kyra waved her hand at the display, closed the terminal, and disconnected her phone. As the door opened, she vanished into the shadows.

THE NEXT MORNING, the lush trees of Germany's Tegeler Forest were showing signs of autumn. Greens transformed into reds, mixing with oranges and yellows. A brisk breeze jostled the docked boats on Lake Tegel. Kyra walked the shore, adding a lone human to the scene. When she reached the pier, she found yachts of all sizes floating there. She strolled up to a smaller boat and observed the name: *The Lakeline*. There she spotted a large, blond, square-headed man with a flat bearded face. He was prepping the ship for a morning on the water.

Jerry's white polo shirt came down to his cargo shorts. His thick feet sported flip-flops. "Kyra?" he said, leaning over the tow bar on the stern. He smiled awkwardly, then looked suspicious. "This is unexpected."

Kyra opened her coat, revealing tattoos, and a lavender bikini. She twirled around. "Just me! No tricks. You know I love boats. I couldn't come to Germany and not see it!"

"Well, hell yeah!" Jerry agreed, "Happy you found your way all the way to Berlin. It took me a decade to get to this country. You're ahead of me by a long shot."

Kyra looked around at the other boats. "You seem to be in fine company."

"Most everyone here owns a yacht," Jerry quipped, "but none of them know how to operate them."

"This is your baby, Mr. Davis?" Kyra asked, pointing at his sleek craft.

He stepped onto the dock. "All ninety feet of her." He chuckled heartily. "Why do you call me Mr. Davis? Jerry, just call me Jerry."

"Just a habit. I did expect your boat to be a bit bigger," Kyra said.

"Mmm," Jerry started, "It's plenty big for a lake. I favor environment over size."

"It's a beautiful boat; I didn't mean to knock it. I think the one I had was about the same size. You've got an excellent V-hull, covered top. Very aerodynamic."

"Oh, she gets some good pickup. I have extra engines. Step aboard," he offered.

"Don't mind if I do!"

Kyra grabbed the tow bar and climbed aboard, nodding down at the engines. "Odd place for them. Won't that stress them with the load?"

"Oh, yeah, if they were the only ones. Those are the auxiliary engines; I know the mechanic at Sun and Water Sports. They refitted her. The speed limit here is 40 knots cruising, but we can break that easily in the early mornings. It's just on the lake, so I wasn't worried about top speed. I just wanted acceleration so I could get that feel of power when I need it." Jerry smiled. "Ya know, when no one's around to see!"

"Of course!" Kyra added.

Jerry opened the portal to the main cabin, "Here is the main interior."

"Lush, spacious, I like it!" Kyra's eyes widened. The interior had white-and-grey seating all around, with assorted wine and champagne glasses to match. There were television screens for multiple viewing angles and a galley with a solar-powered stove. "You're giving me ideas on what to do with my next one!"

Jerry pressed a button on a panel. "It's time to get inspired!"

Hidden speakers pumped out music from every direction, as a deep bass beat rumbled through the floor.

"Wow!" Kyra shouted over the music. "Immaculate. I like how the music doesn't echo around the interior. It's not hollow. The dampeners keep the sound really clean. Good job."

"Shall we take her out?" Jerry blared.

"And end the tour? Only if you say so." Kyra started to move to the music.

"It's fully automated, watch!" Jerry turned down the music and commanded, "*Lakeline*, take us out."

Engines rumbled, anchors retracted, and the yacht pulled away from the dock.

"She'll take us out without wake, and then..." *The Lakeline* smoothly accelerated, "... kick it up a notch. Come on!"

Jerry escorted her to a wide berth chaise lounge near the bow. She settled into blue and grey pillows, as he poured her a drink.

"Here is another dining, drinking area. Usually seats eight, but it's squeezed in a lot more. Shame you haven't been to any of the parties."

The chaise lounge made a U around another table. Kyra let down her hair as the boat headed for open water. She mouthed the word: "Beautiful." As the sun peeked over the horizon on the far side of the lake, light mixed with tree colors, and reflected on the water's surface. It was as if the lake was the mirror for an artistic masterpiece.

"This keeps me going against all of life's stress," said Jerry.

"You're pretty geeky about it," Kyra observed.

"Oh course! So are you."

"Oh yes, I love boats. I love the water. I'm like a dolphin," Kyra claimed, as wind touched her face.

"Well, you came prepared to swim," Jerry said, reminding Kyra of the lavender bikini under her white coat. She smiled.

Jerry pointed up. There, embedded in the deck, was a love seat for two. Kyra went up, and nestled into it, tucking her legs beneath her. "What's a boat like this cost?"

Jerry took a deep breath. "Um... are you trying to persuade me to sell my boat?"

"Perhaps, but I just wanna know what a party on a boat like this is worth!"

He looked at her cautiously. She shifted her body on the love seat. "It's a shame I've never been invited to the party before."

Jerry sighed and commanded the boat to slow down. "It won't happen again," he said. "There were ... protocols..."

"It's okay, Jerry. I know." Kyra stood up.

Jerry sat on the armrest and watched her pace around the bow. He noticed when she stripped off her white coat, revealing the bikini, and the body in it. Wind blew the dress across the bow and into the lake. He then asked, "What do you know?"

Kyra turned to him. "I know why you kept me out of the loop and kept the Shadows doing your dirty deeds." She took a last sip from her drink and threw the glass into the water. Jerry's eyes narrowed as she told him: "I know about Boyacobas and the Reptilites."

Jerry stroked his bearded face, "How did you find out?"

Kyra shrugged. "Does it matter? Boyacabas came with the Reptilites. I honored a man who meant to destroy us. In my ignorance, I mourned him and wanted to avenge him. Now, my memory of my hero is poisoned because I know too much."

"Or maybe not enough," said Jerry.

"Lotus's biggest complaint was that Boyacobas protected me too much. Sheltered me from the truth. That's why Lotus saved me."

"Boyacobas sheltered us all." Jerry looked at her tattoos, and added, "Lotus saved you because Boyacobas trusted you most."

"And what about you?"

"I don't know. Are you here to kill me?" Jerry wondered.

"You'd break me in half if I dared to try. Your fists are as big as my head," Kyra stepped away from the bow. "I'm not here to stop you. I came for answers."

Jerry nodded, squinting at her.

"How'd you meet Boyacobas?" Kyra asked, standing in front of the love seat. "Was he really here to end us all?"

"Boyacobas was the herald of the Reptilites, sent here to sabotage the Earth for their invasion, but he fell in love," Jerry explained as he examined Kyra's body and its markings. "Is it true? Ya know? Between you and Boyacobas?"

"I came for answers, yet you want to discuss rumors?"

"I only ask because it would explain a lot." Jerry shrugged. "But I heard you only date girls."

"Then I guess it isn't true."

"Boyacobas saved us from Mars when the Earthlings would rather destroy everything it took to get us there," Jerry added, leaning back and watching her. "He brought us to Earth. After he came to Earth, he had a change of heart and became an apologist. He refused to help the Reptilites and cut contact with them. We were children at the time. Boyacobas looked after us up until the day he died."

Sadness filled Kyra's eyes. "So that's why he never told me; he was ashamed. How could someone foreign to our planet show humanity better than we do?" Kyra wondered. The news revived her fallen hero but sparked her hatred for the villain who had killed him. "Who is Bishop Kennedy?"

"Some engineer. Lotus was obsessed with the technology he designed," said Jerry.

"So what about after the plane crash - when Boyacobas had the canister?"

"Boyacoba was too conflicted. He got sloppy, and his loyalties became a problem," Jerry said. "Bishop found out who had the canister and went after him. He found Boyacobas, and where the whole mess went down."

Kyra leaned toward Jerry, and barely whispered her next question: "But... how did he die?"

Jerry hadn't witnessed it, but he found the metal shredder covered in blood, and packed with ground up bones. "Not very well," he said.

"Bishop is an evil man, killing the advocate for his salvation. I'll deliver to him the same justice he administered to Boyacobas," Kyra promised. "Then what? Lotus decided to join Reptilites?"

"After Boyacobas died, Lotus took over. He knew the invasion was going to happen whether we were behind it or not. He used the designs in Boyacobas's tablet to build war machines to counter the invasion."

"Wow." Kyra took a step back. "Lotus wanted to fight against the Reptilites? Since when did he become so generous?"

"Hang on," Jerry cautioned. "Lotus was okay with killing humans, but he still wanted to rule the Earth. Let's be clear about that: he just didn't want the Reptilites do it. The six of us agreed. We feared the Reptilite invasion as much as anyone; we were, well... insanely jealous. We wanted a way to oppose the Reptilites, so Lotus used advanced alien designs from the tablet to develop weapons against them. Powerful weapons."

Kyra looked out over the lake. "Then came the Six War."

"Yes! Dimycles led the majority our members to turn on us! ICP got the tablet. We thought we were finished." Jerry's tone became bitter. "We all faked our deaths and fled the country. Everything looked bleak. Lotus realized that without Boyacobas, our fate would be the same as the Earthlings, so he allied us with the Reptilites."

"But you said he didn't want the Reptilites to take control of Earth."

"Right, but he wanted to survive. We were able to salvage a handful of machines. Perhaps enough to win a few battles, but our militia wasn't big enough to win a war. After we allied with the Reptilites, they promised to build us a starship as compensation for taking Boyacobas's place."

"What the hell is he gonna do with a starship?" Kyra wondered.

"He wanted to get to a world with advanced technology, and truly powerful weapons. Lotus figured that if we could get technology powerful enough to destroy the Reptilites he could take back the earth!"

"Whoa!" Kyra started. "Take back the Earth? Why not stop them before they take it in the first place? Is that why you kept this from me?" She hesitated, then said: "So this is all about revenge... for Mars!"

Jerry waved it off. "No, that's not it at all."

Kyra pointed at him. "You want the Reptilites to attack Earthlings the way they attacked Martians on Hellas Basin! You're just trying to sugarcoat it!"

"Kyra, stop it!"

"Why? Because then I'd tell the world your secrets?"

"If you'd just let me explain... it's not that simple."

"That's a code word for 'money.'"

"Yes, of course, there was the issue of money. None of this stuff is free! Dimycles and his sister turned on us and almost annihilated us! Lotus couldn't risk another betrayal. So he got ahead of it. Lotus himself leaked information to the governments of Earth about the invasion; there is nothing you can do to stop it."

The boat came to a halt.

Jerry turned and eyed the stern. Kyra stepped closer to the love seat, looking past him. The engines shut down, and one automatically lifted itself from the water.

"Strange," Jerry noted.

"Are we out of fuel?" Kyra asked.

"Honestly, I'm not sure," he said, making his way sternward.

Kyra sighed, and called after him. "So the secret is out?"

He ducked under some chairs, then came back up with tools. "Yes, he warned every government, and all it did was backfire. ICP doubled their efforts to hunt us down. It was proof that Earthlings will never trust a Martian! They see us as a threat, human or not!"

Kyra made her way back to him. "See you as a threat?" Jerry was on his knees, crawling under the tow bar. She bent low, and said: "They saw you as a cult!"

Jerry leaned over the rail and pulled off the engine cover. Kyra went into the cabin, found a bottle of scotch, and an empty glass, and poured herself a stiff one. She sat down on a plush seat, then heard Jerry's answer.

"Cult?" he shouted. "That was the media! The governments knew exactly what we were up to, but they felt threatened by the weapons we built, so they shut us down. So we found a way to shut them down."

"How?"

Jerry wasn't listening. His attention was on the malfunctioning engine. "It's just... it looks like a few wires were stripped and covered in electrical tape. The tape got wet and slid off. Now the wires are touching, and I think it caused a short... I don't know how that happened."

"That's not what I meant. You said that you found a way to sabotage us," said Kyra. "Isn't that just admitting you figured out a way to let the Reptilites annihilate humans? That's not what Boyacobas wanted."

"Whatever," Jerry mumbled. He lifted himself back up and crawled from under the tow bar. He rummaged through his toolbox for waterproof tape.

Kyra went on: "You realize, by doing that, you proved what everyone said about Martians, right?"

Jerry sighed. "The people of Earth will always hate us. There's only one way to win that war." He crawled back under the tow bar and began fumbling with the engine's wires. Somewhere deep in the machinery, a spark ignited. The engine jerked and automatically lifted itself to its maximum height.

Kyra finished her drink and poured herself another. She breathed in the fresh air and thought about what Jerry told her. "You're right," Kyra admitted, but then she realized he couldn't hear her. She hopped off the chaise and approached him. She found him wedged between the raised boat engine and the tow bar, struggling to get free. He gave her a panicked look, tried to speak, but couldn't. He could barely breathe. Frantically he pointed at the engine's release lever.

"There's only one way to win that war," Kyra said under her breath.

Jerry pushed with all his might, but the engine was too heavy. He groped backward but couldn't reach the tow bar. It cut into his back behind his shoulder blades. He grasped for the release lever, but it was too far away. He stared up at Kyra, his eyes darkening with fatal apprehension

"You mean this lever?" Kyra asked, pointing at it. "What would freeing you do for me? I've done some bad shit. Killed a lot of people, but even the worst human being is still human. For goodness sakes, Jerry, even Boyacobas could see that this was wrong!"

Jerry shook his body in a last-ditch attempt to free himself. Kyra calmly watched, knowing the whole situation dishonored Boyacobas. "Bishop killed him, and Lotus dangled it in front of me to make me his slave. It's all so clear now. Lotus tried to make me just like him. He wanted to get me so disconnected from people that maybe I would, somehow what? Understand his cause? Is that right? The destruction of Earth?"

Jerry stared at Kyra, his last hope fading.

"I felt trapped," she said, "pressured... much the way you feel now. Lotus saved me, yes, but for what? To end the world?"

Jerry's legs were numb. He stopped kicking.

"I cannot believe you want to betray us just to inherit the planet for yourself!" she told him. "Does that sound like a plan that would tempt me into loyalty? I can't say I blame you for keeping it from me, but you had to know I would find out sooner or later."

His face went from blue to purple. Kyra knew time was running out. "I kill Bishop," she said, "and I avenge the only man who saw reason in this whole ordeal. I close that chapter of my life, and I am free." She pointed at him, knowing her voice would be the last thing he heard. "I kill all of you, and I free this planet. I can't possibly express the hatred I have for you."

Jerry groped for her, and she let him pull her close, He reached for her neck, and managed to get his massive fingers around her throat. She wasn't worried. His grip was weak, almost nonexistent. She did not resist but watched him fade away.

She looked out over the water. No one else was on the lake. She took a step back, and Jerry's arm fell. Kyra sat down and took a sip of her drink. The sun rose further over the trees. She gazed at Jerry. He wasn't completely gone yet. His head bobbed up and down in rhythm with his dwindling heartbeat.

She finished her drink. A chilly wind blew over the lake, tousling her hair. The boat floated listlessly.

Kyra looked up at the autumn sky and nodded.

"This is our planet," she told the dying man. "The Six should have died on Mars.

"Hello, Dispatch."

"This is Dispatch, go ahead."

"Yeah, this is Clyde Martin, uh, calibrating at Sherwood Forest. Um... I gotta dead body."

"A dead body?"

"Eh... Yup."

THE MONSTER'S CLOSET

GEORGE STOOD IN the parking lot of the Woodrow Wilson Medical Center watching an agitated crowd of people surrounding the hospital. A line of police officers stood by, ready to intervene should the demonstrations get out of hand. As deputy Ana came up behind George, she wondered if it had already reached that point.

"It's like a firecracker ready to blow," Ana said to him, nervous that the crowd, if left unchecked, could create a bigger problem than the one they hoped to catch.

A vintage car pulled up, and Adrian stepped out.

"There he is." George readied his command.

Representatives of the gawking media saw Adrian attempting to walk from his car to the front entrance, and they attacked him with questions. Before Adrian could answer, screaming protestors swarmed the area and descended on him. A sea of people crowded him and forced him back until he was buried in a thicket of hostility. The police members on duty stepped up to save him from being trampled underfoot.

"Stand down," George commanded, and the officers backed off, allowing the mob free reign over the doctor.

"You can't- pull them back!" Ana screamed in a knee jerk reaction once they lost sight of Adrian. "They will tear him apart! This is outrageous!"

"This is a man on a mission," George noted calmly. "A celebrity doctor wanting to save the one person the whole country wants to see dead – Dimycles."

Ana was nervous but obeyed. Her eyes quickly scanned the area. "A mob is like a wildfire."

"They aren't gonna let him inside that building," George squinted, trying to find Adrian lost in the crowd. "But he knows he's gotta get in there."

"You'd rather send him to the morgue?"

"If Adrian wants to get rid of the fire; he's gotta get rid of the fuel," George said.

Suddenly, his radio came alive. A police officer on duty inside of the hospital radioed to the George and Ana: "Sir, Doctor Blackwell has arrived and is currently head toward E.R. Do we maintain oversight, or stand down?"

Ana mouthed: *What?*

"Stand down; Ana will relieve you," George replied. Then turning to Ana, he said, "This is our guy."

"He was just out here! What just happened? How did he get inside?"

George agreed. "That's what we need to prove!"

INSIDE THE HOSPITAL, Patricia, the red-haired head nurse, ran alongside Adrian, transferring documents to his tablet. Three nurses from Blackwell's surgical team caught up with them and fell into step with the Doctor's long strides. As he scanned the diagnosis, Patricia touched the tablet screen, bringing up x-ray holograms.

"He has sixteen bullet wounds; eleven bullets are still in him. Metallic skin grafts all over his body. Four chains are going into his back and clamping around his rib bones. Here's one of them," Patricia started.

As they boarded the elevator, Adrian questioned her: "What are these? Bite marks? Was he mauled? Did they sic the dogs on him?"

Patricia pressed the panel for the third floor. "Never seen a dog bite do that." She zoomed in on details in the X-ray. One bite mark encompassed the entire shoulder area. Patricia brought up a photo of the chains, and Adrian examined it carefully.

"He has chains beneath both shoulders," She focused on the lower part of the patient's back. "He has two more connecting through his back into his lower ribs. Looks like he was in a torture chamber, but considering what Dimycles did, I'd just as well let him die like this."

Adrian stopped her. "You must separate the crime from the patient. From now on you will call him John Doe. No matter what crimes he's charged with, we do our jobs."

Patricia didn't respond. Though she worked with Adrian for over six months, she was still awed and intimidated by his presence. It wasn't just his size and demeanor; it was his tribal past in Africa. Whenever she saw the T-shaped scars on his cheeks, it struck fear in her.

Adrian's huge hands adjusted the tablet. "Four chains penetrating his back. What kind of metal is that?"

Patricia cleared her throat, and promptly blanked on his question, "What do you mean?"

"How are we going to cut it out of him? Is it just plain iron? Steel? I want to know if it is easier to cut the chains or his ribs." They left the elevator and rushed toward the operating room. "Where are we on his blood work?"

"We still don't have a chart for him," Patricia responded. "Spencer's working on it now."

"Why not Cathy?"

"She – she refuses to work on.... on John Doe. Moral reasons."

Adrian fell silent. For a moment he pondered, then he went on: "No charts? Fingerprints? Arrest records? Prior history?"

Patricia paused, and then said, "His medical history seems to be with the prison that held him."

They entered Surgery. Dimycles lay, face down, his back naked and exposed. Four chains snaked from his back, each color-coded with tabs.

Adrian walked around the table, pulling out his tablet, and passing it over the places where the chains entered the body. Patricia put on goggles to look at the wound and identified the rear portion of Dimycles' shoulder. The area around the chain entry looked metallic, and the skin was reddened.

"Is he developing an infection?" she asked. "Or bleeding metal?"

"Hmm," Adrian was distracted by a thousand details.

Nurse Spencer came in.

"Where are we with that blood work?" Adrian asked him.

"The machine doesn't say anything,"

"What do you mean 'it doesn't say anything'?" Patricia demanded. "Is it dead? Is it off? What?"

"No," Spencer stammered. "It's on... it's..."

"It has to say something." Patricia insisted.

Spencer finally said, "It gives an error like it isn't blood."

Adrian glanced up from his tablet. Pulling on his gloves, he gently probed the skin around one chain, trying to learn something from the puffy redness.

Patricia upbraided Spencer: "Are you telling me he doesn't have any blood?"

"Well, no... er... actually, he does have blood..."

"And you took it?"

Spencer nodded. "I did, but none of the instruments could identify it."

Adrian interrupted with a question for either of them: "Was his skin like this when he came in?"

"His skin was horrible all over," said Patricia. "From the bullets inside of him to the chains, he's a mess, and he doesn't have much time. And I think whatever bit him... poisoned him."

"Put tetracycline in his IV. Prep him for surgery. Let's get these things out immediately," Adrian demanded. He turned to Spencer. "You know what a microscope is?"

"I believe so, yes, of course."

"Go get one. Take another blood draw. Find out his allergies."

Spencer hurried away.

Adrian grabbed a hacksaw, held the chain to the steel tabletop, and started sawing. He kept at it for five minutes. By that time, it was clear that he would fail. The hacksaw didn't even make a mark. Adrian retired the hacksaw and then plugged in various shop tools. Nothing worked.

"Nearly indestructible," Patricia swore.

Adrian thought for a second, pulled out his phone, and scrolled through it.

"Get me this guy," Adrian said, handing the phone to Patricia. "Tell him it's an emergency. Right now I'll just try to get the bullets out, and tend to his wounds."

Once they left, Adrian turned back toward Dimycles. "I need you to hang in there," he said to his unconscious patient. "I have to get these out of you."

Dimycles's breathing became erratic, and his heart rate skipped. Adrian wanted to save the patient, so he grabbed one of the chains and held it firmly in his hand. The chain turned translucent, but before he teleported it away, the door behind Adrian opened.

Ana stormed into the room:"Sorry to intrude."

Adrian let go of the chain, and stammered, "I don't recall summoning another assistant."

"Oh my God," Ana said when she saw Dimycles. "I didn't..."

"Didn't what? Think it was this bad?" Adrain cut in, as he ran behind a control module in the room. "We aren't exactly throwing parties back here."

"I won't be in the way, but I must stand by. Dimycles is as much of a prisoner as he is a patient."

"He's only your prisoner after he's no longer my patient," Adrian reminded her as he programmed the surgical system to remove all foreign objects from the injured body. The surgical robot didn't respond; it didn't know what part of Dimycles to classify as "foreign." Adrian reprogrammed it to remove the bullets, and nothing else. The surgical system errored and reported that metal skin grafts covered all eleven rounds making it impossible to remove.

"I am just here to make sure there isn't an incident," Ana said

"I know what you are here for, but while you're at it, maybe you can be of some use to me," Adrain wondered and then instructed her to join him behind the control module. "See, the machine needs to remove eleven bullets; I figure since you help put them there, you can contribute to taking them out."

"I don't..."

"It's easy, just press this button, the machine can't remove the bullets because metal skin grafts are in the way, so I will manually guide it."

Adrian walked to the patient and watched as needle-like arms dive into Dimycles's body. With manual prodding, he helped the machine dig in and remove the metal callous and bullets from Dimycles.

"What's going on with his body?" Ana asked, watching metal scabs bubble up from Dimycles's wounds, but Adrian ignored her. Not merely as a disrespectful slight, but he truly did not know. The surgery confused him, and the details were bizarre.

Adrian mumbled to himself: "New skin and gangrenous tissue intermixed over metal skin callous. Self-inflicted wounds... and Patricia's right, something's poisoned him." Adrian put all the bullets in a bowl and handed them to Ana, "Try not to put them in anyone else."

He quickly walked toward the door, and Ana called back, "What about the chains?"

Before he left the room, he hollered back, "Working on it!"

Patricia caught up with him and introduced a heavyset man coming up behind her. "Dr. Blackwell, this is Joel,"

"Long time," Joel said with a wink. "What you got for me?"

"Follow me," Adrian told him.

Joel followed Adrian back to the operating room and saw Dimycles for the first time.

"Here's our John Doe," said Adrian.

"Holy shit!" Joel shouted. As he started unpacking gear, he brushed the chain with his fingertips. "You gotta be kidding me," he croaked. "It's inside of him?"

"What do you think?"

"When she said 'pierced' I figured she meant, like.... a body piercing gone wrong. This is so much better!"

Joel pulled out a file, and vigorously attacked the chains over a small dish. He tried various cutting files, then put on his eyepiece and inspected the markings. He poured some solution from a bottle onto a towel and wiped the metal ends.

"What happened to you?" Joel whispered to the patient. He looked up and saw Ana. "Oh, hello."

"Can we cut the metal?" Adrian wondered.

"That!" Joel said, pointing at the metal calluses spotted over Dimycles, "Is metal." Then looking at the chains he said, "I'm not sure this is all metal, but hey, someone had to forge it, right? Destroying something is always a lot easier than making it," Joel chuckled.

"Unfortunately," Adrian admitted.

Joel touched the chain again. "This isn't from our planet."

"Oh?" Adrian asked.

"Our spaceman's chain links are warped, and the alloys are frozen together around the sixth or seventh ring. I'm talking really low temperature." Joel took his pen out and started examining the big end. "Here are the stress lines, and deformities."

Adrian was slightly confused, "Just looks like shoddy metal working. I would have thought it was melted that way."

"It's not all metal, that's why only part of it fused together," Joel said. "They look like that because they were welded – cold. Probably came from the mining on Jupiter." Joel grinned and said, "The drones by Jupiter use the intense gravitational pressure to process their metals, and the zero pressure of space to weld it. I can cut this, but I can't promise it won't hurt him. I'll be making sparks, heat... all that. It'll burn the flesh inside of him."

"Can't damage the patient any more than he's already sustained."

"Oh come on, now that's impossible."

"That's why we called you," Adrian maintained. "If it were easy, I'd get someone else. No further damage to the patient is acceptable."

"I'm surprised Spaceman isn't dead already. What about Plan B," Joel said, but before he continued talking, Adrian' instantly hushed him and dragged him away.

"You are the Plan B," Adrian replied pulling Joel out of the room and into a small conference room.

Joel entered, shut the door, then demanded: "Tell me what's really going on."

"Come again?"

Joel started, "You've got a patient on a death bed under your watch. I worked with you for years when you were in ICP. I know you can make those chains disappear, reappear... whatever you need to do. I've seen you do it; they trained you to do it. Why'd you even call me?"

"Okay. Sure Joel." Adrian replied: "I'll go pull them out right now. When Patricia gets back and asks how the hell did four invincible chains get out of his back, I'll just tell her they fell out!"

Joel wasn't amused.

"And what happens when Deputy Ana spills the word about my power? Once the world knows about me, my name will be attached to every unsolved crime in the last decade as a person of interest!"

"Are you trying to save a life or your reputation?" Joel wondered.

Adrian pounded his fist on the desk. "I will not have a bevy of unanswered crimes pinned on me!"

Joel just nodded. "You'd just rather commit your own crimes?"

"Give me another option," Adrian pleaded.

"Your nurse was half right about them. They're incredible, but nothing is indestructible. Something that's strong in one spectrum is often weak in another," Joel said. "It's diamond mixed it with metallic alloys to make it more manageable. That gives us some chance of cutting it without hurting your boy much. With the right induction frequency, I can massage the electrons, and melt it from the inside out on the molecular level."

"Induction?" Adrian sighed. "That's really overkill isn't it?"

"Yeah, but what do you care? Ana will think it's magic."

Adrian considered this, then agreed, "I'll cut him open, expose the chains, and you can melt those sons of bitches."

Joel smiled and walked away to get ready.

GEORGE PACED BACK and forth outside of the hospital and finally received a call from Ana.

"How'd it go with the Judge?" Ana asked.

"He won't give me a warrant. Says we already have the hospital's cooperation. He also denied seizure of Blackwell's office without a cause because that would give me unlimited access to medical records."

"I feel like we are at a dead end, and I feel like I'm in the way," Ana admitted, "This patient is very damaged."

"That patient should be dead. Follow your instincts. If you need to back off, do so. Let Adrian feel free to be himself. That's what we want."

"I think he's being himself, I just, I don't believe he's the type to do what happened to Mason."

"That's not for us to decide. We just need to do our diligence to collect the evidence. Between Kennedy and Blackwell, they are conveniently too close to suspicious situations for me to let it slide."

"Well, I've got nothing, what did you find out about Kennedy?"

"Nothing. He wiped himself from all systems. So I don't know what connects him with Adrian, or with the Peterson's."

Ana threw out a guess. "Well, what connects the Petersons and Adrian?"

A light bulb flashed in George's mind. It seemed like the missing piece of the triangle that was right in front of his face. He said, "There's got to be some connection between an elderly couple like the Petersons and Adrian. But I think you might be in a better position to know that."

Ana instantly caught on and didn't like the implication. "If I snoop on medical records inside the hospital, that will ruin our lives much less this non-existent case."

"We just need a break. Something to tell us if we're hot or cold."

Ana grunted. "I'll see what I can find."

ADRIAN ESCORTED JOEL out of the hospital then found Patricia.

"I was looking for you," she said. "You have to see this!" She handed him a report and took him into the lab.

Adrian looked over the numbers as he followed her. He commented, "His glucose level is high. It doesn't look like his body produces much insulin. What are these antibodies in his blood?"

"It gets crazier than that," Patricia warned, "... okay... take a look."

Adrian peered through the microscope. "Hmm. He's got a fresh, bright, healthy red color," he observed. "The RBC structure is a bit, well, warped."

"Yeah."

"Maybe he's anemic; we can..."

"That's what I thought too," Patricia warned. "But how is it we have a big strong guy, who both diabetic, and anemic, but seems healthy? Then I looked closer and realized his has no natural immunity to even simplest bacteria our bodies fight every day, so the enzymes in his body have a crazy reaction..."

Adrian zoomed in, picking the cells apart visually. "Is that...? No way."

"His RBC has nuclei," she said. "When Spencer first pulled blood from John Doe, the analyzer gave a count of 15 grams per milliliter. Now it's around 18." Patricia said. "If he has hemostatic properties in his blood that we don't have and no evidence of microbial defense, that means..."

"He's not human?"

"That's right! He's a clone."

Adrain pondered. "Ligation may work to our advantage. He won't bleed so much. We don't have to cut the metal if we can cut his bones."

"That's a hard no," said Patricia, when Adrian shot her a look, she showed him why. "His enzymes! Look what happens when I damage the excess blood cells. See? Enzymes force the metal in his blood to produce a carbon alloy."

"His body is growing a metallic shell around his wounds?" Adrian was astounded.

"I don't know if that's his normal way to heal or maybe a virus caused this. Those metal bits on his body aren't skin graft at all; it's him! If we cut his bones and they cauterize like this, there's no way we can join them together."

"Where did Spencer send the blood samples? Who knows about this?"

Patricia looked nervous.

"What?" Adrian asked. "Who knows?"

"Everyone knows. Even the director is freaking out—says he's flying in tomorrow. He wants us to collect some sample tissue from John Doe. Enough to use for..."

"Shit!" Adrian shouted, standing up. "We need those chains out of him now! We need him awake. We are not experimenting on him; we are trying to save him! And find out what bit him!" Adrian demanded, walking out of the room.

"What bit him?" Patricia followed. "There's no way to get that data," she said. "We can't match his blood to anything, so we can't tell what is foreign and what isn't! The antibiotics aren't doing anything. His infections are getting worse. It's completely new territory."

"Flight 522?"

"What?"

"When corporations face a crisis, they find someone to blame," Adrian told her. "We will be that someone! So don't question. Just do what I say, or we will all find ourselves under a microscope!"

"So? We've got nothing to hide, right?"

Adrian didn't answer, he quickly scanned the blood sample with his tablet and saved the reading, labeling it: "Spiff."

When he finally got a moment alone, he received a call from the hospital director, Bill Russell.

"Do you have any government agents in my hospital right now?" Russell asked.

"No, just local police. What's going on, Bill?"

"Good, good," the director said. "We have a gold mine on our hands. The lab gave me an overview. I want to lock down our financial compensation before we give up the body. Keep him sedated for as long as possible. Keep telling them it's an emergency. I'll be back in the morning."

"Have you lost your mind?" Adrian demanded. "There are ethics, Bill, and we can't just sell a patient to the highest bidder?"

"So you're the poster kid for ethics?" Bill shot back. "Ethics apply to humans, and this guy ain't human. Besides, I'm not talking about selling his body to the government. It's what's in the body that counts."

"What if they do decide he's human?" Adrian demanded. "Then we'll have to explain what we did."

"He's not a human," Russell insisted. "He's a damn clone, and a criminal too! We caught one of their sneaky Martian clones, and conspiracy websites are already claiming that Dimycles was a government setup and that the genocide was an inside job! Whatever you snip off of him is legal gold. It's like printing money."

"Bill?" Adrian asked.

"Let's get something straight," Russell growled. "At some point that body's gonna leave my hospital dead or alive. That will result in an immediate shit storm of media coverage: allegations, investigations the whole nine yards. You play ball with me on this, and you'll get credit for discovering a whole a new human-like species. Do the right thing, Blackwell. I'm hoping you understand me."

Adrian heard a knock. Patricia poked her head in, and said: "The metal guy is back."

Adrian nodded, then spoke into the phone. "Bill, I understand you." He hung up and said to Patricia. "Get ready to move quickly—and send Joel in."

As they left Adrian's office, Patricia informed him: "A police captain, George Wilson, is out front. He wants to speak with you."

"I'll take care of Wilson," Adrian said. "You take Joel, and get him prepped."

He found the officer at the front desk. He gave Wilson a pleasant greeting,

George said, "I hear your patient is quite the challenge. I hope to see another book on how the celebrity doctor protected the monster?"

"My only concern is this patient's health," said Adrian.

"Still hiding behind the pretense of a doctor?"

"Still hiding behind your bullets?" Adrian quipped. "I pulled your work out of Dimycles. You must get paid by the round."

"I get paid by the people. The one's who tried to keep you out of this hospital," George said. "Funny how you got through all that opposition."

Adrian sighed, "What's this about?"

"Flight 522. Kennedy's parachutes crashed that plane. The law went easy on him."

Adrian didn't react to the name. "Are you investigating him?" he asked.

"He should have been locked up, but now he's free to target people because he knows he can get away with it. If you provide some information about some of his targets I can persuade the task force outside to be more cooperative."

"B.K. isn't going to hurt anyone."

"What about stalking?" Wilson asked, showing Adrian a picture. "The Petersons."

"We still have privacy laws in the hospital. I'm not going to discuss patients of this facility," Adrian shook his head sadly. "I think we are done here."

"Okay," Wilson relented. As he watched Adrian leave, and knowing he struck a nerve. George called out:, "Tell your boy, Kennedy. If I catch him by the Petersons' again, he's mine." Wilson made an about face and exited the hospital.

Adrian headed back to see how things were going with Patricia and Joel. As she took Joel's clothes and positioned him in the sanitation booth, he said: "If I can't melt it, that puts me in a bind. Can there be sparks?"

"Nope."

"Metal shavings?"

"Definitely not," Patricia replied. "Can't have anything floating around inside him."

Joel kept grinning and nodding his head.

"You having fun there, champ?" Patricia asked, watching the sanitation booth make its final pass.

"Yeah. I'm not used to getting this kind of attention," he said, "not without paying."

"So how you gonna get the chains off?" Patricia asked.

"Melt 'em."

They walked into the operating room, where Joel had already placed a huge generator.

"Just... stay right there. And don't touch anything," Patricia told him.

Adrian made the incision into Dimycles' back below the scapularis. He slowly cut through the flesh, cauterizing along the way. He exposed the binding link of the chain that wrapped Dimycles's rib bone.

He worked slowly to avoid irreparable damage, but fortunately the bleeding was minimal. Would this blood help heal wounds, the way human blood did? Adrian didn't know. He only knew that he must do all he could to help this patient recover, or they would all be in a lot of trouble. Ethically it was the most challenging operation he'd ever done.

Patricia said to Joel: "You're up."

Beneath his scapula Adrian exposed the binding link around Dimycles' rib. Patricia took photos as Adrian wrapped Joel's induction coils around the link. Joel's deafening machine came to life. Adrian pushed dampening material between the link and Dimycles' bone.

"We're good," Adrian told Patricia, who then gave the nod to Joel.

Joel engaged the machine. The binding link began to vibrate, while the dampening material protected the bone. The vibrations increased, making a high-pitched noise. Adrian pressed a finger to the bone to make sure it wasn't breaking. Under the line where the coils touched, the link changed from metallic gray to light purple. Patricia wanted to ask what was happening, but no voice could be heard above the noise.

Adrian grabbed the chain and held it straight up. The purple brightened underneath the coils, as atoms vibrated in synch with the alloy's critical frequency. Adrian pulled on the chain. It separated at the melting point, and then instantly faded to gray as it started cooling. Adrian handed the chain to Patricia, then fished out the other half of the binding link from Dimycles's flesh.

Patricia stared, wide-eyed. Joel grinned behind his mask.

"Good job, next," Adrian said. As Adrian started on the other shoulder, Joel started getting sleepy. It was turning out to be a long night. He tried to make jokes, but no one could hear him over the generator noise.

It took several hours. By the end their eyes were bloodshot, and their ears were ringing. Nurses wheeled Dimycles into a recovery room, but Adrian wasn't finished. After the surgery team had cleared out, Adrian came back in and injected something into the IV.

"I know you're there," Adrian said to Ana who was peeking into the doorway.

"Just curious, what you're doing is all," she said, meekly stepping inside the room with the doctor.

"Nanomites," Adrian answered.

Ana was silent for a moment.

Adrian stopped and looked at the officer. "Whatever bit him gave him a potentially fatal dose of poison. Just hoping these bots will clear that out."

Adrian pulled out his tablet to measure the nanomite activity within Dimycles's body. The tiny bots started to attack the infections.

"What's that?" Ana asked as Adrian took out another syringe.

"A reagent. In case I need to expel them from his body. Sometimes they try to fix too much," Adrian explained.

The bots cleared the infected tissue, removed the infected cells, and repaired the fresh wounds that had come from the chain removals. Finally, they attached themselves to Dimycles cells and lay dormant.

Adrian shrugged and smiled, putting away the syringe full of reagents. "I don't understand his DNA," he admitted.

Ana asked, "How long do they stay in the body?"

"In us? Only a few months. I don't know the regeneration process of his cells, but eventually, his body will get rid of them."

Ana started out of the room, then looked back. "You're all right, Doc."

ANA WALKED OUT of the room and made it a few steps down the hall before her phone rang.

"Did you get it?" George asked her.

Ana glanced around and nervously looked at her phone to see pictures of documets she had taken earlier. She put the phone back to her ear and sighed.

George was impatient. "That a no?"

"I think maybe we are going about this the wrong way," Ana wondered, looking for another option.

"You found something!" George said, excitedly. "Is it Kennedy? Adrian? What... what? Petersons?"

Ana bit her lip and shook her head. "Adrian's a good guy."

"Tell me what he's hiding in his closet," George requested.

Ana hesitated but ultimately revealed what she found in the medical records: "It's Nicole."

ADRIAN TURNED TO Dimycles with tired eyes in need of sleep. The remaining metallic wounds on the patient told a bitter story.

"Lotus messed you up," Adrian whispered. "No doubt Mason too, and you know where she is."

After Adrian had left, Dimycles slept. He was repaired, but unconscious. The deafening noise had ceased, leaving a lot of complaining patients and staff. Bill Russell would hear all about that the following day. Now the quiet was interrupted only by the soft beeps of monitors.

Dimycles's heart beat steadily at 55 bpm. He'd never slept so well. His IV dripped, keeping him well hydrated. Had he been awake, he might have smiled at the comfort, but he also would've known that the door was opening. A yellow-and-black hand reached down and touched him. Jain looked at the sleeping Exile. She didn't wonder or care why Wuyan had sent this one to Earth. All that mattered to Jain was her mission- plunging a dagger into Dimycles as he slept.

A moment later the patient's heart rate monitor flat-lined. An alarm sounded. Jain pulled her dagger from the corpse. Nurses raced into the room and found Dimycles, still on his back, blood spreading a stain on his chest. The nurses screamed, and Ana raced in behind them.

Jain dropped from the ceiling and Ana saw the black-and-yellow monster. Jain attacked, and escaped undetected by any other humans.

A metal scar started covering the wound on Dimycles chest. The flat-line tone of the heart rate monitor suddenly beeped, spiking up to 120, then dropping to 85. The metal on his chest solidified, and the nanomites returned to his cells. There they lay dormant... waiting.

A ring of dead nurses surrounded the bed, and Ana's body laid torn apart on top of them.

TEARS OF BERLIN

MOTHER NATURE SET the gloomiest of themes, as clouds covered the city of Berlin in a seemingly perpetual fog. Those mourning the death of Mason's young student, Tina, found it difficult to understand the tragedy.

An autumn breeze stirred yellow leaves on the sidewalks as a cab cruised through the streets of the old city. Even the filtered sunlight through the branches seemed yellowed with age. The older buildings contrasted with modern cars and clothing styles. The cab pulled up on Steinstraße. Bishop hopped out and walked to the corner, where Julius greeted him reluctantly.

"This wasn't the way we wanted to receive confirmation that Lotus is still alive," Julius told Bishop.

"But it's the only way he'd want it," Bishop responded. "I take it you aren't very happy to see me here."

As the two men rounded a corner, Julius said, "I've learned to stop asking questions about you. I can't believe you even got on a plane. Did you hack the system, again?"

"I thought you learned to stop asking questions."

"Right, well... Thanks to you, Adrian can't make it. You dropped a half-dead fugitive in his lap. So Sing has to deal with me, and I have to deal with you. Try not to be weird.

"So... here's the deal: The body you found was a rogue terrorist who turned on Lotus during the Six's last stand. His name was Dimcycles. He got sent to prison for genocide and escaped. ICP investigated his escape and realized that Lotus may still be alive. Tina identified Lotus here in Berlin. Sing immediately alerted her team to meet close in on him. When Sing touched down, she instructed Tina to wait for her in a public place—the Maxim bar over there," Julius pointed. "That's where it went down. He got her. Dead in the street."

"I never met Tina," said Bishop. "I feel like the detective who has no real reason to care about a person until she's already dead."

"But, you don't care about anybody, and you're kinda dead inside. So I don't think that should be a problem," Julius said.

A moment later they met Sing. "I want to thank you for coming on such short notice," she said. "B.K., I know you and Julius aren't part of..."

"Forget about it Sing." Bishop hugged her and looked at Julius. "It breaks my heart someone could do this."

"Everyone who knew her, loved Mae, except the animal who stole her," said Sing. "Tina was supposed to wait for us in the Maxim café but died on the street while getting into a cab. Can you believe that? In the street?"

As they approached the bar, Julius added, "They blocked the street off earlier, but they opened it back up." He opened the door and held it for his companions.

Sing was chatty walking inside the building. "Unlike the CIA; the BND works well with us. So Omar's pouring over their data for anything useful in tracking Lotus. That bastard is usually careful, but it doesn't matter. We know he's alive. Nothing short of his smelly casket is gonna convince anyone otherwise. He got desperate and fucked up. There was no reason to kill the poor girl."

The waitress seated the three of them at a dark wood table set with wine glasses. Sing ordered a gamay, and the waitress returned with a bocksbeutel. She poured them each a drink.

Sing sipped her drink, and said, "Ya know, he doesn't scare me anymore. He's made me cold. I'm more afraid of telling Tina's parents their little girl suddenly died in the street from a stroke."

"A stroke?" Bishop asked.

"A stroke? At 22?" Julius echoed, "They'll never believe it."

"She must have been poisoned," said Bishop. "That doesn't sound like a terrorist."

"Yeah, well, what do we know?" Sing asked. "What does death sound like?"

Sing excused herself from the table when one of her operatives called to her. She leaned close, as her contact whispered in her ear.

"It's all pretty sneaky," Bishop acknowledged to Julius.

"More like messy and desperate," said Julius. "He left a trail we can follow. The problem is, maniacs don't leave the kind of bread crumbs you want to pick up.

"And terrorist don't poison people," Bishop added.

"Then he must have an assassin," said Julius. "Lotus probably had someone do it while he was escaping."

Sing sat back down, saying, "You might be right. Omar's working that angle. He's got nothing on Lotus, but he matched a cab request to this location to one that went to a warehouse down south. He did an infrared scan of the warehouse. Nothing's in there, at least not anymore."

Bishop shrugged. "Worth a check."

"Mason is still out there," Sing declared. "I know it. Can you imagine being captive to that monster all these years, with no hope that someone might be looking for you? I'm so ashamed. We won't stop until we get her back."

"Okay," Julius agreed. "Bishop and I will go to the warehouse, see if there are any... crumbs we can pick up."

"Thank you," said Sing, getting up. She gave Bishop a digital scanner. "Let me know what you find."

Bishop nodded, and the two walked out to the street, where they hailed a passing cab. They sat down facing one another, and the taxi sped off.

"Isn't it weird? You have to pay a premium monthly fee to get these luxury cabs back home, but here in Germany they're everywhere," Bishop said, feeling the seats.

"It's a racket. They control the market, and squeeze it for profits," Julius responded, "Everything is packaged for profits. Did you talk to Adrian?"

"About?"

"His patient!"

"I gave him that patient!"

"Did you know you gave him a clone?" Julius asked, "Or it might have been an alien. Hope it's an alien."

"I wouldn't be surprised," Bishop admitted. "I mean, the guy was throwing trash bins around. He must have taken twenty bullets before he went down. If he's not an alien, I want to know what lab he came out of."

Julius laughed, "How many bullets do you think we could take?"

"You mean, assuming they hit us?" Bishop thought, "That's a good question. I'm not rushing to figure it out."

"What's amazing is the profit motive," Julius said. "Adrian's boss, and just about everyone else, want to chop the guy up, and then clone and sell his body parts. It makes you wonder: what's a life worth? Is it okay to take one life so you can clone many more? I mean, if it's one life sacrificed for many, does it make that okay?"

"That's too meta for me right now," Bishop sighed.

"Everything is profits," Julius insisted. "The government, big business. Businesses own the government! Most people don't even own cars anymore. The government owns them all."

"Well, to be fair, car thefts have gone down dramatically," Bishop joked.

"You know what I'm saying. Everything is packaged and centralized and owned by the big guys. Big companies suck up all the talent because the people have no financial backing to make it on their own. Even when someone comes up with their own great idea, the big companies swoop in, take it, package it, and sell it before the little guy can find a single investor. His life's work taken from him—how is that not theft?"

"Sounds a little deep for you. Since when are worried about- oh, you're still mad about your comic book," Bishop said with a chuckle. "You were just a teenager."

"I am still mad about that," Julius agreed, his voice rising. "I don't care how old I get; I'm always gonna be mad about it. I drew a damn good comic."

"But now information is a free-for-all," said Bishop with a shrug. "You text it, email it, search for it, or even just speak it, if it's in the cloud then it's internet domain—anyone can take it."

"But why do the big guys get to win?" Julius asked. "Corporations are bigger than us, and they have more money than us. They can steal, package, and sell my idea before I can even make a prototype. How is that right?"

"You mapped out a VR comic world on the cloud. Someone was bound to steal that. Might makes right," Bishop replied.

"So we're no further than the ancient Romans," Julius said. "Except our profits don't reside in property, they're in stolen ideas."

"Wait till we start traveling to new planets," Bishop raised his eyebrows, "That'll be the next land grab."

"We're already on the Moon, Mars, and Europa," Julius noted. "Sometimes I feel like we should fully commit to ICP, so we could really fight that nonsense."

Bishop's hadn't shaved in a few days, and he rubbed his chin. "Seems that way now, but we have to be careful. ICP charters a shaky definition of terror. What happens when we categorize terror too broadly and call those we oppress 'terrorist' because they have no other means to fight back?"

"I know," Julius relented. "I thought you weren't in the mood for meta."

Bishop chuckled. "You got me."

As the cab reached the warehouse, Bishop added, "This is the first I've been out of the country in a long time. I feel so free right now, less angry. Less depressed. I was devastated by Flight 522. I lost the most important person in my life when Nicole died. I was publically embarrassed as an engineer, but, oddly enough, being banned from technology also gave me a sort of freedom I can't describe."

They exited the cab and walked around the warehouse looking for an entrance. It was not a conversation Julius wanted to have. He and his brother spent most of their waking hours trying to keep Bishop out of jail, and to hear Bishop talk candidly about it brought back the wrong memories.

"Sometimes I feel caged and restricted by what I can't do," Bishop went on. "Then I see you guys, and I can't help but smile. That's when I realize that I have everything I need."

"Adrian told me the cops busted you at the Petersons'," Julius said, peering through a barred window.

Bishop fell silent, then finally said: "Yeah."

Julius sighed. "Unacceptable."

After checking the perimeter, Julius entered the building; Bishop stayed outside to give Julius some space and inspect the facilities management system.

Bishop sighed at the computer readout. "I can't read German."

Footsteps echoed through the empty warehouse as Julius wandered through it. "This place is filthy," he spoke over the phone to his team members while scanning the inside. "Scanner is picking up high concentrations of oxides. And it's not like dust or grime; it's like..."

"Fertilizer?" Bishop asked over the comms.

Julius smelled the foul air, "Not any kind the scanner is aware of."

Julius ran a finger along the floor, got up and brushed his hands. Having worked with the Harold Amos scientists for a long time, he could feel the signs of experimentation but couldn't touch it. "She was here. Lotus must have cleared this out recently."

"I need something more concrete than that," Sing said skeptically.

Bishop entered the building and found Julius. Julius asked, "Find anything?"

"I can't read the reports in another language. Best I can tell, the building complained of its structural integrity being weakened."

"Where?"

"Hang on," Bishop said. He closed his eyes and concentrated. A wave emanated from his body and reverberated off the walls. He opened his eyes, glanced to his left, and pointed. "Those walls feel hollow."

Julius walked over and started tapping the wall with his knuckle. He walked along, tapping until he heard an empty echo. As he glanced back at Bishop, Julius's body phased, fading into translucence. He walked through the wall.

"Damn." From behind the plaster, his voice was muffled. Julius came back through the wall, dragging a dead body in a plastic bag.

Bishop looked down. "Yeah, Lotus was here."

"There's more," said Julius.

"Oh no!" Sing shouted, "Get them all out. One of them might be Mason!"

Julius melted into the wall, then re-emerged with another body. He did this several times, laying the corpses out in a row. "She ain't here," Julius told Sing, as he aimed the phone's camera. "Omar, I'm sending you some photos. Can you get me IDs?"

Julius went down the row taking pictures, as Omar confirmed their arrival on his end. A few moments after Julius sent the last photo; Omar started relaying his findings: "They're scientist, but no Mason. I don't know about the last two. Their bodies are severely decomposed. The system does recognize them. Oh shit! Dammit! Their bodies have trackers! They must be officials! Probably why they were stashed behind the walls."

"German operatives are gonna be on your ass in seconds," Sing warned them. "Get out of there! You're compromised!"

Julius and Bishop heard the buzz of UAV propellers. They looked at each other and headed in different directions. Four small drones flew into the building, cruising at eye level.

They sailed through the warehouse and glimpsed the targets running through the back. The UAVs charged, firing. Several UAVs glided through corridors as three hung back. One shot a door down. Another entered the room.

Julius emerged from the wall, spun, and high-kicked it. The UAV smashed into the wall. Julius phased back through the wall. The other three UAVs charged into the room and scanned it. They found it empty.

As they tracked a heat signature into another room, Julius stepped out from the wall. He snatched the last UAV, phased half of it into the wall on its side, broke off the visible part, and phased into the wall behind it.

The remaining two UAVs went on alert. Their operators suspected vision sensor malfunctions and began random firing. Julius emerged from a wall, stepped between two UAVs, and drew fire from both. As he phased, the bullets went right through him, leaving the UAVs to destroy each other.

Bishop approached him, whispering: "I sense more."

Five field agents entered the building. Crouching low, they crept along the wall. Suddenly arms came out of the wall and grabbed the one bringing up the rear. The man's body turned translucent, and Julius pulled him in behind the wall.

The four remaining agents had gone a few meters before noticing their fifth was missing. They maintained formation and a piece of the scaffolding fell. They turned and fired at nothing. "Nothing" suddenly moved.

A dead body sat up. The agents fired, and their panicked shots tore through it. More bodies arose, seeming to drag themselves along the floor toward the agents. Behind the wall, the fifth officer came to and started banging and kicking. The lead agent called for backup and signaled his men to retreat. The four men ran out, firing back at the corpses who were in pursuit. Bullets riddled the bodies but did nothing to stop them. As the fifth agent finally broke free, he joined his fleeing comrades, and they all escaped the building in a mad rush.

Julius and Bishop laughed. "Nice horror show," Bishop cried.

"You're welcome," Julius chuckled.

Julius dropped into a celebratory squat and bounced his shoulders up and down. Bishop marched in place, with one hand forward and the other behind his head.

A noise echoed faintly, stopping both of them. They assumed fighting stances.

Julius's body was phased. "Hear that?"

"Yeah," Bishop said from inside his shielding. He turned around and saw the noise came from one of the dead bodies. When nothing happened, Bishop whispered, "I don't think it's a bomb." Bishop made the body float toward them and then they saw the device inside of the body bag more clearly. "It's just a radio. When we took him out of the wall, they detected him and maybe trying to contact him."

"Yea, but who is 'they,' because they aren't speaking German," Julius claimed, approaching the body, and staring at the badly decomposed corpse. He tried to understand the muffled words coming from the radio.

"Where is that flag from?" Bishop asked, noticing the uniform seemed to be official, though the rotted body ate away most of the fabric.

"I've seen that before," Julius said, trying to remember the colors. "That's... that's the Sudan." Julius touched the body bag and phased it. The radio fell out, and from there he could hear the words better. It was Arabic. "This isn't a German operative. This man is from the Sudan."

Julius listened to the words from the radio, and shook his head, "They don't seem to be calling for him individually. They are calling for help – from anyone. Is this a recording, or is this happening now? Did... did something happen to the Sudan?"

Omar came back over the phone: "Oh God." He streamed video to the two men. Their screen showed a live feed announcing a massive earthquake had struck the Sudan, sinking the ancient city of Khartoum only moments before.

"Shit!" Julius screamed.

"Can you get us to Khartoum?" Bishop asked Sing, as he punched keys on his phone, summoning a cab. "Whatever game Lotus has set is officially in play."

Omar came over Julius's phone, "Bishop, Khartoum is leveled. I doubt a plane could land at their airport."

"I don't care," Bishop shouted, as he rushed from the warehouse. "Get me there!"

Julius ran next to him, panting: "Can you fly there?"

"Can I fly for eight hours, across ocean and continents without a map? No!" They stopped and looked at the sky – suddenly it was full of military aircraft.

"What's going on?" Julius yelled. "Omar?"

"Hang on. Um…" Sing worked furiously, "I'm trying to book a ticket, but all the flights are canceled, everything is grounded. I don't know how we're gonna get out of Germany."

"He knew this would happen. He lured us here, and knew we'd be stuck here!" Julius stared at the sky and stumbled into the street. German gunships and fighter squadrons flew low overhead. "We got set up! Omar?"

"Hang on!" Omar shouted, "There's a private airfield east of you. We might convince a plane to take us out of here."

"I'll work on that," Sing said. "But no promises."

Julius and Bishop hopped into a cab.

"Don't promise us; promise Mason," Bishop said. "Omar what's going on? This is just like in D.C. Who is everyone fighting?"

"Look, CIA doesn't share data with us. So information's gonna be slow. The BND does, but even they aren't divulging anything. Satellites are shutting down…" Omar sighed. "Information is coming in slow. This is gonna take time."

"This is beyond spy games. This is military?" Julius noticed. "How much time do you need O'?"

"Jules, we aren't gonna fight a war, are we? What's the priority, Sing?" Bishop asked.

Sing took a deep breath, "Mason. Mason's the one-and-only priority. Wherever she is, we get her. We aren't fighting a war unless it means getting her back."

"Then send us to Khartoum."

Sing came back with a flight plan. "Best I could do," she apologized. "There's that airstrip east of you that will get you to Giza. From there you're on your own."

"That will work," Bishop said, as the cab sped off.

"Maybe not," Omar interrupted. "You guys need to hurry. That team you scared off just sent cycle drones your way!"

"I can't make this cab go any faster!" Julius snapped.

"I can deal with that." Bishop broke through the partition and ripped off the top panel to access the test panel. Triggering a maintenance error, he issued an override, kicked out the robot, and took the wheel.

"How long has it been since you drove a car?" Julius asked.

"What do you mean? I just stole a cop car the other day. It's like riding a bike. Who cares?"

"Then why can't you stay in one lane..." Julius spotted all the motorcycles behind them. "Never mind."

The robotic cycles couldn't automatically stop the cab since Bishop broke the robot driving it, so they sent out stern audio warnings in German.

"Do you speak German?" Bishop asked Julius.

"No."

The cycles shot at the cab.

"Drive!" Julius shouted, "Keep this thing going! It's a long walk to that airstrip."

"I'm doing all I can," Bishop shouted.

"Let me drive!"

"You're crazy! I can do this!"

"Yeah, right!" Julius ducked as bullets whizzed through the car.

"I can do it," Bishop breathed a little more calmly.

"Then get rid of these pesky drones," Julius suggested.

"Fine," Bishop agreed. The first row of robotic cycles crumpled as their front tires blew out. The next cycles crashed into them. Soon all the droid cycles had wrecked themselves. Bishop piloted the cab forward. "How far away is the airstrip?" he asked.

"I don't know. Omar hung up."

"Can you look?"

"Yeah, yeah... Where are we?"

Bishop glanced around at signs printed in vague language. "I don't know." He saw a platform ahead. "We're about to pass a fuel station."

Julius peered at the overhead platform. "That's not a toll booth?"

"Tollbooths have cameras; fuel stations have charging rods. I can see the rods from here."

Julius looked at his map. "Found it. It's for fuel and tolls, both!"

As they passed under the platform, the fuel gauge showed they were full, and the toll light blinked.

"Yeah, two hours to destination," said Julius.

Bishop leaned back. "In nothin' faster than this German station..."

"...wagon..." Julius came in "...draggin' trough the countryside. Drones chasin', and gettin' hit."

"Actin' like we ain't shit?" Bishop came in, "Don't know what they facin'?"

Julius nodded his head, and followed, "I run them out, like recess, I'm talking playground...if they don't stay down... I leave them in pieces... scattered 'round."

"Shut it down. J, What?"

"I'm sayin' cops and others... slangin' bullets at brothers... but they can't fade me... cuz I phase thee."

"You phased three..."

"Through the wall, I face them all, then take a chill from the brawl. Yo B' rock up a fifth, we need to sip it to this."

"Nah, save your thirst, so we can pour out the first. Of the liquor... cuz they hit her. We lost a lot of lives liv'n fast and sicker,"

"But it's only gettin' quicker."

"Then we should prolly drink a mixer."

After an hour-and-a-half of freestylin', they pulled up to the side of a domed building with a radar tower on the opposite side. They hopped from their hijacked cab, walked around the building, and saw the airfield beyond. Not seeing anyone, they approached the hangar. They stopped when they heard voices from inside a door.

"Do you speak German?" Bishop asked.

"Bruh… stop it. Why is this happening to me?"

As they entered the hangar, two uniformed men approached.

"Do you speak English?" Bishop asked.

"Yes," the first man said with a thick German accent. "We do. You are from the ICP, yes? We go to Africa?"

"Yes!" Julius piped in.

The pilot pointed at an airplane out on the strip. "The plane is ready. We are rushed, so we must go now."

"Is that your radar?" Bishop asked, pointing to a screen displaying a map of Germany.

"Yes, but we must go," the other pilot said.

"What is this madness?" Bishop wondered as blips filled much of the screen.

"Never seen anything like it," Julius added.

"All airlines are down," The first pilot boasted, hurrying them along. "Nothing is allowed out."

"Except you?" Bishop asked the pilots.

"Why would you risk your lives to get us out?" Julius wondered.

"Money," said the first pilot. "Let's get going."

As they left the hangar, Bishop smelled something. "Pretty gritty garage," he said.

As they all boarded the plane, the first pilot gave them the safety instructions. Bishop cringed when they mentioned the parachute and evacuation system. It was his design. That made him think.

Bishop stared at his friend.

"What is it?" Julius asked.

"Lotus knew the flights would be grounded. He knew we'd be stuck here."

"Yeah, I said that already, but we aren't stuck here anymore."

"I know you said that! But I'm saying, just... listen! All airlines are grounded, but we miraculously find the one plane that can get us out..." Bishop waited for Julius to get it.

"You think Lotus owns this aircraft?"

"I know it," Bishop confirmed. "Not only did he show us where he wants us to go, but he gave us the plane to get there. That odor! This thing has been hauling shipments of fertilizer from that warehouse. This is a trap."

"I dunno if we should abort."

"Why not? We have to," said Bishop. "We're going where he wants us to go."

"But... it's Africa. It's the Sudan?" Julius said. "They need help."

"Why?' Bishop asked weakly. "All we'll find is devastation."

"But isn't that something?" Julius asked, "Whatever he did there, he's gonna do elsewhere. I know our priority is Mason, but I'm sure there are people there need help too."

Bishop sighed, calculating a strategy to end the conversation.

Julius continued, "An injustice anywhere is an injustice everywhere. If Lotus caused it..."

"Alight Sister Souljah," Bishop snapped, "I get the point. Let's split up. I'll see where the trail leads, and you can work with Omar to find out where the trail ends. Mason's gotta be somewhere in the middle."

Julius nodded, then pointed at the cockpit. "Since when are you volunteering to fly a plane."

"It's cool."

"Cool?"

"Yeah, planes basically fly themselves," said Bishop.

"And land?"

Bishop thought for a moment, "Omar should give me a call in a few hours, and we'll go over that."

Julius chuckled. As he started walking to the rear of the plane, Bishop stopped him. "Don't forget the two pilots."

Julius snapped his fingers and walked to the cockpit. Phasing through the cabin door, he unlocked it from the inside. As the pilots throttled forward, the airplane lurched down the runway. Julius leaned back against the door, watching them.

The plane's nose lifted. They took off.

"I've always wanted to do this," Julius said.

The pilots heard him, but it was too late. Julius leaned forward against the g-forces and grabbed both of their shoulders. "Change of plans," he said. He and the pilots phased, flying backward, and out of the plane.

SHEETS OF FROST

A GROUP OF young Reptilites formed a circle in the training room aboard the Kaiman. Those with tails slid them back and forth on the ground, thumping them in unison with those who stomped their feet. To this drumbeat, Kal Kalet drew her scythe. As she stood in the center, her wings opened, and she performed. It was a history lesson for the young ones.

She told them of their ancestors on a planet called Earth. She danced as she sang of the dinosaur, and the Great Abduction. The young ones cheered, as she told them about the Age of Enlightenment when Reptilites gained independence and reasoning. The young Reptilites fell silent as they learned their destiny: a day when Reptilites would wage a world war to reclaim their heritage and the land that had been stolen from them long ago.

After the lesson, students were encouraged to perform the song and dance for themselves, committing the lesson to memory. Kalet watched, listened, and corrected their mistakes. She was in the middle of this when she received a message.

While on its way to the Chunga system, the Kaiman was passing a subspace node. Kalet's scythe returned to a small rod, and she left the training room, heading for the bridge. When she arrived, she connected to the subspace channel.

She neatly folded her dark-reddish-and-golden-brown wings onto her velvety back. Between her shoulder blades was a bright yellow-brown mane of freshly groomed feathers. As Kalet leaned in to her display communicator, Jain's hyperspace link connected. A moment passed, and the channels secured the connection.

"How's everything on the front line?" Kalet asked.

"As expected."

"Tell me about the humans," said Kalet.

"They are confused," Jain explained. "Divided in every way. They seem to embrace chaos."

"Makes them unpredictable, doesn't it?"

"Perhaps, but you should spend more time on the surface. You would know the difference between chaos and unpredictability. They kill themselves for profit. They expect it, and are even addicted to it."

"Sounds familiar," Kalet muttered.

Jain sent the data, and Kalet inspected several photos that accompanied the package. "Are these pictures of the Exile?"

Jain giggled. "You're looking at pictures of five different people. The first is the doctor who fixed him."

"Impossible! How can you tell? They all look the same!" Kalet exclaimed.

"The doctor has a scar on both cheeks. He also has a broader nose," Jain explained.

Kalet zoomed in on the image, "Oh wow. I never noticed. Is it difficult to tell the difference with all of them?"

"Yes. Extremely. It drove me crazy when I first got here. Everyone looked the same. I had tailed someone for a week before I realized I'd followed three different people. They confuse me when they change their clothes. They're like animals who change their skin color to match their environment."

"How do they tell each other apart?" Kalet asked.

"I'm not sure. Maybe by smell or voice. Sarek was a master. He could tell the difference easily. Just a gift, I guess."

"Still, it's for the best," Kalet concluded. "Looking at them as individuals would make it difficult to complete the job."

"How so?" Jain wondered, "Aren't you fully committed to the cause?"

"Of course!" Kalet shouted. "Why wouldn't I be?"

"Killing an individual human should be no different than killing a group," Jain told her.

"Have you ever considered the harm it might cause Reptilia?" Kalet asked.

"No."

Kalet waited for some explanation, but none came. "Okay," she said blandly.

Jain sensed Kalet's continuing discomfort. "What harm will it bring? Reptilites fight amongst each other all the time. That's what the State wants, to stick us in a bucket and watch us climb on top of each other to get out. All this time, what are we fighting for? What's outside of the bucket? To be rulers of destiny? To no longer be slaves? Earth! I tell you, Gedeon is right—Earth is everything. Once you consider the full scope of what our supremacy means to Earth, Reptilia becomes little more than a meaningless pile of rock."

"The concept is just new to me. It's mind-boggling."

Jain reasoned with her friend, "Who is more authentic? The Reptilite who rules Reptilia, or Earth?"

"Reptilia is where we live," Kalet claimed.

"Reptilia is where we were put; Earth is where we are from. There is simply no comparison. Earth is the land where we belong. It is where we have the right to be."

"I agree, but I sometimes wonder about the others...back home...once the war is underway."

"Many won't understand," Jain admitted, "but those are the inferior species we no longer need. They will perish like the humans."

Kalet took exception. "I've read the data. Humans are smart. They can think themselves out of anything."

"That is the source of their reckless behavior," Jain interjected. "They assume they can overcome any dilemmas, so they don't fear the consequence of creating the problem in the first place."

"But what if they can overcome? Can we defeat their combined intelligence? Their hive stubbornness? They won't give their planet up easily. Does it give them a mental edge?" Kalet asked. "Reptilites have a fallback position: Reptilia. Humans don't."

"I can assure you when Rex Gedeon is ready for battle; he will burn every bridge to give us our own mental edge. Fleeing won't be an option."

"So it's a battle for extinction," Kalet said.

"In the past, we've been forced to catch the scent of extinction," said Jain. "Humans will get the final taste of it."

"What about Wuyan?" Kalet asked as she looked at the newly arrived data.

"The Exile is dead. Whatever mission he was to accomplish on her behalf is lost," said Jain. "He seemed surprised I was there."

"What became of him?"

"I killed him in his sleep."

Kalet shook her head.

"Wuyan knows nothing!" Jain insisted.

"We cannot assume what Wuyan knows. For now, you will stay with the Martian until we get back."

"From where?"

"We're going to Chunga to learn of any military plans to ambush us."

"The water world?" Jain started. "They would be the most likely species to contest our right to Earth. They could ruin our effort."

"It's a dangerous game," Kalet warned. "We have no allies, no reinforcements. I hate having to rely on a Martian. I don't trust Lotus. Sarek warned me about him. I didn't take that warning seriously enough. Now, my feathers bristle every time I hear his name. No one's invaded a planet in an Age. The physics make it a nightmare to do, plus it's illegal throughout the Observed Realm."

Kalet saw Jain's full report and a new batch of data.

"It's only illegal if we fail," Jain said. "Laws are for slaves too weak to rise above it. The powerful are above the law. When the humans fall, and we reclaim our homeland, we will write the laws and the history. What is legal depends not on what is right, but who's in power. Read the data I just sent. It will ease your mind. We'll win."

"That's understandable," Kalet agreed.

"Kalet."

"Yes?"

"Either the humans will face extinction... or we will."

Kal Kalet nodded and disconnected the feed. She looked over the candidate applications for science officer. There were only three, and none seemed promising. They seemed willing, but she knew what Rex Gedeon wanted. The real question was: with Sarek dead, did Rex Gedeon know what he needed? He liked eccentric science officers who thought outside the box—officers like Sarek. Gedeon had loved Sarek, whose quick thinking had saved them all many times. Sarek sensed whenever things weren't quite right. He identified problems faster than the ship's sensors. Sarek had overstepped his bounds. He opposed a delicate mission at the wrong moment; Kalet wished he'd never threatened Gedeon in the process. Kalet needed to find a creative science officer who could also obey every order. None of these applicants stood out.

A sharp-beaked Reptilite applicant with a fine row of teeth approached her station. "Kal Kalet, I am Tanga," he said. Tanga wasn't very colorful, but his shoulders, elbows, and knees seemed to contain a natural protective shell similar to Gedeon's. *At least he should be tough,* Kalet figured.

"Why do you want to be a science officer?" she asked.

"I've been fascinated in the world of science since I was hatched," Tanga said, relying on a standard opening. "To be—"

"Sorry," she interrupted. "This position isn't a fantasy. Do you understand the needs of a science officer? What Rex Gedeon wants?"

"He wants someone who is smart, committed..."

"He wants a fanatic." She glanced at his file. "Impressive marks... though I notice you applied for other combat-related fields."

"I have a wide variety of skills," Tanga claimed. "In addition to brains, I have a mean bite."

"You may need those skills," she told him. "There may be a recruitment process. Do you know what that entails?"

"Combat." Tanga brushed his armored shoulders. "I'm not afraid."

Kalet pointed to the science officer's spot on the far side of the bridge. "For now that's your station. Rex Gedeon will determine if you're a good fit."

She watched him take hold of the inner bridge rafters and volley himself toward the station and thought he had little chance of staying there. "Perhaps being around Earth has given me a new perspective on fear," she said to herself. "Maybe our courage is killing us."

The Kaiman dropped out of hyperspace and disengaged its anti-mass field. As they entered the Chunga System, Kal Kalet steadied her controls. The Reptilites took their stations. A communication channel opened, and its message blared over the loudspeaker.

You have entered the Chungassi-controlled territory. We will escort you to Soluca base, where you will be boarded, and processed. If you do not comply, we will destroy you. This is your final warning.

The Kaiman drifted toward the Chungassi system's central star. Kalet's display picked up a Chungassi dome on a path intersecting theirs. A translucent blue-and-white dome appeared on the screen, its hull glowing reddish orange. The hemisphere ship stopped to connect with something- invisible. Enormous bat-like wings appeared on its sides, and the obscured section between them opened, showing long, full, tentacle-like legs. The legs and dome defined the Chungassi's long-range defensive warship: the Kraken. The Kaiman did not comply with the order, and an electrical field sparked wildly around the dome.

"They're preparing to fire!" Kalet warned.

The Kraken floated toward the Kaiman. The tentacles felt for their prey. A leg jutted out through space to snatch the Kaiman. Kalet pumped the thrusters to avoid it. An orb-like projectile shot from the dome's center cannon.

"Charges launched!" Kalet shouted

Gedeon turned to her. "Soft maneuver; avoid the orb's homing field!"

The Kaiman took evasive action. The sphere exploded, lighting the nearby space, but missing the Kaiman.

"Full power to shields!" Gedeon commanded.

Waves of heat and radiation emanated from the explosion. The shockwave hit the Kaiman. The bridge shook as the officers floated in the vacant space. "Give me the damage report," Gedeon ordered.

Kalet scanned it, shaking her head. "No damage. Shields deflected the blast."

Gedeon nodded, and then commanded, "Report 20% damage to the ship's logs, and reduce shields."

Kalet did as she was told. The Kaiman played cat-and-mouse with its opponent. The Kraken's tentacles reached for the Kaiman, but the skull-like ship slipped through. One tentacle grabbed an asteroid, hurling it at the invaders. An electric field danced around the Kraken's dome as the ship launched another charge. A second Kraken approached.

"Two Krakens!" Kalet shouted to Gedeon, as she maneuvered around the asteroid.

The second Kraken decloaked near the Kaiman. Its tentacles shot out to snatch it. Kalet pumped side thrusters and hit the main engines. The Kaiman barely slipped through.

"Watch that charge!" Gedeon warned.

The second Kraken launched another charge, which homed in on the Kaiman.

"Pull back!" Gedeon shouted.

Kalet pumped the front thrusters, and the Kaiman spun around. She hit forward thrusters, and they retreated from the second charge. The first charge came from behind.

"Get centered. Face down, 90 degrees," Gedeon shouted.

Kalet's wings fluttered. The Kaiman engaged right thrusters hard. The second charge swung toward them from the front, while the first charge came from behind. The Kaiman's top thrusters pumped, realigning the ship perpendicular to the charges.

"Full power!" Gedeon commanded.

The Kaiman sped from between the two charges. They met and detonated. Their combined blast shook the Kaiman. Kalet intensified rear shields, deflecting the destruction.

"Damage," Gedeon said.

Kalet looked up. "None, but low-level radiation passed through the lower decks."

Another Kraken appeared.

"Give a report of extensive damage," Gedeon ordered. "Reduce shields to 35%. Disable starboard thrusters."

As three Krakens chased them, Kalet reported her starboard thrusters were down. The Krakens repositioned accordingly, each firing a charge.

"Evade," Gedeon commanded to Kalet.

Kalet had no starboard thrusters, so she pumped her port thrusters, allowing the Kaiman to drift closer to the charges. She pumped them a few more times, trying to spin, but it slowed the ship too much. She engaged the primary drives, but all three charges were locked on them. Her wings fluttered, as she steered the Kaiman away. Two charges weren't fooled, but the third was. Its denotation triggered the others. A massive fireball shook the Kaiman.

Gedeon nodded to Kalet and said: "Shut down defensive shields. Take us to the fifth planet, third moon. Send a distress signal." He turned to his science officer and looked him up and down. "You are with me."

Gedeon and Tanga left the bridge.

The Kaiman blasted its way through the ice clouds of the third moon, landing on its soft surface. Rex Gedeon and Tanga exited the ship and walked on the moist sandy surface.

"What do you know about the humans?" Gedeon asked his new science officer.

"They're dumb, and need to be exterminated," Tanga replied without emotion.

The two of them strolled across the dark surface. A heavy icy mist made it like walking through perpetual sleet. Snowflakes and ice droplets hung in the air. Water beaded on Rex Gedeon's chest, crystallizing into tiny frost particles.

"The humans achieved space flight, and advanced weaponry after only a few thousand years of civilization," Gedeon told Tanga, "Dinosaurs were on Earth for a few million years and still couldn't speak."

"True, but humans still pale in comparison to us. We were made superior in every way," Tanga insisted.

"When two species are so different, how do you measure superiority?" Gedeon asked.

"We are the most varied creatures in the galaxy," Tanga said proudly. "Humans all have the same exact features and body parts. There is almost no difference between them. They are all basically the same color—just different shades. Can you imagine how that would be? Dark greens, light greens, and more green, green, green? We'd all look alike!" Tanga laughed, but Gedeon didn't find it funny. He looked up and saw lights above the ice clouds. A disconnected Kraken dome searched for a hole in the clouds.

"Why are the clouds on this moon solid and floating?" Gedeon asked his officer.

As Tanga tried to frame an answer, Gedeon struggled for breath. With so much ice in the air, it wasn't easy. Icicles formed on his snout, and he shook them off. "Is this air safe to breathe?" Gedeon asked.

"I suppose it is," said Tanga.

Gedeon's scales turned dark orange, and then returned to bluish-gray. "You didn't check?"

"We are Reptilites, we can withstand most atmospheres," Tanga claimed, then felt nervous his response wasn't sufficient. "Y- you commanded me to follow, I just assumed..."

"You let me walk out into a strange planet without checking the atmosphere?" Gedeon scolded.

"O-Of course, I normally would, as a science officer," Tanga stammered. "But I thought hurrying out here was part of your plan. Thought you risked being caught, I assumed you knew that, and I had full faith in your direction."

"Why would I risk getting caught?"

"To find out if the Chungassi know about Earth. Isn't that one of our objectives here?"

It was the correct response, but Gedeon only said, "Mmm."

A Chungassi dome set down nearby, and the commander and crew exited. The Chungassians had large webbed feet, smooth grayish skin, and long multi-colored mohawks. The fins on their backs looked like scaly wings, and they were armed with swords and shields. The females had smooth faces, large eyes, and webbed hair flowing freely around the scaly designs on their shoulders.

"I am Commander Renard," said their leader. "I'm appalled... a Reptilite? Out here? The day the galaxy is free your arrogance is the day I see you chains again."

"How foolish of us," Gedeon responded.

Renard had a dark blue Mohawk. "And you are?"

"I am Rex Gedeon, commander of the Kaiman."

"Indeed," Renard chuckled. "Command your crew to evacuate as they are now our prisoners. Have you gone rogue, or is Apex feeling the need to expand his military campaigns beyond his means?"

"We are alone, and perhaps I may offer something of value to the Chungassi in return for our release?"

"Impossible! A band of Reptilite slaves is all the prize I need," Renard threatened.

Gedeon took the insult, and responded, "Perhaps, you may change your mind, once you see what I have to offer."

The top of Renard's head only came up to Gedeon's chin. Gedeon held out his closed fist, and opened it, revealing a holographic orb. The Orb powered on, showing the image of Earth.

The Chungassian's beady eyes widened. "What is that?"

"What do you know of this planet?" Gedeon asked.

"I have never seen it before," Renard gasped. "It's beautiful."

"It's called Earth," Gedeon told him.

"Is that..."

"Water? Yes."

"Mother of the seas," The Chungassian sheathed his sword and reached forward.

"There's more," Gedeon continued. "The poles are frozen water. There's even water under the ground. You can be the first to discover it for your people. I can give you the location, but only if you find it in your ability to give me my freedom."

"Hmm..." The Chungassian pondered this. "And what will we do with a planet we cannot invade?"

"No one lives on the planet," Gedeon promised.

Renard turned and asked his troops a question in their own language. Their response was negative.

"We haven't yet reported your capture," Renard told Gedeon. "So, as far as anyone knows, your ship could have crashed into the sea floor."

"Sea floor?" Gedeon looked around, "I see no bodies of water."

"You are standing in it," Renard explained. "This moon is poorly terraformed—a financial disaster."

"Terraformed?" Gedeon was genuinely surprised, "By whom?"

"The Merloti, of course! We spared no expense!"

"The Merloti are masters at terraforming worlds. Why did they fail?"

"Ah, the Merloti are masters at giving us exactly what ask for. One must be careful when dealing with them. They are quite pedantic. As you must know, there are very few water worlds in the Observed Realm. We picked this spot, paid the deposit, and they went to work. Of course, it was well into the project that we realized that this moon is too small. Too cold. The atmosphere won't pressurize the water the way we need. We attempted to negotiate the same deal on a warmer moon. The Merloti won't have it."

"Where did you expect to put the ocean?" Gedeon asked

"We are walking in what would be the ocean right here, but the atmosphere isn't right. The droplets just freeze and float in the air. It's foggy and icy all the time. We can't swim here."

"Then the Earth is what you seek," Gedeon said, nodding. He extended his claws, and gave Renard the holographic orb.

Renard commanded his troops to return to the ship, then told Gedeon: "This should never happen again. There are only so many water worlds in the habitable zone. Next time we won't be so lenient."

The Chungassi lifted off, leaving one sentry to monitor the situation.

Gedeon watched the dome rise into the ice clouds. Once they were out of sight he said, "The Chungassi know nothing of Earth. It is more likely Wuyan's pod was sent on an unrelated mission."

"I agree," Tanga echoed.

Without looking at Tanga, Gedeon questioned him. "They left behind a sentry. Why?"

"Clearly to monitor us."

"Yes, but why do we require monitoring?"

"Hmm," said Tanga, realizing the test. "I sense a trap. They will destroy us despite their good faith trade of Earth."

"That is your observation?"

"It is."

"Then why is the sentry still alive?"

Eager to please his commander, Tanga charged through sheets of frost toward the Chungassian. The sentry drew his sword, and held his guard high, with one arm circling. Tanga sprung into the air. The Chungassi blocked with his shield and circled. Parrying with his sword, he hit Tanga, but Tanga's thick armor suffered only minimal damage.

The Chungassian took a low guard. Tanga's jaws snapped several times, and he rushed in. Defending with his shield, the Chunga soldier thrust with his sword, spinning, then slicing down. Tanga ducked low, slipped around, then jumped, and bit into his opponent from behind. He dragged the Chungassian to the ground. A slime oozed from the sentry's body and mixed with the droplets in the air. As the slime bubbled and frothed, Tanga started to choke. The slime was an acid corroding the flesh of Tanga's mouth. Tanga stumbled back. His teeth loosened in the yellow, sulfurous stench, and they started falling out. His face began to disintegrate. He fell to the ground, writhing as he tried to eat dirt, hoping it would stave off the reaction. He was partially successful.

As Tanga lay wounded and gasping, Rex Gedeon shook his head in disappointment.

The Chungassian picked up his weapon and shield and eyed Gedeon. "You are slaves that cannot be trusted!" he shouted, heading for the Reptilite commander. "Was that location for the watery planet a lie?"

Gedeon chuckled. As the sentry closed in, his eyes began to fail. The image of Gedeon faded and all things became shadowed. "The coordinates for Earth are real, but there's something extra," Gedeon hissed at the blinded sentry. "I am sure your eager commander shares your suspicions. He will check the coordinates right away."

The soldier held up his shield, thrust his sword into the air near Gedeon, but found no target.

"Renard will find an unpleasant surprise when he uploads the data from the orb—a virus triggering his self-destruct sequence..."

The soldier stopped his sword in mid-swing. He groped about, and his fingers found his communicator. "Captain Renard!" he shouted into it. "We are the fools! Don't—"

Gedeon snatched the communicator from the blinded soldier. "Yes, Renard," he said into the comms. "You are the fools."

The soldier got a fleeting glimpse of Gedeon's silhouette. He thrust his sword toward the commander, but Gedeon saw it coming. As he kicked the soldier's arm up, he snapped the blade with his tail. He then sent the razor-sharp blade into its owner, and the soldier fell dead at his feet. He looked down at the sentry and said: "Your death was most honorable."

High above them, beyond the moon's surface and clouds, the Chunga Dome lost power. As it drifted down, the hull hit ice clouds and cracked.

Water gushed out, and the self-destruct sequence ended in a vaporous explosion.

With Tanga hobbling at his side, Gedeon returned to the ship. The Kaiman left the moon and wreckage behind. Onboard Kalet sent Tanga to the medical bay, then briefed Rex Gedeon. "Jain filed a report concerning the pod Wuyan sent to Earth," she told the commander.

"What is the status of this life form?" he asked. "Did she learn Wuyan's intentions?"

"Jain tracked the Exile and killed him while he slept," Kalet told him. "She wasn't able to interrogate the subject to find the purpose of his travels."

Gedeon shook his head. "At least Sarek would have had the decency to torture him first, to see if he had information."

"It would be a waste to dwell on such things," Kalet said.

"What about our human contacts?"

Kalet fluttered her wings. "Lotus retrieved the tablet and demonstrated the device in east Africa. An entire city crumbled in a quake. He left to meet Jain in D.C, where he awaits further instructions."

"Good! It works." Gedeon curled his claws. "For a species so young humans are remarkably talented. Where did he get the power?"

"The kidnapped scientist, Dr. Kinoah, developed a plant. She manipulated the thylakoids in their cells to draw and store energy from the ground. When they plant them in bundles, it produces an enormous amount of energy."

"Perhaps this scientist would make a better officer than the ones I've been getting. Where is she now?"

"I believe she is still in the Congo."

"I instructed that she be returned to the Martian. I will need her intact, and fully functioning."

"Yes, Rex Gedeon," said Kalet. "But there may be a problem. A group of humans are looking for her, and Lotus was compromised."

"Those humans must be eliminated," Gedeon replied.

"I need to know exactly what you want," said Kalet. "Are we assisting the Martian? Or simply keeping the scientist in our grasp?"

"We are assisting the Martian. He will retain the scientist in his grasp," Gedeon explained.

"But he's human! Are you sure we can trust him? He kept the existence of a tablet from us until Sarek pushed the issue. What else could he be hiding? And what kind of person betrays their own planet for a ship?"

"The cost of betrayal cannot be measured in money," Gedeon explained. "Morale is often underestimated as a tactic of war. If I defeat the humans, eventually they will rise again and oppose us. We will fight a human resistance for hundreds and thousands of years. Emancipation is a powerful motivator, but I don't want them to be motivated. I want them to be discouraged!

"When the story is told—and it will be—the loss of Earth will pale in comparison to the betrayal committed by the Six. It will hurt the humans in a way we never could. They will take it personally... emotionally. I need that. They must blame themselves for their own fall."

Gedeon's scales darkened. "Humans are not driven by power, but by beliefs. Power is merely the key to forcing others to believe.

"If we control their beliefs, we control them, and I want them to believe in their own extinction."

Kalet acquiesced but had a practical suggestion. "We cannot make it back to Earth without refueling. We must return to Reptilia before going back to Earth."

Gedeon turned to his display and brooded for a moment. "Take us near the border of the Vega System," he commanded.

"Rex," Kalet agreed with a gasp.

Gedeon left the bridge leaving Kalet and the others to look alive at the thought of being near the tumultuous Vega System. Kalet checked fuel and review strategies to balance what Gedeon wanted, with what the ship needed. There is no negotiation when a Reptilite fights a Vega Beast, and Fighting Wuyan's Akolytes was nothing like dodging a Kraken .

SUDAN

MOUZU TALI OPENED his eyes and saw nothing. Everything was still dark. As the tremors subsided, he felt the shock within his body fade. But was he safe? The ground seemed still. He heard coughing and the shuffling of feet. There was the sound of falling debris from whatever was left of the ceiling. Mouzu crawled from under his desk and looked around. Cracks in the walls let in thin shafts of light defined by the thick dust in the air.

"Children!" the Sudanese teacher shouted into the shadows. "Children! Who is here?"

When voices replied in confusion, he stopped them, and began reciting the students' names, and counting the ones that answered.

"Come to my voice," he told them. "Come to me. Suleyman, where is Suleyman?"

"He is here!" A little girl yelled out.

"Yaya!" he called to her. "Bring him forward. Suleyman, come!"

"He won't move," Yaya complained.

"Wait there," Mouzu instructed her. He crawled to a spot along the wall where cracks of light were visible. He started clearing away rubble by hand. Soon he made an opening large enough for the children. They crawled through and stood obediently in the ruins outside the school. Mouzu checked them, then crawled back inside to get Yaya and Suleyman.

"You are okay," he whispered to the boy, "just scared. It is okay." He encouraged Suleyman to move, but the boy would not. "Go, Yaya." He urged the little girl. Mouzu picked up the small boy and followed her out. He lay Suleyman down amidst the boy's friends. Before Mouzu left, the little boy was pushing himself up and standing.

Most of the school was rubble. Mouzu walked the perimeter, shocked by everything he saw. Children followed him, filling the air with their questions.

"What happened?"

"We had an earthquake."

"But why?"

He shrugged. "I don't know."

"Is it coming back?"

"I don't think so," Mouzu admitted. "Stay close."

He saw the Romanian teacher, Sanda Muhly, hovering over a tiny girl's body, performing CPR. She saw Mouzu coming but didn't interrupt her effort. As he got to her, she was depressing the back of the child's tongue to clear a passage. "She's not breathing!" Sanda cried. "Something's stuck in her throat!"

Mouzu pushed on the child's lower abdomen but got no response.

"The ceiling fell on us! Something got into her airway!" Sanda explained.

"Pen!" Mouzu shouted to his students.

Yaya ran up with her pen. Mouzu drew a handle and forceps in the air. When the tool solidified, Sanda held the child's mouth open. Mouzu used the tool to remove a plum seed.

"Give her some air," Mouzu ordered, throwing away the obstruction.

Sanda quickly blew into the child's mouth. She kept this up, and Mouzu helped, pushing on the little girl's chest. After a few minutes, the field patient was breathing a little. Mouzu felt a weak pulse returning.

As Sanda took over the care of the little girl, Mouzu said: "She is young, she will survive. Are there more children to be found?"

"We must check," said Sanda. She looked across the wreckage of the building, then turned, and pointed. A column of heavy trucks approached.

Mouzu ran to the road, waving and shouting: "Stop, please! Help us!"

The trucks halted. Armed soldiers jumped from the backs of the trucks, fanning out to form a perimeter. From the front came three officers, two men and a woman. These three stood, quietly observing what was left of the school. Several of the perimeter soldiers took out sensors and scanned the rubble. One looked back at the officers and shook his head. "No life, Jayln."

Jayln signaled the soldiers to let Mouzu through. He stood before her, and said: "Please, we need your help."

Jalyn shook her head, waving at the children. "Is this all?" she asked.

"All?" Mouzu asked, looking back at the children. "All of mine, yes, but there are more in the building. They are trapped— "

Jalyn quietly conferred with the other officer, Bradford. They pointed at the kids.

"That's not enough," Bradford insisted.

Jalyn shrugged, "I don't care. I don't have time to revive survivors."

"Yes!" Mouzu interrupted, "We have time, hurry, hurry!"

All three officers huddled, and then nodded to the soldiers. The soldiers dug through the rubble, pulling out the lifeless bodies of teachers and students. Jalyn went over them. "Not those with the missing limbs," she said.

Another officer, Saozan, climbed from the last truck's cab. He looked over the bodies and pointed at the live ones behind Mouzu. "Those ten will do."

"Ten?" Mouzu cried. "What ten?"

The soldiers started herding the children onto one of the trucks.

"You can't!" Sanda screamed, but the soldiers pushed her off and kept loading the children. Sanda and Mouzu tried to grab the kids.

Suleyman had climbed aboard, but now he jumped out and ran. Saozan caught him and dragged him by the neck. As Saozan tossed the child back into the truck, Mouzu grabbed his arm. Saozan pinned Mouzu against the rear of the vehicle, then drew his machete, and chopped off Mouzu's hand.

The kids screamed. Sanda leapt from the truck, but Jalyn drew her sidearm, shot the teacher. Sanda's corpse hit the ground. Though he was writhing in pain, Mouzu managed to grab Yaya. Saozan sliced off his other hand. Yaya fell backward into the truck still holding Mouzu's warm fingers.

BISHOP TREKKED ACROSS Khartoum's remains. The city was sand mixed with dirt, holding chunks of debris from former buildings. It all mixed into an uneven pavement of destruction. The city was all but gone. The White Nile flooded much of the western bank all the way to the city center, nearly connecting with the Blue Nile to the east. Bishop felt jumpy, as he answered a call from Sing.

"How bad is it?" she asked.

"I've never seen anything like it," he admitted. "The landscape has changed. A lot of artifacts are damaged. Massive flooding, and many dead."

"I mean, how bad is the plane?" she asked calmly.

"Um... pretty banged up. It was my first time landing one."

"You just press the 'Land' panel," Sing insisted. "It should have done it automatically. How are you gonna get out of Africa now?"

"I pressed the button, but the automated system didn't know how to land in this mess," Bishop said. "There is no airstrip here, and there's water everywhere. I had to step up."

"You were supposed to land in Giza! Now the spaceports are looking for a missing plane."

"That might not be a problem," Omar said, joining the conversation. "The spaceports look like they are going offline..."

"Time's not on our side," said Bishop. "From the looks of it, Lotus' been working on something powerful enough to crush a city, and it works."

"That's bad," Sing fretted, "If Lotus has been using Mae all this time, then he doesn't need her anymore."

Omar said: "Bishop, I'm tracking you via the comms. You're walking away from the epicenter?"

"Yeah," Bishop confirmed. "I thought I heard screaming." He saw a body curled on the ground ahead. "I just found a woman's body."

"Really?" Sing's heart jumped, "Is it Mae!?"

"No. Maybe a teacher." Bishop knelt down by the body and examined the tortured face. On the comm Sing was quiet.

"So, about Mae," Omar started, "What are we guessing? Did she devise plants to cause earthquakes?"

"That's crazy," Sing declared.

"Lotus is crazy," said Julius, joining the call.

"I didn't say he wasn't right. I'm just saying it's pretty insane," said Sing. "What do you think, Bishop?"

Bishop looked northwest. Far away people were wandering, seemingly without direction. The capital of Sudan was in chaos. It pained him. "The earthquake split the city in half," he said. "Most of it is flooded or buried. Yet this body wasn't crushed, or even dirty. She died after the fact."

"What is Lotus up to?" Sing asked.

Bishop took refuge in neutral observation: "I don't see any uniformity in plant life that would cause this sort of destruction," he said. He knelt, and picked up a set of printed forceps. It seemed like an odd location for the instrument. He noticed many footprints of different sizes. A lot had gone on here *after* the quake.

"But what's his end game?" Sing asked, not waiting for Bishop to speak.

"I... I really don't know what Lotus' thinks," Bishop replied. "The Sudanese republics have been at war for years now. How would anyone profit from an earthquake here?"

"It must've been a test," said Julius. "What about the woman?"

"She may have been a teacher," said Bishop.

"How do you know?"

"Because I'm next to a school. Or what's left of it. Plus, there are a lot of kids' footprints, different sizes... things like that." Bishop answered. He checked her feet, and head found the bullet hole and made a holographic image of the trajectory with the scanner. "This is odd. Either whoever shot her was flying..." Bishop walked backward to the firing point, and rotated the image, "... or she was jumping through the air."

He looked down and saw more footprints, and scanned them. "Tell me about these," he said. He then noticed the nearby tire tracks and their deep indention near the firing point. "They were here! Get me information on these tracks!" Bishop insisted.

"I'm on it," Omar reported. "By the way, your man, Jules, helped me get access to some CIA data."

"How'd he manage that?"

"Let's just say those pilots he snatched out of the plane in Germany were a good catch," Omar boasted.

A man in rags approached. "Please," he gasped. "You must help." Bishop followed him to a nearby neighborhood buried in wet sand. He looked around at stunned faces, laboring to step through the soaked landscape. Only a few were able to dig for survivors. The sand was heavy, and each dig profited them little. Defeat hung in the air.

Bishop helped clear debris until a voice came over his comm. "Those tracks belong to a 5-ton military cargo truck. The tire treads are a dead giveaway. The Six designed them three years ago to be amphibious."

"So Lotus was expecting a flood."

"Follow those tracks, and you'll find him."

"Okay," said Bishop, swabbing his face.

"Doesn't sound like I've convinced you," Omar worried.

"You aren't getting the bigger picture I see here. This is beyond devastation. The water all but seals their fate. Rescuing anyone in this sort of mess is hopeless! There's no aid coming anytime soon."

"Mason is our priority, Bishop," Sing urged.

"Yeah, well, what am I gonna do? I mean I'm here," Bishop told her.

"B.K's right," Julius piped in, "We are missing the bigger picture. Lotus flooded this place on purpose to prevent a meaningful rescue. He's probably still there."

Bishop stomped around in the wet sand. "This place is death. Lotus wouldn't be anywhere near here; his work is done."

"Standby." Julius said, "Omar's getting hits on your location from the CIA."

"He's not going back to Germany either," Bishop's voice trailed off. "Either he stays here in Africa or..."

"I said standby," Julius repeated.

Bishop stood up. The general hum of grieving, suffering voices filled the air. "It's no use," he said and headed for the closest sounds of suffering. He found the spot and pointed at some nearby survivors. "Someone is alive," he hollered, "Dig here!"

The survivors used shovels, buckets, and hands to clear away the wreckage. They found the corpses of a man and woman huddled together. They'd died protecting a young girl still alive.

"Get her some water!" Bishop ordered.

The people scrambled. Soon the child drank greedily—a welcome sign of life.

As the rescuers started celebrating, a flatbed truck drove slowly through the sludge to pull up nearby. Workers jumped out and sunk shin deep into the sand. They grabbed the two corpses and tossed them up on a pile.

"We take all we can find," the driver told Bishop. "There are so many—I think they will have to be burned." They found several more dead nearby. Once they loaded the soggy and bloated bodies, the workers placed boards beneath the tires to help the truck rumbled off.

Less than a minute later another truck approached. It slowed as it reached the people, but once it passed them it sped up again. The ease at which the vehicle navigated through the terrain caught his attention.

Bishop heard something from the truck and trotted after it. It was going a lot faster than it should, and he could barely keep up. The back tires looked as if they were ballooned and altered for wet terrain. The truck seemed too clean, as if it had dropped from the sky.

Then he knew what he heard: *Screams.*

Bishop hurried away from the crown. A man shuffled by as the truck passed. Bishop stopped him. "Did you hear the screams?" Bishop asked him, but the man only shook his head.

Bishop ran, but the truck was too far ahead. As he watched it disappear in clouds of mist, Julius came in over the comm, "B.K! We just got an intercept from the CIA. They triggered a hot button on Khartoum."

Bishop didn't answer. He scanned, and found the dark truck's tracks in the sand. He started following them.

"B', did you get that!"

Bishop sighed. "Do they have authorization to put boots on the ground?"

"No," Julius answered. "They contacted flight command in Nevada. It only takes a few minutes to assemble drones. They'll see you!"

"I'm off the grid," said Bishop. "Drones won't recognize me."

"You think the CIA has the same grid?" Julius insisted. "Your face was in the news for a year straight. The people monitoring it will recognize you."

"He's right," Omar agreed. "After Flight 522, anything will put a red flag on your tail. You are not suppose to the leave your city. You left the state, country. You'll go right to the top of the terror listing for this disaster."

"If I become a terrorist, then wouldn't I just be your problem?" Bishop asked.

"No! The CIA doesn't work with ICP. We aren't magically connected to every spy organizations. You will be their problem, and having drones shoot at you from twelve miles away will be yours."

"Got it. I'll stay out of sight," Bishop said.

"Out of sight may not work for a drone. You gotta get out of there completely," Julius told him.

Bishop doubled back to the school site. That's when he found the trails of blood in the sand leading to a severed hand. He then found an area where soldiers, children, and refugees were trying to make some order out of chaos. There was a first aid tent, where someone who'd lost a hand might be. But there were also soldiers herding children into the backs of trucks. Some of the locals were protesting.

"What is this," Bishop asked himself. "Are they stealing children?" Bishop ran up to the tents and found a woman who had an aid worker's badge. "What's going on with those kids?" he asked.

Exacerbated she answered. "None of our aid can get into the country! Everything is flooded, the roads are destroyed! We are following the government's lead. They are taking the orphans."

"Taking them where?" Bishop asked, "Are they sending military?"

She shrugged. "What military? They can't get here."

"Whoa..." Bishop stopped her. "Then whose soldiers are taking the children?"

Nearby, another worker brought in a girl and sat her on a table, then walked away to complete his paperwork. Three officers climbed down from the cabs of cargo trucks. Bishop sent Omar their images, with text asking who they were. He ducked behind the table, and read Omar's response: "The Six."

Bishop watched as the officers ordered soldiers to isolate several children into a group and take them away. Bishop texted Omar: "I thought they were dead." Omar replied" "The devil is a lie."

The girl sitting on the table was dirty, and let out a nasty cough. She spotted Bishop hiding behind the table. With tired eyes, she reached out for him.

Bishop realized it was the girl he'd helped save. "Jules!" Bishop hissed into his comm. "They're abducting children!"

"B'!" Julius screamed in return "Why are you still there?"

"Do you hear me? It isn't just Lotus! They're all alive!"

Julius stuttered for a moment, and finally spit it out, "Drones! They're in the air!"

CAVE OF LIGHTS

TWO PREDATOR DRONES launched from the Gulf of Aden and streaked across the desert sky.

"Get the drones online," The flight commander ordered.

Yani Harris had a full figure, and dark brown hair that curled in a fluffy frame around her head, stopping just below her jaw. She always looked as if she was about to strike a pose. One reason she liked working in drone operations was that her appearance kept most people from taking her skills seriously. She looked like a first-grade teacher or the proverbial favorite aunt. She liked drones because they didn't care about her looks. They just did what she told them to do.

With their internal security checks completed, the drones handed over control to the Captain's Flight Command crew.

Yani had begun her military life in the field. She'd drifted into drone operations, but the more she worked with these machines, the more interesting humans looked. She couldn't quite put her finger on the source of her fascination, but the inherent differences between drones and people intrigued her. Even computers with advanced artificial intelligence lacked something in the human aura. She wanted to learn what that was. Eventually, she couldn't regard drones as independent machines; they were simply an extension of her human spirit—a way to connect with the world. For Yani, a drone was no different from an eye or an arm.

Yani stood at a large table as the flight controller, Erica Bateman, reported. "Strike Command is online."

Yani twirled her hair behind her ear and adjusted her headset to tune in Strike Command.

Born and raised in Nevada, Yani loved her job and loved that it kept her in Nevada close to her family. The only family member she kept her distance from was her father, the commanding general of the SARA military space station. Though she wasn't so fond of dealing with the Virginia-based Strike Command.

Though she was curious about human nature, Yani had a love-hate relationship with other people, particular those outside her command. She was akin to someone who liked the idea of pets, but not the mess that goes with them, Yani thought of herself as liking people, but individually they left her cold.

As Yani pulled the headset over her ears, Strike Command's holograph appeared. The personograph of Agent Alicia Rogers formed in front of her. At first, it was all blue lines in the shape of a human. Then the texture and color loaded. Agent Rogers had thin lips and a smoothly filled out face. Her hair was cut short and pulled back into a reddish-brown ponytail. Yani thought the woman's hair was dyed.

The personograph walked right through Yani. As Agent Rogers went to the table, she barked at the Captain: "Get us visuals. Quickly."

Though Alicia and Yani shared the same rank, Alicia's position came with enough prestige to allow her to bark orders at her Flight counterpart. Suddenly, Yani's simple, straightforward job had transformed into a competitive power grab. Harris dreaded the games.

Political games were like an untranslatable foreign language to drones. They ignored all politics, but Yani didn't have that luxury. Though she didn't like the games, they intensified her urge to learn more about human nature.

The drones zoomed in on Khartoum and began pouring visuals, data, and stats onto the table. Within a few moments, a 3-D version of the Sudan had formed on the table's surface.

"Coming into view," Bateman announced, and the table became a close-up of Khartoum.

"What a mess," Yani said. "Strike, do you see this?"

"I'm standing right here," Rogers quipped. "My intelligence says Lotus left the city by convoy."

Your intelligence? Captain Harris turned around to another terminal window and viewed the report. "Are you sure?" she asked Rogers. "Just because his officers are there doesn't mean he is."

Rogers waved it off. "Fish travel in schools."

Harris commanded Bateman, "Search the outer area of the city. Pan out from there with the alpha drone. I want the beta drone to give me snapshots of everyone alive inside the city radius."

"Yes, ma'am."

The table provided a view of Khartoum and the surrounding area. Dots indicating life forms lit up around the table. Next to the dots tiny people materialized. They walked about on the tabletop.

As Harris glanced over the data, realizing Lotus's desert base must be in the eastern Sudan. Yani was about to issue a command to Bateman, but Rogers spoke first. "Their base is in the mountains; they will be heading east. We should focus our search there."

Yani sighed, then instructed Bateman to give priority to any Eastern travelers. Bateman obeyed, tracking everyone going in and out of the city. An odd military convoy, containing only two trucks, headed east, ignoring roads and other landmarks. Yani walked around the far side of the table and pointed at the trucks. "What are these?" she asked.

"That would have to be the Six," Alicia said. "We're preparing an order to prosecute."

"Rogers, we don't know who's in the convoy yet," Harris reminded her competitor.

Bateman forgot to zoom in while the system was still accounting for Khartoum's survivors. Yani sharply told her to do it. Suddenly the trucks grew bigger, as they drove around on the tabletop.

Rogers edged down the table, and announced, "They're heading for the mountains. Only the Six would be going there. We need you to attack them before they detect us."

"I can't do that," Yani objected. "Not until I know who they are."

Though Yani expected an irate response, Alicia Rogers remained silent.

Strange.

"Captain, look!" Bateman said, pointing at the monitor behind them.

Alicia sent a "No Confidence" signal to the drones.

"Dammit! Strike!" Yani shouted.

With their "No Confidence" signal from Rogers, the drones left the control of Flight Command. Now they operated autonomously. They dropped low, calculating the attack. The drones decided that the convoy probably didn't have Lotus, but probably were carrying enemy combatants. Once they decided to eliminate the targets, they locked onto the convoy and prepared to fire.

Truck flaps lifted in the wind. The alpha drone got a close-up of a child's face in the back of one of the trucks. Identifying non-combatants, the drones disengaged. They returned to cruising altitude, ceding control back to Flight Command.

Once Flight Command controlled the drones again, Bateman zoomed in on the tailgates of the trucks. One truck on their table grew bigger until it was the about the length of a forearm. Yani ran around the table to get a better look. She confirmed the presence of children.

"Are you happy, Rogers? Is Strike Command getting this?" Yani asked.

At first, there was no response; then Rogers said: "Yes... yes, we are. But we still have the threat of the combatants."

"There are children, and possibly other friendlies in the mix," Harris argued. She faced the image of Alicia, "We haven't even identified the full company yet."

"Listen," Rogers snapped, "this isn't about the children. All of humanity is resting on this. I'd rather destroy them all and assure the survival of the human race than nitpick on details. We have credible information Lotus is in that convoy. You are suggesting we wait until they stop-"

"Credible isn't enough," said Yani. "I need to see his face. Until then, we wait. After all, how can we save humanity, if we refuse to protect humans? How can our species be worth keeping if we abandon all that we've learned when we need it the most?"

With the drones operating under the firm hand of Flight Command, Rogers had no choice but to wait. She did so while planning countermeasures. She did not give up.

"Captain Harris," she began, "this is also a national security threat. That gives me the authority to—"

Yani spoke quickly: "The threat isn't imminent, children would die by our hands, not theirs, and you don't have an order from the president."

"We don't report to the president!" Rogers insisted, "but he's aware of this operation. Engage with the convoy before we lose them in the mountains!"

"I report to the president," Yani reminded her counterpart. "So, unless you have a presidential order to eliminate noncombatants, my order stands. There should be no rush to kill anyone. As far as I know, the only imminent danger is the invasion. I command our drone defenses, so I control any air strike. My goal is to ensure that no alien sets foot on American soil! You guys pulled me out of a strategy meeting to track down the Six, so unless this is somehow related..."

"It is related."

"What do you mean?"

Alicia paced, then turned on her competitor. "You may be in charge of our drone defense, Captain, but Lotus may have a device that can disable your drones."

Everyone who heard her paled.

Yani shook her head, "What? That's impossible. Lotus has never had access to any of our designs."

"He didn't have to have access to you. You control too much power with your drones, so we built the device that could shut you down. Lotus stole it!"

Yani took a deep breath. Her voice was small and highly controlled: "Why am I not surprised!"

Rogers shrugged, "It's a simple bug. The satellites transmit it to the Flight Command, and Flight Command instructs the drones to stand down. However, now, if Lotus makes the right moves, he can open up the skies for invasion. Then the aliens can land at will, and face our ground troops. They stronger on the ground; this is their optimal strategy."

"So Lotus is gonna transmit it to the satellites?"

"Not yet," Alicia explained. "He must get the device to the aliens first. They built a transmitting tower in space, and a beacon to communicate with our satellites."

"Transmitter...beacon? In space?" Harris asked.

"That's why we have to stop Lotus now!"

"A beacon in space!" Harris shouted again.

"Once our device is in space, we won't get it back. Those little space saucers the army cooked up wouldn't stand a chance."

"How do you know that there is a beacon up there?" Yani demanded. Rogers did not respond. "How?!"

"SARA," Alicia revealed.

"Dammit!" Yani shouted. After ordering Bateman to track the convoy, she stormed out of the room.

Yani placed a call to the SARA space station, and after a few moments of silence, she spoke to her father, the commanding general.

"General Harris here," said a scruffy voice through the static.

"How could you?" Yani demanded.

"Yani?"

"Dammit, Daddy? Soldiers run blindly into battle because they trust their commanders."

"And commanders have to live with the pain of sending out troops they may never get back. Yani, I've always told you the cost of war. You are really in the safest area, commanding the drones."

"But it looks like the aliens have a beacon that can shut me down—and you knew!"

"Yes," he admitted. "They built a Beacon, and it speaks to our technology. The chain of command kept it from you because we don't want you to hedge your bets. We can't have you thinking about 'what ifs.'"

"Can you take out the Beacon?"

"The Beacon is several hundred thousand miles out in space surrounded by an alien Armada guarding it."

"Oh God."

"Look, the Earth's atmosphere won't allow most transmissions to enter our planet. So they have no way of communicating with our drones from that distance unless they use our spaceports that allow true-space transmissions, or bring the Beacon to Earth and use our satellites. So we are shutting it all down."

"That's dangerous. If the drones get out of my range, they will go auto without satellite relay."

"That's only dangerous to humans. We don't care if the drones accidentally kill more aliens," her father countered.

"But if you shut the spaceports..." Yani gasped, "How will we speak?"

"You have my shortwave radio frequency, dear."

Yani replied. "You aren't coming home, are you?"

"I can't. Several fleets of aliens have started their descents," said the General. "Within a day or two the entire planet will be at war."

Yani wiped away a tear

The General concluded, "From here on out, I need you to focus honey."

"Okay," Yani said, as a lump grew in her throat.

"I love you," her father concluded.

Yani returned to the room and observed the Eastern convoy as it came to a halt near the base of the mountains. Everyone disembarked. Names and profiles started appearing on adjacent screens.

Yani ordered, "Bateman, bring us in closer. Switch from missile sweep to precision laser burst. Mark all friendlies. I need every adult ID'd. Don't worry about identifying the children. If they're tiny, just mark them green."

She then turned to Bateman, "Where does that leave us?"

Bateman pointed at the 3-D images of tiny people running around on the table. "Three officers in front of the company, twenty-three armed guards, all combatants." Bateman answered, "Noncombatants: twenty-six children, one man. One unknown."

"Who's the one man?" Yani asked. Bateman zoomed in. "Why are his hands missing? Is it a glitch or is this guy handless?"

"He's a teacher," Bateman answered as the data came up on the screen. "Mouzu Tali. Non-combatant."

"They must have abducted these kids from a school." She gazed at Mouzu Tali. "Chopped his hands off... who's the guy with the head covering?"

"I don't know; I can't get his face," Bateman answered. The table holograph updated when the man with the head covering turned around. He held a little girl in his arm.

"Twenty-seven children," Bateman updated.

"What about his eyes?" Yani asked her, and Bateman worked on getting a shot of the man's eyes for identification. Yani then continued, "These men are abducting children, and taking hostages. Eliminate them, but I need to know whether the guy in the head covering is a hostage or a combatant."

The drones banked and descended, focusing their cameras on the covered man's face. As she waited for more data, Yani reviewed the list of combatants.

"Strike! Where's the rest of the Six?" Yani asked. "This isn't all of them? We have the physician Jalyn, tactical commander Saozan, science officer Bradford. We have twenty-three guards."

Agent Rogers paced around, then said, "We have credible information-"

"I don't care. Where's Tai? Where's Jerry? Where's Lotus?"

"Captain! They hear us!" Bateman announced.

The soldier had finally heard the roar of the drones. Guards and officers used the kids as shields, as they headed toward the mountains.

The man with the head covering pulled some of the kids away from the guards and shielded the infant. The children scattered.

One of the children, Suleyman, fell and rolled away. Once he was clear of the convoy, he ran off. A guard shot him. Suleyman fell face first into the sand. The convoy disappeared into the mountains.

"Damn it!" Rogers screamed. "You let this happen!"

Yani ran around the table, pointed behind a mountain peak, and ordered Bateman, "Circle the drones around. See if we can get another view."

Rogers pointed, saying, "You can't. They've dug tunnels into these mountains. We'll never see them from the air."

"Agent Rogers?" Yani asked again. "Where is Lotus Daniels?"

"He should have been among the group," she answered.

"He wasn't! Now listen very carefully, Rogers: Nothing requires us to kill children! Don't you get that?"

Rogers' face was like stone, and she remained silent.

"If I executed those kids just now, he'd still be out there, and we'd still be at risk," said Yani.

"Perhaps he was the man in the head covering," Rogers said. "Shielding himself behind children."

"Holding a child? No, that wasn't Lotus." Harris shook her head as she watched the drone feed. "Lotus would just as soon eat a baby than hold it. This guy's body type is wrong, and he was protecting the children."

"Protecting?" Rogers shouted. "He has no legal authority. Which makes him a vigilante."

"The Sudan is destroyed," Yani reminded her. "There is no authority. Vigilante or not, he was watching over those children, and half of them—thirteen—got away."

"Yeah, but one got shot," Rogers insisted.

Yani shook her head. There was no way to get through to this woman. Yani said. "Even through the eyes of a drone, I can read people."

As Yani gazed at Suleyman lying face down in the dirt, the other controllers tried to ID the man in the head covering. Once they'd fed in the data, all they could do was wait.

"We don't know who he is," Erica finally told her commander.

Yani's eyes tightened. Suddenly Suleyman got up and ran in the direction of a village.

Yani stood up straight and exhaled. "Someone knows who he is."

A FRESH BREEZE filtered through the well-lit mountain tunnels. Bishop noticed a set of plants with bright illuminating bulbs growing from the rocky walls.

Another set of plants with veiny and transparent leaves produced nearby. Bishop felt a surge of power coming from the roots.

Power plants.

Pipes collected dripping water from the walls and channeled it along the tunnel. The pipes led to a filtration system that filled a pond with fresh water. The company stopped to rest and take a drink.

Bishop gently let the sick girl he was carrying down, and she crumbled into a ball of pain on the hard floor. He helped her drink some water.

"What's your name?" He asked her, but the girl didn't respond.

Yaya walked up to them and answered, "That's Zahra. She didn't come to school today because she's sick."

Zahra let out a few more coughs, and Bishop continued to make her drink water. He looked around at the company and saw Mouza's served arms bleeding. When he saw Yaya's pen, he asked her to trade with him: he'd take the pen, and Yaya'd take care of Zahra.

Bishop helped Mouzu clean his wounds. Mouzu's face was a pale blank. He was still in shock.

"It's healing," Bishop started to tell the stunned man. "You're gonna be all right. Stay with me. These kids need you."

Mouzu said nothing.

Bishop drew Mouzu a new right hand with the pencil. "These rebels have an interesting setup. The power plants feed the light plants. Power plants give off carbon dioxide and water which should make the air in here poisonous to breathe. Yet, the light plants need lots of carbon dioxide. So the two plants are working together to make in these caves livable."

Bishop looked at Mouzu, but the injured man didn't seem to be paying attention. Bishop drew him a left hand. "Then they have pipes that collect the water from the power plants and channel them to a filtration system. So they can stay pretty well hidden down here for a very long time."

Bishop took a cloth and wrapped it around the hands to give them time to heal.

"I've never seen power plants like that before. Transparent leaves?" Bishop asked in a whisper. "The thing I don't get is: I don't see any connections. How are the power plants getting power to everything else?"

Mouzu didn't answer.

Even when the rebel commander teased him, Mouzu didn't react.

Saozan taunted: "Make him another hand, and I'll just cut that one off too." He neared Mouzu and stopped.

Bishop took a step back to look at Mouzu's newly drawn hands.

Saozan told his men, "I wonder how much ink he has in that pen."

As Saozan pulled out his machete and took a step, Bishop whirled and faced the rebel commander. Bishop removed his head covering.

"Bishop!" Saozan shouted. The entire company seemed shocked. Saozan swung his machete. Bishop blocked the swing, hip-tossed his opponent, and took the blade. As he sliced the nearest guard's gun in half, he also kicked the man's legs out from under him. Using his circular momentum Bishop cut into another defender's chest, spilling blood onto the sand. Shots rang out, and the children screamed and ran. Some guards chased the kids. Another guard aimed a gun at Bishop, spraying bullets. Bishop dove to the ground, grabbed a rock and threw it. The rock hit the guard's face, embedding sand in his eyes. Bishop leapt up and took on two more guards with elbow-and-knee combinations. He finished them off with the machete. When he reached the guard with the sand in his eyes, Bishop touched the knife blade to the man's neck.

"Wait! Hold on!" shouted Science Officer Bradford. "Wait! Dammit!"

The world stopped. Bishop saw the guards had children in execution positions. Bradford grabbed a nearby boy and held him at knifepoint.

"My word... Bishop? Kennedy?" Bradford asked. "What in all of heaven are you doing here?"

"Do I know you?"

Bradford then chuckled, "Oh, you know my work."

"Where's Mason?" Bishop demanded.

"Not the question I expected," Bradford said with a laugh. "Why are you trying to be a hero?"

"She was here! I can tell by the plants. Is she alive?"

Bishop probed the skin of the guard's neck with the machete. Blood oozed out.

"Hang on now," Bradford said. "You say you want to know something. Fair enough, but I want to know something too. Where are the zenomites?"

"Fuck you," Bishop said, resting the blade against the guard's throat.

Bradford shook his head. "Please, Mr. Kennedy... cooperate. These children shouldn't be subjected to such language." He pointed at a guard, and said: "I think we should cut off their ears to spare them from Mr. Kennedy's foul language."

Several overeager guards pulled knives.

"Stop it!" Bishop pleaded. "You know what happened! I gave the canister to Nicole before she boarded the flight. The plane crashed. The canister was lost."

"Not true!" Bradford snarled. "You got it back. Now, are you gonna let these children die for some tiny robots?"

Bishop slowly lowered his machete blade. The guard spit at him ineffectually, shouting: "Die!"

"Why so secretive, Bishop?" Bradford taunted. "I thought scientists were supposed to share information freely." Bradford walked over to the children and stood ready. "The zenomites," he said. "You tell us where to get them, I will phone Lotus, he will collect them, and we will let you all go, no further harm to any of you."

Bishop said, "I disposed of it. There is nothing to collect. The zenomites are all gone."

"You're a terrible liar," he pointed Zahra. "Is she your child? I saw you holding her earlier."

Saozan hurried over, yanked Zahra up, and focused a gun on her.

"Men of science are not butchers!" Bishop said through gritted teeth.

"Men of science are the foremost butchers!" Bradford replied cutting into a boy's thigh. Blood flowed into the sand.

Bishop dropped the machete and raised his hands. "Okay, listen!" he cried. "I'm not lying. I'd lost Nicole, and I was losing everything else because of Flight 522. The zenomites were too dangerous in their raw form, so I figured a way to transfer them into biological entities where they could be controlled."

"What kind of mad science is that?" Bradford demanded, "How did you transfer them?

Bishop said nothing.

"Tell us!" Bradford shouted, "What is this entity that can control zenomites?"

Bishop remained silent.

"I will cut this boy's head off if you don't tell me where the zenomites are!" Bradford said assuredly.

Bishop sighed. "I just realized something."

"What's that?" Bradford asked.

"I know how the plants get power to your lights."

The cave went pitch black.

FLIGHT CONTROLLER BATEMAN shouted, "Captain! The children!"

Yani gulped her coffee and stared at the table. Kids spilled out from a mountain crevice. Putting her headset back, she told Bateman, "Give me a count."

"Six, eleven, twenty," Bateman counted aloud. "There were twenty-seven, so we're missing three."

Yani saw Mouzu carrying a heavily-bandaged young boy. "Twenty-six," she corrected. "One ran away, so I think we're down to missing one."

Guards came out after the kids.

"Engage!" Yani commanded.

Bateman laser-targeted the guards, and the drones shot them. The guards collapsed, holes burned through their bodies.

"Give me a count," Yani demanded.

"Twelve guards... man with no hands... twenty-six kids, with one escaped... man with the head covering and the child still MIA... as are three officers, and the remaining guards."

"Run surveillance till someone comes out," Yani ordered.

"Yes, ma'am."

Not long before sunset, Bateman saw an alert and rushed to the table. Someone emerged from the cave carrying a child. She informed her captain. Yani arrived with fresh coffee.

"Is that our man?" Yani asked.

"Physical stats match, as do those of the little girl. The man's face is still covered, but hang on." Bateman maneuvered the spy craft and extrapolated facial details. She bounced lasers to get pigmentation and constructed a probable face.

"Who is that?" Yani asked, seeing the picture feed.

"Drones aren't finding a match," Bateman responded.

"Run it through a facial recognition protocol," Yani instructed.

"That will take some time."

As Bishop climbed into a jeep and drove north with the infant, Yani agreed to the limitation. "Nothing anywhere near him for hundreds of miles. We have time."

THE SOLAR POWERED jeep carrying Bishop and Zahra drove north through the desert. Though the temperature wasn't very low, Zahra was shivering. Bishop had taken whatever provisions and water he could carry from the terrorist stronghold before leaving, but Zahra wasn't taking it. She not only looked sick but lost.

"How old are you?" Bishop asked, and in return Zahra counted her fingers until she held up seven.

"Do you know where you are?" Bishop asked, but only received a slight shake of the head and a hoarse cough. He stopped the car to give her medicine. "You have to drink this."

"I need to pee," she responded.

After letting her go to some nearby rocks, she hobbled back to him and took her medicine with a twisted face.

"Do you know where you are?" Bishop asked, and she said no. On the tip of his tongue, he wanted to ask about her parents but he couldn't. Bishop covered his face and sighed hard in his hand. They both got back into the jeep, and he drove on.

"Are we escaping the bad guys? Like Portal Porscha?"

Bishop looked at her: "Portal what?"

"Portal Porscha!" Zahra stood up in the seat, excitedly.

"Let's not do that sweetheart; we put our seatbelts on in the car."

"But you're not wearing yours!"

"Ya know what, you're right. That was wrong of me, let's both put them on at the same time to be safe. One, two, three, click!" Bishop watched her restrain herself, and then asked, "Who's Portal Porscha?"

"It's a cartoon. Portal Porscha is a crime fighter who drives a Jeep. Like this!" Zahra coughed, and it sounded improved from before. "And she uses portals to take her to far away places."

"Zahra..."

"I'll be Portal Porscha, and you can be... well, you can be Kron, but he's a dog. He goes on adventures with her."

"I wouldn't call where I'm going an adventure. At least not one made for kids," Bishop thought for a moment, trying to head north as fast as he could, but feeling a nagging pull on him to turn around. He finally found a way to bring it up: "Do you have any family... other family? Maybe, I can take you to, or could come get you."

Zahra's head was doubled over. She was asleep. Bishop sighed, reached over and straightened her so she wouldn't catch a cramp.

AS BISHOP PUT miles between himself and Khartoum, a drone followed him toward Egypt behind the horizon. Eventually, the facial recognition came through.

"It's Bishop Kennedy," Bateman revealed.

"Shit, what is he doing?" Yani asked.

"Do I call it in?" The flight controller asked. "Strike Command has him on their potential terrorist list. They'll pounce on him the moment they find out."

"Screw them. I'm not about to hand deliver their assignments to them," Yani checked with the drone monitoring the Sudan. "Looks like the kids made it back to Khartoum." Yani thought for a moment, balancing justice in her mind. "I believe we're gonna throw this fish back."

AT CAIRO'S AIRPORT, a family entered ahead of Bishop. The airport scanners found their reservation and bid them a safe flight. Bishop walked through. The machine scanned him, but couldn't find a ticket for his child. It told him to go to the screening station.

An officer named Lukas Hanna approached, asking him, "Where are you heading?"

"Back to D.C," Bishop replied with an awkward smile.

Hanna pulled his glasses down over his nose. He looked at Bishop skeptically, and asked Zahra, "Is this your father?"

"No," Zahra answered.

Bishop's smile got crooked; he felt nervous, but in a way relieved, believing the Egyptian officials would take her from him, and find a home for her, and he could go about his business.

"Where are your parents?"

"They went away," Zahra answered. "They went away so I could be here."

When the official looked up at Bishop, Bishop explained, "She's Sudanese, her parents died in the Earthquake to save her."

"So sad. But she is a long way away from home. Do you have custody of this girl?" Hanna asked him, "Mmm. What's her name?"

Bishop looked at the little girl on his knee, and she responded, "My name is Zahra. My parents sent him to take care of me."

Officer Hanna looked at Bishop. "Zahra...? I'll be right back."

Officer Hanna found some fellow officers and told them about Bishop.

"I don't trust him at all, I think we have a kidnapping," Hanna told them. "Can we contact Interpol? CIA? See if he has... what? A history?"

When the others agreed, Hanna sent the request. The reply was almost immediate. After all the officers had read it, they looked at each other in disbelief but shrugged it off. Hanna went back to Bishop in the waiting area. "Have a safe flight," he said.

Bishop found some soup for Zahra. She had finished it quickly, but before they reached the departure gate, she had to pee. In her absence, he sniffed his shirt. It stunk. Zahra returned, and her clothes were filthy too, so Bishop took her shopping for new clothes: a button-down shirt and sports coat from the men's store, and cute dress that fit Zahra. He paid extra to get into a VIP area. There they took a decent shower, and Bishop gave her some more medicine for her cough. Her skin didn't feel clammy any longer, but she still looked worn out. Bishop loaded up on food.

He asked her. "Think this will hold us for an eight-hour flight?"

She just looked at him. Together they boarded the plane. Before they'd taken off, he went online and reserved a taxi in D.C. He looked at her again, trying to gauge if she was happy, sad, or just in shock.

"Let's hope they don't ground the flights before we get back," Bishop told her. Her head fell on his shoulder, and she was asleep on impact. "Good idea," said Bishop. "We've had a long day."

IN NEVADA, Yani Harris sat staring at her terminal. A red message flashed next to Bishop Kennedy's picture. The message directed that Bishop be detained in Cairo. He was a criminal who was banned from air travel. Yani intercepted the message and then sent Egyptian security an all-clear notice for him and the girl. She nodded to herself and called it quits for the day.

THE KAIMAN DROPPED its mass shielding and fell out of hyperspace into Reptilite territory. Gedeon's pupils dilated and changed as they neared the Vega system. The crew hid their edginess as Kalet waved at the controls to bring up her maps. She looked back at Tanga, and he nodded.

"Our spies are sending data as we speak," Tanga reported.

"Wuyan's ships could be anywhere in the Vega system," Rex Gedeon noted. "Keep a watchful eye."

Tanga spoke up, "The border patrol is telling us to leave this system or face grave consequences."

Kalet peered out into space as her maps scanned the area. "But no one's in this sector. Do you think it's a scare tactic?"

"A prerecorded message?" Tanga asked.

"Reply," Gedeon commanded. "Ask them to open a diplomatic channel."

Tanga sent the message. When the only reply was the same constant warning, Kalet said: "I don't see Wuyan's ships anywhere. I'm doing an in-depth scan into the dark matter of space. Maybe they're cloaked."

"Not an entire squadron," Tanga assured her.

"Wuyan is crafty," Gedeon warned.

Kalet squinted at her screen. "I'm picking up some strange particles."

"What kind of strange?" Gedeon asked.

"I've never seen this before. Dark energy particles all around."

"Show them to me," Gedeon said.

Kalet brought it up on the 3D display. Gedeon's pupils narrowed to slits as he observed them in raw form: a collection of bubbles in a circular motion around each other with no identifying information.

"What is that?" Gedeon asked, turning to Tanga.

"I haven't a clue without studying it first," said Tanga.

Gedeon grumbled, curling his claws into a fist.

A troubling alert came up on Kalet's display. She pounded the table, ripped off her visor and shook her head. "The Superiors are demanding to know our position," she reported. "Apex hasn't received a report from Sarek, so he requires an update."

"Apex," Gedeon muttered.

Kalet could see that he wanted to ignore the request. "If Apex doesn't hear from us, he'll send a fleet," she said. "We cannot invade Earth if we're dealing with him."

Gedeon nodded.

Kalet turned the ship away from the Vega system and headed toward Reptilia.

The brown and green planet came into view. Not quite an Earth-like spectacle, Reptilia gave off a dreary view from space as its dusty atmosphere trapped excessive humidity over the dry land. After the Kaiman had descended through the air, the vast trees became visible, and the land stretched to the horizon. The trees had long thick branches into the moist air, and roots plunging deep through the arid soil to the planet's hidden water sources.

The Reptilites laid out a nature-based infrastructure since its atmosphere proved too corrosive for machine designs. There had been a time when they had paved much of their world with concrete roads and buildings, but these structures heated the atmosphere and ceded from the cracked ground beneath it. Fed up with the environmental issue, they returned to a natural style. The sciences were not prestige professions among Reptilites. Though they valued scientific advances, the Reptilites tired of fighting against the elements and easily fell into what they knew best – war, most often against each other. They turned to building their infrastructure with tempered bones and trees native to the planet. They imported most of their manufactured technology from elsewhere, and as payment, they sold themselves to trade their one-dimensional skills.

Reptilia's trees produced tough leaves they used in making their arenas for sport and battle. Reptilite sports always left severe collateral damage. They found nature was a better, cheaper method of repair than using the technological tools and approaches they could not afford. Apex and the other Superiors dwelled in Arena Superia, one of the few arenas with manufactured metals integrated into its design, donated by members of the State gracious for his service and loyalty. Its gold-and-silver lining glimmered in a superstructure of wood and hardened bone. From the sky, it glistened brightly.

There in his Arena Superia, Apex lived and breathed for battle. The Reptilites referred to the arena as "his" because Apex had contributed most of the building material. Whenever he killed another living being, he donated the remains to be cleansed and added. Each addition made the arena grander. Apex took pride in its appearance, and the stage became a physical embodiment of his conquest. Over time, a city grew around the Arena Superia. There was a spaceport, and military barracks housing only the best, most loyal troops.

Kalet landed the Kaiman near Arena Superia on a dock shaped like a giant leaf. Gedeon left the ship reluctant appease his leader.

Kalet noticed her commander did not wear the formal outfit required to appear before the Superiors. Coupled with the rebellious attitude Gedeon left the ship with, it all made her wings fluttered. Her claws closed, and she banged her station table, then she hurried after Gedeon as he disembarked. "Rex Gedeon," she called to him, and he slowed to a stop in the windy mist. "Apex wants your head."

Gedeon turned and eyed her. She continued.

"That's the only reason we are here. The more he fights free thinkers like us, the better he looks to the State. They love it when we kill each other," she went on. "Sarek may have betrayed us, but if you go in there, and get pulled into a fight, where does that leave us? Win or lose, everything you've worked for gets put into jeopardy. The State-"

"The State will face retribution in time," Gedeon interrupted. "As will Apex."

"Just not like this," Kalet pleaded, "The collation of planets will turn on us. Will we fight them too?"

Gedeon brooded, and said, "The problem with Reptilites is that they think power only comes in one... violent... form."

"You saved me, moments before execution, and when you clipped the chains from my wings, you promised me we'd never be slaves again. It is the only type of power that I fear, and Earth is the only hope I've seen."

"I know what I told you," he assured her. "I will not entertain the notion that Apex will ever come between me and my word."

Gedeon walked down the long halls of Arena Superia. A dark gray color tinted his scales, as he passed the Reptilite insignia engraved it stone. The halls were spacious enough to accommodate all the Superiors. Epic columns were decorated with the claw marks and dried blood of those who had failed to please Apex, the Superior Supreme. The design made anyone walking toward Apex feel beneath him. That's how Rex Gedeon felt now.

Rex Gedeon genuflected before Apex, then bowed deeply. "Superior Supreme, Lord Apex." Rex Gedeon addressed him.

"You're late," Apex said, his voice rumbling through the halls. "Where have you been? Why hasn't Sarek updated me on your progress?"

Gedeon said: "I've been protecting the southern region. Kal Sarek is studying strange signals relevant to our kingdom. I came the moment I received your command."

The light barely hinted at Apex's appearance. As he sat on his throne, recessed amidst large pillars, all one could see was his enormous snout. Apex snarled at Gedeon's lack of ceremonial attire.

Apex growled. "Your disrespect for the throne angers me. Your frequent conquest about the Realm has made you bold, and I shall be its end."

As the ruler leaned forward, his massive curved horns were visible above the slits of his eyes. So was the large horn above his nose. "Vyn will take your command," Apex taunted. "He is a true representation of our kind. He has a horn, a buck's horn. A pure physical specimen."

Apex stood, and stepped forward. Large for a Reptilite, he often tried to classify himself as a titan. In truth, a Reptilite could not compare in size with a Titan. Having seen the Earth's dinosaurs of old, Gedeon understood that Apex was closer to the size of their ancestors. As Apex approached, the floor shook with every step. As he walked around the bowing Gedeon, the leader took in the hazy light around the commander.

Apex walked behind Gedeon. Gedeon did not move. Gedeon felt the heat from Apex's breath as the ruler opened his jaws. Apex meant to intimidate others with his thundering steps, but Gedeon regarded each thud as an opportunity. He made a mental note of the frequency of these sound waves. His pupils shifted. The sound waves became visible. Gedeon almost smiled as he pictured his route between each wave amplitude in a rush toward Apex. He imagined using his razor-like tail to split open Apex's gut and watch the half-digested souls spill onto the floor.

Gedeon's eyes morphed to an infrared spectrum. He wanted to identify blood sources he could cut that would kill the leader and those smaller ones that would only hurt him. Ideally, he could manage his attack in a way that would leave Apex alive just long enough so he could hear Rex Gedeon say: *I am Rex Gedeon, the Great Hunter, predator of everything... even you, Apex.*

Rex Gedeon's thoughts drifted to Earth, and Wuyan. He wondered about the strange dark energy particles Kalet had found. His ultimate goal was to conquer something much bigger than Apex- an entire planet. Gedeon decided to engage Apex in battle. He used his leader's biggest fear, Wuyan, as his first weapon.

"Sarek detected strange signals of dark energy in the southern quadrant," Gedeon revealed. As soon as he'd uttered the words, he felt a tingle of fear rippling from Apex.

Apex looked up, and tension crackled through his response, "Strange signals? Dark energy? Wuyan! These could be signs of an attack."

"Our spies report that the Vega Beast have waged a successful counterattack against the Akolyte," Gedeon said. "I don't see how Wuyan represents a threat to our southern quadrant. Her troops are nowhere along our border."

"Fool!" Apex cried. "Your spies are worthless! Wuyan has infested the Vega system, and her army of Akolytes has expanded far too quickly for our comfort. Soon, she will control the Vega system, and the Akolytes will line the border of our southern quadrant! You know nothing of war! It is your fault; your buildup of troops has incited her against us!"

"She's merely a pirate," Gedeon countered. "Pirates don't control systems; they pillage them."

"And where will she go after exhausting the Vega Beast of their resources? Here! Take your simple army and position them at the southern border. You will be our first line of defense. Keep her out, even if you must sacrifice every soul! I demand to hear from Sarek personally regarding this matter!"

"The Vega Beast have made good progress defending themselves against Wuyan," Gedeon assured the ruler. "She hasn't the power to attack us while she loses to them. These dark energy particles and strange signals don't seem to be related to her."

"Vega Beast are no part of the Galactic State," said Apex. "If Wuyan unites them against us, that would be a grave threat!" Apex started lumbering away. "These dark energy signals are their doing; I guarantee it. What you must find out is how."

"As you wish," Gedeon replied.

Apex returned to his recessed throne and dismissed Gedeon. As Gedeon left the battle of wits.

Instead of returning to his ship, Gedeon detoured to the barracks and browsed through recruiter files. He found a long-time student, who had never been recruited. It was odd. She had degrees and published writings. He glanced over her work and was impressed. He had her summoned, and when she arrived, he understood the problem on sight.

"I thought Vega Beast hated Reptilites," Gedeon gasped.

"I'm more than just a Vega Beast," she responded. "And I'm not xenophobic."

"But Reptilites think you are," Gedeon said. "Why would you even come here to this world?"

"I was brought here to aid the scientific advancement, and to find ways around the elements to make Reptilite technology more competitive."

Gedeon read off her name and then looked at her. "Natalyze?" His Earth studies had given him an appreciation of life's repetitions. Throughout the galaxy, he found similarities in everything. "You look like a talking cat."

Natalyze's head snapped up. "A what?" The name took her back, "I've been insulted a many different ways, but never a... a cat? If you want me to feel bad, call me a name I'm familiar with."

"Do you know who I am?" Gedeon asked her.

"I do," Natalyze answered. "You are the freedom fighter. You are Rex Gedeon, who sparked the rebellion. The Great Hunter."

"Your files show that you've attended several recruitments but you've never actually been hired," Gedeon noted.

Natalyze sighed. "Typically, commanders summon me for the combat part of the recruitment – if nothing else."

"How's that working out for you?"

"Painfully," she admitted.

"Then I must inform you. This is a recruitment," he told her.

"Is it? I can smell molted feathers on you," Natalyze said after sniffing the air. "Either you have an officer who is a fowl, or you work in close collaboration with one. I don't imagine you want me to be a part of your crew. I can tell, I won't be fond of this recruitment."

"You are not fond of showing your strengths?"

"Reptilites value strength and power over brains," Natalyze said. "Recruitments are just an effort to kill me rather than useful ability."

"Are you questioning the tradition handed down to us to prove how great one truly is?" Gedeon asked.

Natalyze's look of resignation morphed into a visage of evil. Her hands opened. Her claws emerged. The smooth black fur on her back stood up. She showed her fangs. "I do question it."

"Good," Gedeon replied, walking toward her. "Do you know what dark energy is?"

She maintained her defensive posture, but her eyes sparkled with curiosity. For a moment she was silent as she gauged his motivations, then she risked an answer. "Yes, I do, Rex Gedeon."

"Tell me," Gedeon commanded.

Her back fur smoothed out as she said: "Dark energy comes from dark matter, which means it comes from space."

"Space isn't matter. It's nothing," Gedeon said.

"I don't mean the off-planet areas we refer to as 'space'," she said. "Space contains all existence—the worlds we pass through, the air we breathe. We don't notice the air, but if it wasn't there, we couldn't exist. We only call something 'dark matter' because we can't see it—too dark." Natalyze chuckled at her geeky joke, but Gedeon ignored her wit. She cleared her throat and continued: "Enormous amounts of energy are needed to stabilize dark matter, but that allows the propagation of everything in space. That's what we call 'dark energy.'"

Gedeon showed her data from his ship. "Then what do you make of these?"

She studied the display. "What's that? It can't be right. It appears to be anti-dark energy particles."

"Explain," Gedeon directed.

"Dark matter radiates particles of dark energy," Natalyze said. "However, if there's a tear, or rip in the fabric of space—if space is torn apart—that creates an explosion of dark energy particles."

"But you just said these are *anti*-dark energy particles," Gedeon protested.

"A wave of anti-dark energy particles precedes an explosion of dark matter," Natalyze answered. "From our perspective, when dark matter explodes, it leaves a blast radius void of all space-time. The dark energy particles from the explosion balance the anti-dark energy particles that existed before the explosion. That balancing creates new dark matter, which, in turn, fills the void. That's all entirely theoretical, of course. No one has that kind of technology."

"Take a walk with me," Gedeon commanded her, "You are my new science officer."

"What about the recruitment?" Natalyze wondered.

"The recruitment is over. I already know what your strengths are."

With Gedeon leading the way, they exited the personnel offices and went through the barrack halls. They were passing through the maintenance depot when a voice called: "Unbelievable."

An older Reptilite with a crest for a head came out from a maze of equipment. Gedeon recognized him as Shelzei. Six soldiers followed their older leader. Shelzei glanced from Natalyze to Rex Gedeon, and back again. He looked genuinely confused.

"A fur-beast, Rex Gedeon?" he asked. "I wondered the first time you recruited one, but now I'm convinced you've lost your mind."

One of the soldiers scoffed: "Vega Beast can't function with Reptilites. They think we're too stupid."

"Isn't that the truth?" Shelzei agreed, with a nod of his crested head. "Why would you join his team when you think we are inferior to you?"

Natalyze shook her head in denial. She said, "Reptilites and Vegas came from the same place."

"Vega's were never slaves, though," Shelzei countered, "Your ancestors were considered royalty, while we were forced to fight everyone's battles. Yeah, you think you're better than us!"

Shelzei approached the two slowly. Long ago Natalyze had learned the best way to handle these situations was to leave once that subject came up.

"You think you can force us to live in a society where the Vegas rule us?" Shelzei asked Gedeon.

Rex Gedeon folded his arms and stared at Shelzei. "If I forced you to do anything, you would no longer be obliged to live."

"Reptilites are warriors," said Shelzei. "Vega's were bred a little different. They want to be us."

"That's... that's..." Natalyze found herself speechless in the face of this insult.

"She knows it's true," Shelzei said, chuckling.

She found her tongue long enough to protest: "I know it's ignorant, xenophobic, bullshit breeding logic," she said. Then she pleaded to Gedeon: "We should go."

"No one's going anywhere," Shelzei countered, signaling his troops. His soldiers spread out around Gedeon and Natalyze.

"Let me tell you something, hon," said Shelzei. "You think fur-beast came from the same place as us?"

"Don't call me a fur-beast," Natalyze demanded.

"She feels insulted!" Shelzei taunted, drawing chuckles from his soldiers. "Fur-beast were bred as slave patrollers. They caught Reptilites who escaped and returned them to their masters. So you can call that bullshit logic as much as you want, but it's the truth!"

"What is your business with me?" Gedeon interrupted.

Shelzei sighed. "Ya know, I never said much. I let you do your thing. Didn't like it, but I let your actions slide. Now you have to face it: the boss is the boss. Apex changed his mind. You won't be patrolling the border anymore. Now I see why."

"You are playing the wrong side," Gedeon warned.

"Tell me, will you utter the Vega Beast pledge as your last words?" Shelzei drew his gun. "*I am.*"

Shelzei fired at Gedeon at point-blank range, but the commander swatted the shots away with his powerful tail. Four soldiers charged him, putting themselves between Shelzei and Gedeon. Gedeon was too nimble for them. He leapt at Shelzei, spun, kicked, and sliced with his tail. Two throats tore open. He landed, and whipped his tail- wrapping it around Shelzei's neck. Shelzei's arm trembled, and Gedeon stared him down. Shelzei quickly drew his gun to shoot, but with a yank, Gedeon's tail tore Shelzei's head from the shoulders.

The surviving Reptilites ran off. Shelzei's headless body fell next to his crested head. As Gedeon walked out, Natalyze followed, but they didn't make for the ship.

"Where... where are we going now?" she asked.

"To see Vyn," Gedeon explained.

Near the arena, they found a large vintage bar, constructed from concrete, metals, and other traditional materials. The place was somewhat busy with music and conversation.

When Gedeon walked in everyone went quiet.

"I think we should go," Natalyze urged him. "Back to the ship.... Apex will be looking for us, and this won't be a good place for him to find me. What's the point, Commander? We'll be gone soon, and Vyn... he's probably gone too. This place is full of hate."

When the bartender saw Natalyze, he warned: "She's not welcome here,"

"Hate?" said a voice. It was Vyn in the back corner with some comrades. "Here? Not hate." As his table cleared, he stood up. His massive jaw came to a point in the front. Two horned skin points rose over his ear holes, and he had a beautiful curved buckhorn curving back from the middle of his head. "The only ones who hate are you, Vega."

One of Vyn's allies spoke from the shadows, "Tell us why the fur-beast ceded from the State!"

"Gedeon knows why. The Vegas were mad they lost their prized position to hunt us down," Vyn added. "Of course, Gedeon has been kind enough to do their jobs for them. Who here believes her was out there freeing slaves?"

"He was taking them away from their jobs!" one of Vyn's comrades said.

"Rounding us up to send us right back into war." Vyn stood up and started toward the couple. "Let's be real. There's nothing great about him. He's just a hunter, and he hunts our kind," Vyn preached. Others nodded, and raised their glasses in toasts.

Someone in the back called out, "And here he stands with a fur-beast!"

"So don't point at us, and accuse us of hate. You want to be slaves again! What more proof do we need?" asked Vyn. "You are hate!"

Gedeon kicked Vyn in the chest. Vyn's head snapped forward then back, as he felt the sharp pain of whiplash. As he hit the floor, Rex Gedeon's foot stayed on him.

"Already, you are slaves in the mind," Gedeon dug his foot claws into Vyn's chest. Vyn tried not to scream. "Because you find it easier to live in the world they gave us," Gedeon punched him away. "Then fight for the world we lost."

Vyn struggled up and tried to charge. As Gedeon waited, he hissed: "You don't know your history."

As soon as he was in range, Gedeon snapped his attacker's head down. His tail caught Vyn's horn and whipped him around by the neck. When Vyn hit the floor, his horn dug into the concrete. Gedeon stepped on Vyn's, protruding jaw, and listened to his opponent scream. Vyn's horn wrenched against his head.

"We broke our backbones under their yoke," Gedeon jeered. "We are not free. We are only comfortable with the limited existence they provided us! Gracious to leave our fettered life, we consent to their power over us."

Gedeon's tail sliced flesh from Vyn's arms. "The kingship of Reptilites," he said, "Prohibits me from to consenting to their authority."

Admiring Vyn's stuck buckhorn, Gedeon forced Vyn's jaw with his feet. The concrete cracked. Gedeon's swung his tail, cutting the horn from Vyn's face. He kicked Vyn away and pulled the horn out of the concrete. "You must gain knowledge of self because without conviction you are lost," he said and walked off.

Vyn turned around, bleeding from his chest and his torn appendage. "You first, fur-beast... slave," he gasped, gripping his chest.

As he was leaving, Gedeon leaned into Natalyze. "I lied. Your combat recruitment isn't over. Finishing him earns you a place on my ship."

Natalyze's green eyes flared with wickedness. Her fingers stretched. Out of the shadows of her paws her claws appeared.

"I would cut out my father's testicle as my mother bore me before I'll lose to a fur-beast," Vyn vowed, getting up.

Natalyze leapt from table to wall. From there she flew at Vyn. Vyn punched her away, and she went over the bar, right into a tub full of ice water. Everyone laughed. Natalyze emerged from the tub, her black fur soaked. The laughter grew louder.

She hopped onto the bar counter and attacked. Vyn kicked twice. She slipped and ducked. Vyn pulled a gun and fired as he spun around. He missed, and took another swing at her. She retreated. Vyn shot wildly, hitting friends and furniture, but not Natalyze. She was bouncing between walls and ceiling when she finally landed on him. He butted her with the gun, then spun and kicked her. She went flying. As she flipped wildly through the air, one of his shots hit her in the leg. She smashed against the wall, then crashed onto a concrete table.

Vyn kept shooting, but she rolled away. As Vyn closed in on her, she swatted him with open claws, knocking his gun aside. He hoisted up a concrete table, and slammed it down, just missing her. As he lifted it again, she sprinted away. He threw the table at her. She dodged it, but Vyn reached her and knocked her back. When he pounced, she didn't avoid him. Raising all four claws, she nailed him as he landed on her. Despite the pain of his impact, she dug her claws into his flesh. He thought she was crushed and nearly helpless, but when he got up to finish her off, she held onto his back, still ripping at him. He couldn't reach her.

Natalyze tried to tear the high nostrils on either side of what had been his horn, but they'd been toughened by all his ramming and training. Vyn backed up, smashing Natalyze into the wall. When she hit the floor, he grabbed another table and hit her. Swinging the table like a club, he knocked her behind the bar, then threw the table at her. It shattered against the wall, debris hitting her. Natalyze could barely move.

Vyn jumped up on the bar and looked down at her in triumph. She edged away on her back. Vyn followed, walking along the bar top. She stopped moving. Vyn raised his fist and hopped down. As he aimed a fist toward her head, she managed to dodge. His fist caught in a wooden bar support. Natalyze opened her jaws and bit into his throat. Her fangs sunk deep, squelching his howl of pain. He jerked his arm from the wood, sending splinters flying. He stumbled around punching her, but she locked her teeth to his throat. Her feet felt the wall, and she pushed off hard. As she twisted in midair, she flipped him. As she landed, she yanked Vyn's head down, dunking it into the water.

She held him there.

Vyn swung, kicked, and struggled. Natalyze clawed at the chest wound Rex Gedeon had left. Vyn flopped about, but Natalyze' powerful jaws held his head in the water. Soon he struggled no more. When she could no longer feel a pulse, she released the corpse. Blood dripped from her mouth and wounds as she hopped over the bar. She exited through a gauntlet of hateful stares. When a few Reptilites approached her from behind, she whirled and faced them. They halted. She turned and left. No one tried to stop her.

REX GEDEON COMMANDED the Kaiman to return to the southern quadrant for another deep scan. He demanded an update from his crew.

Tanga spoke first. "We received a message from Earth. Lotus retrieved Boyacobas's tablet and verified the results of the device, but he reports he's still hunted by an organization that's bent on foiling his plans."

"Rex Gedeon," Kalet put in, "if we don't invade soon, we'll lose the element of surprise."

"We aren't relying solely on surprise," Gedeon argued. "We have other tactics. I must be confident that Wuyan won't attack us on Earth. She's up to something. What have our spies learned of the Vega Beast war against the Akolytes?"

"The intel concerns me," Kalet reported. "The Vega Beast are giving the Akolytes a difficult time. Our spies say Wuyan is losing this war."

"Why does that concern you?" Gedeon asked.

"The logistic numbers don't seem to match," Kalet replied. "It appears that she's only using 18% of her army. Either she scrapped most of her forces, or we don't know where they are."

"What about economic factors?" Gedeon asked.

"Those numbers look strange as well," Kalet reported. "Wuyan wasn't hurting for money, so financial woes wouldn't force her to reduce her military. Her economic picture seems healthy. But the Akolytes are spending money on something."

"Something?" Gedeon asked.

"Something big and expensive," Kalet said. "But it isn't coming from the military budget."

"So she still has her army?" Gedeon wondered. "Do you think they're hidden?"

"I think so," Kalet confirmed. "Yes. Yes, she must."

"Does she plan to turn around and attack this sector with her full force?" Gedeon asked. "If she'd done that before, we wouldn't have seen it coming."

"We would be outnumbered in this sector if she attacked with any more than 30% of those missing forces," Kalet said. "I doubt that Wuyan is losing the war. She simply isn't fighting it."

"How is that possible?" Gedeon turned to Natalyze. "Why would Wuyan attack the Vega Beast, but not fight them? What does she want in the Vega system?"

Natalyze shrugged. "I wouldn't know. I haven't been in the Vega system in years. I just see Wuyan as a pirate leading pirates. For all I know she could have selected her target by rolling dice."

"But she didn't," Gedeon snapped, annoyed by her casual tone. "Wuyan has amassed an enormous mercenary army. You don't gain that sort of loyalty without a plan, without a purpose... a creed her people can follow. What's her cause? What draws her to the Vega system?"

"Nothing scientific," Natalyze insisted. "Nothing other systems don't have. She's a pillager, and the Vegas must be easy targets."

"Easy targets don't make high scores." Gedeon studied the sector map. Apex controlled most of the resources near the southern border as a part of his personal wealth. Apex hated Wuyan.

"Apex's fears about Wuyan make him suspicious," Gedeon said. "His suspicions are probably wrong, but they've led us to something. It's not an easy target. Tell me more about the dark energy particles." He aimed this last request at Natalyze. The new science officer felt nervous. She'd never worked on a spaceship, and she was still recovering from her bout with Vyn.

Kalet looked at Natalyze with disgust.

Natalyze tightened her bandages and corrected Gedeon, "The anti-dark energy particles...are utterly astounding. Never seen anything like them, at least, not in nature. I need more time to evaluate the data."

"Give me an educated guess," Gedeon commanded. "What caused the wave of anti-particles?"

Natalyze thought for a moment. *It's not a wave.* She said to herself. She hesitated, wanting to avoid any further possibility of showing disrespect, but then noticed Gedeon's impatience. She said. "Something will impact this area."

"How do you know?" Gedeon responded.

Natalyze explained. "Dimensionally, it has already happened. These are anti-particles, so the phenomena doesn't depend on time. In the future, something ruptures the fabric of space within this area, yet we observe it now. "

"What sort of thing ruptures space?" Gedeon wondered, recognizing his gap in understanding. He skipped to his core question, "How bad is it for us?"

"A lot of things might rupture space," she said. "This one might be a wormhole or the explosion of a dark energy propulsion system."

"What about the destruction of an army?" Gedeon asked. "Or a bomb?"

Natalyze gave serious thought to the question. "Well, yeah, if there were a dark energy bomb, it would produce an event like this one."

Gedeon was intrigued. "What's the extent of the event?"

Through Gedeon's interest, Natalyze could tell he didn't fully understand. She added, "Imagine dropping a stone into water. It creates a splash, and because of the splash, we will see the ripples. That is causal. Now imagine if I drop that same stone, but I see the ripples happening before the stone hits the water? That is non-causal. In this case, we're seeing the ripples before the splash. Judging from the area cover, this one will be catastrophic. Something awful is going to happen here; we can't be here when it does."

Gedeon turned to Kalet. "Report to the Superiors that this phenomena is being investigated. Tell them a radioactive meteorite collision caused it, and there's no danger."

Kalet responded, "Yes, Rex Gedeon."

Natalyze tried to cover her confusion.

"You said Wuyan is building something big," Gedeon said to Kalet. "Let's find out what."

Kalet instructed the crew to prepare for a red alert. From the border of the Vega system, they crossed into territory heavily covered by Akolytes. They got no warnings and met no resistance as if they were alone. It felt quite eerie because they knew they weren't. Kalet studied the holographic map. She steadied the ship, maneuvering around signals that had any potential to betray their position until they were deep into Akolyte territory.

As Rex Gedeon looked out the portal, his pupils changed shape, and he saw latent hyperspace residual particles. He noticed a line of particle clusters stretching in one direction. He directed Kalet to follow it, and they ended up at a construction hangar.

"What can we deduce there?" Gedeon asked.

"She's building ships," Kalet said, "but not warships, more like transport ships."

"Is that where all her money's going?" Gedeon asked.

"Who spends that kind of money to build a transport vessel?" Tanga asked. "You'd have to create another army to escort them."

"Not unless those transports are carrying something very valuable," Gedeon thought aloud. "The point is she is not building warships."

Natalyze mumbled to herself, "Taylots? On Na'tan?"

"What's that? Speak up," Gedeon insisted.

"Sorry. It's...well...I was scanning around to see if the anti-dark energy particles were out here," Natalyze explained. "In my scans, I realized that Na'tan gave off some strange temperature readings. I did a bio-scan of the planet, and I'm picking up odd life forms. Including Taylots!"

"What's a Taylot?" Kalet asked.

"Terraformers," Gedeon answered, but Natalyze quickly jumped in.

"Not just terraformers. Taylots are rocklike, crystalline, life forms—basically living rocks, which are rare. The Merloti harvested the Taylots a long time ago to help them terraform planets, but Taylots can build anything. You give a Taylot enough resources; it'll build this ship. They're worth a fortune! The most valuable mineral in the realm."

"So she's terraforming a planet?" Tanga wondered. "In a system that isn't hers?"

"She doesn't have nearly enough Taylots to terraform a planet, but like I said, they could build anything. That is, if you tell 'em what to make, and provide the resources. Maybe she's here just for the Taylots?"

Kalet eyed Natalyze as Gedeon commanded them to orbit Na'tan. As they approached the planet, Gedeon put up the display and streamed data. When they reached the dark side they saw it: city-sized spores were connected to incubation units scattered on top of a sheet of ice covering a third of the planet. Only, that massive sheet of ice was alive.

Gedeon's pupils widened, and his mouth dropped.

Natalyze gasped, "Oh my god!"

"This war is a farce!" Kalet shouted.

"So that's what the Vega systems has!" Gedeon sucked in air, and said, "The Frost Titan!"

"How did she capture the Frost Titan?" Tanga wondered.

"And what's she doing with it?" Natalyze shrieked. "Harvesting its body to make more? She's breeding titans!"

"She has several incubation units," Tanga started and turned. "Does she plan to capture more Titans?"

"Impossible! She could never control them!" Kalet shouted.

"She wants to unleash them," Gedeon responded.

"On what? On who? The Vega Beast?" Kalet asked. "Reptilia?" For a moment no one spoke.

"I've never heard of someone growing Titans," said Tanga. "Like a farm? That's suicide. Even if she attacks the Vega planets with Titans, what good would that do her? She'll still be stuck with a Titan on a planet she could never use. She would bankrupt her entire empire trying to get rid of it. That no plan at all."

Natalyze agreed. "This is confusing. The Vega system simply isn't worth this much effort, even if it has Taylots!"

"This isn't about the Vega system," Gedeon snapped.

"Reptilia?" Kalet gasped. Gedeon looked beyond the globe at the spores on Na'tan.

"If Wuyan attacks Reptilia with the spores from the Frost Titan, it is finished," Natalyze warned. "Our army will never ever get to Earth. We'll be forced to defend our home."

Kalet corrected her. "Reptilia was never our legitimate home!"

"Wuyan is attempting to bring back a scourge the Realm cleansed itself of long ago," Gedeon announced.

"A scourge that will consume her as well?"

Gedeon eyed the titan spores greedily. "It doesn't matter. The weapon is being built, and we must either possess it or possess its deterrent. Let's help ourselves to a few of Wuyan's titan spores."

"How? We wouldn't dare put a titan on this ship, much less a spore. What if it were to hatch?" Kalet asked. "Usually, ships are designed to escape titans, not transport them."

Natalyze spoke up: "Wuyan conveniently has the spores contained for transport. If we could build a transport ship, it's feasible."

Kalet looked at her. "And maybe the new girl would like to pilot it?"

"Why make our own ship when Wuyan is building some for us?" Gedeon asked, "I want them. Instruct a small contingent to enter this territory and stake out Na'tan. Steal a ship and bring me a spore."

"Bring it? Where, Rex Gedeon?" Kalet asked, dumbfounded.

"Earth," Gedeon commanded. "Call all troops and all ships to arms. Rendezvous in the Earth System."

Gedeon shut his station and left the bridge.

"What are we doing?" Natalyze whispered, floating down to Kalet.

"Obeying our orders," Kalet responded.

"Are we conspiring to abandon our post just when we know Wuyan could attack Reptilia?" Natalyze cried, her voice rising. "That could be considered desertion. Even treason!"

Kalet corrected her, "This is the true direction of the Reptilites! There is no legal authority that can countermand an order for the reclamation of Earth!"

As Kalet left her station, Natalyze followed. "No legal authority? Apex will kill us all! What about attacking in waves? Contingency plans? Retreats? Is Earth a one-way trip? A suicide mission?"

"You don't seem supportive."

"But this is a forced migration to a new planet when there are humans living on Earth! They will never agree to this!" Natalyze complained, trying to grasp her own words, but she smelled something: an odor of anger and intent- but it didn't come from Kalet.

Large hands grabbed Natalyze, and she froze in surprise. Kalet nodded to Tanga, who dragged Natalyze off into a strange room. He put her in a metal box, where the sudden change of atmosphere frightened her. She started pushing, but the walls of the box were lined with spikes that could pierce her paws. The box smelled of blood and innards and felt like despair.

Kalet spoke to her from beyond the box: "I don't know why Rex Gedeon promoted such a useless, inexperienced Vega Beast to be his science officer."

Natalyze felt her fur rise from fear, and from a latent static charge. Tanga balled his fist and hit the box. It created an electric charge, shocking Natalyze. She screamed. When the pain subsided, her knees buckled. She reached out to keep herself from falling. Razor-sharp spikes cut her paws.

"Are you a spy?" Kalet asked her. "Where does your loyalty lie?"

Natalyze regained her composure. She felt dizzy, but her legs eventually straightened out.

Tanga punched again, electrocuting Natalyze. Her muscles locked and her insides boiled. When her screams died down, she fell onto the spikes. "R-Rex...!" she mumbled, trying to pull herself up.

"Are we to deny ourselves the spoils of Earth and return to Reptilia?" Kalet shouted. "Why do we fight for this planet? Tell me!"

Tanga punched the box again. Natalyze's knees buckled from the electric assault. When her thoughts returned, she screamed out, "We will never go back!"

Tanga threw another punch. Natalyze's scream was cut off as her muscles contracted. Again she fell onto the bloodied spikes. Her mind screamed: *Make it stop!* "For the glory of the Reptilites!" she cried.

That brought a moment's relief. She caught her breath, and her body shook uncontrollably. She heard a footstep, then a grunt and another punch rocked the enclosure. If she could just stay standing. "For the wrongs to our ancestors!" Natalyze shouted.

Kalet paced and snarled: "To where is our destiny! To what is our Holy Land?"

Tanga punched again. Natalyze collapsed, and as the spikes pierced her she choked out: "Earth!"

Kalet nodded to Tanga. When he opened the container, Natalyze fell out, battered and bleeding.

Kalet spoke: "We were the first to rule the Earth, and we will be the last."

IN ANOTHER PART of the ship Rex Gedeon walked to his quarters. The halls were pitch black. Power levels were reduced so the Kaiman could avoid detection, but Gedeon saw everything like it was daylight. His red pupils glowed in the dark. He felt focus and excitement. His tail switched back and forth with every step. He opened his mouth in the darkness.

"I am Rex Gedeon. The Great Hunter."

DRIVEN

BISHOP AND ZAHRA touched down in D.C and disembarked. Bishop had smooth muscular arms from constant training. The dapper outfit he'd purchased at the airport at Giza fit snuggly over his upper body. Despite his physical fitness, hours of holding a sleeping child had worn him down. His arms felt useless and weak, making him question his entire level of fitness.

"How do you do it?" he said to himself, as he watched a couple of women carrying their babies. Bishop tried to mimic them, but couldn't master the hip-to-arm technique.

Their pre-booked cab approached the front exit, and the doors opened. Clumsily, Bishop tried seating himself while he stumbled backward into the cab. As the door shut, the cab muffled the airport wind and noise. The taxi sped off as the speakers played an orchestral piece. Bishop was surprised to see a woman in the front seat facing them.

"How was your flight?" she asked.

"I'm sorry," Bishop said slowly, "I didn't realize this cab was occupied."

"Let's just say I'm the driver," Kyra told him.

She had a gun in her lap, and Bishop didn't have to guess her intentions. He went to snatch it from her, but feeling Zahra in his arms make him rethink his strategy.

"You could have just shot the plane down if you wanted to kill me," Bishop told her, adjusting Zahra in his lap, "Save a lot of time."

"Bringing down planes is your thing, besides I wanted you to know it was me," Kyra claimed.

"And you are?" Bishop asked.

"I'm Kyra Garret,"

Bishop thought for a moment, and couldn't place the name, "Well, Kyra Garret, where are we heading?" Bishop looked around.

"JFK," she told him.

"An opera?" Bishop asked.

She squeezed the gun tighter in her fingers, "A metaphor."

"Ah, you must realize that I am no relation to the former president," Bishop reminded her.

"Your casket won't know that," Kyra said, with a steady gaze.

As the car drove on, Bishop watched the pavement roll by. Kyra seemed uncomfortable. She looked at him as if he'd just wiped oil-stained hands on her fine white linens.

"What's with the kid?" Kyra asked. "I read everything about you. Nothing about a child."

"Apparently, you didn't refresh your news feed last night," Bishop mumbled into the window.

"Is that Nicole's daughter?"

Bishops ears tingled, "No." He looked over at Kyra, "What do you know about Nicole?"

"I know you gave her the canister of zenomites before she boarded that flight."

Bishop's head flopped back against the seat. He couldn't stand hearing this. "Not again. You're after the zenomites too?"

"I'm not after any stupid zenomites! You fucking bastard!"

Bishop hushed Kyra, "There's a child here." Zahra was starting to wake.

Kyra's voice grew louder in defiance. "I was always told that I wasn't ready to face you, so seeing you now makes me laugh. I could have ended you a long time ago and saved myself the worry."

"If you only brought a gun, you have something to worry about."

"It's just, now, I've waited so long for the honor of killing you, but I never considered what to do with your daughter. I guess she can just watch."

Bishop didn't mind the banter, but her rudeness wore into him. "And to what do I owe the honor?"

"You killed Boyacobas."

He rubbed his hair and set his hand on his lap. "After Flight 522, I made an effort to memorize the names of all two hundred and three people who died on that flight, so whenever I get cornered by a family member who wants to fight me, or a loved one who wants to kill me, I can sympathize with them, knowing who they lost. I get hate mail every day. I'm talking hand written letters of people who want me dead." Bishop nodded, then shook his head. "I'm sorry for your loss, and I apologize for any involvement I had with that, but I don't remember any Boyacobas. Was that a nickname?"

"Save your pathetic canned speech. Boyacobas wasn't on the damn flight."

"Excuse me?"

"He was the one you killed for the canister of zenomites?"

"Oh..." The memory came to him. He'd had the right circumstances, but the wrong event.

"The one sent by the Reptilites," she said.

"What's a Reptilite?" Bishop asked. "Lizard food?"

Kyra gasped. "I don't believe this. All this time, people talked about you like some next-level genius, vicious enough to require every precaution; but you're no more than a blade of grass blown by the wind. Your kills came from ignorance, not brilliant intent, and you only live now out of the graces of my curiosity."

As Bishop patted Zahra with a calming hand, he responded: "During the court proceedings they tried to pin the parachute deployment on bad design. I thought it was the zenomites that triggered the parachutes and crashed the plane."

Kyra shook her head in disbelief. "You don't know what you're talking about."

Bishop squinted. "And you would?"

"I know, because Lotus knows," Kyra sneered.

"Something tells me you don't know everything Lotus knows."

"You are right about one thing; I don't know why zenomites are so important to him," Kyra said. Her mind went blank trying to think of it losing her moment of superiority quickly.

"Zenomites are like nanomites powered by zero-point energy," said Bishop, taking a professorial tone. "These tiny robots feed off the energy in all the space around them. By feeding on that energy they can control the matter within that space."

"Interesting."

"Ya know, at one point in time, scientist figured out how stars worked. Then people died from nuclear weapons. We tried to understand how debris in space could damage our space crafts, and next thing you know, we're building a hypervelocity missiles. No way were we ever going to let society, much less a psychopath like Lotus, have my designs, but they wanted them.

Before the crash, strange men would threaten and attack Nicole for the canister. Nicole got worried, and we devised a plan to keep them safe. We failed. After the crash, I assumed that the canister was intact. Otherwise, the entire city would have been obliterated had it not. I rummaged through the wreckage to reclaim them, but it was nowhere to be found. Eventually, I tracked it to a rescue worker who found it with a surviving child. When I learned the worker was going to give it to Lotus, I had to move on him."

Kyra shook her head, again, "Boyacobas was no rescue worker."

"I'm sorry," Bishop said, sincerely.

"Not sorry enough," Kyra insisted. "Do you have any idea what killing him means to the world?"

"Boyacobas made a mistake, but I didn't kill him. He mishandled the zenomites."

"Liar!"

"Really, how?"

"Zenomites don't do shit! They don't crash planes, and they don't kill people!" Then Kyra demanded. "How'd he die?"

An image flashed into Bishop's mind: Boyacobas's body being pulled into the dual-shear metal shredder. He heard the crush and saw the blood... "Not very well," Bishop breathed.

"That's sounds a lot like the way Nicole went," Kyra mocked in a tight voice. "For a moment you had me going. You lost her, then went on trial for her death, among so many others. I almost felt sorry for you, but now..." Kyra looked at Zahra. The little girl squirmed in Bishop's lap. Kyra ignored the child, saying: "When you die—"

The car braked, and made a sharp turn onto Interstate 395. Kyra glanced at the road ahead. "Where are we going?"

"How would I know?" Bishop demanded. "You said you were the driver."

"This isn't the route I programmed. What did you do?"

"Nothing," Bishop claimed. "Finish what you were saying..."

"Shut up! Where are we going?" Kyra picked up her phone and dialed a number. As it rang, she watched the road carefully. They were going south when they should've turned north.

"It grieves me that you lost your mentor," said Bishop. "I've faced loss, and it made me do awful things. I've had my share of grief, guilt, and I've made horrible mistakes I can never take back. I despaired, knowing I'd lost everything. I thought I had nothing to fight for."

As Bishop spoke quietly, Kyra sat, cursing her phone, and shaking it. Her attempts to contact anyone beyond the cab were futile. "Damn it," Kyra said, punching another button, "why isn't she picking up?"

Bishop kept talking, and his calm tone soothed the infant. "I was wrong. You always have something to fight for and you always have a lot more you can lose."

Kyra's face went blank. "Where are we going!"

"I don't know, but I know when someone's been set up," said Bishop. As he watched her lose control of the situation, it occurred to him that he was talking to a professional assassin. "Did you kill Tina?" he asked her.

"I don't know what you are talking about," Kyra claimed, and she shook the handle, but failed to open the car door. Up ahead she noticed what appeared to be an abandoned warehouse.

"This is set up. Tell me what you do know about his operation," Bishop urged after his minded burned with curiosity about the missing pieces of the puzzle. "I can help you, but—"

Kyra tried kicking the door; then she pounded her fist against the partition. She broke through to the driver section and ripped out the electrical paneling. The cab kept going. She glanced back at Bishop. "Don't play yourself. You don't know shit."

"You think the joke's just on me? Lotus played you," Bishop mocked back. "Most likely, this car will stop wherever he plans to kill you."

"Then that makes three of us because I'm not dying alone." Kyra pounded the windows, to no effect. "He wanted me to kill you," she hissed, but her words were like the air seeping from a shrinking balloon. "He was training me to kill you…" Finally, she sat in the debris of the driver section. She wondered: *What was this man saying? How could it all possibly fit together?*

"I don't know who he was training you to kill, but it certainly wasn't me," Bishop stated.

"Shut up!"

The cab came to a stop in the warehouse, where everything was dark. As their eyes adjusted, something clamped onto the cab, holding it. Armed men surrounded them. Kyra kicked at a window, then rapped it with the butt of her gun. Nothing happened. She dove into the back, covered her face, and fired at the windshield. The bullet ricocheted, then went into the seat just inches from Zahra's head.

Kyra's mouth fell open. "Holy shit!" She gasped. "That's why they're so afraid of you."

The armed men were pushing the car into a compactor. It settled. As the machine started crushing the car, the men began firing into it.

"Bishop!" Kyra shrieked, diving to the floor.

"Whoa," Bishop shouted. "This is a damn Rumbula!"

"What?" Kyra could not hear him over the noise, "Bishop!"

The car was collapsing around them as bullets flew everywhere. Zahra got agitated and clung on to Bishop. It was as if she knew danger abounded, but he was her safety that kept her from panic. That was enough for Bishop to extend his hands, and everything blew out. The car's panels exploded, and the armed men retreated. Bishop made a tearing motion, and the compactor fell apart. He stood, holding Zahra, as Kyra crouched by his feet. She hugged his leg, burying her face in the crook of his knee. The men kept firing.

Bishop reached out, sweeping up bolts, screws, and metal shreds. When he pointed his finger, the debris tore into the gunmen. The bullets stopped. The only men left alive fled through a door leading to stairs and took refuge on the upper levels.

"Next time you have the upper hand," Bishop told Kyra. "Make sure no one is pulling it down into a grave."

He reached, and one of the automatic weapons on the floor jumped into his hand. He gave the gun to Kyra. Sensing power plants nearby, he ducked into a room and saw rows of the same plants he'd seen in the cave near Khartoum.

"He's here!"

Kyra had ducked into the stairwell, where she shot three gunmen who were trying to get up the levels above. When others above them returned fire, she ducked out of the stairs and took cover. The attackers who'd reached the highest levels were coming out on walkways, ready to try again. She poked her head out and shot at them. Though most of her shots hit the rails, three men fell. Then she saw it: *The rails.*

She leapt out and rolled behind a stack of boxes. The men shredded the boxes with bullets. She could see their reflection off the metal rails.

One, two.

She ducked her head in and out, and cut down more gunmen.

Three, four. Shit! They are moving. Don't move!

The gunners fled up to the next level and returned fire. Kyra crouched down, as the boxes began to disintegrate.

"They have the higher ground!" Kyra shouted.

Bishop emerged from deep concentration and put Zahra on her feet. Kyra's screaming echoed through the building. Bishop hesitated to reason how to proceed with this would-be assassin.

Bishop reached forward and balled his fist. Columns crumbled. The upper floors collapsed. The gunmen fell with the structure.

"That's more like it!" Kyra cried, positioning herself to take aim at any surviving shooters.

Bishop concentrated on things he couldn't feel. Where was the pulse of power he'd felt in the caves of Khartoum? In the cave, things had been crowded together, but here it was all wide open—too expansive. Pinpointing a power source seemed impossible.

"I need to go back to the beginning," he told himself. Bishop pushed his hands forward, and suddenly bricks fell, and there was a wide, high-opening into the sunlight. Empty utility and cargo trucks were lined up outside. Bishop reached up, opened a driver door, and help Zahra onto the seat. He pulled himself up; they buckled up and he gently brushed the dust off her new dress.

"I knew this would happen. This is no life for you," he said, and he drove out to the highway. Instinctively he aimed toward the South Mackey gym. He walked in and looked around at the men who were training.

"Hey, B.K! Babysitting?" Rod said, in a cheerful voice, "You two here to train?"

Bishop chuckled. "Have Adrian, or Julius been in?"

"Haven't seen them."

"Old Man Mister Mackey?"

"He's not here either."

Bishop left, hopped back in the truck, and drove off. When he reached Sherwood Forest neighborhood, he headed for 34th Street and slowed near the Petersons' house.

"Where are we going?" Zahra asked.

Bishop looked at the little girl, "Look. The people who live here are sweet and kind, and they don't have any kids."

"I want to go home!"

"We can't go home!" Bishop told her. "Home is gone, and there isn't place safe enough for me to just leave-"

Drones! They are looking.

Bishop threw the truck into gear and drove on. He hadn't seen the drones, but he felt them. He imagined Officer Wilson waiting in the shadows.

As they traveled through the city, Zahra started to cry while looking around for somewhere to go. Ultimately she clutched his finger. Bishop pulled up to a fire station and parked in front. Everything was quiet.

"Do you know what almost happened back there? The assassin? The warehouse?" Bishop asked, and she shook her head. Bishop continued, "I don't want you to get hurt. This is me trying to save you, I'm trying to help you. I can't run around with this level of responsibility... with a-"

Zahra looked at him lost. Bishop stared up at the sky.

"I've already lost too many people. I can't... take you. Cuz then I can't help anyone else. I need to stay sharp. An assassin got the jump on me, so, yeah, I can't take you. Cuz everyone else, ya know... needs... No way can I take care of you. I can't... " Bishop muttered.

"The chair hurts," Zahra said, as she tried to seat herself in a comfortable position in the utility vehicle.

Bishop's head bowed. "I can't." He wiped the tears from his eyes, "Someone's cutting onions in here." He put the truck back in gear and left the fire station.

The temperature dropped as the sun set. He felt the rain coming and covered the little girl with his coat. He arrived at a house, carried Zahra to the door, rang, and waited. The door opened.

"Oh my god!" Liza tied her robe. "Bishop?"

"Hi, Liza," Bishop said weakly.

"I'm not gonna ask what you're doing here. Who's child is she? She's so cute," Liza said, inviting them inside.

"Um... she's mine?" Bishop answered.

Liza tried to stifle a laugh but failed. Her laughter stretched on too long. "What... in God's name, did you cover her up with? A coat?" She took the girl from him. "She has her dress on backward!"

"I told you," Zahra said.

Going into the bathroom, Liza helped the girl out of her dress. Bishop turned his head. Her husband, Kevin came down the stairs.

"Hon? Is that Bishop," Kevin looked at his friend. "Hey! B.K. Nice to see you, glad you stopped by. You never come by anymore. What did you do to the li'l kid. Play dress up?"

"I thought the tag goes in the back," Bishop admitted.

"She doesn't look anything like you," Liza said, and then she really looked at the girl. "Where have you been?"

"Sudan."

"Don't say Sudan," Liza whispered. "How'd you make it out?"

"It's all over the news; they've never seen anything like it!" Kevin said.

"Well, the world is gonna see a lot more like it," Bishop said.

"What?" Liza asked.

"I was there on recon. It had Lotus fingerprints all over it!" Bishop told them, as he turned back and looked at Zahra. "I – I helped the villagers pull her out from under a watery grave of debris. Her parents died shielding her. The aid workers took her from the villagers. I tried to leave her, but there was just nowhere for her to go."

"Bishop," Liza gasped, hiding tears.

"The Six was there."

"The Six?"

"It isn't just Lotus," He explained. "They abducted kids and took them to a base hidden within the caves. Caves powered by plants Mason created. The leaves act as antennas to direct where the power from the roots go, but the leaves are very delicate. The rebels channel water away from the plants and all I did was redirect the water back onto the plants to short out the leaves. The cave went dark, and hostages escaped. One of the rebel commands had Zahra. So, I took him out to get her back."

"Thank goodness you stopped them."

"They would have stolen those children," Bishop said. "Why does Lotus want to kidnap children?"

"He's never gonna stop?" Liza buttoned up Zahra's dress appropriately. "What's wrong with him?"

"I can't fathom anything he might be thinking. I don't know what he could gain from such destruction."

"That's cuz you aren't a psychopath. I'm a psychiatrist, and I would kill myself if I had him as a client," She watched Zahra pull away and go to Bishop and hug around his leg. Liza cracked a smile of pity. "Lotus is the least of your worries now."

Bishop shrugged. "I don't even know what to do."

"Here's a hint," Kevin said. "Nobody does when they first get em."

"Yea, but don't most people get at least a six month prep time?"

"What's her name?" Liza asked.

Bishop tapped the little girl on the shoulder, and Zahra said her name in a quiet and shy voice.

"What a beautiful name. You must be tired from all of your travels."

Zahra nodded in agreement, and then added, "An assassin tried to kill us, but we got away."

"An assassin!?" Liza shrieked.

"I was gonna get to that part," Bishop added. "My home is probably not the best place right now for us to go."

Kevin joked, "Can you imagine, another Kennedy assassination? What a metaphor!"

"Inappropriate!" Liza snapped. "But you're right about Lotus. He's a madman, and he must be stopped."

Bishop looked at them. "I have to end this. I think he's planning something similar for D.C. I'd brace this house, or have an exit strategy."

"You got it," Kevin said.

"I just need a few hours, if we have that long."

Liza reached for Zahra, "I'll call up Sing, this is a Red Alert."

"I'm sorry if I imposed."

"It's okay," Kevin assured him, "She'll be here when you get back. I'm just impressed you didn't—ya know—drop her off on someone's doorstep. You completely shocked me, and I feel honored you trust us to look after her."

Bishop blushed as he left. He walked out into the quiet night and after a few paces down the walkway he heard a piercing scream come from inside the house. The front door burst open, and Zahra ran out with her shoes in her hand. She ran past Bishop and hopped into the truck, full of tears.

Bishop went to her as she hastily tried to put her shoes on backward.

"You're not going to leave me. I'm not gonna be left out."

"I'm not going to leave you."

"Then where are you going?" Zahra said, trying to get her feet into the shoe the wrong way. Bishop took it from her and turned it around to put it on her foot while she asked, "Why can't I go?"

"I'm going to a place little girls can't go."

Zahra wiped away a tear and pouted. "Can little boys go?"

"No," Bishop said. "Only bigs boys and big girls."

"I'm a big girl," She argued. "You don't want me to go because you want to leave me?"

"I don't want you to go because I love you," Bishop told her. He hugged her and brought her back to Liza.

Darken Skies

AS THE STORM threat receded, the streets of Washington cooled. It was the humid cold of autumn, just frigid enough to make people uncomfortable. A utility truck rumbled through the D.C. streets. Bishop gripped the steering wheel with his right hand, hanging his left elbow out the driver's side window. As the breeze washed through the cab, Bishop's mind cleared. He went back to the beginning- the airport. The large truck barely made it under the overpass as he went back over what had happened.

"The cab picked us up at the airport," he said to himself, "so it must have had my reservation, but Kyra was already inside. Then it took a different route." He drove up the George Washington Memorial Parkway. "She didn't try to kill me inside of the car, which I thought was strange, but she must've wanted me to know. Hmm, she wanted a metaphor."

As evening fell, the cloudy sky brightened in the west. Bishop raised his hand to shield the sun from his eyes. Instead of detouring onto the 395 interstate, as the cab had, he followed the parkway up to the JFK Opera House, as she'd intended. The opera house was closed.

"That's odd." He got out of the truck and walked around it. He checked the sign showing hours of operation. Something about everything felt wrong.

"Where would the shooters be?" Bishop wondered. "No book depository, no grassy knoll, where's her metaphor?"

It was getting dark. He walked the late evening streets, passing a few beggars on his way to the Watergate Complex. He saw a homeless woman, stoned out of her mind, watching the stars, and stumbling around.

"The car was bulletproof, so a shooter would be pointless. She didn't shoot me, so how did she plan to kill me? Hmm, she wanted me to go the same way Boyacobas did. Yuk. So the opera house was just a rendezvous point. She missed it." Bishop kept searching and talking to himself. "Cabs aren't bulletproof, and cabs won't drive their passengers into danger. So it wasn't a cab. Lotus pulled a switch. That's why nothing happened when she ripped out the paneling. He didn't want her to escape- just dead. Can't say I blame him after meeting her."

Bishop walked back to the truck, mumbling to himself: "But he knew I was with her. Did he want me to save her, or perhaps kill her myself? Regardless, whomever she was planning on meeting either had to be tricked as well or killed!"

When he saw the beggar again, he got an idea. He hopped into the truck, drove north a few blocks, and turned onto Highway 29. He parked, taking up several spots in front of the Fats Domino Pool Hall.

He walked in and wandered around until he found the man he was looking for. As Bishop approached, the man leaned over a pool table, prepping his next shot. "Logical?" Bishop said.

"Where were you man, I waited for you. Tardiness. Not a good look." Logical tried his shot and missed. He straightened up and looked Bishop over. "What happened to your clothes? Got a little dusty."

"Long story. So I see the money I gave you is going to good use." Bishop nodded to a stack of cash on the corner of the pool table.

"This is called 'investing,'" said Logical. "Besides my li'l man is all right. His doctor bills are paid. Since when do you fall up in the Fat?"

"Since I got desperate for information. Did a truck go by here earlier today?"

Logical laughed. "A... truck."

"Big... maybe a tow truck or a big rig? Anything out of the ordinary."

A player at the adjacent table spoke up. The speaker, Vigil Anan, wore a black beret. His big ears framed puffy cheeks and a wild beard. "You mean the hearse? Two girls were in it. They shot that car up good."

Logical eyed the man suspiciously, but Bishop asked, "They shot up a hearse?"

"Yup," Vigil confirmed. Others nodded in agreement. "That's why the Opera House is closed now."

Kyra planned to stuff me in a casket and push me into a shredder? "Classy girl," Bishop muttered under his breath.

"What you say there?"

Bishop spoke up. "Did you see the shooters? Where they went? Any video? Anything?"

"You a cop?"

"No!"

"Reporter?" Vigil asked.

Logical spoke up: "He's on parole, and Senator Donald wants him dead."

Vigil spoke up: "In that case, I followed their asses, and I know where they are. But information ain't free."

"This is a matter of life of death," Bishop insisted.

"Don't listen to him, Bishop. He's just trying to hustle you," Logical warned.

"A lot more people are gonna die if I don't track them down," Bishop said.

"Tell you what," Vigil said, clearing the pool table. "One ball. One shot. You shoot the 8 up the table and get it into right corner pocket behind it. Whoever misses loses, whoever does it in fewer bounces wins. If you win, I tell you what you wanna know."

"Okay!" Bishop agreed, grabbing a stick. When he looked at the table, Vigil was laying down five thousand.

"Wait a minute..." Bishop said, "I don't have that kinda money."

"Oh?" Vigil shrugged. "I guess I don't know anything."

Logical fronted Bishop the cash, saying, "Don't say I didn't warn you."

Vigil smiled, leaned over, and hit the 8 off the front side wall. It bounced three times before rolling down into the right corner pocket behind them.

"Beautiful," Vigil smiled. "You go."

Bishop set up the shot, double-checked his angle, and hit it off the front wall. It bounced twice before rolling down into the right corner pocket behind them.

"I win." Bishop said, "Now where'd they go?"

Vigil didn't answer. Bishop looked at Logical, who just shook his head.

"Rules of the hall. The game isn't over until the loser gives up," Vigil chuckled, and put another ten grand on the table, "Unless you want to reneg your winnings?"

Logical fronted Bishop the cash. Bishop leaned back to Logical, asking, "What if I purposefully lose?"

"Then you owe me fifteen grand," Logical demanded, "And you figure another way to find out where the shooter went. You aren't fighting in the cage, B.K. In the pool hall, we don't fight with gloves."

Vigil leaned over, picked his shot, and got the corner pocket behind him in one.

Bishop asked Logical, "Are his pockets deep?"

"Real deep, I saw him lose to a cat named Duke for six hours. Vigil continually upped the bet the more he lost until he came back and beat the pants off the guy. Duke lost a hundred grand that night. I'm not front you a hundred g's."

"Is he a trick shot?"

"I don't know him like that," Logical shrugged, "Damn, he hit it in one. You can't hit it in two, or you lose. If you hit it in one like he did, then we have to raise the stakes to stay in the game."

"Then it becomes a game of whoever misses first? Winner takes all?"

"Unless you keep raising the stakes. Yeah."

Bishop chalked up the stick and leaned over for his shot. His bottom teeth grazed his top lip. He stood up and reassessed.

"Don't over think it," Vigil suggested, with a smile.

"What's to over think?" Bishop asked, taking his position again. "It's just math."

Bishop hit the 8 at an angle, and the ball went forward, spinning, and rolled backward into the corner pocket behind him. The spectators chuckled.

"I win," Bishop told Vigil, again.

"So we are doing trick shots, now?" Vigil chuckled. "Is that the game?"

"I got lucky."

"Lucky?" Vigil hid his feelings behind his dark eyes. "You couldn't make that shot again in million years.

"Wanna bet?"

"That's a bet!" Vigil charged, but the spectators all got to their feet when he said that. Vigil looked around at the tense mob and fell silent.

"You didn't do your shot," said one man. "Either you sink it in zero or raise the stakes. Can't change the game in mid-stroke." His friends shook their heads in disapproval.

Vigil set up his shot, leaned in, and hit the 8 ball at an angle. The ball spun forward then curved off wildly to the right and bounced off the wall. It came to a stop on the lower half of the table.

The spectators collected the thirty grand and gave it to Bishop. He handed the wad to Logical. "Every cage has rules," he told him.

Bishop turned to Vigil, who said, "Yeah, I followed the shooters up to the Waterfront power planet."

Bishop thought aloud, "Power plant? You mean on South Capitol?"

"No, the dam," Vigil corrected him.

"Dam?" Bishop asked, "There's no..."

"On the river, just...just go up Canal." Vigil pointed Bishop toward the riverfront. "You can't miss it. Snake Island."

"I didn't realize there was a dam."

"How long have you lived here, and you don't know about the dam? It's powering most of the neighboring cities."

Bishop put the ball back on the table. He eyed the ball. "That's a lot of power to come from one small dam."

"The states along the Potomac agreed to increase the river's energy generation capacity immensely when they reengineered the river," Vigil explained

"Sounds dangerous and silly. Why would they ever do that?" Bishop asked, and sunk the ball behind, as he had before.

"Clean Energy America," Vigil shrugged.

Bishop looked at Logical and gasped, "Senator Donald?"

Bishop left the pool hall troubled. He hopped back in the cargo truck and took it up Canal. That's when the pulsating power of the plants he'd found in Khartoum tingled his skin. He drove off the road and closer to the river's edge to hop out and walk down the embankment across from the moon's reflection on the water. Islands dotted the river.

"Oh no," Bishop said. The dam blocked the river upstream, but down where Bishop was, there were many tiny islands near the bank. He saw the transparent leaves reflecting the light all along the shore. "Power plants!"

He hopped back in the truck and headed north. He found Snake Island and parked nearby. He walked through the trees, toward the embankment, to get a look at the dam.

"Lotus sowed the entire Potomac island chain with power plants," Bishop said to himself. "He could send power throughout the whole city,"

As he walked around Snake Island, he felt a different sensation. He saw a blinking light and crouched down. He thought it strange until he realized the glow came from land mines all over Snake Island.

The last glow of sunlight disappeared and the night came.

The sound of a firecracker echoed across the water. Trees rustled nearby. He dropped to the ground as a bullet tore the bark off the tree next to him. As the shooter kept firing, Bishop moved through the thicket. He stepped on a pressure plate. It activated.

"Don't move!" A voice came from high in the trees.

He found himself standing in a sea of red dots. He'd activated an entire minefield. He started to turn.

"I said don't move!" The voice had a sickly foreign accent. Bishop couldn't place it.

"Senator Donald?" Bishop shouted, but there was no answer. "Lotus?"

"No Lotus. No you. No nothing. Don't move!"

The words didn't make sense. Bishop saw the spread of land mines connected by charges.

"Domino effect... to... to what? To the dam? You will flood the city," Bishop reasoned. Looking around for his stalker, and mumbling to himself. "Prevent any military advancement. No aid to the people. No rescue. No rebuilding. No stable government."

"Yes. Just... to die," The voice said, getting closer. It wasn't a man, and it wasn't human. "Die. Not too early! To die on time!"

"Senator! You built this right under their noses. I won't let you do this!" Bishop shouted. "You won't break this city!"

"Die," the voice repeated.

Bishop couldn't see the shooter. He extended a field and felt a large rock. Bishop spread his field wider and felt the shooter in the tree—bigger than an ordinary man, or any human for that matter. It moved toward him.

That is not Senator Donald.

Bishop shifted the large rock, using it to replace his weight on the pressure plate.

As he did, the one from the trees—Jain—attacked. Bishop stumbled back and tripped on a land mine. The mine popped into the air and exploded. Bishop shielded himself from the blast and heat. The echo rang across water and land. Had he triggered the dominoes? No. Everything went quiet.

Jain attacked with two kicks, and a thrust of her dagger. She spun with her tail and came down with open claws and jaws.

Bishop ate the first kick so he could get his footing. He slipped her second kick, blocked her dagger, and made a shield as she attacked with her tail. Moving from her claw strike, he flew back, avoiding her jaws. She leapt after him.

Bishop flew up into a tree, but Jain scaled it. As she pounced, he met her, kicking her face. As she took another swipe at him, he leapt out of the tree. He descended, reaching his hands out, and using the field to grab Jain. She hit the ground as he floated in midair.

When Jain jumped up at him, he kneed her in the face, elbowed her in the jaw, and caught her with a roundhouse kick. Jain's head snapped back. As she clung to the trunk with one arm, her sniper rifle fell to the ground. When she regained her bearings, she pulled herself onto a branch. Bishop balanced on the branch in front of her.

She had a foot-and-a-half on him, but as she raised a clawed foot, he grabbed it. Jain cut him across the chest with her dagger. She thrust twice more, and he slipped down to get on the inside. A spherical shock wave burst from him, blasting her away. Tree bark flew, as Jain tumbled into the darkness.

Bishop eased down off the tree and landed softly. He listened. A rustle started on his left, then moved behind him. His chest wound closed.

Jain attacked from behind. He turned, extending his arm, and the shockwave blasted her back. He jumped at her, but she went higher. She skipped through the minefield, with Bishop on her heels. He summoned up two mines, but she jumped high to avoid the blast. He leapt, kicked her twice, clinched her from behind, and threw her to the ground while creating a shock wave. She hit the ground but jumped away from the shock wave. Bishop flew at her, clinching her neck. He flipped around and slammed her to the ground. She swung at him with a dagger. He kicked her arm, grabbed her knife, and stabbed her in the leg. She roared, and her jaws opened to bite him. Bishop summoned a mine into her mouth and flew away. When her jaws snapped shut, the mine exploded.

Bishop returned to the body and stared at what was left.

"What is that?" he wondered.

Everything was dark and quiet. He exhaled, then sat on the ground trying to stomach the answers to impossible questions. The mines posed an easier solution: He pulled them up. This took most of the night, and as the night sky gave way to light in the east, he brought the cargo truck around and loaded it with the land mines.

After the island had been cleared, he returned to what was left of Jain's charred lower body. A beeping noise came from her wounded leg. He found a communicator strapped to one of the holsters. Bishop opened it. "Lotus!"

Bishop ran to the truck and sped south to Capitol Hill. He got out and started walking to relieve his anger.

Lotus stood near the Capitol. He opened his arms as if to embrace an old friend. He held Boyacobas's tablet. A stiff wind blew. As Bishop approached, Lotus could feel his ears popping. He smiled and held his hand out. Bishop shook his head.

"You knew this was coming," Bishop started. He raised his arm. Lotus felt pressure on his spine, and Bishop told him, "Today you'll learn the true meaning of hate."

Lotus lifted Boyacobas's tablet. "I mean," he started. "Would you really kill me? That would make you just like me, and could you stomach that? After all, Kyra put a gun to your head, and you didn't kill her."

"What is that?" Bishop demanded, looking at the tablet.

"If you'd just let her die, life would be better for us both," Lotus said.

"Kyra? What were you thinking? You tried to get her crushed in a metal shredder!"

"Didn't bother you when it happened to Boyacobas," Lotus countered. "Look at you saving Kyra—like you're a hero!" Lotus writhed from the pressure on his neck. "You aren't a hero! Not to her!"

"She is hell bent on getting revenge. Why does she think I killed Boyacobas?" Bishop scoffed. "Give me the tablet."

"I mean, it was a good kill. Damn good kill. You should take the credit. You're a killer, just like me, and every other Earthling. You have blood on your hands and Boyacobas knew it."

"I don't even know where to begin with you. Cults, murders, Nicole!"

"Kyra knew about the flight. Is that why you couldn't let her die? Cuz you figure you might have to kill me, and she'd be the only one who'd give you closure? She hates you more than I do... and-"

"How did she die?" Bishop demanded.

"Which one?"

"Nicole!"

"Better than I will, I expect."

Bishop's rage sent a shock wave at the Capitol gates, bending them. "You have no remorse!" he shouted.

"You want me to cry for them, and yet where were they when the bodies were rotting on Mars?"

"Wha...?" Bishop's mind reeled at this logic. "Mars? I was 14! Mars was a - what are you talking about?" Bishop demanded, "I was too young to even understand what happened. You were too young!"

"I wasn't too young to watch it happen!"

Bishop covered his mouth.

"What? You think all the Martians are supposed to be dead?" Lotus held his arms out wide, "Well they missed one. Hell, they missed six!"

"You're all Martian?"

"I sure as hell ain't an Earthling," said Lotus.

"No... no, this can't be."

"And neither is that Reptilite you just killed. I may not be strong enough to exact my revenge... but they are."

"This is all revenge for Hellas Basin?" Bishop wondered. "Lotus, it wasn't just you that got hurt, we hurt ourselves, the entire human race hurt with what they did. Laws had to change. That wasn't out of hate, Lotus..."

"Yes, it was!"

"It was out of ignorance..."

"People hate what's different!" Lotus screamed. "You hate me! How does revenge feel? You came for the justice that pours from every drop of my blood. There was no limit your anger from the loss of your wife. Is there a limit to the vengeance you would seek if your whole planet was executed?"

Suddenly Bishop wanted to ease his enemy's pain.

"Give me the tablet," Bishop pleaded. "You kept this a secret for so long. Don't give in to revenge. Your plan crosses every line of reason. There are aliens-"

"When you stormed down here to kill me, was that revenge?" Lotus asked. "What would humans do if they suddenly realized they'd come from another planet? How hard would they fight to reclaim their rightful home? Would they let anyone stop them from reaching the holy land?"

Bishop felt his anger draining into sadness. "Is that what the Reptilites want?"

Lotus laughed, "That's what I want!"

"Lotus..."

"*You knew this was coming,*" Lotus mocked, "*Today you'll learn the true meaning of hate.*"

With that, balls of energy blasted from the sky, tearing up ground. Bishop shielded himself. The wind gusted, and Kalet landed hard behind Lotus. Her golden brown wings padded her landing. Her glorious feathers wrapped Lotus, and she held him in her arms. Her yellow-black hawk-like eyes peered at Bishop, as he watched in awe. Spreading her wings, she flew off on a gust of wind, taking Lotus and the tablet with her.

That's when Bishop heard something he didn't expect: a million wings beating chaotically, like a storm of locusts. Bishop turned to the rising sun and saw drone insects coming in like a dark fog. Bishop watched as they dropped from the sky, and burrowed into the ground.

"Drones," Bishop said, "Insect drones. *Zahra!*"

The ground shook.

The Capitol crumbled, the ground rumbled, and debris flew everywhere. Whenever Bishop tried to stand, he fell. Tremors led to a spreading line of explosions. The drones fed off the pulsating power of the plants.

As more drones sunk into the ground, they gained more power from the plants bringing more shockwaves and quakes. The people of Washington woke to find Earth was rejecting her children. Powerful shocks crushed cars, broke limbs, toppled buildings, and killed people.

Bishop levitated to keep from being thrown about. His mind raced. "The flowers give them power." Bishop flew north to Snake Island. He recalled how he'd disrupted the leaves from transmitting while in the cave. Now, he tried to divert power from the plants lining the riverbank.

"I have to short these plants out!" Bishop looked far ahead and realized the magnitude of the task. He pulled water on top of a power plant, shorting them out one at a time. "So many!"

The insect drones gorged on the complex power array. The ground shook. Waves built in the river. The Sudan had been a test for this. He kept hearing Jain's broken English: "Die on time."

"The dam!" He thought, and bit his lip trying to shake the conclusion. "If I don't stop these plants, this quake will continue until there is nothing left of the coast."

He landed at the base of the dam, and could feel the quake's impact gaining strength. The more drones, the more the shock grew. He raised his arms, balled his hands, and pulled in his elbows. The dam crumbled, unleashing the deluge.

Bishop flew over the flood. The river consumed Snake Island and the entire island chain. As more plants drowned, the quake weakened, but the flood threatened to engulf the city. He flew ahead and stopped at a bend in the river.

He summoned cars, trucks, dirt, and anything else nearby, and built a dam. He slammed everything into the river trough, and as the waves came in, he flew off. He looked back and saw his dam failing. The waters washed it away, and everything rushed toward the city.

Bishop flew down and tried to stop it head on. The water slammed into his force field, as gravity mocked him. The river refused to cooperate. The water overtook him. Bishop tumbled inside rapids as the flood charged toward the river bend. The water burned his nostrils. His head crashed against the rock, opening a wound.

Under the water, a giant bubble burst up from a detonation. Bishop willed himself up, and out of the water. He flew ahead of it and stood on a shallow bank downstream.

Bishop summoned the cargo truck and tore it to pieces. He directed the mines to the earth around him, and dirt, trees, and other debris became his raw material for a new dam. As he packed the last of it tightly, the ground rumbled. This wasn't an earthquake. It was the waters of the Potomac rushing toward him. He flew up higher and saw the enormous deluge pouring toward his new construction. "The dam has to hold," he whispered.

He traveled upstream, and probed the ground and water, feeling what he must do. He stood on the dry riverbed, and, as the tidal wave approached, he blasted it. This time, when the water slammed into his field, it felt heavy. As the water rose up, he expanded the field. The weight of the water increased, and he began to let some seep through. Rivulets formed around his feet, and soon he was standing in a few inches of water. As the water rose, he lifted above it and hovered higher and higher. The water level rose until it reached the top of his dam. He let go. The dam held.

Settling back on the ground, he watched a graceful waterfall that he'd created. He surveyed the destruction around him. The drone insects were still flying in, but without the power plants, they had little effect. Bishop stole another truck and sped off. When he got settled on the road, he made a call. Adrian didn't pick up.

Bishop drove through broken streets and stopped at the Anacostia. The bridge was out. Pieces of highway protruded from the waters. Witnessing what had happened to Lotus had spiritually drained him. He felt ashamed for not doing enough, though he wasn't sure what he might have done. He searched his mind for reasons. The Hallas Basin incident had nothing to do with him and simply wasn't enough. The deaths in these earthquakes were terrible, yet Bishop felt no guilt for them. What he felt was a deep regret that he'd wanted to kill Lotus. Bishop thought that if he'd had the same experience, he might have leveled a planet, but he hoped and prayed that Lotus's level of evil and hatred could never exist in his own heart.

Bishop flew across the Anacostia and landed at a private therapist's office. He ran around the building and saw Liza's car. He went into the office.

Her receptionist was on the floor picking up books and plaques. She turned to say, "We're closed..." her voice trailed off. She saw Bishop, covered with dirt and debris, running past her.

When Liza saw him, she put her hand to her mouth and uttered: "Oh my God." She waved Bishop into her office. "Oh my God. What was that?" she asked when she closed her door.

"Where's Zahra?" Bishop asked.

"Right here," Liza pointed. Zahra ran at him wearing jeans and a sweater, but Liza stopped her. "Bishop! I just bought her new clothes! You're soaked and filthy. Take a shower. I'll get you a box of fresh clothes. Then you can hold her."

Bishop's followed her and went into the bathroom to shower. Liza phoned someone who agreed to bring a box of fresh clothes.

"I'm sure we can fix what happened," Liza called to him as he showered.

"We can't fix anything. We built this mess!" Bishop replied.

"Lotus made it," she insisted.

"And we made Lotus!" Bishop said, lathering his hair. "He's a Martian!"

"What?"

"We built our extinction."

"Oh no, no no..." Liza said. "That's why he's so... so disconnected!"

"Did you hear what I said? His actions aren't just about killing people; he's helping aliens kill the human race!"

"Aliens?" Liza questioned. "You mean... immigrants from out of this country or out of this world?"

"The ones from other planets," he said.

"Why would aliens come here?"

"Why would armies march thousands of miles to Jerusalem?"

"But this doesn't look like a crusade."

Bishop stepped out of the shower and put a towel around his waist. "Who rules the Earth?"

"I guess, you could say that humans do."

"Who else?"

"What?"

"We rule it now. Who else ruled the Earth?"

"What do you mean?"

"65 million years ago it was dinosaurs, but then something big happened. All we seem to know about it is that the dinosaurs were suddenly gone. Where did they go? And what happens when, after 65 million years of breeding, and evolution, they want their planet back? Hmm?"

Liza looked at him quizzically. "Dinosaurs?"

"I love dinosaurs!" Zahra shouted from watching a show on a tablet.

"Not just dinosaurs, but something much more advanced," Bishop said, drying his face and hair. "And as long as we're talking about claims, what happens when the Martians we left for dead, want their home back?"

At first, she had no response. Finally, she asked, "Where's Mason?"

Bishop stared out the window, not hearing her. "I enabled him," he breathed.

"Stop it!" Liza said, "Don't you dare go down that path. He has to be stopped. For goodness sakes! Where's Mason?"

Bishop watched a commercial drone fly by. "It's too late. With my own eyes, I looked at a beast fly down and whisked him away. It's too late; they're already here."

The secretary buzzed, and Liza retrieved the box of clothes. Bishop got dressed.

"So the Six have been alive this entire time?" Liza asked.

Bishop nodded.

"And Mason's been... oh no."

"Seems that way," Bishop added, sadly.

"She's the one in the most danger," said Liza. "If they no longer need her, she's dead. I'm calling Sing again. We need to find Mason, now."

BISHOP SUMMONED A cab and left the office with Zahra. He checked the backlog of messages on his phone. There were texts from Adrian about the overwhelming volume of patients. Bishop directed the cab back to Sherwood Forest, stopping at 34th Street. There he watched the Petersons in their front yard. The yards were full of debris with decimated shrubs and grass. The Petersons were outside with their neighbors. He wasn't surprised to see Jacqueline talking animatedly, her gestures contributing as much to the story as her words.

Bishop hugged Zahra close. A smile crept onto his face. Then someone tapped on the opposite window. He rolled it down.

"Step out of the cab, Kennedy," Officer Wilson said.

Bishop sighed and balled his fist. "This is not the time."

"I'm not going to tell you again," Wilson commanded.

Bishop took a deep breath, looked down at Zahra, and relented. When Bishop stepped down, Wilson saw Zahra and shook his head.

"You are full of surprises. Where'd you get the girl? She's not yours."

"How do you know she isn't?" Bishop countered. "Been spying on me?"

"I've been doing more than spying on you, I've dug so deep into your life, I feel like you're my ex-wife," Wilson told him.

"Dig all you want. I got nothing to hide," Bishop replied, adjusting the infant in his grasp.

"You got a lot to hide, and you know it," Wilson growled. "Ya know, you got me good. I'm here trying to figure out the connection between you and the Petersons. You're a smart guy. You didn't just pick a random neighborhood, throw a stone, and decide to watch some people did you? They don't even know you. I checked every possible lead I could. There was nothing, no connection whatsoever."

"Then you should let it go," Bishop recommended.

"I'm talking!" Wilson shouted. Zahra barely seemed to hear him. "I didn't let it go. The answer was staring me in the face the whole time. The connection wasn't yours, it was your friend, Dr. Blackwell, and the Petersons, right? Ole Jackie there was born with a congenital heart defect. That has to be a bull's eye to any medical student trying to stake his claim. No amount of nanomites is gonna repair that, and you'd have to be a lucky sonofabitch to get an organ clone to work."

Bishop leaned back against the cab and let Wilson go on.

"How many hearts did Jackie miss out on? How close did she come to dying a painful death? But she got lucky, didn't she? She finally got an organ donor, and Resident Adrian Blackwell performed the lifesaving surgery."

"Officer..." Bishop's face flushed with the embarrassment of truth.

"I know this girl isn't yours because the only woman who loved you is dead, and that isn't her child," Wilson continued. "Not since your wife died on that same flight, I'd say you got it just as good as you gave. Nicole died when Flight 522 went down, but the crash isn't what killed her. Somehow she got off that plane."

Bishop listened carefully as Wilson went on.

"You didn't know that, did you? Adrian never told you the whole story, and he didn't need to because nobody ever saw the body. When rescue workers found her, they immediately tried to revive her. Her heart was as strong as a freight train, but she was brain dead from the impact the ground. They couldn't revive her, so they did the next best thing- and that's how Jacqueline got herself a new heart."

Bishop's knees went weak.

George shook his head, "When you found out Jackie had Nicole's heart, you couldn't let it go."

"Every time I see Jacqueline, I feel happy," Bishop said hurtfully. "I see Nicole's life force in action, and know she's safe."

"Because her heart belongs to you, always, right?" Wilson said. "As much as that story breaks my heart, I told you, if I caught you here again I'd bust your ass. Now get in the car."

"You don't want to do this with me."

"Get in the damn car!"

Bishop hesitated, but something was different in the officer's eyes. There was a pain seeping through his demeanor. Bishop walked to the front of the patrol car. He hopped in the passenger seat and secured Zahra.

"Where's your partner?" Bishop asked, but George didn't respond.

They rode in silence until they reached the outskirts of the city. Wilson turned left into a long driveway and passed a sign: Istrouma Cemetery. He parked, and said, "Let's go."

Bishop followed Wilson through the graves until they came to a simple headstone. It hurt Bishop to look down, but Wilson forced him to do it.

"This is Nicole," Wilson told him, pointing to her gravestone.

Bishop dropped to his knees, hugging Zahra. He reached down and touched the earth. "She's cold," he cried, and his tears fell on the soil.

"Bishop, you're a smart man. I've been doing this for 13 years. I've seen perfectly healthy people break down and go crazy over stuff like this. You think you're rational now, and day-to-day it might be true, but sooner or later, you're gonna lose a grip on reality. When that happens you won't be able to tell Jacqueline from Nicole."

"It's so cold."

"If you want to say something to Nicole you have to do it here."

Bishop looked up. "But... her heart doesn't beat here!"

"You're losing touch with reality, Kennedy! You're gonna hurt someone. You keep obsessing over that physical heart, and you're gonna blur that line so badly..." Wilson shook his head. "People die all the time. The families of the victims of that flight had to deal with it like everyone else. You think you can cheat, and connect with someone else to save yourself the grief? Nah, it doesn't work that way. You need to learn how to deal with the loss. You need to understand she was laid to rest for a reason. Let her rest. You created the evil that caused it, and you don't want to deal with the fact that you hurt a lot of people- even yourself."

"I created the evil that killed her," Bishop admitted, "But I wasn't the only one."

"Jacqueline Peterson isn't the woman you fell in love with," George insisted. "She isn't your wife. You can't see the Petersons anymore."

Bishop stared at the ground. "In death, you still manage to save a life." He stood up slowly. He looked at Wilson, and said, "Nicole's gone; I know that. It hurts, but in time, I'll learn to deal with it."

Wilson walked back toward the car. Once he was gone, Bishop broke down. He looked at the grave. "I lost it," he whispered. "When you died I lost everything. I lost my nerve- my edge. I lost my life." He felt the rustle of the breeze. "Lotus got to me. He broke me. We broke him too. I just... I just wanted peace, because I didn't want to lose everything that I had. And he just wanted war, because he had nothing left to lose."

He looked down at Zahra and finally cracked a smile. "No one can steal the happy memories."

He stood up. Though the day was beginning, the sun did not shine. A stiff autumn breeze touched the cold part of him. He knelt back down and felt the pain growing. He understood.

Bishop settled on the ground for a moment, then bent, and kissed the earth itself. Her heart would always be with him, and in time, his heart would find a home.

Bishop exited the Istrouma Cemetery on foot and flagged a cab. Before climbing in, he looked up toward the east. There the sky was dark; then the clouds seemed to split open. Droves of military drones took to the air. Far above, in the upper atmosphere of Earth, alien battleships entered the Earth's atmosphere.

Roaster

ADRIAN COMPLETED THE long and innovative surgery on Dimycles. The procedure had exhausted him. Simply doing the operation had left him open to constant questions. There were ethical challenges, legal hurdles, and almost two days without sleep. When surgery was completed, and Dimycles was safely in his hospital bed, Adrian stood, looking down at the sleeping patient.

"I can't help you anymore. Four nurses and a police officer died in the hospital. Inside your room! I can't keep the cops out now." Adrian let out a long yawn and rasped: "They can do whatever they want. If you think what they did to you at the Seson Midway was horrible, just wait till they get their hands on you now that they know you aren't human."

Dimycles inhaled softly, then let it out in a quick puff, like an escaping dream.

"They're going to cut you into pieces, and all the work I did on you will go to waste. Hmm?"

Dimycles didn't stir.

Adrian shouted, "Wake up!" but got no response.

After a quick knock, a nurse stuck her head in the door.

"Yes?" Adrian said, rubbing his eyes.

"Hi, um, a lady's here, in the ER, demanding to see you," said the nurse.

Adrian waved her off, "I really can't. I'm off for the day. For the week in fact."

"She's stable, but she has bruising and some deep lacerations where bullets grazed her." As the nurse continued, Adrian's ears perked up. "But she's also belligerent, going on and on about crazy stuff... and I think I might have to report something to the police."

"Like what?" Adrian asked.

"Paranoid stuff about terrorism. She says people tried to kill her, and she won't speak to anyone but you."

"Where is she," Adrian asked, starting for the door.

"Bed 18."

Adrian went to the ward at the end of the corridor and headed for Bed 18. As he stepped behind the privacy curtain, he found the woman the nurse had described.

"Get out!" he demanded.

Kyra sat up and stared at him.

"What are you doing here?" Adrian demanded.

"I'm hurt, Doctor. Fix me," she insisted.

"I'm not touching you."

Though her face was wild, her manner was calmer than he'd expected. "America's good doctor refusing a patient?" she asked in a voice dipped in sarcasm. "I can't be as bad as the last one. Where are those ethics you preach to the media?"

Adrian felt numb as he reluctantly read her paperwork. He lifted her gown, exposing a shrapnel wound in her calf.

"Your friend is a psychopath!" Kyra snapped, her voice rising. She was still just a step away from hysteria.

"Don't talk to me," he threatened, looking closely at the area around the wound.

"But you have to understand that: he's truly crazy. You should have seen him. He just sat there in a car as it was being crushed. He barely moved! Who does that?"

Adrian took her blood pressure and examined her vitals.

"When a bunch of armed men surrounded us, he just left me," she continued. "Walked out. With a child in his arms. What the fuck! Don't you have to call CPS for men like him? He can't be around kids. That child isn't safe!"

Underneath the tattoos on Kyra's arms, Adrian found old track marks from needle injections. He lightly touched the area. "Histone deacetylase inhibitors. Powerful drugs. Do they help you forget the people you've killed?"

Kyra looked at the tracks. "My wild teenage life… so long ago I don't even remember."

"Some of those look fresh."

"So what? Am I paying you to treat me or to judge me?"

"Are these from before or after you started killing people?" he asked, waving at the needle marks, as he probed her wound. The nurse had left a set of sterilized instruments at the foot of her bed.

"Why do you care? You told me not to talk to you."

Adrian spoke as he removed shrapnel from her leg. "Is Lotus forcing you to do these things, or are you just a fucked up evil piece of shit?"

"Ow! Psycho!"

"What's your business with Bishop? He has no idea who you are."

"He does now."

"Then why are you complaining that the man you wanted to kill left you to die?" Adrian wondered.

"Because he knew I couldn't kill him." Her voice was small and distant.

"Then you should be careful who you target next time," he said, holding up a piece of twisted metal. "This shrapnel could be in your leg now, or in your heart tomorrow."

"Is that a threat?"

Adrian used a laser tool to mend her wound together. "Some scars even a tattoo won't fix."

"Don't bullshit me," said Kya, snatching his laser tool away. "He's the reason I have fresh tracks on my arms!"

"Scapegoat?"

"He killed Boyacobas!" She shouted as she swung her feet over the edge of the bed.

"Quiet," he hissed. "You're just paying the price for every life you've ruined. Why did you come to me if it pains you so much?"

"You're asking an assassin why I came?" Kyra pointed her fingers into his chest and backed away."I want Bishop to know what it feels like to lose everyone he loves."

Adrian looked down at her. "Is that why you killed Tina?"

"Tina was business," Kyra pointed the laser tool at the end of the O2 tank aim at Adrian. "You are personal."

With the laser, she shot the open end of the tank, and the tank violently shot like a rocket at Adrian, where it disappeared, and flew off somewhere into the parking lot outside of the hospital and exploded.

"Oh my god.You too?" Kyra shook her head. "What are you guys?"

"You don't want to know what I am," Adrian grimaced, unscathed.

Just then the floor began to shake.

"What are you doing? Are you doing that?" She cried, grabbing the bed frame. Everything shook. "Stop doing that! You guys are freaks!"

"I'm not doing anything," Adrian shouted. "Stay here!" He stumbled down the corridor and found Dimycles still in his bed—asleep. The shaking got worse. When Dimycles still didn't stir, Adrian stared at him, then toward Kyra's room. "Earthquake!" he breathed.

Screams filled the corridors. Everyone who could move poured out and most of them filled the stairwells. As the quake intensified, Adrian stared back at Dimycles. The ceiling broke apart over the bed. Adrian grabbed the bed just as the roof caved in. Amid plaster and dust, Adrian disappeared.

He reappeared outside of the hospital, Dimycles and the bed in front of him. He pushed the bed into a parking lot. People were falling over themselves. The ground rocked, and threw many to the ground. Adrian looked toward Capitol Hill, but all he saw were smoke and dust.

"What's going on?" Adrian asked himself.

Screaming people rushed out the hospital doors. Adrian teleported to Kyra's room, but she was gone. Nurses were hurrying patients out of the hospital. Adrian helped.

"What kind of earthquake lasts this long?" he wondered, but he knew the answer. "Lotus?" He questioned under his breath.

As Adrian searched for trapped survivors, he saw nurses carrying infants out of the building. He teleported to the nursery and saw several parents trying to get to the incubators. Two nurses stood in their way, trying to keep them back. The shocks hit harder.

Adrian stepped in, and parents and nurses retreated in opposite directions. Parents fell to their knees crying. The ceiling cracked. Adrian knew there wasn't much time. He pushed the incubators together and turned to the nurse and parents. "Hold my hand!" he shouted.

The parents obeyed expecting a prayer.

As Adrian touched one of the incubators, the quake got worse.

"We're gonna make it!" Adrian shouted over the noise.

The floor cracked below them, then gave way. Light fixtures crashed down, then came huge chunks of the ceiling in a roar that silenced the screams.

Then the quake stopped.

Everyone looked up and realized they were standing outside. Adrian saw the building was still standing and went searching for Patricia. When he found her, he said: "Find me a structural engineer as fast as you can. And make sure everyone left alive is out here." He then found Spencer and told him, "Get tents set up all along the hospital ground."

Adrian found Dimycles in the lot, moved him into a tent, and then helped organize patients into groups corresponding with wards. Just as he got portable generators up and running, Patricia showed up with an engineer. The engineer carried a sledgehammer and tape. Adrian took her into the building, and they started careful exploration, marking off areas that were beyond unsafe.

As Adrian left the building, a strange man ran up, crying: "You gotta help me!" In his arms lay a little girl covered in blood.

"Patricia!" Adrian shouted, but she was nowhere nearby. "Come with me," he said.

The man followed Adrian to a tent. "Thank you so much," he sobbed. "She's all I got. My wife, she's dead. My wife's dead. She pushed me away, told me to save li'l Victoria."

Adrian checked the girl. "She's not breathing. I want a code red here!" he turned back to the girl's father. "How old is she?"

"Seven," the man coughed.

Nurses came into the tent and prepped the girl. As they escorted the father away, he kept looking back.

Adrian held his tablet over the girl's body. "Bleeding internally. We need to stop that up, fast." Most of the damage looked worse than it was. She needed attention but didn't seem critical. Then he waved the tablet over her head. There he found a dark spot he didn't like.

"Get me Patricia!" He told one of the nurses. Then to another, he said, "Find Dr. Rushani."

Adrian told the other nurses to prep the girl; then he reentered the hospital where he found Patricia.

"There you are!" Adrian said, "Follow me. Seven-year-old girl on her deathbed."

Adrian climbed over debris to the lab. His safe was still there. He punched in a code, and it opened. He pulled out a box.

"What's that?" Patricia said.

"Nanomites," Adrian said.

"I didn't know we had nanomites here." Patricia's voice filled with awe and excitement.

"All D.C hospitals have them, just in case they need them for the treatment of the President or the First Family." Adrian checked the box, then he and Patricia left the lab.

"And you're gonna use them on a seven-year-old girl?" Patricia asked.

"I'd rather not cut her head open, and risk a six-hour surgery in a tent," Adrian said. "You have issues with this?"

"Oh no. I rather like the idea of using the President's personal medical stash to save a little girl's life. I didn't vote for him."

"We need some reagents," Adrian said, handing his tablet to Patricia. "She's young; her body is pretty tiny. One of these capsules is enough to repair three men—too much for her. We need to taper them through the IV, so only a few nanomites enter her body. Then expel it from her body. Found it!"

"Where did you get this tablet?" Patricia asked, passing her fingers over the screen. "Why don't you ever pay attention to the holograms? This tablet gives you special info?"

"A friend made it for me as a keepsake." They were back outside now, walking through the tents. As Adrian saw unattended items he needed, he took them.

Patricia gazed thoughtfully at his tablet. "This may sound crazy, but I don't know any other way to take it, Everyone with prenatal babies swears something teleported them off the tenth floor."

"Sounds crazy," Adrian agreed, pairing the nanomites to his tablet.

"It was a long earthquake," she went on. "A lot happened. But these stories don't just come from nothing, right?"

"Right," Adrian agreed.

"So how did you get off the tenth floor?"

As they re-entered the girl's tent, Adrian ignored Patricia's question and gave her the nanomite capsule to put into the IV bag. They tapered just a few drops into the little girl's bloodstream, then waited for the nanomites to enter her body. It took only a few moments for his tablet to light up. Under Adrian's direction, the nanomites healed her bruises, then stopped her internal bleeding. Finally, he had the nanomites target her brain hemorrhage.

"I don't want too much activity on an underdeveloped brain. The nanomites may inadvertently try to 'fix' something that's not broken," Adrian told Patricia.

Once he saw the spot go away, he gave Patricia the go-ahead to get the reagents ready. She connected the reagent into IV bag.

"The reagents will send the nanomites to her stomach, where they'll deactivate themselves," Adrian told her. "She will probably vomit them up shortly after that, so get a bag and vacuum ready."

Patricia left as Dr. Rushani entered.

"Dr. Rushani," Adrian greeted her.

"Are you doing brain surgery?" Rushani asked.

"I'm cheating," Adrian said. "Sorry I know brain injuries are kinda your thing, but I didn't want to take the chance and wait."

"Good for you," she said. "Let me take a look."

Dr. Rushani examined the tablet.

"Nice tablet," she commended. "You always have these neat little gizmos. I need to snoop through your office and see if I can steal one."

Though Dr. Rushani spoke in jest, Kyra had already snuck back into the hospital and was looking for Adrian's office. She ducked under the restricted tape and walked along debris-strewn corridors in the dark. When she got to the office, she had to climb over chunks of the ceiling to enter. When she found his phone, it only took her a few moments to hack into it.

She tethered her phone to his and transferred his data. She then put in a bug to monitor his calls and messages. She flipped through the photos. Here was Adrian with his brother, Julius, along with their friend, Bishop. As Kyra zoomed in on Julius, she heard screams outside. She tilted her head to listen the odd commotion.

Outside the hospital, an ambulance had pulled up. Adrian and some staffers gathered around as the driver, and another EMT spilled out. Both men were nearly hysterical.

After Adrian had calmed them a little, the driver spoke: "I don't know! A man came out of nowhere, just... pow! Then he fucking threw me, and beat up Lance too!" He nodded at the bruised EMT. "Where are the police!?"

"He spoke some weird language and walked funny!" Lance added.

"Oh no!" Adrian gasped. He ran back to Dimycles's tent to find it empty. When he got back to the crowd around the ambulance, the ambulance was gone.

"He took it!" Lance screamed, nursing his busted face. "Bastard!"

"Call the police!" someone said.

"Lines are flooded," said a nurse as she worked her phone. "I keep dialing, and nothing's going through."

"Where are they?" someone cried. "We're under attack!"

Lance added, "Someone else was in that truck. We were delivering a patient. Now everything's gone."

Adrian ducked under the caution tape and pushed through to his destroyed office to collect his phone. A few minutes later he came back out, hurrying toward the parking lot. "Patricia," he shouted, "I'm gonna go talk to the authorities... see if they can get that ambulance and patient back. You have to take over."

Adrian climbed into his old car and drove away while making another call.

"Hey, Omar. Yeah, it's me," he said. "Can you track down an ambulance for me?"

Omar's voice boomed through, saying something about it being "truck 52."

"Yeah, truck 52," Adrian said. "Okay, thanks."

Adrian saw that Bishop had called. He messaged his friend while driving home. Adrian surveyed the passing city. "Bad," he said to himself. "Manmade or not, that had to be one of the longest earthquakes in history."

Adrian showered and ate, and when Omar returned his call, he left. Adrian felt he needed a much sleeker car for what was ahead. The floor in his garage slid open, and a lift brought up a gunmetal gray powerhouse. He hopped into a plush, off-white driver's seat. Once the gyroscopic cockpit calibrated, the car rolled out of his garage. He told it to go to the first point Omar had given him: a shopping center. He sped off with a roar.

A few minutes later he parked in the shopping center lot and walked toward a cluster of people. They were gathered around the patient from the ambulance.

Adrian pushed through the crowd, and asked the man: "Did he say anything to you?"

"Yeah, a lot of mumbo jumbo. I couldn't understand a word he said. Where'd he come from? I've never heard a language like that before. Is he a terrorist? I think he's a terrorist."

"Where'd he go?" Adrian asked.

"Beats me. He kicked me out of the truck, then he ran into the clothing store butt naked, and got himself some clothes. He beat up the attendants on the way out, then he ran into the parts shop over there and robbed it. Then, um, I don't know. He drove off. Where are the cops?"

"They're busy," said Adrian. "Are you okay? Why were you in the ambulance?"

"I ate some fast food, right? That place on Guada St. Ya' know that Burger Gurgle spot. I couldn't walk; I was puking and shitting so much. I thought I was gonna die…"

Adrian's next stop was the parts shop. The worker's face was wrapped in a bloody towel, but he was upright. "What happened?" Adrian asked him.

"He came in, wearing this ridiculous outfit. Then he saw my phone on my hip. He punched me in the face, grabbed my phone, then he pointed at people and pushed buttons like it was a gun. What the hell?"

"What'd he take?" Adrian asked.

"Tools. Wire. Stuff like that," the sales clerks reported, "Then he just left."

Adrian got a message from Omar: *He's heading northeast. Could be going anywhere.*

Adrian texted back: *I gotta find this guy!*

Adrian tracked his target to the outskirts of Philadelphia. Dimycles had dumped the ambulance after it ran out of fuel. Adrian hopped into the abandoned ambulance. It had been gutted.

"What's he building?" Adrian asked, examining the cracked dash. He called Omar. "This guy pulled out the GPS system and gutted the defibrillator," Adrian told him. "He used wire he got from the parts store and took several medical supplies."

"I don't know what he's doing," Omar admitted. "Maybe he's trying to find something. How much of the GPS device is left? If you get me the serial number, I can try to cross reference its address."

"What's that buy me?" Adrian asked looking around for it.

"If I know the address, I can reverse track him. That is if he's using it," Omar answered.

Adrian gave him the number.

"It's gonna take some time. There are millions of these things, and for some reason, satellites are going down. You might want to take a break in the meantime," Omar recommended.

Adrian drove into Philadelphia and checked into a motel. In his room, he drifted to sleep. He woke to a call from his brother.

"Hey. It's me. Got your message," Julius said. "Gotta head outta town."

"And 'outta town' means?" Adrian mumbled.

Julius replied, "Congo."

Adrian sighed. Though he was too exhausted to ask why, Julius told him.

"I've been data mining the CIA ever since Khartoum," said Julius. "They fronted a drug cartel a few years back, shipping product through the Congo. One day, during a shipment, they lost all contact with their carriers."

"Mm, hmm," Adrian mumbled.

"They figure it was an ambush, but the product came up on satellite still in the Congo. Near the Sudan border. So, they sent a team in to retrieve the product."

"That team goes missing?" Adrian asked, in a raspy voice.

"That team goes missing!" Julius confirmed. "So they said, fuck that. They move another team to the border and send in drones. The drones get ex-'d."

"Sounds like dinosaurs," Adrian exhaled wearily, "The Congo is teeming with clones."

"That's what they thought too. So they wrote it off, and closed the operation," Julius finished.

"So...you want to go get the drugs?" Adrian asked.

Julius paused. "I didn't think about that."

"Jules!"

"One of the operatives was ICP," Julius clarified.

"Really?"

Julius started sounding rushed as if the rhythms of his speech were being ruled by the rhythms of his motion. "I checked the roster. Kyle Saul: ICP mole in the CIA. He never checked back in."

Adrian sat up, "Dinosaurs don't usually attack people. What happened to him?"

"Nah. No, no, just hang on," Julius said, panting. "Let me finish, cuz you're bout to blow your shit. I got curious too, so I did a signal sweep of the area. Big ass jungle took forever. Found Mr. Saul lit up a distress beacon..."

"How long?"

"Hang on."

"How long!"

"Three months," Julius answered.

"Oh man, he's probably dead now! How'd they lose their own op?" Adrian wondered.

"Two reasons. They don't maintain contact with deep cover moles. So no one was looking for him there. But the biggest reason is... because... he really is dead! He's recorded as being killed in action during that mission, so no one would bother to look for his beacon!"

"I don't understand, if he's dead then who lit up the distress signal?"

"Listen to this." Julius played a message from the signal: "This is...hello?...my coord...four six... by...point five. I'm..."

"MASON!" Adrian sat straight up.

"She found his beacon and lit it! She also tampered with it. Mae didn't send a standard distress call; she encoded a video from a drone in the signaling. That's why it's so broken up. I had Omar decode it. I'll send you a clip."

Adrian stared at the blurry image of ground while speeding. Something had grabbed a drone from behind and walked with it. Adrian saw the foot and leg below the camera. It seemed to be a hybrid of human and reptile. Adrian felt awe. The creature holding the drone knelt. Another creature came out from behind a tree. It looked about like Adrian thought it would: the same species that had produced the foot and legs he'd just seen. The creature said something in an indecipherable language. Then the feed stopped, and the screen went blank.

"The fuck is that?!" Adrian screamed.

"That's what I intend to find out," Julius responded. "No one has ever cloned a dinosaur that can do that."

"Who's your team?" Adrian asked.

"I'm taking the Beaker twins," Julius said. "They're experts in tropical animals and jungle environments."

"Damn it, you need more people. If Mason's being held there, it might be a death trap."

"I don't have time for that," Julius said. "I was trapped in Germany, and the twins were the only ones available."

Adrian sighed, "How fast can you get down there?"

"I'm already in Uganda," Julius answered after a pause.

"Fucking bad idea," Adrian spat.

"Right," Julius shot back. "And you can be the one to tell Mason we couldn't get her because it wasn't convenient. Good luck chasing your naked man,"

"He's not naked!" Adrian protested.

Julius hung up.

Adrian let go a long sigh and considered what he'd just seen. As he fell into dreams, he wondered who'd taken Mason to the Congo. Then his phone rang again.

"He's about two hours away from you, northwest of Allentown," Omar revealed. "Who is this guy?"

"Who is…? The guy? Why?" Adrian shook the cobwebs away and tried to focus on what he'd heard.

"He's close to a USoFT research facility," Omar said. "That's not good. USoFT was an underground society that grew into a government weapons contractor while making weapons for the Six behind everyone's back. This could reignite a war."

"We're already at war." Adrian sprung up from the bed. "Just tell me where he is."

"I sent you the coordinates, but be careful. They'll have Roasters everywhere."

Adrian smiled big, looking himself over in the mirror. "What's a roaster?"

"Their RObotic ASsaulT MembERs," Omar told him. He heard Adrian splashing water and brushing teeth.

"Death bots?" Adrian said as he left the bathroom.

"Shit, you tell me—if you get there in time."

"Other than that, should I cure cancer while I'm doing the impossible?"

"You better fly."

Adrian hung up as he left the motel, got in his car and punched in the coordinates.

Adrian made it from Philadelphia to Sugarloaf, Pennsylvania in the ten minutes he wanted. He drove around the beautiful hills until he found the USoFT headquarters.

The visible signs of Dimycles abounded: A smashed front entry gate and a wrecked truck lying upside down. He got out of his car and walked through the destroyed entrance. There were fresh footprints in the grass leading around to the side of the facility. By the prints, he found leftover parts of the defibrillator, and the parts Dimycles stole.

"Whatever he was looking for, it must be here," Adrian guessed.

He followed the tracks around the building. Broken robot arms and robotic body parts were scattered along the way. Adrian picked up a severed robotic arm and eyed the perimeter. Lights flashed. He'd tripped an alarm. He ran up the hill and around the back.

There he is.

Dimycles stood at the back of the building's hangar. Using another robot arm, he tried to pry open the door. Then he turned and saw Adrian.

"What are you doing?" Adrian asked.

Dimycles paid him no mind and kept prying at the door. Dimycles's attire astonished Adrian, so he approached the strange man slowly.

"What's that you're wearing?" Adrian called out as he neared him. Despite his woman's blouse, sweat pants, and leather boots, Dimycles said nothing. Adrian went on: "Didn't you see a mirror? Those boots are nice. Hey, Dimycles..."

Dimycles looked at his visitor. "I can't go back. Not after what I've done."

"Listen, I'm not here to bring you in..."

"Stay out of my way!"

"Well? Where are you gonna go?" Adrian edged closer. "You hurt a lot of people, and they are all gonna blame me if you hurt anyone else."

Dimycles finally pried the door open, triggering a second alarm. He turned to address Adrian: "Then go save them."

Dimycles disappeared into the room. Adrian tried to run in after him.

Skeleton roasters poured out from everywhere, cutting him off. As two robots came at him, Adrian picked up the torn arm. He bashed one in the head, cracking its frame, then he kicked it. He broke the legs off the other, and when it fell to the ground, he stepped on its neck, severing its head from its body. A pair of robotics drew weapons and fired solid light cannons at him. He teleported behind one, took its gun and shot three more robots in front of it. As another shot at him, he teleported away. The blast tore through another robot. Adrian spun around and shot two more roasters. Three dropped off the roof, and Adrian shot them as they fell. Finally, he ran through the door after Dimycles.

Dimycles stood in front of a transparent barrier.

"Whoa," Adrian gasped at a space ship.

Dimycles heard the rumblings of more robots and ran to the stairwell. Tank-like machines rolled around the corners and passed in front of the wall. Dimycles ran up the stairs, and skeleton roasters chased him. He grabbed them and beat the parts out of them. He then used the parts to beat the others. He ran up two flights, entering each floor to see what might be coming. When he reached the eighth floor, he kicked down a door and found nothing. He felt a shock to his side as another roaster shot him with a stun gun. Dimycles took the gun and stomped the robot until it didn't move. On the tenth floor, he kicked in the door to a conference room, where board members had huddled together. When he aimed his stun gun at one man, a roaster tackled him. Dimycles accidentally shot the chairwoman. She fell to the floor unconscious. Wide-eyed with shock, he shoved aside the machines, grabbed the chairwoman and threw her over his shoulder. Before leaving the room, he turned around and shot the man he'd originally intended.

Dimycles ran through the halls and found an elevator. As he pressed the "Down" button, skeletons surrounded him. They didn't attack. He realized they wouldn't shoot him as long as he had the chairwoman over his shoulder.

The robots did not extend Adrian the same courtesy.

Adrian teleported outside and maneuvered between groups of seven. When one shot at him, Adrian spun around to disarm it, but the gun stayed locked to its appendage. Adrian jumped up, put both legs to its chest, and tore its arm off. He sprayed shots everywhere, then leapt over the broken bodies and ran behind the building. When the robots gave chase, he suddenly appeared behind them, still shooting. When they turned, he vanished and flanked them. He nailed the roasters from the side until his blaster ran out of juice. He spun and smashed another with the butt of the gun.

His assailants recalibrated, and adopted a multiple-attack strategy. The heavier tanks engaged, while the skeletons fell back. Two tanks crashed through the wall, shooting missiles. Adrian teleported to the top of a tank and held on. The tank turned translucent, then teleported, reappearing up in the air. Adrian dropped it so that it would land facing the other tank. Adrian teleported to the rooftop. The two tanks collided. Waves of roasters chased him onto the roof. Adrian jumped off the building, grabbing robots in mid-air, and pulling them to the ground. Before they hit, he'd teleported back to the rooftop.

When the elevator doors opened for Dimycles, he didn't enter the car. He looked into the empty elevator and felt chills. He'd felt this sensation in the Martian prison, Peering into the elevator he saw the darkness of the Seson, and the eerie lift at the end of the hall. That lift only led to two things: torture or death. There, in USoFT, the elevator's open door beckoned, but Dimycles turned and took the stairs.

A flood of robotic guards secured the rooftop. They were constantly recalibrating, unsure of the number of targets. A few recorded malfunctions and shut themselves down for maintenance. Adrian appeared. He cracked one's leg shell. They turned to shoot. He disappeared. He stood on top of another, twisting its head off. As they all fired at the headless Roaster, Adrian stole another blaster. When two others shot at him, he was suddenly behind them. Their blasts hit two other roasters. When they failed to lock onto to him, Adrian ran across the roof until he was over the hangar. He teleported down into it.

He halted when he saw the spaceship. Its black material was contoured in bubbly wave patterns.

"Incredible," he said, lightly touching the surface.

It was a medium-sized ship, shaped like fat stubby X lying face down. At the intersection of the X were gun turrets. The legs of the X were lined with thrusters. The ship had no discernable up or down orientation. Everything looked perfectly symmetrical from all four axes.

The whole thing felt surreal. As Adrian studied the ship, he saw Dimycles on the other side of the barrier. He was horrified to see a woman slung over Dimycles's shoulder. All his work had saved this criminal to do more damage. Adrian burned at the thought. He'd often defended those like Dimycles as people who had gotten bad breaks, and been misunderstood. But here was Dimycles, using this poor woman's hand to gain him access to the inside of the enclosure.

"Not again," Adrian muttered.

At the bottom of one leg, a ramp automatically extended out for Dimycles. As Dimycles carried the woman onto the ship, Adrian ran to the ramp. Despite Adrian's shouts, the ramp retracted and the doors closed. Adrian closed his eyes and teleported inside. The ship boasted a spacious, but plainly decorated interior. Different rooms lined the outer boundaries, with stairs and open space in between.

At first, Adrian was confused. When he heard Dimycles's footsteps coming from the upper levels, Adrian ran up the nearest stairs. He saw the woman lying on the floor, unconscious. Dimycles powered up the ship and then turned, and pointed his gun at Adrian.

"Hey!" Adrian protested, raising his hands.

"You don't belong here," Dimycles said.

"Neither do you, but here you are. So let's start with what we don't know..."

"You don't know anything," Dimycles argued, as he toggled the ship's controls. "You can't even comprehend what's happening. Your mind is still trying to grasp the concepts of good, and evil. There is no good; there is no evil - only self-interest."

"What about her?" Adrian pointed to the woman. "What about her self-interest? And what about me? I'm the one who took those nasty things out of your back. You aren't doing me any favors! I stand culpable for your actions because I saved you when everyone wanted you to die! How does that sound for my self-interest? Why don't you give me a chance? This isn't how we do things here. Now that we can talk to each other let's work with each other."

"What's good for the State, is not good for me," Dimycles told him, lowering the gun. "Why would you save a monster like myself? Why couldn't you just let me die, and cease this torture? The dead aren't aware of their chains. Only the living suffer because only they are afraid to say goodbye."

Dimycles ripped off the blouse and pointed at his wounds.

"Yes. I've seen your scars, and I'm not sure you will live long if you get many more of them," Adrian told him. "I saved you because I know Lotus. He may not be to blame for every callus, but I know his work. I saved you because my friend asked me to, and after seeing how single-minded you are in pursuit of your cause, I understand how Lotus could take advantage of you. You've been through a lot. I can't imagine the trauma you've experienced. Maybe time is of the essence, perhaps others you care about are in danger..." Adrian edged toward Dimycles, saying: "Whatever it is, nothing you are going through gives you the right to come to our planet, and abduct someone."

Dimycles bit his lip, then raised the gun. "Wrong," he said and shot Adrian.

Adrian had teleported out of the ship before the blast hit him. The engines rose to a full roar, sucking the air from the hangar. Adrian materialized in his car just in time to see the back half of the garage blowout. The ship blasted off.

Adrian threw his car into gear, squeezed the accelerator with his hands, and sped off - taking it up to 180 mph. His tires squealed on even the slightest curves. As he pressed buttons, he watched Dimycles' ship, keeping track of its direction. The car windows folded in, and the driver's seat shifted to the center. The front end reformed, coming to a point, and the sides pinched in. The bumper exposed a new set of thrusters. They engaged. As the wings emerged, his tires left the ground at 350mph. With his car turned into an airship, Adrian put on his helmet, pushed the throttle full forward, then pulled back on the wheel, and went airborne in a rush.

Adrian banked right through the G forces, circling until Dimycles's ship came into view. The large X continued its ascent, heading east toward the ocean.

"Shit!" Adrian muttered.

As they approached New York City airspace, Adrian's radar lit up. Dimycles' ship was slow, and Adrian closed in quickly.

Adrian's radio crackled: "Unidentified aircraft..."

"Oh man!" Adrian already heard the scrambled warnings from drone pilots on his comms. After what had happened to Washington, he was amazed to get any warning at all.

They asked him to reduce speed and altitude. When he didn't, they fired at him. Adrian's radar sparkled.

"Shit. Are they sending drones?" Adrian gasped.

A pair of K-29 drone fighters dropped in on Adrian before he could check his rear. Missiles locked and fired. Though Adrian couldn't bank at that speed, the missiles could. They aimed straight at him. He tucked in his wings, and opened his thrusters, pushing his ship to its limit. When the missiles detonated, Adrian outran the shrapnel. He slowed down and banked around.

"No!" Adrian screamed. He got on his radio and shouted: "Do not engage the pilot! There is a friendly onboard!"

Adrian sped toward Dimycles' ship. It crept through the sky surrounded by a horde of K-29s.

"I'm sure your ship works fine in space, Dims, but in an atmosphere, you need some aerodynamics," Adrian huffed. He closed in on Dimycles. Alpha K-29 fired. Adrian flew in front of the missile and banked hard, slowing down. As he dove, the missile closed in on its natural target. Adrian's ship glowed for a moment and then teleported away. When its target vanished, the missile detonated. The K-29s re-engaged, and Adrian again told comms not to engage a friendly.

"Fucking drones, don't you get it?"

An array of weapons locked onto Adrian, and he banked hard left. As they homed in, he teleported to his right. More missiles caught his signature and came for him. Reappearing behind them, he got trapped in the air draft created by his teleporting, flipping his ship around.

Bullets whizzed by, and an energy pulse blast narrowly missed him.

"Guess they're through with missiles," Adrian said to himself.

Adrian positioned himself between Dimycles and the scrambled fighters. He tried to pose no threat and fly without any aggressive actions, but the fighters locked in on him. Adrian acted as if he were alone in the sky. The drones detected compliance. The K-29s held their fire, giving him an immediate escort. Though the drones stood down, Dimycles did not.

Dimycles fired at the K-29s. Beams flew past Adrian's ship, targeting the drones, but the drones' return fire went at Adrian. Suddenly the ship auto-ejected him. The ship blew up underneath him, but Adrian was already floating toward earth.

Adrian looked back at Dimycles's ship and screamed: "Son... of... a... bitch!" Seeing the charred wreck of his beautiful airship, he felt embarrassed. Bits of it scattered in the wind. As the burning remains reflected in his eyes, Adrian's embarrassment turned to anger. He stared at Dimycles' ship floating away. "You think this is over?" Adrian hissed.

The shattered parts of Adrian's airship began acting on their own. Charred metal and burnt plastic pieces folded over themselves. Adrian maneuvered toward the gathering wreckage just as wings and thrusters reformed and connected. His airship quickly put itself back together. Adrian fell toward it, and flipped himself around, as the cockpit reconfigured itself. His thrusters heated. He teleported into the ship and fully engaged them.

Still, after Dimycles, Adrian maneuvered through the scrambled fighters. The K-29s shot at him. He dropped countermeasures. They dropped air mines. When one detonated, he teleported ahead, spun through bullets and banked around their pulse blast. He then teleported far ahead of them and climbed into the atmosphere. Adrian's thrusters burned bright as he and Dimycles flew further over the Atlantic, the scrambled fighters returned to New York. Dimycles climbed higher with Adrian closing in - almost touching the hull. The sky went dark, and the temperature plummeted. The condensation around his ship froze into particles. The ship compensated with shielding. Adrian looked back. The flat horizon was starting to bend. It curved, and soon he wasn't looking at an Earth that seemed flat anymore. He could see the yellow sun turn white.

He was in trouble.

Alarms blared inside of his car revealing high levels of ozone and mercury. Adrian pushed his thrusters harder, but Dimycles's slow ship picked up speed, leaving him behind.

"Shut up!" Adrian shouted and wheezed. He coughed as he turned the shielding to the maximum, but he could feel the air escaping out of the seams of his aircraft. The cream plush seats began to bubble up and deform.

"No!" Adrian panicked. In the black sky, the white sun The X-shaped ship escaped further away, and Adrian tried to turn to follow, but nothing happened.

Dimycles' ship suddenly spun a quarter turn. Blaster turrets emerged from the center of the X. They shot at Adrian. The alien ship sped off, putting distance between them. Adrian tried to bank, but couldn't. His wing flaps moved with impotence. The blast barely missed him. He pumped his front thrusters to move his nose right to align with Dimycles's ship as it sped further from view. Adrian tapped his rear thrusters. Dimycles's ship spun in the opposite direction and cut left with ease. Adrian side thrusters engaged repeatedly, but Dimycles's ship disappeared.

I'm losing them!

Adrian's communications system fell dark with static and interference. Adrian teleported his ship toward the spot where he'd last seen Dimycles. Upon rematerializing, he felt as if he would pass out, and heard the metal of his ship bend violently. He reached around for a bag and vomited. Everything got dark. He felt as if he were chasing a ghost, but finally, he saw a far-off glint of light. Adrian went after it and Texas tailgated the alien ship trying to match Dimycles's orbit.

Letting the lack of gravity maintain course, he teleported himself aboard the ship.

"Motherfucker, you shot me!" Adrian shouted, "After what I did for you?"

"How'd you get on my ship?" Dimycles asked, pushed off a wall toward Adrian.

Adrian hovered in place. Across the way, he saw the USoFT chairwoman still unconscious. Adrian took off from his wall and collided with Dimycles. He punched Dimycles in the face. Dimycles grabbed Adrian's neck and slammed him into a wall. Adrian pressed his back against the wall and shot his legs up, kicking Dimycles in the face. Adrian grabbed him, and yanked him down, but as soon as Adrian lost his grip, he floated off from Dimycles. He took a swing at his opponent, but Dimycles was already too far away.

Dimycles shouted. "You shouldn't have followed me! I can't turn back now."

Dimycles pushed away from the wall and slammed into Adrian. They rolled through the air punching each other until they hit the other side. Adrian turned and wrapped his legs around his opponent's waist.

Dimycles couldn't float away. Adrian pounded him. Dimycles reached for a blaster, but his target teleported behind him, next to the woman.

"You can go to hell for all I care," Adrian screamed, "but not with her." Adrian grabbed the woman and teleported them both back to his ship. Once inside, he let the airship fall back to Earth while the woman remained in the jump seat.

Silently they drifted, and Adrian held an oxygen mask to her face until he heard sounds again, and the sounds weren't good. Frozen paneling from the outer hull of his craft rattled, and the woman suddenly she woke up with a start.

"It's okay," Adrian assured her quickly holding the mask to her face. He took her hand and replaced his with it.

The woman frantically looked around, and with a wheezy voice she asked, "Was that Dimycles?"

Her words shocked Adrian. "Why? Do you know that man?"

"Please," She answered, "Just call me Yaliz."

"Yaliz? Wait, you knew—" Adrian choked on his words as he looked out of his airship. He pointed, and gasped.

Clusters of alien spacecraft were entering the atmosphere with them. At first, it looked like meteorites, but they were in formations. As they drifted closer, he could make out shapes and designs.

"It's an invasion," Yaliz told him, shaking her head.

Adrian thought aloud. "Who's attacking Earth?"

After the words had left his mouth, Adrian wished he could take it back. Echoing in his mind, it seemed like the most irrelevant of all questions considering there wasn't a damn thing he could do with the answer. Having teleported aboard an alien vessel ranked as one of the weirdest things he'd ever done. Falling back to Earth in a car, that was moments from collapsing in on itself, told him that he should just go with the flow.

"No, but seriously, who!"

"Take me home," Yaliz said just as worried. "We should talk."

THE CONGO

JULIUS SAT, crammed into a hovering copter circling the western Congo jungle. With engines roaring, he and his two companions wore helmets equipped with communicators so that they could talk with each other, and the pilot. The pilot made the copter swing down over the foliage, as all four travelers looked for signs of Mason. All they could see was dense trees, rolling hills, and cliffs. The pilot steadied the copter. Julius turned to the rear and spoke to the older Beaker twin, Rebeca, a woman with a square jaw, light brown hair, and a cheeky smile.

"I can't see anything," Julius said into his mic.

"Whose idea was this?" Rebeca shouted above the noise.

Rebeca and her brother, John, loved hunting and were happy to come along on this jungle excursion. Though they were twins, their differences went far beyond gender. John was a freckled-faced redhead.

Julius looked down past the windshield to the ground. Little was visible through the jungle growth. Now and then a sauropod looked up, alerted by the engine noise. The dinosaur would lift its head above the trees, and watch the copter passing.

"The idea sounded a lot better in my head," Julius shouted, answering Rebeca's question.

"I'll try to get us closer," the pilot offered. He flew down until they practically brushed the treetops.

"That won't help!" John Beaker shouted. "But we can see the treetops better. Thanks! Why not just get us closer to the beacon signal and we can pod jump somewhere in the area."

Julius agreed, and the three searchers suited themselves in the jump pods.

The pilot saw an abydosaurus poke its head out of the river. "You should drop your pods around here," he told them. "Shouldn't be any predators down there. Those usually don't attack humans, so you should be good. Just... stay out of the water. Anything in the water will kill you."

The pilot banked for another pass as his passengers strapped themselves into harnesses. To ensure a safer jump, the copter increased altitude. As they ascended, spiked missiles shot up from the trees, tearing the quadcopter to pieces. A rain of debris fell into the foliage.

Due to the sudden drop in altitude the jump pod chutes opened instantly. As pods crashed through branches, the chutes snagged in the dense growth. The twins struggled out of the pods. Once on the ground, they found Julius pulling his gear from his pod.

"What was that?" Julius asked, finally speaking in a normal tone.

"I don't know. Where's Dan?" Rebeca wondered, referring to the pilot.

"Can't be too far," Julius replied.

"Let's go find him," Rebeca suggested.

John said nothing. With a pain in his back he was trying to grit his teeth and bear it. The three survivors headed toward the plane wreckage. Suddenly John's pain amplified. He screamed.

"What's wrong?" Julius asked. He approached John cautiously. "Don't move. You might have hurt yourself when you were landing."

"Could be a pinched nerve," Rebeca suggested.

"Don't worry about it," John said, waving them off. "I'm fine."

"That scream didn't sound fine," Rebeca observed.

"Leave me alone. I'm good," John grunted.

They glimpsed smoke billowing into the sky, and headed for it, assuming it would lead them to the wrecked copter. Rebeca was the first to discover Dan. The pilot had fallen without a pod, and from such a small height, his chute had been useless. He hung from a thick branch, strangled by a parachute cord.

"Someone shot us down," Julius said, keeping his voice low, gathering his weapons.

"We have a retreat problem," Rebeca noticed.

"We have to abort," Julius told them. "We'll go back to the pods. They have automatic beacons. Someone will find us."

"Anytime soon?" Rebeca asked skeptically.

"My brother knows we're out here," Julius reminded her. He looked up at the pilot. "I'll get him down before something eats him. You two find a place to bury him."

Rebeca walked a few paces, and stopped, "You coming, John?"

Her brother stood, staring at nothing.

"John!"

"Huh?"

"Let's go!" Rebeca demanded.

Walking almost like a zombie, he followed her.

Rebeca found a small clearing where the ground was relatively flat. "This spot should work," she said. "Ground's soft enough to dig. Let's get to it."

"I'm thirsty..." John complained, "...a little dry."

"Canteen?" Rebeca suggested.

"Mine's empty."

"Oh." Rebeca handed him her canteen, then went back to her inspection of the ground.

John poured water over his head, looked up, open-mouthed, and drank from the flow. Rebeca didn't notice this extravagant gesture. Something on the ground caught her attention.

"Show me your shoes," Rebeca demanded.

She compared her brother's soles to marks in the earth.

"These are fresh tracks," Rebeca whispered. "Come on!"

They hurried back to Julius, who'd laid out the pilot on the ground. Julius was just arranging Dan's arms across his chest.

"I found fresh tracks over there," Rebeca told him. "Small feet. Possibly female. Might be Mason."

"Let's check it out."

When they reached the spot, Julius adjusted the assault rifle on his back and got down to inspect the footprints. As he crawled about, a bigger print caught his eye. He stood, and traced the shape of a large footprint in the air. "That's not human," he said.

"It's not a dinosaur either," Rebeca added. "At least none I've ever seen. Think it's one of the ones from the video?"

"Could be. Check for more," Julius suggested.

As John stood staring at the ground, Julius and Rebeca followed the tracks in opposite directions, then stopped, and returned to the spot. They'd identified what seemed to be five sets of footprints, but only one set was human.

"The rains come often," Julius said. "The ground is moist. These prints wouldn't last long. So you're right, definitely fresh tracks. She might be alive."

"Why would they keep her alive?" Rebeca wondered

"I don't know. Why do we keep anything we catch alive?" Julius asked.

"I'd rather not answer that," Rebeca admitted.

Julius said. "Let's get the pilot buried and head back near the pods. We are severely understaffed for this."

"No! W-We go," John stammered. "Forward. For... ward. For w-her. Find her!"

"Yo!" Rebeca got to her feet. "Chill out, John. Everything in this damn jungle might wanna eat us. We didn't even land, and already we've lost a plane and taken on a causality. Jules is right."

"I agree, too dangerous," Julius added. "Plus, you might be injured."

"Fucking pussies!" John kept stomping the ground. Then he jumped up and hit with both feet as if to emphasize his point. "Fucking pussies! I'll fuck everything up. Kill everything. I'll murder this forest! Find her!"

John stomped off, exaggerating every step.

Rebeca ran after him and touched his arm. "What the hell is wrong?"

"Stop! Ow!" John screamed at the touch of her fingertips. He turned to her, and she saw his sunken eyes, baggy and discolored.

"John. What's happening to you?"

Julius came over and eyed the injured twin. "He looks swollen."

"John –" Rebeca cried, instinctively reaching for him, then halting.

"Don't touch me..." John warned.

"John, please, just turn around," Rebeca begged.

"His back is swollen," Julius said, pulling out his knife. He looked at John. "You might be poisoned."

John swung wildly, trying to ward them off. Julius ducked, then sidestepped. As he approached John from behind, the injured twin was trying to hit his sister. With one swipe Julius cut the back of John's shirt open.

He stared at the swelling, bubbling back. "Wow. We have to get out of here."

John had two large bite marks on his left side. Pus oozed from the punctures.

"Water..." John whispered meekly, then, with a rush of manic energy, he ran off. As he stumbled through the brush, he tried to express himself. "I need... I just feel... dry."

As his arms swelled up, he ripped off his shirt. His shoes were almost bursting off his feet as he kicked them away. Crashing barefoot through the forest, he reached the riverbank. His body bloated. His skin sagged, and turned to a yellow, mucus-like substance that melted off his body. He fell and clawed his way to the water. He found a shallow pond near the riverbank and struggled to submerge himself.

Julius and Rebeca found him floating on the water. He let out a long, rattling sigh. His eyes went blank, his body convulsed, and something bubbled up through his neck, then burst out of his body. A long, slimy creature emerged and formed a coil in the water.

"Holy shit!" Julius gasped.

"Don't let it get into the river! It'll infect the other animals," Rebeca hissed.

Julius and Rebeca grabbed tree branches and fished the parasite from the water. One end was still oozing out from John's body. When they were done, fifteen feet of parasite flopped and coiled on the ground. John's remains had deflated into a bloodless bag of skin. As the creature twitched and shook, Julius stomped on what appeared to be its head. Just as it attempted to wrap itself around his leg, he cut the head off.

Rebeca went at the creature with her knife and sliced it into pieces. "Who's doing this? Who's out there!" she cried softly. "You will die in the river, just like that!"

"Strange. This water isn't part of the river. It's just a crater."

"What?" Rebeca asked.

"This is a crater," Julius repeated. "A hole collecting rainwater, but how did it get here?" He knelt down and crawled to the edge. "It isn't too fresh. I've got new ground and muddy runoff on top... This is at least several weeks old, maybe even a few months."

Rebeca stepped back to get a clearer view. "Well, it isn't a footprint," she said. "Looks like someone moved a boulder. Who moves boulders?"

Julius shook his head sadly. "Let's head back to the pods. We are asking too many questions. I didn't count on this. We need a bigger team."

Another missile—a five-foot spike—shot out from behind the trees, whizzed over Julius's head, and struck Rebeca. She flew backward, and the spike impaled her to a tree.

The sky darkened. A shadow formed over Julius and grew. A boulder crashed down on him, debris flew everywhere. The earth shook. The block sunk into the soft terrain, forming a new crater. A long and thick chain connected to the stone like a leash with a Reptilite, Menoush, gripping the chain at the other end. He looked at the results of his surprise attack and smiled.

Julius phased through the boulder. Standing on top of it, he became solid again and across at the Reptilite. He pulled his assault rifle from his shoulder. Another Reptilite rushed at him from the side. Julius turned and squeezed large rounds between its eyes. The carcass fell to the ground and slid to the boulder.

Menoush pulled the chain, yanking up the boulder. Julius crouched down, and held on tight, as he and the rock flew through the air. As he passed Menoush, Julius leapt off. Pulling his sidearm, he pumped four shots into the Reptilite and landed on the other side of him. Julies emptied the rest of the clip into the creature. Menoush buckled, losing control of the boulder. It fell to the ground, but Menoush regained his grip on the chain.

"You swing like a bitch!" Julius shouted, sidestepping his opponent.

Menoush composed himself and swung the chain-and-boulder like a lasso. Julius shouldered his assault rifle again to shoot as he dodged the boulder. The huge rock splintered branches, tree trunks, and earth. As it again neared Julius, he rolled out of its path. The rock crashed into the ground nearby. The sound was deafening. Julius was thrown a few meters. Back to his feet, he looked around, his gun ready. Menoush was gone.

"You don't get off that easily," Julius swore, then he saw Rebeca.

The spike had gone straight through her body, then pierced a tree. Rebeca had been cut in half, with her legs and lower torso falling to the ground, and the rest of her slumped over the spike. Julius touched the projectile. It felt light and strong. He closed his eyes, and dragged her off of it. He took the halves of her body and phased them into the ground with what remained of her brother. There he said goodbye, then started after the Reptilite.

Trotting through the forest, Julius stayed level, pointing his weapon. He watched the ground, following the Reptilite's tracks. Soon the trail grew fainter and disappeared, but far ahead he heard leaves rustling. Animals cried. A barrage of spikes shredded nearby trees. As Julius dropped to the ground, a spike pierced the tree above his head. He rolled sideways as another whizzed by, then he hopped up and ran toward the shooter. It was another Reptilite, Krome. He was firing a shoulder-mounted cannon.

From high off the trees, a winged Reptilite dove at him. He fell to his back, shooting into the air. The beast crashed next to him with a thud and Krome fired again. Julius ducked and dodged a new flurry of spikes, tossing away the empty clip and reloading another. The enemy fire increased. Julius looked up to see a troop of monkeys leaping between the trees.

Julius glanced back toward Krome, saying to himself, "He must be protecting something."

A moment later another Reptilite, Prexe, shot a fleshy white projectile from the trees. As it homed in on Julius, it grew a set of fangs and tried to take a bite of him. When Julius phased, the white missile passed through him and buried itself in a tree trunk. The monkeys pelted Prexe with sticks and rocks, but she ran off.

Julius phased into a tree trunk and floated to the top. From the high ground, Julius shot at the enemies surrounding his location and drove them back. Mimicking the monkeys, he leapt through the branches to close in on the Reptilite defensive line. He saw a small enclosure behind it.

"Is that what they're hiding?" he wondered.

As the cries of the monkeys created a distraction, Julius slipped through the branches overhead. He came down the closest tree and peered into the enclosure. Leaves covered something. It moved.

"Mae," Julius whispered. "Mae!"

His voice drew attention from the Reptilite, Sobika, who started toward the intruder. Julius shot but fell back when his rifle went empty. When he reached the splintered remnants of a tree Menoush had destroyed, Julius grabbed a long piece of bark. With his knife he whittled one end, making a long pike. Sobika spotted him and called to the others. When Julius fled, they chased him. Julius turned, faced his attackers, and shuffled away.

Charging ahead of the others, Sobika aimed her claws at Julius and cut off his retreat while Krome fired spikes from a distance. Julius parried the shots with his pike. Trees to the right of Julius exploded into splinters. Menoush appeared and charged him, swinging the boulder. Julius jumped sideways, evading it. Sobika took another swipe at him, but Julius phased through the impact hemorrhage of the boulder and her claws. He phased back and raced behind the boulder.

Sobika gave chase, and Krome jumped high above the boulder, sending another barrage of spikes downward. Julius parried them with his pike, deflecting one into Sobika. She stumbled backwards bleeding. Menoush swung again. Sobika staggered, then charged at Julius. He whirled and stabbed the wounded enemy in her chest with his pike. He jammed his end of the pike into the ground, with the monster impaled upon its point. Sobika tried to free herself, but Julius pulled his other side arm and kept shooting her. Julius saw Menoush's boulder coming. As he phased through it, the stone hit Sobika, smashing her to bits.

Julius materialized, looked around, and wondered: "How many of them are there?"

Another Reptilite, Thumlyn burst out of the foliage. He swung wildly as Julius, who slipped the punches, shot and got behind him. Thumlyn stumbled forward from being shot.

Julius saw that this one was taking it personally. He tossed away his empty gun and pointed back at the spot where Sobika had died. "You look mad as hell. That boulder busted the shit out of her dome."

Menoush, Krome, and Thumlyn surrounded Julius. Julius caught his breath, reached down, and pulled his long blade from its sheath.

"Someone's gonna bleed," he promised them.

From the corner of his eye, he saw Prexe hiding in the trees.

"There you are!" he called to her. "Sneaky!"

Julius rushed Krome, who answered with a volley of missiles. Julius dodged the return fire. He high-stepped over the shots as the missiles tore into the ground.

While Menoush prepped his boulder, Julius hopped over a spike. He grabbed it, phased it, and pulled it from the earth. Moving it just a few feet, he phased it back into the ground on the opposite end, with its point jutting up at an angle.

Thumlyn swung a claw at him. Julius dodged the behemoth. Menoush swung. Thumlyn stepped away from the incoming boulder.

Julius pulled more of Krome's spikes from the ground, phasing it with their points up next to the others.

Julius kept an eye on Prexe hiding in the trees. He dodged the constant bombardment from the others while pushing more of Krome's spikes into the ground.

Menoush prepped his boulder, looking for the winning shot to brag about. Julius barricaded himself behind the reverse spikes. Seeing Julius sitting still, Menoush saw the oppurtunity to crush his opponent.

Julius leapt away as the boulder crashed down. He jumped on top of it. "Mine now!" he taunted.

When Menoush yanked back on the chain, Julius phased the boulder. The thick chain disconnected and snapped back like a whip. The end of the chain smashed into Krome's face. Julius sunk half of the block into the ground and solidified it in the dirt. He stood on top of the dome as Menoush whipped the chain at him. The chain hit, spraying debris, while Julius jumped down between the rock and the spikes. These created small a fort for him, with the stone shielding his back, and a field of spikes deterring any frontal assault.

Krome retreated. Menoush kept swinging the chain, but it did nothing to penetrate the defense Julius built. When Thumlyn attacked, his fists were too big, and the row of spikes kept him at bay.

"Only one more of you bastards," Julius announced.

Prexe, seeing Julius comfortable in his fort, took advantage of an idle prey. She emerged from the trees, snuck around behind, and started climbing the boulder. Julius was still busy fending off his other two attackers. Prexe reached the top of the dome and loaded another poison pill. he inched forward until she saw the human.

All three Reptilites attacked at once. Menoush snapped his whip, Thumlyn charged the barrier, and Prexe stood up and took aim. Julius ran forward, stepped on a spike, and leapt into the air. Prexe locked on him and shot. The white fleshy pill flew down on Julius, forming a mouth with fangs. It connected with tender meat, sunk its teeth in, and injected its parasitic poison.

Julius landed outside his fort and saw Menoush stumble. The parasitic pill was biting into his chest. Julius solidified and ran.

"He must not escape!" Prexe cried. "Rex Gedeon will execute us all."

Thumlyn chased Julius down into a cave. The Reptilite leapt into the darkness, fell, and hit with a thud. Ribbons of dim light streaked the cave walls and floor. Getting his bearings, Thumlyn turned right and saw Julius. Julius ran, and the Reptilite pursued him. He got near, and pounded his fist against the floor, just missing Julius. As Thumlyn chased him, Julius dodged and maneuvered, always evading his foe. The alien threw a huge handful of dirt at his prey, but when the dust cleared, Julius was disappearing around a corner. The ribbons of light faded and nearly went out.

Thumlyn got on all fours and crawled through the darkness. He came around a bend, heard something, and snatched at the air. He pounded the cave floor in frustration and charged forward.

Then he slowed down.

Not knowing where he was, or what twists and turns there might be, he began to worry. A retreat came to mind, but which way was "back?" He crawled one way, and then another- then felt a draft. He turned left, and the last light was gone. Everything was pitch black in all directions. Was he ascending to the surface, or traveling into the earth? He didn't know.

He had no idea which way he'd come down. With no visual clues, he sniffed the air. One moment, a cool draft led him one way, then the damp cave air led him another. He thought he saw a light behind him. He backtracked but found only more darkness. Though his path seemed level, he couldn't help thinking he was going further down into the earth.

He quickened his pace, but the walls began to close in on him. They'd been wider behind him, right? With great difficulty, he managed to turn himself, but when he crawled in that direction, the passage narrowed even more. No matter which direction, it kept getting darker and more cramped. Soon he couldn't even turn around. Thumlyn panicked. He felt himself suffocating. He looked about, but couldn't see. The Earth had swallowed him. He screamed. Echoes of his screams came from in front of him. Did that mean there was an opening? He crawled after the echo and reached a wall of rocks. There the tunnel seemed to stop. He felt along the jagged rocks of the cave wall. He dug. He didn't know what else to do. Soon he couldn't breathe. He pounded the cave walls. If he could make just a little more room... The walls resented his pounding. The earth filled in around him. He was buried alive.

Though Julius also felt fear, he didn't let it rule him. He stood still, kept calm, and slowed his breathing. The walls hadn't caved in on him yet, and he still had room to move around. Nonetheless, he too was lost, and in total darkness. "This is gonna take a lot of concentration," he said, sitting down on the ground.

He felt around, grabbed a rock, lifted it up, and dropped it. He stood up and took a breath.

"I swore I'd never do this again."

He phased into the cave wall and floated in the direction he believed was up. The surreal darkness inside the Earth confused his perceptions. Julius could sense the Earth moving away from him the more he floated. He compensated his trajectory to keep his momentum moving along with Earth. He hoped that he still floated upward.

"This is taking a while," Julius thought, "Maybe I'm floating down... or sideways. No. Stop it! It's okay. You're still good. You still got this. Don't stop your momentum. Up is perpendicular to your momentum. But so is down! No. The Earth only spins one way. We can do this. Focus."

As Julius floated, he began to feel a dizzy spinning. He concentrated, wanting to avoid any sudden actions like phasing back into a rock. Though he felt nauseous, he kept in tune with the Earth. The consistency of the Earth's outer layer changed, and he sensed roots that led him to a tree.

A moment later he stood on solid ground. His heart pounded. A snake coiled around a nearby tree. Only a few tree trunks were visible through the thick foliage. He started through the jungle and soon reached higher ground. He reached a bluff and looked out over the surrounding area. He didn't recognize any of it.

"This jungle his huge," he muttered.

He listened. The sound was far away: a herd of Corythosaurus to the west of him. He was much further east than he had thought. He trekked westward until he reached a point overlooking marshy terrain. Behind him was a cliff wall. He thought he heard weird sounds of commotion from above. He climbed the cliff wall. When he reached the top, he peered over the edge and saw Menoush swinging his chain wildly at Prexe and Krome.

"That parasite must have him good," Julius guessed.

The other two started to fight but then fled from Menoush's rage. Menoush stopped and stared at them.

Julius saw this as his chance. He crept up on Menoush. "You got to pay," He threatened.

Menoush didn't pay him any mind.

"Thirsty?" Julius blared.

Menoush's face was blank, but he still gripped the chain. Julius threw a rock at him. Menoush screamed and beat his chain against the ground. Then he saw Julius. Manoush charged him, whipping the chain. Julius jumped away, flipped back over it, rolled, and ran forward. He attacked Menoush without mercy, with every blow finding its mark. He drove his knife into the monster's eye. Menoush went down, then teetered to his feet. He couldn't stand straight, and when he swung the chain at Julius, he missed, and the chain wrapped around his neck in a noose coil. He struggled to get it off, but couldn't.

 Julius dodged the strikes and ran off. When Menoush chased him down the hill, the chain followed, still looped around his neck. Julius leapt into the air then kicked off from a tree trunk. He rolled, then leapt to the cliff's edge. Menoush stumbled and fell over the cliff. As Manoush flew by him, Julius phased the chain, bringing the last links into solid rock, and making them one. With the rocky ground gripping the chain, the coil around the monster's neck snapped, tearing his head off. Julius went over too, but grabbed the chain, arresting his fall.

Julius watched Menoush's headless body disappear into the foliage below. The long parasite spiraled up out of his body and flopped on the ground. It slowly withered and died.

Julius hung onto the chain as he caught his breath. After a moment, he climbed back onto the cliff, and surveyed the area, quickly spotting the Reptilite encampment. Trekking through the dense foliage, he arrived at the enclosure at the far end. When he reached the gated entrance, his fingers wrapped around the bar. The pile of leaves parted, Mason's face popped out with dry, flaking mud covered her skin.

Her mouth twitched. "Jules?" She pulled herself to her knees and crawled forward to the gate. Julius phased through the gate and starting toward her. Terrified, she scampered to the wall and cowered there. Julius approached carefully. Julius touched her, and she let him, only because she was afraid. Her skin felt cold. She coughed.

"That doesn't sound good," he said.

Mason sat back on her heels, bewildered. Her dark skin was rough and peeling. Her hair puffed out in all directions, snarling through a crown of twigs and leaves. Julius knelt down by her. Something smelled putrid. "We have to get help," he said.

Mason put a fingertip to his face as if to see if he were there. "It's me," he said. "I'm real." He got her to her feet and walked her to the gate. "Hold on," he said. Keeping her close, they both phased and walked through the gate.

"You came by yourself?" she asked.

"Unfortunately, not," Julius said, "but I'm alone now. They shot our ship down and killed the others. We lit a beacon. Adrian should get here soon, so we should go to the drop point."

AFTER A LONG trek through the Congo jungle Kyra found the clearing with the charred remains of the quadcopter. She headed over to the charred pieces of metal - the crashed plane that brought Julius and his fallen comrades to the jungle. In the northeast sky, a waxing moon was rising, it's grayish white crescent barely visible in the blue sky. She found the beacon Julius had set. It anchored to the ground with the tiny dish pointing to the heavens. She opened the back panel, pressed a few buttons, and the dish closed. She pulled a small chip from it, and the unit went dead. She put the chip in her pocket.

In the sky above she saw gray dots, like daystars. A rustling in the trees caught her attention. A weak voice croaked: "Kill her!"

Kyra turned and saw an enraged Mason pointing at her. Then there was Julius drawing his gun. He shot twice at Kyra, but she dropped, and rolled through the foliage

"She works for them!" Mason screamed, hobbling to the beacon. "She disabled the rescue signal."

Kyra got up to run, but Julius kicked her. Her legs went out from under her, and her face hit the dirt. When she tried to get up, her hips wouldn't move. Julius pinned her from behind, forcing her face down into the dirt. The cold barrel of the gun nudged the back of her head. Mason ran up, and kicked Kyra in the ribs.

"Animal!" Mason screamed. "Shoot her!"

"Where is he?" Julius said, looking around cautiously, "Where's Lotus?"

"Far from here," Kyra grunted into the dirt.

"Liar!" Mason screamed. "You can't let her live. She's one of them!"

Julius felt the trigger.

"I don't work for him anymore!" Kyra screamed. "He tried to have me killed! I didn't know about you, Mason! You know that! Lotus never let me in on this side of the operation."

Mason shook her head in confusion.

"What operation?" Julius demanded, using his free hand to press Kyra's face into the earth.

"The Reptilites sent an alien spy to Earth to sabotage the military before their invasion," Kyra gurgled, trying not to eat dirt.

Julius expected as much but felt obliged to question her. "Lotus is crazy, but even that sounds farfetched..." He looked at Mason. "Right?"

"Lotus is a Martian!" Kyra cried.

Julius stopped. "Not possible." He relaxed his grip just enough so that Kyra could speak more easily.

"An alien named Boyacobas rescued Lotus off of Mars. When Boyacobas died, Lotus took up his cause," Kyra explained. "They kept me in the dark! They didn't want me to foil their plans!"

Julius looked at Mason. Mason stood wavering as if she might pass out.

"You have to believe me when I tell you. My loyalty was never to Lotus," Kyra said.

Julius started to let Kyra up.

"Why'd you disable the beacon?" Mason asked weakly.

"Look at the damn sky!" Kyra pleaded. They looked up to see the faint daystars growing bigger than before.

"What are those?" Julius asked.

"Reptilite ships," Kyra continued. "If they see your signal, we'll be dead!"

"You expect me to believe you came here to help us?" Mason coughed. "Why are you here?"

Julius stared up at the sky. "We have to stop this."

"It's too late," Kyra insisted.

"Mason, we can't stay here," Julius snapped. He glanced at Kyra. "Enable the beacon. I must contact my brother."

"Are you mad?" Kyra shouted. "I have a jeep. If we go now, they won't see us."

"We're not going anywhere with you!" Mason hissed.

"Do you want to stay here and die?" Kyra countered.

Julius intervened. "Mason, you're sick. I think you're poisoned."

Ignoring Julius, Mason shrieked at Kyra: "I don't want to go anywhere with a killer!"

Mason lost her footing, but Julius held her up. He glanced at the sky. "Mason ... trust me, I'm on your side, I'm always gonna be on your side, but we're stranded in the worse possible place. Everything here wants to eat us. An army is dropping on our heads. You need medicine badly."

"That changes nothing!" Mason insisted, "We aren't moving until I know why she's here."

"You're the only one who knows what we're up against," Kyra told her. "You made the plants; you saw the drones. You know all about the Reptilites. You lived with them. You know how they can be stopped."

Julius nodded slowly and looked at his companion. "Mae, if there's anything here that can level the playing field, now's the time to get it."

"The plants can power whatever they need to power, but we never seeded the plants here. The humidity kept shorting out the leaves," she said.

"That's barely helpful," said Julius. "Then where would he sow them?"

"Just in the places the aliens wanted to attack, or regions they wanted to destabilize," Mason said. "I tested the plants further north. The Six have heavy weaponry stored in warehouses up there."

Kyra's eyes lit up.

Mason continued, "Those machines have devastating power, but it's not enough to fight a war."

"Maybe it's sufficient to stop one," Julius suggested.

Kyra looked up. As the first of the ships neared cloud level, she became insistent. "Let's go!"

The ground rumbled. Birds swarmed up from the trees. A stampede of dinosaurs broke into the clearing, frightened at the incoming alien ships.

"GO!" Kyra shouted.

Julius carried Mason on his shoulder. Kyra got her jeep transport, they hopped in and sped off. Kyra floored it, breaking away from the stampede. The rough terrain sent jolts through all of them.

"There should be medicine in the back!" Kyra shouted.

Julius tried to cushion Mason as he fished through the supplies. He found what he needed, and did his best to work on Mason's wounds. He looked back. The dinosaurs kept coming, and they were gaining on the jeep.

Kyra skillfully maneuvered around obstacles, but her zigging and zagging slowed them down. The herd closed in on them. As Kyra aimed for any haven, the galloping dinosaurs closed in. It seemed hopeless. Kyra cut the wheel hard to avoid a boulder. The body of an iguanodon slammed into the side and sent the jeep flipping through the air.

The vehicle crashed, rolled, and came to rest on its side. Julius grabbed the Jeep chassis and phased the entire thing. When Mason looked up, dinosaurs were racing through the dematerialized jeep and her body. She held her breath, looked over, and saw Kyra face down, knocked out cold.

Blood trickled down Kyra's temple where she'd hit her head. Throughout the stampede she was motionless. Afterward, Julius pushed her into the back seat and started the jeep, she was totally unaware. Mason took the front passenger side, and they drove away. Kyra began to regain consciousness. As she raised her head, she saw the other two in front, as well as a broken windshield, a dented fender, and the passing jungle.

"How do you feel?" Julius asked Mason.

"Not so good. I don't think the medicine is working," she replied.

"It's working. You'll be okay." Julius touched her arm.

In the back seat, Kyra laid her head back, and looked up at the crumpled roof. She murmured: "What happened?" and passed out again.

She awoke in a bed in a cabin. There were two other beds. Both had been slept in. Kyra got up and went into the bathroom. She inspected herself, gingerly touching the place where she'd hit her head. She undressed, showered, then put on a romper she found. She went outside, and saw the jeep, and a huge entrance, apparently to a cave. She realized she was at the Six's warehouse further north in the Congo. Trees with enormous leaves camouflaged several hangars, making them look like cave entrances. Kyra inspected the damage to the battered jeep. She reached into a rear compartment and pulled out a small gun. She took it inside, hid it where she knew she'd find it, and came back out.

When Kyra heard voices behind the cabin, she went around and found Mason and Julius talking.

"Should my ears be burning?" Kyra asked.

"We were just trying to figure out the best way to get extracted," said Julius. "That armada could be heading our way."

"Of course," Kyra said doubtfully.

"I think I should get cleaned up," said Julius, and he headed for the cabin, leaving the women alone.

"You look a lot better," said Kyra.

It was true. The American scientist's skin had fresh milk chocolate glow. It was a complete transformation from the sickly creature she'd been just hours earlier. Her strong jaw line brought out her full cheekbones, framing her face beneath black hair. Her thick lips curved when she spoke, and her brown eyes had the spark of curiosity. The microbiologist's intelligence and inquisitiveness were obvious.

"I'm better, no thanks to you," Mason quipped.

"If you noticed, I got us out of there," Kyra reminded her.

"I noticed you almost got us killed, but then again, that's what you do so well."

"I still came to your rescue," said Kyra.

"That doesn't change anything."

"Doesn't it?" Kyra asked. "Look, I was being used... just a gun for hire."

"Unbelievable," Mason scoffed.

"Why?" Kyra asked.

"You're just looking for scapegoats. You pulled the trigger. You knew they had me!"

"I didn't know anything. I had to steal a passkey before I learned the Six had pictures of talking dinosaurs. I thought it was just comics at first. I had no idea what they were doing with you."

"There you go again, pleading ignorance."

"Okay, yes!" Kyra cried. "I did a lot of bad shit. I killed a lot of people. Most of them didn't deserve it. I did that! Happy? But people can change." Kyra shrugged. "My life was a mess. It wasn't like yours. I don't have a Ph.D. I can't..." she looked around "...make plants that can think. But I have talents just like you do."

"I don't kill people," Mason replied.

Kyra shook her head, her interest in the argument waning. She looked up at the warehouse behind Mason, "You realize what all that stuff is for right? We are talking extinction for the human race right about now. My talent for killing is about to be in high demand."

"But you only kill for profit, or revenge," Mason sneered. "You don't protect the weak. You've never fought for anyone other than yourself because you've never had a conviction worth killing for."

When Kyra failed to respond, Mason sighed, and nodded. "I need to work on that extraction," she said, and she headed for one of the cave-like entrances. In the front were rows of equipment, plants, and cabinets. She walked through and entered the cave hangar. There she found herself staring at an armory of weapons. "Maybe we don't need to be extracted," she said to herself.

Before her was a cavern filled with Auracles—menacing attack warplanes built by the Six to counter the Reptilites. The planes lined the walls. As she approached these, she passed bionic suits, walkers of the Earth, standing two stories high. They were armed to the teeth with cannons on both arms. They had no heads or eyes but didn't need them. They could see fine. Just looking at the Terredrones gave Mason motion sickness. She tore her eyes away and started toward the warplanes.

Meanwhile, Kyra had returned to the cabin, where she heard Julius in the shower. She went into the steam filled bathroom from the shower and pulled back the curtain to find Julius with his head under the water. He held his face up to the spray. Kyra watched him for a moment, then let the shower curtain fall back into place. She left and closed the door. She heard the shower stop. A moment later Julus came out wearing a robe. He lay back on one of the beds—the one where Kyra had slept—and relaxed. Kyra stood in the doorway, looking at him.

He propped his head up on a couple of pillows and looked back at her. "Mason?" he asked.

"She's working on the extraction," said Kyra. "I don't think she likes me."

"This is the first time in years she's been around people who aren't trying to kill her. Give her some time."

Kyra nodded and sat down on the bed next to him. "How'd we survive the stampede?"

"Guess we got lucky."

"Hmm. How'd I survive Mason? Didn't she want to leave me to die?"

"Mason's not a killer. She's got a second chance at life now. So do you. Or is this your first?"

"I don't get firsts anymore," she said. "People don't usually help me unless they want something from me. It was good of you to keep searching for Mason. Maybe if I'd found her first, I could've saved her. Then she would see that I wasn't the one who sent her there to die."

"You would have had some trouble. Finding her wasn't easy. Remember, I arrived with three other people."

"Reptilites?"

Julius nodded.

Kyra scooted closer to him. "How many were there?"

"Seven or more."

"Monsters?"

"Large but not huge. Still beatable. You'll get your chance soon enough. Then you can say you had a first."

Kyra giggled. "Well, there aren't many things I haven't done."

A sound like thunder came from the sky.

Kyra jumped. "You heard that?"

"Yeah," Julius said, looking toward the window.

They heard more crackling sounds in the air far away.

"What is that?" Kyra asked, moving closer to Julius.

"Antiaircraft fire," Julius said. "That's what a war sounds like." his expression deepened.

Kyra crawled onto the bed and lay close to him. "The world's gonna end. This is really happening."

"We have to stop the Six, whatever it takes," Julius mumbled.

"I don't wanna think about it," she said. "I don't care about Lotus. I'm on the other side of the world. I wanna be free of his bullshit, even if it's just for a moment." Somewhere far off something exploded. She closed her eyes. "I don't wanna fight. I don't wanna be tough. I want to be soft. I want to be vulnerable. Tomorrow this place might be rubble." Kyra stroked his arms. "You look fucking pumped after fucking up those aliens. We can't be enemies anymore. I mean, fuckin' aliens? We gotta stand together."

"Shit was wild," Julius said.

She smiled, "How many did you fight? Hand-to-hand?"

"Fought five, killed three," he murmured.

Kyra breathed deeply, reaching across his chest. "When you moved, I could see the muscle lines in your arms under your robe. Is it like that everywhere?"

"What do you mean?"

"Like..." Her hands slipped under the robe, and she ran her fingertips across his chest."

He sat up and opened his robe.

"Oh. Okay. Yeah. Lie down," she breathed, as her excitement mounted. She stroked and kissed him everywhere. When she started sucking him, Julius let out a long sigh.

"You're overdressed," he said, reaching down.

Julius ran her hands over her romper, looking for a zipper, button, or clasp of some kind. He found nothing.

"It's a one piece," Kyra told him. "The whole thing has to come off."

Julius tried again, pulling at the shoulder, then searching around her waist. "Your outfit defeats me," he admitted.

Kyra smiled and stood up on the bed. Julius watched her snake her way out of the romper. When it fell onto the sheets, she kicked it way. Julius looked up at her tattooed body. She stepped over and straddled him at his waist. She played with him, trying to fit him into her. It wouldn't go.

"Let me," said Julius. "I know how to use it." He flipped her onto her back and got between her legs.

"Don't hurt me," Kyra said with a gasp. "I don't know if that's gonna fit. It's... It's a little too b... Oh my God! Don't you dare stop!"

Julius slid himself in slow, then quickened the pace. He dropped down on top of her, and she felt his weight. When the explosions started again, his thrusts seemed even more powerful.

Kyra breathed heavily and then nudged Julius up. "I wanna..." She reached down and touched herself. "Yeah. That feels good."

As she brought herself to orgasm, she screamed. "Oh my God! That feels so much better than a dildo."

After they were both finished, Kyra collapsed on her back. She put her hand on the pillow beneath her head and felt the gun. Startled, she panicked, then she calmed, recalling that she'd hidden it there.

"I can't remember shit. My head's gone," she said, trying to fix her wild hair. "My girlfriend's gonna be pissed if she finds out."

Julius walked to the window completely naked, and the sky looked red and dusty in the distance. He ate a peach.

"These fruits here are beyond delicious," Kyra said.

Kyra stared at his body, sat up on the bed, and faced him. A low rumble came from large military ships flying low overhead in droves. Julius stood staring out at the war up in the sky. When he looked at Kyra, she was aiming her gun at him. His lips parted. He bit into the fruit. As she watched him, she lowered the gun and pushed it back under the pillow. She walked to him and slapped the fruit from his hand.

"I was eating..."

She pulled him back to the bed, grabbed his head and, as they fell onto the sheets, she pushed his face down between her legs. "Eat!" She commanded.

As he obeyed, Kyra wiggled, squealing with pleasure. All of her pain and worries fell away. Her pleasure was building when explosions startled her. Her eyes opened wide, then shut. She pushed her hand under the pillow.

Her thought crystallized in stages:

Bishop is going to know...

Julius slid his fingers inside of her. His tongue lapped gently and steadily between her lips. With his other hand, he caressed her, stroking her hips. She raised her hips up, then came back down. Julius sent pulses of erotic joy through her body.

...what it's like...

She opened her mouth and exhaled. Moving her hand from beneath the pillow, she pointed the gun at his head. His face stayed buried between her legs. She wrapped her finger around the trigger.

...to lose everyone he loves.

She felt the intense sexual heat. Antiaircraft missiles exploded. The combination was like a drug. Her heart raced. Pleasure spread through her entire body. She screamed. As she orgasmed everything tightened, including her trigger finger. The gun went off with her climax, and suddenly her body went limp.

She felt her gun hand fall to her side, and her legs trembled. She lay back, basking in the poetry of her sadistic pleasure. Her lips formed a crooked smile, and her eyes fluttered, then closed. For about a minute she lay motionless. This was her theatrical piece, and she meant to savor every moment. There would be no encore. Her eyes half-closed. She didn't move. She wanted to enjoy every moment of her theatrical piece. There could be no encore.

As she dozed off, the explosions returned, rousing her. Her heart jumped every time she heard the echo of blasts. The explosions grew more frequent. Finally, she looked down between her legs. She sat up suddenly. Where was her victim? She glanced from the bed to the floor and saw nothing. She got up and found the bullet lodged in a dresser.

She bit her lip. "A first!"

She shimmied back into the romper and snuck out of the house. Mason was nowhere in sight, which was fine with Kyra. She trotted around the back of the cabin to the warehouse entrance. She struggled to open a greenhouse door and slipped in through the darkness. She went through the rows of power plants, her fingers grazing the clear leaves. At the rear of the greenhouse, she came to several rows of black trunks. She opened one. Inside, insects, collected in a hive, awakened, and raised their wings. Kyra smiled.

First Born

AS THE KAIMAN drifted toward Earth, Rex Gedeon stood before the assembly of troops. His pupils shifted into a circle, and he watched the crest of the Earth, letting it fill his mind. This vision inflamed his passion as he addressed his army before the final plunge.

"Sons of Reptilia. I, Rex Gedeon, the Great Hunter, commander of the Kaiman, and chief of the Reptilites come before you with a decree. Earth will be home to humans no longer. Whether by land or by sea, from the first drop of blood you shed, to the last, this mission will be the salvation of our kind. This moment sets us apart from all others in the Observed Realm. The necessity of taking back our home, and reclaiming our nobility, transcends the laws that have oppressed us. I command it."

His troops responded with a roar.

"In our absence, the humans have flourished. Fueled by the oil from our skin, they lifted themselves to the lofty place. As they've raped our home planet, they've shown no regard for the priceless treasures they've stolen. We must save our throne from further desecration. I condemn the humans and command you: Drive their arrogance from the skies, bury them in the soil from which they came. Let the worms do to them as they have done to the Earth. This proliferation of human life has gone on for too long."

"Too long!"

"We were seized from our rightful path, only to become a degraded species fighting for land that has no meaning. We were robbed of our native land, our birthright ruined by the human infestation. For many generations, our children have come of age with no knowledge of their real place or purpose. For those of you who are still ignorant of history: Today, I, the Great Hunter, will show it to you."

As the company saw the image of a nearby Earth, they erupted in a collective shout.

"The coalition of planets that form the Galactic State abducted us to fight their wars millions of years ago. The State has ruled that invading a sovereign planet is a crime. They will call us criminals. But the crime was our abduction! The crime is genetic modification! We, the sovereign rulers of Earth, cannot invade what is already ours! The State is the criminal!"

"Criminal!" cried several voices.

"They stole our link to our home! They robbed us of our history! Even the name, 'Reptilite,' was forced on us by the State! We did not choose this title! Millions of years ago they used us as slaves to fight their wars! They exploited us for their gain! Will the State consider that a crime? Will the State side with us in reclaiming the Earth? I ask you this, why should we seek their permission?"

Angry shouts erupted into an enraged din.

"The more they try to control us, the faster we slip through their grasp. We will use the atrocities they committed against us for our benefit! I tell you, by the rise of the Earth, we didn't become warriors to bring peace to the Galaxy!"

"No peace!"

"We didn't survive our abduction to be the tools of their morality!"

"Long live Gedeon!"

"They would NEVER give me eyes to see our destiny!"

"Destiny!"

"They would NEVER pass a law forbidding me from claiming that destiny by the only means I know best...WAR!"

"WAR!"

"They forgot to change us back into dumb, brutish animals, and now their exploitation has developed an unexpected result: our interest in, understanding of, and passion for our true legacy. I did not ask our ruler, Apex, to back our cause. He is a puppet, afraid of losing the pathetic position the Galactic State has granted him. Instead, I traveled the Realm, recruiting enslaved warriors; I hunted for despairing souls who'd been taught that their only purpose was to fight in the name of their masters. I gave them the truth and amassed this great army. Together we will see it through! No longer will your feathers line the battlefield. No longer will your scales peel for another's benefit. You are worth more than that! You will force the State to recognize the horrors of its actions, or face annihilation from its own weaponry. We are the First Born of Earth!"

"First Born of Earth!"

"We are the First Blood of the land!"

"First Blood of the land!"

"And we will be the last." Pointing to the Earth, Gedeon gave them their war cry: "Reclaim our legacy!"

GEDEON HURRIED FROM the projection room, his clawed feet gripping the floor as he pushed himself into the bridge node. As he floated through, his operators sat up, looked alerted, and kept busy. Holographs of Earth showed troop positions and readiness.

Kalet announced, "K-29 defense around the Earth is very haphazard."

Natalyze studied her holograph of the Earth. "I always imagined they would put up a more unified defense," she said, "But apparently some nations only protect their friends. Do the humans not see themselves as one?"

"They will after today," Gedeon promised, stepping onto a hover platform that took him around the bridge.

Kalet added, "The most advanced nations stand waiting for us."

"Is the beacon ready?" Gedeon asked the Vega scientist.

Natalyze started, "The Beacon is ready, but..."

"The humans are shutting down the satellites!" Tanga shouted.

"They know," Kalet added.

"But... Lotus refuses to cooperate until he is safe aboard his ship," Natalyze continued.

"We need the beacon to get through those drones," Tanga warned.

"The tablet controls the chip," said Kalet. "Get it!"

Natalyze shook her head. "I have the tablet, but only Lotus knows the password!"

"Override it!" Gedeon said.

"I- I can't, It's of unknown origin. It would take years for me to hack into it."

Kalet studied her holograph. The Reptilite Armada entered the atmosphere. "Shall I pull back the forces?"

Natalyze noted, "They've left true space and are under the Earth's atmospheric protection. Communications are down!"

"We move forward!" Gedeon commanded, "The humans aren't stupid, just nationalized. We can't risk them uniting their drone fleets. Attack the advanced countries first, and make them protect themselves. That way we can slip into the undeveloped lands, and exploited their divisions."

"What about Lotus?" asked Tanga.

Gedeon glanced about. "Find the other Martians; Lotus is not leaving here alone," he told Tanga. "Contact the outer fleet. Bring us his ship. I need that beacon lit!"

As Kalet surveyed the Earth holograph, dots on her display turned red and disappeared. "The North American contingent has engaged in high atmospheric combat!"

"Status?"

Kalet looked up from her display and shook her head.

AS ADRIAN FELL through the atmosphere, with Yaliz on board, he had no illusions as to why the shadows over the Earth changed the beautiful sight of the planet into a grim portrait. Like the painting of a soldier, ready to plunge his dagger into the beast, as they both stood over a pit of inevitable death. The clouds seemed different. The sky felt sad. The Earth looked cold and eerie.

A wall of small, human-controlled, high atmospheric drone air fighters formed a tight blockade over the American airspace as they awaited the Reptilite Armada. As Adrian tried to maneuver south of the military barrier, Reptilite ships approached from all sides blocking his way. Unblinking drone airships remained in a densely packed square, as the left and right formations broke off. These two flanking wings scattered through the sky like swarms of bees.

The multitudes met the alien armada head on, reassembling themselves as a rectangular blockade facing the Reptilite ships. The remaining square below moved up closer, behind the front line.

Adrian saw the airships change position. "Let's go!" He flew through the upper atmosphere and asked. "Are these the dinosaurs Julius found in the jungle? Or are they clones?"

"They're as far from dinosaurs as you are from an ape," Yaliz told him. "These are Reptilites in these ships. And no, they aren't clones,"

When the Reptilites engaged the front line, the K-29 drones fired back. The front line gradually widened, as the rectangular blockade below thinned, making its remaining components harder to hit. At first, this confused the Reptilites, but then they concentrated their fire at the embargo's center, hoping to punch a hole. As the same time, the drone formation in the rear tightened, thwarting the Reptilites' attempt to pierce it.

"Dimycles?" Adrian asked. "Did he do this?"

"He's of no concern to you," Yaliz promised.

"Yeah, but you know him," Adrian said. "So I want to know how."

"How unfortunate for me to have a lapse in judgment, for just a moment, and say his name. Yes. I know him, very well." Yaliz said sadly, "There is a history here between us that would need an equal number of years to explain."

"Where is he from? What is he?" Adrian wanted to know. Trying to avoid fire from both the drones and the Reptilites, Adrian retreated higher but his flaps were frozen shut, and he sluggishly relied on puffs of air from this side thrusters to move. "We're never gonna get through this. These drones aren't letting anything by!"

Yaliz said, "If we stay up here we will die."

The Reptilite ships collided with the blanket of drones. With no maneuvering room, the Reptilites had to break ranks, circle and double back up through the formation. The cost of energy to fight against gravity depleted many of them so that a few Reptilite ships lost power and fell back into a drone onslaught.

Adrian maneuvered through the retreating ships, as the K-29 front line spread over hundreds of miles. The drones pursued the retreating Reptilite ships, hoping to deter them from returning. The atmospheric conditions wreaked havoc on Reptilite mobility, the drones' rear flank took advantage of their enemy's confusion. They flew up and engaged the wandering ships.

"Dimycles isn't from Earth?" Adrian asked.

"He is from Covarra. A planet that was once a part of the Sunil," Yaliz answered.

"The Sunil?"

"The Sunil form a brotherhood of hidden planets sworn to protect life from the most dangerous weapons and technology.

The drones' rear flank surrounded a sphere-like formation of Reptilite ships, cutting them off from the main armada. The drones concentrated their firepower, annihilating all Reptilite ships caught in the sphere, then they regrouped, pushing the Reptilite line further into the ionosphere, as they cut off sections of the invading fleet.

"A brotherhood of hidden planets? Dangerous technology?" As Adrian evaded oncoming missiles, he tried to comprehend. "But, what happened to Covarra?"

"Pay attention! You're gonna get us killed! Yaliz shouted. "You want a history lesson, but I don't know every answer! Covarra was destroyed when Dimycles was a child."

"If the Sunil is such a close brotherhood, why couldn't he just go to any of the other hidden planets and build a new home there?"

Yaliz sighed and said nothing.

"I mean, why Earth?" Adrian continued. "Why wouldn't he want to be with his own kind?"

More ships fell into Earth's atmosphere to reinforce the Reptilite line. Their formations pushed back toward the Earth's surface. The enemy line met every obstacle with more firepower. Some drones dodged, while others exploded and fell to earth. As the drones broke rank, some formed a long line to oppose the Reptilites. The aliens engaged this line, but a second line flew forward, backing them up. When the Reptilites attacked the second line, a third drone offense came from the side. The sluggish Reptilite ships couldn't counter this.

Yaliz struggled to remain upright as Adrian circled the drone. "The Sunil became suspicious that Covarra had survived, separate from the Brotherhood. So all Covarrans are blackballed as renegades."

"Tough break. With all those weapons the Sunil must be paranoid."

"That left Dimycles and his sister, Damyae, homeless and desperate. They followed every possible lead that might link to hidden planets."

"And they thought Lotus knew?" Adrian asked.

Droves of Reptilite ships descended. With new reinforcements, the drones split into eight sections: three in the front and two in the middle, two flanking, and one in the rear. The three front sections met the Reptilites and fought. The front sections spread out, and the two middle sections came up, so five formations directly opposed the invaders. Two of these suddenly retreated, attracting Reptilite pursuit. The retreating drones then turned on their pursuers, destroying them. The few surviving Reptilite ships were picked off by the drones above them.

Yaliz squeezed her seat tightly as Adrian steered wildly through the melee.

"Yes, Lotus knew," she continued. "Dimycles and Damyae came to Earth looking for answers about their home planet. Thinking he knew something, they followed Lotus, but he had lied."

"Welcome to Earth – the land of the lies," Adrian said. "Sounds like that's all we have to offer."

Adrian slipped through one flank, only to be faced with drones from another. Eight air fighters broke from the rear to stop Adrian before he reached the surface.

"You still don't get it do you?" Yaliz said

"Get what?" he asked. "A bunch of uppity aliens want to hide. So what? Let them hide. Do they want to walk around in white robes, with their hands folded together? They'll fit right in. I'm not that worried about Lotus and Dimycles. Our real problem is this Reptilite invasion. He zig-zagged downward, trying to avoid the same fate as the retreating Reptilite ships.

"But Lotus has a lot to do with the Reptilite invasion," she insisted.

"Why? What would that profit him? He's human."

"But he is not from Earth," Yaliz explained. "Lotus was born on Mars."

Adrian groaned, and dove straight for the drone blockade, dodging heavy fire, "Then he lied to everyone."

"It's not just him," she started. "All of The Six came from Mars. Of course, they lied! They lied to me, and they lied to him. But now Lotus knows about the Hidden Planets. The Reptilites built him a ship. Now that he has a way to reach the Sunil, he will go to them."

"Oh, is that right?"

"If he gets his hands on anything on one of the Hidden Planets, he could wipe out entire systems," Yaliz concluded. "Earth and this war are just distractions. The Six are diverting their enemies, so they can slip by them, and grab real power."

When Adrian hit the front line of drones, everything in his path disappeared. He teleported far behind the line, into a waiting section of heavy artillery. Adrian's ship disappeared, reappearing far lower, underneath the clouds. Anti-aircraft shells peppered the air around them, but soon he was close enough to teleport just above the surface.

Adrian dropped his landing gear and the ship transformed into a car. He drove on the Pennsylvania back roads until they reached Yaliz's mansion. Out front was a man standing with a little girl.

"Bishop?" Adrian said, jumping from the car. "Who's this?"

"My daughter," Bishop answered, "Zahra."

Adrian gave his friend an odd look, then peered at the child. "Hi, Zahra."

"I couldn't find you; your phone went off the grid. So I tracked your car here," said Bishop. "You got the message?"

Adrian looked at his phone, but it no longer received any signal. "My phone must have been damaged in the high atmosphere."

Bishop nodded toward Yaliz, raising an eyebrow, then told Adrian, "Julius found Mason," handing him his phone. Adrian looked at the screen. It was Mason's request for an extraction. His heart leapt.

Bishop held his hand out to Yaliz. She smiled warmly and shook it. "I know who you are," she said. "Bishop Kennedy, right? Lovely daughter. We have a lot to talk about."

"Not yet," Adrian interjected. "We have to get to Mason."

"Mae should be okay," Bishop said. "Jules is with her."

"Not if the Reptilites are making landfall in Africa," Adrian said, opening the car door. "And, I'm sorry, but I don't have a child seat."

"I don't have ends on gas," Bishop said. He hopped in the back and secured Zahra in his lap.

Yaliz looked to a sky darkening with drones. "Will there be a next time?"

Adrian's tires peeled, as they sped off.

As the hood started angling up, the car reconfigured itself into a flying ship. They soared into the sky. G forces hit, and the passengers sank back into their seats. The ship banked, then headed north toward Canada. As they rose above the clouds, drones pursued them.

Bishop recalled the plants on the Potomac, and said, "There's an army out there."

Adrian nodded. "We just gotta get stronger."

Bishop made Zahra comfortable in his lap, then looked out to see the drones approaching. "Story of my life," he muttered.

Adrian's eyes tightened into slits.

A slight glow formed around their car-turned-spacecraft. K-29s attacked, but ran into an invisible wall. As drones fell from the sky, Adrian's ship went to afterburners. Adrian gripped his steering column. The entire aircraft turned translucent, and they vanished in a flash of light.

THE FALL OF AFRICA

THE AFRICAN CONGO treetops swayed in the wind from the East. A heavy pulsing rumbled from the sky. A contingent of alien ships took advantage of an undefended gap over Africa. It was one of the few large land areas on Earth that held no strategic advantage to any of the powerful nations. Though the Congo held many natural resources, other nations saw it as a place to be exploited, not defended.

The Congo's neighbors organized their forces for a counterattack, but those efforts meant little to those caught in the jungle. Down below the swaying treetops, two people ran from a collection of cottages, toward warehouses and hangars built like caves.

Mason entered the hangar and saw a line of fighter jets painted matte black. These weren't ordinary aircraft. They were Auracles, specifically developed by the Six for assaults on the Reptilite Armada. Though there were still too few of them to make them the salvation of the planet, they were powerful warplanes not to be trifled with.

As Mason ran toward an Auracle, Julius entered the hangar. Spotting Mason, he went after her, passing a brigade of Terredrones. The Six had designed the Terredrones for ground or space conflicts with the Reptilites. These bionic humanoid machines stood two stories high. Their arms had large cannons, whose barrels ended at the machines' hands. Shaped roughly like an hourglass, each Terredrone had broad shoulders for mounted weapons, a large back for thrusters, and a chest opening where the human sat. The Terredrone's large feet had enough power to stabilize the machine and provide mobility.

Julius grabbed Mason and tried to turn her around. She pushed him to the floor where he slid away from her. "You... slut!" she screamed.

"Mae, listen," Julius pleaded as he got up. "Don't be mad."

"I'm furious!" Mason shouted, "How could you? I mean, of all people!"

"Listen," he said, "I know it wasn't the smartest thing to do. It just seemed okay at the time."

"She's a fucking assassin! She tried to murder you... while you were fucking!" Mason shouted.

Julius put up his hands to ward off any potential physical attack. "Mae, it was an accident!"

"W-What!"

"She seemed scared."

"So your dick is supposed to make people feel safe?"

"That's not what I meant!"

"There's a refugee camp north of here. How about we pass you around. So you can fuck them all to safety!"

"Mae, you're taking this a bit personally, don't you think?"

Mason gasped, "Look where've I been for the last two years! Who was responsible for that? How does it not get more personal than that?"

"Sorry."

Mason shook her head, "I hate you so much right now."

"I fucked up," he muttered, staring up at the Terredrones.

Mason hopped in the Auracle's cockpit, sealing it. There in the isolated silence, she started to calm herself.

Suddenly Julius's voice was on her radio receiver. "What are these things?" He'd mounted a Terredrone and was talking to her through the comms. He started to apologize again, but she ignored him.

He waited a few moments, then tried some idle chatter. "So this is what Lotus built? Kinda cool. Quite claustrophobic. I can't see out of this thing." He perched himself in the chest cavity of the Terredrone.

Mason didn't reply. In the dark cockpit, a blinking status light flashed an intermittent glow across her angry face.

"You ever flew one of these?" Julius asked.

She hadn't, but she refused to answer. As she gripped the controls, the light stopped flashing and came on full. The cockpit came alive with a 360-degree display. At first, it made her dizzy, but she quickly got her bearings. She waved her hand, bringing down a menu of mission options. Meanwhile, the cockpit scanned her body and adjusted the environment and seating to fit her.

She stared at a map, still ignoring Julius's voice. After a few moments, she realized what she saw: enemy positions across central Africa, with suggested flight paths and attack patterns.

"Adrian and Bishop are coming in from the North," Julius said through the Terredrone comms. "We need to meet them. They've got no weapons in that car-plane, and they'll be toast without our support."

"Wait here," she answered.

Julius raised an eyebrow, "Mae?"

As Mason powered up the Auracle, she pushed her right hand forward. The front of the plane dipped and lurched ahead. As it shot from the hangar, Mason felt a rush of g-force. She quickly pulled back. The Auracle cleared the trees. The 360-display made her feel like she was floating in a bubble. She banked to the east, just under cloud level. All the gauges and indicators overwhelmed her at first; then one caught her attention. A window popped up on her right, then shifted to the front of her, showing a Reptilite fighter plane on her tail. She dipped low. It followed. Panicking, she climbed. It climbed after her. She dove straight toward the ground, as the Auracle alerted her to decelerate. She decelerated, but the alien ship couldn't follow. It overshot her vector, and she pulled up behind it. The Auracle auto-locked onto its prey. Her weapons menu dropped down, she armed and gripped the controls to shoot.

Then, from her comms, she heard the voice of her target. "Kung sana te!"

Mason's fingers froze. Weakly, she said, "T'ana te."

As she faltered, the alien shook off the lock and escaped. Mason drifted through the air, watching the ship fly away. "What am I doing?" she wondered. "Where am I going? What am I thinking?"

She engaged her thrusters and chased down the rogue ship. In her mind, she started counting. She controlled her breathing as she reassured herself, "Just pull the trigger. I am human. They are the enemy. They deserve it! What they did to me?" As she closed in on the craft, her radar beeped wildly. A fleet of Reptilite ships approached. Her hands shook, and she screamed. The Auracle fell toward earth. She wanted to escape, but her cold arms and numb legs didn't respond to the alerts popping up everywhere.

Her plane stabilized automatically. As she found herself back in the open sky, she felt horribly exposed. Mason spotted a clearing and landed. Above, the Reptilite fleet flew over, no longer mindful of her. She ducked her head into her lap and sat there shaking.

G-get up! They are gonna bomb me!

But they didn't.

The air rumbled, and the trees bent in the wind, and finally everything went silent. Mason felt claustrophobic. She pushed the button to pop the hatch. The cockpit opened and the ladder extended. She stumbled out and fell all the way to the ground. She landed with a thud, stumbled off, and leaned on a tree trunk for balance. After she had caught her breath, she stood on her own two feet. The morning sun peeked over the trees from the East.

"You're free, Mae," She told herself. She walked around, gradually getting her bearings. She breathed slowly and moved rhythmically. She heard music and drumbeats in the distance. She headed that way. Soon she came upon a village. The villagers were performing a ritual, so she kept a respectful distance, but did not hide herself. Men and women wore big masks and held large hammers. They were dancing around a white pile of some kind.

"Eggs?" Mason whispered, edging nearer. The villagers smashed the eggs.

"No. Don't!" Mason shouted, running toward them. "Those are innocent eggs! They don't have anything to do with this!"

The villagers paid her no mind and continued crushing the Reptilite eggs. Mason screamed, grabbed an egg, and ran off with it. As the villagers gave chase, she fell. They tried to wrest the egg from her, but she crouched over it, screaming hysterically. She didn't stop until an old village woman pushed through the crowd and touched Mason's face. The touch of the woman's fingertips seemed to soothe Mason. Her screams stopped, and she relaxed, though she still clung to the egg.

Suddenly the ground shook. Mason tumbled over, landing a few feet away. As Reptilite ships flew overhead, their bombs were exploding nearby. Mason stood, then fell again, the egg jarring loose from her grip. It fell to the ground, and broke, its contents spilled onto the ground. Mason rushed back to her ship. She climbed the ladder and plopped into the cockpit headfirst.

When the Auracle rose over the trees, she found herself perfectly situated behind the bombers. Her Auracle locked on each target as if serving them up on a silver platter. She flexed her shoulders and tensed her biceps, but her finger refused to pull the trigger. She watched as the Reptilites pounded the village below.

She screamed for them to stop. The Auracle's alarm told her to fire. Every detonation frightened her more. She screamed at herself to shoot.

The invaders leveled the area, leaving nothing but smoldering rubble, then they flew out over the north coast of Gabon to rejoin the main armada. From there they were soon hammering the West African Gulf Coast.

The Auracle's maps showed the human defenders spraying antiaircraft fire at the ships, but it did little damage. When Mason altered her display spectrograph, she saw the Armada had a deflecting shield lessening the damage of any human attack. She flew off after the Reptilites.

On the cliffs of Gabon human infantry fired at the Reptilite fleet. The people concentrated firepower on a single carrier to pierce through the shields. The aliens answered by bombarding the heavily forested areas. The ground forces kept up their fire, and support came in the form of Egyptian fighter jets. They engaged the Reptilites in a wild melee. An alien carrier ship swooped in near the coast.

Mason flew low over the trees. Thinking she was an enemy, the humans below fired missiles at her. After maneuvering around them, she pulled up and circled back around.

She glanced down at the earth. The Egyptians targeted the alien carrier, but couldn't get close enough. Would the Reptilite shielding hold against the Auracle's firepower? She checked her controls and found the menu options for charging a cannon blast.

As the Auracle soared, light sparkled through the ship. The indicator turned green. She bit her lip and pressed the trigger. A beam of solid energy shot out. Her ship jerked as her blast hit the alien carrier out over the ocean, tearing through its hull. The ship fell from the sky and broke apart when it hit the ocean. African soldiers cheered her as she flew over their lines.

Mason's hands shook as she saw what she'd done to her former masters. Suddenly she noticed something odd. Just before her blast had broken through the alien shields, something had repelled it for an instant.

"That has to be a localized field."

She flew low toward the Reptilite fleet. The morning sky darkened with more human jets.

After she sunk the carrier, the Reptilites were more cautious. Their fleet spread out over the African coast.

Human bombers pushed out over the waters, unloading depth charges on the remains of the fallen carrier, sending wreckage to the bottom.

Mason advanced past the gulf out to the ocean. She banked around and took a reading of their shields. "Looks like its surrounding the whole fleet."

The analysis showed her the shield barrier. She flew beneath it, to find the shield generator. It was a large box-like craft floating with the Armada.

"If I manipulate the frequency of my ion blast, I can punch a hole through the barrier and slip in, then blow the shield generator," she guessed, tweaking her weapons.

The sun rose high over the forest to the east. Human fighter jets filled the skies, but their enemies remained safe behind their shield. Mason dipped low and flew over the water. She pulled back on the throttle and shot up toward the fleet. She charged her ion cannons.

"They look so confused and uncoordinated," Mason noticed, as she gauged the Armada's position. "Why here? Of all places, why Africa, I don't see what they hope to gain."

She looked back and saw the aliens were hammering the human forces. She bit her fist, trying to gather courage. She circled beneath the shield generator, her cannons fully charged.

They can't hurt you anymore.

She got on her comms, but the satellite feed was weak. She sent out a shortwave broadcast.

"Hello? We need help. We need support!" she announced. At first, she heard nothing.

A human answered. It was a military communication. "What is your location?"

"Location?" she said, looking around, "Um... one degree south and um... twelve degrees... east?"

There was silence.

"Your location is too far for assistance."

"Too far? Too far for what?" Mason cried. "We only have one planet! They're counting on us to be divided—each country holding back. Do you want them to win? Does anyone hear this?"

Silence and static were her only replies.

"If you don't help, they will take control of this continent. From here they'll spread throughout the world. You'll never defeat them that way. Don't let the birthplace of our civilization be the source of our extinction."

She adjusted her bandwidth further and added. "Just so you know. You won't live if everyone around you dies! The fall of Africa is the fall of Earth."

Looking up at the shield generator, she pulled back on the steering and surged upward. She returned to her comms and changed the dialing,

"Julius, you gotta stay there and stop them from digging in. No one's sending support. We won't get another shot."

She shot a disruptive ray, tearing a hole through the shield. It sent their navigation systems into confusion. Once they diverted, she targeted the shield generator.

"Stay tight," Mason said to herself. "They can't hurt me anymore."

Her energy beam tore through the shield generator, disintegrating it. Debris scattered across the ocean, as African jets penetrated, and counter-attack.

A squad of Reptilite fighters poured out of a transport carrier. Mason evaded the worst of their fire, but a few shots grazed her. She dipped low, and to her left, nearly bottoming out over the water. To avoid any further damage, Mason headed north at full speed, pulling higher. Searching the weapons menu, she dropped air mines to ward off her pursuers. They chased her to the shores of Cote d'Ivoire, where the human forces defending Abidjan fired at her. She fled from humans mistaking her aircraft for an enemy by flying over Ghana and back out to sea.

On the horizon, she saw battle cruisers floating in a row. They looked like a row of toys painted against the sky. As she headed toward them, the Reptilites caught her signal and went after her. As she approached the row of cruisers, she saw the floating city of Tarov hidden behind the horizon. She sped north, parallel to the horizon. The Reptilites kept up their pursuit. The cruisers attacked the Reptilites. Mason took evasive action, spinning straight up to avoid the cruise missiles. They destroyed the Reptilites below. She leveled out and saw that the forces on Tarov were ready to fire.

Mason held her breath and went into a dive.

The floating city unleashed anti-aircraft lasers, destroying Mason's pursuers. She flew dangerously close to the military floating city, then banked and cut across the water heading northeast. She saw a collection of Reptilite aircraft spread out, heading toward Nigeria's shores.

Mason recharged the cannons and flew up behind the descending forces. She let loose a blast, tearing a hole through another carrier. The damaged carrier hit a wind shear, splitting the ship in half. Reptilites fell from the sky.

Mason examined the map of enemies from her radar and image scans. As she expanded the area, she saw a much larger force of Reptilites descending into central Africa. Approaching Nigeria, the country tried to repel a full-scale attack. She followed the coast south into Cameroon.

One and one, it wasn't a contest, Mason's aircraft was far superior to the enemy, but as time went on, more of Rex Gedeon's fighters descended to the Earth – and they just kept coming. "This defense is hopeless!" Mason worried.

The sun came up over the land, but the sky was dark with invaders. Alien ships cast an eerie shadow over the Gulf. A new set of ships descended, surrounding the area.

Though the human fighters had superior agility, their numbers dwindled along with their firepower. Mason inhaled deeply and tried to steady her hands.

She banked away from the Cameroon coast, heading straight out to sea. The Reptilite fleet approached the coast through a fog of smoke and destruction. Mason felt queasy as she tried to understand the action she was taking - flying toward the Armada as if she were a go-cart playing chicken with a Mack truck.

As she fired her long-range weapons, human bombers and fighters engaged from the north. Mason gave a joyful shout to see the reinforcements.

Drone fleets came from the west, surrounding the area.

The carrier Mason had downed was now sinking into the Atlantic. The few surviving Reptilites pulled themselves from the remains and swam away from the wreckage. Human submarines hit them with a sonic blast, leaving only entrails. The once beautiful beachfront was now just another scene of destruction.

Quadcopters and attack helicopters flew up from the city of Tarov. Swooping low over the water, they attacked the Reptilites over Nigeria. Another massive fleet of drones took to the air from northern Cameroon. Naval vessels launched a barrage of cruise missiles from just over the horizon.

Though the Reptilites suffered casualties, alien reinforcements poured down from space onto the Cameroon coast. Carrier bays opened, spilling out Reptilites paratroopers.

"Don't let them on the beach!" Mason shouted.

She banked her ship around the island of Bioko and coasted to sea level. Angling upward, she attacked the Reptilite paratroopers in the skies. Seeing them brought flashbacks of her imprisonment. They dropped through the skies like living tanks.

She shook off her paralysis and fired on the descending troops. The Reptilites fired back, still descending near the Pico Basile. A Reptilite swatted an African fighter jet out of the sky with its tail. Other Reptilites had parachutes with propulsion that carried them to the coast of Cameroon.

She saw copters getting too close. "Watch it," she warned in vain. "Get back!"

When Mason shot up some parachutes, their Reptilites missed the target and fell into the ocean. Two more submarines came up from the south and went after the submerged combatants.

Mason skimmed the treetops of Bioko, targeting more paratroopers. She blasted them to pieces before they could reach the thick foliage. Thick smoke and debris clouded her vision. When she got clear, soldiers were popping out of the water, going onshore, and scaling the trees.

Mason flew out to sea, did a vertical climb, and turned. She dove back to sea level and drifted toward the island. Tilting the Auracle left to skim the coast, and shoot Reptilites off tree branches. She then bombed the coastline.

Mason found herself climbing through crossfire between drones and Reptilites. A gunship fleet divided over Bioko, creating zones of control to prevent a Reptilite landing. As Mason maneuvered, her console alarm went off.

"I'm hit!" Mason screamed.

The sun blinded her when her Auracle listed. She wrested control over her aircraft, positioning herself in the shadows of the Reptilite fleet, but her ship took more flak from the crossfire. She banked sluggishly, eyeing the coast of Cameroon through the fog.

"Can I make it?" She was still over open waters, with more fighters speeding her way. Her heart jumped. "I won't make it!"

She turned southeast toward Bioko. More shots hit the hull. She lost power and glided, becoming a sitting duck. The flak got thicker.

"Damn it!" she shouted.

Mason ejected just before the Auracle exploded. As she shot downward, bullets and laser blasts whizzed by. She balled herself up as Reptilite aircraft spotted her. She crashed into the water, going deep. Kicking her legs she struggled to reach the surface. She emerged, gulped air, and found herself caught in the ocean current.

Mason still had her chute on. Now she deployed it, and the current pulled it open. As it dragged her, she pulled a knife, cut the chute lines, and engaged the propulsion system on her backpack. It pushed her toward the island cliffs until the ocean water shorted out the propulsion unit.

Waves crashed into shore at the base of the cliffs. She pulled off the jet pack and paddled through the water. The waves tossed her forward. She grasped for land, but was pulled back under and out. Another wave took her, and she emerged even further out. She tried to catch a wave, and finally one tossed her into the mouth of a cave.

She gripped sharp rocks at the cave's mouth, waiting for a break in the waves. None came. When she pulled herself from the mouth, a wave smashed her against the cliff, and she was hurled back out to sea. She dove to the bottom—airless, but calmer. She gripped a rock, then slipped, and got caught in the currents again. She finally surfaced, swam out, then north, and finally caught a wave that took her in. It threw her onto the black soil. Her hands and arms were cut up, and she saw her own blood mixing into the receding wave.

Finally, she stood. She steadied her wobbling legs and started to walk. Bits of Reptilites had washed ashore. Monkeys watched her from the trees. She hurried through the dense foliage. Human gunships over Caldera were fighting off Reptilites. A gunship faltered in the sky over Mason. As it caught on fire, it began falling straight toward her. Voices screamed, hands grabbed, and suddenly she was being pulled into a trench. The gunship skimmed the ground and came to a stop.

Mason stood up, muddy and wet. Villagers surrounded her. As they all climbed from the manmade trench, she tried to thank them for saving her life.

"You are... fighting them?" she asked in English. These people looked timid and peaceful.

A large dark man with a button nose stood and answered her in heavily accented English. "Everyone is a fighter now. I am Seibou."

"I'm Mason," she said. "Seibou, you can't stay here. You all have to leave this island. It isn't safe!"

"We know, isn't safe! That is why we cannot leave this island," Seibou agreed. "Who will fight for the suffering animals? Come, this way!"

Seibu showed her a nest of defenseless sea turtles among the island's exquisite flowers. "What will happen to them?"

Mason sighed. *What would happen to everyone?* From the north came the sounds of an explosion, then gunfire.

"Quickly, to the fort!" Seibou shouted, and they all ran, Mason following. They fled through the trees and up a hill.

On the hilltop villagers fought off powerful Reptilites, protecting their makeshift fort. There was a pile of dead Reptilites, but now the invaders were arriving in much greater numbers. Mason saw a massive gun partially obscured in the stack of Reptilite bodies. She climbed the pile, kicking off the Reptilite corpses. Soon she'd uncovered a gun twice as big as she was. She gave it a shove, and it tumbled down. She jumped down after it, and villagers ran to help her. They dragged the gun inside the fort, where the managed to stabilize it, and aim it at the enemy.

"Fire!" Mason rasped.

Four villagers held the gun, and two others squeezed the trigger. They blasted the Reptilites attacking the fort. Though fewer invaders were dropping from the sky, more alien ships were flying west over Cameroon.

"Is there no end?" Mason wondered.

The sunset, streaking the western sky with yellows and reds. A haze of battle smoke created even richer hues. Still, the Reptilite forces came from all sides.

"They're not that big," Seibou said. "Nine feet at the most, and smaller."

"You're assuming they don't get bigger?" Mason asked.

"Well, do they?"

"No one sends their best troops first," Mason warned. "Trust me. There are bigger ones than what you see."

"Then it will be a battle between a man and a mouse."

Mason signaled for the soldiers in the fort to charge. Infantry poured out, charging against the Reptilites. The Reptilites started stomping them, but then the guerillas began ganging up on each separate invader. Soon the humans were winning, but Mason worried that theirs would be a short-lived victory. There were too many human casualties, and night was falling. "Ten of our dead to one of theirs is not a viable strategy," she thought.

She peered over the fort wall and saw the Reptilites setting up a camp east of them.

"They're digging in," Mason called down to Seibou. "Can we shoot them from here?"

"Too far, and through the trees... our shots will never reach them," Seibou replied.

"Then we have to get closer."

"Excuse me?" Seibu asked.

"Get everyone together!" Mason commanded. "Tear down this fort. We can't stay here."

Seibou relayed the command.

"They surround us," one villager shouted. "We will be overrun!" cried another.

"We can't let them have our land," Seibou called out, "and if we stay it will be theirs for the taking."

Immediately the villagers started pulling the fort apart.

Seibou asked Mason, "What do you have in mind?"

"We need to get within firing range before it's nightfall," Mason replied.

With the fort disassembled, the village fighters inched toward the Reptilite encampment. When they got within sight, Seibou whispered to Mason, "Is this close enough?"

Mason nodded affirmatively. "Reconstruct the defensive block between the trees in a semi-circle," she told him.

The villagers hammered in stakes and pikes and piled sandbags in a concave formation. Mason told them to leave the center open.

"The trees will slow their charge," she said. "If we can funnel them into this hole, we can kill them one-by-one."

When a few villagers complained, Seibou ordered them to press on with the plan. Mason put some guerillas high in the trees to fire at any alien aerial support. She also needed these treetop fighters to start the action. When everything was ready, they fired on the Reptilite encampment. The Reptilites responded with their version of cavalry: charging beasts with armored heads and horns.

"You were right," Seibou said. "They do get bigger."

The treetop fighters rained down fire on the charging warriors that did no damage and emboldened their mad charge. Other alien cavalry joined in the vicious assault, but by doing so, they ran into each other, slammed into trees, and tripped over bushes and vines. Committed to their goal, they edged forward toward the human defenders, but their charge had lost momentum due to the confusion. Their final push against the human line was weak. Defensive pikes held steady, skewering the beast leading the charge.

Once it was evident the defenders had held, Mason commanded the Bioko on the front line to unleash everything. The guerrillas emptied their clips and battery stations, killing the remaining Reptilites.

The aliens who survived were disappointed in their weak charge and retreated to the encampment for another try, but to the Reptilites who had stayed behind, they couldn't make out who ran toward them. Their commander feared the worst and assumed it was the humans charging the base, so the leader quickly summoned the front line of infantry to prevent them from getting through. Retreating Reptilite cavalry smashed into their own advancing infantry, and it took a few moments to bring order to the pandemonium. Eventually, the infantry regrouped to complete their orders. They formed a line and pushed toward the human fort.

The damp, soggy earth wasn't fit for a march – especially not after the constant cavalry trampling. The heavy aliens sunk into the mud with each step. As the land turned into a swamp, they quickly tired. But these fighters had been hardened in battle. Despite the mud, broken trees, and dead bodies, they pushed on. When they saw the hole in the human line, they formed up to take advantage of it. The stumbled toward it, and then the slaughter began.

Scores of humans became fodder in the desperate fighting. The Reptilites swatted and smashed them, but since the terrain and confusion had diminished the enemy's strength, the courageous villagers swarmed over the aliens. Human victory seemed feasible, but Mason was not happy with the odds.

She signaled the fighters to come down from the trees and reinforce the line. Under her command, they formed up on the ground and punctured the center of the Reptilite infantry. The humans effectively cut the invading force in two. They surrounded one group, then poured in on the invaders, slaughtering them *en mass*.

Reptilite ships in the sky wanted to help, but darkness, foliage and smoke made action impossible. As the battle raged below, human planes arrived, and started blasting the Reptilites from the sky.

A Reptilite ace played chicken with a human jet fighter. They charged each other head on. Mason saw them approaching, then lost them in the smoke and trees. The human lost control and crashed into the jungle, exploding on impact. The Reptilite pilot barely landed in a clearing before dying.

Mason pointed at the Reptilite encampment, and told Seibou: "We have to get them off this island." As if to punctuate her thought, one dying Alien hurled his last grenade into a crowd of villagers. The blast blew them to pieces and tumbled Mason into nearby sandbags. She staggered to her feet, her ears ringing. For a moment she was deaf, but gradually her hearing recovered.

The guerillas were in chaos, and Seibu was screaming for a medic. As the medic arrived, Seibu pushed Mason to the ground.

"What—" she started

"Just stay still. It will be good," Seibu hissed.

Mason looked down and saw shrapnel about the size of her foot piercing her abdomen. Shock froze her. The medic quickly cut off her clothing and pulled out his kit.

Mason grabbed the metal shard with her bare hands.

"No! Don't pull it out!" the medic screamed.

Mason yanked it out. Red fluid ate into the metal. She looked down in horror. Her insides no longer contained a stomach. Everything down there was bionic.

The medic stumbled back. "Qui etes vous?"

By now the darkness was total. Mason stood up in the starlight. Though blood covered her from human and Reptilite, she knew the dripping stinging red substance was neither.

Sarek!

Mason crawled from the chaos, stood, and fled east. Villagers shouted at her to stay down, but she didn't listen. Bullets and laser beams whizzed by her. She hid behind corpses and scurried through bodies and trees until she came to the abandoned Reptilite aircraft that just landed. Red acid still dripped from her bionic middle.

I need help!

She hopped in the cockpit and fell into the oversized seat. She pressed what looked like an ignition switch, but all she did was blast the trees ahead of her. "Oops. Not it." She stood up to look over the dash. "So... if I were a Reptilite, how would I start a plane? Not all of you have tails, and some of your heads are oversized. Hmm... you all are huge."

She got on her knees, dug behind the seat, and found a weight sensor. She hopped down from the cockpit and found the dead pilot nearby.

"Please don't be diseased," she begged. She hauled the body back to the plane and got it into the cockpit. The fluid from her wound was eating away at her clothes. She felt lightheaded and stumbled backward, then righted herself. With the Reptilite pilot in the seat, the plane's controls lit up. Panting, she hopped on top of the corpse and took off.

The left wing had blast damage, and bullet holes riddled the windshield. The main control panel indicated only 5% power. She barely got enough altitude to make it over the mountainous hills of Bioko. The aircraft puffed along so low over the ocean's surface that it was almost like poling a raft on a river.

A larger Reptilite ship approached. She ducked down and lifted the dead animal's arms, so it appeared to be steering.

A voice came over the comms.

"Sul ko le?"

Mason tilted her head back and thought.

"Um..." Her mind went blank.

"Sul ko le?"

"Sec!" she remembered.

When the ship left, Mason breathed a sigh of relief, but then it came up on her rear and latched onto her ship.

She screamed.

Mason looked around for a weapon. The larger craft was connecting to the hull, refueling her plane. After the indicator had shown a power increase, the fuel ship detached and flew away. She resumed her place at the controls.

Mason stood in the dead alien's lap, using both her hands to steer through the Reptilite formations landing all over Central Africa.

"This is really happening," she breathed. Her vision faded. Her hands dropped, and she fell forward. She looked down at her empty abdomen. The red liquid was gone, leaving only stained tissues. "They must have hit a battery or something. I feel slow -Sarek... what did you do to me?"

She adjusted herself, and flew east, toward the Congo.

CONGO SKIES

ADRIAN WRESTLED HIS aircraft south, over the desert areas of Libya and cruised into Chad. The round gauges on the roof of the car-plane helped him maintain control, giving the smoothest ride possible under the circumstances. The damage received from the high atmospheric chase left the comfort from his car-sized aircraft barely tolerable.

The car was one of the few toys Adrian had where Bishop hadn't lent a hand. Bishop thought to himself that he definitely would've improved the airflow in the back if he had a say. He coughed in the stuffy air and looked around for a water bottle.

Bishop had just asked Adrian: "Do you want to save the world?"

After a long silence, Adrian replied: "I just want to get Mason back, then I'll think about being a hero. You?"

Bishop looked down at Zahra's head, her face glued to the window, watching the countryside pass by. Her big brown eyes slanted up at the ends over her tiny dark nose. She had fat cheeks and a crooked smile. Her lips lifted higher on her left when she giggled.

Adrian and Bishop entered the airspace over the Congo and flew low over the trees. Zahra pointed whenever she saw an animal below.

"I wake up each morning just to live 'till the next," complained Bishop. "Gotta be more to life than that. Right now, Zahra's all the hero I need to be."

Alien ships had landed, infesting the Congo. From a distance, they appeared like dots in the fields.

"Where'd Mason say she was?" Adrian asked, "We'll have to grab her and dash. I've got no real weapons on this plane."

"The mind is a powerful weapon," said Bishop. "It will tell you when you are strong, and when you are weak. It will always be right. The zenomites will listen if you just tell them what to do."

"Yes, but will my body withstand it?"

Bishop fell silent. A few Reptilite ships broke off from the Armada. "I think they see us," said Bishop.

Some of these Armada outriders flew nearer, but they never ranged too far from the fleet. Bishop reached for Zahra to move closer to him.

"If we get close, and drop in fast, they'll still have a chance to bomb us," said Adrian.

"Strategize."

Adrian banked toward the fleet, away from the extraction point.

"We'll create a diversion, and then ghost when it gets dark," Adrian said. "That should give us enough time to fly to the target, touchdown, rescue, and lift off. Agreed?"

"You're the pilot."

Adrian accelerated toward the Reptilite outliers. They responded as he'd expected: missiles followed by an energy blast. Adrian spun the plane, rolling through the barrage. When missiles detonated nearby, he teleported then far from the explosion.

Zahra gasped.

"How'd you do that?" Bishop asked him.

"Been practicing," Adrian said, feeling a bit light-headed.

Adrian took them into a steep climb. Flanking ships attacked him broadside. Bishop threw up a field, blocking the worst of the assault.

Facing megaton denotations, he galvanized a force field so strong it threw out superheated sparks.

Adrian took them into a dive, as more ships closed in. He rolled right into their center. "What was that?" he shouted above the noise when he saw the sparks. "Bishop, are you squeezing the air? Do that again!"

Bishop cradled Zahra in his arms as Adrian maneuvered. Bishop concentrated again and forced a chunk of air into a massive pressurized ball, sparks flew but it did nothing to stop the missiles that headed their way. He abandoned his experiment and used his power to force the missiles back toward the alien ships.

"It's not giving me much of a payload," Bishop said. "A gun would be so much easier."

Adrian steered an erratic course toward a carrier. He turned to Bishop. "You want to take the wheel?"

"Why? Where are you going?"

"To get a gun!" Adrian disappeared.

The doctor teleported into the carrier helm and landed on a Reptilite commander's face. Crew instantly attacked him. He teleported behind them, tripped a guard, took the gun, and blasted the creature's face off. As he took off down the corridor sirens went off.

"I'm the invader now!" Adrian shouted, shooting every creature in sight could until the clip was empty. He teleported up a few levels and attacked a guard crew. When five huge Reptilites came at him, he cut the first one off with a crack at his knees. Adrian vanished, and wrapped himself around the second one's neck, snapping it. He grabbed the dead guard's gun and blasted the other three.

"This is a big ass gun!" he exclaimed, heading for the engine room. "Delicious!" he yelled, firing at the engine core. Sparks flew everywhere. Adrian teleported to the hull and ran on top of the frame as it exploded.

"You see that ship, yeah?" Bishop told Zahra as he steered with his mind. "That's Uncle Adrian having all that fun!"

When invaders started firing at Bishop, he shielded and dove. "Whoa!" he cried. "Maybe we're having a good time too!"

Still gripping the big gun, Adrian jumped from the exploding aircraft. He went into free fall. A smaller fighter went after him with a barrage of laser blasts. Finally dropping the gun, Adrian teleported onto his attacker's fuselage.

Bishop groaned. "Showoff... and look! He dropped the gun!" Bishop aimed the car-plane at the falling gun. "Toy!" he told Zahra. "Let's go get it!"

Reptilite fighters peppered the area with blasts, and Bishop changed his mind and retreated. "We'll be patient, and wait for Uncle Adrian to bring us a present."

Adrian clung to the Reptilite craft, pouring his energy into the plane. He teleported the entire fighter plane into a nearby carrier, and let it tear through the vessel.

Adrian looked for his next target. Another carrier approached and let loose an artillery barrage at him. From behind him came a light beam that cut the carrier in half.

Clad in his bionic suit, Julius flew up and caught Adrian.

Seeing the suit, Bishop shouted, "Now that's a toy!"

"If you wanna play, get to the extraction point!" Julius shouted over the comms.

"Let's go," Bishop said to Zahra.

Adrian gripped the Terredrone arm, as Julius swung by another carrier. Julius phased them and flew onto the enemy ship. Adrian rolled, hopped, bounced and spun, kicking a Reptilite's teeth out.

Julius blasted out of the carrier and faced a squadron of fighters. As the Terredrone charged its arm cannons, it tore the wing off of the lead plane with its robotic arms. Using it like a sword, Julius cut the other fighter to pieces. When the pilot ejected, Julius threw the wing shrapnel like a javelin, slicing the Reptilite in half. Then unleashed a cannon beam destroying the others.

Teleporting to the bridge, Adrian slammed the pilot's head into the console. Sparks flew, as current electrocuted the Reptilite. Adrian picked up a gun as big as his body and shot every Reptilite in sight.

Julius saw Adrian running on top of the falling carrier, As he swung near, Adrian teleported to the Terredrone, and they flew off together.

"I think that counts as a diversion! Let's go!" Adrian communicated.

The Terredrone landed with a thud back at the rendezvous point, and Julius phased out of the suit. "They should've stayed extinct," he boasted.

"Yeah. Let's hope they do," said Adrian. "Just let me get suited up in one of those. Where's Mason?"

Julius nodded to the west. "She flew to the front lines."

Adrian froze in horror. "You let her go? The only reason we came here was to get Mason! Why? Why did you let her leave?"

"I couldn't stop her," said Julius. "She needed to get away, and told me to stay here."

"Get away from what? What did you do?" Adrian demanded.

"She's been a captive for two years," said Julius. "If she wants to go, I can't do anything!"

"What if she's in trouble?" Adrian shouted.

"She told me to stay so I did until you guys showed up. Why's everyone on my case?"

"Because you lost what we came to get!" Adrian screamed.

"Didn't you get her broadcast? This is a war!"

"It's not a war we have to fight," Adrian insisted. "For every one we destroy, twenty more will make landfall. These guys are ready to take the whole planet. How can we stop them?"

Bishop emerged from the hangar. He might've joined the argument, but instead he smiled down at Zahra. The other men fell silent.

"You brought a baby into a damn war zone!" Julius retorted.

Bishop covered the child's ears. "She's not a baby, and watch your language."

"Sorry, Zahra," Adrian apologized for his brother.

Bishop smiled and nodded to the hangar behind him. "Follow me."

Inside the hangar, Adrian and Julius stared at all the artillery: seven Terredrones and five Auracles. Bishop looked up at a bionic fighter. "These suits are remarkable."

"Now," Adrian started. "We will use their own weapons against them."

"Reptilites didn't build these," Julius explained. "Lotus did."

"How?" Adrian wondered.

"That tablet. The one you stole for ICP. The one they stole back. It has secret technology in it," Bishop said. "I saw it in D.C, right after an assassin named Kyra tried to kill me." Bishop looked sternly at Julius when he said the name.

"Kyra," Adrian shook his head, "What a menace. She came to me afterward, but fled during the earthquake."

"Ah," Bishop said, still eyeing Julius, "Perhaps, she was just scared and needed comfort."

Julius stared at the hangar floor.

Adrain looked at the machines, though remarkable, there was only a few of them. "This isn't nearly enough to fight a war."

"Are we here to fight a war or find Mason? We can only protect the ones that matter most," Julius said.

"How do you decide who matters?" Bishop asked.

"No one wanted to stand against the militia that killed our parents. It would've been nice," said Adrian to his brother. "We may not be able to save the entire world, but if we do it one person at a time, maybe things will be different." A powerful noise came from outside. A vessel was landing. "What's that?"

"I told you she was coming back!" Julius shouted, realizing it was Mason.

Adrian smiled, but then said: "You still let her go, dammit! I hope she's not pissed!"

As Adrian left the hangar, Julius turned to Bishop. "Why is he always so touchy about Mae?"

"Wait till he finds out about what you did with Kyra," Bishop said, sharing a fruit with Zahra.

"Mason told you?"

"Damn right! She's furious," Bishop said sternly.

"I take it you didn't tell Adrian."

"No way! If I had, you'd be fighting a different war right now. What were you trying to prove? Kyra? Oh man, you're dumb as shit. Never let your guard down around her! Adrian's gonna come unglued. He's got some weird guardian angel complex over Mae. I guarantee you, when he finds out about you and Kyra," Bishop chuckled, "I got tickets to that fight."

"I feel like a dumbass."

"We all do things we regret," said Bishop. "It'd only really be dumb if you died."

Mason landed her wounded alien jet near the hangar. Adrian grinned when he finally saw her peek over the cockpit. He ran to her.

"Mason!" Adrian cried, as she jumped down to the ground. "Mae?"

Her clothes were torn, and she was covered with blood. "I'm okay," she panted.

"You look--" Adrian stopped, then said: "Let me check your vitals." He pulled out his tablet.

"No!" Mason screamed, pushing him away, "I'm fine... just tired."

Adrian put the tablet away. "Okay," he whispered.

"You hungry?" Julius asked, emerging from the hangar, "You probably need some food."

"I'm not hungry," she said and walked toward the warehouses.

Given her wounded condition, Adrian went to protest, but held his tongue.

Mason slowed and turned. "Okay. Some food would be nice."

"This place has amazing fruit!" said Bishop, emerging from the hangar. "I'll get you some."

When Mason saw Zahra, she grimaced, then shook it off. "I'm seeing a lot of weird shit today. Give me some privacy. There are clothes in that warehouse. I just... I need to freshen up."

"Be my guest," said Adrian. With a lot of effort, he stood still.

As she walked off, he whispered to Julius, "If she's not out in five minutes..." His brother nodded.

Mason walked, head high, into the warehouse. As soon as she'd closed the door behind her, she fell to her knees. She coughed, and struggled to breathe. Crawling to a set of cabinets, she clumsily typed in codes. After several failures, the door swung open.

Dammit, Sarek!

The cabinet had bionic parts stored neatly in rows. She'd seen these often but never paid them any mind. She pulled down a battery pack and fell on her butt. Digging into her abdomen, she unlatched a punctured cylinder and tossed it away. An alarm in her head warned of danger, but her lungs begged for air.

She inserted the new cylinder and instantly felt re-energized.

Mason's head fell back against the cabinet. As she stared up at the warehouse ceiling, she realized she'd been holding her breath the entire time. The burning in her lungs was real. She closed her eyes, exhaled, and drew in air. She sighed as her body gave into relaxation.

Hero

BEER IN HAND, Omar walked into his house and headed straight for his basement. He rubbed the bottle against his arm, trying to relieve an itch. Beads of condensation rolled off the bottle onto his tattoos. In his basement, he kept a paradise of electronics and surveillance equipment. It was a hacker's work of art unknown to the world he was watching. When he saw his stolen top secret documents scattered about on his coffee table, he gathered and stacked them. These were corporate secrets, unreleased songs, and unpublished novels, and other works the world had never seen. He read everything he stole and was always amazed at how many great ideas never saw the light of day. The same was true of the scandals he uncovered, touching companies and politicians.

Omar neatly piled the documents next to a bowl of pumpkin seeds. He sat down at his console, unlocked the screen, put on a pair of headphones. As the physical world faded, he dove into his virtual planet. The default screen popped up, and a three-dimensional virtual platform of apps and scripts appeared. The war intrigued him. After the D.C earthquake, the military cleared the skies, making way for rescue workers, and airlifts. This created a defensive hole the Reptilites would have been wise to exploit. It was a small hole, but a hole nonetheless. Now Omar saw the skies were filled with sentries, and the city had some protection against any new alien attacks.

He commanded his system to locate Adrian. The mapping zoomed out to show the whole Earth, but it complained about the lack of satellite communication. The locator found Adrian somewhere in Washington, D.C.

"Hmm. What? Call Bishop," Omar instructed his machine.

"Hello?" Bishop's voice was choppy on the speaker.

"Kennedy?"

"Hey, Omar!" said Bishop's voice. "Hey guys, it's Omar!"

"You got Adrian with you?" Omar asked.

"Yeah, sure, hang on."

"Hello?" It was Adrian's voice, "Omar! Just the savior I need to talk to!"

"Yeah?" asked Omar.

"You have a miracle to get us out of here?" Adrian asked. "We have Mason!"

"I don't know," Omar answered. "I think we lost what little opening we had. The military owns the skies right now. Even a bird would have trouble getting into this city. The drones are up there 24/7, but I'm glad you found her."

"Yeah!" Adrian said. "Mason's alive. She's pretty banged up from battle, but she's okay. That's all that counts."

"Well, if anything happens to her, I'm sure you will be the first to jump on it," Omar chuckled. "I'm glad you agreed to help us get her back. I knew you'd pull through."

"What other options do we have to get out of here?" Adrian asked. "The Reptilites are in the Congo. The sky here is pretty clear. We can make a break for it anytime."

"I'll see what I can do," said Omar, "but I'd rather not say much right now. Do you have your phone with you?"

"Yeah, it's in my hands. I think it got damaged high in the atmosphere."

Omar scratched his chin, supremely worried as the map on his displayed showed Adrian's phone was still in D.C. "Has your phone been out of your possession anytime recently?"

"Not that I can recall. Why?" Adrian asked.

"Just being cautious," Omar said. "Can you open the back of your phone for me?"

"Okay." Adrian complied with Omar's request.

"Is there a small chip in the corner?"

"Yes."

"It's not supposed to be there. Someone bugged your phone. Can you read off the numbers to me?"

Adrian read the numbers, and they both hung up. Omar searched for the ID Adrian read off from the bugged chip.

Omar started checking alarms on his monitor. Almost immediately he saw a security breach tied to Adrian's phone. When he acknowledged it, more alerts popped up. He bulk-closed them all. He felt tired and took another sip of beer. With so few satellites operating, he had to track the clone the hard way. "We rely too much on satellites," he said to himself.

He ran a trace program. As data polled on the screen, he went to his bathroom and washed his face. Bags were forming under his eyes. Feeling his headache, he reached into his medicine cabinet, but the pill bottle was empty. He stretched his neck and wished for sleep, but his compulsive nature never let things go. A moment later he was back at his terminal. He saw the chip's address. "A Teltel chip? Who does that anymore? That's ancient."

He pried further, accessing his last personal call to Adrian. He hacked into the nearest phone, found the four addresses connected to the call, and scrolled through to match the number Adrian had read. Omar sighed and scratched his cleanly shaved chin. His fingers had run down the back of his tattooed neck before he scrambled through his files. He was looking for an older script he'd made to track the discontinued chip.

"What the hell did I name that script?" he asked. When he finally found it, the addresses traced to a call he'd placed to Adrian a few days earlier. He listed the four addresses and transferred them to a map on another monitor, but the map only showed three.

"What?"

He expanded the map over the US, then the world. Still only three points.

"Uh?" Omar moaned and rubbed his eyes. "This script must be old." He returned to the previous screen and recoded his script to get more details. It would now show numbers next to each location. He saved the script and executed it again.

Now the map showed the number "2" next to the dot indicating Omar's location during the call. The script placed a "3" by the carrier that connected the call. Over Adrian's position, it showed a "1" hidden beneath a "4."

"Oh shit! Were they in the same spot? At the hospital?"

Omar thought a government worker must have snuck into the hospital during Dimycles's surgery. If that were true, he could reverse-track them.

"I hope it's a CIA op," he said to himself, but then he recalled that the CIA had stopped using Teltel chips long before. He traced the address to its real phone number and then traced the number to the carrier. He accessed the carrier's database to match the name. Ignoring the name, he matched all the data to the Internet cloud, allowing him to view pictures, live chats, and run a facial recognition program on the data. Unfortunately, Omar already knew this face - it was Kyra. He gasped.

He called Adrian. As the phone rang on the other end, Omar watched the map. The number "1" moved from the hospital to the Congo, as expected, but the clone's destination gave him a shock. "4" moved from the hospital, and came to rest over "2." That was right here—his home. He sprung up from his chair as Adrian's voice came over the speakers.

"Hey O', you got my phone working!" Adrian's voice came over the speakers.

"Call the police!" Omar shouted. On a second line, the computer dialed 9-1-1, but the line was busy.

Kyra sprang from her hiding place and shot the phone box. Omar's secondary box took effect, keeping the line of Adrian open.

Adrian heard the shots. "Omar? You okay?"

"It's Kyra!" Omar cried. "Stop! Kyra please!" He stumbled backward, raising his hands. She tripped him, and he fell back over the couch, landing behind it.

"Kyra? Omar!" Adrian's voice echoed through the lab. "OMAR!"

The voices of Bishop, Julius, and Mason filled the background.

Kyra knelt on the couch, staring down at Omar behind it. He was twisted like a pretzel between the sofa and the wall.

"I didn't... I never did anything to you," Omar said squirming.

She nodded in silent agreement. "You have video?" she asked.

"V- video?" Omar repeated, and his system added video to the call.

"Hi, Adrian," Kyra said, looking where she assumed the camera must be.

Thousands of miles away Adrian froze at the sight: Kyra kneeling on the couch, looking down. Adrian knew she must be looking at Omar. "Kyra, he's got nothing to do with this."

"Is he like you?" Kyra asked, looking Omar up and down.

Omar tried to move his arms, but couldn't.

"No!" Adrian shouted.

She shot Omar in the leg. He screamed. Blood spurted from the wound.

"Kyra!" Adrian cried.

"I guess not," Kyra said.

"Stop!" Omar begged. "Please!"

"What do you want?" Adrian pleaded. "Just name it."

As Omar struggled, she pushed the couch, wedging him in tighter. He gulped air.

"You aren't like Bishop either?" Kyra curiously noted, "Are you there Bishop?"

"Please don't!" Omar whimpered. "I swear. I'll do anything."

Kyra glanced at the screen and saw Bishop looking over Adrian's shoulder. Now she knew where her enemy was. She turned back to the man behind the couch. "How well do you know Adrian?" she asked. "Is he a good doctor or a bad doctor?" She pointed the gun at him.

Omar was so scared he couldn't talk.

"How many people have died under your care, Dr. Blackwell?" she asked Adrian.

Adrian knew the number all too well. "Thirty-two," he breathed, stifling an anguished sob. "I remember every one of them."

Kyra hadn't expected that. She'd assumed he would boast of having none.

"Wow. That's a lot. I don't remember half the people I killed," Kyra admitted. "How do you deal with it? When they pass? How do you live with yourself?"

Adrian recalled all the ways he'd dealt with death, starting in his childhood. "I remind myself that I'd done all I could to save them," he told her. "Sometimes that's how life is."

"That won't work in my business," she told Adrian. "I need more drastic measures. When you saw those tracks on my arms you insulted me. That really hurt my feelings."

"You tried to kill me!"

She saw Julius behind him. "Yeah? I tried to kill Jules too, but he didn't make a big deal out of it." She giggled. "Right Jules? I missed you, I guess. Sorry about that. Your dick was so good; I almost forgot why I was there. That's gotta make you feel like quite a man."

"What do you want?" Adrian asked.

"I want you to save him, doctor," Kyra answered putting Omar in her crosshairs.

"Anything."

"Tell us your secret," she said.

"What?" Adrian asked. "You already know about the zenomites."

She shot Omar in the chest. Omar beat his fist against the couch. Adrian fell to the ground, staring at the image on the phone screen.

"Tell us your secret!" Kyra screamed.

Omar coughed up a bloody shriek: "Your book!"

Kyra nodded. "Omar here has an absolute treasure trove of unpublished work. Amazing stuff. He even has the original drafts of your book and all of your diary pages you kept about your addiction."

Adrian went pale.

"Tell us, and you'll save him," Kyra said.

Adrian's eyes filled with tears. "You're going to kill him all the same."

"Are you giving up?" she asked. "Is that what happened to those thirty-two patients? Did you decide they were hopeless and walk away?" She turned to her most immediate victim there on the floor. "What do you think, Omar, now that you know who he is?"

Omar gurgled blood and tried to breathe. Kyra stroked his head, "Ssh. It's okay. He's a good doctor; he'll save you." She turned to the monitor. "Won't you?"

"I was uh, I was selfish," Adrian stammered

Kyra shot Omar again. His screams accompanied his foot pounding the couch.

"Dammit!"

"You are a filthy evil person!" Mason shouted, her voice wavy with fear. "I should have fucking killed you when I had the chance! Someone should put you out of your misery!"

"Hold on to that thought, sweetheart," Kyra said.

"Kyra, this isn't right," said Bishop. "Why go after him if you're mad at me?"

"Because I want you to die internally first, Bishop. I want to squeeze the life from your soul. I want you to understand, but you still don't! I'm beyond furious! And right now, so is Omar. It isn't fair you get to be okay, and people like us get hurt. Omar needs some of that special robotic nano-stuff, yet you're stuck in the Congo pretending to be heroes. Meanwhile, Omar slaves all day in a basement, doing all he can to help you. And you can't even get him some super nerdy powers? Why is the special nano tiny bots just for you three?" Kyra watched as Omar tried to hold his body together. Blood poured from his chest and leg. She looked at Adrian. "Those bots are just for you guys, right, good doctor? Like everybody else, I'm just not good enough. You call me a piece of shit!"

"But... you're just gonna kill him."

Kyra shrugged. "You don't know that. You might save him."

With that, Adrian's pride died. He turned and looked behind him. "I left you to die."

Mason flinched at the words, not expecting his secret to involve her.

"I could've saved you from Lotus during the Kennesaw bombing, but I... I didn't want to the police to know."

Mason stood fast there in the phone camera's view, but she felt her soul fading and wanted only to flee. These were the first humans she'd seen in years. They obviously had no intention of harming her. She felt threatened by the truth. She backed away, shaking

"...To know that I was the second man in your room that night," Adrian confessed, hoping it would keep Mason from running. "You never had sleep paralysis. You didn't make it up. I took away all the evidence. You were r-raped. I saw it, and I kept quiet about it. When Lotus kidnapped you, I didn't save you because I didn't want the police to know... my powers, because they would pin me for a rapist."

As Mason opened her mouth to spill the hateful feelings in her stomach, Kyra cut her off. "Bishop," She asked. "How fast can you fly?"

At once, Mason felt a rush of betrayal and compassion, as Omar started to thrash, and Kyra shot him in the head. His eyes closed, as his head fell back.

Adrian screamed.

"Let it go, Adrian," Kyra said. "You did everything you could. Sometimes that's how life is." She walked around the room, saying: "The next time you try to judge me, you'll realize I made you a better person."

When she sat down and peered into Omar's laptop, the screen locked. She pulled it from the dock, plopped onto the couch, and grabbed Omar's hand. An old shirt lay in a heap, and she used it to wipe the blood from Omar's forefinger. Holding the laptop over his face, she peeled back his eyelid and pressed his finger to the keyboard. As the laptop started, she reached into a bowl on the table and helped herself to a handful of pumpkin seeds.

In the Congo, the others stared at Adrian in shock. He was deep in sorrow. Mason felt her heart sink and realized that Sarek must've failed in his attempt to make her entirely bionic.

"Hang up," Bishop told Adrian. "We have to go, and all she's going to do is toy with us."

Across the ocean Kyra busily typed into Omar's computer, initiating a program. She glanced at the last image of the faces in Africa and said: "I wish I could be there to see the insects pick the flesh from your bones, and know that you-" The line disconnected as all global communications shut down.

In Africa, the four stood, avoiding each other's eyes. Bishop felt a tingling under his feet.

"We have to get out of here," he said.

They stared blankly, as if in a trance.

"Move!" Bishop shouted. Zahra started crying. The floor began to shake. Julius took a deep breath and phased into a Terredrone. Adrian glanced at Mason. A chill shot through her body, and she hid from his gaze. He stepped back and teleported into a nearby Terredrone.

"Mae," Bishop pleaded as the shaking increased. "We have to go."

A crack opened in the ceiling.

Mason crossed her arms on her chest. "Shall I die with the monsters who violated me, or live with the men who became monsters?"

"Every life is unique, but every death is the same," he shouted, flying into a Terredrone's opening with Zahra. "Please, just live another day."

The three human-controlled Terredrones powered up and ran out of the hangar. The night sky seemed to move.

"What the hell!" Adrian shouted.

"Earthquake drones!" Bishop announced, and the Terredrones lifted into the air. Insects covered the land but did not drive into the ground. No shock waves followed.

"You sure about that?" Julius asked. "They don't look like drones."

Julius was right. The insects weren't drones, but real, and among them, the only hunger was an appetite for Reptilites.

"Mason," Adrian mumbled in disappointment before flying off.

Mason ran through the warehouse and raided the bionic cabinet. After tossing extra battery packs and bionic equipment into a large bag, she returned to the hangar. She stowed it into an Auracle and blasted off.

As the team flew over the Congo, they saw Reptilite bodies covered with feasting insects.

"The bugs ate them," Mason said, in a flashback of realization to when Sing first showed her the strange sample of manure. At that moment it all made sense, Lotus was indeed making a biological weapon, she was just analyzing the wrong thing. The insects were the weapon. Mason followed the other three Terredrones high into the sky – away from the plague that teamed over the land.

Voice of Insanity

KALET PUT HER talons to the bone textured floor and raced through the halls of the Kaiman, anger bursting from her green-and-yellow face. She broke through the door to a visitor's room, and there was Lotus. She rushed him and punched him across the chamber.

"You betrayed us!" she screamed. She hadn't listened to Sarek. He'd known what Lotus was up to, but she'd failed to heed. She hated everything.

Natalyze charged in behind her commanding officer. "What are you doing?"

Lotus wobbled to his feet, wiping the blood from his lips, "You'll pay for that. How do you expect to win this war without me?"

"Shut up!" Kalet shouted, "You were supposed to use the insect drones to sink the human defenses. Instead, you used them against us!"

"What?" Lotus wondered. "Impossible!"

"You designed them to eat us!" Kalet screamed. "Sarek tried to warn us!" She kicked him.

Lotus felt his ribs crack and crumpled, coughing blood. Kalet pulled her scythe.

"Stop!" Natalyze shouted. "If you kill him, we can never access the tablet!"

"He cannot live! You fool! Gedeon will execute us all!" Kalet shouted.

Natalyze shook her head, "He will understand!"

Lotus coughed up more blood, and said, "Tell that to the last two science officers!"

"Don't you dare speak!" Kalet threatened. "You are the voice of insanity—" She grabbed him by the throat, and sliced into it. Lotus kicked and gurgled.

"Stop!" Natalyze screamed. "He's saying something!"

Kalet cut his throat, yanked his tongue out, and cut that off. She threw him down and kicked him again. His hands went to his throat, and blood sprayed from between his fingers. Kalet backed him into a corner and thrust Boyacobas's tablet at him. "Open it!"

Lotus couldn't begin to comprehend her words. She sunk the tip of her blade into his abdomen. From his mouth came a crimson liquid scream.

"Please stop!" Natalyze shouted. "He can't!"

"Of course, he can. I will bite off a finger for every moment he refuses to type in the password."

"Then it will last all but ten moments because the tablet isn't password protected," Natalyze explained. "I've tried. It's... it only opens to authorized users."

Kalet didn't buy it. "Then why doesn't it open up for him?"

Kalet waved the tablet near Lotus's body.

"He's not an authorized user," Natalyze explained. "Probably to prevent this very thing!"

"Where are the others?"

"The others?" Natalyze asked.

"The other Six, one of them has to be it."

Natalyze quickly searched through her system. "I think... I believe that they're dead."

"You'd better tell me something a lot different than that!"

Natalyze brought up the profiles, and Kalet stared at the display with her.

"Look," Natalyze directed. "It's impossible to reach Tai! Bradford and Saozan show dead. Jalyn is missing!" The map moved from the Sudan over to Europe and another profile popped up. "Jerry is dead... but I think-"

Kalet noticed an alarm as the scanner checked over the Earth. "What is that?"

Natalyze was taken back by the request and examined the alarm. "A hyperdrive trail?"

"From who? I didn't authorize any travel out of this sector."

"I will investigate."

"Now! If a spy has left this system, our problems have increased."

"Yeah, but Kalet, what about the Six?" Natalyze wondered.

Kalet turned to Lotus. He clawed at the wall, scrawling something in blood. She stared back at Natalyze. "He doesn't leave this room. I will get Tai!" She stormed out.

Natalyze turned to Lotus and read the cryptic words in his blood.

A SINGLE REPTILITE ship dropped from space. As it hit the atmosphere, it glowed brightly against the night sky. The heated light caught the attention of North America's air defenses. Drones formed up to stop it, but traveling at Mach 23, the tiny capsule cut right through them. Missiles exploded without consequence.

The capsule approached the East Coast. Cruisers engaged their point defense systems and lasers touched the sky. It was like hitting a flying grain of sand with a bullet, but soon the algorithms lined up, and the lasers burned through the capsule. It exploded.

When jets took to the sky to confirm the destruction, they met a swift end. Kalet landed on a jet, pulled her scythe, and cut through the plane and its pilot. As she leapt into the air, two more aircraft tracked her. She pulled her wings back and dove. The jets strafed her, but she dodged them.

As she reached the eastern shore, SAM batteries below used their radar to track this speeding alien. Kalet flew under the antiaircraft fire, swooped low over the city of DC, and caught sight of her target. She soared, and dove into Omar's home.

Kalet blasted through the wall, splintering it. She charged down to the basement. Kyra grabbed her gun and shot Kalet, but the alien blocked the bullets with her wings. Seeing the digital equipment and Omar's body, she yanked Kyra up by the hair, and flew up, blasting her way out to the backyard. Kalet saw the Auracle Kyra had stolen from the Congo. She threw the human in back, hopped in, and launched into space.

Kyra's attempts to escape halted when the Auracle soared up into space toward the skull-like ship. The sun reflected off three-quarters of the hull, making the rest invisible. The Earth's moon and the alien ships nearby were only partially visible. It was Kyra's first time in space. She was in awe.

Kalet dragged Kyra through the bowels of the Kaiman. Kyra threw a protest, though she gained no footing being carried by a being twice her size. Kalet threw her into a room. Kyra tumbled in and sat up on her butt. She looked around and saw the room's door was gone, apparently torn off, and a feline, black-furred alien was in view.

Lotus lay in a pool of blood in the corner. That should have pleased her, but instead, she only felt fear. It was all too real.

The ten-foot Kalet gripped Boyacobas's tablet in her hand and commanded a report from her officer.

"The ship is of unknown origin, definitely not human," Natalyze said.

"Where did it go?" Kalet asked walking toward Kyra, with the tablet.

Kyra remained on the floor, in a dazed state of confusion, staring at Natalyze's display. It showed profiles of the Six, yet her picture was right there among them, under Tai Cao.

"W-what?" Kyra asked.

Natalyze looked up from her station. "It went to Mars."

Kalet stopped in her tracks. "The Exile!"

"The who?"

"He went back for her," Kalet put it together. "Did the ship take on a passenger? Did it stop?"

"No, it merely scanned the prison, and continued."

"She wasn't there. Wuyan must have taken her."

"Taken who? Who are these exiles?"

"The Sunil."

Natalyze hit the podium. "You have to be kidding me!"

"Time is of the essence," Kalet turned to Kyra and continued to walk toward the human cowering on the floor. "Open it! Or the line of Martians ends with your head."

Kyra shook her head – *No.*

Kalet forced the tablet into the prisoner's hands, but Kyra refused. The Asian mercenary opened her mouth to speak her defiance but was cut off.

"Tracking its trajectory," Natalyze hollered out. "I believe the Exile heading to the Go'Din system."

"To that thieving pile of scum. They won't help him," Kalet said. The rod in her hand extended at full, and the blade of the scythe came out.

Kyra saw her face in the reflection of the blade. Breathing became difficult for Kyra as she kept what little stance she had. She placed her arms on the ground to keep from falling backward as the blade inched closer to her neck. Kyra glanced at Lotus, but all he could do was bleed.

Kyra looked up, once again, at Natalyze's display of the Six. The pictures of all the members were familiar to Kyra, except, of course, the sixth- her. The name had the wrong face. A wave of confusion and disbelief battled each other for supremacy in her veins trying to remember Tai Cao.

Kalet's scythe touched Kyra's face. In the reflection, she saw her odd tattoos that she realized this was the same lettering as the etching on Boyacobas's tablet. With trembling hands, Kyra wondered. She touched the screen.

The tablet unlocked.

Kalet relieved the tablet from her dazed prisoner and confirmed access to the beacon. She turned her scythe toward Lotus, and blasted him, spraying half his face against the wall. "Clean that up," she told Natalyze.

"And what of Tai?"

Kalet looked Kyra up and down. "Tai stays." Then she left the room.

Though the sense of danger faded, the confusion and disbelief both lost the battlefield of emotions to the anger that welled inside of Kyra. Kyra couldn't take her eyes off the display with her face as one of the Six, and she put together the rest of the horrific story of her life in her mind.

"I killed...him," Kyra muttered. In her mind, she saw Jerry and heard his voice.

Boyacobas saved us from Mars... he took us to Earth.

Lotus saved you because Boyacobas trusted you.

Kyra slowly got up, feeling shameful. Natalyze stepped aside as young Reptilites entered the room to collect the body Kalet shot.

Kyra watched Lotus's body get hauled away; the display crossed a red X through his profile. She read the bloodstained message Lotus left on the wall, and with a depressed voice she uttered, "I am."

"No one steals from the Sunil."

THE PRISON OF HOLICE

A PRIVATE COLLECTOR willed a renovated fort called the Holice to the Galactic State. Previously, the fort had been built as a science outpost dedicated to the study of nearby irradiated asteroids, but eventually its focus turned to war. The Din species renovated the outpost, fitting it out as a military installation. They saw it as an asset in their battles with their close cousins, the Go'Din. Though both of these societies were of the same species, philosophically they could not have been further apart. The Go'Din held up wealth and luxury as their ideals. They sneered at the Din and their more modest lifestyles.

Though the fort took the name Holice, its namesake was not a warrior. Holice was a philosopher who'd been killed during an intense argument with Felpo of the Go'Din. With tensions already high, the murder was merely a tipping point for the inevitable – interplanetary war. The Din redesigned and expanded the science outpost, seeing it as a strategic point in their offensives against the Go'Din.

The Go'Din's expensive war effort required its citizens to lower their standard of living, but the payback was an eventual triumph. They repelled the Din's forces, took control of the Holice, and, feeling quite superior, they returned to their lavish ways. The two nations remained officially at war, but for many years neither side took action. Then rogue Reptilites swept through the system and took the fort in an unprovoked attack. The Go'Din retreated, the Reptilites occupied the fort, and then, when they realized they had no use for it, they abandoned it.

Generations passed. The Din reclaimed the fort, renovating it to accommodate guests and diplomats passing through their system.

Accommodations were straightforward and comfortable. As it became a likable stop, the Go'Din became jealous, feeling the modest Din had squandered a great opportunity for notoriety and riches. The Go'Din inserted a spy, who incited a revolt. When the uprising began, the Go'Din laid siege; the Din held off the assault, but the spy kidnapped the base commander and held him for ransom. They demanded the fort. The Go'Din knew the Din would see the leader's individual life as worth more than any fort or weapon. When the Go'Din threatened to kill him, the Din surrendered the base, and the Holice once again became the property of the Go'Din.

Reptilites returned and attacked the Go'Din's home planet as they were distracted. The Go'Din appealed to the Din for aid, but none came. To pay for an unexpected war, the Go'Din had to go into debt. Despite their vast military expenditures, the Go'Din lost their war, and a part of the settlement was a tribute payment to the Reptilites. The Go'Din had to sell everything. They were going to sell the Holice, but instead, they gave it to the Reptilites as part of their tribute payment. In the end, the Go'Din were left beaten and impoverished. That's how things stood until the Galactic State intervened.

The Galactic Coalition, as they were known at the time, joined their military force to contain the Reptilite aggression. The Reptilites, still bitter from their long bout to achieve emancipation, opposed their former masters. The Vega Beast and the Galactic Coalition had a falling out over how to handle the former slaves, and the Coalition renamed itself the Galactic State in an attempt to erase their past.

Without the help of the Vega Beast, the State sought a more diplomatic and economic tactic rather than military. They proceeded to unify currencies and scientific knowledge, thereby forcing the Reptilites further into poverty. The nomadic aliens could only find work doing the same jobs they had done as slaves- dying, and so they relinquished the Go'Din home world and found themselves back on Reptilia.

That is how a private collector purchased the Holice, and on his death, willed it to the Galactic State who then thought of using it as a fortress, but it was too remote to be of any strategic value. Instead, they turned it into a prison. The inmates mined nearby asteroids and the State used the products for fuel or sold them for profit. The Holice was soon one of the most profitable prisons in the Galactic State. It remained heavily guarded. The guards routinely inspected all cargo, and the shipments were strictly scheduled. So it was terribly odd when an unidentified X-shaped spacecraft arrived nearby and requested docking privileges.

When the mysterious ship was sighted, the Holice went into partial lockdown- sealing off its wards. Wondering about the commotion, the hairy shipping commander lumbered to the control room.

"What's going on?" he asked.

"Supply order," said the multi-limbed bay controller.

"We have no deliveries scheduled," the shipping head said.

"The order came from the lab."

"Dispatch sentry ships!" the commander barked. "Lab? They don't get to go around me. They should've had my authorization. I want that ship boarded, searched, and held until I get to the bottom of this."

"Right away." The bay controller sounded the alert and ordered sentry ships into orbit.

"And another thing," the shipping commander continued. "If they find drugs, I want it confiscated. I know about their little smuggling operations, and party favors. That's the problem with being so far from the headquarters. Corruption! You hear me? That's why I rule with a tight fist and lead with my eyes open. Gotta catch—"

"It's gone."

"What?"

"Ship's gone," the controller told him. "It left the sector."

"Hmm." The shipping commander stood up straight and rubbed his hairy face.

"The ship reported problems with its docking gear and aborted its landing. They turned around and left."

"I wasn't born yesterday. They must think I'm stupid," the commander said. "Tell the sentry ships to remain on high alert. Put guards with heavy artillery at the hangar door. Nothing goes in or out without my knowledge."

"Yes, sir."

"The lab will just deny everything, but I'll get to the bottom of this."

The guard ships went into orbit, and the hangar-docking gate closed. None of them knew Dimycles was there. He peeked out from behind a crate. His space suit's magnets anchored him to the floor. After the hangar had depressurized, he watched the workers entering the central facility through the main door. Dimycles looked around.

"One way in, one way out," he muttered to himself. He felt disappointed.

He floated up to the ceiling of the oval hangar and hid upside down behind more crates. When he saw the entrance a safe distance away, he drifted down, slipped behind a spaceship, and crept along the wall, but his magnetic boots were noisemakers. He wiggled out of his suit, and shed the boots, forgetting how cold it could be in the Holice.

Dimycles floated over to a cabinet where he grabbed cold weather gear. He replaced it with his space suit and helmet. When he started pulling on the coat, he realized it had more than two arms.

Great.

He floated through the entrance door into the second ward. His feet touched the ground inside of a UV lighted corridor. In the strange light, everything glowed. Gritty walls reflected specks of dirt as Dimycles walked forward. As he rounded the corner, he heard guards approaching the hangar door behind him.

Leaving won't be this quiet.

Dimycles had walked through here once, long ago, and he could barely remember the layout. The ultraviolet light hurt him, making it hard to see. Slowly he edged further into the second ward.

He saw a guard coming and waited for the sentry to round the corner. Dimycles struck him repeatedly until the guard until it fell to the floor limp. Dimycles felt around the glowing body. That guard's eyes were set low on his hairy face, one on each side of his nose.

"You're not exactly my species," Dimycles panted, as he took the guard's goggles off its smelly face. He fit them onto his face as well as he could and adjusted the visual modes to filter the light, helping him see more clearly. An ergonomic handle connected to a claw blade. The handle's decorative design glowed in the light.

"Nice knife," Dimycles said. He took the guard's utility belt, radio, and pistol. He removed his coat and took an oval canteen from one of the pockets. He popped off the top, sniffed, and sipped it.

Water?

The taste of it made Dimycles cough. He checked his pistol. *Six shots.* "Can't do much with this," he complained.

Dimycles walked back to the entrance door. Two of the three stations had a guard parked in front of it. Dimycles knew he might've just killed the third guard, and these two might worry when their coworker didn't return.

Dimycles knew his six bullets would be of little help against them, they were much better armed, and a frontal assault would prove suicidal. He might get one, or he might not, but he would surely die at the hands of the other. He reviewed his inventory and thought.

Water.

Peering up at a heating vent, he turned his goggles to infrared and spotted the path of the induction coils. The heat traveled through tributaries and came out in a junction behind him. He retrieved the dead guard's corpse and set it down by the heating vents. Pulling off the floor panel, he cut into the duct and shoved the body down into it.

For a moment, Dimycles pondered if his plan would work.

I just shoved a dead body into the heating duct. It's gonna stink in here!

He closed the panel, returned to the spot near the entrance door, and crept around the corner on his hands and knees. He inched closer, specks of blood glowed on his body, and eye'd the large guns of the guards.

I need to get out of that door behind them, and those are some big guns.

Dimycles poured out the contents of the canteen to create a small glowing puddle on the floor. He retreated to where the guards couldn't possibly see him.

With the heat blocked, the area cooled quickly- then it stunk. One guard radioed in: "Maintenance, this is Carver Hangar Patrol. Do you mind checking zone 9 for climate? It's getting cold."

"Hangar Patrol, this is maintenance. We see zone 9's climate issues, and we're coming to investigate."

Dimycles hopped up and raced through the central commons toward the maintenance area. Two maintenance orderlies were coming out the doors. Dimycles pounced, and slammed one guard's head into the floor. He grabbed the guard's fallen wrench, and swung it at the other, smashing his face. He took their badges and radio and slipped through the doors before it sealed shut.

With white light filling the maintenance room, Dimycles removed his goggles and took a deep breath. He thought for a second.

"They're gonna be missing these guys soon," Dimycles worried. "Should I get the jump on it?"

Glancing around the maintenance room, he grabbed a handful of metal balls meant for cleaning. He got on the support radio and gave an update: "Medical, this is Maintenance. We have a guard down by zone 9, possibly comatose due to the intense cold. He needs immediate medical attention. Control room, can you divert heating collateral to that area until I get back to maintenance for an override? Over."

"Medical responding," said a voice. "We are en route."

Dimycles threw on his goggles and zipped over to the medical bay. After sprinkling some metal balls on the ground, he hid behind the doors. A medical team exited. A few members slipped on the balls. He used the distraction to duck into the medical bay.

Control came over the radio: "We are showing full power to 9, Maintenance. Confirm divert."

Dimycles found a computer, pulled up the mic, and said: "Control, this is maintenance. That is confirmed. Over."

Dimycles frantically searched the prisoner manifest.

"Where would we divert from, over?" Control requested.

Dimycles found his target. *Damn.* He inhaled, and tried to think.

"Maintenance?" The voice from Control crackled over the speaker. "Do you copy? Over."

"Uh... Maintenance here," Dimycles answered. "We copy. You are correct: full power in zone 9. Please divert from the hangar. Over."

"Shut power to the hanger? What's the problem Maintenance? Over."

"Blockage in the connecting ducts from the second ward. It needs fixing. Possible dead animal," Dimycles told them

Without waiting for a reply, Dimycles trotted out of Medical. He tightened his coat and approached the third ward partition. Biting his lip, he pressed the button to summon his enemy – the elevator.

Hearing the gears clank as it descended made Dimycles feel light headed. As the elevator door opened, spots of dirt shone under the UV aura. Dimycles stood still, then drew his pistol. He pointed it into the lift, held it steady, then took a step inside. He quickly pushed the button. The doors closed, and opened again a moment later. He jumped out and waited until the cold tingles left his body.

Dimycles snuck up on the sentry guarding a pressurized chamber. He had shot four times before the guard went down. Dimycles toggled his goggles and everything still looked black in infrared. He took the dead guard's credentials and accessed the nearby control panel, disabling the chamber. Cold liquid and gas expelled from creases around the housing. A cloud of glowing blue gas filled the hallway. Dimycles took a pistol and another pair of goggles from the dead guard. When the chamber depressurized he looked up, taking a step back. The room grew warmer as the mist faded away.

A bright reddish-orange spiked pole punched through the door. It morphed into two blades, cutting the door on a diagonal. Someone kicked the door open, sending echoes through the empty halls. Ambient light filtered through the gas and steam from the chamber. Dimycles took off his goggles and saw a figure emerge. The newcomer sparkled red-orange made from a diamond lattice. The blade morphed into a hand, and the mesh character morphed into a young woman.

Her irises and hair were white. They reflected the UV glow. Grime covered her fair skin, and she wore prison clothes that remained dull even in the light of the ultraviolet.

As she neared him, condensation dripped from her skin. "Dimycles?"

"Ina," Dimycles answered. He smiled and shielded his eye from seeing her better.

"But why?" she asked.

"Childish games and silly drama aren't reason enough to leave a friend," he said. "You never deserved to be in here. Besides, I need your help."

Ina looked around. "Where's Damyae?"

"That's my problem," Dimycles said putting on his goggles. "That's why I need your help."

Ina touched his neck and felt a strip of metal along the side of it, then taking his hand, she followed him back down the hall. An alarm sounded. She pulled closer and felt the pistol on his waist.

"Blasting our way out?" she asked.

"I've got two shots left in there, and six in the one I took from the chamber guard."

"Not much," she thought aloud.

"These guards use small clips because of people like us. We might kill a guard, but we won't get much ammo from him."

They reached the lift. Dimycles gave Ina the other set of goggles. She looked at them and shrugged.

"Also, without much ammo, a guard can't do much damage to the structure," he said.

"So I shouldn't expect to walk right out of here?" She asked. As the lift doors opened, she put on her goggles, resting them above her forehead. She stepped into the lift, pulling Dimycles in after her.

"We're still in the middle of nowhere," she said as the doors closed.

"I have a ship."

"Really? What ship?"

"My ship," Dimycles said.

Ina seemed unimpressed. "They'll freeze me for good if I get caught. They'll put me under a piston and shatter me into dust."

When the lift reached the bottom floor, Dimycles stopped the doors from opening. He raised his goggles and faced her. "Do what's right for you."

"I've got nowhere to go," said Ina. "Where's Damyae?"

"I don't know."

"Be honest."

"I am. I don't know where she is," Dimycles repeated. "But I know who has her. I know how to get her back."

"I swore that if I escaped that cold cell, I would never go back," she told him. "And I meant it. What ship do you have? Your old one? The Chyee? Old Nimble?"

"Yes. I just need to get to the hangar," Dimycles said.

Ina sunk her fingers into the fur-like surface of his coat. "I had a sister too."

Dimycles felt himself soften. "Ina..."

She hushed him with her finger and pulled the goggles down over his eyes. She turned around, pressed the button, and the lift doors opened. Guards opened fire the moment they saw her. She ran out into the shots, her body morphing into a lattice, as her arms turned into blades. The shots had no effect as she charged forward. She cut a guard in half, formed back into her body, and grabbed the dead guard's gun. A platoon of guards chased her through the hallways. Dimycles covered his eyes and ran around the back way to the entrance door. Shots and alarm lights obscured their vision.

As guards poured into the second ward halls, Ina backed herself to a wall and shot at them. She grabbed another weapon from a fallen guard, emptying its clip the moment she could aim. When pain burned through her shoulder, she turned into a lattice. As guards sprayed bullets from a balcony, the shots ricocheted off her sparkling body. She turned, and found more guards opening a linked net to catch her. Blocked in, she formed a blade, cut the right wall open, and ran into the inner section.

Inside, Ina cut through the guards as if they were paper dolls. Torpedo bullets pierced the air. Their tips opened, and clamped onto her lattice, then grappling hooks shot from the bullets' bases, and stuck into the floor. Ina formed a blade and cut herself loose. More missiles latched onto her body, firing chains into walls and floor, trapping her down.

Dimycles blindsided the Hangar Patrol and armed himself with their heavy weapons to repel an assault. "Ina! The hangar!" Dimycles screamed, looking around.

Guards rushed from the third ward, rolling a machine into the room where Ina was trapped. As they aimed it and fired, she cut through the chains trapping her down and managed to dodge the strange blast. She looked up and saw the wall behind her had frozen over where the blast had hit.

"Ina!" Dimycles's voice echoed down the halls.

Ina cut herself free of the remaining chains and ran toward his voice with guards chasing at her heels. Just as she saw her partner, she hit the patch of ice left by the water he poured earlier. She slid, and Dimycles took a knee.

"Open the entrance door!" he shouted.

The guards chasing after Ina hit the ice too, and Dimycles shot them one-by-one. Ina formed a blade to cut the door open. "NO!" Dimycles shouted. "Don't damage it! Just use the guard! This door has to seal shut for the hangar gate to open!"

Ina retracted her blade, grabbed the guard, and morphed into a lattice, then into a clone of him. With fingers identical to the guard's, she touched the panel and opened the hangar.

"Go! I'll hold them off," she cried, as a small army rushed toward them.

"Not a chance."

"We'll both die!" she screamed.

Dimycles grabbed her and dove into the hangar.

As the entrance door closed, the guards shot an ice blast. It missed the two fugitives but froze the outside gate at the far end. The entrance door sealed shut after that.

"What the hell is that thing?" Dimycles asked about the ice blast while trying to disable the entrance paneling.

"It's how they caught me the first time," said Ina. Her voice was the guard's. She morphed into a lattice, then back into her own shape. "Where's your ship?"

"Out there." Dimycles pointed toward the frozen hangar gate. He floated to the cabinet to retrieve his space suit.

"Out where? On the asteroid?" Ina sounded worried.

"Hiding, yes," Dimycles replied, putting on his boots.

Ina looked disappointed.

"What?" Dimycles defended. "They weren't just gonna let me in! Look, if we can open the gate, I can remotely land it in here."

The guards were manually opening the entrance door, and appendages started reaching through the cracks. Ina grabbed a weapon to push them back. "Get your suit on!" she shouted.

Dimycles suited up and hobbled over to the control panel to try to open the outside gate, but the system returned an error message. He hit the console. "The gate won't open if the entrance isn't sealed!"

"The hangar gate is frozen shut!" Ina shouted.

"We're stuck!"

Once the guards got the entrance way open, they poured into the hangar. They refrained from firing, not wanting to damage the garage or the equipment.

The fugitives backed up to the frozen gate.

"You sure your ship is out there?" Ina asked.

"Yes," Dimycles assured her, "But..."

Ina morphed into a giant hammer and banged on the frozen part of the gate.

"Ina! No!" Dimycles shouted, pulling on his helmet. The panicking guards dropped their weapons and tried to crowd back into the second ward. Ina banged repeatedly. The ice gave way, and the gate cracked. The vacuum of space tore off the gate, crumpling the hangar. Everything flew out into space.

With the inside hangar door still ajar, the wall separating the second ward from the hangar cracked and pulled apart. The rotating asteroid flung everything inside the Holice into space. Inflated bodies tumbled through the air vortex into the void. A protective wall slammed shut between the third ward and the second ward, saving the prisoner section.

While Dimycles flew into space, surrounded by debris, he used his wrist controls to summoned the ship. A tractor beam pulled him aboard. Detaching his gloves, he floated up to the pilot controls and began looking for Ina.

He saw a glint from her diamond lattice body. He reeled her in and got out of his suit. He floated down to his bay and waited. The lattice morphed back into Ina. She coughed and breathed slowly.

"Space hurts," she groaned.

"You gutted two-thirds of the Holice," He reminded her.

She tried to giggle. "Now that's payback."

Proximity alarms sounded.

"Well," she gasped, rubbing her arms, "I did my part. Time to do yours."

Dimycles floated up to his pilot station. Sentry ships approached. He engaged his thrusters. The ships opened fire. His agile ship dodged, and the shots missed. Dimycles fled to the nearest asteroids. He banked around one. One fighter followed while the other sped around to the opposite side to cut him off. Dimycles' ship spun and slowed. He fired a delayed missile. When the enemy crossed the asteroid's horizon, the missile detonated, destroying the fighter. Dimycles turned, and destroyed another sentry ship as it passed his bow.

Dimycles banked low over the giant asteroid. As his hull nearly skimmed the surface, two pursuers fired wildly at him. The irradiated asteroid stopped their guidance systems. As Dimycles retreated from his attackers, he lined up a shot that destroyed them.

As Dimycles sped off, five more ships closed in. He steered in close to a larger asteroid, then orbited until they swung in around him. They tried to cut him off. The asteroid was large, but not big enough these close maneuvers. Dimycles varied his orbiting vector. One ship followed, but the others didn't. When he again changed direction, another ship followed, but the rest held their courses.

As they tried to keep from crashing into one another, Dimycles picked them off one-by-one. Only two got away. Both took defensive positions high above the asteroid.

Dimycles heard Ina floating up to him. He thought about just leaving the two fighters and escaping while he had the chance. He looked at Ina. She shook her head no. Dimycles slowed, drifting closer to the asteroid. On the return, as the horizon neared, he switched to missiles, manually taking aim.

"What are you doing?" Ina asked.

"Too much radiation," Dimycles explained. "Can't trust the guidance system."

Dimycles had nearly completed the orbit, and he knew the two ships were just over the horizon. He shot two missiles. They flew low and then curved out and up toward their targets. The pilots saw them coming, but it was too late. The ships exploded.

"Sling shooting?" Ina asked.

"It's a lost art," Dimycles said.

Ina nodded. "Nice."

Dimycles typed in new coordinates. The ship changed course and entered hyperspace. He turned his artificial gravity on. It was quiet for a few moments. Things started to settle to the floor.

"Are you okay?" he asked.

"I'm fine," she said. "Just a little shaken. Dirty too."

Dimycles laughed and touched her hair. "Let me show you where you can get cleaned up."

While Ina cleaned up, Dimycles looked at himself in the mirror. He hadn't shaved in a while. After taking a shower, he couldn't find a blade. With his face lathered, he grabbed the large knife he'd stolen from the Holice and scraped it along his cheek. The blade was too dull. Giving up, he washed off the soap. His face felt tingly and fresh, but still supremely hairy. After he had patted his beard dry, he dressed in clean clothes and found Ina tucked in and sleeping. He watched her for a moment.

"I failed Wuyan's test," Dimycles cooed, not wanting to rouse her. "I couldn't escape Earth with what I wanted. How can I possibly survive the Sunil with what she wants? If I fail, I'll lose Damyae...and now you?" Dimycles returned to his navigations and brooded in silence.

Several hours later, Ina came up behind him. She noticed he was looking at his fuel cell pump shaft- it was broken. "So what's the plan?"

"I need your help to fix this."

Ina chuckled. "You traveled across the Realm, and risked your life to break me out of jail just to fix your fuel cell pump shaft?"

Dimycles nodded and admitted it. "Yup. Actually, I did."

Ina's hair grew long in one section, and then it formed into a rod. She broke it off and gave it to him saying, "May you always have a piece of me where ever you go."

Dimycles replaced his broken shaft with the rod she gave him and smiled: "I will cherish it till the last."

Ina giggled at the silly response and asked, seriously, "So where are we really going?"

"Rested?" Dimycles responded, ignoring her question.

"Yeah. I feel a lot better, and you smell better than you did!" Ina touched his hairy face. "But you still need a shave."

"Thanks! It's been a while since I've had a proper bath. I'm shutting down the gravity. To save some power until I can get my fuel cells charged."

He got up, and Ina watched him walk away. "Your clothes need work too," Ina called out.

Dimycles laughed and shut off the gravity.

"You still didn't answer me," Ina said, her feet leaving the floor.

Dimycles didn't respond.

"Where are we going?" Ina asked, a bit more irritated.

Instead of answering directly, he said: "Ina, please. I can't lie to you, so I think it's just best I take you wherever you can start a new life. Because where I am going there are powerful secrets that you will not survive."

"I don't believe that," Ina snapped. "If it's a secret, then it can't be powerful."

"You have to trust me on this," Dimycles insisted as he floated to data station to check reports.

"I broke a piece of myself off to help you fix something that probably wasn't even broken, and I don't even care. But this... ignoring me, and playing dumb, actually hurts my feelings."

"Wuyan," Dimycles said. "I'm reading up on Wuyan."

"Who's she?"

"She freed me from a Martian prison under the condition I do something for her—get something—and she took Damyae as collateral."

"So that's where you two have been all these years? Why can't she get this thing herself?"

"She doesn't know where the planet is."

"And you do?"

Dimycles nodded. "I do."

Ina floated to the navigational units and checked their destination coordinates. "Where?"

"Calare," Dimycles answered, nervously biting his lip.

Ina checked the navs again.

"Looks like we are going to the middle of nowhere," she noted. "There's nothing out there."

"Calare is a Hidden Planet," Dimycles informed her.

Ina hung there for a moment, thinking. "What's a hidden planet? I mean, why are they hidden?"

"They are hidden because they don't want anyone to find out their secrets." Dimycles rubbed his beard. "I don't know if any of this makes sense to you. On Mars, the guards were going to execute me, and Wuyan showed up. She said she'd free me if I would tell her where Calare is she wants something from the planet. I said that it was forbidden for me to tell, but I could steal it for her. So she freed me, sent me to Earth to get my ship, and out of nowhere the Reptilites attacked me!"

"Whoa! Reptilites?"

"Twice they tried to kill me! I fought to get my ship, but when I left Earth I saw that the Reptilites had invasion army surrounding the planet,"

"Hang on! Invasion? Has anyone ever invaded a whole planet?"

"It's been ages. Not since the formation of the Galactic State."

"This is all confusing."

"All I know is that I need to get Damyae back."

Ina morphed into a lattice, floated to Dimycles, and looked at him in his eyes. "You won't lose her. Wuyan is the one who's gonna lose." Her lattice changed shape. She morphed into Damyae: same blue eyes and dirty blonde hair, just like Dimycles. "What does she want that we can get?"

Dimycles gasped at the vision. Finally, he answered, "The core of the Midnight bomb."

"Never heard of it."

"Because it's not something anyone lives to tell about—not even the user. It's a dark energy bomb... completely erratic. All time and space continuity are destroyed within the blast radius until space folds back over itself to close the rupture."

"Why would ever want such an indiscriminate weapon?"

"Now you know why Calare is a Hidden Planet."

"But you don't know how she'll use it," Ina noted. "The only thing you know is that getting the Midnight core could save a life."

Ina's Damyae morphed into a lattice, turned to the side, and looked out of the front window. "Could we rescue Damyae from Wuyan first?" Ina asked.

"I thought about that." Dimycles said. "I don't know where Wuyan is keeping her."

"What if you give her the location of Calare as a trade for Damyae?" Ina asked.

"Calare is a highly advanced planet, so Wuyan can't go there even if she finds out where it is."

"If they're so advanced, how you gonna rob them?"

"They're sophisticated but predictable," Dimycles answered. "Their organized methods are as much of a weakness as a strength."

"Wuyan's probably not stupid, and it doesn't sound like she's suicidal," said Ina. "Will she attack them for it?"

"Calare's been hiding doomsday devices from the Observed Realm for generations. Their defenses are second to none."

"Okay, that makes sense. Maybe that's why she wants the core: To build a bomb that will win her war."

Dimycles shrugged. "We know what she wants, even if we don't know why she wants it. If can get Damyae back, that's good enough."

"A planet that keeps the most destructive technology in the Galaxy to themselves sounds suspicious. All of this is news to me. Maybe she wants to expose Calare?" Ina speculated. "It's all sounds kinda shady. If their goal is so noble, why hide?"

"And risk being constantly assaulted by violent species bent on domination? Better to stay hidden for that exact reason."

"I don't agree. Calare just needs to keep those weapons out of the wrong hands."

"Those devices are dangerous in any hands. They have to stay hidden!"

"Hmm, you make it sounds like they are a blameless race," said Ina. "What happes if Calare decides to be the bad guy?"

"The other Hidden Planets won't let them." Dimycles answered.

Ina was a bit shocked, "Other... Hidden Planets?"

The ship's nav system sounded an alert. They were closing in on Calare.

"Last chance," Dimycles warned her. "After this, there's no going back."

The lattice morphed into Ina. She peered out at the stars. "Let's go."

THE HIDDEN PLANET

BEYOND THE DARK nimble space ship, about a missile-throw from the spot where two friends sat looking and waiting, was the forbidden secret. Only a select few knew of it. It was a fold in space.

"How did they ever find something like this?" Ina wondered, staring out the window like a child at the zoo, looking into the lion's cage.

"The same way you make most discoveries - by looking for something else."

Dimycles moved the ship closer, and then Ina saw it. Her eyes popped, and she gasped. The lion poked its head out of the tall grass.

"Long ago, a woman named Yizekia went looking for naturally occurring wormholes," Dimycles said. "While drifting in space near her test site, she turned her dials like so... and realized that she'd discovered something entirely different."

"A fold in space," Ina whispered.

Dimycles nodded. He maneuvered the starship closer to the faint ripple and entered the fold. To Ina, it appeared that the stars had warped into a bubble and then straightened back out.

"Trippy," she said. "So weird. Everything looks the same looking out—"

A flash of light streaked nearby.

"What's that!" Ina wondered.

"I think it's just an asteroid."

"Oh." Ina shrugged, unimpressed. She looked over at the navigations, and where there was nothing, now showed a full planetary system. "This is it. Let's go to Calare!"

"You want to get us killed?" Dimycles stammered. "This system is not what it seems. You don't explore Sunil territory."

"This system looks normal," Ina said, browsing through the technical readouts.

"Yep," Dimycles agreed. "Looks that way."

"Then why hide it?"

"Hang on," Dimycles urged her silence, while he went over the plan in his mind.

While Ina counted the planets in the system, she noticed two switched places. "What just happened!"

"Those planets aren't real. They are just decoys. Visiting or even nearing them can suck you into a wormhole that will spit you out somewhere else in the galaxy, or tear your ship apart. Depends on how sturdy the ship."

"Do you know the combination? Which of these planets is the one we want?"

"I'm not quite sure. There is, however, one man who has their secrets at the touch of his fingers. Let's hope he's still around," Dimycles said. "The Sunil's first military order is to protect their home world. I was hoping to track their battle cruisers heading to Calare, but they remain cloaked. Which means they haven't completed scanning my ship."

"So..."

"Wuyan was right. The only way to bring them out of hiding is to threaten them. They will scan my vessel for anything worth confiscating and then they'll find it."

"Find what?"

"You."

A voice came over the comms, startling her. "This is Admiral Kahlan, from Calare's outer rim defense. You are in strictly controlled space carrying forbidden contraband. Please identify yourself and head to coordinates which we will provide."

Ina mouthed, "An admiral?"

"We'd better get ready," Dimycles replied. He looked at Ina and bit his lip, "And you are okay with what we discussed?"

Ina nodded, stood tall, and her body morphed into a lattice, then became Dimycles. Dimycles looked at the mirror image of himself with a teary eyed smile as Ina's version of him had no metallic scars. "I've gone too far to turn back now."

Dimycles sent identification as an explorer from the Hidden Planet, Togales. As soon as he received coordinates, he flew directly to the assigned meeting point. There the Calareans boarded, questioned Dimycles, and escorted him into an orbiting station near the home planet. He waited in the visitor's area, by a window. He could see that Calare's clouds covered the entire planet.

Dimycles gasped, "The white planet."

The room had no visible doors; wall sections opened and closed for entry and exit.

A voice came from behind him: "Welcome. I am first Captain Gajra."

Dimycles turned to find a tall, tanned, older woman. They shook hands.

"How are things on Togales?" Gajra asked as she escorted Dimycles through the terminals to the transport area. "It's a gorgeous place, I hear. Lots of snow and sports. Is Kunkel nice this time of year?"

"Unfortunately, Kunkel was buried under a volcano eruption many years back," Dimycles answered. "It's not so nice anymore." Dimycles followed Gajra through walls and down corridors.

"What plans do you have while you are here?" Gajra asked, leading him to a sealed tube connecting to a taxi area.

"I've done a lot of transportation back home, carrying goods as a transporter. I'd like to live here for a few years, and learn about your cultures and peoples," Dimycles explained.

"We have one culture, we are one people," Gajra said dryly.

"Of course," Dimycles responded, trying to cover his error. "That's why I think I will feel right at home."

Gajra looked over the records and added, "Seems you've been here before. Welcome back. Your credentials are in order, and you have already made transportation arrangements with a local named Gama. Until the arrival of your official records from Togales, you will not be allowed on the planet surface for any reason. Any attempt to go would be a capital offense."

"Official records?" Dimycles asked.

"Yes, of course, we've started a new verification process for immigrants. We will have Togales verify everything about you. I'm sure, given that you were here before, everything will be just fine. Your fuel crystals are a bit flat too; I imagine you must have been doing a lot of traveling."

"Here to there."

"Pick up anything along the way?"

"How's that?"

"When we initially scanned your ship, we detected a piece of the Herlon Colossus inside of it and conducted a closer inspection, I hope you don't mind," Gajra said apologetically, "That's contraband under our laws."

Dimycles covered his worry.

Gajra looked suspiciously at the traveler, "Fortunately, it just a small piece, like a rod. It was lodged in place of your fuel cell pump shaft."

"Oh, the rod? I had no idea that's what it was," Dimycles insisted. "I just thought it was spare junk."

"How about we make a deal: I'll send your ship to the docks, get that pump shaft fixed, and recharge your crystals, if you would be so kind as to give us the rod."

Dimycles smiled. He knew the "deal" was an order. "My pleasure," he said, nodded and smiled.

Gajra did not return the smile. "The Colossus was a titan that devastated the people of Herlon. After its defeat, it was broken apart and its pieces scattered. The Sunil has not officially classified it as hidden treasure, but we do our diligence to collect the relics as we find them."

Gajra noticed Dimycles had no response to her lecture, and added, "I don't know how the educational system works on Togales, but they should have taught you that. I can excuse an errant relic, but if you want employment as a driver, I shouldn't have to remind you that transporting any of our hidden treasures without authorization is punishable by immediate death." At that, she gave the order to her troops to process his ship, and then she walked away.

Dimycles unnerved himself and went to the edge of the last tube, where a car met him. He got into the passenger seat next to a rotund fellow with short black hair.

"You look like shit!" Gama said as soon as he laid eyes on Dimycles. He punched his passenger in the arm. "What have you been eating? Rocks?"

"I haven't been in the nicest neighborhoods lately."

"No shit! You look like you been living in a trench!"

The car disembarked from the orbiting space station and descended into the atmosphere of Calare.

"Hey, so, are they gonna check my credentials with Togales?" Dimycles asked.

"Yeah, they changed it last year. Lots of changes went down, ya know?" Gama answered. "Don't worry about it. I got you covered."

"I didn't know."

"You been gone so long."

"It's a good thing my initial paperwork checked out."

Gama scoffed, "Will you chill out? You're here two minutes, and already you make me want to take you back. I got my fingers in everything. You want to question my connections?"

Gama descended into the upper atmosphere. "So, where you wanna go? Get some girls? Get some drinks? Looking like that, I know you haven't gotten any action. Your game ain't that strong."

"I wouldn't mind taking a look at, well, you know?"

"Relax! That's golden! You haven't been here in years. You beefed up, and it seems like you've been living in a cave, but all you want to do is peek at my stash? Got your priorities mixed up. We'll get to that later. You hungry?"

Dimycles shrugged, "Not really, so... do you have it?"

"Of course, didn't I say relax?"

"On you?"

Gama patted his chest and pulled out a screened device. Dimycles took it and turned it on. Gama glanced over. Dimycles was scrolling through records.

"What are you doing? Give me that," Gama demanded. He snatched the device and put it back in his pocket. "You're gonna mess up my data. What do you want to eat?"

"Whatever is good," Dimycles said, typing into his watch. He handed Gama some money.

"Where did you get that?" Gama asked with a laugh. "A museum? Put that away. We don't use those paper bills anymore."

"No more currency? What hasn't changed here?" Dimycles asked, sheepishly pocketing the cash.

"I like your watch," Gama hinted.

Dimycles was tapping information into the watch. "Thanks. It was a gift. I'm not selling it."

"Well, it ain't a free world. That hasn't changed. It's just that don't no one take that old money anymore. So that's what we'll do. Make some money. Yeah? Fill your pockets with some legit cash." Gama laughed again. "I know just the place we can make that happen."

As they flew, Dimycles saw puffs of clouds lined with janky ghettos. The kids in their torn clothes were housed in outdoor cages, playing wind sports with makeshift equipment. They passed a floating apartment complex. He asked Gama about what he saw.

"Forget about them," Gama said. "That's Slimm City projects. Broke losers, drug heads—you know the type. We won't get any money out of them."

They arrived at a domed arena in the clouds.

"A game?"

"Not quite."

Gama pulled around the backside and went in a secret entrance.

"A casino?"

"Yeah."

"Aren't they illegal?"

Gama stared at Dimycles. "No!"

Gama nodded to the parking attendant, who tipped his hat, allowing them to slip through another driveway. Gama looked back at Dimycles. "Okay, yeah."

GAJRA LEFT THE space station, returned to her mothership, and reported to Admiral Kahlan on the deck.

"Everything okay with the new guy?" Kahlan asked.

"I have my eye on him for now," Gajra said. "Wants to be a driver."

"So he aspires to mediocrity, and that bothers you?" Kahlan asked.

Gajra answered: "What bothers me is that he thinks anywhere he rests his head is home."

Not one to ignore the gut of his first officers, Kalan requested a status on Dimycles from the ship crew. "He went to the Chelsa Dome," Fyzel replied.

"Gambler. Figures," Gajra scoffed. "I should go arrest him."

"Calm yourself," Kahlan replied, "He's a vagrant, doing what vagrants do. We spend more resources arresting them than they give to us. Besides, those games suck you in. He'll be in there for a long time."

"Long enough to get his credentials back from Togales, and his ship back from repair," Gajra mumbled.

"I find it pathetic that career hitchhikers call themselves explorers," Kahlan added, lost in thought. "He's just a bum. I bet he's probably broke, with nowhere to live. He's burned all his bridges with people who felt weary of his couch surfing, and his only real home is his smelly ship.

He comes here, and does he want to work? No, he goes straight to a game. What a drain on society. He'll be broke and out of here in no time."

"Good," Gajra replied, "At least he won't be staying long."

DIMYCLES WALKED THROUGH the casino into the domed underbelly and viewed the games. He showed little interest in gambling. At every station, Gama gave him a coin to play, and Dimycles always lost. Gama just shrugged it off and trotted through the casino like a kid at a playground. Eventually, Gama asked about Dimycles's somber mood.

"The house always has the advantage," Dimycles complained, as they walked to another station.

"Well, yeah! Otherwise, it wouldn't be gambling," Gama shouted, slapping his friend on the back, and then nursing his hand.

"They have a bigger bank. They control the environment," said Dimycles. A nearby attendant offered him a drink. He took one off the platter, and took a sip, "The dealer is just a distraction."

"Man, let that go! The joy of gambling is winning something from nothing! Of course, the odds favor the house. If it were fair and easy, everyone would do it, and no one would win much. You can't think like that if you are gonna win, boy!"

"Why do they have a casino in a dome? Especially if it's illegal? Wouldn't it be better on the surface?"

"That's because this is the only casino that has the Dive Or Chase game!"

"Dive or Chase?"

"Follow me."

They went through a door into the arena below the dome.

"An aviary?" Dimycles gasped, walking into the bright light. There wasn't any floor. Dimycles could see straight down to the planet's surface. It made him dizzy. He looked up to see a row of floating chariots, all in different colors. One was red, another yellow, the one each of blue, and green. Enormous birds of prey perched on the riders' outstretched arms: The predator birds.

"Each host has a diver-bird branded with its master's colors," Gama said, leading Dimycles to an empty seat. "The red one is Pole Dive. The blue one is Misty Haven. The green one... is... um. Ya know, I don't even know," Gama flipped through the program and found their names. "Cook! The yellow is Goober."

The diver-birds glared, their eyes piercing and devious; contoured to artistic perfection. The birds had lethal beaks and razor-sharp talons. Feathers coated their bodies, and their plumage glistened in the spotlight. Dimycles had never seen anything so exquisite.

The arena was nearly full. A single cage hovered in front of the chariots, housing a smaller, rainbow-colored, token bird. Wind gushed up through the open floor, creating a powerful draft. A scoreboard across the field showed the number of catches for each diver-bird. Pole had the lead.

Dimycles sat down. A large display was showing the prior round. Pole's red image dove down through ringer markers, capturing the token bird before it could get to safety.

The screen cleared. Gama placed a bet on Goober. A loud buzzer sounded, and the token bird darted out from the cage. Chariot riders released their diver-birds to go after it. The token bird darted and dove toward the surface through the ring markers. The divers made a steep descent, opening their majestic wings to change course, flying through the markers after their prey.

Pole soared high over the other three, then pulled its wings back and swooped down. It twisted into a barrel roll and passed the yellow leader. Gama screamed at his bird. A ring marker approached. The token bird opened its wings, but the red diver did not. Pole dove straight through the token bird, shredding it, and flew past the ring.

The crowd erupted. Bettors holding red cards held them up in victory. Gama was unhappy.

Dimycles sipped his drink and commented: "Savage."

"Pole always wins!"

"Then why do you bet on yellow?"

"Because the odds are higher, so the money's better. Okay, next round." Gama typed in his bet: Goober to win. "He betta show up this time."

Pole took the next three wins, and Misty took the other two. Dimycles pitied the token birds, and Gama pitied his pockets. They were emptier every time.

"You did nothing to deserve this," Dimycles whispered as if the tokens could hear. "The path was set before you to face those who are clearly better than you."

"What?" Gama said over the noise. "The hell are you talking about?"

"I can see why this game is illegal. How can it win?"

"Oh, give him time. Goober pulls out a win or two."

"No!" Dimycles said. "I mean the token bird! You only see this as a game of chance between four birds, but for the token, it's just a sadistic punishment ending in death! The token is an exquisite bird. In any other environment, we would savor its beauty. It didn't choose to be here."

Gama stared at Dimycles as if he were a stranger. "Never mind."

When Pole won another, Dimycles wanted to leave, but Gama hesitated. "Just one more," he said. "I have to win this time. My odds are good. Pole can't win them all!"

Dimycles looked up. As a new contestant was readied, a green-and-yellow token went into the front cage. When Dimycles saw it, he stood. "That's a Brenner. Didn't know they had Brenners here."

"What? Now you want to bet?" Gama asked.

"Yes!"

"The red is on fire, it's a sure bet," Gama said, giving him a coin. "You will at least get your coin back."

"There is no such thing as a sure bet in a casino," Dimycles replied. "I want to bet on the token."

"That coin is worth a lot!" Gama shouted, "Don't you dare bet that on the token bird. I've been doing this for 20 years, and I..."

Dimycles pushed the coin through the slot and typed in his bet. Gama looked at him oddly, mumbling under his breath, "Waste my money. You owe me."

The buzzer rang. The Brenner bird sped from its cage, but it didn't look good. Instead of pulling its wings back for a faster dive it flapped its way down.

Gama rose to his feet; Goober was on the attack.

Dimycles screamed, "Don't flap! Dive! Dive!"

The crowd shouted for the kill. The yellow bird dove. The Brenner flapped, barely getting through the first ring marker. The more it flapped, the slower it flew.

"Oh no!" Dimycles slapped his forehead as Gama crumpled the program. Goober closed in.

Goober gained speed, but beyond the first ring, he cut too hard. Misty overtook the yellow bird and neared the token. Misty's neck tightened, as it pointed its beak for a clean impact. The Brenner dodged. The blue diver missed and streaked by. Flapping furiously, Misty tried to stay in but careened out of bounds. The Brenner flew down through the second ring marker.

"That... was not graceful," Dimycles complained. "At all."

The Brenner didn't look pretty. It was like an insect next to these diver birds. Dimycles watched the display as the Brenner bird flapped its four wings, and headed for the third ring. It flapped a little too slowly. Pole saw Misty's failure and began circling. With exquisite timing, Pole barrel-rolled through the markers into the path of the token. The Brenner nearly stopped, balancing itself in the air currents. It then turned, and flew toward the red diver.

"What the hell?" Dimycles shouted.

Instead of attacking, the red diver opened its wings, caught a gust, and decelerated. Pole showed its talons, snatching at the token. The Brenner darted sideways, dashing behind the red diver. As the wind increased, the red diver flapped harder, but couldn't stay up. As Pole started to stall, it spread its wings wide and glided. As it floated by, it snapped at the Brenner, but, unaffected by the wind, the Brenner easily dodged. It darted in front of Pole as if to entice it. When Pole remained in one spot, the Brenner flew away.

Goober and Cook took control. The Brenner dodged erratically, then went into a full dive.

The Brenner approached the sixth ring. Goober and Cook pulled up alongside it, but they couldn't all fit through the six ring. Goober and Cook collided, missing the ring marker entirely. The Brenner pulled its wings back and dove through.

Pole regained its position, then fell, and gained speed. Its dive would be shallower this time, as it assumed the Brenner would pull back and dodge. The Brenner didn't. Instead, it dove faster, into the seventh ring, and through the safety tunnel. The red diver flew past the tunnel, missing its prey, but it displayed incredible grace, and the crowd still rooted for it. The crowd threw red confetti and cards.

Dimycles clutched the arms of his chair, as his dispenser poured out tokens. Gama grabbed a bucket and started shoveling money into it. Dimycles didn't move. Even moments after the finale, he wasn't shocked or relieved; he was inspired.

"Do you have any idea how rich you are?" Gama asked, now on his knees, as he plucked the last coins from the floor. "You had thousand-to-one odds."

Dimycles scooped out a handful of his winnings and gave them to Gama. "I think my win streak has officially started."

"Let's go do irresponsible and dangerous things with this money," Gama suggested.

The two reentered the casino and got another round of drinks at the bar. As Dimycles sipped his, he suddenly got serious. "Hey," he said to Gama, "about that... that thing I was asking about."

"Oh yes, yeah, right. Don't worry about it; I told you. Have some fun first. It's all right here." Gama patted his coat pocket.

"Everything?" Dimycles asked.

"Every... thing," Gama repeated. "I have Calare's entire inventory cataloged and mapped out. I don't play, but this ain't the place to talk about it. Eyes everywhere."

Gama went to a gift shop and bought Dimycles a carrying bag. Then he grabbed Dimycles's unkempt and wiry beard. "You look like you just escaped prison. You got money, but you don't look like it." They went through the air tunnel to Gama's car.

Further down the clouds, they stopped at an upscale mall. Gama paid the parking fee, and they walked through the air tunnel. Before entering the mall they had to scan themselves in.

"What's that all about?" Dimycles asked.

"Security."

"You can't do anything about that?"

"Oh, come on. I pick my battles. This is a ritzy mall! I can either catalog every weapon on this planet or spend my time getting past a mall scanner. Which would you prefer?"

"Okay, I see," said Dimycles.

"Thank you! Besides. I like scanning in. If a fire broke out, they'd know I was there!" As they reached the entrance to one business, Gama steered Dimycles inside. It was a shaving and hair salon. The staffers had perfect manners and were elegantly dressed. They soaked Dimycles's face, shaved him, and cut his hair. Gama then took him to a men's clothing store where Dimycles brought a custom-tailored suit and a tie.

"Nice! Now, you look like a Sunilian," Gama told him.

"Thanks, I needed this. So now, about the inventory," Dimycles said.

"Oh, man, you still on that. Okay, just... follow me."

After finding a cigar shop and music bar, they sat down in a comfortable corner. Gama chopped a stogie, ran it under his nose, then lit it. He gestured to a young female dancer, directing her to find some friends, and then come back to the table.

"Now, we can talk business," Gama said, handing the tablet to Dimycles.

Dimycles took it, but said, "This is the one place I don't want to talk about this."

"Relax," Gama assured him. "These girls don't give damn. They're illegals. Who are they gonna tell?"

As Dimycles scanned the inventory, his eyes widened. The sheer magnitude of the Calare arsenal was staggering. He stopped on the Midnight core.

"What's that?" Gama asked, looking over Dimycles's shoulder.

"Nothing... just browsing."

When the dancer returned with her girlfriends, a woman wearing blue took a liking to Dimycles. Setting the tablet aside, he let her sit on his lap and ordered her a drink.

"So what's the plan?" Gama asked him. "I know you're up to something. You got some buyers, some sellers?"

The woman in blue sipped her drink and raised her eyebrow. "You smell nice," she told Dimycles.

Dimycles pulled out a cigar and asked her to get it ready for him. Caressing it, she snipped off the end, then gave it to him. He put it between his lips, and she lit it for him. Dimycles leaned back, lost in sensual pleasures.

"I love that look," she said to him.

"What look?" He asked.

"The look of experience, and expectation," she said. "You seem like even though you've been through the worst a thousand times, you still take every moment like your first."

"Not the first," Dimycles answered. He sipped his drink and savored the taste. "It's like every moment is my last. It's like taking one long, luxurious breath between birth and death." Dimycles touched her behind her ear, then traced a line along her jaw.

Gama watched from across the table. "So young. So bright-eyed. So beautiful."

"I used to feel like that," said Dimycles. "I still remember the first and the last time."

She touched his thighs, running her hands up to his hips. She leaned into his chest. "I can make you feel that now," she whispered.

Dimycles chuckled. Gama raised his glass and proclaimed, "I'm all for pleasure before business."

Dimycles bit his lip, and said, "Ya know, looking at the inventory, there's way more items than I expected."

"Business is good."

"Ya, but remember, we used to do nothing more than protecting the devices already on our planet."

"Yeah?" Gama started paying attention.

"Then things changed."

"Of course," Gama blew a line of smoke rings. "Constantly adjusting our understanding of our purpose, and our policies."

"So then what?" Dimycles wondered. "We go to other planets, and take their doomsday devices?"

Gama eyed Dimycles.

Dimycles continued, "What gives us the right?"

"What do you mean? We're the damn Sunil. The right is ours!" Gama insisted.

"But who gave us the right? Did we give it to ourselves? These aren't just doomsday devices. I see conventional weapons and advanced technology in this inventory. Who gave us the right to dictate to other planets? Why are we the ones who can tell them what they can have and what they can't have?"

Gama threw his cigar down, "What!"

"Whoa! I'm just asking. I didn't mean to offend you."

"But you did," Gama snapped. "Offense taken! You don't question..."

The lady in blue squeezed Dimycles's shoulders and arms.

"Calm down," Dimycles said. "I was just asking."

"Look! You think every planet should..."

"Dammit! It was just a question!"

"If we let every planet decide how to use their own devices, we share the blame for their mishaps," Gama said. "Only six planets were hidden in the folds. So only six planets have the right to protect them."

"I thought there were seven," Dimycles murmured.

Gama gasped, then stood up, and left.

The lady in blue shook Dimycles. "You have to get out of here!"

Gama was heading straight for the guards up front.

"Hang on," Dimycles said. "What did I do?"

The lady in blue grabbed his hand and stood. Dimycles checked his watch. He tossed the last of his cigar into his glass, grabbed his bags, threw the tablet inside, and walked after her.

"Is there any way out of here?" Dimycles asked. "Backdoor?"

"No! We're miles in the air," she reminded him. "This building is completely sealed. We have a crawl space the girls use to avoid troublesome clients, but it doesn't go anywhere!" As she pushed him along, they saw Gama talking to the guards, and pointing back at the now-empty table.

Pushing him down behind a counter, the girl in blue said, "There are questions you just cannot ask." She left him there and reconnoitered. She slipped by Gama, who barely acknowledged her. She saw guards searching for Dimycles. Finally, the girl in blue darted behind a column. There she turned into a lattice, and then into Ina.

"Dims?" Ina shouted into her watch, "Dims where are you!"

"I'm on the surface," came his answer. "What took you so long?"

"Ran into some trouble," Ina huffed, hurrying along through the mall corridor.

"Trouble indeed! Where's Gama? Just stick close to him. We'll need him."

"Um... I don't think that's an option."

"W-What? What happened? Is he with the authorities?"

Looking back, she saw the guards deploying. "Well, you could say that."

"Dammit! We need him!"

"Don't you have anyone else?"

"No!"

"Great," she gasped. "I – I gotta go hide. Let me call you right back!"

"Ina? Ina! No, listen! Come get me!"

She didn't wait.

Ina ran to the exit doors, but they wouldn't budge. She heard guards running behind her so she quickly walked away and ducked into a store. There she shifted into Dimcyles's appearance. As Dimycles she returned to the exit door. He'd been scanned, and she knew that would gain her entry to the air terminals. She looked around for Gama's car but couldn't find it. She hopped into a taxi.

"Where to sir?" the automated cab asked.

"Um... the- the casino!" she demanded.

"I'm sorry, but casinos are prohibited destinations. Where to sir?"

She saw barricades going up. Alarms were blaring.

"Oh, the... uh... the uh um um... surface?"

"I'm sorry, but the surface is only allowed for legal and non-temporary immigrants. Where to sir?" Guards were stopping other cars nearby.

"The - Dammit! I'm messing everything up. The – the Sim slim..."

"Do you mean. Slimm City?"

"Yes! Slimm City!"

"Calculating.... Is your destination on the map correct?"

"YES!" she screamed shaking the partition in front of her.

"Please deposit funds."

She rummaged through her purse and shopping bag. Not knowing the currency, she started shoving coins into random slots. The air cab again asked for money. Fed up, her hand turned into a blade and pierced the partition, cutting out the middle. Once she was in the front seat, she reformed as Ina. She took out the logic unit and manually sped away.

THE SECRETS OF CALARE

A RECTANGULAR TRANSPORT vessel touched down on the Calarean surface. Three workers hopped out. Compartments lined the chassis, and the workers removed three of these, loading them into a hovering crate. After they'd pushed the crate away, another compartment shook itself loose, and thudded onto the ground. Dimycles popped out, clutching the Herlon rod.

It was humid. Everything was silent. An ancient temple loomed up ahead. It was covered in vines, and concealed by the trees. Large stones covered in ancient carvings made up the outer structure. It had several domes, as well as steeples rising from the roof at various heights. He put the compartment back in place on the transport and walked up to the temple entrance.

When he checked his watch, he saw he had an update. As he entered the temple, he read, whispering the words: "The core is in the Vima Gami." A long hallway stretched before him. It was well-lit and constructed of gray stones. Dimycles glanced around. Stone doors lined the walls at intervals. "Which room is the Vima Gami?"

Using his watch, he scanned the area. He pointed the instrument up to burn the scanned image into the security cameras, but he could find none. He examined the side stones, looking for trigger switches, lasers, or sensor mechanisms. His hand slid across the smooth rock surface and did not feel a single unnatural indention. He felt suspicious of this ancient hallway of secrets with no security system.

He stepped into the corridor and edged forward, passing doors on either side. Admiring the designs on the stones, he wondered how the hallway remained so bright. He didn't see any torches or light sources, so he raised his arms to look for a shadow. When he turned around, he noticed the corridor leading back to the entrance had gone dark.

He stopped. Ahead of him, the hall shone brightly, but behind him, everything dimmed. Curious, he took one big step backward, toward the entrance, and the hallway behind him brightened with that motion. He backed up a few more steps, and light flooded the entire corridor. "Okay?"

Dimycles took a deep breath, returned to walking forward. He took the leftward passageway, and the light continued to surround him. The darkness creeping up behind him made him uncomfortable, and he abandoned mission to think things through. Dimycles turned around and walked back toward the entrance. The dark hallway brightened as before, but as he rounded the corner, he found only a stone wall where the entrance had been. He pushed the wall, but it would not budge.

"What happened?" he asked, backing up against the stone wall.

When Dimycles went back down the corridor, the darkness followed behind him. He tried each door, hoping for a signal or sign of the Vima Gami. The hall seemed to curve endlessly to the left. The darkness crept up so close, that when he slipped his foot was lost in shadows. The floor was invisible. He had to scramble back up. He turned, faced the darkness, and reached out to touch it—nothing! When he walked into those shadows, no light came. Instead, the hall remained dark.

He felt as if he were at the edge of a cliff overlooking a dark abyss. If he walked away from the edge, it followed him. He turned and ran through the brightly lit corridor ahead. Choosing a random door, he entered a new room.

Dimycles took a moment to catch his breath. Looking around he realized he was right back in the same corridor, but now it was fully lit.

"Did the room get smaller?" he wondered.

The same thing happened. Whenever he turned around, the corridor behind was dimming. When he tried moving sideways, the darkness crept toward him. He found another door that opened into another hall. This one was smaller: the roof was lower, and the doors seemed shorter than before. What was he supposed to do?

He scanned Ina's data, and let out a holler. "How do I get out of this place? Vima Gami? Row 24, column 12. That's it? What the hell is a Vima Gami? "

Dimycles shook his head, and took another step forward.

The wall behind him immediately dimmed. As he passed the next door, the darkness seemed to race to keep up with him. By the time he passed the second door, the hall behind him was almost black. He shrugged and went through the door. Everything looked the same.

"Okay? Progress?" He wondered aloud. "So why did that work? Huh? You just messing with me, or did I get the code?"

Finally, it came to him: the code of Ancient Sunilian numbers. This was numerology he had long since forgotten. He tried to remember how all that worked. Finally, he decided the vimagami numerology must amount to 21435341. Having already gone through the second door, in this new corridor he took the first. Once more, it all looked the same.

"Yeah! Got you figured out!" he cried, trotting along to the fourth door. As he entered the shadows behind him seemed uncomfortably close. Next, he took the third door. In the corridor, the darkness was right on his heels, and he wondered if he could make it to the fifth door. Taking tiny steps, he crept along, hoping a slow speed would keep the darkness at bay. As he opened the fifth door, his foot slipped into darkness.

He breathed easier in the new hallway. Five was highest number. "Three more doors," he said to himself. "Three, four, and one."

Knowing he could make it, he calmly walked to the third door and entered—only to bump his head. The new corridor was exceedingly small.

"What the hell! Why... what? You're cheating!" Dimycles screamed. He hunched over. "I had it right, and you know it! You cheating hater! Vimaaaa Gaaaaami! A is three, and it is always thr-"

He thought about it again, and looked over his numbers, realizing that the combined A and M made a seven, not a three and a four. Dimycles had to get to the seventh door.

The corridor was already dim, giving him little to work with. Reluctantly, Dimycles accepted his situation, and slowly ventured to between the third and fourth door. The emptiness was close behind, and his own shadow melted into the dark stone floor.

"Unbelievable."

By the fourth door, his foot was already slipping over the edge behind him. He barely made it to the fifth. The ceiling in this corridor was so low he had to crawl. He found himself wondering what exactly it was in the darkness that scared him so. He imagined a floor of spikes awaiting him, or maybe he would fall into a dark purgatory and remain there until he withered away. What scared him the most was monsters. Something about the dark unknown seduced his imagination into creating creatures that could only do harm to him.

He considered his predicament.

He needed to reach the seventh door. His road had run out by the fifth. Dimycles lifted his feet, steadied himself, and pushed off from the phantom ground. He rolled and jumped, but the darkness ate away the floor. He reached out, and clung on to the sixth door handle on one side, and the wall on the other. His feet dangled in darkness. When he tried to stand, he could feel only a hint of the surface. Ahead along the opposite wall, was the seventh door.

To leverage the jump, he opened the sixth door, and clung to it, as it swung out. Once the door opened all the way, he put his feet to the stonewall and leapt to the far side, where he slammed into the seventh door. He swung it open and entered, just as everything faded away.

Though the seventh door was correct, opening the sixth door had tripped the temple's security system. Guards were roused, though Dimycles didn't know that yet. The new corridor was so small and tight; Dimycles could barely crawl. When he exhaled, he blew the dust on the floor.

With the ceiling so low, only a child could stand, Dimycles started hyperventilating. It was like being in a miniature elevator that wasn't going anywhere. He crawled and waddled forward trying to reach the first door. Instantly his knees and feet slipped into the darkness. The floor faded, and he fell into the abyss. He barely managed to grip some partial floor, but it was enough to save him. He pulled himself up, sweating, but the forward movement of his hands caused the darkness to creep along ahead of him. He scrambled against the disappearing cliff and reached the first door, but the ceiling was too low. The door opened, but the stones on the ceiling caught the top of the door and impeded his ability to open it all of the way. He tried to slip his fingers between the door and the wall to pry it open, but there was not enough room. He pounded against the low ceiling, but the stones felt solid and heavy and didn't even echo the sound. He reached into his backpack, pulled the Herlon Rod, and used it to pry the door open, little by little, as the top of the door scraped against the low clearance. The movement he made caused the darkness to descent upon him, and he realized just enough space to squeeze his body through the tight opening. He thought everything went black, but his eyes were closed. When he opened them, he gazed about the the outer chamber.

The room was dark gray marble from floor to ceiling, with hundreds of the pillars scattered around. The entire room formed a circular corridor that wrapped around the inner chamber.

Dimycles wandered through the pillars, looking for a way into the inner chamber. Suddenly, he heard a noise from the outer wall. He saw the marble separate, revealing a door. Dimycles ducked behind a pillar and watched four guards emerge. The marble door closed behind them, vanishing into the wall.

When the guards walked into the center of the outer room, the inner wall opened. They passed through, and it closed. Dimycles ran to the wall and dug his fingers into the marble. He found no openings. He looked about and spotted a curiously broken pillar. He approached it and realized it was actually a platform. He stepped up onto it.

The watch on his arm alerted him. It was Ina.

"Dims?" Her voice came over the watch line. "Dims where are you?"

"I'm on the surface," he whispered. "What took you so long?"

"Ran into some trouble."

"Trouble indeed," he echoed. "Where's Gama? Just stick close to him. We're gonna need him."

"Um...I don't think that's an option."

"W-What? What happened? Is he with the authorities?"

"Well, you could say that."

"Dammit! We need him!"

"Don't you have anyone else?"

"No! I don't have anyone else!"

"Alrighty, great, I – I gotta go hide. Let me call you right back!"

"Ina? No, Ina, listen!" Dimycles looked at his watch. She'd already hung up. "Hide?" he wondered.

Dimycles heard the inner chamber wall reopen, followed by a single set of footsteps. He knew it must be one of the guards. Dimycles hopped off the platform to hide. The guard heard something and looked around. Not seeing any trouble, the guard disabled the platform and started back to the inner chamber.

Dimycles jumped out from behind a pillar and bashed the rod into the guard's head. He dragged the unconscious guard to the spot where the opening had been. Now it opened up for them. He took the guard's badge and gun and entered the inner chamber. Three guards manned holographic stations inside of a light gray marbled foyer surrounding the inventory room.

Dimycles aimed the gun at one, but the stock lit up, beeped, and the trigger locked. All three guards turned. Dimycles hurled the gun at the furthest one, then bashed the nearest one's head with the Herlon rod. He kicked the second and punched at the third, but this last guard dodged.

The third one slammed Dimycles on his back. Dimycles threw his legs up trapping the guard's arm and head and swept him to the ground. Dimycles came to his feet. The second guard shot Dimycles twice in the chest and once in the shoulder. Dimycles rammed the shooter, knocked the gun away, and knocked him out with the rod. The first guard pulled his weapon, spraying bullets at Dimycles. Dimycles bored through the salvo, grabbed the man's arm, and forced him to shoot the third guard. This third one was quick. He pounced onto Dimycles, who couldn't help but wince from the pain.

The three of them struggled on the ground, as blood flowed freely from Dimycles's wounds. Dimycles pushed himself up from the guards, causing one to shoot the other. The injured guard fell onto his killer, and Dimycles finished him off.

The station holograms were already up. As Dimycles hobbled over to one, he noticed metal cauterizing his wounds. He used the access codes Ina had sent. When he saw the data, he noticed the inventory had more than quadrupled since last he observed it. "Interesting," Dimycles whispered. "I guess they've been busy."

Forgetting his mission for a moment, he perused the inventory. It had items he'd never heard of, and others were weapons of legend. None were particularly world ending, but many were dangerous. He pulled himself away, saying: "Let's get this over with."

He checked his watch for the location of the Midnight core, then thought for a moment. Using the watch, he cloned the authorization from the guard's access badge. He grabbed a clean suit and mask and put them on. He went through the decontamination chamber into the inventory room. It was all clean white marble, lined with rows of large columns.

Dimycles counted the rows. He found the 12th column, touched the fourth section, and the compartment opened with a rumble.

He looked inside the compartment. "What?" The compartment was empty. He ran from the room, and pulled off his mask.

He double-checked his location, then snarled: "She tricked us!"

Dimycles screamed in anger and then hopped back on the terminal. He read the recorded location of the core, then spoke into his watch. "I'm in hell. She tricked us!"

He pounded the terminal desk, but then a message sounded. It was Ina.

"What did you say? You were breaking up. I don't think I can hear you unless you stand in specific spots."

"I got nothing, Ina. The core is gone," Dimycles hissed.

"You sure? Wait... maybe Gama had the wrong coordinates. What do you think?"

"I double checked their computer here. It's labeled 'In Storage,' and it's checked in. So someone definitely stole it!" Dimycles pulled at his beard. "What is she up to? Why would she send me here to find something that's not here? Where are you, Ina? Can you get here?"

"No, but let me see what I can find out."

"You still have Gama's tablet?"

"Yup."

"Wow. 'Mal must like you; he never lets anyone hang on to it."

"Ooh, well, you know me. I just say all the right things."

Dimycles slouched back in the chair and huffed. He looked around the room and said, "I don't even know how to get out of here."

He flicked through the list of devices in the inventory, hoping the Midnight core might be miscataloged.

"Without it, do you have another exit plan from the planet?" Ina asked.

"No."

"Maybe Wuyan just wanted to know where the planet is? Or was it all for nothing?"

Dimycles searched the system files, looking for whatever data Calare had on Wuyan. He thoughtfully stroked his beard. "Well, she well wants something. She didn't get me for the fun of it!"

"Okay, what issue does Wuyan have against the Sunil?" she asked.

Dimycles shrugged. He'd found nothing to connect Wuyan with the Calareans. He checked records of military excursions. Apparently, Wuyan had never engaged the Sunil.

He felt stymied. "She wanted the Midnight core. I know that. Her eyes glowed whenever she spoke of it. I felt it. That Core was everything to her, but we got nothing."

"Her eyes glowed?"

"We need to find something else," Dimycles said, "but there isn't anything else! That's all we know. We have to get out of here."

Ina started looking through Gama's tablet. "Look, I'm gonna level with you Dims. We can't leave empty-handed. Escape will be hard enough, but if we don't have anything to barter with, we're dead."

Dimycles went over it in his mind, speaking his thoughts: "Vegas, the Reptilites... no, no... none of it makes sense."

"What's the deal with the Sunil and the Watchers?" she asked, browsing across numerous sites on Gama's tablet.

"Nothing... what do you mean?"

"I found a shared site hosted by the Watchers – for the Sunil."

"The Watchers?" Dimycles echoed.

"Two secret societies working in tandem for their interests." Ina sent Dimycles a link.

He accessed the new Watcher surveillance. "Ina, they just detail information on all sorts of races."

"They are doing their jobs," Ina said, impressed with a wealth of information. "Are they selling this?"

"I doubt it. Watchers just observe and record. What kind of money would you get for selling stuff that already happened?" He checked the database for surveillance on Wuyan. "Where's Wuyan? There she is. Wuyan invaded the Vega System. So, let's see how you are fairing against the Vega Beast."

Dimycles paired his watch to gather the information. The Watcher's reports on the military status of Wuyan's wins, losses, and troop positioning was blank.

"Wuyan's army is... missing?" Dimycles was taken aback. "That can't be right."

"What's the point of invading the Vega System if she isn't even there to fight them?"

"It' not that. They don't know where she is. This isn't right. She can't just show up and disappear," said Dimycles. "Where could she take her military?"

Ina gasped.

"What?" Dimycles demanded.

"She took it across the galaxy..." Ina said.

"Where do you see that? I don't see any tracking logs on her movements."

"That's because she wanted to sneak attacked the Watchers!"

"What!" Dimycles frantically scanned screens, catching up with Ina. "Where you see that?"

"Right there in big letters," she said. "'Suspect imminent attack on the Realm of the Watchers.'"

"No way! She is bold!"

"Is that bad? Is that where she took the Midnight core?"

"I don't think she has the Midnight core," Dimycles said.

"Then who has it?

"I don't know!"

"That doesn't get us anywhere, so can we pretend she has it? What can she do with it?"

Dimycles shook his head, "She can kiss herself goodbye, as well as everything in its blast radius."

"Blow stuff up." Ina adjusted herself in the back of her cab, setting the tablet on her knees.

"Beyond blowing things up, it completely nullifies all space, time and reality within its blast radius," Dimycles told her. "She would effectively erase the existence of everything around her."

"Does that help her? What are the Watchers doing to her?"

"Nothing! They can't. They're Watchers, not Doers. The Watchers just watch. They record the activity of all life. If she destroys them, she will destroy all knowledge of all civilizations that have ever lived."

"That doesn't sound very promising. How does that give her power?"

"I don't know, which is why it doesn't make sense."

"Well, dammit, think! What do the Watchers have that would make her want to destroy them?"

"Nothing! The Sunil has every device she could possibly-- Oh no!" he cried suddenly.

"What?"

"The Cube of None!"

"Cube of who?"

"It's the one thing the Watchers have that the Sunil could never get their hands on!"

Ina was completely confused. "So she wants to destroy the Watchers to get the Cube of None?"

"Yes! No, no, she doesn't want to destroy the Watchers at all; she just wants the Cube of None! You were right, Ina. She was just using us to find out how to get here."

"I was just blowing hot air. Why here? What's so special about Calare?"

"Because," Dimycles turned back toward the inventory room, "she can't open the cube, without the key!"

He searched the system again and explained, "Those who defeated the Cosmic Titan locked its source of power into the Cube of None. Then they gave the cube to the Watchers, but for the safety of the realm, they never revealed to anyone where they'd hidden the key..."

"That makes sense if they didn't want the two pieces in the same place, and even if you got the cube, who would ever find a hidden planet?"

"Exactly, and Covarra has it!" He said, masking and decontaminating again, and running into the Inner Chamber. Tearing through the inventory, he found what he was looking for: "The Key of Titans." Dimycles whispered looking at it.

Unlike a typical key, this was a cylindrical disk with a handle at the center. It was a combination of dark, wood-like material, crystal, and several layers of intricate symmetrical designs that came up into a thin dome on both sides.

"This is everything." He dropped the box and ran, gasping into his watch. "Ina! We got it! Now let's get out of here!" He heard no reply. "Ina, did you copy?"

When he got no response, he realized there was no signal within the inventory room. As he tried again, he saw the guard he'd knocked unconscious standing at the inventory room door, blocking him.

Dimycles asked sweetly, "You wouldn't know where I can find an exit, do you? I followed this map, and, I kinda got lost, and stumbled into..."

The guard stepped back and closed the inventory room door.

Uh oh.

Alarms sounded. The room rumbled, as the large columns sealed over. The marble columns sank into the floor, and the room cleared. Now it was an empty white marble room.

Then the floor moved.

"Um?"

ADMIRAL KAHLAN STRODE through his ship onto the bridge, Gajra running close behind him. Kahlan asked Fyzel, "Where's Dimycles?"

"Last we checked he was shopping at the mall," Fyzel replied. "He triggered a renegade alert and a lockdown."

"Confirm that," Gajra shouted. "Get me eyes down there!"

Within moments Fyzel reported, "The police assembled in the malls and blocked the emergency tunnel exits. They contacted a local named Gama and determined that Dimycles snuck into a secret tunnel at a cigar bar. That's the last."

"He must not escape," Kahlan commanded. Gajra nodded and then left the bridge to board a shuttle down to the planet.

Admiral Kahlan issued orders to his crew. "Lock down the main hangar. This vagabond renegade is not going anywhere without his ship."

DIMYCLES SECURED THE Key of Titans in his backpack and ran for the clean room door. The floor shifted, and his legs buckled. He fell flat on his back. Above him, the roof transformed into a translucent dome. Though he couldn't see through it, he assumed anything above it could see in. Bumps popped up in the marble flooring.

"Is this room alive?" Dimycles wondered.

He looked at his watch, but couldn't get a signal. Again he tried for the door, but the shifting, spinning room disoriented him, making him woozy. The floor was like a sea, and out of it, wave-like marble hand formed, grabbing him. When he tried to kick it off, he hurt his foot against the stone and he fell onto a few items he'd emptied onto the floor earlier when he'd been searching. He snatch an amulet bag and looked inside of it.

"The cuffs of Sabosin?" He stashed the amulet bag, and then saw a club; he reached for it, but it moved away before he could grab it. "What? What's happening?" He crawled forward to get it, but the club just distanced itself further.

Getting to his feet, Dimycles ran after it, but his steps felt like he was in a dream. Though his legs pumped furiously, he couldn't get anywhere. The club seemed infinitely far away.

As the floor kept morphing, he twisted his knee; then his feet started melting into the marble. When he pulled them out, they were gooey blobs, but they solidified. He had to lift his feet high to make any progress.

Marble tiles formed into a monster as tall as the ceiling. A marble fist punched Dimycles across the room. When he hit, he felt his bones crack, and he stifled the urge to vomit. He felt his diaphragm lock up. Dimycles staggered to his feet, he took a deep breath and coughed violently. When he tried to steady himself, the wall moved, throwing him down again.

The monster sent down a storm of marble boulders. Trapped beneath the heavy rocks, Dimycles heaved and pushed them off. As he stumbled forward, a spike shot up in his foot. He hollered, tearing his foot from the point. The monster kept hurling boulders and raising new spikes. Dimycles dodged, as the nanomites stretched metal across his wounds.

Seeing the club again, Dimycles ran toward it, but the room shifted, giving the illusion that he was upside down. When he pulled out the Sabosin cuffs, he fell upward and crashed to the floor. A spike caught him below the jaw, tearing his neck.

He stood up and closed his eyes, envisioning the room as he last remembered it. It didn't help. None of this was an illusion. The room was moving. The monster reappeared from the floor, grabbing him and throwing him the other way. Dimycles landed on his head and slid into a wall. Fist-size fireballs rained down through the dome.

"Ow!" Dimycles said, pushing himself to his feet. Pain wracked his body, but the hole in his neck was healing.

When he pulled the Sabosin from his backpack, the stones were glowing with psychedelic colors. The bag seemed to melt through his hands. He closed his eyes and drove his hand deep into the bag. He pulled out a pair of green stones. The monster grabbed Dimycles, and more fire rained down through the ceiling. As Dimycles thrust the green stones into the Sabosin cuffs, the monster threw him, and the cuffs activated.

Dimycles flew through the air. The cuffs charged his body with a burning sensation. The pain was so great, it drove him to laugh like a madman. Then came a surge of energy. Now his heart burned, but it felt so good. The world slowed, but only because his perceptions and movements had accelerated. He floated toward the far wall. His heart throbbed like a turbo engine. The marble monster was still stretched out from throwing him. A new gale of fire bullets rained from the ceiling, but now he could evade them. With a quick shake, he changed direction. His foot touched the floor and in one hop he traversed the room.

Dimycles picked up the club. He ran through the rain of fire, clubbed the monster, sparking a flash from the club, followed by an explosion. It blasted the monster to smithereens while tossing Dimycles across the room. The explosion charred the walls, destroying part of the roof. Rubble filled the exit. He looked at his watch. It had a signal. He could see the sky through the punctured dome.

Choppers hovered there, continuing the rain of fire. Dimycles hopped up and tightened his backpack. It was getting hard breathe because of the smoke. The heat was too much. Dimycles scaled the marble wall, jumped off at the top, and grabbed the edge of the opening in the dome. He pulled himself up, climbed over, and ran across the roof. Soldiers shot at him with handheld tractor beam cannons. Dimycles ducked between the steeples, dodging the beams. Adjusting the bag on his shoulders, he hopped from the roof.

He dropped, muttering, "Oh, this just keeps getting better."

When he landed, he started to sink into soft, swampy ground. When he looked up, he was confronted by an army of hovercraft. Soldiers in high-powered jet suits swooped low to contain him. They were almost as fast as he was. Dimycles had to run in circles to keep from sinking.

He called to his watch: "Ina!!! Where the hell are you? Can you even hear me?"

There was no response.

The troops gave chased, then retreated. Hover tanks laid out a spreading carpet of fire. The retreating troops re-engaged, and then came in waves. Dimycles fled as they closed in, his fist gripping stones.

"One of these stones has to make me fly," Dimycles said to himself.

He pulled out the green stones and replaced them with the yellow ones. The troops were suddenly a blur as Dimycles slowed down and they zipped by. His cuffs reactivated yellow. He jumped high in the air, but instead of continuing upward, he quickly landed.

As soon as he hit, he started to sink. A soldier had doubled back. As he flew by, Dimycles grabbed him. The soldier's momentum jerked Dimycles up from the swamp.

Dimycles was trying to remember each color's function. He stuck his arm out, and light came into his body. His arm emitted a blast of energy, blowing away the pursuing troopers, but it also blasted his ride! As they tumbled into the swamp, explosions tore up the ground around them. Dimycles spotted tanks. Raising his hands, he blew holes in the tanks. More troopers poured in from the flanks. Choppers arced over the horizon.

He trudged through the swamp and started pulling the jet pack off a felled trooper, but the man wasn't dead, and it developed into a fist fight. As he knocked the soldier unconscious, his watch signaled him. It was Ina. She gave him a rendezvous point.

"Yes! I gotta get outta here," Dimycles cried. Replacing yellow stones with green, he got a supercharge and ran off through the swamp.

WE HAVE EVIDENCE the suspect escaped in taxi 402.

Scanning.

Taxi 402 is offline. Residual sensors detect northeast vector.

Scanning. Taxi 402 at Slimm City projects. Intercept.

Roger.

"I've never seen a place like this," Ina said, as she brought her knees to her chest in the back of the cab. She'd hidden at the Slimm projects in the clouds but knew it couldn't last. She heard the police cars closing in.

The residential building looked like a cage in a mental institution. She shook her head. "I'm sorry Dims," she whispered. Her hand began forming a blade, as she prepared to attack. She could hear the police radios. They were searching for Dimycles.

Don't they know where he is?

Ina morphed into lattice then into Dimycles.

"Better than dying in the Holice," she resolved in her male form.

The stench in the projects was grim. She ran across feces-covered floors, past residents who slept on beat-up mattresses and hard floors - sitting up. An older man pulled a gun from under his mattress, and feebly aimed it. She snatched it from his hands, turned to shoot the robotic police, but then saw that they weren't exactly robotic.

Not exactly.

"What the...?" she gasped, lowering the gun. "Ghosts?"

Holographic police chased her down. Ina/Dimycles shot, but the bullets went straight through them. As they approached, their hands materialized to grab her, but she shot the hands off and ran.

Electricity crackled around her, and the ghost force appeared in front to cut her off. She bashed through the walls on her left and hid behind the partitions. A ghost came through a wall. She shot wildly, backing deeper into the rooms, blasting holes in the walls around her. As the ghost cops closed in, a methodical tapping came from above. A young man was signaling with his hands. In her male form she looked up questioningly, and the young man dropped a gun into her hands.

Ina/Dimycles shouldered the new gun and shot. There was no kick, and she lurched forward. A static charge singed the wall. She figured it out, shot again, and the ghost police shimmered, faded, and reformed. Suddenly a group of residents appeared, fighting alongside Ina/Dimycles. The charged the phantom cops, and confusion reigned.

Ina/Dimycles took advantage of the melee to slip away, but she ran into a dead end. The form of Dimycles morphed into a lattice. The lattice cut the wall open and morphed into Ina. She ran outside, where the wind nearly blew her off the platform. She gripped the walls and looked down.

"Long way," she chuckled. Still hearing the commotion inside, she scurried along the platform.

She reached the parking area and spotted her stolen taxi surrounded by police. A gang of Slimm guerrillas chased off the ghost authorities. She was about to make her move when she heard footsteps. Again she morphed to her lattice, ducked low, and then changed to Dimycles.

When Ina/Dimycles looked up, she saw the young man who'd thrown her the weapon. His bright eyes were set in a pleasant face.

"Thanks," she said, crawling out from behind a car.

The young man raised his arm, and with his thumb and index finger, he motioned to Ina/Dimycles, and then pointed at him.

"Oh, um..."

The young man pointed at his own head, made a fist, traced his thumb along his jaw, and pointed at Dimycles.

"My name, my name is Dimycles?" she said, not sure what to make of it all.

The young man laughed, crouched low, and picked up a handful of clouds. With his finger, he wrote his name in the air.

"Perilous," she read. The cloudy name blew away in the breeze. "Pleased to meet you. I – you can't speak? I figured in a place like this, something like that would never, I mean-"

Perilous started another statement, but Ina/Dimycles waved it off, saying, "Don't bother explaining, I understand. Poverty is the same on every planet."

Perilous nodded, and then pointed to the taxi.

"Yes, that's mine." She reached into the car and grabbed the shopping bag and purse containing coins from the casino. "Thanks for stepping in," she said. "I was really in trouble. Let me pay you something." She opened the purse to show Perilous the gambling winnings. Perilous' face lit up. "Maybe payment would motivate you to help me one more time?"

Perilous shook his head, and snapped the purse shut. He glanced around suspiciously.

"It's yours!" Ina/Dimycles said, pushing it on him.

Perilous took a step back.

"Okay." Ina/Dimycles took back the purse. "I get it. Sorry."

She returned the purse to the taxi, adding, "My life isn't all about the money either. I just wanted some way to make it worth your while."

Perilous motioned with his fist in the palm of his hand, and then touched his nose. Ina/Dimycles didn't quite get it. Perilous approached her.

"Well, you could earn it," she said. "Or you could just help me out. Is there any way you could meet me down on the surface? I have a couple of bags down there, and I desperately need them."

Perilous shook his head, no. He touched Ina's Dimycles face and with his thumb, running it along the jaw. Ina/ Dimycles sighed mournfully. She morphed into a lattice. Perilous smiled and watched the lattice morph into Ina.

"If you could meet that guy on the surface," Ina said finally, it would help. I'm Ina."

Perilous gratefully made an "O" with his thumb and forefinger. When he got in the car, she leaned in to set the rendezvous coordinates. As her face neared him, she could feel his breath on the back of her neck. She punched in the data, withdrew from the driver's window, and watched Perilous speed away. She returned to her taxi feeling sad. Her steps were shaky. The idea of getting off this planet was impossible. They couldn't do it—at least, not together.

She reached into her stolen taxi, then stopped, unsure of herself. She sighed, and pushed past the hopeless feeling. She started the taxi, hopped in, and sped off.

ADMIRAL KAHLAN READ the confusing data. "The mall showed Dimycles check in, and then he checked out. The ground forces reported engaging him moments later. Then he disappeared from the surface to the Slimm projects. He must have a teleporting device. That's the only way he could make it from point to point so fast."

A call came in, announcing: "Dimycles was spotted reentering the mall just minutes ago!"

"Fool, why would he go back to the mall?" Kahlan growled. "Tell the ground troops to regroup. Gajra will secure the mall. We will close in on him."

After giving the order, Kahlan contacted the main space hangar, and told the general manager, "Dimycles is in the atmosphere... Yes, in a mall. Regardless, he cannot get off the planet without his ship. I think Dimycles' only hope will be to teleport back to the hangar. I am sending a small team to secure the hangar. Do not let anyone in or out until I arrive."

ONCE DIMYCLES WAS alone in a field, he slowed and took out the green stones. He then tried the red stones. A heated charge filled his body. He jumped, but he came back down, landing in a surge of red energy and flames. He noticed the ground was burnt around him.

He looked at his arms. "Dammit!"

He made a fist and a red glowing haze of fire emitted from his hands. He looked in the bag. "Really?" Dimycles complained. "Four sets of stones and I have to go through three of them before I learn that the fourth is what I need." He put the red stones back and took out the blue ones. He tried to remember how the rhyme of the Sabosin went.

"I played that show so much it made my parents sick, but now I can't even..." He felt a hand on his shoulder. He turned to strike and stopped.

Perilous jumped back, folding his fingers together. Dimycles did the same. Perilous pointed to the Dimycles's backpack on the ground. After swiping an open hand across his palm, Dimycles nodded to him, and Perilous looked in the bag. When he saw the contents he turned pale.

Perilous touched his forehead, and extended a fist to Dimycles- slowly extending his pinky and thumb.

Dimycles sighed and pointed at Perilous. Then with both hands, he pointed at both sides of his own chest, touched a thumb to his jaw, and touched his pointed fists together.

Perilous nodded, but shrugged, putting his fist on the backhand of his other fist.

Dimycles face saddened, and he raised both hands in the air to Perilous – a surrendering expression.

"My sacrifice," Dimycles said.

Perilous turned and walked away with the backpack. He got into the car and sat alone. Dimycles watched. Finally, Perilous turned and nodded. Dimycles jumped in back.

Perilous piloted the car into the air. Dimycles glanced around nervously. The mute driver drifted high into the sky, avoiding ground forces. Suddenly Dimycles realized they weren't stopping. They were headed straight through the upper atmosphere into space; Dimycles felt his stomach give way.

"Ina?" Dimycles said sheepishly.

Perilous looked back and smiled meekly. He raised both hands toward Dimycles in a surrendering fashion.

"Her sacrifice."

GAJRA STRODE THROUGH the mall, and into the cigar bar. Her men had detained the lady in blue.

"The trail goes cold from here, captian," a soldier told her.

Gajra strolled around, assessing the layout. Turning her attention to the seating area, she sat across from the Jvee.

"Who are you working for?" Gajra asked.

"N-No one," Jvee stammered. "I don't know what they're talking about. I don't know anything,"

"What's your name?"

"Jvee"

"You look nervous, Jvee"

"Your men scare me," she complained.

Gajra gestured to her troops. "Give us some room." The men retreated. "That better?"

Jvee nodded.

"Tell me about the guy," said Gajra.

"What guy?" Jvee asked.

A cigar smoldered on the table. Gajra grabbed it and held it like a weapon. It was still burning. "This guy," Gajra said.

Jvee shrugged, "I wouldn't know. He stood me up."

"Men like him are trouble," Gajra told her. "Did you like him?"

"I didn't know him," Jvee answered. She thought for a moment, and offered: "He smelled nice."

"What kind of smell?" Gajra asked.

Jvee shrugged, "Like trouble."

"What did he talk about?"

"Same thing men like him talk about: themselves, money, power."

"Did he have money? Did he say anything about the Sunil?"

"We are the Sunil!" Jvee gasped.

Gajra balled her fist. "I'm asking if he spoke treason. Was he a renegade?"

"I would never sit on a renegade's lap," Jvee asserted.

"Mmm, well, the gentleman over there has a different story, and even though our cameras didn't get a good angle, the man you entertained appeared to have something in his hands." Gajra leaned forward, staring into the eyes of Jvee, but the girl in blue said nothing. "I noticed your papers aren't exactly up to par," Gajra added.

"Please," Jvee pleaded. "I didn't do anything. What do you want from me?"

"I don't want to hear it!" Gajra scolded. "Follow me!"

Gajra grabbed Jvee's arm and escorted her from the bar. While they walked out, Jvee gave Gama a scowl. The bar quieted and the troops waited for their captain.

Moments later, Gajra returned alone and asked, "Where are we?" The soldiers wore blank expressions.

"Captain?" one asked.

"Status!" Gajra shouted. "What have you been doing, just standing around in a bar?"

"Captain. No Captain," the soldier said. "Dimycles isn't anywhere to be found. The mall is clear." He leaned toward Gajra, and added, "You spoke to the lady, yes?"

"What lady?" Gajra asked.

"The lady in the blue dress..."

"Blue dress...?" Gajra questioned, but he then received a call from Kahlan.

"Report," Kahlan demanded.

"We have the mall secured. The troops on the ground haven't determined the level of vandalism yet, but they feel the perpetrator is already out of their custody. If he has teleported, he may already be at his ship," Gajra explained, "Dimycles isn't here in the mall."

"Well, he isn't here either! I'm at the hangar now," Kahlan told her as he entered the space hangar. "The hangar is too far from the surface for any teleporter. So where else could he be?"

"The hangar?" Gajra gasped.

"Where's the ship?" Kahlan asked the hangar's general manager.

Hearing this, Gajra screamed: "Dimycles's ship isn't in the hangar! It went out to the docks for repairs."

"Where?" Kahlan snapped.

DIMYCLES'S SHIP LEFT the docks at max speed; He was the only occupant. He felt nervous. His mind couldn't focus, caught in a constant cycle of self-reassurance and disbelief. Death was ahead. If he were lucky, he wouldn't live long enough to feel the pain.

An angry Admiral Kahlan called his troops to arms. The same organization that made Calareans so predictable also made them efficiently dangerous. Starships from every corner of the fold appeared moments later. Some starships decloaked, and then rallied to the planet.

Dimycles saw the ships go by– not bothering to detain his vessel. As he watched from his portal, a Battle-class starship followed protocol. They were on their highest alert, and they would protect the planet before chasing after relics. Because of that Dimycles knew he could make it out of the fold, and he also knew he could never last a moment longer than they allowed.

The Calareans still didn't know what he'd been seeking, or if more ships were coming to attack the planet. Dimycles knew they'd protect against an attack first. Stacks of starships rallied to the planet in groups of five. Five groups stacked themselves into larger units, and so on until a mesh of warships formed a blockade around the entire planet.

Dimycles felt his heart sink trying to avoid the realization that cut away at the core of his heart. Ever since he lost his home world, being apart of a society that put itself above all others had always been a warm secret he cherished. Though never thought the day would come he would ever be considered a renegade.

Admiral Kahlan's eyes looked as if they would pop a blood vessel. Gajra came back onboard from the clouds. She nodded to the Admiral, indicating that the planet was locked down, and no longer in danger.

Kahlan's response was a shout: "Get him!"

Fleets of Calarean ships poured out of the fold, while others remained by the planet, defending. Dimycles understood he needed to take action. Tired of his nervous pacing, he turned off the gravity and floated. At that moment he didn't like being alone.

"It's probably for the better," he sighed.

A shopping bag floated up, and Dimycles grabbed it. He reached in and pulled out a suit.

"Ina," Dimycles said weakly. With a half smile, he gazed at Ina's gifts for him. He put the suit back in the bag and pulled out the tie. Ina's scent mixed with the aroma of cigar smoke. That relaxed him, but the scents quickly faded away. He put the tie back and pulled out a card.

Dimycles,

I thank you for burying whatever happened between us in the past, and coming to rescue me from the Holice. You did give me another chance at life, and I was willing to give it to help you in return.

You asked for a piece of me to repair your fuel pump, but when the Calareans found it, they said it was a piece of a titan. Did you know that's what they would find? I never had a reason to question my origins before, but now I can't stop thinking about it. Am I just a reanimated piece of titan? I bid you farewell on your journey, as I will stay here to see if I can find out how mine started.

Please enjoy the suit, I think it will look handsome on you. I tested it out. The ladies love it.

There is also a razor in the bag. Shave!

Oh yeah! It's a gift. Don't pay me back!

You already bought me enough.

Always,

Ina

Dimycles pulled out the razor and returned the card. He floated to the washroom, wet his face, and slathered it thick. He grabbed the razor and ran it across his jaw. With his other hand, he wiped the hair into a towel. After repeating this on the other side, he finished and wiped his face with a wet towel. His skin felt tingly. He wet his hair and pulled it up into a top bun. For a moment he forgot his predicament.

His solemnity gave way to focus. He floated away from the washroom toward his lockers. He pulled out a pencil, a compass, and a star chart. He closed the locker.

"I've got something for them."

STAR CROWS

AFTER PURSUING DIMYCLES across the Realm the fleet of Calarean ships dropped out of hyperspace. The starships all bore the Sunilian insignia: a pentagon of planets surrounding one. In groups of five, they powered forward toward a floating cloud of space dust.

A vexed Admiral Kahlan rode in the lead ship. He was angry with himself for allowing Dimycles to come on his planet. Even more infuriating was allowing the fugitive to penetrate so far into the fold. The Admiral asked for a report.

"He's disappeared into the Volcaroo system," Fyzel announced. "We are nearing it now. It shouldn't be difficult to catch him."

Kahlan looked at his display. "Volcaroo is a nebula?"

"Admiral?" Fyzel wondered.

After double-checking, Kahlan said, "We are going into a nebula. What is Volcaroo?"

"Volcaroo is a class C star system. It has six planets and three..." Fyzel stopped. None of that was in the visual. Fyzel tried to reconcile the discrepancy by refreshing the map. The new version still had them entering the Volcaroo system- but there was no system.

"Their star must have collapsed, yes?" Kahlan said, his voice sour. "You need to stay on top of these things."

"It was too young to collapse," Fyzel protested.

Fyzel ran a deeper analysis. The Volcaroo system was indeed a nebula. The analysis revealed that the nebula consisted of the remains of

Volcaroo's exploded star and pieces of its planets. A destroyed planetary system.

Gajra asked, "Who lived in Volcaroo? Anyone? Or was it barren?"

Caryna answered, "Various life forms lived on two of the planets. Not very advanced. We would never have tracked any of their distress calls or migration requests."

Fyzel turned and smiled at Caryna. She'd saved him from further embarrassment. The analysis graph spiked. Life form detections sounded alarms throughout the nebula. Fyzel's smile turned to an expression of horror. He turned to the admiral. "Star crows!"

"Full stop! All ships!" Kahlan commanded. Caryna relayed the order to the other ships.

"Star crows?" Kahlan asked, leaning forward. "Dimycles went in there? Such devastation. What's he trying to do?"

"Die?" Fyzel wondered.

"Don't be silly. Nobody does something like this unless he has a plan." Kahlan stood up. "What are his options?"

Caryna said, "He either is going to dump the key to hide it or maybe wait us out and try to escape."

"Track him," Kahlan ordered.

"He's running on low power or no power," she explained. "Probably trying to avoid waking any of the star crows. Either way, I can't track him."

"Ion field? Track his gravity signature," Gajra suggested. "He must have life support running."

"He has no ion field," Caryna replied. "His ship is too small, at least, for me to detect any latent power through the nebulous debris. We're too far out. His gravity must be off because I see no errant fields from it. He's as invisible as a pebble."

"Well, that's at least one part of his plan," Gajra added. "He wants to keep us away from him. Can we send a ship in after him?"

"To do what?" Caryna asked. "We'd have to run on low power just like him. We'd have no way to capture him without disturbing the star crows. He's probably close to the nest core anyway."

"Pretty ballsy. Mark all of the nests on our display," Gajra commanded. "With his shields down, he's vulnerable. How close can he get to the nest core with his ship in that condition?"

Fyzel highlighted several nesting spots throughout the nebula. He then highlighted the nest core - the harvested core of the lost Volcaroo sun.

"He can get pretty close," Fyzel replied. "As long as they're dormant, they aren't that hot."

Kahlan thought for a moment. "Scan for anything coming out of that nebula. Whether he dumps the key or leaves, something has to come out of it."

"Wormhole?" Gajra asked.

"Can a ship that size open a wormhole?" Kahlan asked.

Caryna responded, "Even if it could he'd have to power up."

"Then we'd detect him," Fyzel added.

"You mean then the star crows would detect him," Caryna corrected him. "Those star crows would destroy him before he could manage it."

"Give me a worse case. Even if he succeeded then what?" Kahlan asked.

"Star crows can go through wormholes," Caryna answered. "They would follow him in to protect their territory. The danger is that they could disrupt the hole's signature, and he would emerge at a random point in space."

"If he comes out at all," Fyzel added.

Kahlan said, "Let's focus more on what he is going to do with that key."

"Admiral, the Galactic State!" Fyzel snapped.

"What about them?" Kahlan asked.

"A fleet of State forces are approaching the far side of the nebula," Fyzel said.

"What in the stars does the State want with him?"

"Says here he busted a prisoner out and destroyed the Holice in the process," Caryna said. "They want him bad."

"If they catch him, they'll kill him," Gajra added.

Kahlan thought for a moment, "That's how he did it; he had a partner we missed."

Gajra said, "If they catch him first, it will get political. We need to prepare for that."

"Send word back to Calare to dispatch a diplomat to the Galactic State headquarters," Kahlan instructed, then asked. "We can track the key, right?"

"Yes," Caryna answered. "He removed it from its container, but the key itself has an unmistakable signature. We just need to get close enough to scan for it."

"Too small?" Kahlan asked.

"That and all the interference," said Caryna. "It's just a tiny key. Maybe if we were on the same planet or close to it but not in this open space."

"Then he knows that. I want all navigational systems tracked," Kahlan commanded. "What other options does he have? What's on his ship? Escape pods?"

"Admiral," Fyzel said, "he has two escape pods on his ship, and an escape capsule."

"What's their speed?" the Admiral demanded. "Load capacity? Signatures?"

"The escape capsule has a solid state dark energy drive," Fyzel told them.

"How the hell...?" Gajra asked.

"We were going to confiscate it when it came back from the docks, but it never came back," Fyzel said.

"His best option is to eject that key in the damn pod, and that's a pretty good option," said Kahlan. "So here's the deal, the pod will have a destination route in its navigational systems. I want that information. I want to know whatever his pod knows. I want to know where his pod is going even before his pod knows!"

Seeing that Kahlan misunderstood, Caryna clarified, "We can't track dark energy drives."

"Nonsense," Kahlan said. "Of course, we can."

"They pull from the fabric of space itself, not fuel sources. They don't send exhaust into our space," Caryna insisted.

"What?" Kahlan asked. "Get a way to track it. Right now!"

"It's true," Gajra confirmed, speaking for the subordinates. "It makes slight ripples into the dark matter, but we're talking needle-size. Personally, I think his best plan is to pod the key and launch it."

"That's still no plan," Kahlan said, "How would he escape? We'd still catch him. Then we'd find the pod."

"That's if the star crows don't destroy the pod first," Caryna objected.

Kahlan stared at her. "They can destroy the pod, but I doubt they can destroy that key."

"A-Admiral," Fyzel stuttered, "the State is sending four ships into the nebula after him."

Taking his command chair, Kahlan shook his head, frustrated.

Gajra told him, "They are walking into a trap."

"Shall I warn them?" Caryna asked.

Kahlan brooded for a moment and then shook his head. "Only the key matters!" He pounded his hand against his armrest, and gave the command: "They will dig their own graves. Leave this sector."

TOAH WALKED THROUGH the spaceship corridors behind his father, Captain Proto. His little 8-year-old legs worked to keep up with his father's aggressive strides. They entered a room big enough to hold 30 people. Blue fabric covered the dark walls. Toah's father handed him a visor, along with a stern instruction to wear it. Hesitantly the boy put it on, and the room was suddenly white, vacant, and much bigger. Toah found his father standing next to a small table. He had a gun in his hand.

Captain Proto put the gun on the table. "Why did you shoot Carty?" he asked.

"I didn't mean to shoot him. I... I don't know. I just- "

"Did you want to kill him?"

"I just wanted to show him something," Toah explained.

"Show me what you wanted to show him. Pick up the gun."

Toah looked at the table and picked up the gun. Armed icons popped up all over the room. Startled, Toah dropped the gun and stumbled backward.

"The moment you touch a gun, the decision to kill is at your fingertips," Proto told him. "Do it again. Pick it up."

Toah nervously complied. He held the gun awkwardly by his waist.

"Point it at something."

The boy pointed it at an icon of a generic robot. He looked out beyond the barrel, and the gun went off. The kickback buckled his arm. The gun fell.

"Why did you shoot?" Proto demanded.

"I don't know, I didn't... I didn't mean to!"

"You told the gun to shoot!"

"I just held it. It shot by itself."

"It does not shoot by itself. Pick up the gun. When you put your finger on the trigger, you are telling the gun to kill whatever it sees. Now aim again."

Toah aimed the gun, instinctively curling his finger around the trigger. When he removed his finger from the trigger, he still held the aim. He left his index sticking out. His dad leaned over and guided the boy's finger to the index hold. After Toah had held the position for a few moments, Proto gave the order.

"Shoot."

Toah shot at the icon. When the shot went wide, his father made him repeat the actions. They did this several times until Proto received a call.

"Go ahead," he said into the comms.

"Captain, we've tracked the fugitive to Volcaroo. We're outside the system now awaiting your orders."

"Volcaroo? Who owns it?"

"Uninhabited. It appears to be a nebula. There's hot gas and debris from the area."

"They probably went there to hide. Dispatch four armed scouts to root out, or engage the target. Determine a route through the nebula so the fleet can cut off any escape."

"Yes, captain."

When the line went dead, Proto turned back to Toah, "If the gun hadn't been on stun, Carty would be dead. You must understand: this is not a toy, and it is not for show. It is for death and nothing else. Now I have to meet with Carty's parents and smooth this out. Keep practicing."

Toah watched his father leave and took off the visor. He looked at the fabric-covered walls, and then at his empty hands. He closed his small fingers and stared at the door. Pulling the visor back on, he gripped the gun. The icons reappeared. He aimed and fired.

FOUR SCOUTS LAUNCHED from the fleet and flew deep into the Volcaroo nebula. In tight formation, they sped through the area, but the expansive system dwarfed their search efforts. After several scans a winged officer named Wiper spoke up. "Biometrics are picking up life, but they can't tell me what kind."

The other wing commanders repeated their scans, drawing the same conclusion. Dotted life forms appeared at random spots within the cloud.

"It's all over the place," Taema said. "These fugitives picked a good place to hide. Heat and debris everywhere- totally messing with my scans."

"Call it in," wing leader Reed commanded.

Gysree got on her comms. "Fleet command? This is right wing, Gysree. There are indeterminate life forms in this nebula. This maybe a hideout or an ambush of some kind."

The four wings cruised through the area and the response came back. "This is Captain Proto. Proceed with the pursuit. The fleet is entering into the nebula to do a full sweep. Life form readings confirmed, but threat readings are minimal."

The three wing commanders waited for their lead, but Reed still gazed at his map. He confirmed the threat readings, and turned his scanners at full, looking for any sign of manufactured technology.

"Where to?" Wiper asked.

Reed said, "Let's try for the center. If they're sweeping the rim, we can start from the inside out."

Wiper's scans blipped only for a moment. "Hey. Hey!" he said, "I had something—just for a second."

The squad followed him toward the nest core, where the glint of light showed up on their displays.

Wiper added, "Yeah. There it is. That them?"

Gysree called out to the idle craft: "Fugitive spacecraft, you are under arrest by State law. Do not resist and you will not be harmed."

"Split up," Reed commanded.

Gysree tried another warning: "Fugitive spacecraft, you are now targeted for termination. If you do not comply with our escort, you will be destroyed."

"No response. Are they playing dead?" Taema asked.

"I hate that game," Gysree muttered.

"You would think they would know better."

"They're powering up!" Wiper shouted.

"Fire warning shots!" Reed commanded.

Gysree repeated: "Fugitive spacecraft, you are targeted for termination. If you do not comply with our escort, you will be destroyed!"

Wiper watched the ship steer away. "They're on the run!"

"Close in on them!"

Taema watched her display. "They're aiming for a large heat source of some kind—possibly the depleted star core. Our sensors are losing calibration due to the gravity field."

"They're trying to lose us. If they get close enough to that depleted core, our sensors may lose them. Take 'em out before they get away!" Reed warned.

Wiper shook his head and stared at his scanners. "I'm picking up a lot of life forms on that core."

"Double check that. The radiation may throw off our sensors," Reed explained.

"Roger."

"They are in range."

"Engage."

"Roger that."

PURSUED BY TWO major fleets, the Chyee listed aimlessly in the cosmic dust of the Volcaroo system. Dimycles had little means of escape. Floating in his silent cockpit, he counted his stolen Sabosin gemstones and sighed. "So the blue ones make you fly? These things should come with directions." He put the stones back in their bag and pushed off from the wall.

As he floated his mind wandered to thoughts of his dad, then to the things he'd told Ina about the Sunil. He recalled the Inner Chamber on Calare.

Then he thought of his sister.

"Our father was the best sling shooter around, wasn't he Damyae?" Dimycles spoke to the air. "He would have been known across the Observed Realm, but we were part of the Sunil. Just because we were born on Covarra." Dimycles clutched the bag of stones. "The forgotten."

He thought of how much he missed his family. "What happened?" he wondered aloud. "Why did we lose our home? None of this should have happened."

Dimycles remembered his boyhood. One minute everything was there. He sat at a table laughing with his family. It was a normal day. His father made a joke about 'pee' soup, while his mother brought dinner. The next moment a light flash, blinding heat, and he blanked out. When he regained consciousness, everything was dark, as if someone turned off every light in the world. He'd blacked out again, and awoke on a strange barren planet.

His sister lay face down in the sand next to him. Neither of them knew how they'd gotten there. No one else was there. He spent the next few years growing up on a desert planet dotted with mountains and rich oasis.

"Milana!" Dimycles gasped as he floated closer to his escape pod. "I don't understand how that place supported life. Probably why nobody knew we were there."

Dimycles put the Sabosin stones in the pod, followed by the wrist cuffs.

"Milana was just another rock in space. It wasn't even on record as being a life-bearing planet." He shook his head, "There is life there." He frowned. "And a lot of death."

Dimycles glanced over his body- tatted with metal. Even when he lived on Milana, he had no problems healing normally except in extreme circumstances. It seemed being imprisoned on Mars aged him by the decade every night he tried to stay alive. He touched himself but felt nothing on his metallic calluses. A wandering thought asked what will become of him if it covered his whole body?

Clearing his mind, Dimycles looked at the key to the Cube of None and turned it upside down. He shook it, rubbed it and tried to twist it; then he put in inside an escape pod after nothing happened.

He packed other gear into the pod, including a helmet. He closed the pod, pushed himself back to the cockpit, and cleared his thoughts.

Dimycles plotted the stars with his compass, and manually set a course for the pod. Then he placed three tiny round markers around the nest core on his navigation charts. He powered up a control panel, looked out the window, and then back at his navigation chart. The three markers triangulated a permanent target near the nest core. He grasped the controls, as his ship floated through the adjacent nebula.

He breathed slowly hearing his father's voice in his head. *Let's skip some rocks.*

Dimycles counted his heartbeats in between his breaths. He tuned his mind to his bio-pattern. He watched a star disappear behind the nest core. As he neared the nest core, a second star disappeared. Dimycles fell into a trance. His rhythm matched the beat of the universe. He saw the star he wanted. He took a deep breath and counted heartbeats until the star he wanted disappeared behind the nest core. He'd done this with his dad many times, but it hadn't meant this much, and he'd certainly never tried to slingshot an object around a nest core. Now he merely exhaled.

Then he fired.

The turret adjusted itself to aim between the triangulated points. The ejection pod silently launched, pointing far from his intended target. Propelled only by momentum, its navigation controls were deactivated. With no gravity controls, nothing could guarantee it would take the right course before its dark energy drive took effect. Dimycles realized his dad had been right: this was a lost art.

As the pod closed in on its target, it picked up speed and started to curve. Dimycles waited - caught in the rhythm of the universe, but something was different. A distant glimmer disrupted the flow.

"No," Dimycles gasped, identifying two State ships.

"They aren't even running on low power," he said to himself. "They're giving off too much signal!" He saw his pod curving toward the nest core. It was picking up speed. "Good, good. Come on!" Two State fighters came at him. He prepped his engines for a fast power up. "This is gonna be dirty."

The fighters were almost in range. The pod moved dangerously close to the nest core. Dimycles' palms grew moist. *Please don't wake up.*

The trajectory had to work. State fighters were closing in fast. He prepared to jump to full power so he could drop at a 90-degree angle from their attack. He turned on his navigation.

"These guys are reckless," he muttered.

He pulled himself over his navigation panels to scan the outer area of the nebula. An entire fleet waited. He scanned for the Calareans. "No sign of them... I know you're out there."

His ship alerted him to a pulse from the nest core. "I expected them to be reckless, but not stupid."

Dimycles didn't know what part of the nebula he should target. He rather Calareans catch him than by Galactic law enforcement. *The Calareans would kill me, but only after they got the key back. The State just wants me dead.*

Again he scanned for Calareans, with no results. "Where are you guys?"

Dimycles' navigation sounded another alarm; the incoming ships were in range. Now there were four, with two coming up behind his ship to block any escape.

"Damn it!" Dimycles shouted.

The fighters closed in.

"No systems, no shields, not even basic hull integrity," Dimycles worried. "Their first shot could burn straight through my ship."

He glanced back, and saw the pod had cleared the core, but not the nebula. Dimycles powered on all systems. The controls engaged slowly, and the State scouts were on him, firing again and again. They already had the jump on him, so he struggled to abort the ship's power-on routine. He manually overrode the system and got the engines and shields up. He sped away.

Dimycles fled toward the nest core. His weapons powered online.

"So reckless." Dimycles complained, arming a gun turret. He sighed, shook his head, and admitted. "I never expected this to be easy."

Under withering fire, Dimycles swung his turret toward the fighters. He patiently gauged his shot, aiming, and tracking velocity. Finally, he fired.

"Shit!" Dimycles stared in horror. He'd forgotten to remove the three navigation markers. His turret automatically readjusted and shot at the nest core. He cringed. His missile detonated. "Oh...shit!"

Dimycles punched his console in frustration and pushed himself from the cockpit. He floated down to his lockers and jerked them open. He dug furiously through the contents and found a bulky heat-shielded suit. Dimycles heaved it out and pushed it toward the control center. He launched himself past the suit and back into the control pit.

Dimycles grabbed the controls and changed course directly for the scouts- shutting down all systems after the course set. The master system flat-lined, and everything went down—even life support. Dimycles grabbed the heat-shielded suit and pulled it on in the dark.

He barely had it up to his waist when a bright light peered through, and he saw his own shadow. He looked out at the nest core. Its colors were changing.

WIPER SQUEEZED HIS trigger, pumping laser blasts at Dimycles's ship, and each shot got closer to connecting. With his other hand, he engaged his thrusters to adjust the angle. As the blasts closed in, Dimycles's ship engaged and evaded. Wiper adjusted, and then saw his target firing a missile back at them.

"Incoming!" Gysree shouted, "Oh, wait..."

The missile changed course, turning away from them and heading for the depleted core of the Volcaroo star. The detonation produced an odd rippling effect. The entire core went from a soft purple glow to a bright red-orange. Gysree's pupils shrunk.

Taema and Reed tried to cut off the target's escape routes. Wiper saw the nest core expanding as debris left the core. It looked as if the tail of a red comet was aimed right for them. "Are ... Do you see this?" Wiper asked.

"What the..."

"What is that?" Gysree asked. "Is it exploding?"

"Evac!" Reed shouted, "Evac now!"

Gysree pumped her thrusters to spin around, and then pushed the throttle to maximum. She got on her comms. "Fleet command, the core of the nebula is rupturing. Pull back! Heavy debris, high temperatures!"

Wiper's bio scanners showed moving life. His mouth opened, but no words came out. The ship grew warmer as fiery debris gained on them.

"Is it... following us?" Taema asked.

"What kind of explosion is this?" Gysree wondered.

Wiper zoomed in on the debris and thought he saw an eye - black pupils dotted within the sea of fire. Red flames spread like wings around fiery talons. A beak opened, yet there was no sound. Something hit. All his scanners went dead. Wiper screamed into dead comms. The star crows' super-heated fire tore through their ships.

Dimycles waited and watched.

THE STAR CROWS headed straight for the escaping fleet.

"Get me four groups! One formation!" Proto shouted. His fleet reassembled into four sections. "I want a suppressive fire; hold them off while the rear lines escape."

As the state fleet formed a defensive posture, Proto's carrier ship took up a distant position so he could see the action. The rear flank opened fire. The State fleet began its suppressive maneuver allowing other ships to retreat.

The attacking starcrows changed from fiery red to bluish white. A powerful heat wave rippled through the bridge, the environment controls attempted to compensate.

"Did you feel that!" The pilot screamed.

Proto's plan crumbled.

Star crows dove at the rear flank. They attacked in three waves, each one on top of the other. Their heat started killing the fleet's crew. Solar flares from the third wave annihilated the flank. The ships twisted and buckled under the flames. The crows' talons clutched the ships, tearing them apart. The fleet went into a scramble.

A group of star crows attacked in a linear fashion, piercing the retreat formation. Once they'd penetrated, the crows formed up in a nautilus pattern, spiraling out, as they melted ships with their body heat.

"There're people aboard those ships," Proto muttered, sinking to his knees. In all his years he'd never seen such slaughter. Thousands of crewmen gone in a beautiful show of lights.

A rogue collection of State ships formed a last-ditch defensive line.

"What are they doing? Get them out of here!" Proto shouted.

His communications manager sent the message but got no response. The formation held ground, firing at the killer birds. The crows formed into a "V."

"Why aren't they leaving?" Proto demanded.

"Too much debris," gasped the pilot. "They wanted to make a last stand."

Proto watched the star crows pierce the line into the remains of his fleet. Their talons tore through hulls. All was consumed in fire. They started melting whatever remained.

"They're getting pulverized."

The star crows reformed and headed for Proto's command ship.

"How do they do that?" The pilot asked. "Banking around in space? How are they flying like that?"

The star crows opened their beaks. A flare rocked the ship.

"Get us out of here," Proto commanded.

The pilot looked down at his navigation systems, but the flares scrambled his feed.

"I'm blind!"

Proto screamed. "Go!"

The pilot bit his lip and engaged the thrusters. The force reversed their momentum, and the large ship slowly turned. At full throttle, the ship picked up speed, rocketing forward. The weapons specialist shot debris out of their way, and rubble smashed against the ship's hull, spinning them around. The pilot regained control and corrected the vector. As the star crows gained ground, the pilot readied the hyperspace drive.

"Get me a clear route!" the pilot screamed.

The weapons specialist laid down a heavy spray of firepower to clear a path. Stray debris kept hitting the ship and bumping it off course, forcing the pilot to correct the vector.

"Get us out of here!"

The star crows flared up, ready to destroy the ship. The pilot saw a clear path; he engaged the hyperdrives.

A stray boulder hit the starship, lodged itself into the hull. The anti-mass field failed, and the ship swung wildly. The gravity field failed, sending everything inside flying. As the carrier spun, the boulder dislodged, and the vacuum of space threatened to suck all of them out. The fail-safe partitions slammed down, saving the ship from imploding.

The bridge members floated aimlessly inside of the command center. Finally, the gravity realigned, and they dropped to the floor.

Scrambling to his feet, Proto screamed, "Report!"

"The solar flares threw off our navs!"

"Our engines are damaged!"

"Captain, we're stuck!"

Proto's heart pounded, and he felt light headed as looked around the bridge. All eyes were on him. "Abandon... abandon ship," he rasped.

"How?"

Proto looked at the display showing the crows forming a parabola, then a layered circle. The entire formation glowed as one.

"Captain!" everyone shouted.

Proto turned around and calmly walked off the bridge. Then he ran. He stumbled through corridors and stormed into the VR room. His son stood there, shaking and pale.

"What's happening?" Toah cried. His father hugged him and took his hand. Toah felt safe.

"Put this back on," Proto said, giving his son the visor.

Suddenly, the two were no longer standing in the blue room, but in a sunny field of flowers stretching to the horizons.

Toah glanced around—no guns, no threats. Toah looked up, happy. He'd finally learned how to fire a gun. Suddenly he appreciated the impartial nature of power. "Dad, I'm sorry I hurt Carty," Toah blurted. "It won't happened again."

Proto got on his knees and smiled.

"I believe you. I forgive you, son," Proto said hugging his little boy. Then he playfully wrestled Toah to the ground, and they rolled around in the field, as Proto tickled his boy.

Toah laughed until his gut hurt. The more he laughed, the hotter it got. Suddenly all went cold. The sunny field warped, engulfing him in a huge sphere. It was like a round room of flowers, spreading infinitely. He'd never seen the room do that before – it was cool. His dad smiled, and everything disappeared.

DIMYCLES PULLED OFF his gloves to get a better grip on the controls.

"Dimycles," he said to himself, "please move faster."

Though he was far away from the main destruction, the hot air in his ship was too thick to breathe. He wrestled through it, hoping the crows would ignore his powered-down ship. Now he desperately needed a way out.

Power came on, generating shields. The engines whirred, and the ship accelerated. His nimble craft darted through the rocks seeking a way out of the nebula. Dimycles didn't want to look back.

Something happened. The scanners went blank, and his navigations went offline. Glancing back, he saw the star crows formation glowing as one. Then came the thermonuclear explosion. As he gripped the hot controls, his hands felt as if they were burning. He fled at full speed as the heat wave reached his ship.

Once the Volacroo system was behind him, he breathed easier. Life support balanced the ship's atmosphere, and he powered up the rest of the systems. With paper and pencil, he mapped a path to the sector's edge. As his navs came back online, an alarm sounded.

Three star crows had followed him. They were right on his tail. He dove. They dove. He pumped his thrusters hard and fled right. Two crows banked after him, while the other dove, then came around and cut him off.

I am the token bird.

His ship spun, and thrust left then right. The crows followed. He tried spinning around. They went by, then dove under him, and came up following on his tail.

"How do they bank in space?" Dimycles asked. They disappeared from his display, but a dark purple one appeared outside his window. "Are they toying with me?"

He did nothing, allowing the ship to follow its current vector. The three crows surrounded him, and the ship's environmental controls compensate the temperature.

"Do I gotta keep you guys entertained?" he wondered. "Or you get mad?" He readied hyperspace coordinates, then thought better of it. "I'd rather them think they are playing with me, rather than chasing me."

Dimycles executed flying tricks. They followed. The temperature cooled, as the birds followed all his moves. As they were having fun, Dimycles was seriously trying to lose them. He accelerated, did a full reverse, and the crows sped past him. They'd almost disappeared, but then returned. "How do they fly like that?"

Suddenly, Dimycles felt his ship shudder and jolt back.

"We've got him!" Fyzel cried, as the Calarean tractor field caught Dimycles.

DIVINE RIGHT

CARELESS, GAJRA THOUGHT as she walked through the halls to the prisoner interrogation room.

For years, the Calareans had been falling deeper into social negligence. They'd grown bored with their existence as a hidden race. Their grandiose halls on the planet's surface no longer inspired pride. As their sky cities fell into poverty, their citizens turned to crime as a means to survive. While no one could find a Hidden Planet, that meant no one would know who or what they were. They would have no legacy. They hid both their treasures and their vices.

As Gajra entered the interrogation room, she noted the symbolic shield that hung on the wall. An ornament engraved with a pentagon of five planets, bearing the sixth planet in the middle with a galaxy spiral etched into the bottom. The décor hung with pride, a fine symbol for the Sunil, but a hurtful reminder to Gajra that they had failed in the essential task of preventing Dimycles from stealing one of their precious treasures.

Dimycles hung suspended by his neck. He gripped the energy band around his throat, keeping himself from strangulation. Gajra stopped and stood in front of him. Dimycles stared at the ceiling, trying to wiggle his neck higher. His feet dangled and kicked. He still wore the suit Ina had bought for him.

Two guards walked in and stood on either side of Dimycles. The air was fresh but tense. Below Dimycles' dangling feet was a round metal plate. It controlled the gravitational pull on him.

"What does she want with the key?" Gajra asked him.

"Who is she?" Dimycles choked.

"Are we going to play this game?" Gajra sighed. She increased the gravitational pull.

"I need...I need a lawyer..." Dimycles pleaded in between the gasps.

"It would be pointless," Gajra responded. "We're not subject to State authorities nor any other power in the Realm."

"Keep me alive," Dimycles rasped. "You need the key."

"Whether you stay alive is entirely up to you," Gajra assured him. "We will find the key one way or another."

"Not if she finds it first!"

"Oh? So now we are back to 'she?'" Gajra noted. "What's in it for you? What do you want with it?"

"Maybe I am c-c-curious?" Dimycles stammered.

"Maybe you're stupid!" Gajra snapped. "You know? I think you are."

"I'm smart enough... to get past your security," Dimycles retorted. His feet were like lead, and his fingers burned against the noose.

"Don't be so proud. Your little heist is short lived. As with all things dangerous to the galaxy, we will possess the key once again, and you will be the loser," Gajra asserted. "Whatever she promised you, she won't give you. You must understand. Whatever she tricked you into believing was a lie. We can protect you from her. The daughter of Sun Chi can never stand against the might of the Sunil."

Sun Chi?

"Wuyan is an Akolyte?" Dimycles asked.

"And that is all she ever will be!" Gajra cried. "The daughter of a pirate. A nomad. A scavenger with no code! If you were smart, you would deal with us, and cast aside your petty life of plunder. Instead, you could lavish in a kingdom with real riches."

"Y-Your laws demand my execution," Dimycles gasped. "Why protect me?"

"In the interest of justice," Gajra said with a smile. "Maybe we can see this incident in another light. You know where the key is, right? You work for us to reclaim it, and we set you free."

Dimycles kicked harder trying to get blood to his head. His legs felt heavy and tired.

Gajra continued to press: "Wuyan is weak. She's desperately looking for more power to save her dying fleet. What difference does it make to you what the daughter of Sun Chi does? We will hide you from her, and she will be powerless to oppose it."

"Hide me?" Dimycles asked. "To what end."

"You will be free. Save yourself. No more prison. Stop this nonsense, and come down from your noose. Name your price. There is no prize greater than the freedom of choice," Gajra argued.

A fading Dimycles pulled himself up against the weight. "How can I be free if I'm hiding?"

"You had a good look at our inventory. You know we are powerful," Gajra boasted. "We exist to stop people like her."

"I saw technology stolen from other planets and races. You're scavengers too," Dimycles spit out.

"It is our right to accumulate these weapons. We determine what is dangerous, and what is safe for the Observed Realm. You must understand, we have adjusted our view over the years. It is not just doomsday devices we need to control. We also must appropriate harmful technology as a whole. We keep everyone safe by reducing the impact of war. No star system should have to endure the troubles of another. Who will protect them? Certainly not the daughter of Sun Chi."

"You won't either," Dimycles said in a croaking whisper. "You would just stay hidden."

"You know so much about us. Where are you from? We could find no history of your birth."

"I am... Covarra." Dimycles gasped these words, then lost consciousness.

Gajra frowned at the motionless prisoner. Dimycles's words angered her and made her head shake head in futility. She motioned to the guards.

The band around Dimycles's throat disappeared, and his limp body fell to the floor.

When the prisoner began to stir, Gajra went on: "So you knew what you did was wrong? You rebelled and opposed the eminent domain that the Sunil hold sacred above all else—our divine right. Unforgivable."

"I don't want forgiveness," said Dimycles, as he tried to stand. "Nor do I want protection. I just want answers."

Gajra balled her fist. "You are the one who must answer!"

Guards dragged the prisoner away. When they threw Dimycles in the brig, he tumbled to the floor and passed out.

Gajra nodded to the guards and commanded, "Prep him." before making her next stop at Kahlan's quarters. After sitting down with the admiral, she reported, "Dimycles is one of us."

"I could have told you that. No way could he sneak through our systems so quickly were he not. The question is: what planet is he from? It isn't Togales. We checked."

"He is an Exile."

A dead silence fell.

"Perhaps this is the proof we needed that Covarrans were renegades," Kahlan speculated.

"But he wants answers," said Gajra. "I'm not sure he knows what happened to his planet."

"It doesn't matter. He's been out for too long. He can never return. This is exactly why we don't allow people to leave the fold. The influence of the Realm is insidious! Now, what shall we do? Kill the last of a forgotten people? We can't keep him."

"He's meaningless to us," said Gajra. "I'll have Brooks finish him. We can find that key ourselves, given enough time."

Kahlan shook his head. "Given enough time, someone else might find it."

"Even if Wuyan gets it. She can do us no harm. She'll just roam the galaxy with a band of Titans."

Kahlan rubbed his temple – frustrated at Gajra's lack of understanding.

"Wuyan isn't our worry. The Watchers are," Kahlan insisted. "We cannot allow them to control both the key and the cube it opens! The daughter of Sun Chi attacked the Watchers, so she must have the Cube of None by now. We must control the key, and that is why Dimycles must stay alive, and that is why we will take him to the Galactic State!"

Gajra thought for a moment. "A cover-up?"

Kahlan leaned forward. "Whoa, who said anything about a cover-up?"

"We can't transfer a prisoner to someone outside our fold," Gajra warned. "Dealing with the State only puts us at their mercy and complicates our goal. We will keep him here! I must advise against striking a deal with-"

"We cannot go home without the key!" Kahlan insisted. "They will execute him immediately and put us under review for the whole thing! Losing our treasures to a renegade? We will be lucky to survive the hearing! So, yes, we will deal!"

"How will we explain it?"

"Here's how it happened. We tracked the Exile to Volcaroo. We left under threat from the star crows. The State captured him in our absence."

"Admiral, with all due respect, that sounds like a cover story," Gajra said. "It's likely that every crew member recorded the real situation in their personal logs."

"Then everyone on the ship will be given a new understanding of the situation. Every passenger aboard will expunge their logs, and follow our new directions. Questioners will be executed as renegades!"

"As you wish," Gajra replied.

"Insubordination will not be tolerated," Kahlan reminded his understudy. "The State will keep the renegade alive and protect our interest, as we will protect theirs."

"Is it necessary for us to assist them in the expansion of their sovereignty?" Gajra wondered.

"Diplomacy requires us to walk a fine line," the Admiral answered. "We seldom interact with the outside Realm. We cannot expect to stay hidden all this time, then suddenly show up and boss them around. That will only reawaken questions of our elitism, and contempt for their laws. Not only will they stop working with us, but it may incite them to come searching for us."

"How often do we need them to work with us?" Gajra asked. "By the time we deal with them again, a new regime will be in place. It will have new laws, and this system will be long dead. Besides, the State acts above the law all the time."

"A dog will bark at it's on reflection in the mirror! You think the State will be sympathetic if we do as they do? As a mentor, I can tell you, the worst part of this deal is knowing the State gets away with the same pretentious attitude that they penalize in others. One day you'll be an admiral, facing troubling situations just like this, where there's no easy solution. The trick to cooperation is balancing the illusion of power."

Gajra bowed and walked away.

DIMYCLES AWOKE TO a tingling sensation in his ears. When he reached up to scratch, he found a tight band around the back of his head, attached to inserts that went into each of his ears. Guards flung open the door and seized him. Dimycles fought them, but they beat him and stuffed him into a cloth bag. The guards dragged his struggling body down the corridors. They hauled him into a lift, and ascended, kicking and punching him. At a higher level, they pulled him off the elevator into a room. There he heard his thoughts echoing from walls. It was as if he were shouting. Speakers were amplifying his words, making him feel mentally naked.

He heard Gajra's voice asking, "Where is the key?"

Dimycles shut his eyes. He tried to suppress his thoughts, but every word that came to his mind reverberated through the room. His thoughts were betraying him.

Stop it!

"Stop what?" Gajra asked.

Dimycles felt them lift the bag as more guards kicked and punched him. He clawed at the device on his head, trying to tear it from his ears. All he got for his trouble were the amplified screams inside his mind.

"Why don't you think about where you sent that key?" Gajra suggested.

More thoughts poured from the speakers. When Dimycles screamed, "Never!" his body suddenly felt terminally cold. They'd dropped him into a tank of freezing water. He thrashed, but the cloth stuck to his skin. He felt suffocated and tangled. More thoughts came from the speakers. He willed himself to think about unimportant things, but his mind tricked him into thoughts of the key—

The Key of Titans.

"Yes!" Gajra screamed. "Tell me where it is!"

Guards pulled Dimycles from the water and continued to beat him. The wet bag stuck to his mouth, blocking the air. The beating stopped. They paused long enough for him to catch his breath, and then dunked him again. It was shallow, and he struggled to swim to the top, but the wet cloth clung to his body and making it impossible. His lungs burned, and his mind raced. They pulled him up again. Obscure, confusing, meaningless thoughts spilled from the speakers. He tried to catch his breath and contain his mind. Instead, he panicked.

Where... where am I? I can't breathe!

The sound of his voice confused him. He clawed at the bag, his gasps turning into hyperventilation.

"The key, for breath!" Gajra promised him. Dimycles said nothing, but his inner thoughts still spoke to the spectators

They dropped him in again, and he swallowed water.

Don't! Capsule...Titans...Slingshot...

Dimycles felt furious with himself, but he had little control. The sight of Lotus flashed through his mind. The guards pulled him out and beat him again. His voice no longer sounded panicked. It narrated his thoughts calmly.

His body felt numb. He vomited, and coughed. The voice from the speakers hemorrhaged information as he wildly thrashed in the bag. He felt an inner, bloodless chill pricking his skin. The guards kept assaulting him. His head whipped back and forth, as his words flooded the room.

His desire for numbness echoed from the speakers. His ears rang. His fingers went numb. He no longer heard his voice.

Then the bag ripped open. Dimycles swam for the surface. He emerged in a haze of brilliance. Admiral Kahlan was waiting. Dimycles's dad was behind the Admiral, gripping a rock. When Dimycles reached for his father, his fingertips closed on emptiness. Wuyan was holding her hands out to him. Dimycles reached for her. Her eyes were black, like coal.

"Save me!" Dimycles pleaded. "Like you once did..."

When he tried to reach up, he sank faster. He kicked his feet and felt happy. It was almost over. He could make it.

"Help!" Dimycles shouted again, "Don't let her..."

Dimycles knew he was on the verge of breathing. He got a euphoric rush.

One more stroke to the surface.

But Dimycles was still in the bag at the bottom. They'd never pulled him up. Blood red water settled. The inner voices stopped.

Gajra turned to Brooks, the guard, and asked, "Who is Yaliz?"

GAJRA started toward the bridge and her subordinate commander, North Brooks, quickly caught up. The earrings North wore twinkled, and her armored suit disappeared, leaving the commander in her official uniform. North removed her gloves. Her smoky brown skin glistened from the humidity, and her short black hair stuck to her head in wet waves. Her tiny chin gave her jaw a V-shape. Her eyes and eyelashes were big.

"Yes," she confirmed to Gajra. "He said, Yaliz."

"What is Yaliz?" Gajra demanded.

"I've never heard of any planet named Yaliz. Perhaps a person," North offered.

Gajra walked past the captain's chair to Fyzel and asked the same question.

Fyzel complied. "Twelve planets have people named Yaliz. Thirty-five more have people with similar names."

"Cross-reference them with any planets his ship has visited," Gajra said.

"Yaliz could be anything," North said, "His mom, his school. A kid who picked on him. A game he played. He was saying a lot of nonsense. He could have made up a name."

"But he didn't!" Gajra explained. "That poor soul didn't even know his own name. He was a broken piece of glass. His mind was mush and wanted only one thing- to breathe. Wuyan and the Key of Titans are the only two things that could give him what he wanted. Yaliz is the only sensible word he was capable of thinking at the moment of death. Which means Yaliz is more than just anything—it's everything to him."

"He said 'maybe I missed,'" North added. "He's not sure if he hit his mark or not."

"Mark or not, as long as we get close." Gajra pressed her knuckles to her mouth. "Yaliz."

"Okay, guys," Caryna called out. "Take a look at this."

Gajra, Fyzel and North gathered around Caryna's station as she toggled the search bubbles and watched them connect – to Earth.

"A group of Martians, called the Six, started an uprising on the American continent," Caryna explained, maneuvering the bubbles.

"Right. Dimycles fought alongside the Six," Fyzel added.

"He then turned on them," Gajra told them. "We researched that already."

"Forget about that for a second," Caryna said and inserted another search bubble to the mesh. "So did she."

Caryna zoomed in on the connecting branches. Yaliz's name emerged.

Gajra squinted. "How do you know that? What's the source of that bubble?"

"His own ship," said Caryna. "The ship logs report that Dimycles was in an ambush during the Six War. He saved two survivors from that ambush and brought them onboard his ship."

"Yaliz was one of the survivors?" Gajra asked.

"No. She died in that ambush," Caryna said. "The ship's logs reported the casualty."

"Yaliz and Dimycles knew each other. He saw her die. How does that help us?" Gajra wondered.

Caryna opened a new bubble and typed in: "USoFT."

"What's that?" Gajra asked.

"USoFT was an underground society before they became a major government weapons contractor. She worked for them," Caryna replied. "Looks like USoFT made weapons for both the government and the Six."

"She was making weapons for him while he was fighting with terrorist, and also making weapons for the government hunting him down," Gajra said, pacing back and forth putting the story together in his mind. "Either there is a lot of love there or a lot of hate."

"If she loved him, why did she leave him in prison to die?" Fyzel asked.

"No question about it. She was playing both sides of the table until the one hand folded. So she worked the only play available."

"Yet she didn't rescue him from prison?"

"Maybe she did," North realized. "Check her connection to the Akolytes."

"No connection found, except..." Caryna paused while checking Yaliz's connections to outside worlds, "Well, the technology she used came from none other but the Merloti."

"The Merloti? Dimycles has never visited the Merloti," Fyzel said, double-checking the information.

"No," Caryna agreed, adding the Merloti bubble. A connecting line lit up on Yaliz. "But she has."

"She isn't human?" North asked.

"Well, she sure doesn't look like a Merloti!" Fyzel said. "She's way too tall. Her skin isn't blue enough."

Gajra pointed and nodded. "That's our girl!"

"But she was pronounced dead," Fyzel complained.

"Is she?" Caryna asked.

Fyzel said, "Oh come on; he didn't send the key to a dead woman on Earth. He shot the key out with no guidance; he's not even sure it made it out of the nebula."

"She may not have the key," Gajra agreed, "but she is surely a target. Take us to the Galactic State headquarters, and then bring me Yaliz."

"Yes, Captain," Caryna responded with a bow. She gave Fyzel a stern look, and he began queuing up the destination changes.

Gajra left for another meeting with Kahlan.

GAJRA FOUND KAHLAN sitting in solemn silence. Gajra stood to wait for an opportunity to speak. Kahlan spoke first.

"No response from the Watchers," Kahlan said. "I even reached out to their Ancient Ones, and there's been no response."

The hair on Gajra's neck rose. "That she would be so bold to attack our allies! We will aid the Watchers and crush the Akolytes!"

"Absolutely not!"

"But I thought..."

"Silence! You're not thinking like a leader. I'm trying to train you, and you need to listen! Have I told you nothing about the illusion of power? How many times must I tell you the fine line of control? We are the Sunil, keepers of power, protectors from doom, yet we shared power with the Watchers. They had the cube, we had the key, and now thanks to Wuyan, we now have an opportunity to get both under our control."

Gajra tried another tack. "The Watchers are our allies, and they are well aware of our desire for the Cube of None. They will suspect our motives. If we help them against Wuyan, it will take suspicion off us, and assure them of our good faith in future matters."

"Patience," Kahlan answered. "The time will come. For now, Wuyan's interest and mine run parallel. Both of us want to remove the Cube of None from the Watchers' control. After we're sure she's done that, we will aid the Watchers to defeat her. In the end, we must control both the key and the Cube of None."

"I understand, and real power is controlling the illusion," Gajra said, repeating her mentor's words. "But Lila's Pearl is no illusion. If Wuyan opens that cube, no one will have the power to-"

"The Akolyte would never open that cube," Kahlan said.

"We must prepare for it," Gajra warned.

"Prepare for what? Without the key the cube is useless! With the key, the Perlekai will destroy her! No way. She will never open it."

The comms came back to Kahlan, "Admiral. We have approached the Galactic State Headquarters."

"I'll be right there," Kahlan answered.

Gajra reiterated, "We still need to prepare for it."

Kahlan turned to Gajra. "We are the Sunil. We already have."

AFTER THE INTERROGATION, North smelled horrible. Returning to her room, she passed her friend Zephra. Zephra greeted her, "Commander Brooks?" but got no response. North went into her room, undressed, and stepped into the shower. As the room steamed up, North stood under a hard spray of water. The dirt washed away, but something about what she'd seen and done stuck with her. When she finished toweling herself dry and wrapping her body in the towel, she sat down on the side of her bed.

Zephra knocked on the door. When North didn't answer, her friend came in. Seeing something was terribly wrong, Zephra sat down and gave North a hug. North tried to speak but choked as she couldn't explain it.

Zephra could think of nothing to say. She just wanted to be there for her friend.

Then came a communication from Gajra. North let go of her towel, stood up, and started dressing for the next mission.

HE COULDN'T REMEMBER much of the attack, but Dimycles imagined it was his brain's way of helping him deal with it. He rubbed his head and tried to think. He remembered star crows.

"Star crows!" He laughed at his inexplicable survival.

The laugh made him wince, but he couldn't contain it. Soon he was in tears. Still, he couldn't stop laughing until he felt the tingling in his ears. He still wore the mind reading device. He yawned. His jaw hurt. Finally, he fell back to sleep.

He woke up to the sound of his cell door opening. Guards dragged him out. He was in too much pain to fight. They threw him onto a lift, and he felt panic. Lifts never took him anywhere fun. This time, he could see everything. His main fear was that he would recall every image.

They took him from the lift into a bright room. The room was a mechanical puzzle illuminated by floodlights. This time, they threw him in the water without restraints.

The leader, in a bionic suit, spoke. "What is on your mind?" North asked. Her voice was a mechanized rasp emitting from her helmet.

Food.

"You want to eat? We'll feed you."

"No, you won't!" Dimycles shouted, desperately trying to stay afloat.

"Yes. We will."

His mind wandered, and his voice came from the speakers. *What's in this tank?*

His feet tingled. Water snakes were biting him but many caught a mouth full of metal. They wrapped themselves around his appendages and shocked him with electricity. Losing control of his bodily functions, he sunk, his thoughts still echoing through the room. He struggled to control his thinking. Another snake shocked him, and he inhaled water. He tried to shake them off, but they slithered this way and that, holding on.

Finally, he broke free, and burst up above the surface, only to hear his thoughts shouting from the speakers. Guards stood around, laughing and chanting.

Laugh. Dimycles heard his voice say it, and he forced himself to laugh. The snakes shocked his legs, and his left hamstring locked up so badly, he screamed. He forced himself to cover it with a laugh. When the speakers went silent, the guards stopped laughing. Now the only laughter came from Dimycles. He'd learned to stop the speakers. He was determined to laugh forever if he had to.

The muscle spasms bent his leg. Two snakes wrapped around his left arm, and he laughed as he tried to rip one off. It was like grabbing slippery spikes. Suddenly he realized this was what masochists must feel. He'd found a way to extract pleasure from the pain—even when the snakes wouldn't let go. He kicked his good leg furiously and laughed some more.

In their confusion, the guards approached the tank. Dimycles pounded the water to stave off the snakes, but his effort failed. Two of them squeezed his left arm, delivering pulsing shocks. It felt as if they were going to peel his flesh off. He imagined this in the form of a cartoon and laughed even harder. A snake bit his side looking for sacred flesh. Dimycles screamed in pleasure.

"What's wrong with him? What is he doing?" North asked.

"He's enjoying it. He's going to kill himself!" said another guard.

"Why isn't the device working? Why can't we hear his inner thoughts? Make him stop laughing!"

When another snake wrapped around his chest, Dimycles' laughter went silent. Instead of shock, he felt as if his chest was under a boulder. His pain was replaced by immense pressure. Dimycles sank. The snakes dragged his body down to the bottom, drowning him. They squeezed his body and gnawed at his flesh.

"Get him out of there!" North shouted. "We need him alive!"

Just as they got the prisoner out of the tank, Gajra entered. The guards threw the snakes back into the water.

"What news?" Gajra asked.

North stood at attention, "He said something about a 'midnight core,' then found a way to silence his thoughts."

"The Midnight core?" Gajra pondered. "Take the device off of him. Get him cleaned up."

"We may be able to find another way. Perhaps in his sleep?"

"Subconscious imagery is not usable memory. Last time we tried, we ended up looking for a house that didn't exist because the prisoner's subconscious built it from his childhood insecurities. Then we wasted a month tracking his favorite sports hero looking for insects," Gajra pointed out, signaling her commander to follow. "We're moving on and transferring the prisoner to the Galactic State."

"A transfer? The State will kill him for what happened at Volcaroo."

"Everyone wants to kill him," Gajra replied. "Kahlan brokered a deal with the State to grant a stay of execution...for now. That's why you'll go with him undercover to ensure he lives until we find that key."

"What about the Midnight core?"

"Are you paying attention?" Gajra asked. When North nodded, Gajra continued, "Whatever he stole, Wuyan wants. She'll come for him again. Your only mission is to stick by him, and keep him alive until we can capture the Key of Titans from the daughter of Chi."

North looked back at the wounded prisoner and felt curious. Then she saw ribbons of torn flesh appear to turn metallic. North shook her head to clear her thoughts, focused, saluted to her commander, and accepted her mission.

AS THEY TOOK a break in the Commons, Fyzel told Caryna, "This bothers me."

"Really?" Caryna asked, "What part?"

"The whole thing?"

"Since when?"

"Since the moment we were told to abduct someone. It's just strange to me. We've never done this before," Fyzel said. "It's completely illegal, even by the laws of the State. Article 2 of the Intergalactic Asylum Act expressly forbids..."

"All laws are made subject to our eminent domain," Caryna interrupted. "Besides, this Yaliz isn't innocent either."

"How do you figure? She could still be dead for all we know."

"You keep on about that, but that's why we need answers. This Yaliz joins Dimycles in his fight against the Six; then she gets killed, but somehow she ends up leading a human weapons contractor? With Merloti tech? If she's human, I'm willing to bet she's violating the Intergalactic IP Trade Act, by getting rich on technology she stole from the Merloti. If she isn't human, then I doubt she's on Earth legally – possibly bring foreign disease with her."

"Earth isn't part of any coalition," Fyzel argued. "I'm not even sure Earthlings are aware of anyone but themselves. She doesn't need paperwork to live there. State laws are invalid on Earth, and we have no mandate for abducting people."

"All laws are made subject to our eminent domain," she repeated.

"Yeah, but now we have to change our private logs to say we never caught Dimycles. That's a bit much, don't you think? It seems like a big cover-up. I don't know who to trust."

"We need answers," said Caryna. "Yaliz may have them."

"Sure we need answers and results, but stealing someone from another planet is a slippery slope. It calls into question our right to steal technology without..."

Caryna silenced him. She glanced around to see if anyone had heard. With her finger still on his lips, she gave him a stern look. "Earth is far away. It will take some time to get there. Think about what you say before you say it. Otherwise, you may end up on the wrong end of this. The State laws don't apply out there, but the laws of the Sunil are valid anywhere we see fit. Gajra will get approval for us, and we'll get her in a dignified manner."

"Dignified? And what kind of approval?" Fyzel asked.

"The approval will be for a mission to prevent her from harvesting weapons—weapons we may have to confiscate one day. It's our right and duty," Caryna said.

"What if Yaliz is dead?"

"She isn't."

"But does she have the key?"

"You're just second-guessing me because you don't want to abduct her," Caryna said, laughing. "What-ifs won't hold."

"Haven't we manufactured a connection between her and the key to justify her abduction?" Fyzel asked.

"No. I found a connection between her and the one person who knows where the key is," Caryna answered. "We're just exploring that connection, and most likely she will be instrumental in determining the key's location."

"This ends with her as bait, to catch bigger bait, to get the key."

"I don't see a problem with that," Caryna said, "and as your ranking officer, I don't think you should either."

Fyzel shook his head and sighed. "Of course not. Sometimes I just... like to hear myself think."

Caryna smiled, "I love hearing your thoughts. That's what so great about you. Just don't be stupid and tell anyone else what you think."

Caryna heard a message and told him: "Brooks has cleared the ship. Like it or not, we have a job to do." They returned to the bridge.

COMMANDER TEVVOSE PETRI stepped around the prisoner who knelt on the floor in chains. Dimycles's restraints covered his forearms in a shell, and a chain connected his helmet to his shackled feet. The Galactic State Prison commander chuckled as he reviewed paperwork.

"You must have friends in high places," Petri said to the prisoner, then the Commander returned to his reading, adding, "or enemies."

Petri leaned back against his desk, looking down at the detainee. The commander had bushy eyebrows and the smile of a chubby-cheeked child. His thick neck settled on tiny shoulders over a gut on which he could rest his arms. "I've been commander of this prison for over twelve years, and I've never read a prisoner report so ridiculous as this," Petri swore. "Why were you on Earth?"

Dimycles shook his head mutely.

"Well, it's not like this is an interrogation. Feel free not to answer."

Dimycles nodded, and said, "I got lost."

"Mmm, well, you certainly made yourself at home there, because this report says you joined a terror group called the Six?" Petri cocked his head and waited for a response.

"It didn't start out that way. I, well, kinda got caught up in a situation that wasn't my fault."

"Not your fault?" Petri said with a laugh. "Which part? Genocide? Death sentence? Or how about when the Six conspire with the Reptilites to invade a sovereign planet? See now that's where I start needing a new pair of glasses! Do you ever sleep? Or is your whole life bent on causing trouble?"

Dimycles winced. "It does sound a bit harsh when you read it all at once, but yes, I've had a great many sleepless nights."

"Despite every criminal act, here's the part that makes me laugh: You've brought the great Sunil out of hiding, and they've promised us advanced weapons and ships if we'll just keep you alive." Petri's chuckled to himself and whipped an invisible tear from his cheek. "Alive? Remember: the Galactic State was formed to stop the Reptilites from invading sovereign planets. We were set up to stop people from leeching off other worlds, and non-native species killing others from sovereign worlds. That's our purpose, and despite your crimes against everything we stand for, the Sunil has the gall to ask us to look the other way."

"You said yourself; I have enemies in high places."

"It's quite an offer," said the Commander. "The hardware will double our power, and who am I to get in the way of prosperity? But there is a problem. You broke into our most profitable prison. You then broke out an inmate, and destroyed the place – killing everyone inside—save the prisoners of course."

"Naturally."

"Then we sent a fleet to stop you, but they were destroyed after you hid in a nest of... living stars? Star crows? What is that?"

"That wasn't... that wasn't entirely...100% my fault either. I didn't realize the State would come in after me."

"Well, you must understand, I will honor this agreement to keep you alive, per our deal with the Sunil, but... there are a lot of guards out there with families, and families of families, that are gone all because of you." Petri shrugged and sighed. "I can't speak for them once my back is turned."

Dimycles blinked and took a deep breath, as the frowning Petri gathered his things. "Well, I must be off," said Petri, holding up a document. "Reptilite invasion. I need to investigate this... Is there anything else, you'd like to tell me?"

"I'm sorry if I hurt anyone close to you," said Dimycles. "I do have enemies in high places. My survival came at a severe cost to everyone around me. After all of the unreasonable demands, can I just ask you for one favor?"

The commander stepped backward, startled.

"Leave a key, at least somewhere close by?"

Petri shrugged, popped a key from his pocket, and threw it across the room. It landed in the soil of a potted plant.

Once Petri was gone, Dimycles closed his eyes and inhaled deeply. *Wuyan...where are you?*

Heavy footsteps marched down the hall.

Dimycles scrambled to his feet and hopped toward the potted plant. The door burst open, and guards poured into the room. Dimycles thrust his head into the soil and swallowed the key. Something stabbed his back, blinding him with pain.

A leathery hand gripped his neck and threw him across the room. The guards all wanted a piece of him. Dimycles swung his shelled hands, hopping and charging through the mob. A blast hit his side as bullets tore through his flesh. He got out the door, and they chased him down the corridors. Even as he threw himself into the gated barrier, the guards beat him with fists, pipes and anything else that was handy. His helmet was his only protection.

Finally, Dimycles broke through the railing, plummeting five stories, with several guards crashing right on top of him. He felt his bones shatter against concrete and willed himself to remain conscious. He couldn't breathe. Something grasped his feet and dragged him away.

As the world quieted, he opened his eyes. A sandy-greyish furry figure was looking straight at him. "Welcome to the HQ," said the creature in a breathy, high-pitched voice. "I'm Sofran from Bulmac. You hungry? Food can get scarce here, and those guards up there are pissed. I'm sure they won't be feeding you anytime soon."

The creature pointed a tiny claw at a plate of food. When Dimycles moved, he groaned in pain. He carefully pointed his hands at a cup. With

Sofran's help, Dimycles gulped down its entire contents. The liquid tasted disgusting.

Perfect!

Dimycles stared at the plate, and a strange expression came to him when he saw it.

"It's a plate," said Sofran. "You put food on it. No waitress to do it for you. It's a tough life."

"You guys have beds, lights, and even plates?" Dimycles wondered. "This is a resort. Too bad I won't be around long enough to enjoy it."

"What are you in for?" Sofran asked.

Dimycles vomited. When his watery eyes recovered, Dimycles focused to realized he was in a laundry room.

"I killed a lot of people who didn't deserve to die." Dimycles used his lips to search his vomit for the key. Once he had it in his teeth, he unlocked his arm restraints.

"Wow. K-Killed a lot of people?" Sofran stammered. "Why'd they bring you here? We're mainly political and white-collar prisoners."

"Where am I?"

"You are on the planet Selaus Prime. The Galactic State Headquarters is here. This is the HQ prison."

Selaus Prime?

Dimycles began unchaining himself.

Sofran studied him. "Why did you kill people? Sounds... personal."

"Sometimes that's how it's gotta be," Dimycles said, to the sound of alarms and running guards. "Why are you in here? You seem pretty... harmless."

"Have you ever head of a Livestock Planet?"

Dimycles looked around the room for anything to make a weapon. "A planet where algorithms map the behavior of every living thing into a sellable commodity?" Dimycles said.

"Right!" Sofran confirmed. "Knowledge is power, and knowing the behavior of everything on a planet is ultimate power. I got busted for selling Livestock Planets—which to me is a victimless crime... Right?"

Dimycles was busy breaking a pipe from the wall.

"I feel like I helped them," Sofran continued. "I knew when people were hungry before they did. I knew what they wanted to eat, and they never knew hunger. I knew every word of every conversation they had, their thoughts, desires, all in the palm of my hand I turned every pattern of life into profit for consumption. The whole planet became livestock. Have you ever been to a Livestock Planet?"

"No. I hear Livestock Planets all died out." Dimycles swung the pipe over his shoulder.

"Oh no, they are some still out there!" Sofran insisted, scurrying on top of a pile of laundry. "Here's the trick. Usually the elite on a planet benefit from data mining, but eventually it overtakes everything. Even the ones who think they are in control. Once that happened, I came in. I sought out Livestock Planets and mined them for my profit. Shouldn't be illegal. If you ask me, they do it to themselves. I just collect on it. The Galactic State classified data mining a foreign planet as parasitic. Eventually, they busted my racket and here I am."

Dimycles was ready to leave but hesitated. "Data mining, huh?"

"Yup."

"Like the Watchers?"

Sofran's beady eyes bulged. "Whoa! Now you're talking something of a whole other level! That's some serious data! The Watchers have recorded life for eons!"

"But they have a strict code not to use that data for anything," Dimycles added, "So as not to pollute their records. It's a strict oath."

"That's what makes it so valuable!" Sofran screamed. He swallowed the scream, embarrassed by his excitement.

"So..." Dimycles tried to wrap his mind around it. "There is profit in collecting that information?"

"Come on now! If one Livestock Planet is worth a fortune, can you imagine what the Watcher's data is worth?" Sofran almost choked on his words. "Think about that. Can you imagine the power I'd have if I could make algorithms based on the entire history of every living thing in the Realm? Right? You can't tell me you wouldn't pay top dollar to take a li'l peek inside their records."

Dimycles heard footsteps closing in, and braced himself.

Sofran kept talking. "Maybe that just me. I like info; I like to know everything, but Jui? She likes the muscle."

The noises outside died down. Dimycles crept toward the door.

"Muscle is a rare commodity in this prison," Sofran went on, "and you are beefy... for a humanoid, that is. Don't be surprised when she comes to recruit you. If they let you live."

Blast and bullets rained through the door. Dimycles ducked behind a pile of laundry.

The guards stormed in and met a swinging pipe. Dimycles beat the guards back but remained in the room. "Clothes!" he shouted.

Sofran scurried back and pressed buttons, dropping enough laundry for a cellblock around Dimycles. The guards poured in, but their shots disappeared into the laundry. Dimycles came over the top, swinging the pipe into their heads. He kicked the corpses into a pile filling the doorway.

The rear entrance to the laundry room burst open. It was the reserves. Dimycles hurled a huge pile of laundry over them, then scrambled over the corpses, and out the door. His pipe got caught in the rafters, so he ran through the prison unarmed, as artillery rounds whizzed past him.

A guard dove out and tackled him, whipping its thin tail around to cut his neck. Dimycles put his forearm to what he thought was the creature's jaw, and his other arm behind its neck, then squeezed until he heard something snap. Kicking the corpse away, he ducked through corridors and ran into a rec room.

The creatures on the exercise equipment fled as guards rushed through after Dimycles. Finally, they surrounded the prisoner and opened fire. Bullets and laser blast riddled Dimycles's body.

North Brooks stood by the whole time watching from a distance until she came to realize that Dimycles could take no more. She pushed through the attacking guards to the front and held up her gloved hand.

Dimycles thought it might be a hallucination because she held no weapon.

Brooks's hand grew to the size of a man, and she slapped away a score of guards. She picked up a few stray guards with the large fingers, and the hand detached, sending the guards floating away like balloons. She pulled her sidearm from her thigh and shot through all of them.

The delay saved Dimycles, giving the zenomites enough time to start healing him. He failed to recognize Brooks, though he knew something seemed familiar.

Dimycles knelt shivering, hoping his body had not been damaged beyond repair. North was doing the heavy work, slaying guards as fast as they came at her. He stared, fascinated by her ability to stretch her limbs, and seemingly disconnecting her hands from her body. It didn't make sense until she turned and he saw the official insignia on her chest.

She is Sunil!

When the guards attacked in force, she slipped through their ranks, then retreated. She balled her fist, and the gloves she wore charged up with sparks.

The guards clearly couldn't match her abilities in the fight. Her gloves sent signals that disabled their weapons, and she followed with electric shocks that sent her victims into cardiac arrest. As these guards fell, more rushed in. North twirled and ducked, and then came up with electrical fields crackling around her. Her hands grew, and she flung guards into each other.

The remaining guards fell back and regrouped. They would keep their distance and shoot. It would've been a good plan if the floor hadn't started rumbling.

North felt it first. "Wha-"

The guard's communicators blared, and they heard the sirens. The alarms came from outside the prison. A light beam pierced a hole in the jail roof. Brooks dragged Dimycles under a bench as debris pelted the floor.

Through the hole in the roof, and into the room, one blast of cold air followed a second, everything in it path froze, including the guards. North and Dimycles were safe beneath the bench. A sudden heat wave boiled everything it touched, turning every item into a puff of steam.

A new wave of guards dropped through the roof. They wore white-and-purple suits, round helmets, and large visors.

"Stay down," Brooks told Dimycles. She came out from under the bench, her hands raised. As she approached these new troops, they aimed their weapons at her.

"We just want to leave," North insisted. "That's all. Don't make this worse."

They surrounded her, the tips of their blasters just inches from her face.

"Have it your way," North muttered, and her earrings twinkled. Instantly, a weaponized bionic armor surrounded the Sunil commander who blasted the guards away from her.

A beam of sparkling light formed, creating a body—Wuyan. Wuyan zipped through the room in a flash and came upon Dimycles.

"Stand down!" Wuyan commanded.

North turned to face Wuyan, and after raising her arms, she fired several blasts at the pirate leader.

Wuyan saw the shots coming. The reality and space of the room morphed, and all of the shots went wide – hitting the walls and the equipment around her. The room snapped back to normal, and Wuyan grabbed Dimycles. Together they zipped through the prison as the halls and rooms buckled before them. Wuyan brought Dimycles to the thirtieth-floor conference room.

Dimycles was larger but nearly naked with his jumpsuit torn away. His arms and legs were well torn from battle, and the disfigured prisoner felt weak in her presence. Unlike on Mars, here he could see her clearly. Her eyes were iced. Her black hair, flowed down to her hips dotted with icicles. The blue and light purple icicles had red flames frozen inside.

"You're still alive," Wuyan said in a steady voice.

"You shouldn't have come for me," said Dimycles. "It's a trap."

"So you are the bait?" she wondered. "Or did they keep you alive for some other reason?"

"I'm a survivor," he said. "Does it... disappoint you?"

"Yes! Unless you have the Midnight core, I will have to kill you myself." She smiled with halfhearted pity. "Of course, you don't have it. Do you? Which brings me back to question your survival: Why did they let you live? The Sunil would have beheaded you immediately, so they must have some selfish motive. What do they know about me?"

With a nod, he answered, "They know that the daughter of Chi wants the Cube of None."

Hearing the name of the cube, Wuyan gasped. "What have you done?"

The conference room wall cracked and exploded as North broke it down with a huge fist. Trying to cut off all escape, the Sunilian Warrior make her arms encompass the entire room.

Wuyan froze the room, looked at Dimycles and said, "You took the Key of Titans!"

A hole opened above them; she grabbed him, and the both flew out to the roof – overlooking the land of Selaus. Wuyan bit her lip and threw him down.

"Where is it!" She shouted.

"I can't tell you."

"You left the Key of Titans unguarded? Do you know what Titans lay dormant, scattered throughout the Realm? Who would be so stupid!" Wuyan repeated, "Where is the key!"

"The moment I tell you, the Sunil will know," He warned. "They'll kill me and get it back, and we will both lose."

"Let me deal with the Sunil. If you don't tell me, I will kill you!"

The ceiling cracked open as large hands emerged from underneath and split it apart. North stepped onto the roof as a giant and shrunk to normal size. She shouted into her comms, "The target is in site!"

Wuyan's troops all took to the roof to attack North.

"Let me go!" Dimycles cried to Wuyan. "I will retrieve it for you. Please, just give me my sister, and release-"

"No! I trusted you already, and I've learned my faith was misplaced. Your honor charmed me, and I indulged in that fantasy, like a silly young girl. I believed you could be my champion. No more! Not only did you fail to get the Midnight core; you forced me to accelerate my careful plans."

"I need my sister!" Dimycles insisted. "Otherwise, I have no leverage... I have nothing!"

"Don't hurt him!" North shouted from afar. Wuyan's guards ran up on her, but North closed her fist and swung it into their weapons. The electric shock temporarily disabled the weapons. North ducked low, kicked one guard in the hip, then, with her growing hand, she swept through them, and they tumbled to the floor. She raced to help Dimycles.

Wuyan picked the prisoner up by the neck and held him over the high rise. North stopped. More troops descended on her and attacked. North radioed again to her command, "Please advise! Target is onsite, and the package is in grave danger!"

"I know who you are," Dimycles gasped. "You are the daughter of Sun Chi, from Ako."

She squeezed in on his neck. "And what is it to you to say his name?"

Dimycles stopped and stood his ground. "I speak his name because I knew him!"

"Liar! You only know what the history books say—a contamination of lies!"

"I was picked up by the pirate ship where he was a slave. He worked on the power converters for the water synthesis! I knew him!" Dimycles insisted.

Wuyan stared, then shook off this assault. "That means nothing!" she cried.

"It means that I was there! I know what happened! I saw it all! Your father led the insurrection that took over the pirate ship, and he freed my sister and me."

"And then what?"

"Everyone has a different path in life. Saying that yours is somehow related-"

Wuyan shouted, "And then what happened!"

"He became the leader of the Akolytes, until, well, until... he died, but Wuyan, your father freed me. Enslaving me again thwarts his intention. He led that insurrection to stop things like this."

"My father wanted to stop people in power from hurting those without it! My father led the insurrection to save his daughter. Me! He did it to stop the pirates from doing what they were doing to me."

"I know that," said Dimycles. "I hadn't thought I was the only child sex slave on that ship."

Wuyan slapped him so hard, a hole opened in his cheek. North blasted all of the offending troops away from her and challenged Wuyan.

"You will not hurt him!" North demanded.

"Stand down!" Wuyan threatened.

North radioed to her command for instruction, but none came. She targeted Wuyan, prepared to make a powerful blast on the pirate.

"Stand down!" Wuyan again insisted, threatening to kill Dimycles.

North received a message from her command: *Package has not revealed the location of the treasure.*

The vague instruction frustrated North, and in her reluctance, she stood down. Her earrings twinkled, and the bionic suit disappeared, leaving North back her her official attire.

Wuyan stomped, sending a sheet of ice that encased North's feet. Ice covered her ankles and calves, then slid up her knees and thighs. She pounded it, but it was solid. Her body slipped into the ice cocoon.

"Power!" Dimycles shouted to Wuyan. "It's poisoned you!"

"Silence!"

"No! I was a slave just like you, and your father," Dimycles snapped. "It didn't turn me into a raving pirate, bent on galactic domination. What's wrong with you?"

"Your mind is too small to comprehend what is right with me!"

"I don't remember anyone on that ship who could warp reality like this. How? Where did you get these abilities? Look at what you've become!" Dimycles pointed at himself, "Look what you've made me become!"

"Where is the Key of Titans?"

"Let me go get it, please! Give me my sister, and we will give you everything you want. Power and vengeance have poisoned your mind. What's in that cube isn't worth-"

Wuyan tightened her grip. Her ice fingers sucked the heat from his body, balling her other hand into a glowing fist. Looking over Wuyan's shoulder, he saw North encased in ice. He felt the ice grip that held his neck and understood what was coming.

"My key or everything you hold dear will go the way of your home world!"

He wriggled against her grip. "Go back to the hell where I found you."

Frustrated, she went to kill him, but what he said struck a chord with what she wanted to know. *Go back...* A change came over her. Her cold hand warmed, taking on its natural color, and she gently set him down. Dimycles coughed, and looked up at her.

Wuyan stepped back, *Go back to the hell...* she chuckled, and eyed him. "Clever." She turned into sparkles and flew away with the wind.

Dimycles ran to North, smashing the ice around her body. As she fell to the roof shivering, Dimycles covered her and held her close.

She looked up at him. "Sh- she knows?"

Dimycles nodded and rubbed her arms. When she tried to keep talking, he hushed her and pulled her head into his chest. The remaining troops left alive; all took off after their leader. North's body trembled, and she started apologizing. "I swear... I didn't know you did it to save your sister." North stifled her shivering for a moment. "I thought you were just a renegade."

Dimycles nodded, still holding her.

"Are you two the last... the last from Covarra?" North asked.

Dimycles bit his lip and nodded.

"No one knows what happened to Covarra, do they?" North wondered, nuzzling her face into his chest.

Dimycles set his jaw and stared at the exit where Wuyan had gone. "The Watchers do."

DISCOVERY IN SPACE

FOR MASON NOTHING was quite as unnerving as the awkward silence of space. She flew high through the Earth's atmosphere in her Auracle, sluggishly trailing three Terredrones. She struggled to keep the warplane from falling behind in the thin atmosphere. Not that she was in a hurry. Even in space, she couldn't escape her internal prison.

Adrian flew his Terredrone a safe distance from the other two. He glanced back toward Earth as if looking for an excuse to go back there. Alien's ships covered the upper atmosphere, testing holes in Earth's air defenses. Below was violent war, and above was the endless blackness of space. He thought of diving down into the fight. A cowardly way to avoid facing Mason, but death appealed to him more than the pain of shame.

Julius did not want to face his reality. He'd saved Mason, then ignored her in a wild moment of passion. Bishop faced his share of demons, but the more he tried to rid himself of their vice, the tighter their grip became.

Meanwhile, Mason wondered how many years it had been since her last meaningful human interaction. She looked at the duffle bag she took with her- it was full of bionic parts from the Congo warehouse. She still wasn't sure what Sarek had done to her, but she didn't want to get caught without any replacement parts.

She wondered: *Am I more machine than woman?*

The silence isolated them from each other. Finally, Julius broke the silence with an update. "Everything is holding."

To Julius, the voice sounded like fingernails scratching a chalkboard.

"I'm getting some fluctuations on the biomechanics and sluggishness on the left leg, at least on mine," Bishop said, not allowing Julius to stand alone.

"Yeah. I see that too," said Julius. "I've been compensating. Should probably get it tweaked when we get to a hangar."

Mason pulled up closer to Julius and Bishop but remained silent.

"This war is big," said Bishop, "We can't stay in the atmosphere and make it through. Perhaps if we enter true space, and re-enter directly over the U.S, we might get home with minimal resistance. What trajectory did you follow with Yaliz, Adrian?"

"I passed over Canada, but I never went this high."

Silence returned. The three Terredrones rose far above Earth, into the darkness of space. Julius brought down holographic menus. "Heat, temperate, radiation, all deflected well," he read off his gauges. "Whoever designed this did a good job. I'm getting some unidentified... stuff on my radar? What do I even call it? What is that?"

"Space junk," Bishop muttered.

"We are so dirty when you step back and look at what we've done. Saturn has a beautiful ring of rocks; we have a nasty ring of trash. How awesome are we? Whoa, that trash is coming in fast."

They dodged through garbage. Mason fired into the debris, scattering it. The action gave her grim satisfaction, and she kept shooting.

Adrian praised her efforts. "These solid light blasters are brilliant."

Mason stopped.

"Yeah," said Bishop. "You can adjust how solid you want it. Going slower hits harder."

"We can even combine blast," Julius reminded them. "Wanna match frequency?"

Julius and Bishop charged up and sent a single super beam out into space.

"Devastating!" Julius shouted.

"Reckless. It's gonna hit something important in about two thousand years from now. Ya know that?" Mason warned, with a grimace.

"Nah, we increased the mass. It'll fade!"

Zahra's voice came over the comms, "Can I shoot it?"

Everyone smiled.

Mason giggled and spoke. "Why such a huge beam? Don't get me wrong; it's cool. But don't you think that's overkill?"

"You can kill anything if you have a big enough gun," Julius answered. "And after tussling with those big lizards, I figure, you can never have a big enough blast."

"There's North America," Bishop said. "We should let Mason go in for reentry first. Her ship has shielding that can hold up."

"Shielding that can hold up?" Julius asked.

"No, no, hang on," Bishop called. "Something's not right. I feel an... emptiness... out there."

"Well, 'out there' is space," Mason reminded him. "It's empty."

"I feel it too," Adrian added. "Like scattered nothingness. If I tried to teleport into it, there would be nothing there."

"Yeah, I feel it too," Julius added, "Wow. It feels... void."

Mason's mind overrode her feelings, and she pulled down her control menus to run scans. "You guys are confusing me. I'm running scans out there. I'm getting the basic gamma rays and magnetronic activity I'd expect."

"It's deeper than that," Julius noticed and changed course.

Mason noted they were in true space, and checked her graph. "I don't see anything different."

"It's like tiny little holes all over the place," Julius mentioned.

"Space is emptiness, so what can put holes in emptiness?"

"Space isn't exactly empty," Bishop explained. "A fish swims in water. We walk through air. Planets fall through space. You don't notice the thing you are in, but it's there. It's tangible, and it is very real."

"Our zenomites get power though the energy in free space," said Adrian. "When something's missing, we feel it."

"The only thing I know that causes this is dark energy anti-particles," said Bishop. "We need to be sure. This phenomenon could be dangerous."

"Dark energy... anti-particles? I don't think we have anything that can detect that," Mason said.

"No one does," said Bishop, "at least not on Earth. Only the SARA space station controls that kind of experimentation."

"What if it's them?" Adrian asked.

"We should warn them," said Bishop. "They may not realize what's happening out here."

The three Terredrones changed course and sped toward the SARA space station.

Mason sighed, reluctantly following. "What is the use of dark energy studies? That's not my field."

"It's like a fish that wants to learn about air," Bishop said. "It can swim to the surface and study the air directly, or stay underwater and study an air bubble. We don't need to go to the edge of the universe to explore its exterior. If we tear a hole in space, we can observe the void from here. Instead of traveling billions of light years, we just do it right here in our own backyard."

"How?" Mason asked.

"Scientists bring dark matter to a critical level and... well, detonate it."

"That's not the word I wanted to hear," Mason said.

"It's not a big amount," said Julius. "They take a tiny helping of dark energy particles, but it releases megatons of energy just from the detonation. So that's why they do it out in space."

"Yeah, he's right. It produces a massless, timeless, void inside of the explosion," Bishop added. "Timelessness is key here. Before detonation, anti-particles start showing up."

"Out of nowhere?" Mason wondered.

"Yeah," Bishop said.

"Wouldn't that violate energy conservation?"

"Not exactly, because the system is non-causal," Bishop continued. "Energy is conserved. It just happens in a different sequence from the way we experience time. There are endless theories, but here's how it breaks down: Before the detonation, the anti-particles show up, like magic sprinkles in space. The detonation then expels normal dark energy particles everywhere. But the anti-particles are already there. These antiparticles react with the normal particles from the explosion. They continuously balance each other out until the void closes."

"But never this expansive, and so close to Earth," said Julius. "What we feeling are anti-particles all over the place. We'd need units bigger than megatons to measure the size of the explosion this could cause."

"Are you tell us there's gonna be some enormous explosion of dark energy outside of Earth?" Mason asked. "What happens if Earth gets caught in the void?"

The three were quiet.

"Oh, come on!" Mason shouted.

"I think it's a good question. We need to find out," said Bishop.

They reached the SARA space station in deep orbit. Flying around to a docking portal, they waved at a crewmember through the windows. When the man inside panicked and sounded an alarm, Bishop signaled to him and pointed to the dock.

WHEN CAPTAIN YANI Harris entered the Nevada Flight Command Center, her soldiers saluted.

Erica Bateman provided the status, "The Reptilites are feeling lucky. They brought two large contingents over North America."

"Any descent?"

"No Captain, not yet, but," she flipped views, "the Pulkovo Observatory finally found the alien beacon, and estimate there is another armada defending it."

"About time they found it," Yani said, relieved.

Erica raised her hand, "It was no easy thing to find. It's a big sky. Also, that wasn't the end of the status. The beacon and its defending Armada are moving."

Yani nervously turned to Officer Schneider, "What about sat-com?"

"Our satellites are offline," he reported.

"Good. Spaceports?"

"Offline as well."

"What are they up to?" Erica asked. "If the beacon won't work without our ports, why are they bringing it closer to Earth?"

Captain Harris paced. "If they can't broadcast it, they may try to bring it closer to the atmosphere to use our satellites, or localize the effect. Track them, and let me know where they orbit. Where is the contingent attacking?"

"Based on their current trajectory, they will arrive somewhere over Mexico, Texas, the Gulf, or Florida."

Yani thought for a moment, "They are going to try and pillage our oil rigs. Dille! Contact Gulf Command. We need those ships fully alert. Schneider! What's the ETA of that beacon?"

"I'm not sure Captain. It's on the other side of the world. We're using short wave radio to communicate with the observatory, and they are struggling to keep a clear line of sight on the beacon. It's mostly guesswork right now."

"War is a science of estimation," Yani mumbled. "I need the best! Keep on that. Dille, boost another shortwave line. Get me in touch with the SARA space station. I need better eyes on that beacon."

THE SARA SPACE station closed its hatch and sealed its tubes. After decompressing, Mason exited her ship and watched the others floating out of their Terredrones. They looked around at the flashing alarm lights. Armed soldiers surrounded them. There was a lot of shouting.

"They don't look happy," Julius noticed. "It's been a while since anyone was happy to see us."

The main security hatch opened, and a burly, big-cheeked, wide-jawed man hustled through the hole. This was the base commander. "At ease!" he snapped.

"Sir, they could be spies!"

"They aren't."

Though the men were troubled, they lowered their guns.

"General Harris?" Adrian said, softly, trying to reorient himself to speak.

"It's been a while," said the Commander. "You still a doctor?"

"Well, a lot has changed over the past few days," said Adrian.

"You bet your ass." He glanced at Bishop and Zahra. "You are insane to bring a baby up here. Vicky!"

A female cadet floated up. "Yes, Sir!"

"Escort this man to the nursery; get this baby some food and care."

"Yes, sir!"

Harris eyed the others. "How did you guys get out here?"

"We stole some alien tech and used it against them," Adrian replied.

"Times like this blur the lines between civilian and soldier, and makes some people heroes," Harris said to the remaining three. "Follow me."

Harris took the crew to the mess hall, where they sat on orbed chairs and ate meal sticks. Adrian broached the subject of the anti-particles, "I need to speak with the science crew about their testing."

"Out of the question," Harris snorted.

Adrian cleared his throat, "I know it's a bit unusual..."

"Unusual?" Harris laughed, "You think you're smarter than them?"

"Smart enough to know your space station could be in danger," Julius replied.

Harris scoffed, "You must think I'm blind. I see the wall of aliens around our planet. Of course, we're in danger!" As he lit a cigar and puffed, he asked, "What danger are you worried about?"

"We discovered anti-particles not far out of Earth's orbit," Julius revealed.

"What kind of anti-particles?"

"Dark energy anti-particles."

The general puffed thoughtfully. "That's impossible."

Adrian was quiet for a moment. "Is it?"

"Who is she?" the general asked, pointing at Mason.

"Dr. Mason Kinoah, a microbiologist. She's with us," Adrian insisted.

"Why aren't you eating darlin'?" The General asked, rotating the cigar between his fingers.

"Just not hungry," said Mason twiddling the meal stick in her fingers. "I get that way when I'm worried."

"Get Azher in here!" A soldier jetted off. Harris continued to Adrian, "I gave your book to my cousin. I think it saved his life. We'll see. He poisoned just about his entire body from rum and vodka. You should see him now. Forty-two years old and he looks eighty. Gray hair, skin like a prune. Spots all over. Refused to get help."

Adrian didn't know what to say.

"I read your book," the General went on. "I liked the way you found control over yourself. You looked at drinking alcohol as a super power. That caught my attention right off! I never thought of it like that! And you had to control it, like a responsibility. Mmm... indeed a good approach to managing addiction. I was on leave and found my cousin on the side of the road in rags, and with a bottle. I gave him the book. Didn't know what became of him until my daughter called me up one day. Yani told me that my cousin carried the book around with him for months, and read it bit by bit. Yep, saved his life."

Adrian nodded and turned to Mason, who looked away.

Azher jettin into the mess hall and looked at the two Blackwell brothers. "You know about the anti-particles?" he asked.

Adrian and Julius floated off the their orb chairs, both nodding.

"Follow me," said Azher.

The brothers and Mason went with him to the science operations room. There Azher opened up the chart. "We've tracked the rate at which these antiparticles are rising. We've never seen anything like it."

"Is the Earth in danger?" Mason wondered. "What could cause this?"

"Earth? In danger?" Azher scoffed. "Earth is the least of it." Azher showed an extrapolation of the data, and continued, "The amount of power this many anti-particles can induce would create a void explosion that would extend well beyond the Kuiper belt."

Mason shrieked. "The entire solar system?"

"Extrapolations are risky and often inaccurate," said Adrian, "Especially so far into the future."

"But this is the future! Anti-particles of dark energy are non-causal!" Azher shouted. "What we are seeing is in reserve, and it guarantees an explosive in our future."

"That would annihilate our solar system!" Julius shrieked.

"Where is this coming from?" Adrian demanded.

"Well, we first thought it came from the Beacon."

"What beacon?" Julius asked

Mason said, "You don't know about the Beacon?"

"No."

Adrian shook his head. "Beacon?"

"The Reptilites built a tower way out there. A large army surrounds it," Azher revealed.

"So whatever this beacon is must be important," Julius said.

"Oh, we know what it is. At first, we thought the Beacon caused the anti-particles, but it's nothing more than a broadcast station."

"What's it broadcasting?"

"Our tech language," Azher said. "They want to disable our air superiority."

"How?" Adrian asked.

"Drones don't get tired. As long as the sun shines or the wind blows, they will defend the sky 24/7. The aliens haven't been successful in developed countries because our drones attack them relentlessly. Drones might be smaller in size, but they make up for it with recycled nuclear-tipped hypervelocity missiles that will tear right through them."

"Our game is strong," Julius chuckled.

"We got word from the CIA that the aliens got a hold of a device that is designed to disable any attack drone, and clear the skies," said Azher.

Julius gasped.

"Sounds like Lotus helped them," Adrian said.

"Maybe, but it isn't a foolproof attack method," Azher replied. "The Earth's ionosphere will block almost any radio transmission they try to send. So they need a conduit, like our spaceports, or our satellites. So that's why there's no communication anymore. We shut it all down. Commercial flights. Spaceports. Satellites. It's all down."

"Dammit! We are still picking up Lotus's breadcrumbs," Julius complained. "Worst case scenario- what happens?"

"Worse case scenario?" Azher repeated. "Assuming the beacon has some way to shut them down? We lose all drones, and the skies are clear for an all-out invasion. Human pilots will have to take to the skies, and the boots on the ground will have to fight. The death toll skyrockets. We'd still have a chance. Worldwide, we have a pretty formidable ground force."

Mason shook her head – *no*.

Azher chuckled. "Isn't that right? Even if they get through our skies, our ground forces are solid. They don't have anything to disable that."

"What if they had a way to disable our ground forces as well," Adrian wondered.

"I doubt it. Aliens would need inside help, and no human's about to do that."

Adrian exchanged glances with Mason, then said: "We need to talk. Perhaps you should get the General in here."

Mason backed away from the group, pushed off and floated toward the chamber hatch to leave the room.

MASON NOTICED THE two robotic sentries roaming in front of the nursery. When she asked, they unlocked the heavy door and let her inside. Bishop floated around a board teaching Zahra. He drew two squares and a triangle.

"Which one is different?" Bishop asked.

Zahra pointed at the triangle.

"Good," Bishop then drew a triangle followed by two circles. "Which one is different?"

Zahra looked and pointed at the triangle.

"Good," Bishop drew again: a circle, a square and a circle. "Which one is different?"

Zahra pointed to the square.

"Good," Bishop said. His final draw had three identical triangles. "Which is different?"

Zahra thought for a moment, and said, "They are the all the same!"

Bishop pointed back at the board and asked again, "Which is different."

Zahra understood and pointed to the drawing with no triangles.

"Good." Bishop leaned forward and gave her a kiss. He glanced over at Mason. "Just trying to get her to think outside of the box, ya know. Sometimes you need to look at the big picture." He picked the little girl up. She yawned, and fell asleep from all the thinking.

Mason folded her arms over her chest.

"I know," Bishop softly sighed. "It's my fault."

"How could you do something like this? There is a reason humans don't have this kind of power naturally."

Bishop nodded. "I wanted something to ease the pain, and conventional drugs didn't work."

"You wanted to control the pain!"

"I wanted to control everything," Bishop insisted. "I didn't realize that I couldn't control myself. I know... it sounds too much and too little... too late."

"Even when a prisoner is captured, and put under the worse living conditions, they can survive the hardships by escaping to the peace and tranquility of their mind. The fact that I believed that I was crazy, took the one sanctuary I needed to stay strong away from me. I believed that I made the whole thing up. Bishop... seriously! I did everything they asked me to do!"

"You have every right to be furious."

"I'm furious with myself. I hate understanding why you did it. I hate knowing why he did it. He could have been my protector, and with just a word, he could have saved me! Not from the explosion, but from caving while I was in captivity. He could've told me the truth, and with my sanity, I could've been at peace with what happened to me, and believed in myself! Worst of all, I don't hate him because, I..." Mason dabbed a tear "...I looked up to him. Am I'm more concerned with his reputation than my well-being? Logically, it makes me feel disgusted, and then I look in the mirror and realize, that I too hide secrets. With that realization, I am furious!"

"I created three monsters," said Bishop.

"We're all monsters now," she said. "When I first saw you with that girl, I was too tired to express my anger. Bringing a child into the Congo? You are a piece of work. You know that? But I realize that there is no safer place for her. I look at her and watch you protect her. She doesn't fear anything because... she only knows you are her safety."

"She'd be better off with my parents," said Bishop, "but I can't even contact them."

"Global communication is down to prevent the aliens from using it."

"But what would they use it for?" Bishop asked.

"To control our air defenses," Mason said. "The Reptilites built a beacon to command our satellites to shut down the drones. Then they use the plants I created to clear the ground."

"We should probably let the General know what they're up against," said Bishop.

"Your boys are telling them now," Mason explained.

"You won't say his name, will you?"

"It hurts," Mason admitted. "It really does. The world watched me burn in a fire and then forgot about me. I escaped aliens, to be with friends that are monsters. Seeing you guys lifted me. Kyra's words broke me down all over again."

"She broke us all. Mae," he said. "I don't know how to tell you how sorry I am. All those years, we thought you were dead, but you were in a far worse place. Your strength and survival inspire me. I have nothing to complain about, ever!"

"Of course you do," Mason cleared her throat and reached for Zahra and embraced the girl. "Omar's dead, and we don't get to give him a funeral. At least I got a funeral." She looked at the sleeping child, feeling refreshed. "Something about children makes us feel happy and refreshed. I see why you are so attached." Mason looked around in the nursery. "You're a good man Bishop, even when you don't want to admit it."

"I am a man, but to say I've earned the title of 'good' is a stretch. I've made a lot of mistakes, causing most of our problems. If I'd simply let Kyra die..."

"Then I wouldn't know the truth. I'd rather the truth kill me than live as an ignorant fool."

"Then who am I? I could have killed Kyra, but I didn't. Hell, I could have killed Lotus, but I didn't. Now that everything is out of hand, what was it worth? Was I just being self-righteous? I should have killed them all."

"You are kind and compassionate, but pain puts fear into anyone. It turns you into a selfish monster. You can't just run around snapping necks like some warrior of justice. This war on Earth still would've happened, and you'd still be guilty!"

"I spent a lot of time in the mountains," said Bishop, "away from everyone. I sat in the snow trying to make a snowball with my mind. I caused an avalanche to come down on top of me – twice before I got the hang of it. After that, I did more. I made a snowman, and then I made two snowmen. I animated them. I built a house of snow, demolished it, and built a bigger one; trying to be a master. I did so much to control my powers so that I wouldn't hurt anyone. When I could have killed them, it confused me. I couldn't do it. It seemed unnatural."

"Bishop, it is very natural to respect life. That isn't the problem. It is our duty as humans."

Bishop swallowed hard. "I had a duty to keep her from... I should have gone!"

Bishop covered his face.

Mason floated closer and put her arm around him. "What happened to Nicole wasn't your fault."

"Yes," he wept.

"It was Lotus and his insects. At your trial, they said it was impossible for an insect drone to catch a plane. That's why they wouldn't believe the reports. You can't blame yourself. You tried to help people, and you did. Your evac system saved a lot of passengers. Not just commercial flights, but commercial space flights, anything that went in the air pretty much benefited-"

Bishop looked up quickly, and his mouth dropped.

Mason shook her head confused, "What?"

Bishop reached for the nursery door. It tore off its hinges and folded in half. Two robotic rovers turned in attention, but Bishop flew out of the nursery and right through them. Like a bullet he flew down the halls in a panic.

"THEY'RE ENTERING THE atmosphere!" Schneider's shout echoed through the Flight Command room.

The table at the room's center presented a holographic image, focusing on tiny ships above the table.

Yani leaned in and squinted. "What are they up to? Zoom in, Bateman."

The tiny ships grew.

"Same formation as last time," Bateman said.

"Making the same mistake twice? We can't be that lucky. Dille! What's going on with the beacon?"

"Beacon is still pretty far out there," Dille recited. "Sats are still down. Not a peep."

Yani turned back to Bateman, "Speed?"

"Mach 4, at a much steeper angle. They aren't slowing down."

Yani punched the table. "Dammit, that's what you're up too. That's way too fast for maneuvering. They want to slam right through our drone formation."

"What is this madness?" Schneider asked. "Are they gonna ram us? In mid-air?"

"The Reptilites clearly aren't good aerial fighters," Dille explained. "They're big, and so are their ships."

Yani paced and talked: "They must want to make it a war of attrition, punch a hole through our formation, and have the second block ram straight through to the surface—the ideal battle for a Reptilite. No strategy, just overwhelm the open-field. They want to take this fight to the surface."

"Another contingent's entering the atmosphere," Bateman added

"Formation?"

The table zoomed out to show the whole.

Bateman pointed at the block of descending ships, and reported, "The main section is forming a rectangular block." The table zoomed out further. "The second is coming behind the first, and concentrating at the center rear. The total formation will be a battering ram made of thousands of ships."

Yani leaned over Bateman's shoulder, pointing at the drones directly underneath the Reptilite concentration. "Open up our center line here, and thin it out."

"Captain?" Bateman shrieked.

"We aren't going to win a head-butting contest. Leave enough drones to give them something to hit, but push the main force to the edges on both sides. Give me a dome formation."

Bateman manipulated the drones and then sent the order. The aerial drones obeyed, forming a dome.

Dille said, "This is different. Large transport ships are orbiting above us. They must be confident this will work because they plan on making landfall the moment they get through."

"They won't get through," Yani insisted, double-checking. "They piled up so much on their center their flanks are weak. Attack it immediately!"

Bateman's fingers glided along the table panels. She glanced at Yani.

"Right first," Yani instructed

Bateman initiated commands, asking, "How many?"

"Don't hold back. Give me a 4-to-1 ratio. Get rid of them!"

A flood of drones left the formation and attacked the exposed Reptilite wing. The aliens' aerial battering ram did not respond to the loss of their right flank. They remained tight up the middle and closed in on the drones ahead.

"Soon as it engages, pull back on the drones. Give way!" Yani shouted.

At the tip of the paraboloid, the Reptilites crashed into the drones. The drones opened fire and gave way as the Reptilites pushed into them.

"Pull back! Pull back!" Yani demanded.

The Reptilites rammed deep into the drone formation. They received little resistance as the drones gave way over the Gulf.

Yani saw the enemy's left flank had weakened. "Left flank! Left flank! Pour it on!"

Bateman obeyed, commanding another set of drones to attack the Reptilites' exposed left flank. Without a defending flank, the Reptilites drove their heavily concentrated core toward the surface.

Yani pointed over the table. "Pull those center drones back. Hold the flank! Funnel them in!"

The Reptilites dove into the drones attempting to punch through.

"Observatory still tracking the beacon. It's still way out there. Sats are still offline." Schneider reported.

Dille spoke up, "We have contact with the SARA. No one is answering back yet."

"Stand by," Yani commanded.

"We are standing by!"

Bateman nervously shook her head. "Drones destroyed the Reptilite flank; shall I send the rest to attack the transports?"

"No, turn them around and attack the Reptilite core from the rear."

The drones did an about face and covered the alien rear. The Reptilites suddenly needed an escape but had none. There was no way through the formation.

"Have all drones turn inward!" Yani cried. "Yes, like that. Surround them completely. Exterminate them!"

Drones blanketed the Reptilite core in an oval shell. The drones fired at will, and the Reptilites were formed too tightly to return fire without destroying each other. Their numbers dwindled.

"You have no chance!" Yani said. "This ends now!"

The drones poured it on, then suddenly stopped.

"What happened?" Yani shrieked.

"I don't know!" Bateman cried.

"Are we still online?"

"They're gone!"

"Did we lose comms?"

"No – n- no! They are gone! The drones are falling into the Gulf."

Drones dropped from the sky. The freed Reptilites powered through toward the surface, blasting their way to the Gulf. Earth's cruisers unleashed missiles and antiaircraft fire, but they were overwhelmed. Bombs dropped, splitting ships down the middle, and oil rigs exploded.

"Oh no!" Bateman moaned, adjusting the table display. Tiny ships floated and then broke in half. "The Reptilites are attacking the oil rigs; the cruisers are taking the full brunt!"

The Reptilites cruised low, just as they'd planned, decimating Earth's defenses.

Yani slumped and felt light-headed. A fleet of Reptilite ships went northeast up the Gulf of Mexico.

She muttered, "Houston?"

The daytime sky sparked, as Houston lit up like New Year. They threw up everything they could, creating a devastating net of detonations against the invaders. Debris rained down into the coastal waters. Though the Reptilites pushed harder, Houston's defenders held their ground.

Then a SAM battery operator noticed that the sky in the east was darkening. "What is that?"

Insect drones filled the sky and flew over the city. They landed, bore into the ground, and the Earth shook. Houston cracked into a thousand pieces. The defensive wall opened and disappeared. The alien forces swooped in, dropping bombs and paratroopers. Buildings that had withstood the earthquake now collapsed in flames.

Then came the land war. The towering beast stood up and plowed through the city. Anyone who could- fled. High above they heard the victory roars of thousands of para-dropping Reptilites.

THE GENERAL, his officers, Adrian, and Julius all hung out at the science observation deck. Azher displayed the image of the beacon, and the Armada guarding it. They were discussing options when Bishop burst through the hatch.

"Spaceports!" Bishop shouted.

Adrian and Julius came to attention. Everyone else looked blank. "We have to take that beacon down, or else it will use the spaceports!" Bishop cried.

"Spaceports?" the General asked.

Azher protested, saying: "No way. We already shut down the spaceports and the satellites."

"But not the one for Mars!" Bishop shouted.

Adrian gasped, "Hella's Basin Memorial."

Azher's brown face turned red. He started checking data. "It's been so long; I don't even remember the frequency!"

Some cadets rushed to help. Azher finally tuned into it. Voices blared through the overhead speakers:

...repeat! This is Hellas Basin Colony!! Please! Why are you attacking us! Don't leave us like this! Repeat! This is Hellas Basin...

"Those spaceports are still active?" Julius yelled.

"Shut them down!" The General shouted. "Shut them down!"

Azher worked his controls, as Bishop shook his head. "You can't. Not since they were memorialized years ago. Remember?" Bishop nodded to his two friends. "These aliens have a clear channel to every aircraft on Earth!"

"We attack!" Julius shouted, pushing off from the table. All three raced toward the hangar.

Harris didn't object. A cadet caught sight of a short wave radio message from Flight Command to the SARA. The cadet floated up to the general and handed him a communicator. "It's your daughter."

Suddenly the General's face fell into despair listening to the recording. "Yani?"

"Daddy? Daddy!" The voice broke through. "They shut me down!"

Mason floated to the hangar, holding Zahra. She stared through the window and pressed her hand to the protective glass. She watched as Julius, Adrian, and Bishop went to their Terredrones.

"Wait!" Azher shouted, in protest. "What are you doing?"

The three looked up to the hangar window. "We have to bring it down?"

"The Beacon? Um...how? That thing is well over 240 thousand miles away! It would take you weeks to get there. Forget about it; it's over."

"They can use the L-1," Harris said.

Azher's eyes bulged, and in protest, he asked, "General?"

"What's the L-1?" Bishop wondered.

"It's a ship. The engines will set up a neutral mass field that should push you damn near the speed of light. That would get you there in minutes."

"How do I fly it?" Adrian asked.

Harris spoke into the comms, "It's unmanned. It flies itself. Just hang on."

The three got into their Terredrones and held on to the chassis of the L-1. The bay doors opened, and, with a snap, shot them into space.

Azher, still pale with horror, said, "We've never tested it with humans before."

Harris nodded, "We have now."

"It's a one-way trip," Azher said.

"What? What do you mean?" Mason asked.

"It will take every bit of fuel to get them out that far," Azher explained. "They'll never make it back to Earth. Even if they don't get obliterated by that Armada, they'll be floating in space for all eternity."

Harris made a big sigh, "They knew that."

Beacon of Courage

GENERAL HARRIS RASPED: "Move! Move!" His cadets moved the space station to avoid a collision with an alien carrier. The base picked up momentum and crept out of the way.

As the carrier passed, Reptilites leapt at the SARA.

"We're gonna get boarded!" a cadet reported.

Harris huffed his cheeks. "Tell those pansy sons of bitches to get a move on it!"

The cadet blared an alarm. Soldiers flew to the hangar to board their saucer-shaped craft. The hangar opened and shot the saucers out.

Hull breach alarms sounded. The Reptilites blasted holes and entered the station.

THREE TERREDRONES HELD on to the L-1 as it powered through space toward the beacon, and headed straight into the defensive armada.

Adrian looked over his controls, weapons, and defenses. He wondered out loud, "Do you think this is enough to face off against an alien armada?"

Julius answered, "Lotus built these things to kill Reptilites. I mean, say what you will about the man, but if he designed these things to kill, I'm just willing to bet that's exactly what the fuck they do."

The L-1's fuel diminished. It slowed down and it's mass shielding fell off.

"Well..." said Julius. "Ride's over."

"I can feel them," Bishop warned.

Adrian studied the heat signatures on his scanners, then switched to visuals. He saw nothing but black space. "But where are they?"

"They're out there," Julius assured him.

"Everything's black," Adrian said. "How can we fight if we can't see?"

"They may be hiding," Bishop suggested.

"Hiding behind what?" asked Julius.

"Behind darkness," Adrian shot back. "Shift positions, use the display. We should be nearing them. My scanners are picking them up. We just... we just can't see them!"

The team backtracked and flew up at a different vector, taking advantage of the sun's light. Many of the distant stars now turned out to be nearby enemy ships. The Armada was right in front of them.

Julius's eyes narrowed. A formation of alien defenders moved toward them.

"Spread out!" Bishop hollered, "Move to the edge of their ranks. Don't let them surround us!"

Julius's scanner beeped. Projectiles were heading his way, but he had no visuals. "What's going on?"

"Must be missiles. You're not gonna see a shell until its right on you!" Bishop warned.

"Move!" Julius screamed.

Bus-sized missiles zipped past and exploded. The blasts blew them away from each other.

"We have to close the distance," Adrian commanded.

Another array of spear-like missiles approached.

Adrian twisted, but a rocket came right at him. He had disappeared before it hit. It exploded, and he reappeared, out of breath.

"Close the distance!" Julius called out. "We can't see these missiles! There's no light!"

"If we close the distance, they'll just switch to solid energy blast! That will be harder to dodge," Bishop warned.

"At least we'll see it!" Julius shot back.

Bishop flew near to the Armada's front line and blasted a passing ship. The enemy's shielding deflected most of the blast, and the outer hull stopped the rest. Adrian flew up the rear and hit it with a bigger blast. The ray punched through the deflector shield and finally breached the hull.

"Holy shit! These ships are tough!" Adrian shouted.

"What's wrong? You're breathing hard," said Bishop, as he finished off the wounded ship with another blast.

"That last teleport took a lot out of me."

Adrian spun himself around and counted eight ships forming to attack.

"You just having an adrenaline dump. Calm down!" Bishop thought for a moment, "There's almost no pressure out here. It's gonna take everything you got to pull yourself together every time you do that."

"If I can't teleport I've got no advantage!" Adrian drifted to the edge of the formation to keep them from surrounding him.

"We can't fight these guys toe-to-toe!" Julius hollered. "These are military grade fighters."

"Increase the power on your blast. We may have to combine beams," Bishop commanded, turning toward his friend.

Bishop flew to Julius, tried to stop, but could not. The Terredrones grabbed each other's arms and coasted. They charged up, as three enemy ships broke from the eight, and headed for them. The Terredrones combined a blast into a super beam. The wide blast engulfed the three ships. The shielding deflected the blow at first until the rays overwhelmed the shields and broke through.

"Turn up the heat!" Bishop shouted.

Adrian dropped down the menu and raised the power graph to the max.

A Reptilite ship flew out of the darkness at Julius. It used its side thrusters to position itself, but Julius beat it to the draw, blasting it to bits. Now the other two came, firing rounds of missiles. Julius engaged his thrusters, and as he closed in on the ships, he met a huge spread of blaster fire. He couldn't turn fast enough to avoid it. Instead, he concentrated and phased. The lasers shot right through him.

"I can't move like this!" he cried out.

The two ships descended on him, both firing through his phased body. With Julius unable to materialize, the ships orbited him firing through him non-stop. He floated helplessly, trying to hold the weight of the suit together. Panic overwhelmed him and he felt himself losing control.

"Get them off me!"

The two ships kept up a constant barrage.

Adrian raised his cannons and shot at the orbiting fighters but missed. He engaged his thrusters and went to save his brother. Another set of enemies closed in on Adrian and cut him off. They shot out a spread of missiles that detonated, sending him the other way. Another alien ship came in on him and fired. He teleported away at the last second and felt light-headed on his return.

Bishop and Adrian stared helplessly at Julius. The more they tried to help, the more alien ships came at them. The two split up, and Bishop led the Reptilites off on a chase. When Adrian sought to reach his brother, two more alien fighters attacked him. Adrian charged up, spun around on his axis and unleashed a thick beam. It destroyed one ship, but the wingman fighter persisted.

"Teleport!" Bishop shouted.

Adrian, still winded, shook his head, "I can't!"

"Hurry!"

Adrian hollered and disappeared. He pulled himself together near Julius. The alien fighter attacked him. Adrian fled. The alien ship gained on him, and Adrian veered off.

Bishop got free from his attackers and came up under Julius. His mind made a large force shield around Julius. "Jules!" He shouted, but no response came.

Using almost all his power, Bishop sent the two ships orbiting around Julius into each other. Their collision ended the assault for the moment, but Julius never phased back.

"Jules!" Bishop screamed.

"He's not responding," Adrian cried.

TWO REPTILITES UNMASKED themselves, revealing beady eyes and smooth faces that narrowed into sharp beaks. Their clawed hands gripped guns as their clawed feet gripped the walls of the space station and enabled them to lumber through the corridors of the SARA, shooting soldiers and smashing equipment.

Mason slid from out from her corner; an assault rifle slung over her shoulder. She squeezed the trigger, and felt the vibration, as she emptied a magazine into a Reptilite. The force of the shot made her fly backward. She grabbed on to the wall to stay steady. Bloodied, but still standing, the Reptilite returned fire, tearing holes in the floor.

Mason dodged, rolled, loaded, and planted her foot firmly into the wall. She squeezed. "Fucking die!"

The Reptilite screamed, and a second one appeared in front of him. The new alien swiped, missed, and then kicked her across the hall. She bounced from wall to floor and recovered. She emptied the last of her magazine into the invader. Mason saw a close-quarter rifle with larger ammo floating around, so she grabbed it and pushed herself out to the corridors. As she flew through fallen rafters, she saw the hole in the ceiling. She strapped on her weapon, and pull herself into the roof. There she found Zahra, tucked away in hiding, behind a reinforced steel box.

A clawed hand grabbed Mason's foot and yanked her down from out of the roof. The Reptilite stomped, but missed as Mason rolled away. When Mason hopped up, she took a hard punch, put her foot to the foot and launched herself right back at him, and took a powerful hit in the face from the larger alien.

"A dawa?" the Reptilite growled.

"A dankoo!" she answered.

"Elonchi?"

"Mason!"

"Ah, Boroli!"

Mason shot Boroli in the leg at close range, blowing out a huge exit wound. She punched him in the stomach, sending him flying. She aimed the weapon at Boroli, and said, "You won't live long enough for me to care."

But another Reptilite was coming up behind her. It knocked her in the head with its weapon. She balled up, dizzied, floating around, then spun around as the alien leapt high. Mason raised her feet, grabbed the wall, and kicked her attacker into the ceiling, making tiles blow out everywhere around them.

Mason hopped up, and pinned the Reptilite to a rafter, and shot it point blank in the head. The head blew apart in a bloodied mess.

"Mason!" It was a Reptilite voice from behind her. Boroli held up Zahra in her steel cage, taunting Mason.

"No!"

As Boroli ran off, Mason followed after him through the floating mist of Reptilite and human blood.

AS ADRIAN'S TWO attackers prepared for a second run at him, Adrian took the opportunity to fly to his brother.

"Don't touch him!" Bishop shouted, aiming at Adrian's pursuers to cut them off.

"I can't touch him. That's the problem!"

Bishop blocked the missile detonations with a field but noticed the explosions were pushing him further away from his partners. Bishop compensated with his Terredrone thrusters.

"We need more mobility!" Bishop shouted, firing at any enemies he could see.

When Adrian finally reached his brother, Julius was floating listlessly, still faded. "What happens if he stays phased like this?" Adrian asked.

"I don't know," said Bishop. "This has never happened before!"

"Think! Dammit!"

"He might be passed out from exertion, fear, adrenaline, or all of those things," Bishop said. "At least it happened here."

"What the fuck is that supposed to mean?" Adrian demanded.

"On Earth, he'd sink into the ground, and we might never know it happened. Then, if he woke up and stabilized, he'd die. So yeah, space is probably the best place." Bishop nailed an enemy with a blast. "Just leave him, and get that beacon!"

A larger ship flew toward them, shooting egg-shaped bombs. The Terredrones clung to each other and charged a beam, as Bishop shielded them. A cluster of explosions lit the space around them. They got bounced around until smaller fighters resumed their attack.

Bishop dropped his shield, and together they let loose another super beam. The large bomber exploded.

MASON SWATTED THROUGH a trail of body parts and blood floating around the space station, pursuing Boroli. When she met more Reptilites, her bullets bounced off their plated heads. The lead Reptilite stood in a doorway. She threw her weapon at it. Mason punched the wall, and her fist broke through it, then she grabbed the horned head of the enemy and pulled it toward her. Grabbing its gun, she blasted the Reptilite.

"That's more like it!" she said, hoisting a gun almost as big as she was.

As other Reptilites crowded into the doorway, she blew them apart. She ended up near the hangar.

Boroli called to her. "Fulaa, fondata!"

Mason aimed at him, but he held out Zahra like a target.

"Fulaa!" Boroli said, pounding his chest with his free hand.

"Fondata!" Mason shouted. She threw away the weapon and rushed him. Boroli tossed Zahra away, swiped down at Mason, spun around, and back-swiped at her, tearing her shirt. He punched her square in the chest, and she stumbled back. She recovered, pushed off the wall, and grabbed his neck, hammering him with her fist. The alien clawed, but couldn't repel her. Mason gripped his arm, and balancing off the ceiling, she threw him to the floor. Using his tail for balance, he got upright, but Mason had his neck. She climbed on top of him, and stomped his skull. He curled up, rolled in mid air, and was poised to strike. She pushed away quickly.

Boroli, let out a roar, pushed off with his tail, and charged the human. He kicked at her with clawed feet. Mason punched them away, and hurled a chunk of concrete at him. He head-butted it, and it shattered.

"Come on!" Mason shouted as he came back at her.

As his tail swept around, she hopped over it and grabbed him. He kicked her, and she ducked. He took another swipe with his claw, grazing her side, then he started kicking wildly at her.

Mason ducked and dodged until a kick sent her through the wall. The alien jumped through after her. She pulled herself under an I-beam and came up. Boroli kicked her in the face, then swept his tail under the I-beam targeting her feet. She moved her legs, balanced on the beam, and kicked him in the face. In the darkness, Boroli snapped at her, but his beak came down on the I-beam, marking the metal.

Mason slammed his head into the beam, then punched and gouged, until she'd clawed one of his eyes out. The Reptilite stumbled upside down, screaming. Mason launched into him. As he writhed backward, she pushed off and stomped his head into the ground. Desperately he wrapped her with his tail. When Boroli opened wide to bite, she grabbed his beak, holding it open. She punched him in the face and tried to free herself from his tail. He snapped again. She let his tail wrap her tightly and used that leverage to rip his jaws apart. She freed his bottom beak and used it to stab him through the chest with a piece of his mouth.

Mason wasted no time. As she rescued Zahra, alarms blared, and more Reptilites invaded the station. She heard Harris's voice over the speakers. "Our repair drones are under attack, without repairs this station will implode. Abandon station... full evacuation..."

"I gotta help them," she said, muttered, Zahra under one arm, and a huge alien gun under the other. "Maybe Jules was right." She flew into the hangar with Zahra, and boarded the Auracle. The hangar sealed tight, and ejected her from the space station.

ADRIAN SOARED AWAY from Bishop, attracting another collection of enemy fighters. As they started shooting at him, he turned and returned fire.

"Think of something!" Adrian demanded.

"What should I think of?" Bishop shouted coming up behind the aliens. He shot the rear section off one ship, and Adrian finally nailed the other two.

"Earth's defenses are down!" Adrian said. "We need that damn beacon! What do we have to do to win this?" He teleported to avoid debris and groaned.

"You okay?" Bishop asked.

"Yeah, ya know, teleporting isn't so bad." Adrian gasped. "Much easier to disappear out here, but coming back takes the wind out of me. I wonder if I can just-" Adrian disappeared.

Bishop looked around, but no trace remained. Bishop flew to the nearest alien ship, latched a field onto it, and used the connection like a vine. He swung around to attack the other ships.

Bishop latched on to another ship, and blasted it as he swung away.

Meanwhile, Adrian had reappeared behind the enemy line. He saw the beacon, and practically shouted with joy. Adrian dropped down his menus. He diverted power for the largest beam his suit could produce and then saw alien spaceships heading right for him. There wouldn't be time to charge. He shot out what he could before teleporting back to Bishop. As Adrian reformed, he was panting heavily.

"I couldn't... I – I couldn't get it," he gasped. "Come with me?"

"Oh hell no!" Bishop protested. "Are you crazy? When you disappear, you're in a quantum state. Your body's everywhere at once, but your consciousness isn't! If you pass out and lose consciousness, I don't know what will happen."

As Bishop spoke, a ship flew past, and he tried to catch it with a field. He couldn't turn around fast enough. "Dammit!" Bishop grunted. "We have no mobility."

"Make some mobility!" Adrian demanded, catching his breath.

Another ship attacked with a flurry of shots. They dodged. The two played cat-and-mouse with the enemy as they gradually neared the beacon.

"Make some mobility?" Bishop grumbled. "Really? Do you see a paper clip and some spare gravity lying around?"

"B'!"

"What? There is no gravity! No air! We can't bank! We can't outmaneuver them. They have bigger thrusters, better shields, more soldiers—maybe we can hit the beacon from here."

"We can't see it! It's too dark!"

"Can you teleport again?"

"Not at once, it's too far, I can go undercover again, but this is taking a lot out of me!" Adrian said. "What the fuck is gravity anyway?"

"It's an effect ya know, from mass..." Bishop explained, dodging an incoming barrage.

"Invent some mass," Adrian suggested, shooting back.

"I can't invent mass. Mass is like stabilized energy..." Bishop dropped his menus and changed weapons.

"Don't our zenomites do some something with the energy from the universal fabric?" Adrian asked. "Or some shit like that? What the fuck good is it?"

Another ship was coming. Bishop got set to fire, then stopped. His eyes widened.

Adrian noticed Bishop's delay and shot at the ship himself. He hit it, but not fatally. Two other ships approached. Bishop stayed still, so Adrian spun around, pumped his thrusters, diverting the invaders.

Adrian stared at Bishop, frustrated at his friend's inaction. "The fuck! Are you stuck? What are you doing?"

Bishop called out with a strained expression. "Making gravity."

MASON FLEW OUT of the space station and targeted the carrier. As the carrier fired, she turned right. Instead of banking away, the Auracle rotated in place. The blast hit her.

"Dammit!" She thought she was dead, until she looked at Zahra. Next to the child was a large Reptilite weapon.

Mason checked the menus. The shields were up, but the tactics of space fighting confused her. Engaging her thrusters, she realigned her ship with the carrier.

"This sucks," Mason complained. As she drifted toward the carrier, she examined her menus. She noticed cadets in saucers repairing breaches on the space station, but she also saw escape pods fleeing the space station.

"Let's see if Jules was right." Mason held down the controls, charging the prime weapon. "With a big enough gun, you can kill anything." She wanted to atone for any help she'd given these invaders as they'd prepared for war.

She let loose the cannons. The super beam struck the carrier's shields. The beam pierced the shield, tearing a hole in the carrier, but the carrier still functioned. Mason reoriented to fire again. She pushed the beam along the axis of the carrier, tearing the vessel in half.

The explosions and vapor shocked Zahra. Mason consulted her map.

"Where's your dada?" she asked Zahra. "We should go help him, huh? Yeah?" Mason suddenly felt an overwhelming sadness. "If only we could get out there. There's got to be a way to get them ba-"

Suddenly, an alert popped up on the screen.

Unusual gravitational anomaly detected.

"Huh-" Mason wondered. A tiny dot appeared on her display, along with a warning to avoid the area. She looked out, and saw stars twinkling.

Critical mass detected. Gravitational singularity imminent.

"Bishop!" Mason screamed into her comms, "What is going on?"

All she received in response was more warnings.

Recommended course of action: Withdraw.

Mason cried out: "Please, don't do this, Bishop. Don't leave your daughter like this."

Excessive tidal forces detected.

Impact: Three minutes.

Recommended course of action: Withdraw.

"No, no, no... what does that mean? Tidal what? We can't leave him! Bishop?"

Autonomous system engaging: Recommended course of action initiated unless override.

Mason looked at Zahra, and then out into space. She felt the Auracle automatically engage the thrusters and flee.

ADRIAN SAW SPARKS of light flashing around Bishop. "Wha- what?"

An alarm flashed on his menus, showing an unusual heat source and gravitational fields. As Adrian flew from Bishop, he looked back and saw the sparks increasing around his friend's Terredrone. When Adrian detected an unidentified celestial body, he put up a sun filter over the video. A bright sphere surrounding Bishop grew, and its heat signature set off alarms.

Adrian floated backward toward his friend, along with tiny particles in space. The massive Reptilite ships drifted as well. Bishop pulled huge amounts of energy from space, and ambient heated material formed around him.

Adrian realized what was happening.

"Oh... wait. Yes!" Adrian pulled down his menus and changed weapons.

Bishop squeezed the energy into a super dense space around himself. Adrian sweated, and got light-headed. He orbited Bishop's ship, blasting any nearby aliens. As gasses and rocks formed around Bishop into dense matter, Adrian got his perfect battlefield.

As two ships chased him, Adrian flew around Bishop and ambushed the Reptilite ships. He swung himself around and dove head on into another, dodging spear-like missiles. After the debris had blown out from the explosions, it all settled in around Bishop forming a large sphere; Adrian maneuvered through it all. He disappeared, and reformed inside the ship, and then blasted right out of it.

He charged up and fell back toward Bishop. When ships chased him, Adrian dodged and slung past Bishop. The ships followed, but gravity took their momentum, and Adrian used his cannons to blast them to pieces.

Another ship caught on to the trick and flanked Adrian. Before he could turn to defend himself, another blast came out and destroyed it.

"Jules!"

"I'm up!"

Bishop's exertion pushed him to the limits of his abilities. He packed the nearby space ever more densely. Struggling against gravity, the Reptilites could no longer protect the beacon. Their ships came in, two dozen at a time. With Bishop's star brightening, they no longer had the cover of darkness. Adrian and Julius saw ships heading right at them. Julius shot.

"If Bishop can push it, so can we," Adrian disappeared.

When a large section of the enemy line went after Julius, Adrian and his Terredrone reconfigured on the side of them. He charged and blew a hot blast of energy over the alien line. The energy blast flowed over the ships, eroding their shielding and hulls. Finally, it pierced through, and they were gone.

The duo had increasing trouble with the gravitational pull increasing from Bishop. The Reptilite Armada fared worse than their human rivals. Their destroyers collided into Bishop, and the material from their ships became crushed and molten. The debris started forming a metallic surface around him. The Terredrones diverted full power to shield the humans from the heat. When they saw the beacon, Adrian hollered out, "Go get it!"

Julius phased, engaged his engines, and didn't move. "I can't! It doesn't work that way!"

"Make it work!"

"I can't move out here."

"How do you do it on Earth?"

"I don't know. Earth moves, so I just let it."

Adrian thought about it, "Earth only moves in one direction. I see you walk around all the time! It's all in your head."

Julius phased, concentrated and moved a bit in his purposed direction.

"I'm too slow, you go!" Julius hollered out.

Adrian groaned. He blasted at another ship and then teleported toward the beacon. Teleporting away while so close to Bishop's gravity made it difficult to pull himself together around his consciousness. He struggled to do it, and once he was reformed he almost passed out. While trying to shoot the beacon, he pitched forward, with only the restraints to catch him. His vision faded. He saw the Beacon drifting behind swarms of enemy ships. Carrier ships latched onto it with a tractor beam. They reoriented themselves, ready to jump into hyperspace with the beacon in tow. Adrian put the Terredrone on automatic and tried to recover enough to resume teleportation. He had to destroy the Beacon before they got away.

"Just... one... more... time..." Adrian stammered. He vomited on himself. The Terredrone screeched an alarm.

Bishop's mind drifted off. Rocks and ships tore apart as they neared him.

When the Reptilite carriers engaged their anti-mass fields, Bishop's gravity lost its effect. Adrian pushed his thrusters, headed for the beacon, and weakly called his brother's name: "J – Jules." He took back the controls. "Jules!"

Bishop couldn't hold on.

"I'm on it!" Julius shouted.

Julius engaged thrusters, headed straight for the beacon through enemy fire. He dodged in and out through the barrage of suppressive fire. He moved his hands to charge his cannons as he came to a blockade of enemy ships. "Need to focus!" He flew toward the destroyers, imagining he was on Earth. He visualized his momentum, though he had no point of reference. They fired. He phased and drifted straight through them. He targeted the carriers, phased through their anti-mass fields, and materialized solid again. When he had a clear shot at the Beacon, he fired both cannons at full. The tower station went up in a sudden blaze.

Bishop's lips quivered. The exertion took him over the edge. He let go. Adrian saw the super-dense mass come undone. "Jules! Phase!" he screamed.

Adrian disappeared. Julius phased just as some of the Reptilite carriers sped off. Bishop let it all go, the energy he'd gathered dispersed back into space. The explosion lit the area around him catching the Armada attempting to escape. A silent blast field spread over them as space rippled and quaked. The super-heated mass released its energy and engulfed everything.

The star-like aftermath imprinted itself into the blackness, as everything faded.

Adrian rematerialized, as did Julius.

"Jules?" Adrian groaned. He felt physically and mentally weak. His head felt heavy. "Jules? Where are you? My comms aren't showing anything."

Adrian tried to change the controls, but his hands shook, and a painful sensation crawled over his skin mixed with nausea. Adrian's mouth was dry. He had no water, and no food to cure his depleted body. He felt claustrophobic panicked, and alone. He wanted out. He wanted to get out of the suit, and struggled to open the hatch against the constant blaring alarms.

The stars sprinkled the sky around him. A twinkle in the distance became brighter, and he realized it was another Terredrone coming toward him.

The yellow and red mechanical beast showed itself and Julius made it do hand signals. That's when Adrian realized the final blast from Bishop knocked out their communications. He couldn't see his brother, but knowing that Julius was nearby put him in a calmer mood. Together, they flew through orange dust and gas looking for their friend. In the middle of it all, they found the white and black Terredrone floating about the debris. Inside Bishop lay, unresponsive. Both brothers both grabbed an arm and pulled him along.

They flew out, in silence, toward the tiny sliver of Earth so far away.

The three drifted toward Earth for almost a day in painful silence. Desperately they attempted to catch it, fighting off the ever creeping sense of hopeless mixed in with the chilling physical shakes of dehydration. The planet was spinning hundreds of thousands of miles away from them, and even at full speed, the Terredrones couldn't catch up. The tiny blue spec of Earth became smaller and soon would become yet another white dot into the vast background of space.

The problem with giving up hope was that there was simply no other option to take. There was no food or water. Even doubt itself, though firmly evident, hadn't the soil to flourish. There was no ground the brothers could fall on their knees to formally state their surrender, nor the air to claim their intentions of death, though irrelevant and inevitable. There was nothing but hope, and Julius saw it. A glimmer of light—the Reptilites' mother ship headed the opposite direction, toward the battle site.

Julius tapped his brother's machine and pointed to the blink of light. Adrian gave his last, and in a flash, he teleported them all aboard the ship as the Kaiman zipped through the plane. Their Terredrones stepped into the hangar bay. With the battle behind them, the brothers had little to say. They stripped off their suits, dragged Bishop from his bot, and laid him on the hangar floor. Then they went in search of water.

THE ORDAINED

THE UNDERBELLY OF the Kaiman seemed more of a relic than a machine. The floors feel like they were made of bone and wood, and boasted a texture and décor unlike the smooth, all while, modern feel expected from an advanced race.

Adrian knelt down over Bishop, unconscious on the floor as Julius looked on with worry. Adrian pulled out his medical tablet and scanned over Bishop's body. "He'll be all right. At least physically. There is only so much we can do now. He's- he's in a coma."

Julius lifted up Bishop's head and forced fed him water. Most of it dribbled out onto the ground, and Julius shook his head. Then he heard a voice.

"Let's hope he's dead."

Adrian and Julius looked at each other. They looked up, and in the distance, they saw the strangest sight. It was Kyra.

She walked over to them, and the brothers quickly stood up and got in between her and Bishop. She stopped and appeared disgusted at the man in his weakened state.

"You can't protect him forever," She scoffed and retreated to the far side of the bay.

They watched her typing into the system computers, and then they saw her grab a clunky space suit.

"What are you doing here? I thought you were in D.C," Julius muttered, but she paid little attention to him. The two approached her cautiously.

Adrian quickly thought to ask, "Lotus, where is he?"

Kyra, shrugged off his inquiry, while she dragged the space suit across the bay floor until she finally decided to speak up. "Dead, not that he could talk to you if he weren't."

She started fitting herself into the oversized space suit only to pause when she noticed the two men looking sad, hurt even, at the news.

"You expect me to believe your crocodile tears?" She chuckled.

Adrian noted, "What happened on Mars was a tragedy."

"What would you know?" Kyra asked, "Were you there?"

"No," Julius piped in, "It isn't our place to judge people when we'd do the same thing if we were in their shoes, which is the problem with all bigotry. The point is, it could have been any one of us stuck on that planet, and we would have reacted the same way."

"I thought you said he was insane."

"We all shared a part of his insanity," Adrian explained. "We brought his betrayal upon ourselves. We just always figured, maybe we could reach him and make it right before he took it too far."

"Well," An angry Kyra huffed as she fit herself into the suit. "I'm sure you won't lose sleep over one life. I think we can all agree that you've seen your fair share of death, Doctor Blackwell."

She put on gloves and hobbled over to a pile of gear in front of a bay command terminal.

"Every human life is precious," Adrian mourned.

"Except if you must protect your own, right?"

"You know, it's true. We all failed one way or another because we put our interest first. It was selfish, but I'm happy I lived long enough to prove that I learned my lesson," Adrian wept. "Omar didn't deserve what you did to him. I hope you consider that and change to better yourself. Something I hoped Lotus would have done in this dark hour of humanity. It shouldn't take an invasion from an alien race for us to value another human life."

Julius curiously watched her grab a jet pack and asked, "What are you doing?"

"I'm getting dressed."

"We can see that, but where are you going? Outside?"

"Yes," Kyra confirmed, typing on the command terminal with one finger. "The Reptilites built Lotus a ship. The Reptilites can't use it, and since Lotus is dead, they are giving it to me. Well, he's never gonna need it where he's going,"

The brothers fell silent, and they all heard Bishop speak, "Then I guess our business is done here."

The two brothers turned around, and Kyra's face felt flush with anger when she heard his voice. "We are far from done," Kyra muttered watching their grieved faces turn to joy when the brothers realized their companion awoke from his slumber.

The three ignored Kyra's quip, and the brothers ran to Bishop's aid. They helped him sit up and inquired about his condition. Once Bishop assured them of his good health, they all hugged, but realized the news was premature as Bishop tried to stand. He seemed dazed and unsteady on the floor.

"Tell me we're not actually on their ship," Bishop pleaded, falling back down to a seated position on the floor.

"Well, yeah," Julius told him. "The mothership came by to assess the damages, so we had to hop on board."

"Why am I on the floor? Do they have artificial gravity? How does it work?"

"I think you need to focus on other priorities. Like, at least we are alive," Adrian told him.

"For the time being," Kyra shot in.

Bishop got to his knees and looked past his friends at Kyra, wondering, "You still plan to avenge the loss of your mentor?"

Kyra shrugged. "I'm over it now."

A glow of hope came over his face, and he mentioned, "Good, I'm glad we can finally move past it. Join us? Perhaps we can put what happened behind, and start anew?"

"I'm not that over it," Kyra scoffed. "I would never join your little gang. To be hella honest, I hate you."

Lights on several docking tubes blinked, and Kyra kept pressing a button on the console until only the third docking tube remained active.

"You guys drive me crazy," She continued. "Mourning the death of a murderer. Lotus killed, pillaged, and lied his way to power and all you can do is feel sorry for him. I followed his lead, and you judged me like a worthless piece of shit? All of you can just go fuck yourself."

Adrian noted her complaint and replied, "It was wrong of us to judge, but you must admit, Lotus is-"

"I am Martian!" Kyra interrupted. "As were the rest of the Six! Do you want to know why I have those track marks on my arm? It wasn't because I wanted to forget the people I killed- it was because I didn't want to remember the people you killed! I wanted to forget where I came from; I wanted to blow everything that happened to me, courtesy of the human race, out of my mind. In the process, I lost who I was, and forced myself to latch on to a worthless society that never accepted me. I actually thought Tai Cao was a different person!"

The news startled Adrian.

"Oh...no," Julius wailed when the truth hit his heart. "We, as Earthlings, are forever indebted for what happened on Mars. Kyra, we renounce those actions."

"I can't imagine the suffering you've been through. There will only be peace between us from here on out." Adrian promised, with great lament. "There has been enough death between the two worlds."

"I grieve for the loss of those lives that bled from our sectarianism. We didn't know anyone was still alive. I would have helped?" Bishop insisted from his knees.

Kyra picked up her gear and pressed a button on the console. The third docking tube partition depressurized and opened up. She said, "Of course you didn't know. You didn't even know who Boyacobas was when you killed him. You don't even know what Lotus did to your wife after I took her!"

Like a bullet to his brain, the words hit Bishop, forcing him to post an arm on the ground to keep from tumbling over. "What?" He stuttered.

"She's lying," Adrian protested immediately, not impressed with the mind game Kyra threw out while they were all in a genuine moment of remorse.

Doubling down, Kyra added, "I almost snatched that canister from her at the airport, but she was constantly on her guard while we spoke. Then security agents came to her, and I ran off. So Lotus hijacked the plane, but he also failed to steal the canister from her. I was standing by as insurance, but his stupid insect drones tore off the damn chutes. Because fuck me, right?" Kyra finally admitted, "I flew my jet pack at top speed, do you have any idea of how hard it is to stick a landing on a falling plane? I almost didn't make. But I snatched Nicole out of the plane before it crashed. I thought she had the canister, but she ejected it with a little boy. That's why Boyacobas went to the crash site for it."

Ending it there, Kyra walked off toward the docking tube.

"Then what! Where is Nicole?" Bishop screamed, lightheaded and fell over himself.

Adrian quickly grabbed his friend and insisted, "Don't listen to her! Nicole's dead. I did the heart transplant myself!"

Kyra turned around before she entered the tube. "How do you think you got that heart? You still think Boyacobas was a rescue worker? He was an alien! He was the one who rescued us from Mars! He was the one that gutted Nicole like a fish to throw you off from looking for the canister. You should've just given it to him when they asked for it." Kyra reoriented herself and walked into the tube; she mumbled, "You have no idea what they did to her."

When she turned around, she noticed Bishop's eyes were tightly closed, like a child about to throw a tantrum, gritting his teeth with both hands covering his ears trying to shield himself from the words.

"What are you so mad about?" Kyra set her gear down to initiate the docking procedure, and her arm reached forward to connect the safety tether to the chassis of the docking tube. She had spoken before the partition finished closing. "You killed him. Even if you didn't know who he was, or what he did. Go have a beer."

"Is Nicole still alive?" Bishop shouted, but Kyra ignored him- putting her jet pack on as the partition closed. Bishop pushed Adrian off to get to his feet, and he ran on shaky legs until he reached the barrier where he pressed the communication button. With his cheeks flush against the speaker he pleaded, "Is Nicole still alive!"

Kyra picked up her gear nonchalantly and rolled her eyes. "What do you care? You'll never make it back to Earth to find out. You'll never even see your daughter again." Kyra just shook her head frankly, as she put on her helmet. "I owe you one Mr. Kennedy, and I'm gonna put your daughter through the same hell I went through. I will make her hate every bit of who she is, and suffer every torment I was put through. Let's see how you judge her when she's just like me."

Bishop stumbled backward at the words, watching Kyra seal her helmet, and his right eye twitched. With his cheeks flush red, he asked, "Did you just threaten my daughter?"

Kyra sealed her suit and watched Bishop give her the expression of pain and hurt she'd longed to see. Finally, he showed some emotion to her cause, and she'd found a way to make him care. Watching Bishop raise his hand, she looked past him and saw Adrian and Julius running toward Bishop – frantically screaming at him.

No.

The door behind her unexpectedly opened, and Kyra flung out of the tube backward into space. The safety tether cord, anchoring her to the terminal, tightened at full length. The harness gave Kyra whiplash and spun her around, upside down, to face the starship designed for Lotus on its approach. Kyra used the jetpack to fly away, but the safety harness held her in place. She reached behind to grab the tether cord and turn herself around to see the brothers on the other side of the partition put their hands on Bishop to stop him.

They dragged him to the floor - much too late.

The steel tether cord snapped in two, and Kyra flew backward, slamming into Lotus's ship. The jet pack ruptured from the silent impact and spewed gaseous accelerant everywhere sending her tumbling around the frame until she was on the other side – floating overboard. Kyra swung her arms wildly to orient herself back to the ship, but she could not reason with the gushing jet pack until it was empty and left her floating in a dusty yellow cloud of fuel.

Kyra kicked, but there was no floor for her to stand on. Her hands swung in every direction trying to swim back to the Kaiman, but she fell away. At first, it seemed like she spun around within the emptiness of space, but the further she moved away, the more the Kaiman did the spinning, and she felt motionless. Horrified, she watched her gear float off in every direction. She stood on nothing, but everything else moved and rotated away from her in a manner that made her dizzy. Not understanding how to perceive what happened, she screamed and kicked her legs trying to run after it, but she never seemed to move.

As everything drifted further away, she saw a sliver of the moon come over the horizon of the Kaiman. She looked around, but she couldn't find Earth. Kyra screamed for help and reached all over the place to grab on to something, but only held fistfuls of nothing in the silence.

Kyra panicked, and hyperventilated, as she floated about in the empty chasm, and in the distance, a large white light in the form of a disk interrupted the uniform blackness. Her body got further away from the Kaiman and instantly she felt warm – then tingly hot. The sun seemed like the light at the end of an infinitely black tunnel. It peeked at her, as she weakly asked for help and the visor automatically dimmed her helmet as the heat grew intensely inside of her suit. She kicked her feet to reorient herself away from the blinding light, and she faced the empty galaxy that seemed to stretch around her as she floated off forever into space.

KAL KALET SAT alone in her quarters. She looked into the mirror ball on her scythe and saw the grief on her green and yellow face. She could not hide it. As she finished doing her ritual of song and dance, she rose from her knees. She closed her eyes, and she lifted her scythe high. It turned back into a small rod. She walked through the long bony halls of the Kaiman and took a deep breath as she entered her commanding officer's quarters. Rex Gedeon seemed in a solemn mood as well, in a deep squat by the window, meditating. He did not rise when she entered.

"Losses?"

Kalet had nowhere to run, and nothing good to say. Therefore, she started from the top of it all.

"Lotus created insects to attack us. Our landing party in the Congo has not finished reporting the dead," She said, "If we assume a near total loss in the Congo that reduces us by 20%."

Gedeon asked, "And what of the Martian?"

"Lotus is dead. Natalyze disposed of the body."

Kalet watched, noticed Gedeon had no response, and his scales did not change color. She continued.

"The beacon designed to take out Earth's air defense is destroyed. I don't know how they did it. Earthlings, in specially designed suits, attacked our armada. We have no records of the humans ever possessing the kind of power. Natalyze is still pouring over the data to determine what kind of weapon it was. That catastrophe caused us another 25%. It is a good thing our forces were spread out. Otherwise, that detonation would have cost us a total loss.

"With the fighting over the advanced countries, and the assault over West Africa, we estimate another 15% to 20% loss there," Kalet sighed at the words she spoke, "Rex Gedeon, over half our invasion force is no more, with no hope of reinforcements."

Gedeon mumbled under his breath to himself. "There is no bridge we can cross back to Reptilia."

Kal Kalet went silent, listening, and when Gedeon went silent, she continued, "Tanga reported that the Galactic State contacted Reptilia requesting an explanation of our invasion on Earth. Apex has banished us all and marked us for immediate execution. Tanga also reported that the Galactic State had deemed our invasion over a sovereign planet illegal. They have sent diplomats to Pluto and demanded our immediate audience; else they will attack us in defense of the Earthlings."

Rex Gedeon's scales turned dark red, and Kalet shuttered.

"Are we finished?" Kalet shook her head wondering.

Gedeon whispered to himself, barely audible, "Warfare is ordained for you, though it is hateful unto you."

Kalet, not hearing, took a cautious step closer. "Rex?"

Speaking up to his Kal, Rex Gedeon answered her, saying "War is never easy, nor is it straightforward – and most assuredly, it is never finished. The Galactic State wants to force peace, but there will be no peace."

"But, we've lost so much. We cannot hope to-"

"This is the same peace they forced upon Priang when the Xuxu attacked their planet, and yet now, the Priang are no more," Gedeon told her, "Take us to Pluto. The Galactic State will hear my defiance."

Kalet made note of his command but didn't move.

Rex Gedeon continued, "Instruct the army in the Congo to bury their dead and to regroup to threaten an attack on the Mediterranean, then we will concentrate our next assault on the isolated nations. Do not destroy the humans. We need them alive to force fealty from their legitimate governors. Send another party to the Congo to reinforce our losses, and instruct them to take shelter among the indigenous dinosaurs. When we get to Pluto, I will stall the State into deliberations until we can argue that we have legitimate claim over the land."

"That may not be enough," Kalet worried. "State law says we need a majority control over the planet to have a claim. The humans are arrogant, but they aren't stupid. They will never, ever, surrender, or plead fealty. They will die before they utter the words, and the State will attack us. How many battle fronts will we face if Apex arrives?"

Natalyze came into the room, "Rex Gedeon. We are receiving an urgent diplomatic transmission from the Galactic State headquarters."

Gedeon told them, getting up, "Very well. You have your orders."

Kalet and Natalyze left the room to carry out the military commands. Gedeon approached the hologram, initiating the line to the Galactic State headquarters.

Gedeon stood tall and watched Wuyan's image appeared before him.

"Rex Gedeon," She greeted.

"Wuyan?" Gedeon gasped in shock.

"Venturing to the outskirts of the Observed Realm? Earth? Really now. I've always heard that the Reptilites were bold, but you have added new meaning to it," She began.

"Does the Akolyte have spies among our ranks to have such knowledge?" Gedeon inquired.

"Do not flatter your ambitions with my concerns," Wuyan dismissed. "As there are much more highly advanced races that plague me."

"Perhaps your misfortune is to my advantage," Gedeon gambled.

"I guarantee it."

His eyes tightened. "Go on..."

"The Galactic State has denounced your audacious attack on Earth," She claimed, "The Secretary-General will force you to withdraw."

"Kojuti is a coward; it is a mere political setback in the element of surprise. I will see my grave before I see the State oppress my kind again. What harm can they be to me?"

"It's public knowledge now. The Reptilites will look weak attempting to negotiate terms with the State. Your enemies will double, and the State will never approve of the invasion of a sovereign planet," Wuyan assured him. "They will attack you! How will the Great Hunter afford a battle on two fronts with no support?"

"The Galactic State doesn't care what happens way out here. I will delay their political banter long enough to gain a majority control over the Earth, and send their politics into confusion."

"Not if I can help it," Wuyan threatened.

"How can you possibly influence the State?"

Wuyan smiled, "Do you not realize from where I now contact you? I attacked them, and I have seized possession of the prized Galactic State headquarters on the planet Selaus Prime."

"You have taken Selaus Prime?"

"They are at my mercy. I will force the State to extinguish your invasion!"

Gedeon's scales turned red, "You are a spiteful witch. I can't see how attacking us out here is of any benefit to you!"

"Or... perhaps I will force them to recognize your invasion as a lawful one," Wuyan offered with a suggestive voice, "How do you choose Rex Gedeon?"

Gedeon's scales calmed and turned to a shade of grey, "State your terms, but do not expect an acquiescence!"

"The Sunil, they are a thorn in my side. I have stolen a key from them and hid it on a planet near you. The Sunil are on the verge of discovering it. If I leave to get it, they will surely follow me, but if you get it for me, they will be none the wiser. Rex Gedeon, get me the key! Secure it and I can find it in my interest to help you win Earth!"

"The Sunil? What have you done!" Gedeon demanded. "Your dangerous game will have us both fighting a battle against an enemy we cannot beat."

"What do you say?" Wuyan demanded in return.

"What about Apex?"

Wuyan huffed, "Apex is your problem."

"I won't do it, unless we have a provision against him," Rex Gedeon asserted.

"Time is of the essence," Wuyan begged.

Rex Gedeon resolved his demands, "I will retrieve your key if we can come to these terms."

Wuyan leaned in, and looked him in the eye through the holograph, and clutched the air with her fist, "I will sign a cease-fire with the Galactic State, and I will return their beloved headquarters to them under the condition they recognize you and your armada as the rightful First Born of Earth. You are a sovereign entity lawfully reclaiming what is theirs. That would make your invasion legal," Wuyan proposed to him. "Upon departure from Selaus Prime, I will attack Apex at Reptilia. I will engage him in full. He will be unable to traverse the distance to attack you on Earth."

"All you want is the key?" He confirmed.

"That's right. If the Sunil gets the key before I do, I will consider our terms null and void. I will join Apex, and the Galactic State in your permanent extinction," Wuyan concluded.

"The threat is hardly necessary. Your terms are acceptable." Gedeon closed. "Transmit to me the location of the key."

"I will not risk sending the coordinates to you. They will intercept it. The whereabouts of the key is known only to a few people still alive," Wuyan insisted, "I know that the Galactic State has summoned you to Pluto. Go! There you will meet the State as planned because I have ordained someone that with go along and lead you to the key."

"How long till they arrive?"

Wuyan replied, "My contact is already there."

REX GEDEON'S SCALES turned a bluish grey as he stepped into the outer halls of the grand arena on Pluto. A panic came over the attendees strolling through the area at the sight of him. Armed mechatronic bots instantly lumbered toward him and locked on. Infantry units took positions between the bots and aimed their weapons ready to fire. Bystanders heard the high pitched sound of weapons charging through their panicked whispers. The diplomats looked at his appearance of large claws and fangs with both awe and disgust as they scurried away from him behind the line of protection. Another battalion of armored troops rolled up the hallway forcing the bystanders to give way as the Galactic State military surrounded Gedeon.

Once a quiet hush settled over the highly tense situation, Tevose Petri walked through the troops to the front line and looked Gedeon over. He said, "The Secretary-General didn't think you'd arrive."

"Kojuti does not think."

"Follow me."

Gedeon followed Petri into the inner arena. Behind them, the military crept at a safe distance, and in front of them military drones hovered above Gedeon and locked on to him.

"Listen," Petri started, as he escorted Gedeon to the viewing station. "I'm all for 'live and let live', but how could you violate the first amendment of the Galactic State Constitution of Planetary Sovereignty?"

"Doesn't that very bill outlaw abductions?"

Petri sternly shot back, "That happened in a different era! I know what you're thinking, but none of that is going to fly with this audience. Their delegates had to leave their home planets to deal with your shit. No one is happy- least of all you! I get it, but still..."

"Why are you speaking to me?" Gedeon wondered.

Petri waited for Gedeon to get into his platform and continued. "No one would stand for you as legal representation, so... they assigned me."

"You?"

"That's right."

"I wish to speak for myself."

"Think about what you're doing. You don't want to represent yourself. Not only have you demonstrated ignorance of the laws, but just the sight of you scares-"

"They need to see me," Gedeon demanded.

"They don't want to look at you."

"They need to see me because they made me!" He grumbled.

Petri took a deep breath. "I will petition Kojuti, but you need to understand that no one wanted to bring you here in the first place. I'm not even sure what or who made Kojuti change his mind to allow you to come. The delegates get very nervous being around a Reptilite," Petri looked at the army of military surrounding them. "If you haven't noticed."

Gedeon gazed about his platform. His eyes shifted. He saw a convergence of electrical impulses beneath his station. His eyes shifted further to catch the reflection of explosive materials beneath his assigned place.

"So don't leave your station," Petri added as he walked off.

Kojuti allowed Petri to have the floor and speak to the audience on behalf of the Reptilite. Immediately, upon calling the session to order, members from the Akentu planet threw demands before Petri could make a statement.

"Motion the Reptilite be removed from these proceedings!" They shouted.

"Motion denied," Kojuti said.

The Kalin joined in, saying "Apex is the true ruler of Reptilia, and only he can speak for the Reptilites. Rex Gedeon must be removed!"

"Motion denied!" Kojuti snapped.

"This is outrageous! Reptilites are dangerous and criminally inclined. It's in their genes. I can look at him and see that he doesn't have an eloquent bone in his body."

Petri took aim at the accusations and replied, "The defendant cannot be absent from his own trial!"

"He is no defendant! He's a monster."

"Motion denied! That is the end of it!" Kojuti hammered. "The Reptilite will remain here until I say otherwise."

The two representatives fell silent until others from the Go'Din sounded out. The arguments piled on, one by one until several in the general assembly were all shouting down at Petri.

The Go'Din, fond of material riches and still sore from the Reptilite invasion ages ago, were the first to broach the argument. "This violent act of invasion against Earth must be dealt with-- swiftly! Reptilites are attempting to gain prosperity by relocating to a richer planet."

"We cannot allow Reptilites to gain in prosperity in the Realm!" The Akentu demanded.

The Kalin joined in. "This is proof that we cannot live in a society that gives Reptilites the freedom to act on their own. They must be restricted to the outskirts-"

"Objection," Petri interrupted, flustered at the disorder Kojuti was allowing. "Slavery is outlawed, and the State cannot restrict travel or the freedom of expression."

"Only in the cases of non-violent expression, yet the Reptilites are incapable of any kind!"

"What proof do you have?" Petri scoffed.

"Slavery ended years ago, and Reptilites have yet to gain any meaningful prosperity in the Realm, what is their excuse?" The Akentu charged. "Also, there are studies proving a Reptilite's average IQ is a moron level compared to any members of the Galactic State coalition."

Petri gasped at the assertion. "Objection! You're implying breeding logic as a means to suppress another species?"

"Nonsense, my comments are based on facts! Their low IQ is not a result of breeding; it is in their genes. They evolved in their corner of nature with the traits they have. We, advanced nations, don't function at that low of a level. They are a threat to the order we are trying to maintain, and the peace we desperately need, by definition, they are what's wrong with the Galaxy,"

"You can't integrate our societies."

"Hopeless."

Petri appealed to their senses. "The Reptilites have been successful in establishing themselves on Reptilia."

"But only in mud huts, and stone! Meanwhile, we build great societies and flourish on planets in shorter periods of time."

The Kalin warned that "Reptilites are very robust. They can survive the atmosphere on most planets without the needing to adapt the environment. While this may be good for sustaining their existence as a species, they haven't needed to evolve a higher IQ because of it!"

Picking up, the Go'Din levied, "As a result, we have dumb animals roaming the Observed Realm, and invading other planets."

"I motion that Reptilites be medicated for their violent attributes and restricted from any technology at or above space flight," said the Akentu.

"You cannot restrict the advancement of other species!" Petri objected.

"If their advancement means less crime, absolutely!"

"If we annihilate every Reptilite from existence, only then will we see a drastic decrease in violent crime across the Realm."

"When they were first freed from slavery, the newly freed Reptilites did not cause this level of crime."

"They did indeed commit less crime back then because we dealt with it the way we should be dealing with it now," The Go'Din announced. "Vega Beast!"

The eyes of the Kalin grew wide in realization. "That is what the Vega Beast were made to do! They would control their neighbors and make a fine addition to the Galactic State coalition."

Petri objected. "That will institute xenophobia against Reptilites."

"There you go again; I'm talking hard science."

The Go'Din attempted to put more weight to the Vega Beast by rejecting Akentu's argument. "I object to the notion of medically treating the Reptilites. Another branch of government would have to be created to monitor the administration of medicine to Reptilia. That would levy heavier taxes on our wealth."

"It would be cheaper than cleaning up after them!" The Akentu defended.

Petri shouted, "Then would you propose medicating other species? You are targeting one class of species!"

"Violent crime is disproportionately attributed to them, so we must target them."

"You are clearly targeting them due to bias! That is hateful!"

"Why does that sound hateful? We are utterly disgusted by their uncivilized and violent ways. It has nothing to do with disliking a certain species or anything like that."

"If they didn't act that way, we wouldn't hate their behavior. They can't help it. We don't hate them for that. We feel sorry for them."

"It's proven that most Reptilites suffer from a chronic alkaline deficiency in their brains!" The Akentu continued, pushing their scientific agenda. "They haven't the means nor the desire to develop technology to correct this deficiency. So don't ask us why we hate. You should ask why we aren't doing more to create a cure to fix the real problem!" The audience cheered in agreement. "Medicine that Reptilites can take in order to control their natural, genetic, tendencies. That's what we need!"

"That's what we need!" Others cheered on.

"These things are curable!" The Akentu stated. "If a cure was developed, then Reptilites could join the rest of the coalition as a civilized society. Hate would no longer be an issue because Reptilites wouldn't act like narcissistic, sociopathic, subspecies."

The room got quiet.

Gedeon was missing from his assign place. The audience fell into a low roar of confusion and fear until a voice echoed near Kojuti: "The State commits crimes, but only Reptilites are criminals."

Gedeon's scales flickered and turned a visible deep purple near Kojuti. The low roar of the audience intensified into a frenzy. The military, protecting the diplomats advanced on the center stage.

"Stop! Stop! Get back," Kojuti shouted, preventing the troops from advancing on him, and demanding order be restored to his proceedings. "He isn't going to do anything but stand there looking stupid and uneducated. Let us prove how useless the mental acuity of a Reptilite is. You would like to kill something, wouldn't you? That's all you are-- a killer!"

Petri panicked and entreated the Reptilite, "Rex Gedeon, please! Every nation in the entire realm will unite against you and overwhelm you. You will lose everything!"

"My story will not end in a tragedy," Gedeon promised.

"Wasting your breath, come now, finish me. Reptilites know of nothing else, they hold nothing of value but a scorecard of death," Kojuti said. "Show us your scars, your 'war cred', how many battles have you survived to scavenge what pitiful accolades you've received? Show me why everything they speak about you is true? Speak! Is your translator broken?"

"You perceive Reptilites are war mongers as if the State doesn't own ships," Gedeon charged.

"We own ships because we build them! We are advanced, unlike your violent kind."

"How are we violent, when the State is the one selling us the guns to kill ourselves, and charging us into their wars to die for nothing?" Gedeon asked the Secretary General as he paced. "How did the state acquire their territory? Though gifts and blessing? You are the beneficiaries of theft, making laws to maintain your coercive system of oppression."

"What other purposes would you serve? You are a killing machine, not a thinking machine. You have no other reason for existing!"

"Jealousy."

Kojuti scoffed at the accusation.

"You made us this way because we are everything you want to be," Gedeon continued. "Every part of me came from a fantasy deep down that you cannot bear to realize you have no control over."

"The only one having a fantasy is you and your claims of Earth."

"Xuxu invaded planets, yet they still enjoy free trade throughout the Realm."

"The Priang insulted the Xuxu King! It was against their culture."

"Will you offer an excuse for every crime committed, as long as it isn't from a Reptilite?"

"The statistics prove your kind do it more!"

"The statistics prove you turn a blind eye to the crimes of other species," Gedeon claimed. "If obtaining land through violent usurpation is contemptible, then for what purpose did you enslave us?"

"You speak of slavery as if it were the end of you. You speak of Earth as if you have some claim to it. Your ancestors could not protect it, and you do not deserve it. You would be extinct if it weren't for us," Kojuti challenged. "You want some compensation for fighting our wars? Your bodies wouldn't mean anything without the galactic infrastructure we have built."

"An infrastructure constructed only for your benefit, with our bodies and with our souls as capital for your investments."

"I don't care," Kojuti ruled. "You will never have Earth. You will crawl back to the corner of the Realm where we put you or the entire State will-"

"And if we stand together and defeat you?"

"That will never happen. We have turned your kind against each other for millennia. You will never unite to achieve anything!"

"Yet again we are constantly forced to prove ourselves, against an outcome you don't want us to achieve while being held under a microscope of success."

"Foolish Reptilite, accept what you have become, or deal with the disappointment. You were never meant to do anything but die," Kojuti pointed out. "No matter how good you are, no matter how much you accomplish, it will never be good enough for us. Every mistake you make, and every time you fall, we will attribute it to your kind. Any success you have, we will find a way to degrade it. The only success we will ever attribute to you is your rise from being our property to being our burden."

"In the back of your mind, I will always be just a slave," Gedeon responded, but Kojuti could not make out what the Reptilite said. The words sounded muffled. Rex Gedeon's scales were feathered outward like spikes, glowing a deep red.

Though he didn't fear it, Kojuti noticed he had a shortness of breath. In his peripheral vision, he saw the entire army of guards mobilized in his direction. Kojuti instructed them to halt. He felt his tongue move, but the words did not come out. A short distance away Kojuti saw his body lying on the floor.

Everything faded in Kojuti eyes as his lungs screamed out to him, but he was unable to satiate them. He felt suffocated, but he couldn't take a breath. He winced in pain when he felt his entire head in the palm of Gedeon's paws, and the Reptilite's claw found its way up the exposed piece of his spine. Gedeon leapt into the arena. Kojuti saw blood and bodies torn in half on his way through.

Mobilized tanks engaged to stop the Reptilite.

Kojuti was afraid, but he couldn't feel his heart. His head remained firmly in Gedeon's grip, and he couldn't make sense out of what was happening as Gedeon carried him across the room in a sprinted rush. Kojuti watched Gedeon rip a metal pipe from the floor and impale a dozen infantry with it. A tank targeted them, and everything went blank to Kojuti as Gedeon shoved his head inside of the barrel and held it there. The tank backfired, and blew out the insides of the machine.

The torn pipe breached the facility, and pressurized liquid from Pluto's atmosphere used to stabilize the reactor temperature, spewed forth throughout the arena. Members from all quadrants ran for the doors, but the doors were jammed shut.

"Who sealed the doors?" They screamed, unable to escape.

Fail safe systems activated and partitions sealed over the ruptured pipes. The military units, standing as a barrier to protect the diplomats from the harm, caught the brunt of the liquid nitrogen spray. Their efforts saved the civilians, but their sacrifice turned them into brittle frozen blocks of metal. They stood like statues for Rex Gedeon to demolish at will, and the Reptilite crashed through them as he stomped his way to the huddled masses of diplomats.

"This is... this is what you want! Right? War! Your minds are incapable of reasoning with those you deem inferior to you!"

Instantly, he killed the score of Akentuvian members that opposed him so freely. He approached the Kalin and said, "Earth."

They objected. "Never!"

Gedeon grabbed them and tore them apart, one by one against their protest.

Soldiers trapped inside of frozen tanks broke free and from the shattered pieces they ran, desperately trying to save the hostages. Gedeon collected them like trophies, and with their bodies, he laid them out to spell the word EARTH in flesh and blood.

The diplomats fought amongst each other to hide, wishing the very walls would fall on top of them to save them from the madness.

"How deep-seated is your spite for my prosperity that you'd hold on so tightly to a planet that means nothing to you?" Gedeon moved closer to another group. "Earth," he demanded.

With their courage intact, a few stepped forward and refused the order. "We cannot bow to acts of terror!" and with that, they died.

"Earth," Gedeon spoke to the Go'Din.

Their hearts softened with fear, and they negotiated. "Perhaps, yes we can partition the planet. We will assign 51% of it to th-"

Gedeon rejected the deal by silencing the orators with death. "Earth!" He shouted.

Understanding where the result would head, Tevose Petri was not without his negotiating skills.

"It is yours!" He shouted. The remaining others chimed in agreement. "What good is Earth to us? What hope did man ever have? I will not stand for this senseless violence a moment longer! The Galactic State, from henceforth, will recognize the Earth as sovereign property belonging to the Reptilites. The current inhabitants will be mandated to hand over their occupancy of the planet to the rightful First Born of Earth."

OUTSIDE OF THE auditorium, in the halls encircling the conference room a smaller figure cloaked with a head covering stood alone. Rex Gedeon approached and tried to see her face, but her hood covered it low. She didn't wear the normal ceremonial garb but a plain dark covering. It seemed to keep her warm.

"If not by conquest, shall you inherit the Earth by law?" She questioned.

"Laws are written by those in power to monopolize the resources they have stolen," Gedeon claimed. "Earth will be mine by conquest, and by law, I shall keep it."

"And what law will you write when the nations of those you killed storm this system and wipe Earth from existence?"

Gedeon looked back toward the general assembly he destroyed, and saw those he left alive picking themselves up from the carnage. Gedeon spoke again to the smaller female figure standing next to him, "The law of Titans."

The cloaked figure stood still and remained silent.

"I cannot guarantee your safety," Gedeon told her on approach. "Tell me where it is, and return to Wuyan with your life."

"It is in a place no one wants to go, and a place no knows exist," She whispered to him.

Gedeon breathed smoothly, turning to look down on the messenger, and demanded, "Where is the Key of Titans?"

The woman pulled back her hood, and looking up, she said, "I will take you beneath the sand."

ACKNOWLEDGEMENTS

In 2008 I took a trip to Rio De Janerio, Brasil – a beautiful city with beautiful people. The beaches were a gorgeous sight, but they were equally as dangerous to a guy like me who has the swimming capabilities of a caterpillar. I foolishly waded through the waters and frolicked in the powerful waves. I found myself out by the surfers, who took the challenge of each wave, and rode it away. Unlike those surfers, I, however, didn't have a board. I didn't even have a prayer when a vicious undertow caught me and dragged me further out to sea.

Considering I spent all that day training Brazilian jiu-jitsu and lifting weights, I had zero strength left to fight both the waves that tossed me about and the undertow that pulled me back in for more punishment. Clearly, I'm still alive (I think), yet I mention this story to underscore how my battle back to shore is unique, because unlike anyone else's story of drowning... this one happened to me.

So too, this book series has been an enormous learning experience for myself and the people who have shaped my experience in life. I want to acknowledge and thank everyone I know for giving me the experience to shape the characters in this series.

I am very grateful to Ruxandra Tudorica and her patience with me to craft such beautiful cover. She has been a great help, far beyond just the cover of the book. Thanks to my editor, Peter Heyrman, who very graciously took the job of editing this story. I also want to bring attention to the scientific and engineering community. Of course, all in this book is fiction, but I try to hold to real physics wherever the story makes it possible. Our reality possesses a wealth of intrigue, fascination, and fundamentals like zero-point energy, gravity, and other topics I pivot around in my writing. I hope that something in my writing made someone curious enough to ask a question or two about the world they live in, or perhaps maybe just a phrase struck an idea.

Science fiction isn't always about lasers and adventure (or maybe it is!), it allows us to open our minds and explore our reality and look at it from several, albeit impossible, angles. Yet, that is what engineers as best at doing. So I'd really like to thank the reader for joining this adventure, and I most certainly will give due diligence to bring more engaging and gripping stories in the future.

www.ingramcontent.com/pod-product-compliance
Lightning Source LLC
Chambersburg PA
CBHW030536020726
47494CB00005B/1393